THEY WERE MEN OF HONOR,
MEN OF COURAGE, MEN OF DISTINCTION . . .
WHO MUST NOW FACE THE ULTIMATE TEST

LIEUTENANT COLONEL PAUL "LUCKY" ANDER-SON—His face horribly disfigured in a near-fatal flying accident, Anderson has always been the consummate professional warrior. But suddenly the war has gotten personal: His intelligence-officer fiancée has fallen into the hands of enemy guerrillas, and her fate is unknown.

CAPTAIN MANNY DeVERA—Bitter over a false accusation that nearly led to his court-martial, he is about to learn the true value of loyalty and trust; DeVera has been given a critical assignment, the success of which will determine the safety and survival of his fellow pilots.

COLONEL BUSTER LESKA—A veteran of North Korean prison camps, and respected leader of men, Leska now faces tragedy on two fronts: in the skies over North Vietnam . . . and at home, where domestic conflicts over the war are tearing his family apart.

QUON—The famous North Vietnamese ace has fought with skill and valor against the Americans. But denounced by an insidious rival in his own government, he now lives for revenge and a chance to betray the betrayer.

AND AN EXTRAORDINARY WOMAN

GS-15 LINDA LOPES—Attractive, successful and reunited with the man she loves, Linda has everything. But all of that disappears in a deadly burst of gunfire.

ALSO BY TOM WILSON

Termite Hill
Lucky's Bridge

TANGO UNIFORM

TOM WILSON

BANTAM BOOKS
New York   Toronto   London   Sydney   Auckland

TANGO UNIFORM

A Bantam Book / March 1994

ISBN 0-553-56500-1

Published simultaneously in the United States and Canada

Bantam Books are published by Bantam Books, a division of Bantam Doubleday
Dell Publishing Group, Inc. Its trademark, consisting of the words "Bantam
Books" and the portrayal of a rooster, is Registered in U.S. Patent and Trademark
Office and in other countries. Marca Registrada. Bantam Books, 1540 Broadway,
New York, New York 10036.

PRINTED IN THE UNITED STATES OF AMERICA

OPM   0 9 8 7 6 5 4 3 2 1

Please join me in a toast. Not to war, for war is destructive. Not to protestors of war, for they fail to support their countrymen. Let us drink to those who dare to fight to keep the American dream alive. Water, if you please, in remembrance of our comrades who did not return.

ACKNOWLEDGMENTS

I must accept blame for any faults herein, for I have been blessed with the support of professionals throughout the production of *Tango Uniform*. Literary agent Ethan Ellenberg provided guidance and a periodic nudge in the proper direction. Editors Tom Dupree and Tom Beer kept things on an even course at Bantam's New York offices, juggling and coordinating deadlines and keeping the faith. Don D'Auria and Lise Rodgers provided hawkish eyes and sharp pens. Sales rep Jim Bourne took me under his enthusiastic wing and carted me around the Western U.S. on a memorable promotion tour, interspersed with war tales from a technical grunt's perspective and a measure of Western lore. Jim, Roz Hilden, Rebecca Cleff and Kathleen Clement taught me about the people at the heart of the business, the book distributors, with their hardworking staffs who bring the product to the bookshelves. Without them, the rest of us—authors, agents, artists, editors, publishers and representatives—would toil in vain, for readers could not buy the products.

Jerry Hoblit again graciously exercised his memory for technical details about North Vietnamese defenses and the rugged, prescient and quite extraordinary F-105 Thunderchief. Billy Sparks spent a week telling me about how things were at Takhli during the period of the novel, detailing everything from living conditions and musical renditions, to combat missions and his spectacular shootdown and subsequent rescue. Also of immense help were discussions with, and telephone calls and letters from, officers, enlisted men and wives; commanders, flyers, P.O.W.s, and support people;

Army, Navy, Marine and Air Force; Americans and Vietnamese. I've included a number of their stories in this work. All helped to establish the environment of a rather minor, yet maddeningly frustrating war held long ago in a distant land.

Thanks.

√ Six

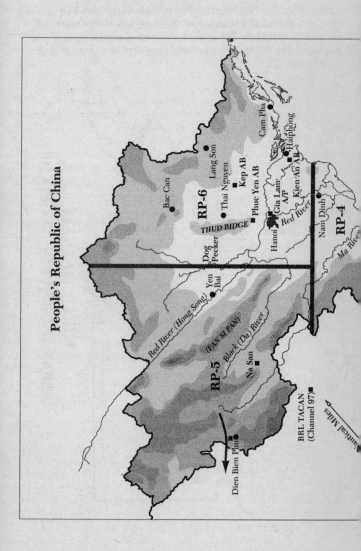

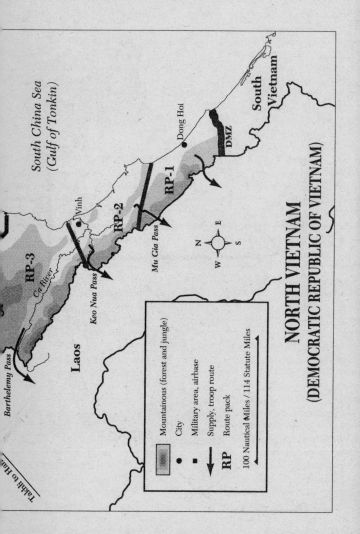

Barthélemy Pass

South China Sea
(Gulf of Tonkin)

Tchin to Hâ...

RP-3

Cả River

Vinh

Laos

Keo Nua Pass

RP-2

Mu Gia Pass

Dong Hoi

RP-1

DMZ

South
Vietnam

N
W · E
S

NORTH VIETNAM
(DEMOCRATIC REPUBLIC OF VIETNAM)

Mountainous (forest and jungle)

• City

Military area, airbase

↓ Supply, troop route

RP Route pack

100 Nautical Miles / 114 Statute Miles

BOOK I

si•er•ra ho•tel [fighter pilot jargon, circa 1965] < phonetic alphabet acronym for "shit hot"— *Informal.* adj. describing something very good, outstanding.

CHAPTER ONE

Wednesday, October 18th, 1967 0550 Local—Route Pack Six, North Vietnam

Light spread in delicate tendrils, reaching westward from the bright sky directly in their paths. Far below, the earth was cast in serene shadow, as befitted the early hour.

The sixteen-aircraft formation flew four miles above the Red River: F-105 Thunderchiefs, the tough, workhorse fighters tasked to fly the most dangerous air strikes into the heartland of North Vietnam. A four-ship flight of two-seat F-105Fs called Wild Weasels ranged a few miles in front of them to keep the SAMs and radars busy while the fighter-bombers did their work. Several thousand feet above them roved a flight of F-4 Phantoms, their MiG-CAP, searching for enemy interceptors.

Altogether, the various aircraft in their various roles made up the alpha strike force. They flew inexorably toward a rendezvous with fire and steel.

North Vietnam was appropriately funnel-shaped, for through it supplies and soldiers were poured to support the hungry communist war machine fighting in South Vietnam. The Hanoi-area was the funnel's vortex, and NVA troops and supplies converged and were massed there before being moved southward along the Ho Chi Minh Trail, which was not a single trail, but hundreds of roads and paths snaking through a dozen mountain passes into Laos, then weaving down to eventually end in South Vietnam.

For two and a half years American fighters had come to nip about the periphery of Hanoi. They'd destroyed much of the city's electricity production and distribution network. Party bureaucrats had hauled in diesel generators to power their lights and air conditioners, and told the peasants and soldiers that they must suffer in support of the war effort. The Americans bombed military barracks about the city's periphery. Ho Chi Minh had evicted hundreds of thousands of civilians from Hanoi proper, telling them it was for their safety, then billeted the troops in the emptied homes, for the Americans did not bomb cities. The fighters had destroyed the road and railroad bridges between Hanoi and the sources of weapons and matériel in China and in their port city of Haiphong. The Vietnamese had enslaved half a million peasants in a massive construction-and-repair effort. They built underwater bridges for trucks and used boats and barges to haul the remainder of supplies from the ports up the Red River to the safety of their hub city.

The North Vietnamese Army was centrally commanded from its headquarters, which the French had called the Citadel, in the northern *quartier* of the city. The government of the Democratic Republic of Vietnam operated in a business-as-normal mode nearby. An emergency underground facility constructed for military and civilian leaders had thus far proved unnecessary. Top military officers and government bureaucrats suffered only heavy traffic congestion as trucks, carts, and bicycles were packed into the city throughout the days—lining streets and alleyways in the southern suburbs—waiting for darkness when they could convoy their heavy loads southward.

The capital city was the safest haven in the country, for it was protected by the American politicians. No American aircraft were to overfly Hanoi; none could venture within twenty miles of the city without the express consent of the American President and his small circle of advisors.

But that Wednesday the American President had given his cautious approval for American aircraft to penetrate the twenty-mile circle. The target was an overpass on the

Doumer Highway, a main artery of north Hanoi. The fighter pilots had been briefed that no bombs were to fall on the city of Hanoi or its suburbs, although they were glutted with supply trucks. They were to attack only the overpass, which if destroyed *might* partially plug a single hole in the sieve for as long as forty-eight hours while it was being repaired.

As the air war over North Vietnam continued, it began to look like no other that had gone before. Aerial warfare had always been a system of weapons and countermeasures, and of tactical wiles to defeat both of those. But with the advent of supersonic aircraft with efficient avionics, computers, and weapons on the one side, and radars, agile interceptors, computers, and missiles on the other, there came to be little room for error. The air war had developed into a deadly game of chess. But the Vietnamese were provided with an edge, for they knew precisely what the American president would and would not allow his rooks and knights to do. On their side of the board, the Vietnamese had safe areas in which to maneuver, build, and position their forces, and their machine gained strength daily as modern defensive weapons poured into the countryside surrounding Hanoi.

The long-range radar at Phuc Yen Air Base, immediately northwest of Hanoi, detected the alpha strike force shortly after it passed into the North Vietnamese airspace, and Phuc Yen radar controllers positioned MiGs north and south of the Americans' route of flight. As the Thuds continued east toward their target, a three-ship flight of MiG-17's was directed to attack from the north, then was warned away as the high-flying Phantoms turned toward them.

The controllers also notified the acquisition radar operators, who in turn radioed position, altitude, airspeed, and heading to the operators of precision radars directing surface-to-air missile and antiaircraft artillery fire. The MiG pilots were ordered to stand clear so the SAMs and AAA would have clear fields of fire at the Thuds.

As the formation crossed the Red River and continued over the wide valley, now in the hot zone dubbed as route pack six alpha, the precision radars tried to paint them and feed information to their weapons systems, the Mach three missiles and big artillery.

Each aircraft flew with an electronic countermeasure pod under its right wing, which radiated a trickle of noise preset to the frequencies of the Soviet-built SAM and AAA guidance radars. The jamming created a series of bright lines that danced on the radar scopes and shielded the aircraft from detection. The radar operators looked for gaps caused by aircraft with weak or malfunctioning jamming pods.

First Lieutenant Joe Walker

Joe carefully craned his neck, first in the dimension to his right, then to his left. He was number three in Wildcat flight, leader of its second element. When they'd crossed into North Vietnam, they'd joined with three other flights to form the sixteen-ship formation, and Wildcat lost its identity, becoming a part of the Takhli alpha strike called Bear Force.

Joe scanned carefully, focusing at various distances from the aircraft. It was not a natural task, but one that had to be learned. If your eyes were improperly focused, you could stare at a distant aircraft and never see it. If the aircraft happened to be a MiG setting up to fire a heat-seeking Atoll missile, the error could be fatal.

Although apprehensive about the current situation, Joe was happy with his lot. He loved flying fighters and had wanted to do nothing else since childhood, when he'd hung models from his ceiling and immersed himself in stories of the pioneers of flight, reading about men like Glenn Curtis, Billy Mitchell, and Jimmy Doolittle.

An only child, born late in their life to upper-middle-class parents, he'd been encouraged to accept no limits upon his life. The fact that they were black, a misnomer in his case, for his skin was the tawny color of café au lait, was seldom discussed in their household. They lived comfortably in a sprawling California ranch-style home located in a quiet suburb of Pasadena. His investment-broker father methodically replaced the family Oldsmobile every three years and kept the aged beater pickup, which they called the "fun truck," in good running condition. Their pool was not the largest in their neighborhood, but it was big enough and was meticulously maintained by a Japanese gardener, who had come around once a week since Joe's earliest recollections.

He'd excelled at team sports in high school, his best games baseball and football, and as a junior he'd been approached by scouts from a dozen major colleges. Instead, his father had helped him achieve his dream by writing, telephoning, and calling upon a dozen senators and congressmen until Joe had gained an appointment to the new Air Force Academy. Although Joe was a diligent and bright student, the prequalification exams had been difficult. And though he did well on the tests and then graduated at the top of his high-school class, he continued to worry until he'd arrived at the new Colorado Springs campus and was being hazed so thoroughly by upper classmen that he no longer had time for minor concerns.

Like most plebes, he'd had his doubts during his first year at the Academy, but there had never been a question as to what he wanted for his future. He was going to fly airplanes, and if providence allowed, jet fighters.

Now Joe was soaring with eagles, his right hand delicately grasping the control stick of the biggest, toughest, sleekest fighter aircraft in the world . . . and at any moment the enemy would begin to try to shoot him down in earnest.

The Phantoms flying above and to the north had been alerted by Big Eye, the airborne radar, that a flight of MiG-17's were positioning for attack, and had run them off toward the Chinese border. The Wild Weasels up ahead radioed the force that three SAM sites were active in the target area just north of the sprawling city of Hanoi.

His adrenaline pumped ever faster as they approached the Lo River, halfway across the Red River Valley.

Bear Force leader, a new lieutenant colonel named Donovan, called from the front of the formation in a cool, businesslike tone, telling the pilots to check their positioning and ensure their music, meaning their jamming, was on. That was the first time Joe noticed that his ECM pod control-indicator lights were alternately flashing between green and amber.

0600L—Senior Officers' VOQ (Visiting Officers' Quarters), Tan Son Nhut Air Base, Saigon, South Vietnam

Colonel Buster Leska

The wake-up call came right on time, yet seemed impossibly early. Buster tossed back the sheet and slid out of bed, still groggy. Although he was conditioned by twenty years of early rising, his days and nights were precisely reversed. Forty-eight hours earlier he'd been halfway around the globe in Washington, D.C.

He stood, stretched mightily to remove the kinks, then began his warm-up exercises, the same ones he'd been taught as a flight cadet in 1947. First the stretches, next the leg lifts, then the bends and toe touches. Thirty of each, done in the fast cadence designed to get a heart pumping and muscles loosened.

Buster remained in good trim for a man of forty-one years. At six three he weighed in at 198, just ten pounds more than he'd carried as a buck captain. He was calm-natured, the way some big men tend to be, and wasn't plagued by self-doubt or a drive to prove his masculinity. He was serious by habit, but couldn't suppress a ready smile when he was pleased, regardless of the somberness of the occasion. A pleasant person, at peace with himself and his place in life.

Leska's neatly cropped hair was shock white, but it was not a result of aging. It had been like that since his mid-twenties when he'd spent seven months in a North Korean prisoner-of-war camp. His captors had known he'd destroyed six of their best fighters, so he'd not been well received. The white hair had appeared during the first weeks of physical and mental torture.

Now there were American pilots in other communist prisons. Buster wondered how they were being treated—he knew it would not be going well for them. He had friends there—too many friends.

Big day today, Buster thought as he finished the warm-ups and stripped off his shorts to step into the shower. If things went right, perhaps he'd help plant the seeds to end a war that had dragged on far too long.

He turned the water to full blast, and as he scrubbed himself, he felt his body coming alive.

0609L—Doumer Highway Overpass (Target Area), Route Pack Six, North Vietnam

Captain Billy Bowes

The first two flights were in their dive-bomb attacks, swooping toward a tiny spot on the ribbon far below. Dark-gray flak bursts blossomed in their midst.

The plan had been to hit quickly, with elements alternately attacking from various clock-positions. Release the 750-pound bombs as high as possible while maintaining accuracy, then wrench the birds around to the north and rejoin over Thud Ridge, the spine of green-clad mountains that pointed to Hanoi like a great finger.

He saw eruptions of dirt and smoke from the first bomb explosions, and from the second. One set was errant, going off in a long string toward and into the Red River. Another bracketed the target, which was fast becoming obscured.

Billy winged over into his forty-five-degree dive attack, then pulled left and let the aiming pipper settle in the vicinity of the target.

The lazy drift of the rising smoke told him there was a gentle wind from the east at ten knots or less. He decided to go direct, to bomb without offsetting to allow for windage. He moved his rudder left and right for a final evasive maneuver, then settled the aircraft and began tracking the target, finger poised on the pickle button.

He was passing through 8,000 feet when it all came together, the sight picture squarely on the intersection of the roads and his gut feeling that he was aiming properly. He held it for a millisecond of final tracking before he pickled and felt a small lurch as the bombs departed. He pulled up ever so slightly for separation from the bombs, then pulled harder, into a nice four-gravity pullout to the north.

A Wild Weasel pilot called a SAM launch from a site in Hanoi, warning the pilots over the target area.

Billy was buffeted a couple of times by flak bursts, but set up an erratic jinking motion while he was still recovering from the dive attack. Finally he rolled the aircraft over on its back and scanned the earth below.

The overpass was covered by too much smoke to tell if his bombs had hit. He looked around and saw first his wingman, then number three, Joe Walker, pulling out and chasing toward him. He looked farther still and saw number four. His flight had made it thus far. A SAM flashed through his view, darting between numbers two and three, then another missile, off to one side at the limit of his peripheral vision. He rolled upright and continued his climb, constantly weaving to foil the enemy gunners.

He eyed the fighters joining to the north, over the ridge, and jinked toward them, then made a wide S-maneuver to slow enough for his men to close the gap. He was within a couple of miles of the formation when the last flight called they were off the target, and that the overpass had indeed been knocked down.

The force commander, a newly arrived lieutenant colonel, gruffly admonished the last flight to hurry and join up, that they'd discuss results on the way out.

Billy came out of afterburner and began to maneuver to the rear of the eight aircraft already in position.

"*Wildcat flight,*" he called. "*Radio check.*"

"*Two!*"

"*Three!*"

"*Four!*"

The chorus had been quickly given, indicating everyone was okay.

"*Double-check your weapons switches, Wildcats,*" Billy called, reminding them, now that the bombs were gone, to set up to fight MiGs.

"*Cut out the chatter, Wildcat lead,*" the new mission commander snapped over the radio. His call sign was Bear Force leader, but he did not give it.

"*Wildcat three's got an intermittent problem with my ECM pod,*" called Joe Walker.

The Wild Weasel flight called a SAM launch at the strike force's five o'clock. Billy scanned back and watched as, one by one, the missiles dropped off their boosters and darted up at them.

"*Keep the SAMs in sight and maneuver at will, Wildcat*

three," called Billy Bowes. If Joe's ECM pod was faulty, the gomer SAM operators might be able to single him out.

"Negative. Hold your position," radioed the mission commander in an angry tone. Before takeoff he'd told them to maintain their position within the sixteen-ship formation . . . period.

The SAMs appeared to track the formation, then zipped by to their right.

Billy breathed easier.

They were approaching 12,000 feet, their prebriefed egress altitude, and Wildcat was closing into place.

They were still vulnerable until the force was joined together.

Billy narrowed his eyes on the RHAW, the radar warning receiver, and the fuzzy grass spiking out in all directions from its center. Interference from their own jamming. Most of the pilots flew with the RHAW audio off, claiming it was a distraction. Billy kept his turned down, but never off. Even if the jamming noise made it less useful, sometimes he could tell when SAMs were launched. Like now, when a squeal sounded in the earphones of his helmet. A powerful strobe lapped at the left edge of the RHAW scope, and the SAM, ACTIVITY, and LAUNCH lights were on and steady.

The Wild Weasels had not called this one, but he had faith that it was real.

"Wildcat lead shows a SAM launch at our nine o'clock," Billy announced, staring out to his left past Joe Walker.

"Maintain formation integrity," snapped the new force commander. *"Let the ECM pods do their work."*

The lieutenant colonel's words were still hanging when Billy saw a SAM, small and incredibly fast, speeding toward them.

Joe had seen it too, for his left wing dipped and the nose of his Thud had begun to come around left, breaking into the SAM, when the missile's warhead exploded in a huge orange flash.

Joe's bird lurched mightily but continued turning. He was reversing to the right as the other two missiles flashed by. He pulled out half a mile below and to the formation's left.

"Wildcat three, Wildcat lead. You okay, buddy?" called Billy.

While there was no response, the Thud was still flying and Billy could see no smoke.

"*Wildcat three . . . ,*" he started again.

He was interrupted by the mission commander. "*This is Bear Force leader. Get into formation, Wildcat three.*"

Jesus, thought Billy. Didn't the colonel realize Joe had been hit? "*Wildcat three's radio's out, Bear lead,*" Billy snapped over the radio. "*He was hit by the missile.*"

Silence answered him. Joe Walker was slowly dropping behind, and Billy thought he saw a slight trail of smoke.

"*Wildcat lead,*" Billy immediately called, "*is descending to join Wildcat three.*"

The mission commander keyed his radio and started to say something, but stopped himself midsentence.

Billy banked and flew out to his left, keeping Joe in sight. He noted that Wildcats two and four joined him. Joe Walker was a good man, and his flight-mates weren't about to desert him.

Again Billy tried to talk to Wildcat three, but there was no response. Sure as hell, he'd lost his radio.

When Billy pulled closer, he saw that Joe's bird was beginning to burn. Red flame trailed along the fuselage. It was hard to spot in the bright sunlight, but if you stared, you could see it.

Joe was leaning forward, concentrating on something inside his cockpit. Finally he looked out, noticed Billy on his right wing, and nodded. He held his fingers up in a zero sign, and Billy wondered if he was trying to signal that he was out of fuel, that he was okay, or that something else was wrong.

Billy made a fist, thumb extended spoutlike, then motioned as if he were drinking from it. It was the query asking for fuel status.

Joe nodded and lifted his gloved hand into view. He extended all five fingers and held them crosswise. Five thousand pounds of fuel. No problem there.

Joe formed the letter *E* with his hand by cupping it into a *C* and extending the forefinger to bisect it, which meant that he'd lost electrical power.

Billy looked up at the larger formation and saw they were continuing outbound at their higher rate of speed. He returned his attention to the problem at hand. The Red River was just ahead, and Billy began to grow hope that Joe might make it that far. If he went down here, on the eastern side of the river, there was little chance for rescue.

"Bear Force lead," he called to the mission commander. *"This is Wildcat lead. Request more fighter escort for Wildcat three down here."*

The response was slow in coming. Finally, *"We're four minutes from the Black River, Wildcat. Once we're across, we'll set up an orbit and wait for you."*

Billy doubted Joe had four minutes. The fire was more apparent, with flames streaming brightly from the starboard side of the fuselage. He stared at Joe, who was watching him intently, pointed at him, then back toward his tail. Joe nodded; he knew he had major problems back there.

"Wildcat lead, four. I see muzzle flashes from the ground a couple of miles ahead."

"Keep it moving around, Wildcats," said Billy. Following Joe Walker's lead, they'd descended through 9,000 feet and were dropping still.

A belch of black smoke puffed from Joe Walker's tailpipe, indicating a compressor stall, which meant that Walker now had problems not only from fire but also with his engine. Joe was still watching him intently, waiting for his signal. The members of the flight had talked about this situation many times. Billy suppressed the urge to tell him to get out now, right now, and to hell with worrying about being rescued.

He sucked an anxious breath as twice more the engine puffed smoke.

Four dark flak bursts exploded ahead of them, then two more clusters appeared off to their left. Close, but not close enough, and they were almost out of gun range.

They crossed the Red River and approached the foothills of the western mountain range. If Joe's bird could make it a little farther, he'd have a chance of rescue.

When Billy moved his eyes back to Joe's ailing bird, the fire had turned a bright blue and was spreading ever closer to the main fuel cell aft of the cockpit. Walker's Thud now left a thick, oily black trail. Joe had only seconds left before it would blow.

They crossed over the first tall ridge of green-clad mountains.

He would wait no longer.

Joe was still watching him closely. Billy pointed a forefinger at him. He nodded.

Billy made a fist, thumb up, then jerked it upward, motioning for him to eject.

Joe immediately pulled his head back against the ejection-seat headrest.

Get out! Billy's mind screamed.

A thruster pushed the canopy up into the airstream, and it was whisked away.

Get out!

The fire blossomed, covering the Thud's entire midsection in a flash-explosion. The nose slewed sideward, but as it did so, there was a sparkle of light and a blur.

Joe's ejection seat?

The Thud torched, burning fiercely, and began to tumble through the sky, scattering scrap metal and parts in its wake.

Billy slid into a hard left turn, followed by the others.

"Wildcat lead, Wildcat two. I think I saw the seat go."

"Weeep! Weeep! Weeep!" wailed the emergency beeper, which came on when a parachute opened.

"Wildcat three is down," called Billy, still in his turn and looking back for the chute. He looked harder, then saw it, small in the distance. Joe was floating down a couple of miles to his east. They'd made it ten miles past the Red River, not nearly far enough to make Billy feel good about Joe's chances for rescue. The gomers responded quickly whenever they saw a bird in trouble.

"I've called for rescue," radioed Bear Force leader, again not giving his call sign.

Billy worried about having a green mission commander when one of his men was down.

"Bear Force leader, Wildcat lead here. Suggest you send two flights back to the tanker to refuel while the rest of us wait here to keep the area clear of gomers."

After a short pause, Bear lead took his suggestion. He ordered two flights to proceed to the KC-135 tankers orbiting over Laos, and said he was on his way to join Wildcat at the rescue scene to take charge.

The beeper was abruptly shut off, although Joe Walker hadn't yet touched down in his parachute. A thrill ran through Billy. Joe was obviously alive and functioning!

Billy descended to 5,000 feet, then called on guard frequency. There was no response.

The chute disappeared into trees.

Two very long minutes passed with no response from Wildcat three.

Finally Joe called. His voice was emotional and he was in pain. He was caught in tree branches, so high up he couldn't see the ground through the foliage.

He also could not move from the waist down.

0645L—Seventh Air Force Headquarters, Tan Son Nhut AB, South Vietnam

Colonel Buster Leska

The driver let him off in front of the headquarters building. Buster passed by two sharp, chrome-helmeted security policemen guarding the approaches to the door, and returned their crisp salutes. Inside he showed his ID at the entry desk.

"The general arrive yet?" he asked.

"Which general, sir?"

"The commander. Lieutenant General Moss."

"No, sir."

A staff officer, ten pounds overweight and wearing military-issue black-rimmed eyeglasses with lenses as thick as Coke-bottle bottoms, approached and showed a security badge to the guard. He peered at Buster, then at his name tag.

"We've been expecting you, sir," he said, smiling. "I'm Lieutenant Colonel Gates, the one you've been talking to on the telephone."

They shook hands.

"Am I still set up to meet with General Moss this morning?"

"Yes, sir. His staff car will arrive at the door at oh-seven-hundred, twelve minutes from now. You can set your watch by it. You've probably just got time for a quick cup of coffee before he arrives. I'll show you the way."

Buster signed for a temporary badge, then followed Gates up to the Seventh Air Force commander's suite.

Gates waved him toward the door. "I'll meet with you after you're through with the general so we can set up transportation for tomorrow morning."

"Thanks."

Gates hurried away.

A fiftyish secretary with improbable red hair busied about Moss's outer office, which was gaudily decorated with fake foliage and artsy, modern paintings. Her back was turned to him as he entered and set down his briefcase.

"Hi, Flo," he said.

She turned, raised an eyebrow, and didn't pause before saying, "You owe me lunch."

He laughed easily.

Flo had been Moss's secretary for the past nine years, following him from one assignment to the next since he'd gotten his first wing commander's job at a fighter base in North Carolina. Buster had been a buck captain then. Each time Leska was promoted a notch, she claimed responsibility and demanded he take her to lunch. He held Flo in a bit of awe, for she ran her outer office like a not especially benevolent tyrant. She kept the keys to the gate and decided who should or should not enter. She was very capable, could simultaneously handle several telephone calls and hosts of visitors, and was the only living human known to be able to keep the cantankerous Moss in his place. Flo took no crap from anyone and unabashedly played favorites. Fortunately, Buster was one of those.

"How is Carolyn?" she asked. She had an elephantine memory when she wanted to exercise it, amnesia when she did not.

"She's fine. Decided to stay in the Washington area while I'm here. We bought a place in Bethesda."

"Mmmm."

"She told me to say hi. You remember our son?"

"Marcus. No father should give such a name to such a nice-looking boy." She arched an eyebrow. "I suppose it's better than Silvester, though."

Buster winced. His given names were Silvester and Tomas, and he cringed at the sounds of them. There'd been grade-school fistfights before he'd established that his name was Buster.

"Mark's not a boy any longer. He's in college. Columbia

University. Wants to be a fighter pilot. I couldn't get him into the Academy." He did not say it was because of mediocre grades. "But he wants to try for his commission as soon as he gets his degree."

She served him coffee laced with one sugar, no cream, as he liked it.

"Lunch," she repeated, pointedly lifting an eyebrow. "After you've done your business with the general, I want to hear all about how things are going for you and your family." She called Moss "the general" regardless of whom she was speaking to, as if he were the only general of any consequence in the world.

"Yes, ma'am."

"So you're finally getting command of a wing."

He smiled.

"I liked it better when we knew you were safely tucked away in Washington," she fussed. "When I heard you'd volunteered to come over here, I could hardly believe it. The general worked hard to get that Pentagon job for you, Buster."

Since Buster was one of Flo's favorites, she felt duty bound to complain when he got out of line. She pointed at a bright-hued, cubist nightmare painting. Flo carted the awful art from one assignment to the next and would tolerate no criticism. "Straighten that, would you?"

He did.

"Major Phillips went to Takhli too, you know," Flo said. Glenn Phillips was likely Flo's favorite of the favorites. He was one of the youngest and certainly the best looking of their group—drove around in a flashy Corvette and dazzled the ladies—had feminine hearts pitter-pattering from Scandinavia to Tokyo. When Phillips had been on the Thunderbird demonstration team, he'd once shown up at Nellis Air Force Base squiring a rising movie starlet, and took her to the Caesar's Palace gourmet room for dinner with Flo—whom he'd introduced as his other girlfriend—General Moss, and two other members of Moss's mafia and their wives. While the ladies asked the starlet about life in Hollywood and the men all secretively ogled her, Flo had sat through the meal with a jaundiced eye, ignoring the conversation. Later she pronounced the girl entirely too shallow for

Glenn. Flo looked out for her flock before indulging in any frivolities.

"Yes, ma'am," Buster said.

"He was shot down, you know."

"Two more months, and it'll be a year. At least Hanoi's listed Glenn as a prisoner of war. There's a lot of questions on some of the others."

"The communists released photos of Major Phillips being paraded through the streets of Hanoi," she said. "He looked very pained and emaciated." Her mouth was taut as she stared at the picture he'd straightened and gave a terse nod of approval. "You watch yourself, Buster. Entirely too many men at Takhli are being lost."

"Yes, ma'am."

The door opened and Moss strode in, followed closely by a colonel who was briefing him on the fly about the night's activities. Moss glanced at Buster and curtly nodded his greeting, as if he didn't know him, then motioned at his door, still listening to the colonel.

Buster followed them into Moss's private office, remaining unobtrusive as the colonel finished.

"Keep me posted," Moss growled, and the colonel turned to leave.

"Close the door," Moss muttered. The colonel did so.

Moss stood quietly, eyeing Buster with a neutral look.

"Good to see you, General." They'd known one another since the early days in Korea, when they'd flown Twin Mustangs, Moss as squadron commander, Buster a lieutenant wingman.

"Just couldn't stay out of it, could you?" said Moss.

Buster grinned. "No, sir."

"I get you the best colonel's job in the Air Force, and you volunteer to go to the asshole of the world. You ever been to Takhli?"

"Never even been to Thailand, General."

"Only place on earth it can rain buckets for two hours, then half an hour later blow up a hellacious dust storm."

"I've heard they fight well at Takhli."

Flo quietly came in and placed a cup of coffee on Moss's massive desk.

"Anything on my schedule this morning?" Moss asked her.

"Nothing until nine, as you wanted."

"What then?"

"You go to MAC-V for General Westmoreland's meeting."

"Get me out of it." Moss rolled his eyes at Buster. "Boring as hell. They talk about body counts, bomb tonnage, and percentages of population affected by pacification programs. Everything's numbers. No one talks about how to win the war."

Flo's mouth tightened. "I told General Westmoreland's executive officer that you'd be there. You missed the last two meetings."

Moss glared but she stood her ground. Finally he sighed. Knowing she'd won, Flo quietly left the room. Moss waved Buster toward a chair.

"How's Gentleman Jim?" Moss asked. Gentleman Jim was General McManus, Chief of Staff of the Air Force. Buster had worked at his right hand at the Pentagon, in the job Moss had pulled strings to get him into.

"The chief's got a bad heart. It's worrisome to his staff, but he keeps charging along."

"He's got a thankless job," Moss muttered. "The politicians still ignoring him?" General McManus, even more than the other service chiefs, was overlooked by the President and the SecDef L.B.J. viewed himself as an expert on aerial warfare and felt he needed no outside advice. He and a small circle of cronies prioritized targets in North Vietnam, established restrictions, and authorized certain of them to be destroyed, without asking for military opinion.

Buster made himself comfortable. "That's one reason I'm here, sir. General McManus wanted me to brief you face-to-face on a matter he feels is important."

"He called and said you'd need a couple of hours."

"The chief's concerned about the way the war's going."

"The air war?"

"The whole thing. He feels it's getting more screwed up with every passing day. He's a strong believer that America should never have become involved in a land war here."

Moss snorted. "Now there's an original thought."

"General Westmoreland is traveling to Washington next month to wave the flag. The chief thinks he'll ask for more troops."

Moss looked surprised. "More troops? Jesus, he's already got half a million here."

"General McManus believes he'll ask for between one hundred fifty and two hundred thousand more."

Moss thought, then slowly nodded his head. "Maybe so. Westy likes big numbers."

"The chief wants to know if you could force the issue over here with air power alone."

"Sure we can. I told him that last time we were together."

"He says the timing was wrong last time you talked."

Moss glowered. "*Politically* wrong, he told me at the time."

"He also wants to know if it can be done without expanding ROLLING THUNDER." ROLLING THUNDER was the OPlan for the bombing campaign in North Vietnam.

"You mean can we win with air power here in South Vietnam and not change anything about what we're doing up north?" asked Moss.

"Yes, sir. The President keeps a stranglehold on air activity over North Vietnam. It's his private show. Every time the chief makes a suggestion about bombing more vigorously up there, he's told to shut up and sit down."

"It doesn't matter what the President or anyone else thinks. North Vietnam is the key. No matter what you read, Hanoi's running the entire show. The NVA regular troops, the Viet Cong irregulars—they're all controlled by politicians and military coordinators sent from up north. All major decisions for both the NVA and Viet Cong come from party leaders in Hanoi."

Buster sipped his coffee and listened.

"A few months ago I briefed Gentleman Jim that we can still kick their asses by systematically bombing Hanoi and Haiphong, like the guys who wrote the ROLLING THUNDER OPlan meant to do in the first place. The original planners said we should hit the enemy relentlessly, around the clock, and not let up until we'd destroyed their infrastructure. It would have been a piece of cake two years ago. Every week that passes, the defenses get tougher, and we'll take more losses doing it."

"Then you feel there's no way to win the war here in the South?"

"Not with air power. Here it's a ground show. Westy uses us as artillery. Mainly close air support and beating up jungle trails." Moss stood and walked over to a wall map, and tapped his forefinger on the red splotch of ink at the top. "Hanoi's the key. The only key. We're fighting two wars, Buster. An unconventional ground-and-air war here and a conventional air war up north, and we're fighting both of them wrong."

0720L—Route Pack Five, North Vietnam

First Lieutenant Joe Walker

Coming down in the chute, he'd been aware that something was badly wrong with his legs. That had been big problem number one. Second had been the fact that there'd been no good place to land. All he'd seen on the way down were trees, very tall teak trees, and they'd extended in every direction except to the east. Since he didn't dare steer the chute toward the dense population of the Red River Valley, he'd had no option but to go down in dense forest.

He knew to hold his knees and feet tightly together and assume a crouching position when he went into treetops, but when he'd tried, his legs wouldn't respond. When he'd finally descended, he was whipped and battered by limber branches, his chute hung up, and he was slammed hard into a tree trunk.

The chute slipped, then caught even more firmly, and again he was battered against the trunk. When the pain from his legs finally began to course through him, he almost passed out.

A previous flight commander had told them all that if they found themselves in a situation like this, as soon as they got on the ground, they should pick a direction and run like hell, putting several miles between themselves and where the gomers saw them go down. Joe Walker, the fastest man ever to play football for the Air Force Falcons, could not even have crawled if he'd been on the ground, and he was not on the ground.

Waves of excruciating pain enveloped him, and he

shrieked, then gritted his teeth together to stop the noise. His teeth chattered from the effort.

It eased finally and he fumbled, retrieved a survival radio from his vest, and called for Wildcat lead. When Billy Bowes responded, he told him of his situation.

Another minute passed, and Bear Force leader radioed and asked about his condition, and he repeated his litany.

The pain swept over him again, and he whimpered over the air, not caring that the pilots up there might hear.

Bear Force leader asked if he could see any unfriendlies in the area. Joe repeated that he could not see the ground, that he was caught in the treetops.

Wildcat lead came back on the air. Billy Bowes asked if he had his tree kit with him.

A few weeks earlier they'd been provided with a thin nylon rope and a pulley assembly, to be carried in a pouch sewn to their vests. Some of the pilots had refused it for the sake of saving weight. But Joe had not, and he wondered why he hadn't remembered it.

Use it, Wildcat lead urged, to lower yourself.

Joe began fumbling at the Velcro tape securing the pouch and, doing so, dropped the hand-held radio and heard it crashing through the branches below. He panicked before remembering there was a backup radio in the vest and another in the survival kit dangling below him on a tether. Finally he pulled the rope out and began lacing it through a parachute harness ring, wishing he'd watched closer when they'd demonstrated how to use the kit. When he thought he had it right, he gave the rig a couple of tugs. It held. He cautiously opened first one parachute release, then the other, and immediately began to slip and fall.

Damn!

He held on to the rope for dear life, dropping several feet, catching, dropping again, with the rope slipping through his gloved hands before his hold became effective, and again he was swinging and being battered against the tree trunk. He held on with all his dwindling might, rope burns smarting his palms. He banged again into the tree and screamed from the excruciating pain.

After hanging stationary for a full minute, he began to play out the line cautiously, ignoring the searing sensation from his hands, dropping in jerks and starts. After fifteen minutes of lowering, he could see the ground for the first time, and the dizzying height made him catch his breath. He was still more than fifty feet up the tree and knew there was not nearly enough rope to make it to the ground.

He heard a buzzing, mosquito sound grow closer. Engine noise from a propeller-driven aircraft. He tied the rope carefully, so he'd be held in position, and pulled out the second radio.

Sandy lead, the A-1H pilot who was the first of the rescue team to arrive at a scene, was calling on emergency guard frequency.

After answering appropriate personal questions to establish that it was indeed First Lieutenant Joe Walker on the other end of the radio, he was told to continue to lower himself.

Sandy lead sounded nervous. They were not far from the hot area, and the quaver in his voice was warranted. Sandy told him the choppers were holding only twenty minutes' flying time away, waiting for authorization to proceed. He advised Joe to lower himself to the ground while they waited.

Joe told him the rope wasn't going to reach.

Sandy grew quiet at that revelation. Since there was no way they could rescue him from halfway up a teak tree, Joe said he'd somehow get the rest of the way down.

0749L—Seventh Air Force Headquarters

Colonel Buster Leska

Over the intercom General Moss asked Flo to call in Lieutenant Colonel Gates, the staff officer who had escorted Buster to the office.

"We can talk freely in front of Pearly," Moss said. "He's my out-of-country expert—stays in touch with the Thailand units and keeps me up to speed on the air war up north."

They'd been talking about the possibility of an air campaign to force the North Vietnamese out of the war, but no matter where Buster tried to lead the conversation, Moss kept returning to the key—Hanoi.

Gates rapped at the door and hesitantly poked his head inside.

"Come on in," Moss snapped. He'd grown increasingly annoyed about Buster's reluctance to understand that the quickest way to end the war was through massive bombardment of targets in and around Hanoi.

Gates started to take a seat to one side of the room, but Moss waved him up beside Buster. "Anything new happening, Pearly?" Moss asked.

"PACAF headquarters ordered increased surveillance of Phuc Yen airfield."

Moss glanced at Buster. "That's their biggest MiG base. We've requested permission to bomb the damned place a dozen times since I got here last year, but each time it's been denied. Maybe PACAF knows something we don't. Think they're going to finally turn us loose, Pearly?"

"I queried PACAF on scrambler phone, but they're not saying. They just say to comply with the message, which directs two photo flights a day over Phuc Yen."

"Anything else?"

"Preliminary results of the morning alpha strikes are in."

Moss eyed him. "And . . . ?"

"They radioed a success code on both targets."

Moss turned to Buster. "We sent forty Thuds and eighteen Phantoms to bomb a dinky highway overpass and a bridge we've knocked down twice before. Both targets were passed down from the executive branch. Both will be repaired within a day or two. That's what's wrong with the war up there. We keep playing games."

"I thought you requested the bridges campaign."

"Sure I did. And it was like pulling teeth trying to get it approved. But if you're talking about winning this thing, about *really* hurting the North Vietnamese and making them rethink what they're doing, we're going to have to do a hell of a lot more."

Buster reflected on what he'd been told. Thus far it had gone as General McManus had predicted.

Moss turned to Pearly Gates. "Losses?"

"An F-4 from Ubon northeast of Hanoi, and a Thud from Takhli to the west. They're trying to get the Thud pilot out, but they're worried about the location, which is only fifteen miles from the Red River."

"A goddam highway overpass," Moss muttered. "And believe it or not, that's a better target than we get most of the time."

Buster was still thinking about the loss of the Takhli bird. "Pearly, Colonel Leska's on a mission from the Chief of Staff. Gentleman Jim wants to know if we can force the North Vietnamese to withdraw their troops by using air power."

The lieutenant colonel grew a happy look of anticipation. "But he wants to know how we'd do it only here in South Vietnam."

Gates's smile faded. He slowly removed his glasses, pulled a cloth from his shirt pocket, and methodically began to polish the lenses. It was not a rude reaction, just a prop to allow himself to think things out. Others might light a pipe.

"I told him there's no way," Moss added, frowning at the thickness of the lenses.

"Hanoi," Pearly Gates said in an even, deliberate tone, "has been the key to Tonkin Vietnam for centuries. It's the center of their culture. The Chinese understood that, and nothing had changed a hundred years ago when the French arrived. Only after Governor General Doumer set up business in Hanoi did the French finally control Indochina."

"Paul Doumer," said Moss, parading his knowledge, "was the guy who showed the French how to plunder Indochina."

Pearly Gates judiciously nodded agreement. "The Japanese invaded in World War II and centered their activities in Saigon, but when Ho Chi Minh took over after the war, he immediately changed the capital back to Hanoi. And when he whipped the French in 1954, Hanoi became his home base as well as the center of the Lao Dong party nervous system. Threaten Hanoi, and you threaten the Lao Dong party. Eliminate the Lao Dong, and you've removed the communist threat to Indochina."

"Our purpose is limited," reasoned Buster. "We want the North Vietnamese to withdraw their troops and support from South Vietnam and Laos, nothing more."

Gates carefully placed his glasses on his nose and blinked. "The key's still Hanoi. If we threaten its destruction, they'll realize they're about to lose everything they've fought so hard for for the past thirty years."

"There's no other way?"

Pearly Gates shook his head without hesitation. "Hanoi's the head of the beast."

"If we bombed there, it would mean killing civilians."

"Most civilians were forced to leave the city proper over a year ago. Hanoi's a military fortress. But, yes, civilians would be killed. It's something to be considered."

"Foreign nationals?"

There are the embassies and two hotels where foreign visitors stay, and we should avoid them. But there are also military advisors, and that's something we'd have to deal with. There would be foreign casualties."

Moss casually waved a hand at Pearly to interrupt. "We're going to have to settle something right now, Buster. Unless we act like we're at war, *nothing* will succeed. That's what's gotten us to this sorry state of affairs, acting like we're not really at war, like all we're after is an agreement between gentlemen. The communists are not gentlemen out to bring better government to the Vietnamese people. They're after domination and control. We've either got to take off the kid gloves and duke it out, or keep hemorrhaging soldiers, sailors, and pilots in a halfway war. If Gentleman Jim wants us to come up with a plan to win, he's got to realize two things. One, it will take heavy bombardment of the Hanoi area. Two, it will involve loss of not-so-innocent lives."

Buster glanced at his watch. It was 0757. Three more minutes. That would provide the hour he'd promised General McManus he'd spend with option one.

"As I told you before, Buster, there are two distinct wars going on. One's the guerrilla war in Laos and here in South Vietnam. That's the one the reporters follow, where the beleaguered, yet honorable and brave Viet Cong are slipping about in the jungle fighting the bullying Americans and the slothful Vietnamese."

Richard Moss had never liked politicians or reporters, but the description he'd just given was one increasingly parroted by a growing number of newspapers and congressmen in the States.

Moss shook his head sadly. "Honorable? Brave? Last week I was taken to a hamlet the Viet Cong had visited the previous night. They'd butchered the headman because he'd accepted supplies from the Saigon government, then they cut off his children's hands so they could never bear arms against them."

Buster winced.

"MAC-V invited the press out to the village, but they didn't want to go, because they said it was contrived by the military establishment and they were onto a hot story. Know what the reporters were excited about? They'd found a couple of South Vietnamese colonels with American air conditioners in their offices and sent in reports about the corruption of the ARVN."

Moss stared at him. "But that's down here in the South. Here our fighters and the B-52's are used to bomb supplies and troop concentrations and provide close air support for our troops. We do a damn good job of it when we can find them, but that's not an easy task. All they shoot at us with are small arms and the occasional thirty-seven-millimeter gun. Up north it's a different ball game altogether. Give him a rundown on North Vietnamese defenses, Pearly."

Gates nodded. "There's a total of about ninety MiGs, counting MiG-17's and . . ."

Buster waved his hand. It was time to drop the facade. "I received briefings on the defenses at the Pentagon, so I've got a good idea of what they've got."

Moss brought home one last point. "North Vietnam has become one hell of an armed camp, with hundreds of SAMs and guns backed up by MiGs. About three fourths of all that's concentrated in one area—Hanoi—and it's well coordinated. Does that tell you something about how much they prize the place?"

Buster slowly stood and walked to the map, studying it closely, then turned and shifted his vision from one man to the other. "I promised General McManus that I'd spend my first hour trying to find another way. He figured you'd tell me what you just did, but he wanted to know if there were any possible alternatives."

Moss glowered. He didn't like games, such as the one Buster had just tried. "Go on," he muttered.

"The chief listened hard when you gave him your JACK-POT briefing and told him we could force the North Vietnamese out of the war with appropriate bombing. As I said, he's concerned about the way the war is getting out of hand,

and he agrees that the best way to do it is through an all-out bombing campaign. His problem is convincing the President. Let me rephrase that. His *first* problem is *getting* to the President, and *then* it's convincing him."

Moss listened, lips pursed.

"There's a certain supporter of an intensified aerial campaign on the executive staff, whom the chief wishes to remain unnamed. Let it suffice to say he's in a position that should allow him to get General McManus in to see the President. But for this thing to work, he'll need your support. As soon as you contact him that we've had this meeting and tell him you're on board, he'll send a note through his contact to the President, asking for a private meeting."

Moss chuckled out loud. "Hot damn. Didn't know Gentleman Jim had it in him. Thought he was too busy trying to get himself appointed chairman of the Joint Chiefs to make waves."

"He realizes there's a chance his career will be terminated as soon as the SecDef finds out what he's doing. A few months ago he had aspirations of being named chairman during the spring shuffle, but the heart attack changed his perspective."

"So he's willing to throw himself on his sword."

Buster raised an eyebrow. "There's something he wanted me to pass on, sir. In private."

"Go ahead. Pearly can keep a secret."

"General McManus said to tell you he's going to nominate you as commander of Tactical Air Command in April, during the shuffle. If he's relieved of his position, that appointment would also go by the wayside. So, as he said, it's not only *his* aspirations at stake."

Moss was quieted. TAC was commanded by a full four-star general, and the post was the ultimate goal of all fighter-pilot generals. The Air Force Chief of Staff job was the private fiefdom of bomber pilots like McManus, had been since the inception of the Air Force. TAC was the coveted top job for a fighter pilot. But Moss had been feuding with "Bomber Joe" Roman, his four-star boss at PACAF headquarters, since he'd taken over at Seventh Air Force, and it was unlikely he'd even dreamed he might be considered for the TAC position.

"I . . . uh . . . thought Gentleman Jim was close with General Roman," he said awkwardly, "and . . . Commander of TAC?" It was out of character for Moss to stumble on words.

"General McManus wants everything we're discussing to be held in confidence, *especially* from General Roman."

Moss peered at him. "I thought they were buddies. Both being bomber pilots and all, I thought . . ." His voice trailed off.

"General Roman has repeatedly stated his support of the SecDef's suggestions, all of them, including the one to cut back the ROLLING THUNDER campaign. He's done so in several memoranda circumventing General McManus. He's very obviously shooting for the chief's job."

Moss's face clouded.

After a short silence Buster continued. "The chief wanted to make sure we considered alternatives first. There being none, and he couldn't come up with any either, by the way, he wants you to formalize your JACKPOT plan for the bombardment of Hanoi and Haiphong. He wants it to be a complete OPlan, with force structure, targets, timing, projected losses, and an addendum that shows costs. He'd like it done in a timely manner. He wants you to include everything it will take to win. His people will polish it on the other end."

Moss slowly nodded.

"He suggests that you include B-52's in the OPlan."

Moss frowned. A superior officer's "suggestion" was tantamount to a direct order. "I was told by General Roman that the bombers aren't to be jeopardized, that they're a limited resource."

"The chief said a few people might oppose their use, but he emphasized that they be part of the picture."

Pearly Gates's mouth curled as a smile threatened to surface. Moss turned to him.

"You had some kind of straw-man plan you put together using a composite force of bombers and fighters. What did you call it?"

"Total Forces Utilization, sir."

"That's the one."

"You had me take out the B-52's. That's when we changed the code name to JACKPOT."

"Well, put 'em back in," Roman growled.

"As you said, it was only a skeleton plan, sir."

Buster interrupted. "The chief wants us to call this whole

scenario JACKPOT, same as the briefing you presented. He'll be setting up back-channel message routines and asks for you to do the same here."

"Back-channel" meant messages sent for the addressees' eyes only, with no copies going to anyone else and only minimal records kept. Back-channel traffic was used by senior officers when they wished to communicate covertly and off the record.

"Can I ... ah ... keep Colonel Gates in the loop?"

"The chief's using a small group of assistants, people he knows he can trust, to help on his end, so I'm sure that would be fine. He'd also appreciate it if you gave him the names of key people in the tactical-fighter business back in the States who he can rely upon. He wants to make sure we've tested and examined every possible detail of the campaign."

Moss remained thoughtful. "JACKPOT," he murmured.

"Yes, sir. He wants all messages to be coded that way. He's set up his end of the comm net, and they'll be looking for the word 'JACKPOT'."

Moss got up and gathered the other two in front of the wall map, and they began to discuss what it might take, studying the areas, pointing at this feature or that, talking strategies and tactics.

Flo buzzed on the intercom to announce that the general should prepare for his meeting at MAC-V.

Moss growled that he was busy with an important matter.

Moss said that he'd put Pearly to work on the project immediately and would recommend contacts at various fighter bases both here and in the States—people they could trust implicitly, as Gentleman Jim said—to make observations and inputs while Pearly worked on the plan.

"Strategic Air Command will be involved too," Buster reminded him.

"I can talk their language," said Pearly Gates. "Who's their project officer?"

"A full bull named Wesley Snider will liaise between here and Offutt. He's got a solid background in plans, and before that he flew B-29's, B-47's, and B-52's. I met him when I spent my year in the exchange program. General McManus trusts him and says you can too."

"From bombers." Moss's eyebrows were furrowed, as if it

were difficult to think of a bomber pilot he could possibly trust.

"I flew with Wes Snider at Barksdale," said Pearly Gates. "He's a smart officer, General."

"Flew with him?" Moss seemed to remember something about Pearly he'd forgotten. As if he'd been reared by apes and only recently civilized. "In B-52's?"

"Yes, sir. Colonel Snider's a good man."

"Okay," Moss muttered reluctantly, as if giving in to a demand to allow the enemy access to vital secrets.

"Then you're aboard?" asked Buster.

"Damned right. It's the first ray of light I've seen out of Washington since I got here."

"I'll provide any support I can from the trenches, General."

"We'll need to maintain a good picture about what's happening up north. Keep your eyes open when you get to Takhli, Buster. Share any insights you run across."

"Will do, sir."

"You'll have a group of good guys working for you. One of them was shot down, and now he's off on R and R, recuperating." He emphasized his next words. "I *suggest* that he be assigned as one of your squadron commanders."

"Yes, sir." The "suggestion" was noted.

"His name's Lucky Anderson."

Buster brightened. "I met him once. The guy with no face?"

"He was burned in a bent-wing F-84 accident a few years back. He's a hell of a fighter pilot and has a good head on his shoulders. I trust him, like I trust you and the other members of my mafia." Moss peered narrowly. "He'd be a lot of help on something like this."

"There's another young pilot at Takhli I want on my team. We'll send a weekly message, if that sounds appropriate."

"When does Gentleman Jim want his first message from me?" Moss asked.

"ASAP. He'd also like a couple of names. He picked Wes Snider to coordinate between here, the Pentagon, and SAC. He wants you to pick the liaison for the tactical side. Someone already stationed in the States."

"I'll give him two. Gordie White's the two-star running

the Fighter Weapons Center at Nellis, and he's got Benny Lewis working for him. Those are two of the best. That way he'll have the test ranges at Nellis at his disposal to try out any new tactics he wants to use."

Buster knew both men and agreed. "As soon as he gets your message, the chief's going to send out his initial message to the small band of players; then he'll try to set up the first meeting with the President."

"How many in this small band?"

"Pearly here and the two in the States bring it to twenty-three, I believe."

"Why so few? This is going to have to be a very big effort."

"There are a lot of wolves around who'd love to scuttle what the chief will be trying to sell, and there've been entirely too many leaks recently. He says you can add people as required, but to send in the names and make damn sure they're reliable."

Moss mused for a moment. "I'm concerned that we're going out of the chain, straight from a numbered air force commander to the top. We're not only bypassing General Roman, but also Admiral Ryder at CINCPAC."

"Only at first. They'll all be briefed at the appropriate time."

"What's Gentleman Jim waiting for?"

"He feels there's no plan until we get a positive reaction from the President."

"Another problem we'll face is streamlining command-and-control on a big effort like we're talking about. At present it's fragmented. Approval comes from the top, authorizing the strikes, then CINCPAC sends target lists to both us and the Seventh Fleet. The Navy plans their thing and we plan ours, and the coordination is terrible. That's a definite concern." Richard Moss grew quiet in his introspection, trying to think of more problem areas.

"General McManus will ask you to forward all of those within the next few days, but first he simply wants to know whether you're aboard."

Moss turned to Pearly Gates. "Go down to the comm center and get out that first message. Tell him I'm aboard without reservation, and give him the two names I mentioned for liaison officers. And while you're there, set up the back-channel procedure. Anything coded JACKPOT is for my eyes only, and only you or I can pick them up."

Lieutenant Colonel Gates prepared to leave.

"And, Pearly, I want you to bring me back the only copy of the message. I'll keep the file in this office. I don't want another kept *anywhere*, understand?"

"Yes, sir." Gates hurried out, quietly closing the door behind him.

Moss eyed Buster. "If Gentleman Jim can pull it off at his end, we're going to save a hell of a lot of lives, Buster."

"We'll lose aircrews over Hanoi in the air raids, General."

"Fewer than if this thing keeps dragging out. There's been no end in sight." Moss continued to stare steadily. It was an old habit of his, to pin a person with his gaze when he spoke. Buster had picked it up and sometimes found himself doing the same with subordinates. Moss's voice softened. "You always were a damned good wingman. Looks like you did well for Gentleman Jim. This is fine work, Buster."

"Thank General McManus, sir."

Moss chuckled. "Oh, I do, I do. But it's funny, him changing his mind about the idea shortly after you were named to his office."

"All I did was answer the questions I could and give advice when he asked for it, like a proper staff officer."

Moss had trouble couching his next words. "When you get to Takhli and start flying?"

"Yes, sir?"

"Watch your ass."

Flo opened the door without knocking, a stiff and determined look on her face. "Your car's waiting at the front entrance."

Moss sighed, then rose and warmly shook Buster's hand. "Flo's got your day set up. First you get a tour of the control center and they'll go over the air tasking routine, then . . ."

"General!" Flo admonished.

Moss retrieved his hat. "Dinner tonight at my quarters. We'll play a set of . . ."

"I'll let the colonel know his schedule," Flo snapped, her jaw set.

Moss gave Buster a helpless smile and departed.

0850L—Route Pack Five, North Vietnam

First Lieutenant Joe Walker

The agony came and left in ever-intensifying waves.

Both legs were dangling uselessly, and he was at the end of the nylon line he'd threaded through the parachute harness rings. If the rope had been just ten feet longer, his boots would have touched the ground. He hung there, biting his lip apprehensively every time he thought about the fall that must come.

The prop-driven A-1H Sandy buzzed in the distance, the pilot unwilling, this near the Red River Valley, to venture closer for long.

"How you doing down there, Wildcat three?" his hand-held rescue radio crackled with the now familiar voice of the Sandy leader.

Joe's voice was low and monotone. *"No change, Sandy lead. I can't lower myself any farther."*

The Sandy pilot had advised him to cut the rope with his survival knife. He said the Jolly Green helicopter's pararescue corpsman, called a PJ, wouldn't be able to get to him if he remained in the tree.

But Joe knew that after he dropped onto his injured legs, he would surely pass out from the pain. He said he'd cut himself down as soon as he saw the whites of a corpsman's eyes.

"Wildcat three, this is Sandy lead. You hear the chopper yet?"

Joe listened, endured a wave of pain, then croaked, *"Yeah, I hear it."*

"Change to button Charlie on your survival radio and check in. If you get no radio contact, come back to me on this frequency."

"Roger," he muttered through gritted teeth. Sweat ran profusely down Joe's face as he endured another agonizing wave. He moaned low, for he couldn't stand it. This time it was longer before the pain subsided.

He huffed a few breaths, then looked closely and selected *C* on the survival radio's leftmost rotary switch.

"Sandy lead," he uttered with a gasp, *"this is Wildcat three."*

A cheerful voice joined him. *"This is Jolly Green four-one. Reading you loud and clear, Wildcat three. You ready to get outa there?"*

"Yes, sir," he moaned, hurting again.

"Wildcat three, select tone on the right wafer switch on your radio and press the transmitter button for one minute. Then I want you to change back to voice and call me again."

"Ah roger, four-one."

He did as he'd been told, holding down fiercely on the transmitter switch. As he did so, the chopper approached, hovering overhead, the downwash of the rotor blades making the tree limbs thrash wildly. The chopper moved, but the engine and rotor noise remained loud as it hovered close by.

. . . fifty-seven, fifty-eight, fifty-nine, sixty, he counted to himself.

He heard the crackle of a radio . . . not his . . . and looked around down below.

A man in jungle fatigues and blackface approached cautiously, talking into his radio, looking up and scanning around the tree branches.

"Here," Joe croaked to get his attention.

The PJ found him. "You gotta come down, Lieutenant, 'cause I got no way of getting up there."

Joe Walker fumbled in the g-suit pocket for his survival knife, then opened the blade and began to saw on the nylon cord.

He did not pass out when he fell to the ground, both feet crumpling beneath him at unnatural angles. The pain was so intense that he couldn't stop screaming and sobbing.

The PJ sergeant scooped him up in a fireman's carry and hurried through the forest. They quickly arrived at a small clearing over which the chopper hovered.

Joe Walker continued to blubber with the awful pain as the pickup device was lowered, and as they were reeled upward together into the open doorway. They pulled him inside and the chopper ducked and the engine screamed defiantly as they sped westward toward safety.

As they secured him to a canvas litter, Joe heard the medic tell others to take care because both legs were badly fractured. He felt the pinprick of a needle jabbed into his arm, and then the warm sensation of something entering his system.

The pain began to subside.

At least for a while, First Lieutenant Joe Walker's war was over.

CHAPTER TWO

Thursday, October 19th, 1225 Local—Base Operations, Takhli Royal Thai AFB, Thailand

Colonel Buster Leska

The meticulously polished and maintained silver-and-white T-39, the executive jet normally reserved for General Moss's use, was taxied to a spot directly in front of base operations. As the pilot shut down the left engine, Buster stared balefully out the porthole window at the banner draped across the front of the mustard-yellow control-tower building.

WELCOME TO TAKHLI, PRIDE OF PACAF, COL SILVESTER T. LESKA

A colonel stood in front of base ops, staring at the aircraft and idly tapping his hand-held radio against his pants leg. After a closer look Buster confirmed him to be B. J. Parker, the man he was replacing. They'd met a few times before, but he didn't really know him. Pearly Gates had given him his impression, and at dinner General Moss had told him some, but it had been Flo, the general's secretary, who'd given him the snapshot judgment of B. J. Parker that

was easiest to remember. He has a little man's complex,
she'd said, that has nothing to do with his size. Something
inside Parker drove him to impress upon others that he was
one of the big boys.

Moss had said that Parker's reputation was mixed, that
he'd never really made up his mind about him. He was an
adequate manager of men, but too obvious in his zeal to
make general. Most of his superior officers thought well
enough of him, but many peers and subordinates were less
impressed. On the whole, though, not a bad leader. The
people he commanded delivered results. The 355th Tactical
Fighter Wing, which Parker had led for the past year, was
known as a unit that could be trusted to get the job done.
Moss often used them for the toughest missions, against the
meanest targets. Not long before, for instance, after numerous tries by various units, a pilot from Takhli had been first
to knock down a span of the heavily defended Doumer
Bridge in downtown Hanoi. That was just one in a long line
of achievements. Certainly a can-do outfit, but the 355th
also suffered higher losses than other units.

So what did all of that tell Buster? He'd better learn
B.J.'s secret to success, then cut the losses. *Would that be
possible?* he wondered.

There were two junior officers and an NCO on the aircraft with Buster, hitching rides back to Takhli from Saigon,
and he waited until they'd deplaned before hefting his bag
and moving toward the door.

A sergeant poked his head inside. "Help you with that,
Colonel?"

"Careful, there's breakables inside." He referred to the
bottle of Chivas Regal, placed there by Carolyn, who knew
how to pack a fighter jock's bags.

The sergeant took the B-4 bag and stood out of Buster's
way so he could get out and down the steps. When he was
on firm ground, he saluted Parker. B.J. was still wingco,
which made him the man in charge and the ranking colonel
on base, regardless of dates of rank.

Parker returned the salute and smiled as he stepped forward to grasp his hand. "Good to have you aboard, Colonel."

"Buster. Call me Buster," Leska said, eyeing the banner.

"I remembered"—Parker smiled—"but General Moss
called last night and said he wanted it like that. Something

about keeping you in your place. We'd already put one up reading S. T. 'Buster' Leska, so the guys had to take it down and make a new one."

Buster grimaced. Moss had a strange sense of humor. "It worked. I'm in my place. Now do me a favor and have them take it down, okay?"

Parker called over a colonel he introduced as the base commander and told him to remove the banner.

"Better get a move on, Mike," he told him brusquely. "Colonel Leska's been known to get downright mean when his people don't listen up, and as of tomorrow your ass belongs to him."

Leska frowned. Although Parker was joking, Buster treated subordinates differently.

"How about a ride around the base?" asked Parker. "Show you what you're stuck with."

"I'd like that," said Buster as Parker led him toward a waiting staff car.

The staff sergeant had placed his B-4 bag in the back of a pickup and was giving instructions to an airman. B.J. gestured. "He'll take it to your temporary quarters. I've got you set up in the trailer next door until they've got my things out of the commander's trailer. Tomorrow it's yours."

"Long as there's a bed of some description, I'll be grateful. My body thinks it's the middle of the night."

"Takes a week to acclimatize."

The sergeant returned from the pickup to open B.J.'s door, then hurried around to get Buster's. They waited in the backseat of the air-conditioned Ford sedan as he slipped into the driver's seat and turned to B.J. for instructions.

The base tour took two hours, for they stopped at every construction site, and there were a dozen building and paving projects under way. Parker showed him two new barracks for the enlisted men, then those for noncommissioned officers, staff officers, and finally the windowless sixteen-man quarters for company-grade combat pilots.

"They call 'em Ponderosas, like on the television show."

"How come?" asked Buster.

Parker opened his mouth to answer, then furrowed his brow. "Got me," he finally answered.

"Where do the field-grade officers live?" he asked.

"In trailers adjacent to the Officers' Club," responded Parker, still pondering the previous question.

"How about the WAFs?" asked Buster.

"We've got no suitable facilities on base for women. It's an all-male society. Except, of course, for Thai women who work on base."

"What do the guys do for entertainment?"

"There's the bowling alley, recreation center, and base theater I showed you, all new. Then there's a new service club for the airmen, and of course the officers and NCO clubs."

"Female companionship?"

"The town of Ta Khli's only a couple miles from the main gate. They pronounce it as two distinct words like that. It was a sleepy little place before we got here. Now the west side's been turned into a sin city with a couple dozen cheap clubs, bathhouses, and such, and a bunch of farm girls eager to earn the family fortune. Our flight surgeons check 'em for diseases and issue the girls cards to show they're clean."

"You have any trouble with the people there?" Less than desirable entrepreneurs were drawn like magnets to military installations to prey on service men.

Parker shrugged. "Once in a while a club owner gets uncooperative. That's when you take it to the Thai base commander, and he straightens it out. Usually sends 'em packing back to Bangkok."

"Thai base commander?"

"We're a tenant unit, Buster. Takhli's a real, no-shit Royal Thai Air Force Base. They built the original runway back during the Second World War. They were on the Japanese side, by the way. Flew Zeros out of here to attack our transports flying the Burma Hump. When it became apparent the Japanese were losing and started to pull out, they switched loyalties."

"I'll be damned."

"The Thais fly a squadron of F-86's located on the other side of the base. Not a bad organization, but they have to work like hell to keep the old birds flying."

"They get along okay with our guys?"

"One thing you'll find about Thailand, the people here really like Americans. Very different culture, but they think we're okay and they treat us with respect. They know that if we leave without finishing the job, the communists are going to end up next door in Laos and Cambodia and cause a lot of trouble. There are already bands of communist terrorists—they call them CTs—operating in some areas of Thailand. Not many around here, thank God."

Buster nodded.

"Tonight we're having dinner with the Thai base commander, if that's all right with you. Thought you should get to know him right away."

"Sounds like the thing to do." Buster had wanted to spend the evening talking with a longtime friend, Mack MacLendon, who was stationed here. Now he'd have to delay it until after dinner, which he'd leave a little early.

"Watch out for the Thai base commander."

"Oh?"

"He's got four daughters by his number-one wife, and a couple more by his number two. Buddhists are polygamous, you know. Anyway, so far he's only gotten one daughter married off. His goal is to get them all happily wed, and American airmen are considered good catches."

They completed their look at the base by slow-driving the perimeter of the flight line. First Parker showed him row upon row of sleek F-105 Thunderchiefs.

"We've got eighty birds assigned right now. Seventy-one D-models for the strike pilots, and nine two-seat F-models for the Wild Weasels. Got two shipments flown in from the States last week. Since they shut down the production line at the locomotive factory, Thuds are becoming a limited resource, Buster. We've lost two hundred and fifty in combat so far. We keep taking losses like that, we're going to run out of airplanes."

That was true. The Thunderchiefs in Europe had been replaced by F-4's and shipped to the war zone. Besides the ones at the Thai bases at Takhli and Korat, there were only those at the training bases in Kansas and Nevada, and the few in the logistics-and-repair facilities.

"A hell of a lot of fine pilots have been lost," murmured B. J. Parker. "The month I got here, a single squadron lost twenty-four aircraft." He stared out the window with an expression that Buster could not readily identify as sadness, guilt, or nostalgia. Perhaps it was a mixture of all three.

He gave him his moment before asking another question. "How's the morale?"

"The crew chiefs and most of the support people reflect the attitudes of the combat pilots, and I'd guess you'd say their feelings are mixed. They're pros, so they'll keep flying and fighting as long as they're told to. The biggest problem is they can't see an end to it. They fly up there and see the good targets, but they're not allowed to bomb them. They watch MiGs taxi out at Phuc Yen and can't attack them. Instead they're sent to penny-ante targets in the middle of the world's toughest defenses. If they get shot down, they don't know if they'll ever get out of prison, so when they're hit, they try like hell to make it back far enough to have a chance of being rescued."

B. J. Parker stared at the F-105's without expression. "Considering all that, how's their morale?"

"Like I said, they're pros. They want to get on with it, go out and kick ass and win, but if they're told to shut up and keep bleeding on two-bit targets, they will."

"How many quitters?"

"Three in the year I've been here. One during the raids on the Thai Nguyen steel mill, one during the bridges campaign, and another with a questionable medical problem. Two were experienced fighter jocks, and one was a retread from SAC. Every time it's a surprise. A guy'll be a tiger one day, and the next he'll refuse to fly."

"Three's not bad."

"No. We had as many or more in World War II and Korea."

They drove by the tanker operation. Ten KC-135's were assigned to refuel the fighters on tracks designated by colors, such as green, orange, and red anchor routes. Parker explained there were also brown and tan routes, located out over the Gulf of Tonkin, mostly used by the F-4's flying to North Vietnam out of Danang.

They were across the base now, and Buster viewed the Thai F-86F Sabres with a smile.

"I've got eleven hundred hours in those," he said, "including ninety and a half missions out of Osan in 1953." The half mission was the one on which he'd lost his engine and been forced to bail out over hostile territory.

"I was at the Koon," said Parker, meaning Kunsan Air Base in South Korea, "in F-84's."

A Thai pilot was at one of the Sabre's boarding ladders, reading over a form on a clipboard as he prepared for flight. He erupted into a heated argument with a maintenance man and ended the discussion by raising the clipboard and chasing him around the aircraft, swinging it at him and shouting.

Buster and Parker both chuckled.

The pilot began pointing at the aircraft, jabbing his finger and screaming, and the maintenance man was scurrying frantically about to do his bidding.

"Like to try that with one of our crusty old line chiefs?" asked Parker.

"No way," said Buster, and he saw the staff-sergeant driver grinning to himself.

"What's over there?" asked Buster, pointing at a motley collection of C-123's and C-130's.

"C-123's are Air America. C-130's are Bird and Son Company. CIA contractors. They do their covert thing. Their operation's controlled by MAC-SOG, which is directly under MAC-V, another name for Westmoreland's bunch. They also get inputs from the spooks at the various embassies. They're supposed to work with our Special Operations, Army Special Forces, and the Navy SEALs on their unconventional wars, but from what I hear, they're pretty independent. They've got their own hierarchies and lines of support and generally keep to themselves, but they can do good work when it comes to helping get a downed pilot out of Laos, things like that."

"I'll keep that in mind."

"The Air America people also maintain and keep Channel Ninety-seven on the air. That's a TACAN navigation station on the border between Laos and North Vietnam. We use it for a checkpoint and to update our Doppler nav equipment when we go up to pack six." B.J. drew back and looked at Buster. "You know about the different route packs?"

"We were briefed on them daily at the Pentagon. Pack one's at the southern extremity of North Vietnam, along the DMZ, and they keep going up in number until you get to pack six at the northeast end. Pack six is getting a reputation among the pilots. Good place to avoid, they say."

"Hanoi and Haiphong are both in route pack six. That's

the real badlands. Never been anything like it, Buster. I saw flak over Germany and Korea, but nothing like you'll see here. We can handle triple-A if we keep jinking and fly above the majority of the stuff. The MiGs are tough, but they're also manageable. Then you add the SAMs, which they've got by the bushel. Things come at you fast, and the SAM operators are damned good. We're briefed the gomers are better operators than the Soviets, and that makes sense because they get a lot of practice."

"Gomers?"

"That's what the guys call the enemy."

"Like we called the North Koreans slopes and gooks."

"Something like that. Doesn't mean anything ethnic, just a name for the bad guys. Anyway, individually we can handle everything the gomers shoot at us, but when you put it all together, you've got SAMs when you fly up high and AAA when you get down low, and MiGs trying to do their thing everywhere in between, and it gets damned hairy. Our losses have dropped since last spring, because we're learning. I just hope we learn enough before . . ." Parker grew silent again, slipping into the odd reverie.

"Who owns the big hangar over there?" Buster pointed.

"More of the spook operation. Every few days a U-2 lands and they park 'em in there to keep 'em out of sight."

B.J. directed the driver to return to his office.

"I've got a few guys waiting to give you a rundown on combat operations. You up to it?"

"Sure." Buster was determined to stay awake until the normal bedtime and not give in to his body's confused clock.

When they arrived at the wing commander's office, they were greeted by a burly chief master sergeant who gave Parker a rundown on what had happened during his absence. The briefers were waiting for them, he said.

Buster looked about the outer office, which was sterile and militarily correct, and made up his mind about something. He'd give civilian personnel at Seventh Air Force a call and see if they couldn't help rectify the male-only situation. Perhaps Lieutenant Colonel Pearly Gates could help raise the priority to send a few female secretaries their way.

When they entered the briefing room adjacent to the commander's office, a group of waiting officers sprang to attention.

The first speaker was Major Max Foley, the lanky, scarecrow wing weapons officer. Foley's credentials were complete. Before coming to Takhli he'd been an instructor at the elite Fighter Weapons School at Nellis, and after he'd arrived, he'd killed two MiGs. He'd already been awarded a Silver Star Medal, and Parker said he'd been put in for a second.

Buster knew Max Foley relatively well. He, like Leska and several others, was a member of the group who called themselves Moss's mafia. They could call upon one another, discuss sensitive matters, and gain support when the going got tough on a worthwhile project. General Moss kept track of them all and tried to help out in their promotions and assignments. Max was known as the brashest among the group.

"I'll need your expertise, Max," Buster said at the start of the presentation.

"Sorry to let you down, Colonel, but I'm flying my hundredth mission tomorrow."

"Good for you. Where are you being reassigned?"

"Fighter ops at TAC headquarters."

"You'll like Langley Air Force Base and the area. Nice place to live."

"My wife's from Virginia. She's pawing the dirt to get back home."

Parker motioned restlessly. "Go ahead with your briefing, Max. We've got a lot to tell the colonel and not much time to do it."

Foley gave a pitch about their standard combat munitions loads, the formations they flew, and the tactics they used. Buster listened intently, keen to pick up every possible nugget. He had Max go over the SAM evasive maneuver several times, to make sure he had it down.

When Foley was finished and started to leave the room to make room for the next briefer, Buster held him back. "What's the biggest problem you see flying up there? By that I mean something we should be working on."

Foley didn't hesitate. "Our radio chatter. We've got the worst radio discipline in the world when we get up there. We brief the guys repeatedly about staying off the air unless it's necessary, and about using clear and concise words, but when the shooting begins and the SAMs start flying and they start to see bogeys, the guys chatter like magpies. I find myself doing it. Somehow we've got to change that."

"Anything else?"

"Getting the guys over the twenty-mission hump."

Buster was puzzled.

"Fifty percent of our losses are new guys, and I don't mean low-time pilots or guys who haven't been in combat. I mean the pilots who don't know *this* kind of combat. By the time they've flown twenty missions, they've generally learned the ropes. They know how to jink, how to spot SAMs and judge their distance, how to bomb a target, all of that, because they've done it."

"So what's the answer?"

"Same as the solution to the radio-discipline problem. We're giving 'em the wrong kind of training before they arrive. We've got to improve things so they won't come here as cannon fodder."

Max Foley was in high gear, obviously angry.

"We're not fighting World War II or Korea. We're not even fighting the same war we were six months ago, because the threat keeps changing. Somehow we've got to prepare them."

Parker remained silent through the harangue, and Buster let it soak in.

Major Foley started to leave, but again Buster held him up. "I'm going to need a tactics expert to replace you as weapons officer. Someone who can take what you've learned and work with it. Do you have any suggestions?"

Max thought on that for a moment. "There's Major Lucky Anderson. He's damned good."

B.J. interrupted. "Not Lucky. General Moss wants him to take over a squadron when he gets back from Hawaii."

Buster smiled. "He made that suggestion to me too."

Max was still looking at Buster. "Does my replacement have to be a major?"

"I don't care if he's a colonel or a second lieutenant. If he's good, I want him in charge of tactics."

"We've got several pilots here who graduated from the fighter-weapons school. Most of them would be good. There's one guy who helped me on a few projects here before he got into some legal trouble."

"The Supersonic Wetback?" asked Buster.

Max did a double take. "Yes, sir. You know him?"

"I knew Captain DeVera in Europe. He was one of our instructors at the gunnery base in Libya."

Foley glanced at B. J. Parker and hesitated before continuing. "Manny DeVera is damned good with weapons and tactics, and he's a hard worker."

Parker cleared his throat and nodded his approval. "Captain DeVera would likely do a good job. You . . . ah . . . know about the hot water he was in? Being charged with bombing the wrong target and sent to the Philippines for court-martial?"

"It was a daily topic at the Pentagon."

Parker's lips became tightly pursed. "He's been cleared of all charges and should arrive back here at Takhli in the next day or two. I'll tell you about that incident later."

There was something in the way B.J. said it that told Buster he wasn't proud of the way he'd handled the Manny DeVera incident. It made him curious.

"Thanks, Max," said Buster, and Foley gathered his notes and left. Replacing him was a jovial-looking officer wearing a class-B uniform with no wings. "I'm Captain Boye, sir, and I'll give a short rundown on weather conditions here and in the North Vietnam target areas."

"Smiley Boye," said B.J., "is our weather magician."

The captain displayed a wide grin, explaining the nickname. "Weather on the subcontinent consists of two seasons, both driven by the Asian monsoon wind phenomenon. During the summer monsoon, from April to October, we get hot weather and heavy rain coming up from equatorial regions to our southwest. During the winter, which we're about to enter, the monsoon wind does a one-eighty and comes down from the northeast, and it gets drier and cools off a few degrees. . . ." He continued his canned spiel.

After the briefings were completed and it was just the two of them, Buster asked Parker about the support he'd received from higher headquarters.

B.J. said he'd had no problems with that aspect. Then, too cautiously, Parker asked if he knew General Roman, the four-star who commanded PACAF.

Buster said he did not, that he'd heard about him but had never met the man.

Parker said General Roman was interested in the fighter

operations at the Thailand bases. "Calls us fucking cowboys," he added gingerly. Then he grew silent, and Buster knew he would say no more about superior officers.

Before they left the now-quiet briefing room, Parker told him about a full colonel named Tom Lyons who'd been shuffled off on him by General Moss.

Moss had already warned him about Lyons, but Buster listened politely.

B.J., cautiously indignant, said Lyons had fabricated evidence that Captain DeVera had bombed a restricted target. "The man is amoral," he said darkly.

Buster knew Lyons. He'd run across him in other assignments. He was from an obscenely wealthy and politically powerful family, and on previous occasions only his father's interference had saved him from disgrace. That same political clout was the only reason Buster could think of to explain his rapid rise to colonel.

"What're your plans for him?" he asked.

Parker's face clouded. "I'd like to court-martial the bastard for lying, but he covered his tracks too well, and the PACAF judge advocate general's office told me to cool it. I've got him working for Mike Hough, the American base commander in a job just as demeaning as I could make it— hoping to hell he'd get the message and retire. But I dunno. I think he's working something behind our backs. Yesterday we got a message from PACAF asking if he's excess and available for reassignment. I put my neck out and answered that Lyons is filling a critical position in charge of an important project."

"Anything we can do to get him out of the Air Force?"

"If there is, I can't think of anything. I asked him to resign, but he just gave me a fish-eye look and said no. I gave him a rock-bottom efficiency report, but the man came out and told my personnel shop he's been able to have others like it eliminated from the system. If he swings the reassignment, you'll be passing on a bad apple to someone else, but I'm not sure you can stop it."

Then Parker told Buster the rest of the story, how Tom Lyons carried grudges for certain pilots and enlisted men and connived to get even. There'd doubtlessly been other losers, but his primary victim at Takhli had been Captain Manny DeVera, the Supersonic Wetback.

"This is likely going to ruin Manny's career," B.J. concluded. "Too many people will remember he was almost brought to court-martial, and few will care that he was exonerated."

"Maybe I can help," said Buster.

Parker droned on, as if he hadn't heard. "The war the guys are fighting should be enough. The restrictions, the crummy flying weather, the god-awful threat." Again B. J. Parker was staring at something in the distance that Buster could not imagine.

1645L—Vietnamese People's Army Headquarters, Hanoi, Democratic Republic of Vietnam

Colonel Xuan Nha

The colonel in charge of North Vietnam's sophisticated defenses was a short and compact man who displayed a placid demeanor despite his maimed body. His face was scarred, accentuated by a small, sharp nose and a patch covering his empty right eye socket. His left arm had been severed at the elbow. Both the eye and the missing limb were casualties of a Mee air attack, when they'd bombed and strafed the guided-rocket command van he'd been in.

A hero of the great Viet Minh victory at Dien Bien Phu during the War of Liberation, Colonel Xuan Nha was also a highly decorated hero of the ongoing War of Unification. He was regarded as the man most knowledgeable about the technical systems provided by their Soviet allies. He'd studied them and knew them—knew the circuits, every electron tube, switch, spark gap, and resistor. He knew rocket fuels, both solid and liquid, their burn rates, and the attack trajectories they provided. He'd learned to position rocket and artillery batteries to gain the greatest advantage. He knew the long-range radars, and how the controllers must coordinate their information to the interceptor pilots and rocket-firing batteries. Xuan Nha was responsible for the tools and methods that integrated the air defense system and was extremely good at his job.

He stood at the rear of the Hanoi command center, slightly hunched over, for the effects of the Mee bombing still plagued his body. Six months earlier the doctors had not believed he would live, let alone return to duty. But Xuan Nha had a tenacious spirit and ignored their pessimism . . . and proved them wrong.

During his recovery he'd performed his important job from a room in the sprawling Bach Mai Hospital, under the watchful eye of a medical team; but that would change. Tomorrow he'd move back into his home and only periodically visit the hospital. Today Xuan Nha had wished to visit the headquarters and view the current situation from the command center. It was time to return to full life and breathe fire into the defenses.

His protégé, Lieutenant Colonel Tran Van Ngo, was with him, as was his communications officer, Senior Lieutenant Quang Hanh. They were not subservient in his presence, as most senior officers demanded. In the past they'd worked together like a finely tuned machine, Xuan Nha leading and they carrying out his orders. Colonel Nha demanded results and successes, and they strove to provide him with those.

"Would you also like to see your office?" asked Lieutenant Colonel Van Ngo.

Xuan Nha thought of the walk to the upper floor and replied in a rasping voice, which was also a result of his injuries. "I cannot get up the stairs." He despised mentioning such weaknesses.

Quang Hanh, with a baby's face that betrayed his youth, spoke proudly. "We have moved our offices to the first floor. The intelligence people were not so willing to leave at first, but General Luc suggested they reconsider." He smiled. "I have set up my radios and telephones in a room adjacent to your new office."

"Very good," croaked Xuan Nha.

"Would you care to see it, comrade Colonel?" Quang Hanh limped toward the door. He had been caught in the same attack as Xuan Nha, his leg badly mangled.

"One moment." Xuan pointed at a new aircraft track being drawn on a glass plotting board, superimposed over a wall map of the Democratic Republic. The track paralleled the Hong Song, the great river that ran through the northern sector of Hanoi. "What is that?" he rasped.

A nearby captain turned his head. "It is a Mee recon-

naissance Phantom, comrade Colonel. This is the third one
overflying that area in two days."

"Phuc Yen?" muttered Xuan Nha. The air base located
only twenty kilometers north of them was restricted from air
attack by the Mee politicians. Was it about to be targeted?
He thought about that, then *almost* rejected the idea. Normally the Mee were not so obvious. The reconnaissance
Phantoms had new side-looking sensors and could observe a
target from some distance. So unless they were looking for
something specific and needed great camera resolution, why
would they fly directly over the base?

Puzzling.

"Let me know," he croaked, "if they return there."

"Yes, comrade Colonel," the captain said obediently.
They were accustomed to following Xuan Nha's dictates in
the command center. Although he'd been away for several
months, it was as if he'd never left.

General Tho, the two-star commandant of the People's
Army Air Force, entered the command center and immediately came over to greet him.

"Welcome back, Xuan Nha." He eyed Xuan's painful,
bent posture. "Are you well enough to be standing?"

"It is such a pleasure to be out of the hospital that I will
endure it. It is so grim there that you wish to heal quickly."

"Sit. There will be no formalities until you are well, my
friend."

My friend? General Tho and his officers of the VPAAF
had always maintained judicious distance from officers of
the VPAND.

"Thank you, comrade General." Xuan Nha grimaced
painfully as he cautiously took a seat behind a scarred
wooden table.

General Tho flicked his wrist at others in the area, indicating he wished to speak privately. They moved away
quickly, leaving the two alone at the back of the large room.

Tho lowered his voice. "I attended a meeting of the general staff yesterday, and your name was mentioned. They
spoke about your being released from the hospital."

Xuan Nha waited. Discussion of one's name was not always desirous.

"General Luc is not well," said Tho.

"I had not heard," Xuan replied. Luc was the one-star

general, Xuan Nha's immediate superior, who commanded the Vietnamese People's Army of National Defense. The VPAND included the guided rockets, antiaircraft and antishipping artillery, and the vast home-defense militia. They and General Tho's Air Force were assigned the task of protecting the Republic.

"Few know about it. He became very ill yesterday morning, and the doctors at Bach Mai are still examining him. He has had stomach problems in the past, but nothing so severe as this. He was vomiting blood."

Xuan nodded, withholding expression.

"General Dung asked about a replacement. He wishes for you to attend the general staff meetings in Luc's behalf until he is well. There are important matters about to be discussed. Even I do not know the subject—it is that sensitive. I told the general that I would approach you and see if you would be able to attend."

General Van Tien Dung was second within the People's Army only to General Giap, the Minister of Defense. Xuan Nha responded without hesitation. "I would be honored to attend, comrade General."

"But are you able? Sometimes we must sit for hours, and your condition may not allow it."

"The Mee bombs and bullets hurt me badly in many places, comrade General, but they did not affect the muscles of my buttocks. If I am not required to stand for long periods, there will be no problem."

"It is your thoughts we must have, Xuan Nha. I will advise General Dung immediately of the soundness of both your buttocks and your mind."

They smiled together.

Xuan Nha gestured at the plotting board. "We have been discussing the Mee reconnaissance flights."

General Tho stared at the board. "I was told the Mee were showing interest in that area, but that it also may be a bridge they are looking at."

"Possibly they are preparing to attack Phuc Yen airfield, as they did Kien An last month."

Tho nodded. "Perhaps. We have heard nothing yet from intelligence. They are normally reliable in such matters."

"Who commands the air regiment at Phuc Yen?" asked Xuan Nha.

It was a sensitive question. The previous commandant, a legendary fighter pilot and Hero of the Republic named Quon, had been accused of negligence to duty. He'd disappeared, as if from the face of the earth. In such matters one didn't question the wisdom of the Lao Dong party, nor was it wise to discuss the wrongdoer's name. But Quon was married to General Tho's cousin, daughter of the powerful politician Le Duc Tho. It was unlikely he'd remain in disgrace for long.

General Tho cleared his throat. One walked cautiously when discussing party matters. "I have assigned a *temporary* commandant to the air regiment."

The carefully couched words confirmed that Quon might not be gone much longer. Xuan Nha smiled, wordlessly conveying that he was happy the general's relative might soon return.

General Tho again said he was happy to see him up and about, added that Xuan would be advised of the time of the next general staff meeting, and departed.

Xuan Nha mused as he stared at the doorway. He decided it would be judicious to spend the remainder of the day in his new office, going over the various dispositions of his forces. He was pleased to be selected to attend the high-level meetings and didn't wish General Luc an especially rapid recovery.

CHAPTER THREE

Captain Manny DeVera

The Band of the Pacific, the group of Air Force musicians
based in Hawaii who played at various functions throughout
the command, struck up a single chorus of "Ruffles and
Flourishes," then, after a short pause, launched into the "Air
Force Hymn."

Captain Manny DeVera watched and listened. The band
was good, accenting the lively tune with cymbal clashes and
booming bass drums. But Manny was in no mood to be
roused.

He'd arrived at Takhli an hour earlier, from the Philippines where he'd been sent for court-martial for bombing a
restricted target. Even though all charges had been
dropped, he felt betrayed. It was embarrassing that anyone
could think so lowly of him to believe he'd lie. Not that he
thought they shouldn't be bombing more meaningful targets.
Of course they should be. But to think they believed he
could look a fellow officer in the eye and lie about anything
at all was demeaning. It would be difficult to forget the ex-

perience, impossible to think well of the colonels who had believed he was guilty even after he'd told them differently.

When he'd gotten off the C-130 and heard about the change-of-command ceremony to be conducted outside base ops, he'd decided to hold off checking back onto base, a procedure about as pleasant as getting teeth drilled by Dr. Payne. It hadn't been hard to delay going to personnel and waiting in line until some airman was kind enough to let you fill out a hundred forms, then take a checklist around to every minor office on base and get it signed and initialed as you dropped off various of your voluminous records, then go to the squadron, where you'd be assigned at the bottom of the list for a room, the best of which were already taken. It seemed unfair to have to repeat the procedure he'd completed when he'd first arrived at Takhli.

So he'd decided to procrastinate and watch, with a sense of perverse satisfaction, as Colonel B. J. Parker was replaced. He'd known the outgoing wing commander and the new one about equally well and had once thought highly of them both. No more. He could never again think well of B. J. Parker, for the colonel had been the one to prefer charges. He'd told Manny about pressure he'd received from the four-star at PACAF headquarters, but no matter what he said, he was the one who'd signed the papers saying that Manny DeVera was a liar.

Since he'd been betrayed by Parker, he was reluctant to think Buster Leska would be any better. Fuck 'em both. He'd be content to be left alone to lick his wounds and quietly fly out the remainder of his hundred-mission tour as Blue four. Blue four was what they called the most obscure fighter jock in a flight of fighters. Number four was the least experienced, least responsible, and often most ignored position.

He glared at the ceremonial platform as Colonel Parker raised his eyes to watch a four-ship flyby. Manny lifted his head and also stared. The F-105Ds were in a tight diamond formation. As they passed the end of the runway, the Thuds pulled up to perform a bomb burst. Number two was too quick with his pull-away, spoiling the symmetry, but they generally looked good. Only the fighter jocks watching would be critical.

Manny lowered his eyes and caught Colonel Buster

Leska looking at him, having somehow picked him from the crowd. After a moment's hesitation Manny lifted a hand and made an "okay" circle with his thumb and forefinger. It was one of those automatic things he sometimes did without thinking, and he instantly regretted it, even though Leska smiled and nodded.

B.J. started to speak, stopped when the amplifier squealed and a technician hurried to fix the problem, then told the gathering about how it had been an honor to lead "the great 355th Tactical Fighter Wing," and how he'd never forget how the men from Takhli had served with courage and dedication. Then he talked about passing the baton of command.

A clean Thud, returning from a combat mission and devoid of bombs and fuel tanks, streaked down the runway so low and fast the noise was ear-shattering. The pilot pulled into a slight climb, performed a crisply executed eight-point victory roll, followed by a second, and the gathered crowd began to cheer.

It had to be Max Foley's hundredth mission, thought Manny; he was the only one in the wing with two MiG kills. He found himself wanting to yell with the others, but the sad feeling, the lump in his stomach, kept him from participating. Foley turned and came back around for another flyby, this time at 2,000 feet, and tapped his afterburner as he approached. *Uh oh!* Manny clapped his hands over his ears just as Foley's bird went supersonic and the wave swept over the base with a tremendous boom. The tower swayed and nearby buildings shuddered.

"There goes the booze at the club," lamented a pilot. Every time someone fucked up by going supersonic near the field, windows were broken, but the jocks and crew chiefs didn't give a damn about that. They mourned the liquor bottles and glasses that fell from perches at the O' Club and NCO Club stag bars, and the fact that another pilot was now in deep shit.

B.J. glared at the sky, then turned to Colonel Leska with an apology, which was unintentionally transmitted over the PA system. Leska said to forget it, and that was also amplified. Parker finished his speech, unable to suppress his anger at being upstaged. He did not pause or look up again as flights from the morning combat missions began arriving home.

When it was Leska's turn, he told the group that he was happy to be there, freed from the musty bowels of the Pentagon. He told them he expected good work from everyone because it had to be a team effort. He said loyalty was a two-way street, and if they gave theirs, they could expect his in return. Finally he said he'd buy a round for everyone at the NCO and Officers' clubs, and that brought a *real* round of cheers.

As Leska stepped away from the mike, Manny saw his eyes light on him again.

He remembered Buster Leska from Europe. He'd been a lieutenant colonel on the staff at the headquarters at Wiesbaden, Germany, and paid several visits to the gunnery base in North Africa where DeVera had been assigned. He'd seen no pretension in the tall pilot, only a dogged dedication to duty, and they'd found agreement in most things they'd discussed. He'd worked with Leska on several weapons projects and spent a couple of evenings drinking with him at the rowdy Wheelus Officers' Club bar. He'd even shared his insights and complaints about overly cautious rules governing flying training in Europe. Manny remembered that he'd been outspoken, as he often was, and that Leska had listened closely. He wondered if he remembered and was holding a grudge. His recent experience with Parker made him wary of colonels he'd once admired.

As the group dissipated and Manny walked toward base ops where he'd left his bags, a staff sergeant hurried to his side. "Captain DeVera?"

Manny returned his salute. "Help you?"

"Colonel Leska would like to see you in his office after the ceremony, sir."

Shit, Manny thought. "I just got in, Sarge. I've still gotta sign on base."

"He asked that you meet him there as soon as he sees Colonel Parker off."

"Goddam it!" Manny exploded. He wanted it to be over, to be left alone!

The sergeant drew back nervously. "He asked me to tell you, sir. I'm just . . ."

Manny sighed. "Not your fault, Sarge. I'll be there."

As the staff sergeant disappeared into the crowd, Manny watched the two colonels, Buster Leska and B. J. Parker, standing and talking together. A shiny T-39 Sabreliner was parked in front of base ops, probably waiting until all the combat aircraft had landed so it could take Parker to Bangkok or wherever he was going. Manny DeVera wondered what kind of shit he was in with Leska. Probably something Parker had passed on. He'd likely tell Manny that he knew what he'd done, and not to step out of line again. He decided to say yes sir and bear it. *Fuck 'em all.*

He left his bags at base ops after asking a sergeant there to look after them, then walked down a newly paved sidewalk toward the wing commander's office.

When he'd departed two weeks earlier, there'd been several of the old boardwalks left, but now it looked as if they were trying to pave the entire base. New parking lots were scattered here and there, and concrete sidewalks, some of them still roped off so they could dry in the high humidity, made it look almost like a stateside base. No more walking the boardwalks and watching snakes slither underneath.

At the wing commander's office, the chief master sergeant in charge of admin asked him his business, and Manny said he was waiting for the new commander. The chief said the colonel would be busy with meetings scheduled with the various deputy commanders all day, but Manny said he'd wait anyway. He settled into a chair in a corner and read a dog-eared copy of *Airman* magazine. A few minutes later he watched as several full colonels arrived, got their cups of coffee, and gathered into a group not far from Manny to discuss their new boss.

Not many knew Leska. The Deputy for Maintenance said they'd attended the same class at the Air War College in Alabama, but he hadn't really gotten to know him. The base civil engineer said Leska was an ace, that he'd shot down six MiGs in Korea. Since then he'd been serving mainly in various headquarters. The Deputy for Logistics said he came from some kind of job on the JCS staff in the Pentagon. The Deputy for Operations said Leska had only recently been checked out in Phantoms and then in Thuds. He'd seen his records and confirmed that he had six kills in Korea. He had 2,000 flying hours in fighters, both prop and jet. But, he added meaningfully, he'd amassed a lot of hours flying support aircraft, which confirmed that he'd spent a bunch of time in staff jobs, and . . . his Form 5 showed a few hundred hours in BUFs. By that he meant "big ugly fuckers," bombers assigned to Strategic Air Command. That silenced the group and made them thoughtful. Anyone who'd flown bombers had served in an altogether different world.

Colonel Leska came in before the deputies could discuss that interesting point. Manny noted he was now carrying the portable radio Parker had brandished half an hour earlier. To commanders, changing radios was like passing a royal mantle. Colonel Leska was now Eagle One, call sign of the man in charge.

Leska stopped short and looked about impassively at the gathered colonels. "I feel overwhelmed," he finally said, his tone friendly. "You guys got nothing better to do?"

The vice commander spoke for the group. "Colonel Parker liked to meet with us as soon as he returned from a trip, so we thought . . ."

Leska interrupted, his jaw now set firmly. "Don't try to second-guess me, okay? I want to talk with you, I'll call. I set my own agendas."

The colonels stared awkwardly, suddenly ill at ease.

"I'll come around and visit each of you in the next couple of days, and you can tell me what you do and how you do it. I like stand-up staff meetings every Monday and Thursday, and that's when we'll get together and talk business. You'll all get a memo outlining all that this afternoon. Now, any of you have pressing problems that require my *immediate* attention?"

After a moment of silence the civil engineer spoke up. "We've got a question about siting the new gym, and Colonel Parker said he wanted to be briefed on it. The ground is unfirm and the soil samples show . . ."

"Hold it!" Leska turned to Colonel Hough, the diminutive base commander. "*Your* problem, Mike. *You* solve it." He glanced about again. "Any others?"

Hough cautiously cleared his throat. "There's considerable damage from Major Foley's flyby. Broken windows and such. The estimates are just starting to come in, but . . ."

Leska nodded toward the Deputy for Operations. "Apologize to the base commander because your guy screwed up. Then call Foley in and chew his ass. Tell him about all the grief he's put you through and all the damages, then threaten him with article fifteen punishment. Soon as you're done with that, I'd like to see both you and Foley here in my office."

"Yes, sir." The DO hurried toward the door as if happy to escape, pulling his blue cunt cap squarely into position.

The rest of them stood about awkwardly.

"We've got a lot of work in front of us. You're big boys. You handle your business, and as long as you do your best, I'll be satisfied. That way we'll get along fine, and maybe we can even get the job done. But don't waste my time with minutiae and bullshit, okay?"

Before anyone could answer, Leska motioned toward Manny. "Let's go into my office." He nodded to the staff sergeant clerk typist standing beside the chief master sergeant. "I like my coffee with one sugar, no cream. Captain DeVera?"

Manny started. "Sir?"

"How do you like your coffee? We may be in there for a while."

As the colonels silently filed out, glancing back at the two of them, it was apparent to all that Colonel S. T. "Buster" Leska had taken command. Manny trailed after Leska toward his inner office and realized he really didn't know this guy. He prepared himself mentally, grimly wondering what kind of bad news he was about to receive.

1015L

The discussion was not at all what Manny had anticipated. As soon as the door closed, Leska dropped all trappings of rank. He shook his hand warmly and said it was great to see a familiar face—someone he *knew* he could trust to help him get his new job done. Next he chatted about how he'd gone from Europe to SAC, of all places, in a program some idiot in the Pentagon had come up with to place pilots with fighter experience in bombers. He said he'd been like a fish out of water when they'd checked him out in B-52's. But, he said, he had to admit he'd found out what it was like on the other side of the fence and had grown a new respect for BUFs and Strategic Air Command.

After six months in bombers he'd been selected for colonel and sent to the Air War College at Maxwell Air Force Base. When he finished, he'd been sent to the Pentagon. He wasn't sure, he joked, which was worse duty for a fighter jock, bombers or the five-sided circus. For the first twenty minutes Manny hardly had a chance to talk, because Buster Leska carried the conversation. Then he asked where Manny had gone since he'd seen him last.

Manny told how he'd extended for another tour at Wheelus AFB, Libya, and had set up the new tactics range that he and Leska had discussed during the colonel's last visit there.

Leska gathered his eyebrows quizzically. "When are you up for major, Manny?"

Manny DeVera wondered where the conversation was leading. "Two more years, sir."

Leska stared for a moment, then dropped his bombshell. He wanted Manny to replace Max Foley as wing weapons officer. He said he'd normally follow the chain of command and let the decision come from the Deputy for Operations, but he'd wanted to make this particular call himself so he'd know he'd have someone he knew and trusted in the sensitive job.

Manny went through a period of slack-jawed silence, then of trying to compose himself. He nodded periodically, stupefied, not adding much to the conversation because he didn't know how to respond except with words that sounded like mundane horseshit. Leska charged Manny with the task of coming up with new ways to minimize losses while destroying the targets directed by higher headquarters as efficiently as possible. He told him to keep the Deputy for Operations and the squadron commanders filled in on what was going on with those efforts, but not to allow them or the system to interfere with his judgment.

"Manny," said the colonel, "everything else that goes on here—building new facilities, maintaining morale, feeding the troops, keeping the supplies coming in on schedule, maintaining the airplanes, the running of the organization—none of it means a damn if we're not flying and fighting to the best of our potential. I consider what you'll be doing as one of the most important assignments I'm going to give out in the next few days."

DeVera remained dumbfounded. Everything had been turning to shit, what with the official charges and the bleak trip to the Philippines. His outlook had been so bad for so long that he hardly dared to believe what he was hearing. A couple of days before there'd been doubts, official doubts, about his integrity. Now he was being entrusted with lives and given the best damned job in the wing.

Colonel Buster Leska

Buster enjoyed building Manny up and watching the sour expression evaporate. From the first time he'd worked with him at the base in North Africa, he'd found Manny DeVera to be not only capable, but also one of those rare people who unflinchingly told it like it was. It had galled him when he'd heard about the charges. The Air Force needed to nurture young leaders like DeVera, not try to destroy them. He observed him closely as he talked about teamwork. Manny was a handsome guy, with powerful shoulders, dark eyes, and an expressive face. Since he'd last seen him, he'd grown a Pancho Villa mustache that drooped at the corners of his mouth. Half an hour earlier he'd looked defeated. Now he was alive, like the guy Buster had known in Europe.

He remembered stories about the Supersonic Wetback being one of the foremost womanizers in the fighter pilot corps and wondered how many were deserved. Likely quite a few, he concluded. But as great as Manny might be with the ladies, he had a lousy poker face. Buster could *see* Manny's spirits rising, *see* him losing the frown he'd worn when Buster had picked him from the crowd during the change-of-command ceremony.

While Manny was digesting the news that he was to be the new wing weapons officer, Buster eased in a second hook. "There's another matter, that's got to be held strictly between you and me." Manny was still staring, but he'd regained some of his old composure. *God, but the young are resilient,* Buster thought.

"Every few days I want you to come by my office and we'll talk, just like this. I want you to be my eyes and ears, a window into the combat arena. Let me know whenever you see or hear of anything new going on with the North

Vietnamese, any insights you get that aren't covered in our normal intelligence briefings."

Manny looked puzzled.

"Any weaknesses we might be able to exploit. Any target that we could destroy to really hurt them. We've got to learn the North Vietnamese's Achilles' heel and don't have long to do it."

DeVera narrowed his eyes before he said, "We're restricted on what we can and can't hit, Colonel. Targets in pack six are specified in the air tasking orders sent from Seventh Air Force."

"I understand all that. I still want the information."

Manny's brows remained gathered until a knowing look crept over his face. "What you want to know is what it would take to win?"

Buster Leska nodded. "That's precisely what I mean."

DeVera was perceptive. He was also the sort who had to think things out for himself and disliked doing something unless he understood it. In a nutshell, Buster thought, he was the kind of officer who'd be needed to lead tomorrow's Air Force. In order to rise through the ranks in the military world, it was best if an up-and-coming young officer had a "sponsor," a senior officer to help guide and nurture his career, just as General Moss was doing for Leska. During the long plane ride to the Orient, Buster had decided to do the same for DeVera. He couldn't think of a better man to put his trust in.

The chief master sergeant called from the outer office that the Deputy for Operations had arrived with Major Foley in tow. Leska paused, then spoke in a terse voice, loud enough to be overheard by Foley. "Tell them to take a seat and wait."

He turned back to Manny. "It'll do Max good to cool his heels and worry some. That was a dumb-shit thing he did, lighting his burner over the field at low altitude." Manny couldn't suppress a grin, which Buster ignored as he glanced down at notes on a scratch pad.

"What do you know about Major Paul Anderson?" Buster asked.

Manny answered without hesitation. "I consider him the finest man and best combat pilot in the wing, Colonel."

"That good?"

"Lucky Anderson's a superb pilot, he's a good leader of men, and he's got rock-solid judgment."

"We're going to be working closely together, the three of us. You two are going to help me on the project I was speaking about. We're going to find that Achilles' heel, and the smartest way to chop the damned thing off."

"The rumor's around that Lucky's taking command of the 354th squadron," Manny said. "Is that true, sir?"

"No. The Deputy for Operations assigned Lieutenant Colonel Donovan as interim commander of the 354th, but I'm making it permanent. That squadron's gone too long without a squadron commander, and they can't wait around while Anderson plays on a beach in Hawaii for two more weeks."

Manny looked crestfallen, as if it were he being bypassed for the job. He fidgeted uncomfortably in his chair. Quite obviously, he thought a lot of Anderson.

"Lucky Anderson will get a squadron," Buster said. "Probably the 333rd. They've had good leadership, so it'll be a better place for a new squadron commander to try his wings." He watched DeVera's face brighten. He hoped he received the same kind of loyalty.

"You want me to fly with any squadron in particular?" Manny asked, a touch of his old cockiness growing in his voice.

"Fly with them all. Keep 'em up to speed on the latest tactics and pick up what's going on. I'm placing a lot of faith in your judgment, Manny."

DeVera glowed each time Buster mentioned his trust. The legal battles had eaten away at his indomitable pride, but it was fast returning. Buster picked paperwork out of his in-basket and waved at the door. "You've got a lot to do, so go ahead and get started. Learn anything you can from Max before he leaves, get settled in your new office, and fly a couple missions. When you've got your feet back on the ground in a few days, I'll want you to check me out on the flying here."

"You want *me* to check *you* out?" Again Manny looked amazed.

"Yep. Put me on your wing and show me the ropes."

Manny stood. "Yes, sir." His salute was very proper.

When the door closed behind Captain Manny DeVera, a

smile played across Buster Leska's face. There were aspects of command that he especially treasured. At the forefront of those was rewarding men who deserved it.

Buster looked out the window at the fighters parked in their neat rows, baking under the relentless sun. He stared for a full minute, savoring the new job. Then he glanced down at the list of the wing's key personnel, past the deputy commanders to the names of the squadron commanders he'd penciled in at the bottom.

His eyes lingered on the name of Lieutenant Colonel Mack MacLendon. On Buster's very first operational assignment, fresh out of flight school and just a couple of years after World War II had ended, Mack had been his flight commander. Although Mack had flown P-47 Jugs in Europe during the war, he'd piloted the nimble P-51 like a maestro with a fine violin. He'd taken Buster under his wing and shown him the intricacies of the P-51H and how to get the most out of it. Buster had developed a sort of hero worship for the man. Now here *he* was, Mack's commanding officer. Lesser men than MacLendon might have been upset by the twist of fate, but when he'd dropped by his trailer the previous night, after leaving Parker with the Thai base commander, Mack had broken out a bottle of single-malt Scotch and they'd celebrated.

It was a matter of luck, his passing Mack in rank and position. At the start of the Korean War they'd both started with two aerial kills in F-82 Twin Mustangs, but then, in 1951, he'd been assigned to F-86's while Mack had gone into F-84's. Buster had gotten four more enemy kills in Sabres while Mack concentrated on dropping bombs and dodging flak in his Thunderhog. Subsequently Buster had been assigned to headquarters jobs, impressing generals and giving speeches at civic gatherings, while Mack had remained in the squadron trenches, leading men and teaching them the finer points of flying fighters.

Mack would be leaving Takhli in another week, and Buster wished to hell he was not. He needed his kind of steady support and leadership where it counted most—in the squadron. The previous evening he'd learned much more about the fighter operation in the two hours with Mack than he had during the full day with B. J. Parker and all his briefings.

His mind returned to the matter at hand. The Deputy for Operations, George Armaugh, was waiting in the outer office. He had to do some fine pussyfooting to establish the right rapport with the man whose authority he'd just usurped, and which he intended to bend just a bit more.

He paused thoughtfully for a few reluctant heartbeats before calling on the intercom, "Ask Colonel Armaugh to come in—alone, please."

The colonel paused at the door and started to salute, but Buster waved him to the chair vacated by Manny DeVera.

"Need to talk to you for a few minutes, George." The Deputy for Operations took his seat. He was a serious man, and from all Buster had heard, capable. He also outranked Buster by two years' time in grade as colonel. Both of those were reasons to play this one carefully.

He attacked it in a direct fashion, as he did most things. "I just did something I will try not to repeat in the future. I jumped the chain of command and appointed Captain DeVera as wing weapons officer. I don't apologize for the wisdom of selecting DeVera, since I have great faith in him and have reasons for my action beyond that, but I apologize for not consulting with you first."

The DO's face clouded and his jaw set firmly. Buster had stepped squarely onto his turf. The weapons officer worked for the Deputy of Operations.

"I wanted to tell you at once so you wouldn't hear about it secondhand."

The DO nodded, but it was a curt motion.

"I saw the list you forwarded to Colonel Parker. The one regarding your recommendations for commanders of the flying squadrons, and I'd also like to discuss those with you, George."

"You're making changes?" Armaugh asked too abruptly.

"Suggestions. I do the suggesting, you do the changing."

The DO's brows were knitted and low, his look dark. Buster knew that if he were in his shoes, he'd be feeling much the same. There was little worse than a boss who interfered.

"You're going to have to bear with me, George. No matter what anyone thinks about the importance of various organizations within a flying wing, the critical elements of a combat unit are logistics, maintenance, and operations.

We're here to fly and fight, and those three functions are the keys to making it happen. I'll be working very closely with my three deputies in those areas and calling some of the shots there."

"If you don't trust my judgment, Colonel, I'll request—"

Buster interrupted sharply. "I didn't say that, Colonel. I don't know you well enough to know if I do or don't trust you. If I find we can't work together, you won't have to request a transfer or another job, because you'll be history."

The DO looked as if he'd been slapped. Buster continued without pause. "Now let's discuss your squadron commanders."

"Yes, sir." Armaugh, who Buster had heard was generally quiet and unassuming, wore the look of an angry bulldog.

Buster read from the key personnel list. The DO had recommended that Mack MacLendon be replaced in the 357th by Lieutenant Colonel Obie Zeigler. Leska knew Zeigler from Europe, and he was an amiable and capable, if overly cautious, manager of people. Not nearly the leader Mack was, but there were few of those around. "I know Obie," he said. "You made a good choice there and I agree. You tell him yet?"

"No, sir."

"Go ahead and cut the orders." He went back to the list. The DO had picked Lieutenant Colonel Yank Donovan, a new arrival, as acting commander for the 354th squadron until Lucky Anderson arrived back from R and R. For the reasons he'd told Manny, Buster objected to the temporary status. What he'd not told Manny was that he'd talked about Yank Donovan with Mack MacLendon the previous night. More than anyone, Buster trusted Mack's judgments of men.

"You've got Donovan down as the acting 354th commander. Why not put him in full-time?"

The DO hesitated.

"Tell me about him," Buster prodded.

"Very capable pilot. A lot of experience in fighters."

"He comes from McConnell, right?" McConnell AFB in Kansas was the replacement training unit, or RTU, for pilots upgrading into the F-105.

The DO nodded, obviously still displeased that his recommendations were being second-guessed. "Yank was an instructor there."

"When I went through McConnell a few months ago, he was considered somewhat of a pompous ass."

The DO was quick to agree. "Yank's favorite words are "I" and "my." He's quick to take credit and slow to give it."

"That why you're not giving him the command job?"

"I want people leading the squadrons I can be damned sure are taking care of the pilots. I don't trust Yank Donovan to do that."

"How will you know if you don't try him? He's a senior lieutenant colonel, and he's got more flying hours in the Thud than almost anyone in the wing. My *suggestion* is that you put him into the job full-time and give him a try. He screws up, we'll get rid of him."

"Yes, sir," said the DO with a sigh.

"How about the 333rd squadron? You didn't have a recommendation there."

"Colonel Parker told me General Moss directed that Lucky Anderson get command of a squadron. That's the only one left for him now."

Buster began his little bit of playacting, to boost the DO's ego that he'd just trampled. "I dunno. He's only a major, and that will create problems. If you don't think he's the right man for the job, I'll call the general and argue for someone else." Buster felt his charade was safe enough. Mack had told him that George Armaugh thought highly of Lucky Anderson. He also knew that changing General Moss's mind about giving Lucky Anderson a command would be next to impossible. When Moss made a decision about his men, he stood by it come hell or high water.

"Tell me about Anderson," he said.

The DO reflected for only a couple of seconds. "He can handle anything you give him. He's that kind. I think we should give him a shot at the squadron."

"That good? He's only a major."

"I trust him."

Buster looked thoughtful, as if he were making up his mind. "Okay," he finally said, "I'll go along if you think he's the right guy for the job."

The DO looked somewhat mollified, as if his toes felt just a bit less trampled.

"How's the base commander reacting to Major Foley's flyby?"

"He called three times before I left my office, to update the damage estimate. The total was up to five thousand dollars and climbing. Every time he called, his voice got a little louder, I'd tell Max his tab was going up, and Max would shrink a little lower."

"Anything serious?"

"Blew down a couple of sheds around the base perimeter they'd put up to keep the Thai guards out of the rain and the noonday sun. Otherwise it's mostly broken glass.

"Dumb-shit thing for Foley to do."

"Yeah."

Buster cocked his head. "You ever do it?"

"Once. I was flying F-89's, and it was damned hard to go supersonic without really trying. I buzzed the SAC base at Upper Heyford, over in the UK." The DO *almost* grinned. "They never caught me and I never told."

"I did it just once too," Buster said. "After my sixth kill I made a low pass over Osan in an F-86. Couldn't sit down for a week for the multiple ass-chewings, and they were seriously considering an article fifteen."

"How'd you get out of it?"

"The following week my engine quit on me, and I spent seven months up north, courtesy of the North Koreans. When I was released, they'd forgotten about it. At least I guess they had. I sure as hell didn't ask."

The DO chuckled for the first time since Buster had called him in.

"Tell you what," said Buster. "Drop back by this afternoon, and we'll figure a way to calm down the base commander and still get Max Foley on his way back to the States." Five minutes later the DO was gone, to check on the afternoon's combat-mission preparations.

Leska picked up the key personnel roster and marked it up the way they'd changed it. Then he put it aside and sat back in his chair. His mind dwelled on the matter that was seldom far from the surface of his thoughts, the task he'd been given by the chief. He had never been entrusted with a mission of such consequence, and although primary responsibility was now passed to General Moss, Buster continued to be concerned. *If Moss provides the proper ammunition, and if the chief can be convincing enough with L.B.J. . . .*

He wondered if the North Vietnamese leadership had an inkling of what might be about to befall them, whether they were weighing the threat of a balls-out attack by the American air forces. They should be worried. No two-bit dictatorship should think they could get away with what they were doing. Surely the President would grasp at the chance to end the fighting, once he understood the awesome pressure the Air Force could bring to bear on the North Vietnamese. When he gave the green flag, the nature of the war would quickly change.

He savored the thought.

1945L—Hanoi, DRV

Colonel Xuan Nha

The homecoming, after spending more than six months in the Bach Mai Hospital, was more satisfying than Xuan Nha had dared to hope. His wife, Li Binh, made it so.

When the aged black Peugeot delivered him to the driveway of their villa, Li Binh waited in the lighted entryway, a dutiful and serene expression stamped on her face. His car door was opened by the driver, and Xuan tried hard to maintain dignity as he turned and slowly emerged. Lieutenant Quang Hanh, who had ridden with him from the hospital, limped painfully around the vehicle and grasped his arm to help support him.

Li Binh followed them to the front door, held open by a comely young girl hardly out of puberty, who looked on with wide eyes.

"Welcome home, my husband," said Li Binh. As he made his way inside, Xuan passed six new servants lined and awaiting his inspection. Li Binh had expanded the number of household help, as befit her new positions in party and government.

"There," Xuan Nha croaked to Quang Hanh, motioning at a rugged chair fashioned of coarse strips of water-buffalo hide.

Li Binh pointed, and the young maidservant was quick to

go there and hold it firmly in place as Quang Hanh maneuvered him. Xuan felt perverse satisfaction as he took his seat. The chair was Spartan and uncomfortable, but it represented his life prior to the Mee bombing attack that had crippled him. A symbol of normalcy and return.

"Tea," barked Li Binh, and the girl bolted toward the kitchen. Xuan Nha watched her go as Li Binh curtly motioned Quang Hanh toward the door.

"I have assigned Lieutenant Hanh as my aide," Xuan rasped. "I would like him to be assigned a room." Xuan Nha and Quang Hanh had shared much in the past year. The lieutenant had been his communications officer and courier throughout Xuan's triumphs and promotions. He'd also been there when the Mee fighters had found and bombed them, and had lain wounded at his side.

"Of course, my husband," Li Binh murmured. She motioned to a manservant. "Show the lieutenant the quarters at the garages."

Prior to his injury that room had been assigned to Xuan Nha's driver. He'd disappeared soon after Li Binh learned he was a sometime lover of her nephew, Nguyen Wu, now an official in the Ministry of Internal Affairs. Li Binh had obtained the position for her nephew prior to hearing of his preference for males, when she'd used him for her own sexual gratification. She'd banished Nguyen Wu from her life . . . and her bedroom . . . and had his known male lovers killed.

Li Binh was powerful, secretive, and very vindictive.

She stood before him, the dutiful smile still on her face. Capable Li Binh, member of the Central Committee and advisor to the politburo, just assigned the title of Deputy Minister for External Affairs. The title was symbolic. She personally and zealously supervised the highly successful propaganda efforts abroad, interfacing with antiwar and other dissident groups around the world, her fingers in so many foreign pies it was dizzying. She was one of few who was not only a favorite of Ho Chi Minh, the Enlightened One, but also most of the others within the highest government circles . . . because she obtained results. Surely the most influential behind-the-scenes member of the government, she worked to *remain* in the background. Vo Nguyen Giap, Pham Van Dong, Le Duan, Le Duc Tho, and others were known to the world. Li Binh was a shadow who often made their political successes possible. It was Xuan Nha's belief that, although the Vietnamese People's Army was dedicated and capable, Li Binh and her offices had the only real chance of forcing the Mee from the war. The People's Army must withstand and endure, destroy as many Americans as possible, but only through quiet, judicious application of international wile could they win. Secrecy and political cunning were Li Binh's fortés.

If Giap grew upset about the effectiveness of a particular Mee weapons system being used against his troops, she could orchestrate a peace-group demonstration outside the manufacturer's munitions plants, cause delays, create exposés to appear in American and European newspapers, and even contrive political investigations by representatives of the American government.

If Le Duc Tho called for a change to the image of Viet Cong savagery, articles would be released to the world's media by press services. The Viet Cong would be shown as dutiful, courageous soldiers, the atrocities committed by corrupt Saigon puppet soldiers who tried to blame them on the communist rebels.

Li Binh provided results. She'd become indispensable to the party, infinitely more powerful than her technical-minded husband, and certainly didn't have to maintain charades of respect or politeness toward him. But they'd lived together, shared secrets never to be told another, and developed a familiarity and easiness together. He supposed those were the reasons she greeted him back into the household. She didn't need him for any purpose he knew of.

When he'd been gravely injured, she'd visited only once, then left him to die in the Bach Mai Hospital without even a semblance of grief. She'd resumed visiting only after it became apparent that he might survive, when he'd resumed his duties of overseeing the country's sophisticated defenses from his hospital room, but she'd displayed open repugnance at his hideous burns and missing limb. The feeling of familiarity had been slow to resurrect.

He settled in the chair, hunched to protect his still-sensitive abdomen, and regarded her. With a nod she banished the remaining servants.

"You look well, Li Binh."

"Thank you, husband." She bobbed her head, a tiny caricature of the traditional act of wifely obeisance, then pointed about the room. "It is as it was when you left."

"But you are not."

Her expression sharpened.

"You have had many successes. I know how you have proved yourself again and again. I smile when I hear of each glorious victory. You bring honor to me and to your family."

Her smile was genuine, for Li Binh was tremendously vain. She enjoyed exercising control and being told of her power. Xuan Nha knew to use that key. They were similar in that regard.

"I see you have a new household staff," he said. As did other high officials, Li Binh drew political prisoners, who for a variety of reasons suffered the wrath of the Lao Dong, for use as servants. She felt the ones who'd fallen furthest, who had once held positions of power, were best, more fearful, and thus reliable, for they were sufficiently intelligent to know the alternatives.

She shrugged. "The old ones grew complaisant."

Which meant she'd either had them eliminated or shipped to labor units. The thought of their fates didn't bother Xuan Nha. The reason for her decision interested him. Complaisant? They'd been constantly terrified and would have done anything not to anger her. It was more likely they'd learned too much about Li Binh's personal life. He decided they'd been executed by secret policemen from Internal Affairs and tossed into a killing pit to ensure their silence.

Tea arrived, borne by the meek young girl who served and immediately hurried out. Xuan's eyes followed her with interest.

"Her parents," Li Binh said of the departed girl, "were lawyers, her father a people's magistrate in Haiphong. Western books were found in their possession. They were about to be sent to carry supplies on the trails when I asked for them."

Xuan looked at the closed door and wondered about Li Binh's desire to surround herself with failed success.

"The servants know to assist you," said Li Binh. "I told them to be helpful."

He nodded, uneasy that he was so dependent. Xuan Nha had his own vanities.

"I had your things moved to the south room," she said quietly, "for I felt you should not be jostled while you sleep."

"That was thoughtful," he responded. He felt no surprise. He'd known she wouldn't wish to share his bed. The spacious guest quarters in the south wing were quite sufficient for his needs.

"I must return to my offices, husband. You will find I am even busier than before."

"I understand your duties are important."

"If you wish for anything, tell the servants." She departed.

Xuan Nha sighed and settled back in the uncomfortable chair.

After he'd spent half an hour of quiet contemplation, Quang Hanh cautiously peered into the room. "Colonel Nha?"

He motioned him inside.

"I have the radios set up in my room, comrade Colonel, and I have established contact with the command center. They know to call if they have anything requiring your attention."

Xuan grunted his approval. Quang Hanh held a distrust of telephone lines.

"If you no longer need me . . ."

"Just keep me informed," Xuan said. When Quang Hanh had departed, Xuan blew a breath and began the arduous task of rising from the chair. He'd fumbled at two attempts when a male servant appeared. Xuan settled back in the chair, failed in his task and panting from exhaustion.

The man stood quietly, obviously too frightened to speak.

"My room," croaked Xuan Nha, and the man hurried to help.

When they entered the south bedroom—Xuan lightly supported by the manservant—the young cleaning maid was inside, turning down crisp new sheets. She regarded Xuan with a fearful look and tried a smile.

"Out," Xuan whispered to the man, and both servants bolted to leave.

"You." Xuan lifted a hand at the girl. "Stay for a moment." She was visibly trembling as the man carefully shut the door.

"Who was that?" he asked, casting his eye toward the door.

"My father, Colonel sir," she answered in her timid voice.

He nodded, wondering if she was repelled by his disfigurement. During the past two weeks he'd noticed a certain slight stirring and had been curious to find if his body still functioned properly in that regard. He'd seldom been satisfied rutting with Li Binh, and the present sleeping arrangements were satisfactory, as was the frightened girl. Xuan curtly motioned with his hand to draw her nearer, then leaned on her child's body as he hobbled toward the bed. She was trembling with fright, which made him anticipate his experiment all the more.

Never a sensuous man, for he viewed that as weakness, before the bombing attack Xuan Nha had nonetheless occasionally enjoyed a female—preferably when the conditions were correct, such as after the killing of an enemy, and when there was a handy receptacle to dominate. This time it would be different, more of an exploration to prove he'd not lost that masculine capability.

As he cautiously lowered himself onto the mattress, he grasped a handful of her hair. He tried to will the stirring sensation to return as the girl whimpered and followed his grasp. *It would be better if she fought,* he grumbled to himself. Then he remembered that he was far too weak for that.

First things first, he thought, and had her pull down her trousers and stand on shaky legs as he reached harshly into her with his blunt fingers and reamed, grunting with his effort. He withdrew his hand once to hit her and angrily order her to stop wailing. He groped harshly in her for several minutes, until the hymen was torn and the orifice stretched to his satisfaction. Finally he grasped her arm and pulled her onto her knees.

Xuan sat silently for a moment, huffing and regaining strength, satisfied that he'd eliminated that initial barrier. He forced her mouth open with bloody fingers, again grasped the handful of hair, and brusquely pushed her face onto his lap. He'd grown fond of the French way as a university student in Paris, and wondered if he could succeed in building the sensation by using her that way.

For the next few minutes, until he grew impossibly tired, the terrified girl worked relentlessly, her objections reduced to snuffling into his sparse pubic hairs.

To no avail. Finally, he groaned unhappily and ordered her to leave.

Had the Mee taken even that away? He heard the girl crying outside the door, her sounds drowned by the anxious voice of her father, the former people's magistrate, asking if she'd pleased the colonel.

2015L—O' Club, Takhli RTAFB, Thailand

Captain Manny DeVera

Manny emerged from the phone booth with mixed emotions. He'd called the Peace Corps camp near Nakhon Sawan where his girlfriend from before his trip to the Philippines worked, and struck out. At first their conversation, especially her coolness, had puzzled him. While she was pleased that Manny was free of his legal nightmare, she wouldn't drive over to see him. She said she knew how *that* would end up.

He'd had pleasant visions of the way she grasped her ankles and rocked and crooned her orgasms. She was one of the horniest females he'd ever known, and he'd looked forward to their celebrating his return in bed.

And no, she'd said, she wouldn't come by if he made his way to Nakhon Sawan and rented a hotel room. When he began to argue and sweet-talk her, she revealed the truth. During the past week she'd gone bonkers over the camp supervisor, and her new love was both a pacifist and a jealous man. If he caught her even *talking* to a warmongering fighter pilot . . .

She'd said she didn't remember saying she'd wait for Manny. She'd ended the conversation abruptly, saying she was busy. Gotta get back to work. Good hearing your voice, hon. *Click.*

Manny had stared at the warbling phone in his hand, then tried to make light of it.

Too bad. So Sad. . . . Next? He wandered into the stag bar, feeling some of the gloomies returning. Upon reflection he realized that every time he'd gotten into trouble in the past, a female had been involved in some manner. It would be prudent, he decided, to avoid intimate contact with women for a long while, except maybe a periodic, therapeutic visit to one of the whores downtown. No more round-eyes until he finished his combat tour. The thought didn't thrill him. The Thai ladies in Ta Khli fucked so halfheartedly the pilots often joked that the only difference between screwing one of them and beating off was that you had someone to talk to.

DeVera went to the bar and downed a single MiG-15, the sticky mixture of Scotch and Drambuie called a "rusty nail" by civilians. Then he made his way toward the dining room, fighting against the current, for most of the guys were on their way to the stag bar to get an early start on Max Foley's hundred-mission party.

He surveyed the dining room, looking for someone to join for dinner.

"Hey, Manny!" Captain Billy Bowes and Lieutenant Smith, two guys from his old flight in the 354th squadron, motioned to him. There were already four at their table, so after he'd shaken hands all around, he pulled up a spare chair from another table, moved a battered guitar case to one side, and sat. They were ordering chicken-fried steak and fried rice from the Thai waitress, so he told her to add another to the list. The dining room's menu was limited to basic selections.

Billy, who now commanded C-Flight, and Smitty, a C-Flight member, were seated on either side of Manny. Dusty Fields and Animal Hamlin from the 333rd squadron were across the table. They all welcomed him back and commiserated his getting the shaft; then Smitty asked when he'd be coming back to the squadron.

"I'll be bunking with the guys in the 333rd squadron," he said, motioning his head toward Dusty and Animal, but withheld the announcement about his new position.

"Well, hallelujah," kidded Dusty Fields in a caustic tone.

Billy Bowes, who was half-Cherokee and looked it, seemed somber. "We were talking about Joe Walker, Manny. You hear about what happened?"

"I heard he got hammered by a SAM, but he made it out far enough to be rescued."

Billy nodded. "He was fortunate. The Jolly Green had to go in a long way to pick him up."

"I hear he got busted up pretty badly."

"Broke both legs and his pelvis," said Animal. "He'll be laid up for a while."

Animal Hamlin was a quiet type, but he'd not always been that way. He'd gained his nickname as a wild lieutenant bachelor at McConnell AFB, Kansas, and couldn't shake it. His fellow fighter jocks continued to call him Animal, saying that he'd shown his true colors as a lieutenant and sooner or later they'd reemerge. Animal couldn't convince them he was a reformed, happily married man with a family. He was from New Jersey—pronounced Noo Choizey—and spoke with that odd, part New Yorker, part moon-man accent.

Dusty Fields asked, "Where'd they take Joe? Clark Hospital?" Clark was a big base in the Philippines and had the largest military hospital in the region.

Billy Bowes shook his head. "They flew him directly back to the States. Probably to either Travis or Wilford Hall in San Antonio."

"Hope it's Travis," said Smitty Smith. "Joe's from California."

"Then they'll ship him to Texas for sure," said Dusty. "The Air Force takes pride in fucking things like that up."

Billy mused. "Walker's a good man. He's also one smooth pilot. We're gonna miss him in the flight."

Dusty leaned forward, eyes pinned on Manny. "Any truth to what I hear about your being assigned as wing weapons officer?" Rumors spread as quickly among fighter pilots as in any ladies' bridge group.

Manny gave Dusty a look brimming with humility. "Colonel Leska said he wanted the very best, so what could I do? I told him I'd help out."

Dusty didn't hesitate. "You should've told the truth and nominated me."

"If I told the truth about you, he'd have you reassigned to Piper Cubs. You be good to me, and I'll tell him you're not as mediocre as everyone thinks." Dusty Fields and Manny had run into one another numerous times during their tours in Europe and the States. Both were better than adequate pilots, and both were devout bachelors with exag-

gerated and nefarious reputations. They competed mercilessly . . . and were friends.

"Whaddaya t'ink a da new wing commandah?" asked
Animal Hamlin in his Noo Choizey accent. He was a good
pilot and also a fine musician, and the guitar went with him
whenever he was off duty. When he sang, the moon-man accent was transformed. He played a mean git-fiddle—which
for some reason he'd painted Day-Glo fluorescent orange—
and when he crooned a ballad, it came out soft, clear, and
melodious.

"I knew Colonel Leska from Europe," said Manny. "He
had a shit-hot reputation. When I talked to him this morning, he confirmed it. Man's got his act together."

"The rumor's going around he's from SAC," said Dusty,
wearing a frown. Fighter pilots distrusted bomber people.

"He spent a few months in B-52's after he left Europe,"
said Manny. "That's all."

"I heard it different," Dusty argued in a low voice. "I
heard he's got a lot of bomber time."

Manny's face grew hot as his anger rose. "For Christ's
sake, Dusty, he was an F-86 ace in Korea. Spent the last
months of the war in a POW camp. They sent him to SAC
on some kinda exchange tour, then to the Pentagon, but the
first chance he got, he came back to fighters."

"He was a POW in Korea?" Billy asked. He sensed that
Manny's disposition was heating. Bowes was good at tem-
pering arguments.

"Yeah. He was treated pretty bad. That's where he got his
white hair. He hates commies with a passion." Manny stared
malevolently at Dusty, still angry that he'd poor-mouthed
Leska. He pulled his eyes away finally and looked at Billy,
who'd taken his job when he'd been relieved of duty. Bowes
had developed into a capable flight commander. "Where's
Henry Horn?" Henry was another member of the flight.

"Finished his hundred missions two days ago. Said he
was meeting his wife at Don Muang airport and they'd
spend a day or two in Bangkok, then drop in and check on
Lucky in Hawaii."

They talked about Lucky Anderson and how fortunate he
was. He'd been shot down, then rescued from North Vietnam after spending nearly two months on the ground. Intell

reports said he'd spent the time with a hill tribe near the Laotian border, but somehow it didn't ring true.

"He's going to take command of the 333rd squadron soon as he returns," announced Manny. "When I talked to him in the Philippines, he thought he was getting the 354th, but they assigned it to another guy." He thought he was breaking the news, but Smitty piped up that they'd been told that afternoon. The new 354th squadron commander was a light colonel named Yank Donovan.

"What's he like?" asked Manny.

"That's him over there," Smitty said, nodding to a corner table. A meticulously groomed lieutenant colonel was seated, talking with Colonel Tom Lyons. He glanced at their table, and his eyes met Manny's for an instant. The look was cool and neutral.

"He doesn't care much about who he talks to," murmured Manny. Tom Lyons was the one who had "discovered" the trumped-up evidence that had almost hanged DeVera.

"He's the only man on base who's friendly with Lyons," said Billy. "Even before Colonel Parker relieved him, it was common knowledge that Lyons fucked you over."

Dusty Fields frowned. "How come he's got it in for you?"

Manny blew out a sigh. "First time I ran across him was down in North Africa, at the El Uotia gunnery range. I was in the range tower watching a flight of F-100's on the dive-bomb circle. One guy pulled up into the leader, and they both went down. Lyons, he was the one who screwed up, made it out okay, but the other guy was killed. Lyons tried to get me to lie to the accident board, but I wouldn't go along, so he's had me on his shit list ever since."

"And that's a very long list," Smitty said.

Manny nodded. "Anyway, when he got here, he found a chance to get even by making it look like I was deliberately attacking the wrong targets up in pack six."

"I heard about that," said Dusty. "You better not give him another chance at your ass. The looks he's giving you aren't exactly friendly."

"What's Donovan like?" repeated Manny, not wanting to discuss his previous woes.

"Impressed with himself, but not much with the rest of us," Smitty said.

Dusty spoke up. "Give him a chance. I watched his

bombs hit yesterday on a target down at Vinh, when he took out a loading dock. Little bitty target and they were shooting, and he still took it out clean. He's a good pilot."

"You can say that," Smitty said woefully. "You're not getting him for a commander."

Dusty grinned at DeVera. "As for his ego trip, how about all the stories we hear about the exploits of the great, one-and-only Supersonic Wetback?"

"That's different," Manny said with a straight face.

Dusty Fields laughed. "Welcome back anyway, asshole." He raised an eyebrow. "When's Lucky Anderson coming back from his R and R?"

"Couple weeks, I'd guess."

Animal Hamlin spoke up. "Be glad when Lucky gets here and takes over our squadron. We heard the new wing commander's gonna be flyin' with us until he does, and he's gonna be adjustin' to combat."

Manny was quick to defend Colonel Leska. "Shouldn't take long."

Billy Bowes shrugged. "Doesn't matter anyway. Since Leska's the new wingco and Yank Donovan's been named squadron commander, we don't have much choice, do we?"

Manny watched as Tom Lyons leaned forward and said something to Yank Donovan. They both chuckled low and glanced about the room. *Like conspirators,* Manny thought. Since Tom Lyons's connivery had been found out, he'd be in no position to make trouble for Manny or anyone else for a while. But what about Yank Donovan? He decided to keep an eye on him.

Dinner arrived and they ate quickly and efficiently, as professional military men do. They made the standard comments about the lousy food and bemoaned the fact that Max Foley's hundred-mission party was obviously getting under way without them. The noise level from the stag bar was growing by the minute.

"Foley's leaving big shoes for you to fill, Manny," Dusty Fields said with happy malice.

DeVera finished his mouthful before speaking in a quieter voice than normal. "Then I guess I better grow big feet." There was no way Manny was going to betray the trust Colonel Leska had shown. No way at all.

Animal Hamlin hefted his battered guitar case, and they

headed for Max's party. As they left the room, Manny felt Colonel Tom Lyons's cold glare. He turned and stared back for a moment, then very slowly gave him a "fuck you" grin. The Supersonic Wetback had returned.

The stag bar was packed. Max Foley was at the other end of the room, fending off questions about his foul up earlier in the day when he'd tapped afterburner and trashed the base. Two sets of songsters competed loudly from different areas. Laughter and shouted conversations added to the general din. Animal took his brightly colored guitar out of its case and plunked a couple of notes in anticipation. Dusty took orders, wormed his way through the crowd to the bar, and a few minutes later returned with drinks for the five of them.

"Thanks," shouted DeVera over the hubbub.

"Thank Max. The drinks're all on him!" Dusty yelled back.

"I think I will." Manny tried to get to Max Foley to tell him how much he appreciated the information he'd passed on that afternoon and wish him well, but couldn't make headway through the mob.

A stern face appeared above the others. Colonel Leska had entered the bar, flanked by Colonel Armaugh, his Deputy for Operations, on one side, and Colonel Mack from the 357th squadron on the other. The pint-sized base commander glowered about angrily in their wake. Leska understandably had less trouble getting his group through than Manny had experienced. He pushed his way to a position directly in front of Max Foley, and the clamor lessened a bit.

"Quiet!" yelled Colonel Mack.

Buster Leska tried to say something but was drowned out by the noise level.

"Dammit, be quiet!" Mack roared. Mack MacLendon was regarded as a superb leader of men. He could also get downright mean if his orders went unheeded. The group grew silent. Leska motioned Colonel Hough forward. The tight-jawed little base commander brandished a sheet of paper and waved it in Max Foley's face.

"I have here a list of the damage caused by Major Foley's flyby. It comes to more than nine thousand dollars, mostly in broken windows and collapsed guard shacks." He held it high, then carefully handed it to Foley, who took it and read with a woeful expression.

"This is no place for an ass-chewing," Dusty Fields grumbled angrily. "He's . . ."

"Quiet," Mack growled in their direction.

Colonel Hough glared at Max for a long moment, then stepped to one side. Buster Leska carefully removed a second sheet of paper from a zippered flight-suit pocket, slowly unfolded it, and held it out to Max. His voice emerged in a deep rumble. "Major, I think you'll find the disciplinary action in order."

Right here in the club? It bothered Manny too. Foley looked troubled as he gingerly took the sheet. Animal Hamlin muttered something about fucking bomber pilots. Buster Leska, the Deputy for Operations, the base commander, and Colonel Mack wore stern looks, all directed at Foley. Max, looking contrite and embarrassed in front of his friends, cautiously opened his mouth to speak. But his mouth drooped as he stared at the sheet of paper.

"What've you got to say to the nine thousand dollars, Major?" asked the Deputy for Operations.

"It's . . . uh . . . a lot of money, sir." The fact that the corners of Max's mouth began to twitch, that a grin was curling his lips even in the face of his tormentors, was mystifying.

"You damned right it is," muttered Colonel Hough, the base commander.

Mack, the light colonel commanding the 357th, agreed, "An example had to be made."

"Now," said Buster Leska, "read what Colonel Hough, Colonel Armaugh, and I put on the paper you're holding. I want *everyone* to hear."

Max glanced at the wing commander, then cleared his throat. "You sure, sir?"

"Read it, dammit!"

Max tried to maintain a straight face. "It says . . . 'From this date, the twentieth day of the tenth month, of the nineteen hundred sixty-seventh year of our Lord, and forever hence, the official words to the ballad of the lovely lady called Mary Ann Burns are as follows. . . .'"

Muttering filled the room. "Mary Ann Burns" was the name of a favorite fighter-pilot song.

"Well?" asked Leska.

"Sir?" Max was grinning from ear to ugly ear.

Colonel Armaugh, the Deputy for Operations, pointed his finger directly at Max's nose. "Sing the damn thing! And I don't want you to get any of the words wrong and embarrass me in front of our new wing commander."

"Animal!" said Mack, motioning to Hamlin. "Give us some notes." Hamlin hastily pulled up his Day-Glo orange guitar to render the musical background. Max led off in a terrible, nasal voice, then Colonel Leska joined in, his voice deep, loud, and sonorous. Soon the thunder of fifty-odd fighter-jock voices filled the confines of the barroom.

The song was rendered to the tune of "Reuben, Reuben, I've Been Thinking," but the words were:

> *Mary Ann Burns, queen of all the acrobats,*
> *She can do tricks that can give a man the shits,*
> *Roll green peas through her fundamental orifice,*
> *Do a double back flip and catch 'em on her tits.*
> *She can shit, fart, fight, fuck!*
> *Fly a jet! Drive a truck!*
> *Mary Ann Burns is the girrrl for me.*

The gathered voices boomed as they chanted the finale:

> *She's a great big son of a bitch! Twice the size of me!*
> *The hairs on her ass are like the branches on a tree!*
> *She can shit, fart, fight, fuck!*
> *Fly a jet! Drive a truck!*
> *Mary Ann Burns is the girl for meeeee.*

Whoops and catcalls filled the bar. "Shit hot!" a pilot yelled in exuberance.

Leska raised his hands high and the noise dwindled. "I want everyone here to remember. If you're ugly as sin, kill two MiGs, and know the official words to 'Mary Ann Burns,' you can fuck up a flyby and get away with it. If you aren't ugly, haven't killed two MiGs, and can't remember the words, don't even *try*, or your ass is grass and you better be ready to pay the bill."

Max Foley was laughing too loudly to conceal his relief.

"Wipe that smile off your face, Major," growled Colonel Mack, "and get ready to do some serious drinking."

"Congratulations," said Leska, shaking Foley's hand and admiring the bright red, white, and blue hundred-mission patch on his shoulder. A few minutes later, after a single drink, the colonels slipped quietly out the side door and left the pilots to enjoy themselves without the hindrance of brass.

Manny DeVera grinned at Animal Hamlin and Dusty Fields. "*Now* tell me what you think of our new wing commander." No one disagreed that Buster Leska had established himself as a shit-hot fighter-jock commander. One of *them*.

An hour later Manny also left the party, to go to his newly assigned room at the 333rd squadron's Ponderosa and get a good night's sleep. He decided to go on foot, to clear his head from the effects of the alcohol and do some private thinking. He walked briskly. The Supersonic Wetback felt reborn, and there was a happy lift to his step as he started to walk the half mile.

He intended to take his new job seriously, to show Leska his faith wasn't misplaced. The next morning he'd finish clearing onto base, then fly a combat mission in the afternoon. In a couple of days he'd begin giving Buster Leska his combat checkout, and he wanted to be damned well prepared.

CHAPTER FOUR

Sunday, October 22nd 1255 Local—Nellis AFB, Nevada

The day was bright and sunny, and the temperature hovered above the seventy mark. Sol, relentless in the summer months, swept the sky in gentler arcs during the late fall. October and November were the best weather months in the low desert city of Las Vegas.

On this balmy Sunday local rock hounds, picnickers, campers, and four-wheeler enthusiasts swarmed over the desert. In those families who'd decided to stay in the city, a goodly number of females were badgering their men to take them to the strip to catch one of the several matinee shows featuring America's top entertainers. A similar number of males used delaying tactics so they could watch the Packers-Colts game.

TFWC, Commander's Quarters

Major General Gordon S. White

"Gordie, it's for you," called his wife.

The Baltimore Colts, his favorite team, had lost the toss

and were about to kick off. The odds were even up, and he didn't want to miss a minute of the game.

"Tell 'em I'm out," he yelled back. If it was something life threatening, he'd have been called over his hand-held Motorola radio, which they called "the brick." His never-ending penance was to lug the thing around with him as if it were handcuffed in place.

"It's the message center," she said, "and they say it's important."

He couldn't think of anything short of a declaration of general war that should warrant the people at the message center to his call his home in the middle of a big football game.

"I'll call back," he tried, forlornly eyeing the television.

"Gordon?" His wife had assumed *that* tone.

He started, glanced over his shoulder, watched the kick . . . the Packer receiver took it on his five, then ran straight ahead into Baltimore tacklers the size of Kenworth semis.

"Way to go!" he yelled gleefully, watching the pileup.

"Gordon!"

He sighed and went into the living room, where he picked up the receiver. Two minutes later he was out the door, not hurrying as he might in response to an aircraft accident, but not dawdling either. It was not often that a two-star general received a couriered message from the Chief of Staff of the Air Force.

It was only five blocks to the large, box-like concrete headquarters building of the Tactical Fighter Weapons Center. The officer courier was supposed to meet him at his office with the message, which was to be placed in his hands—only . . . and to be read by his eyes—only.

As Gordon White turned into the circular drive in front of the headquarters building, he noted that a few vehicles were parked at the south entrance to the basement, where the Fighter Tactics branch was located. Working on Sundays and holidays was not uncommon for that group while the air war was burning hot in Southeast Asia.

The pilots there were a sort of conduit to introduce new weapons and new tactics, which they tested in the deserts of Nevada, into the war effort. They were led by Major Benny Lewis, whom White considered to be one of the finest young leaders in the Air Force.

·   ·   ·

It was a good football game. In the second quarter Johnny
Unitas's relentless passing game pushed Baltimore ahead
fourteen to seven, but the world-champion Green Bay team,
coached by Vince Lombardi, bounced back after halftime
and was doggedly chewing up the field. Bart Starr alternately passed to Paul Hornung in the flat and gave the ball
to Jimmy Taylor for short yardages, all the way down to the
nine-yard line, where the Colt defense stiffened for three
straight plays. On fourth and goal Taylor battered his way
straight ahead through the Colts' formidable line and
dragged three men into the end zone. After a short runback
on the ensuing kick, with the game tied at fourteen-all,
Unitas took the field to the wild cheers of Baltimore fans.

Gordie White missed all of that.

1340L—Fighter Tactics Branch

Major Benny Lewis

In the basement of the Fighter Weapons Center building,
the four military members of the air-to-ground team had
seen neither the clear sky nor a glimpse of a football game
since they'd arrived at eight o'clock that morning to catch
up on work. Since it was a nonduty day, they wore civvies,
toiling in a large underground vault that had been sectioned
into small offices, hurrying so they might at least catch the
final quarter of the big game.

Lewis, chief of the team, was in a melancholy mood that
was hard to shake. He'd been like that since Friday, when
he'd been told by the flight surgeon, a fellow officer he'd
once thought a friend, that his request for a review of his
flying status had been denied.

Six months earlier he'd ejected from a jet and received a
compression fracture of the spine. Not a break, he'd emphasized in his request, merely the compression of a couple of
spinal disks. In his formal letter he'd told the flight-surgeon
buddy that he was healed, that he felt fine, that there was no
reason to further delay being placed back onto flight status.
The answer had been simple and direct; he'd have to wait

three more months until his case would be reviewed, and first reviews were seldom encouraging. Most likely it would then be *another* three months and another review before they seriously considered his request.

Six more months!

The flight surgeon "buddy" had told him he might be looked at more favorably if he'd taken better care of himself and had not insisted on returning to work so early.

He'd promised to take better care in the future if the flight surgeon would just *please* forward the request. He'd been told to resubmit in three months, *after* he took all that good care. The full-colonel hospital commander had made up his mind about the matter and wouldn't relent.

Damn! Benny Lewis missed flying like a ballerina might miss her toe shoes, a painter his easel, a plumber his pipe wrenches. Flying fighters was what he did, what he was good at. His back still pained him a bit, but he could cope with the periodic twinges that came mainly when he failed to wear the back brace.

Benny was out of the bulky brace they'd initially given him, and the one he now wore, usually anyway, was much lighter and limited only sideward movements, which he had to admit were not pleasant. But he was better—*much* better—than he'd been before. Doctors, he'd decided, were among the least understanding people alive.

He'd reluctantly started work on an officers' evaluation report for one of his men when Moods Diller, the young captain he shared his office with, caught his attention by repeatedly clearing his throat.

"You got a cold or something?" Benny grumbled.

Diller was working on refining his two "smart weapons" concepts. It presently took an average of forty fighter-bomber sorties to destroy a point target, one that required a direct hit. His smart weapons held out the promise to destroy the same target with a single bomb. The laser project, which the Pentagon assigned the preliminary code name of Pave Dagger, involved a laser illuminator that radiated a pinpoint of bright light onto a target, and a 2,000-pound bomb equipped with a sensor to detect the light, and electronics to move the bomb's fins and steer it into the target.

"I'd like to fly down to Dallas tomorrow," Moods said. "Meet with the Texas team and watch a demo they've put together. If it works, we're going to get new lasers for the target illuminators, and new transducer material for the bomb sensors."

Benny grunted and went back to reading from his in-basket.

Moods worked with a Texas team and a California team, both consisting of top engineer-scientists. The California team was working on TV-guided missiles called Mavericks, while the Texas team worked on the laser-guided bombs: Pave Dagger. Neither project was "quite there" yet, but the Texas team was closest. Both guidance methods entailed extremely technical concepts, and Benny glazed over and responded in incomprehensible grunts when Moods started talking about pixels, pulse rates, photons, and auto edge tracking.

"The trip okay with you?" Diller asked cautiously. They'd been told to curtail unnecessary travel.

That part Benny understood. "How're you going to get there?" he asked.

"Commercial. There's no military flights going to Fort Worth tomorrow."

"No way. We're already low on travel funds for the quarter, and we've got a month and a half to go. Tell your engineers to come here if they want to talk."

"Dammit, Benny, they can't bring their lab here. Pave Dagger's the most important project in the Center, probably in the whole Air Force, and I can't even go to Dallas for a demo?"

"What's the subject again?" Benny awaited the answer, which he doubted he'd understand.

Moods sighed and started over again. "The Texas team found a new source for lasers and a completely new transducer material for the bomb kit, and they think they've solved the modulation problems. They want me to help them get it approved with the guys from the Armament Lab. I've gotta see it if I'm going to help 'em, and we don't have much time."

"No way." Benny lowered his eyes to the AF Form 77 he was working on and began to fill in the rating blocks.

"Just this one trip, Benny?" Moods was pleading. His project was important to him.

"How many trips have you been on so far this month?"

Moods thought. "Three or four, I guess."

Benny fished around in the clutter of his in-basket and found the paper he was looking for. He added the numbers. "Nine trips in five weeks, six of 'em on commercial airlines. You're spending more travel funds than the rest of us combined."

"That many?" Moods was genuinely surprised. His mind worked in another stratum from the mundane.

"You've got to start cutting back, beginning right now."

"Benny, this one's important."

Lewis glared, wanting to get back to the captain's OER, which was overdue.

"The Texas team says this is the breakthrough they've been after. The material we've been using has been unstable. They found this little company in Germany, and the pulse rate is dead on. *Perfect* for what we're doing."

"Germany?"

"Yeah. They've got the new laser and seeker set up on a test bench in Texas, and it's operating right on frequency, Benny. No more screwing around, varying the bias voltages on each individual seeker to try to compensate for pulse-rate anomalies."

Benny stared.

"It's the anomalies that have been slewing the results. The rate changes from seeker to seeker, and there's no reliable way to compensate."

Benny was getting a headache. He grunted.

Moods recognized the sound. He slowed his machine-gun speech rate. "What I'm saying is the new material will make it work the same way, every time. The bombs will all have the same error, so once we adjust for it, they'll be dead on."

Benny smiled at something he understood.

"I won't ask for any more travel before I leave for Danang."

Benny sighed. Moods wanted to conduct a combat test, which he was against until Moods had achieved better results on the test ranges.

"Benny, we've got the circular error down to less than sixty feet, and all of that's in the anomaly. They also break lock because they drift off frequency, and that would be fixed too. I told the Texas team it was unacceptable, that if they couldn't find the solution, the whole project may have to go back to step one. They listened, and they've put half a million dollars into a materials study, looking at everything produced by man in the free world. Now they think they've found it, the breakthrough we've been looking for."

Benny brooded for a moment, then sighed again. "Sorry, Moods. We just don't have the funds."

One of the captains from the room next door peeked in. "Unitas just threw a pass for a touchdown. Score's twenty-one to fourteen. I'm taking off, boss."

"You caught up?" Benny growled. Moods Diller's wheedling hadn't helped his temper.

"Pretty much. I'll be in late tomorrow, because I'm flying on a weapons test in the morning. Dropping thousand-pounders with the new time-delay fuzes."

Two weeks earlier a similar test had ended in airborne disaster when a TD fuze had inexplicably armed and set off the bomb load while it was still on the F-4. The Phantom as well as the aircraft commander and pilot-systems officer had been vaporized. There'd not been enough of anything scattered across the desert floor to investigate the problem properly.

"They've found the problem?" asked Benny.

"Mercury corrosion in the fuze . . . they think." The captain looked anxious to depart.

Benny waved him out. "See you after you land. We've got a U.S. senator and a couple staffers coming in Wednesday on a boondoggle, and you'll be doing the briefing."

Politicians liked to visit Nellis Air Force Base, located beside the fun capital of the world. The hotel-casinos vied for their business. Most preferred to stay at suites in Caesar's Palace or the Desert Inn, which were not shabby digs for a "working" trip, and their tabs were either comped or picked up by American taxpayers.

"I'll be prepared." The captain was already hurrying out before Benny had a chance to ask how he'd learned about the latest developments in the big game.

Moods scribbled on a notepad, examined what he'd written, then tapped his pencil methodically on the paper. The sound was increasingly irritating. The second captain from the adjacent room poked his head into the doorway. "I'm done for the day, Major."

"Sure you are," Benny said caustically. He knew the captain wasn't caught up. He was working on changes to the Three Dash One manual, the tactics bible for fighter aircraft, and they were never done making changes to the mammoth-sized tomes. Fighter tactics were changing weekly with all the lessons being learned in Southeast Asia. They had an impossible deadline, two weeks hence, to make the newest updates.

"Hornung opened up the fourth quarter with a twenty-yard run. The Pack's on the fifty-yard line."

"How the hell do you know that?"

The captain grinned and looked about to see if anyone was listening. "We snuck a radio in this morning. It's mostly static down here, but you can hear if you listen close." For some ridiculous reason—something to do with security—radios were prohibited in the vault.

"The Packers are on the fifty?" Benny asked. He was a Green Bay fan.

"Yes, sir. Taylor's running good today, dammit." The captain favored Baltimore, and they had a two-dollar bet on the game.

Benny tossed the unfinished evaluation report back into the in-basket. Jimmy Taylor, fullback for the Pack, was his favorite power runner. "Let's lock up the classified and go over to the club so we can catch the last quarter."

"I'll be there in a bit," muttered Moods Diller, looking at his doodling as if it were doing something wrong. He might show up, but on the other hand, he might become immersed in his technical doodles until well after dark. Moods's Pave Dagger project meant much more to him than any football game. It rated right up there with sex and flying airplanes.

Benny gathered the classified papers from his desk, double-checked that he had them all, and secured them in his safe. Then he picked up and examined the scrap of paper stuck into the corner of his desk pad. It gave the flight number and time of Julie Stewart's arrival on Friday. His backseater had been killed when they'd been shot from the skies of North Vietnam seven months earlier. Julie was his backseater's widow, and she'd be bringing her month-old daughter, little Patty, to live in Las Vegas for a while. He'd feel better after she arrived, as he always did in her presence. Sort of warm and at ease, as if things were as they should be. She said that his being nearby helped give her strength.

Benny stuffed the paper into his shirt pocket, thinking about her. Also he thought for the hundredth time how he had to make sure nothing appeared improper about their relationship, what with his being recently divorced and her husband having just been declared killed in action. It would distress him if anyone was to think poorly of her. Regardless of how much he felt for her, and he wanted her so badly he hurt inside, nothing improper had happened between them. He'd never even kissed her, except the way a guy might peck his sister on the cheek, and if people were to think . . .

The captain was back at the door, exulting. "The Packers had to punt. The Colts have the ball on their own twenty." They talked about football on their way to the parking lot.

As he was walking toward his car, Benny heard a voice hailing him, and was surprised to see General White on the lawn, in jeans and a polo shirt, motioning at him.

They didn't leave the general's office for more than an hour, and not once did they mention football. Instead they spoke at length about a project General McManus called JACK-POT. The stated goal was to force the expeditious withdrawal of the North Vietnamese Army from South Vietnam through the use of sustained aerial bombardment of the Hanoi and the Haiphong regions.

Major General Gordon S. White was to provide all necessary testing and analysis required to support the project. Major Benjamin L. Lewis was specifically named as a project officer and would liaise between the Pentagon, TAC, SAC, Nellis, and Seventh Air Force in Saigon.

"Since travel's involved, that may be a problem in your case," White said.

"My back is feeling much better, sir."

"The hospital commander doesn't agree." Benny Lewis had recently created an uproar at the Nellis hospital by taking an unauthorized trip to Southeast Asia on another project.

"If you wish, sir, I can stay here and coordinate while someone else does the traveling." As much as he wanted to participate in the project, Benny didn't look forward to being constantly away after Julie arrived in Las Vegas next Friday.

"Maybe." General White reread the first paragraphs of the CSAF's message and shook his head. "Nope. He's specific about naming you as liaison officer. I'll speak with the hospital commander. Tell him it's an operational necessity that you travel, and that we'll send you first-class, commercial. The seats are bigger and more comfortable."

With that settled, they went back to the remainder of the message.

They'd been provided with a list of individuals who were currently cleared, and who could be contacted or involved in the project. All others were to be regarded as lacking the need to know. On the list were a total of twenty-eight names: seven at the Pentagon, two at Headquarters SAC, two at Headquarters TAC, two at a research and development lab at Wright-Patterson field, three at Seventh Air Force Headquarters in Saigon, and twelve others scattered around the various headquarters and operational bases. The number of stars on the list was impressive, but equally so were the generals who were not included, like the commanders of PACAF and Logistics commands.

While it was recognized that more personnel would be added to the list as the project progressed, names of nominees were to be provided, via back-channel message, to the office of the CSAF. Throughout the initial planning phase of the project, the numbers must remain minimal. All travel and research projects were assigned CSAF priority 1A. Three funding-program element numbers were initially provided: 11211F for strategic bombers, 21211F for tactical fighters, and 61611F for tactics-and-ordnance development. Those were all approved fund codes, established for and monitored from the office of the CSAF. Additional funds would be diverted as required. The Chief of Staff set a preliminary timetable—the target date for forces deployment was set for NO EARLIER THAN FEBRUARY 15TH AND NO LATER THAN APRIL 1ST, 1968. That gave them from four to six months to prepare.

Additional instructions would follow. General White was to acknowledge receipt and understanding ASAP via back-channel message. All such messages would be coded as

Secret—Immediate—JACKPOT, and would receive special cryptographic handling.

As Benny returned to the basement, he had a thought. If they worked as Moods said they would, the Pave Dagger smart bombs would be a definite advantage for a campaign of the sort the CSAF envisioned. Losses might be minimized, and target results improved.

Moods Diller looked up with a surprised expression as Benny entered the small office. "I thought you went to the club to watch the game."

Benny shook his head. "You still want to do that combat test with your smart bombs?"

Moods's jaw dropped. "At Danang? Yeah," he finally croaked. "I want to do it bad. That'll give us the real proof."

Benny nodded. "You're on. Get the test plan together."

"I've already got it. We'll send thirty bombs and kits to Danang and . . ."

"How about your trip tomorrow?"

Moods grinned wider yet. "It's on?"

"If it's necessary to get the bomb project on track, it's on."

"How about the money?"

"I'll find it. You just get those bombs working as soon as possible, okay?"

When Benny left the basement vault, the football game was long over. He went to the club, where a bartender told him the results as he sipped a cold beer. His Packers had lost a close one, but it couldn't quench Benny's enthusiasm.

In the *really* big game, Vietnam, they were finally going for the win.

1535L—Sixteenth Tee, Base Golf Course, Offutt AFB, Nebraska

Colonel Wes Snider

"I think we should move the tee-box back a bit, so it catches more of the dogleg," Wes was saying.

The course was closed for the winter, but he was giving

a few more pointers to the guy who'd be replacing him as chairman of the base golf committee. Wesley Snider had once faced the tough decision whether to take a commission in the Air Force or become a golf pro. The game had been good to him—a golf scholarship had helped him through his four years at Ohio State. The lure of flying had only barely won out, and although he enjoyed it, there were days when he wasn't sure he'd made the right decision. He still carried a ridiculously low handicap and was judicious enough to back off some when he was playing with superiors. General officers enjoyed playing a round with Wes, and his career hadn't suffered because of the sport.

He was a youthful colonel, and two weeks earlier had received orders to report to U Tapao Air Base in southern Thailand as Deputy for Operations. The next step would be as wing commander of a bomber wing, and after that he figured he had a good shot at wearing stars. He knew he was a capable officer, and the golf certainly hadn't hurt.

"Colonel Snider?" A man in civvies, carrying a brief case, approached them. The telltale bulge of a shoulder holster under his windbreaker revealed him to be a classified courier.

"Yes," he said.

"The command post told me I might find you here. Could I speak with you alone, sir?"

"Sure." Wes nodded to his replacement and told him he'd be right back. He walked over to one side of the fairway and motioned the fellow in civvies over.

The courier quietly introduced himself as a captain from the office of the Chief of Staff of the Air Force and indicated the briefcase.

"I'm carrying a message for your eyes only, sir. Could we go to the command post?"

"It's classified?"

"Yes, sir."

Wes had handled couriered messages before, but had never been called into the command post like this. "Why all the secrecy?"

"I really can't say, sir. I'm just following orders. I can say that the message was given to me by General McManus, and he gave me the delivery instructions."

Fifteen minutes later they were in a back room at the

Offutt command-and-control center, and Wes was reading the personal, informal note from the CSAF.

His orders were being changed. No longer was he going to U Tapao, Thailand. While he would be officially reassigned to the CSAF office in the Pentagon, Wes was to report to the commander, Seventh Air Force, in Saigon, and he was to do it ASAP. He could expect to travel often for the next six months, as a project liaison officer on something called JACKPOT. He could not, General McManus wrote, speak that code word aloud for the present. Prior to his departure from Offutt, he'd be briefed in by the four-star CINCSAC, who was also on the project. He would be further briefed by Lieutenant General Moss upon his arrival at Saigon.

His important task, McManus wrote, would be to help provide a bridge of understanding between the strategic and tactical forces involved in JACKPOT. That would be a major chore, but a most critical one.

Although he was mightily let down that he would no longer be running operations for the composite strategic wing at U Tapao, Wes Snider was a good soldier . . . and was increasingly intrigued about what JACKPOT might be. As the instructions on the note demanded, he ran the two sheets of paper through the nearest shredder.

The captain in civvies nodded. "I'll be leaving you now, sir. I've got to catch a flight back to Washington." His task was completed.

A few minutes later Wes started out of the command center, but he was held up by the security guard on the desk. "CINCSAC's in briefing room three, sir. He'd like to see you."

Things were moving rapidly in Wes Snider's world.

CHAPTER FIVE

Monday, October 23rd, 0435 Local—Command Post, Takhli RTAFB, Thailand

Captain Manny DeVera

The four pilots of Buick flight spent almost an hour in the six-by-eight briefing room. On the table before each was a small, canvas map-case containing their flight plan, flight-data card, and charts. Manny stood at the blackboard, carefully going over details of the indoctrination flight. The two captains, who would fly in the second and fourth positions, listened more intently than they might have otherwise, because Buick three was their wing commander. As Manny spoke, all took notes on the backs of their flight-data cards and interrupted when they had questions.

This was the first of their one hundred missions, their initial flight over North Vietnam. They were to air refuel from a KC-135 tanker on Blue Anchor, the easternmost of the racetrack routes, which began a few miles north of Ubon Air Base. After tanker drop-off they'd fly southeast into route pack one, then survey the South China Sea coast northward into pack two.

"We'll remain south of the city of Vinh today, to avoid the

SAMs and guns there," instructed Manny, "but I want you all to monitor your RHAW receivers for radar signals and call out what you see and hear."

He refreshed their memories about Firecan radars, with their dish-shaped antennae that fed information to antiaircraft artillery. "They control fifty-seven- and eighty-five-millimeter guns," he said. "The smaller stuff, like fourteen-five-, twenty-, and thirty-seven-millimeter, are visually aimed and can't reach up very far for you anyway. The big stuff, like hundred- and hundred-twenty millimeter, is too unwieldy and awkward to track a maneuvering jet. But fifty-seven- and eighty-five-millimeter guns are nimble as hell, and they can reach up and grab you, especially if they're directed by a Firecan. Watch out for 'em.

"If you hear a rattlesnake sound on the RHAW, look again and see if the SAM light's illuminated. That means a Fansong radar's painting you and feeding information to a surface-to-air missile launcher." He went over the simplest SAM evasive maneuver, just in case. "Long as you see the missiles in time and you maintain your maneuvering energy, you can dodge 'em by turning hard into them. Remember, wait until they're damned close, then . . ."

"How close?" asked a captain.

"So close you can read the fine print on the warhead. You'll know when he's overcommitted. Then, when you're about to crap your pants, break into 'em hard, like you would a MiG, and they'll overshoot just like a MiG would. The stubby little wings just can't turn the missile fast enough to keep up with you.

"We shouldn't see much of either big guns or SAMs today, but keep jinking and moving it around or you may be unpleasantly surprised. When we get there," said Manny, "we're going to take a good look around so you can get the coastal terrain and the Ho Chi Minh Trail imprinted on your brains. When you fly combat, you want to know where you are, anywhere over North Vietnam, just by glancing out at the ground. It'll surprise you how quickly that knowledge comes once you realize that sure as hell, someday your life's going to depend on it."

They went over the day's objective, which was to bomb either supply barges they might find on the Ca River, which dumped into the sea just south of Vinh, or suspected truck parks on the Ho Chi Minh Trail.

"You probably won't *see* any trucks on the trail, so you'll have to take intell's word that they're there. They travel at night and hide under trees and camouflage during the daytime. Unless they're carrying ammo and you get a secondary explosion, you likely won't even know if you've hit anything when you drop."

Manny was pleased to see that Colonel Leska was frowning at his description of the suspected truck parks. They were the least favorite targets of the combat pilots, who generally considered them a waste of both their time and taxpayer money.

"On our way back we'll climb up to twenty thousand feet, and everyone will practice flying at fifteen hundred feet out and forty-five degrees back from one another. That's the way you'll be doing it in pack six, when you get into sixteen-ship ECM pod formations."

"Why fifteen hundred feet?" asked a new captain.

"That's how close a SAM radar operator can distinguish you from another aircraft. His resolution at his favorite firing range is fifteen hundred feet. If everyone has their ECM pods on, and if everyone's in proper formation, he can look at the formation from any angle and all he'll see is jamming. That gives him a big blob on his radar screen instead of individual targets. Today it doesn't matter if you fuck it up, but when you get to pack six, you'd sure as hell better get it right."

As they all went out of the briefing room, headed for the personal equipment shop to check out and put on their flying gear, an unpleasant memory came to Manny. Several months earlier he'd allowed fears to get the best of him when he'd flown combat. An all–consuming terror had taken over his mind and paralyzed him. It was not likely to happen today, since they were going nowhere near the big guns in route pack six, but he wanted to make damned sure of it. Even before he entered the PE shop and went to the counter, he began reinforcing himself with the ritual he'd learned to beat the shakes and jangles.

Lucky Anderson had told him it was the same method practiced by fighter jocks since the beginning of aerial combat. *Remain calm by staying on the offensive and keeping*

*your mind busy with what you're going to do next to beat the
enemy,* Lucky Anderson had told him. *Remain calm—stay
on the offensive—think of what you'll do next,* Manny's mind
would chant to him when he was flying combat. *Calm—
offensive—what next?* Captain Manny DeVera began the ritual as he slipped on his helmet and tested for oxygen leaks
at the test bench. By the time he'd collected the rest of his
flight gear, his face had become hard. His eyes had narrowed and grown calculating, like those of a warrior.

0640L—Blue Anchor Air Refueling Track

Colonel Buster Leska

The refueling went smoothly. They'd hooked up with the
tanker just north of Ubon Air Base and were dropped off
over western Laos with full tanks. Then they followed
Manny DeVera's lead and flew the short jaunt into the
southern panhandle of North Vietnam.

Manny began his running narrative at Dong Hoi, a
coastal fishing city thirty miles north of the demilitarized
zone, and described various landmarks, like the fishhook—
which was a curved spit of land that jutted insolently into
the sea—as they continued up the coast.

They flew at 4,500 feet, just above the effective range of
small arms, so the terrain features, villages, and boats would
be easily discernible.

Thirty-seven-millimeter flak exploded in random white
popcorn bursts over one coastal town, and Buster found
himself grimacing. It was no different from what he remembered seeing in Korea, but there he'd flown at 20,000 and
30,000 feet, searching the sky for MiGs in his Sabre, as the
fighter-bombers rooted around down below doing the dirty
work with bombs and rockets. The previous night Mack
MacLendon had joked with him that his turn had arrived.
"Glad you're finally going to help out with the real work,"
he'd said, grinning.

When they were thirty miles south of the city of Vinh, at
the mouth of the Ca River, Buster picked up first a Firecan
AAA radar, then a Fansong SAM radar on his RHAW receiver, and Manny confirmed they were being tracked but

said the radars were too distant to be a threat. It was when the strobes grew out to the second and third concentric rings on the scope that you had to worry, he told them. As they drew closer, they encountered a few bursts of 57mm flak, but Manny held them away and narrated over the radio.

"Buick flight, note the shape and color of the flak bursts. Fifty-seven comes up in groups of fours and sixes. It's gray like that when it's all high explosive and shrapnel. If it's got phosphorus in it, it's bright red or white, but you won't see much of that."

When the SAM radar signal grew stronger and more persistent, Manny turned them away, westward, saying the SAM lessons would be given at a later date.

They flew to the high green mountains, where DeVera showed them the canyons through which the twisting Ho Chi Minh Trail meandered.

"There are three main routes through the mountains," Manny radioed as Buster looked down at the solid-green canopy of treetops, *"and there are thousands of hiding places for the trucks in each of the passes. Trying to pick the right truck park, that might be in use at the moment, is like finding the pea in a shell game."*

Buster thought he saw something on one of the roadways below. *"Buick lead, Buick three. I've got something in sight on the open roadway down at our two o'clock."*

After a slight pause Manny answered. *"Roger, Buick three. That's a truck all right, but notice it's parked out in the open and it's not moving? It's likely a broken-down hulk they're using for a flak trap, trying to sucker us down into range of their guns. I want the remainder of the flight to stay up high here, while I show you what I mean."*

The novices circled in an orbit, watching the truck as Manny left them and flew northward, descending. When he was down to 3,000 feet above the treetops, he turned back toward them, coming fast, jinking, heading straight for the truck on the road.

Furious lines of red and yellow reached upward from several sources, traversing the sky and searching for his twisting, turning aircraft. DeVera was quickly by them. He flew in a climbing turn back toward Buick flight.

"That's what I mean by a flak trap, Buicks. Don't let them

*sucker you in unless you're carrying cluster bombs and plan
to take 'em out. Even then you want to release high, because
you won't know how many guns will be shooting, or where
they're shooting from."*

Five miles west of the flak trap, Buster spotted something
moving on a roadway.

*"Buick lead, three's got something just off the road at our
ten o'clock."*

*"Roger, three. I saw it. I think it's water buffalo. Whatever
it is, there's a line of them in the trees down there. Set up
your switches for dive bomb, Buicks."*

The flight released a total of twenty-four 750-pound
bombs on the creatures, and when they came back around
for a strafing pass, Buick two called out that they were
horses and pulled off high without firing his gun.

Manny DeVera gruffly called for two to get back into the
strafe pattern, that the horses were undoubtedly carrying
supplies. They circled and wheeled in the sky, diving and
machine-gunning the specks that ran about wildly below.

On their return flight to Takhli, they practiced flying the
ECM pod formation, forty-five degrees back and 1,500-feet
separation. No one talked about what their bombs and bullets had done. No one wanted to think about terrorizing and
mutilating horses.

As they continued homeward, Buster thought about the
mission. Except for the altitude and the jungle, it had looked
and felt much as it had when he'd flown combat in Korea.
He knew it would be more dangerous and much busier
when they flew in pack six, but the pumping of adrenaline
when you knew that other men were trying to kill you was
certainly the same.

0920L—VPA Headquarters, Hanoi, DRV

Colonel Xuan Nha

The general staff meeting had been in session for twenty
minutes. General Giap sat at the head of the large table and
ran things. General Van Tien Dung was at his elbow, periodically scanning the attendees but seldom adding arguments
or commenting.

For the past three months a plan had been in place to mount an energetic spring offensive. Seventy-six-year-old Ho Chi Minh's health had rallied, but they all knew he wasn't going to last more than another year or two. Before his death, he wanted an end to the war he'd urged his people to fight for five, ten, twenty years or more. His goal was a united Vietnam, under the hegemony of Hanoi and his creation, the Lao Dong party. It would be his legacy that the subcontinent be dominated and guided by the Lao Dong.

His armies and their Pathet Lao allies were marching victoriously through the vast Laotian plains and were preparing an offensive designed to run the Laotian Army from the battlefield. They operated freely in Cambodia. They were doing well enough against the ARVN puppet army, and there was such political confusion under Saigon's laughable attempts at Western-style democracy that he *knew* he could prevail there, but only if the Americans withdrew.

The Washington politicians must be convinced to stop providing weapons and training to their puppets, but even more, they must disengage their troops. He knew it would take considerable military and political pressure to make it happen.

On October 1st the Enlightened One had called for a closed-door meeting of key members of the Central Committee, including the seventeen-man politburo and selected others who led the Lao Dong party. Xuan's wife, Li Binh, had been there, and she'd related what had happened.

Ho Chi Minh had told the Minister for External Affairs that he and his people were doing well, that his work undermining the war effort in the United States was just as effective as what they'd done with the French in the War of Liberation. Li Binh swore that he'd looked directly at her when he spoke the compliment.

Then he'd turned to his Minister for Defense, General Vo Nguyen Giap, and stared. He'd said nothing, but Li Binh said more was voiced in that long, quiet look of the Enlightened One than he could have uttered with a thousand words. He'd motioned, and his nurse had lit and handed him a filtered cigarette. He'd drawn on it and coughed, the sound of a rasp on wood. All of that time he'd continued to stare at Giap.

"In late 1953," he'd finally said in his high-pitched poet's voice, "I asked for a great victory, and three months later you gave me Dien Bien Phu."

Giap, the Enlightened One's friend and confidante, had silently nodded. Dung, Giap's right hand, had kept his eyes judiciously lowered, unable to break the intensity of the moment with his usual gross jokes because of the gravity of the situation.

"Thus far this year," Ho Chi Minh continued, "the Americans have won every battle."

Giap found his voice. "The same was true in 1953 with the French." Cautiously, he'd added that he was positioning forces, gathering strength both in the demilitarized zone and the Mekong delta.

"It is late 1967." The Enlightened One paused to cough again, this time sounding much weaker. "Mark this date on your calendar." The room had become so quiet that Li Binh said she could hear her own breathing.

Ho Chi Minh wheezed and was successful in suppressing another cough. Then his high, melodic voice had emerged in a whisper. "I ask for a great victory. Another Dien Bien Phu. Give me ten thousand American prisoners, as you did with the French. With that, the American presidency will fail. Other men will say that if they are elected, they will stop the war. Johnson will become afraid, for he is a politician, and American politicians are much more frightened that they may lose an election than a war in a distant land. Then he will tell the people that he will immediately end the war if they will just elect him again."

Li Binh said the Enlightened One had not waited for Giap's response, that he'd beckoned and his nurse had helped him to his feet. He'd left with no further word.

Following that meeting Giap had called a series of discussions with his senior staff. The previously planned spring offensive was to be reviewed. They must find an American weakness. He was determined to perform another Dien Bien Phu miracle. Since this was Xuan Nha's first time to attend such a meeting, he didn't know what had transpired before, but it was apparent that Dung and the others were apprehensive about the gamble Giap was contemplating.

"We must not be premature," Dung cautioned. "If we are to attack successfully, we must first assure that we can sustain and supply our soldiers." Foremost, Dung was a careful logistician.

"See to it," Giap told him. Dung licked his lips thoughtfully. Then he turned to General Tho and Xuan Nha, who were seated in adjacent chairs down the table.

"We will be moving great quantities of supplies from Hanoi. You must protect them as never before." Both men agreed. Xuan Nha said he'd move additional defenses to the southern side of Hanoi, and series of AAA and SAM batteries as far southward as they dared. Tho said he'd tell his pilots to concentrate their interceptors in that area.

Dung told his colonel of logistics to move his convoys more boldly, to double their present tonnages. When the colonel looked astonished at the order, Dung said they should be able to do it with the increased protection during the first, critical part of their long journey.

The colonel said he'd need more people, to repair or circumvent the many bridges destroyed by Mee air attacks, to ferry supplies across waterways, and to actually do the hauling. Thousands of new bicycles were on their way from China, he said, but they didn't have the manpower in place at the Cambodian base camps to use them.

Dung turned to Xuan. "How many militia can you spare, Colonel Nha?"

Xuan Nha had studied the home-defense forces. They were pets of General Luc, especially the elite units manning the beaches against attack, so he knew to be judicious.

"Ten thousand," he finally croaked in his ruined voice.

Dung mused for a moment. "Make it twenty thousand." He waited for Xuan's response.

Xuan banished all emotion from his face. Would General Luc argue at a time such as this? Should *he* argue? General Dung had already mobilized fifty thousand other militia and sent them south to fight. Taking 20,000 more from their posts would leave only 200,000 to defend the perimeter of the People's Democratic Republic. The militia of the People's Army of National Defense were poorly trained and often thought, especially by those who believed there was a low probability of invasion, to be useless. If they *were* invaded, they argued, People's Army regular units must be quickly called home to fight.

Xuan Nha finally broke his silence. "Has the general considered that if the Mee are subjected to a defeat such as you are planning, they might bomb more vigorously here in the North? I think it is worth considering."

"More vigorously than they are already doing?" asked a colonel on Giap's staff.

"The Mee pilots are restrained by their politicians. If they were to lose a major battle, the politicians might think differently. They might believe that if they attacked us with everything they had, brought B-52 bombers up here, perhaps even bombed Hanoi, we would disengage."

Giap pondered the point. Xuan Nha was known to be uncannily accurate in his forecasts about American reactions.

"Perhaps," Xuan added, "they might even invade with their Marines."

Giap suddenly shook his head, his mind made up. "The Minister of External Affairs assures me that if we achieve a stunning victory, the Americans will lose heart in the war and stop bombing altogether. He says the danger of increased bombing attacks is more likely if we attack and fail. That *must not* happen. And he says no matter *what* we do militarily, there will be no land attack. I must believe him."

Xuan acquiesced. The time for argument was past. "I will provide the twenty thousand militia immediately, comrade General."

Dung turned to General Giap. "If we double the numbers of shipments for the next two months, we will deplete the supplies we have on the docks at Haiphong and in the warehouses in Hanoi. Should we ask the Russians for more shipments of weapons and supplies?"

"Yes, but I don't want even them to know that the offensive will be as massive as we are planning. If they increase the numbers of ships coming into port too quickly, the Mee might be alerted. I want complete surprise." They studied and argued over the map of South Vietnam for the next hour. Where would the Mee Dien Bien Phu take place? When should they attack?

Xuan Nha's own mind turned in a different direction. It was likely that General Dung's people would ask for more of the VPAND militia to help in their massive supply efforts. He tried to think of an argument to prove they were critical to the war effort and must remain under the control of the Army of National Defense.

The generals continued to debate about where to mass their troops and how many should be placed in jeopardy by striking at the Americans. Finally, General Giap decided that the matter was of such importance that he must call on certain leaders operating in the South.

"I have already requested that Le Duc Tho come north to attend our meetings," he said. "He should arrive within a week." Le Duc Tho was a member of the Lao Dong politburo, the highest-ranking politician operating in South Vietnam. He was Ho Chi Minh's personal representative there, coordinating the war effort with the party, as well as with the Ministries of External Affairs and Defense in Hanoi. Half warrior, half politician, he held the authority of a supreme on-scene commander. He was also General Tho's uncle and the source of his power. He seemed pleased that Giap was calling upon his famous relative for advice.

Giap surprised them all then, for he said he would also call for General Tran Do, deputy commander of all communist forces in the South, and Colonel Tran Van Tra, commandant of Vietnamese People's Army forces in the Delta and Saigon regions. *Is Giap thinking of taking Saigon?* Xuan wondered. What a bold stroke *that* would be.

The meeting did not adjourn until 1400. Giap and Dung departed first, followed by the remainder of the senior officers. As Tho began to rise, Xuan struggled painfully to his own feet and asked for a moment of the general's time.

"Yesterday and this morning the Mee reconnaissance Phantoms continued to overfly Phuc Yen," Xuan Nha croaked.

Tho mused. "When the flights began, I alerted the acting air-regiment commandant to prepare to evacuate the aircraft north into the Chinese restricted zone. I also asked intelligence to verify whether and when they will attack, but so far there has been no response."

Xuan Nha brooded. "The Mee may be bluffing, but I feel they are not. They have bombed your auxiliary fields, and it seems logical that Phuc Yen will be next. That is the way they do things, one cautious step at a time. They will attack," Xuan Nha said confidently.

Tho appeared more concerned.

Xuan touched his forefinger to his chest. "I feel it here. My men shot down one of their reconnaissance Phantoms.

When the Mee pilots were interrogated, they both said they were ordered to take very precise photographs of the base at Phuc Yen."

Tho sighed. "I also believe they might attack. But when?"

"May I suggest that the critical time might be when the reconnaissance flights are stopped? They might do that to let us think they have changed their minds and *won't* attack."

General Tho considered his words.

"And may I also suggest that when that happens, and"—he pinned his eye on Tho—"you evacuate your aircraft from Phuc Yen, that you tell the pilots to remain silent on their radios and to fly very low so the Mee will not know they are gone or the destination."

Tho nodded very slowly.

Xuan Nha felt a glow of satisfaction as the general departed. Tho had listened and would heed his advice.

1620L—Command Post, Takhli RTAFB, Thailand

Lieutenant Colonel Pearly Gates

Pearly had landed only fifteen minutes before, brought to Takhli on his round of the bases to participate in the next morning's bombing attack. Before coming to Takhli, he'd visited Ubon and Korat. The bases would be bombing in that order: Ubon, Korat, then Takhli.

Assembled in the room and seated before him in the briefing theater were the key operations personnel; the wing commander, his vice commander, Deputy for Operations, weapons officer, and the three fighter-squadron commanders. They waited for Pearly Gates's words with full attention, for General Moss sent his representative to the bases only before important missions.

"During the past few months," Pearly began, "we've been permitted to attack the auxiliary MiG bases, such as Kep and Hoa Lac, and the smaller deployment bases. A month ago the Navy began pounding on Kien An, the MiG base just south of Haiphong. But we've repeatedly been denied permission to hit Phuc Yen, their biggest base, or the command and control facilities there. That permission is now anticipated to arrive tonight by courier from Washington."

Several grins appeared on the faces before him. "About time," breathed Colonel Armaugh, the quiet Deputy for Operations. Pearly went to the back-lit map of North Vietnam and tapped his forefinger on Phuc Yen, just north and across the Red River from Hanoi, and well within the red circle marking the twenty-mile restricted area surrounding the North Vietnamese capital city.

"How many MiGs are hangared there?" asked Colonel Mack, whom Pearly remembered from prior trips.

"At one time we estimated seventy-five. More than forty MiG-17's, a dozen or so MiG-19's, and about twenty MiG-21's. They've also had two IL-28 light bombers based there, but we haven't seen them around for a while. We've seldom counted fewer than thirty-five fighters on the ground. It's their primary MiG base, with full maintenance-and-repair facilities."

"Pearly," asked Colonel Leska, "when I was at Tan Son Nhut a few days ago, you were concerned about the higher-headquarters-directed recce missions over Phuc Yen. Any chance they'll be alerted and fly out the MiGs before the strike?"

Pearly nodded, his face grim. "Yes, sir, there certainly is. When we received this preliminary alert, to stand by for tasking, I requested that the recce missions be terminated. The last photo run occurred at oh-seven-thirty this morning. We're hoping they didn't give everything away. We'll continue to monitor for a mass evacuation with our airborne radars and the Motel long-range radar at Udorn, and if we see them fly out, we'll advise you."

One of the new squadron commanders motioned a hand for attention. He was neat and well-groomed, with eyes that constantly shifted about the room. His name tag read DONOVAN, and he'd worn a sour frown throughout most of the meeting.

"Any idea why the dumb shits at higher headquarters are making it so apparent we're about to bomb there?" he growled.

"I have no opinion that wouldn't be conjecture," Pearly Gates replied.

"Who ordered the photo missions?" demanded Donovan.

"The silly bastards at some headquarters trying to kill me or something?"

Me? wondered Pearly. Why not *us?* "The directive for recce was passed down by PACAF, but the original order came from the Joint Targeting Office at the Pentagon."

Donovan snorted.

The wing commander fixed the light colonel with a withering glare. "We'll talk about that later, Yank," Leska said. He faced Gates. "What's the anticipated timing, Pearly?"

"Oh-seven-hundred for the first time over target. That'll be F-4's from Ubon. Korat will hit with their Thuds fifteen minutes later, and your TOT will be oh-seven-thirty."

Several attendees jotted down the times.

"There are to be no cluster bombs carried," continued Pearly, "and anyone who isn't sure of hitting his target is to pull off high and dry. They want minimum collateral damage, because it's known there are foreign nationals on base."

"Russian advisors," Donovan muttered derisively.

The briefing lasted for fifteen more minutes, at which time Colonel Leska excused everyone except Pearly and a captain wearing a fierce-looking mustache, who'd listened intently but said nothing. When the door was closed, Leska gestured.

"Pearly, I'd like you to meet Captain Manny DeVera."

Pearly smiled as they shook hands. "So I finally get to meet the Supersonic Wetback."

"The one and only." DeVera grinned.

"There was a big-time ruckus at Seventh Air Force when they tried to hang you for bombing the restricted target."

DeVera had been smiling, but he tensed at the mention of his previous troubles.

"All the support was on your side. General Moss was pissed off. He made inquiries until he got a telephone call telling him it was out of his jurisdiction and to butt out."

"That call come from PACAF?" Manny asked quietly.

Pearly nodded. "I'd better stop talking out of school, but I want you to know we were all happy as hell to see you on your way back."

Colonel Leska spoke in a low voice. "Manny's my choice to work with us on the JACKPOT project. When Major Anderson gets here, the three of us will be feeding you all the supportive information we can."

Pearly started to speak, but DeVera interrupted. "JACK-POT?"

"Remember when I told you to gather target information? To find the Achilles' heel?"

"General Moss," said Pearly, "had established contact with the Chief of Staff, like you said, and I've got two of my people pulling out different ingredients we'll need for the OPlan."

While DeVera's eyes grew wider, Buster Leska's narrowed. Pearly picked up the wing commander's concern about secrecy. "My people don't know what they're working on. We build a lot of plans, and most of them just go into the musty files."

"JACKPOT?" repeated Manny DeVera.

"A large-scale bombing campaign designed to end the war," said the wing commander. "Don't breathe a word about it outside of our discussions," Leska said firmly. "Period."

"This decision to bomb Phuc Yen have anything to do with it?" DeVera asked.

Leska considered. "Probably not. This one's been a long-running hassle between the SecDef and the military. Every time General McManus or the Chief of Naval Operations suggests bombing Phuc Yen, the SecDef's people argue it would be a dangerous escalation that isn't worth the effort. They say we're overstating the numbers of MiGs, and that we'd endanger foreign nationals." He gave Pearly an inquisitive look. "Did General McManus get in to see L.B.J.?"

Captain DeVera's eyes grew wider yet.

"Yes, sir. Two days after we sent him our first JACKPOT message, he called General Moss on the scrambler net and told him they'd met and he believed it went well."

"Then perhaps General McManus did convince him to make the Phuc Yen decision."

"I don't think so," said Pearly. "The Joint Targeting Office directed the photo recce missions before General McManus got in to see him."

"Those may have been directed by the SecDef's office, trying to prove there are fewer MiGs there than we're stating. The SecDef's people didn't want this mission to take place."

"Yesterday morning's photos," said Pearly, "show a

MiG-21 near the takeoff end of the runway and two
MiG-17's parked in a maintenance area."

"Where are the rest of 'em?" DeVera asked.

"In hangarettes and under camouflage," Pearly told him.
"When you study the target photos, you'll see nets strung all
over the place. It's going to make it difficult to get accurate
bomb-damage assessment." Pearly's glasses slid forward
onto the bridge of his nose, and he absently pushed them
back into place with a forefinger.

DeVera glowered. "I hope to hell the MiGs are there tomorrow morning."

"If they're not," said Buster Leska, "it's going to make us
military warmongers look awfully foolish for beating our
drums and asking for the mission."

Pearly glanced wistfully at the map. "If they leave them
in place for just one more day, we'll have 'em. We'll knock
out half their air force in a single mission."

Buster nodded and got to his feet. "How about joining us
for dinner before you go?"

Pearly quickly shook his head. The food at the Takhli
club was rated as the worst in the combat zone. "I'd better
get on back to Saigon, Colonel. The courier from Washington should arrive by the time I get there, and we'll have to
issue an amendment to the air tasking order. We want this
one to go off without any hitches."

CHAPTER SIX

Tuesday, October 24th, 0420 Local—Command Post Briefing Theater, Takhli RTAFB

Colonel Buster Leska

Buster had flown only the one mission over North Vietnam and knew he wasn't proficient to lead the important strike on Phuc Yen. He would have preferred that Mack MacLendon lead it, and Mack would have done so gladly, no questions asked, but it was neither fair nor right to ask it of him. He'd completed 112 missions up north before someone had noticed and Buster had ordered him taken off the flying schedule. Now he was busy briefing his replacement, Obie Zeigler, and preparing to depart. Buster had picked George Armaugh, his quiet Deputy for Operations, to be force commander. Yank Donovan had volunteered and was leading one of the middle flights. Manny DeVera had also come forward, so he was bringing up the rear, shepherding the last flight in the sixteen-ship formation.

The remainder of the pilots selected for the mission were their canniest and most accurate dive-bombers.

The pilots whooped happily when they found they'd finally be able to attack Phuc Yen. When they learned that

Takhli would be third to strike the target, they complained
that the others might not leave any MiGs for them. From
the back of the room Buster watched and listened, wishing
he were going along. He didn't like the idea of sending his
men out to fly and fight on a big one without participating.

A command post ops specialist was finishing with his
neat print on the Plexiglas mission board, and Buster read it
carefully, pausing at each nugget of information.

OCTOBER 24

Takeoff	Time:	0600L/2300Z
	Altimeter:	30.05″
	Temperature:	35° C
	Weather:	Scattered
Pri Tgt #1	JCS 31:01	
	Phuc Yen Airfield/Runway & Acft Shelters	
	Air Refueling:	Green Anchor
	Tgt Coord:	21°13′ 20″ N
		105°48′ 12″ E
	Tgt Alt:	415′
	TOT:	0030Z
	Altimeter:	30.01″
	Weather:	Scattered/ Broken
	Defenses:	Heavy AAA/ SAM/MIG
	EXECUTION WORD:	LEMON DROP
	RECALL:	LOBO
	SUCCESS:	MAVERICK
	UNSUCCESS:	KING GEORGE
Pri Tgt #2	JCS 31:12	
	Phuc Yen Control/Radar & Facility	
	Air Refueling:	Green Anchor
	Tgt Coord:	21°13′ 17″ N
		105°48′ 09″ E
	Tgt Alt:	415′

TOT:	0030Z
Altimeter:	30.01"
Weather:	Scattered/ Broken
Defenses:	Heavy AAA/ SAM/MIG
EXECUTION WORD:	JAWBREAKER
RECALL:	LOBO
SUCCESS:	COWBOY
UNSUCCESS:	HOT PEPPER

Alt Tgt   Vinh Ferry (Submerged)

Air Refueling:	Blue Anchor Ext.
Tgt Coord:	18°41′ 22″ N 105°41′ 53″ E
Tgt Alt:	S/L
TOT:	0020Z
Altimeter:	30.00"
Weather:	Scattered
Defenses:	Medium AAA/ Poss SAM
EXECUTION WORD:	NIGHTFALL
RECALL:	JASMINE
SUCCESS:	DUNGEON
UNSUCCESS:	BLUE BOY

The primary targets were both at Phuc Yen, as Pearly Gates had told them. The first eight aircraft would bomb the MiGs in their revetments. The third and fourth flights, Donovan's and DeVera's, would attack the Barlock long-range radar and the adjacent control building, the eyes and brains behind the enemy's interceptor operation.

Buster wondered how many pilots had sat in this room and others like it at other airfields, wishing they could be flying this mission. Taking the fight to the enemy. Knocking out North Vietnam's biggest airfield as they should've done the first day they'd gone up there.

The pilots filled in their data cards from information on the board and spoke in low voices. Two argued about tactics to use if MiGs were launched to defend their base. Another spoke about the possibility of the MiG pilots taxiing their aircraft away from the revetments where they were normally parked. Yank Donovan argued that they should swing around and strafe the MiGs after the bombing attack, but George Armaugh told him they'd stick to the plan—make a single pass and get out of the area. The four Wild Weasel crews, the SAM killers, discussed missile sites that had been active on their last flights up there.

A lieutenant from intell came in and circled the words "Lemon Drop" and "Jawbreaker." The mission was on. Chatter from the pilots grew and filled the room. As the Deputy for Operations took the podium and glanced about to ensure all flight leaders were present, Buster started to leave.

Colonel George Armaugh spoke. "Did you want to say anything to the men, sir?"

The room grew quiet. Buster turned and eyed them, scanned from one side of the room to the other, then shook his head. "You guys are professionals. Just do the job."

He left the room, closing the door behind him, and turned to go to his office. Battles and wars could be won or lost, but paperwork kept growing at the same relentless rate.

0714L—Route Pack Six, North Vietnam

Captain Manny DeVera

Remain calm—stay on the offensive—think of what you'll do next, Manny's mind chanted.

The sixteen-ship formation crossed the Red River two minutes ahead of schedule, close on the heels of a similar gaggle from Korat Air Base. The F-4's from Ubon had been first to attack and could be seen in the distance at their eleven o'clock, headed back west toward safety. Throughout the Phantoms' bombing, Wild Weasels had called multiple SAM launchings, and the sounds of the emergency beepers of an F-4 crew shot down over the target area still rang in Manny's ears. Both beepers had been shut off, so he supposed they were alive.

"Good luck, buddies," he muttered for the sake of the downed pilots. Then Manny looked out at the group about him and felt a shudder of anxiety course through his body. *Remain calm—stay on the offensive—what's next.* He sucked in a breath and steadied himself.

He was flying with a flight of old hands from the 357th squadron, the can-do bunch trained by Colonel Mack. They were all in place. Pros, like Colonel Leska had said. The flight just in front of him was led by the new 354th commander, and he flew with men from his squadron. Smitty was on Yank Donovan's wing. Billy Bowes led the second element, off to the other side. Another captain, a solid pilot named Ron Wilshire, who had a sort of hero worship for Donovan and had been an instructor in his section at McConnell Air Force Base, was his number four.

Manny took another good look around for MiGs, then glanced again at the clip of recce film he'd brought with him, which showed where the radar and command-and-control building were located just west of the northern end of the runway. The photo was mostly incomprehensible because of all the camouflage, but features of the layout had been marked by photo interpreters. Donovan's target was the command-and-control building. Manny's four would go after the radar itself. Both were just X's shown on top of the indistinct maze of nets.

The F-4's, being first to attack, had flown south of the target, feinting as if they were headed down the Red River toward the Doumer bridge, but turned up on their left wings and dived toward the runway to put their bombs along its length and crater it. If they'd done their jobs, the MiGs couldn't take off and escape.

A Wild Weasel flight called out a SAM launch in the direction of the Korat formation, and Manny strained his eyes in vain, then pulled them back to the airspace surrounding his own group.

The sixteen-ship formations from the two Thud wings flew directly toward Phuc Yen, not bothering to hide their intentions as the Phantoms had done. The shortest way between two points was a straight line.

A cacophony of voices sounded on the radio as Korat attacked the target. There was a lot of flak, they said. Manny looked about at his flight again, a queasy feeling rising in his gut.

Remain calm. He swallowed and shook his head to clear it, and a numbing sensation invaded his emotions like a thick, protective cloud. He stared ahead, looking for the target area, and saw a blanket of white popcorn puffs down low, and darker bursts in groups of six, just north of the Red River. Smoke and dust from bomb explosions rose from the airfield.

Closer now. *Think of your next move.*

Time slowed and Manny made corrections in still, snapshot frames, checking his lights and gauges, looking out toward the target, taking a last glance at the target photo. Click . . . click . . . click. The strike force began to climb up to delivery altitude. The mission commander called for his flight to begin their roll-in.

Manny began to react mechanically. The second flight of four left them, diving toward the revetments and cloaked parking areas. *Stay on the offensive,* his mind growled at him. After the single twinge of apprehension, there'd been no more. He'd not allowed his mind the luxury of feeling threatened.

It was Donovan's turn, and Manny watched closely, time still passing slowly, as the four aircraft turned earthward. They'd briefed a forty-five-degree dive. Yank's dive angle looked to be precisely that. Manny waited until Donovan's fourth aircraft entered the dive, then sucked in a shallow breath. He'd told his flight to make it quick and dirty, to dive-bomb with minimum sequencing—bam! bam! bam!— so the gunners would have too many targets.

Don't delay. Take the offensive. Get 'em! He abruptly rolled upside down, nursed the control stick back and settled at forty degrees plus, then rolled back upright. He steadied the big aircraft in its dive, jinking slightly, eyes glued on the target in the combining glass before him.

The first Thuds in Donovan's flight were releasing. Bundles of flak searched and settled about the rearmost one, a bit off to his right. Ron Wilshire? At 8,000 feet and almost at release altitude, a burst found the bird and covered it.

Manny passed through 10,000 feet, past other angry explosions, no longer jinking.

Wilshire's aircraft was still in its dive. Pieces of the airplane began to shed, trailing behind in an obscene tail of debris.

"*Get out!*" Manny yelled hoarsely over the radio. Aircraft parts continued to fall away, now joined by a thick streamer of dark smoke. Bombs and fuel tanks somehow popped loose and accompanied the airplane as if they were flying in formation toward the ground.

Oh Jesus! he thought momentarily, but then the numbing sensation returned, and he concentrated on the earth coming up at him. Smoke, dust, and debris from the hundred-odd bombs already released on the air base drifted about in thick clouds. Light wind from the west . . . eyes fixed on the part of the obscured area that was supposedly his target. Smoke there too.

Manny's aircraft shuddered from a near miss. *Steady.* The sight picture came together. He pickled, felt the lurch of bomb release, waited a heartbeat, then pulled the stick back smoothly. Another buffet from a burst of flak reminded him to jink. *Dummy!* He pulled the stick harder and began to move the aircraft in random motions to provide a more difficult target for gunners.

Manny looked up toward the aircraft in front of and above him, corrected toward them, performed a slight roll, and stared back to observe the target area.

Bombs from the last aircraft hit where they'd been aimed, bright flashes in the midst of heavy billows of smoke from other explosives.

A snapshot of Ron Wilshire's burning aircraft blinked before him.

He'd not especially liked Wilshire the few times he'd met him. A wiseass. Maybe it had been Yank Donovan's influence. But now . . . *Jesus!* The scene replayed in Manny's mind—the airplane and bombs hurtling earthward. He'd been too busy with his dive bomb to watch the impact. *Gotta remain calm. Gotta stay on the offensive.*

0945L—Wing Weapons Office, Takhli RTAFB, Thailand

Manny was weary from the long mission, and still a little hyped from the rush of adrenaline, but he was also angry. The only MiGs they'd found in the open at Phuc Yen were a couple parked far from the revetments, and those, they were willing to bet, had been a couple of hangar queens the gomers couldn't get off the ground. As far as they knew, without benefit of analysis by the photo interpreters at Saigon, the MiGs had flushed before the arrival of the first strike force.

The debriefing had been cautious and downbeat. Just before they'd begun their dive, three SAMs had zipped between a couple of Thuds and would have taken them out if the gomer SAM operators had judged their altitude better and detonated the warheads properly. The bombing itself had gone pretty well, with most of the bombs landing on or near their targets. They'd lost one, confirmed as Ron Wilshire, to antiaircraft gunfire. On the way home they'd had another near miss with SAMs.

At the debriefing Yank Donovan said Wilshire had been out of his prebriefed position, and that was why he'd been hammered. He'd acted as if the death of the captain who'd followed him around like a dependent pup had been an act of suicide.

Manny had disagreed. Wilshire might not have been in the precise position Donovan would have liked, but he felt it was something else. Slow timing perhaps? Donovan's mouth had twitched angrily as he'd spoken, but he'd not responded to the criticism.

Yank was a cold one, Manny decided, and entirely too confident. Donovan had been positive that his own bombs had taken out the control center—although there was no way to know with all the camouflage, smoke, and flying debris down there.

Manny sat in his office, sipping hot coffee and staring at the wall, which was still adorned with a photo taken from a frame of Max Foley's gunfilm. The photo lab had blown it up to fill a twenty-four-by-thirty-six-inch frame. It showed a stern view of a MiG-17 with fire torching brightly from its wing-root. Foley's second MiG kill. Max Foley had been a superb weapons officer. Could Manny *really* fill his shoes?

He thought back on the mission again and wondered if they could have done anything to make it better, to increase their odds of survival and still get bombs on target. Foley had despised the big formations that were ordered to fly by higher headquarters. He'd said that fighter pilots were supposed to fly in flights of four, not in gaggles like geese and bombers. And a goodly number of the wing's pilots, Manny included, had taken his lead and agreed. So, he pondered, did they really give enough thought to the formation they flew?

The gaggle, as they called it, was a result of tests conducted at Nellis Air Force Base, where they'd tried to optimize the effectiveness of jamming pods against SAM and AAA radars. And—like it or not—they were going to continue flying it on their way to and from the tough targets around Hanoi. If all that was so, then shouldn't they concentrate on making damn sure they did it right? He'd noted that almost half of the formation had been poorly spaced. So . . . *concentrate on training the pilots to fly at precisely the correct distances and angles.*

Secondly, how about the ECM pods they relied on to mask the big formation? Too many were failing on a long mission. So . . . *jack up the ECM maintenance shop and find out what's wrong, then correct it.*

Sounds easy, Manny, he told himself, and wondered.

His mind returned to Ron Wilshire. The gunners had been able to concentrate on his bird. Perhaps if Donovan's flight had done as Manny's had—rolled in and bombed the target almost simultaneously so they'd confuse the gunners, a matter of tightening up only a second or two between aircraft—maybe that would have saved Wilshire.

There was another thing. One of the Wild Weasel pilots wanted to increase the numbers of SAM killers accompanying the strike force to two flights on the toughest targets. They'd been getting more Wild Weasel aircraft and aircrews, and he said they could provide better protection that way. Manny decided to speak with the Weasel pilot again, then maybe go see Colonel Armaugh and try to get the change pushed through.

Perhaps there was work for him to do after all.

1725L—Hale Koa Hotel, Honolulu, Hawaii

Major Lucky Anderson

The Hale Koa was a hotel in downtown Honolulu operated and maintained by the U.S. Army at Fort DeRussey for military personnel stationed in the Pacific. Since Fort DeRussey occupied some of the prime beach frontage along Waikiki, the Hale Koa was extremely popular. As the Vietnam War wore on, it became impossible to get a room on short notice, for war-weary soldiers, sailors, and airmen used it as a haven, a place to meet with wives who flew in from the States, and to forget about combat.

Lucky was fortunate, for General Moss had personally called the commander of Fort DeRussey, and he'd felt embarrassed at the way the hotel staff had greeted him, ushered him to a suite on the top floor, then treated him like some sort of royalty. He was not royalty at all, just a fighter jock who'd been dumb enough to let himself be shot down and spent too long running around North Vietnam trying to get himself rescued. Which made the suite and the good food and the company—*especially* the company—even better. They'd been there for five days, and would remain for the rest of their two-week leaves of absence. Right up to when they *had* to leave, and then he'd want to stay longer. Only a fool would want to return to combat.

Linda called in to him from outside. "Paul? When you gonna bring a girl a drink?"

Lucky finished swizzling her boozeless mai tai, grabbed a beer from the refrigerator for himself, and walked out on the balcony. She was stretched out on her tummy, straps of the bikini top loosened and lying to either side. Linda spent an hour of each day either on the beach or the balcony, soaking up rays.

He grinned and held the mai tai up high, so she'd have to raise and expose herself. She foiled him, holding her top in place with one hand as she took the glass.

Lucky frowned. "How do you do that?"

"A gal's gotta learn to cover her assets."

He leered. "Why don't we go inside and *uncover* your assets."

"You're insatiable," she said, sipping and sighing. She

looked his rugged body up and down, then giggled, sounding more like a teenager than a government official responsible for multimillion-dollar budgets. When they'd first arrived in Honolulu, she'd been the one to initiate their frequent lovemaking. Now they were both into the game, and neither could get enough.

"You're going to bake out here anyway," he observed as she stood, bra still held firmly in place, and followed him into the living room.

"I don't burn," she said, jauntily tossing the top aside as he closed the blind. "My daddy's side's Mexican, and we just get browner." It was the truth. Only her breasts were pale, the rest of her evenly tanned. She rose onto tiptoes to stretch lazily, and he admired. Linda moved in fluid motions, like a cat. She was tall and trim, perhaps not beautiful to all others, but certainly perfect in his eyes.

"Let's go build up an appetite for dinner, hunk," she said in her sexy tone, then twitched her hips suggestively as she started for the bedroom.

He didn't need encouragement.

A *rappedy-rap* sounded at the door.

"Damn," Linda muttered.

"I'll get rid of 'em," he said morosely. The three times they'd made love that day was not nearly enough. Lucky waited until she closed the bedroom door.

The rapping came again.

He cracked the door, then opened it wide. First Lieutenant Henry Horn was there, a cute brunette at his side with a papoose carrier on her back.

"I'll be damned," Lucky muttered. He grabbed Henry's hand and began to pump it energetically.

"Sure good seeing you again, Major," Horn said, beaming.

Lucky ushered them in as Henry introduced his wife and their infant daughter. He said they'd gotten in the previous morning and planned to spend a week in Honolulu before going on to his assignment at Luke Air Force Base, near Phoenix. The couple were about to sit when Henry's wife, who carefully avoided looking at Lucky's face, noticed the bikini top on the floor and reddened.

Lucky deftly scooped it up. "My fiancée is . . . uh . . ."

Henry explained how Major Lucky was engaged to this

nice lady who ran the USAID office in Bangkok. His wife smiled weakly, still trying to avoid looking at Lucky. His face had been badly burned and scarred in an aircraft accident several years before. He was accustomed to uneasiness and looks of horror.

Lucky went to the bar, hid the bikini top, and asked if they'd like a drink.

She passed. Henry said he'd take a beer.

Linda appeared from the bedroom, wearing a flowered muumuu and white sandals.

Lucky grinned at her. "Hon, this is Lieutenant Henry Horn, from Takhli."

She smiled graciously. "I remember seeing you there. You were in Paul's squadron, weren't you?"

"I was assigned to his C-Flight, ma'am," Henry answered. He introduced his wife again, and Linda made a fuss over the baby.

Lucky looked on, thinking how much he loved her. "Anything new back at Takhli in the last few days?" he asked Henry as the women continued their discussion.

"Joe Walker was shot down." Joe and Henry had both been assigned to Lucky's flight. They'd been close, graduates of the same class at the Air Force Academy.

"Damn," Lucky muttered.

"They picked him up, but he was badly banged up. Legs and pelvis broke all to hell from the ejection. It'll be a while before he's back in the cockpit."

"Good man, Joe."

"Lemme see. Oh yeah. They got in a new wing commander the day after I left."

Lucky gave him a questioning look.

"Guy named Lasko, Lesko, something like that. I saw the banner they put up for him. He's got an uncommon first name. Sylvester?"

Lucky brightened. "Buster Leska. I met him once. A big guy with white hair?"

"Got me. I was busy clearing out of the place."

"If it's Buster Leska, he'll bring a lot of clout. He shot down a bagful of MiGs in Korea and speaks with authority. Won't be long before he'll be wearing stars."

"I hear you're getting command of one of the squadrons."

"Wonders never cease," Lucky murmured, thinking Leska would be a good change of pace for Takhli.

"You'll do well. The guys like working for you."

Linda broke in. "Let's all go to dinner."

Henry's wife, who hadn't looked Lucky in the face after a single, horrified peek outside the door, tried to mumble an excuse.

Henry ignored her. "I think it's a great idea."

Linda, having sized up the situation, shook her head at Henry, then placed her hand on his wife's arm. "Hon, Paul may not look pretty to you, but when you get to know him, he's precious."

"Precious?" echoed Lucky.

"You go change while I entertain our guests," said Linda.

"Precious!" Lucky muttered as he dutifully went to the bedroom.

CHAPTER SEVEN

Colonel Buster Leska

The intell debriefings were held at tables in a room adjoining the command post, and Buster looked on quietly. Manny DeVera was going from one group to the next, asking questions and generally being nosy. Buster was content with his selection. Manny was working hard at it.

That afternoon the Takhli strike force had paused in their relentless bombing of Phuc Yen and gone after the Doumer Bridge, on the north side of Hanoi, and when they'd left it, two spans had been knocked down. A good day's work, even if they knew the North Vietnamese would be quick to repair it. They'd knocked down spans several times in the past.

Manny had talked his boss, George Armaugh, into trying something new, sending out a Wild Weasel flight both in front of and behind the strike force on the hairy missions. Armaugh had immediately come to Buster, who'd called Pearly Gates and asked him to speak with his bosses at Seventh Air Force *toute suite* so they'd get the change added to the air tasking order. The increased protection from the

SAMs and Manny's constant railing to the pilots about flying
the formation precisely and getting on and off the target
quickly had contributed to the fact that they'd suffered no
losses during today's tough mission.

Yank Donovan, commander of the 354th squadron, came
into the briefing room and took a seat, speaking with Captain Billy Bowes, who'd flown the mission with him.

Buster observed him. Yank's face, deeply etched with red
creases from wearing his oxygen mask pulled taut, was animated as he spoke to Bowes. He seemed to be doing a good
enough job with his squadron, but there was something
about him that was troubling. He was changing in some
manner Leska couldn't quite explain to himself. Yank maintained his reputation as a self-centered asshole, but every
time Buster had seen him the last few days, he'd worn a
sour expression and was talking intently with one of his
men, as he was now doing with Bowes.

Fright? He didn't think so, although such an emotion
would be forgivable. Donovan placed himself on the schedule for every tough mission that came down, and from what
Buster overheard, he was putting his bombs squarely on target. Yank was uncannily accurate.

The previous morning, when he'd landed after losing one
of his flight members at Phuc Yen, Donovan had acted almost light-hearted about the loss, but a bit later he'd found
him brooding, so tense he'd snapped at Buster. He wondered if it wasn't his egotism and maybe the thought that
since he was infallible, he should never lose a member of his
flight.

After a pause Buster tried to shrug the matter off. The
guy was doing his job, and there were other, bigger concerns. He left the command post and walked toward his office, tapping the portable radio on his leg, thinking about
Donovan and wishing to hell that Lucky Anderson would
get finished with his R and R to Hawaii and return. Squadron commanders, the good ones anyway, were the key to a
combat operation. The unit pilots often reflected their attitudes.

Colonel Mike Hough, the short and abrupt base commander, pulled up beside him in his blue staff car and gave
a quickie salute. "How ya doin', boss?"

Buster nodded his greeting.

"Seems cooler than normal today."

Cooler? The heat was stifling. He waited, knowing Mike had something on his mind.

"You know about a full bull we got here named Tom Lyons? The guy Colonel Parker caught lying about one of the pilots?"

"B. J. Parker warned me. He works for you now, right?" He'd spoken with Lyons briefly a couple of days before, and he'd seemed subdued, as if he was lying low and minding his business.

"Colonel Parker told me to give him a horseshit job. During General Roman's last visit his guys bitched about the base being dirty, so I put Lyons in charge of a bunch of jailbirds cleaning the place. Picking up trash and rocks, planting grass, washing down buildings, stuff like that."

"Sounds like a good job for him."

"A message came into personnel this morning telling us to cut orders reassigning him to PACAF headquarters."

Buster frowned. "Was it time for a transfer?"

"Nope. He's on a year tour, and he's only been here six months. You got any suggestions?"

"You say the message came out of PACAF headquarters?"

"Straight from their chief of colonels' assignments."

"Does Lyons know about it?"

"My admin guys haven't shown it to him, but yeah, I think he does. He's been bugging 'em, calling two or three times a day to ask if they've got something for him."

Buster sighed. "I'll phone PACAF and try to get it changed, but somehow I doubt I can swing it."

"The son of a bitch is pulling strings."

"More than likely. Anything else?"

"The lieutenant colonel promotion list just came in. We've got three people on it."

"How about Paul Anderson?"

"Lucky's at the top of the list. He'll pin 'em on in a couple weeks."

Saturday, October 28th, 1855 Local—Command Post, Takhli RTAFB

Lieutenant Colonel Pearly Gates

This time Pearly's briefing to the Takhli wing staff wasn't well received, for he brought news that the raid on Phuc Yen had produced no good or lasting results. Upon close analysis it had been determined by the photo interpreters at Tan Son Nhut that no operational MiGs had been destroyed on the ground, and even the long-range radar had been moved south into Hanoi and was back in business. The command-and-control building had been demolished, he said, but now the same function was being handled out of Gia Lam, the civil airport adjacent to Hanoi.

The new squadron commander, named Donovan, interrupted and said he'd known he'd taken the command-and-control building out. It was bragging of the most obvious type. Pearly paused only briefly before continuing. He announced targets for the next day. Another strike at Phuc Yen to take out hangars, then a sweep of the MiG auxiliary bases where the MiGs had most likely been dispersed. When the briefing was done, Colonel Leska and Captain Manny DeVera stayed behind for a private meeting, as they'd done the previous time he'd visited.

As soon as the door closed behind the last man, Pearly shook his head gloomily. "We received a bad-news JACK-POT message from General McManus."

"Go ahead," said Leska.

"The SecDef's office was openly pleased that we found no MiGs at Phuc Yen, especially after we'd been requesting to bomb there for so long. They say we're still overstating the numbers of MiGs, and all we did was cause the deaths of foreign personnel."

"If there's foreigners there, they're Russian advisors," Manny DeVera erupted angrily. "I think we oughta kill every damned . . ."

Colonel Leska raised a hand to silence the Supersonic Wetback. Pearly continued. "They're trying to use that as proof that there's no profit in bombing *anywhere* in North Vietnam."

Leska maintained a neutral expression, as if he'd heard it

all before. Which, Pearly decided, was likely the case, since he'd just come from the puzzle palace.

"General McManus says it would help tremendously if we'd locate and destroy the MiGs. He says it's become as much of a political issue as a military one, and the JACK-POT project's going to be more difficult to sell if we keep missing them."

Buster Leska mused. "Does he realize that it was likely the recce missions flying across Phuc Yen that tipped them off?"

"Yes, sir. But General Roman at PACAF agreed with the requirement for the recce missions. General Moss thinks he's also in agreement with the SecDef about canceling bombing in the Hanoi and Haiphong areas. He's indicating he doesn't like the way things are going with the ROLLING THUNDER campaign and doesn't want more escalation."

Leska sighed mightily. "We don't need that kind of in-house opposition."

"General Moss thinks it's because he believes B-52's should be doing the job up north."

"I believe they should be a part of it myself," Leska said, "Perhaps a big part."

Manny DeVera looked uneasy with the suggestion.

"Has Wes Snider showed up at Seventh Air Force yet?" Leska asked.

"The colonel came in two days ago. He's still receiving briefings about our operation and getting his feet on the ground."

"Did he bring anything new from the States?"

"He says SAC has had a plan for the heavy bombardment of North Vietnam for two years now. He's going to get me a copy of their OPlan."

"Like I said in Saigon, Wes will be a lot of help. He's well-known in the bomber business, and just *maybe* he can get General Roman aboard."

"I hope so, sir, but there's a lot of bad blood between General Roman and General Moss. General Roman thinks everything should be done with bombers, and General Moss thinks they just get in the way and flatten a lot of jungle."

"We're after a combination, Pearly. It'll take both to do the job right."

"Right now we've got to bomb the MiGs if we're going to maintain our credibility."

Buster Leska nodded. "We'll do our damnedest, Pearly, but first we've got to find 'em."

"And so far," Manny DeVera added darkly, "the gomers aren't cooperating."

Monday, October, 30th, 1812 Local

Captain Manny DeVera

Manny listened in on yet another series of pilot debriefings, going from table to table and wishing he'd hear from *someone* that they'd found MiGs on the ground. No one had, as they hadn't for the past two days, and they'd now attacked all the enemy's known auxiliary air bases, even including Yen Bai and other smaller ones, which weren't located in the Chinese buffer zone. That was where the operators at Motel, the over-the-horizon radar at Udorn, believed they were now operating, for the MiGs they watched on their scopes dropped below their radar coverage headed north, in the direction of China.

Colonel Leska had flown his first pack-six mission on the afternoon go, but when he'd returned, he was grumpy and wanted only a one-word report from the intell debriefers. Yes or no? Had anyone reported seeing MiGs on the ground? He hadn't liked the answers. Yet no one was sure they *hadn't* destroyed MiGs in the attacks. The target bases were heavily camouflaged, and nothing could be positively confirmed either way. There'd been several fires left burning beneath the netting, but they couldn't be confirmed as aircraft. Most of the pilots felt it was support equipment left behind, such as mobile generators or vehicles.

Could they have been MiGs?

Sure, and Jane Fonda *could* be out pitching for people to buy war bonds.

By seven o'clock, after flying the morning mission and sitting in on the final debriefings for the afternoon go, Manny decided that following fifteen hours of work he was entitled to dinner and a couple of drinks at the bar. As he trudged along the concrete path toward the club, he la-

mented about what Pearly Gates had told them regarding
the Air Force Chief of Staff's difficulties with the Secretary
of Defense, and the feud between Generals Moss and Roman.

Politics, jealousies, and petty bickering. It was a terrible
shame that their leaders were arguing like that while men
were betting their asses. He'd always thought of American
leadership as something finer. He'd believed that the politicians knew and cared about the shitty things that the guys
walking through bad-ass jungles, sitting on ships off hostile
coasts, and flying in the unfriendly skies had to go through.

He read in the papers how some politicians were turning
against the war—listening to flag-burning demonstrators,
even marching with them. Yet even that hadn't made him
believe less in American leadership. Those were just a
bunch of cowardly dope-smokers, unpatriotic assholes who
went along with the biggest crowd. The ones in charge, the
men who *made things happen*, were august, fatherly, and
caring men.

Welcome to the real world, Manny DeVera, where generals argue about using this World War II tactic or that one
while fighter jocks try to tell them that for Christ's sake the
gomers are down there firing Mach three missiles. Where
politicians on one side told them to keep on betting their
asses, but to make sure they didn't bomb the important targets, and politicians on the other side told reporters that
draft dodgers were doing their patriotic duty and the military was filled with baby-killers. Where the Chief of Staff of
the Air Force, with his thirty-plus years of military experience, was having to shut up and get lessons on flying combat from the President.

He emerged from his thoughts as he noted activity at
Colonel Tom Lyons's trailer; enlisted men carrying boxes
while Lyons and Lieutenant Colonel Yank Donovan chatted
and looked on.

Lyons was leaving?

Donovan saw Manny and nudged Tom Lyons, who
turned to see who it was. Lyons's smile faded, and he grew
a stony gaze. A hard, mean look, like Manny had been the
one to try to screw him over instead of the other way
around.

DeVera gave his "fuck you" smile and walked on, remembering the time Tom Lyons had slapped the girl in front of another trailer, not fifty feet away from where he was standing, and how Manny had thoroughly whipped his ass. That had been the morning before the charges had been made. His face burned at the memories of the outrageous lies. Yet Lyons was still wearing the uniform, with eagles on his shoulders and command pilot's wings on his chest. Which just showed you what you could get away with if your father was rich and powerful.

"Captain," he heard, and turned to see Donovan hurrying resolutely after him.

"Yes, sir?"

"You didn't salute."

"Sorry, sir." He saluted Donovan, who glared harder.

"I meant Colonel Lyons. You looked right at him and didn't salute."

Manny grinned, holding his salute and waiting for Donovan to return it. "It's starting to get dark, sir. Guess I thought he was a fucking post or something."

"Don't be insubordinate."

"I don't mean to be insubordinate to you, sir."

Donovan chewed on that for a moment, then turned to leave.

"Sir!" Manny roared in his loudest voice.

Donovan turned back to him.

"Are you going to return my salute, sir?"

Donovan gave a curt motion with his hand and stalked away.

Manny continued walking toward the Officers' Club, wearing a grim expression.

CHAPTER EIGHT

Colonel Xuan Nha

The day was a glorious one and would not soon be forgotten. He should have known it would be so when it began so well. He'd risen early and walked about the perimeter of the grounds in the darkness, trudging more than half a kilometer before returning just as the orange morning sun peeked over the high stone fence surrounding the villa. As he'd entered the rear door of the household, servants were just beginning their labors, and he'd beckoned for the girl to follow.

She'd balked and begun to cry. He'd turned wordlessly to the father, who'd scolded and pushed her to follow the colonel.

Xuan had motioned for her to close the door as he painfully sat on the bedside. She'd known what was expected, for twice daily for the past ten days he'd exercised her mouth long and vigorously, each time with the same discouraging results. This morning had been different, a result of determination and hard labors, as were other successes of the day. The Mee had not taken his malehood. The thirteen-year-old girl was no longer a virgin!

She'd mouthed him to partial tumescence, then lost her remaining innocence by perching birdlike over him, anxiously fingering him and herself, squatting and grunting aloud as she stuffed him in. Reacting with sharp cries to his punches and slaps, she raised and lowered herself until . . . a stirring . . . a growing urge . . . a tremble . . . a spasm and emission. The task was complete.

When Lieutenant Quang Hanh had arrived at the villa entrance in the old Peugeot, Xuan Nha felt jolly. He'd joked and even crowed some about fucking the girl as they'd driven to the VPA headquarters buildings. Soon after arriving there and hobbling to his office on the first floor, he was again made happy.

General Tho, commander of the VPAAF, had entered his office, flanked by his aide and smiling widely. He did not dismiss the aide, so Xuan knew the meeting was official. Before taking his seat, General Tho had casually mentioned Quon, the disgraced commandant of the air regiment at Phuc Yen. Surely, he said, he'd completed his reeducation. His transgression had been minor, and his services were needed.

Meaning, Xuan Nha knew, that General Tho's uncle and Quon's father-in-law, Le Duc Tho, was going to make that "suggestion." Had he finally arrived from the South? No one except the Enlightened One, Giap, or Le Duan would dare deny Le Duc Tho.

The enigmatic Quon, hero of the people and the best-known pilot in the VPAAF, had been cocky and outspoken. Xuan wondered if that would still be true, if Quon would now be cautious, speak tentatively, and exude the odd serenity he'd seen in other powerful men who'd been politically disgraced. Quon's treatment was undoubtedly severe, for the man who supervised his program was Nguyen Wu, and the two men despised one another.

When Xuan Nha had been wounded in the Mee attack, Nguyen Wu had replaced him as commandant of rocket-and-artillery forces. He'd done such an awful job that the guided rockets had become a threat to their own MiG pilots. Quon had become outraged and arranged with General Dung that Wu be shipped to the South "to study the NVA

air defenses." Wu had returned unscathed, but had not forgiven him. Later Xuan Nha had learned something else—
that Wu had also engineered the death of Quon's only son,
a lieutenant fighter pilot who had devoutly revered his famous father. He'd made certain that Quon heard rumors of
Wu's duplicity, but the fighter pilot had refused to accept
the fact as truth, believing Wu was too cowardly. He should
have heeded Xuan's warnings, for there was little treachery
the conniving Nguyen Wu would not stoop to. Now that Wu
had Quon in his grasp, Xuan Nha was sure he was brutaliz-
ing his old enemy.

Nguyen Wu, now an assistant to the widely dreaded
Commissioner of People's Safety, in charge of the Lao Dong
party's reeducation program, was Li Binh's nephew. She'd
used her influence within the Central Committee to gain his
appointment, which was undoubtedly why General Tho
brought it up to Xuan: to pass on through his wife to
Nguyen Wu and begin the process of releasing Quon without embarrassing pressures being brought to bear by Le
Duc Tho. The small group of officials who ran the Lao Dong
party, and therefore the country, often used third parties to
pass potentially embarrassing messages.

General Tho paused to lend the Quon matter appropriate
weight before turning to a happier theme—praise for Xuan
Nha's advice, which had saved the VPAAF from destruction
by warning him of the impending attack upon Phuc Yen.
Tho had ordered the MiGs to be evacuated to dispersal
bases, flying very low and exercising radio silence as Xuan
had suggested.

He went on about how the Phantoms and Thunder
planes had arrived the following morning to bomb only
empty hangarettes and parking ramps. They'd lost two
MiG-17's and a MiG-19, and those only because they were
so battle damaged they couldn't be repaired in time to be
flown out.

Next Xuan Nha had advised Tho also to evacuate the dispersal bases at Hoa Lac, Kep, and Yen Bai, saying that since
the Mee had missed them at Phuc Yen, they'd try to find
MiGs at bases they'd previously been authorized to bomb.
He said he'd provide early warning with his radars. Tho had
accepted that advice as well. As soon as enemy fighters were
seen approaching the great Hong Valley, his pilots would fly

their assigned missions, then drop low and recover at the small airstrips near the Chinese border where American fighters were strictly prohibited.

As if Xuan was able to foretell the future, four days after they'd bombed Phuc Yen, the Mee had attacked the auxiliary bases.

Xuan Nha had maintained a neutral expression throughout Tho's words of effusive praise, but his chest almost burst with emotion. Not only was he being heeded by the generals, he was receiving praise from a man who, only a few months previously, had denounced him when he'd failed to stop the Mee from destroying the national steel mill.

Before Tho had left his office, they'd discussed the next move the Mee might make. Mee commanders would be so frustrated by their failed attempts that they'd ask for new, perhaps even bolder, targets. It would be up to their politicians whether permission would be granted.

As General Tho rose to depart, he'd looked about and asked why Xuan hadn't moved into General Luc's elaborate offices. Perhaps even into the new underground facilities for senior officers being completed north of the present headquarters. Those were air-conditioned, safer from attack, and would, he added pointedly, be appropriate for a man with Xuan Nha's heavy responsibilities.

Xuan had answered humbly that since he was only *acting* commander of the VPAND, he didn't wish to be presumptuous. Tho had raised an eyebrow, as if to say it was only a matter of time until Xuan was named permanently to the position.

In the afternoon Xuan attended yet another strategy meeting of the senior staff, this one headed by General Dung, to discuss the spring offensive demanded by the Enlightened One. At the outset of the meeting, General Tho repeated his praise of Xuan Nha. He was finishing when Le Duc Tho, personal emissary of the Enlightened One and second only to Le Duan in the Lao Dong party, entered. He had his nephew, General Tho, repeat his words, and this time Xuan Nha was lauded to a man who would undoubtedly relay the words to Giap and the Enlightened One.

A glorious day indeed for Colonel Xuan Nha.

It was difficult for him to concentrate on the meeting as Le Duc Tho told about the fight in the South, describing the present, mobile situation and the concentrations of power. Four full regiments of his best VPA forces were being positioned in the central highland near the Cambodian border, in hopes of annihilating the thousand Mee soldiers and six hundred puppet militia at the large supply base at Dak To. If they could maintain their surprise, the battle would be swift and the outcome sure. If they were detected, they'd hasten the attack before the Mee could reinforce.

Victory at Dak To, he said, should be complete within the week. If things went as planned, they would indeed win a major battle against the Mee. Perhaps not as grand as the one over the French at Dien Bien Phu, but impressive nonetheless. The Enlightened One was entirely correct, he said. They *must* achieve a widely publicized victory, and it could not come too soon. The Mee were winning *every* major ground battle, and that fact wasn't lost on the people in the South. If the Mee continued to succeed, the people would be increasingly unresponsive to NVA and Viet Cong demands for support. But provide a single, decisive communist victory—show them, as they'd done in 1954, that even with their technology and vast resources, Westerners were human and beatable—and people across the puppet nation would rise up to help.

It was a powerful speech, given by a masterful orator.

Le Duc Tho then launched into a discussion about possible locations for the great battle. He felt the area around Dak To was appropriate. After the People's Army won the initial battle, the Americans would reinforce in great numbers. If they could annihilate the replacements as well, it would be an even greater victory. When General Dung mentioned Khe Sanh, a town near the demilitarized zone where Mee Marines maintained a base of operations, Le Duc Tho solicitously said that was also a possibility. The mountainous regions south of Dak To and surrounding Khe Sanh both reminded him greatly of Dien Bien Phu.

Le Duc Tho was extremely pleased that Giap had called for the buildup of troops and supplies. Regardless of where they attacked, if the effort was to be as massive as it must be, they'd need plentiful stores of soldiers, weapons, and ammunition. They began to speak of the supply effort. A colonel from Dung's office said they were shipping half again as much as normal. Within two more weeks they'd succeed in doubling the tonnage. Intelligence sources in Saigon reported that, at least so far, the Mee were unaware of the dramatic increases.

Thursday, November 2nd, 1845 Local—Wing Commander's Office, Takhli RTAFB, Thailand

Colonel Buster Leska

Buster hand-printed the message, reluctant to have it typed by the chief master sergeant's administrative crew in the outer office.

```
SECRET—IMMEDIATE—JACKPOT
7 AF CC EYES ONLY—NO FURTHER DISSEM
DTG: 02/1200ZNOV67
TO: HQ 7 AF/CC, TAN SON NHUT AB, SVN
FM: 355 TFW/CC, TAKHLI RTAFB, THAI
SUBJECT: JACKPOT INPUTS
1. (S) RESTRICTIONS ARE ADVERSELY
IMPACTING COMBAT EFFECTIVENESS,
ESP. BEING UNABLE TO FLY IN NUMEROUS
AREAS, I.E., TWENTY (20) NAUTICAL MILE
RING AROUND HANOI—WITHIN TWENTY-
FIVE (25) NM OF CHINESE BORDER, ETC.
RESTRICTIONS SEVERELY LIMIT TACTICAL
OPTIONS AND INGRESS/EGRESS ROUTES,
MAKING OUR TURNS AND ROUTES
PREDICTABLE. ALSO, NUMEROUS
LUCRATIVE TARGETS OF OPPORTUNITY ARE
CONTAINED IN THESE AREAS (INCLUDING
TRAINS, CONVOYS, WAREHOUSES,
LOADING DOCKS, VEHICULAR TRAFFIC,
AND AUXILIARY MIG BASES).
2. (S) FEELINGS AT THIS LEVEL INDICATE
BELIEF THAT THERE ARE VIABLE
MILITARY AND NONMILITARY TARGETS
WHICH HAVE BEEN RESTRICTED WHICH
WOULD HAVE GREAT IMPACT UPON NVN
CONDUCT OF WAR, BUT ARE NOT
INCLUDED ON THE JCS TARGET LIST.
```

THESE INCLUDE DIKES AND DAMS. REQUEST
LTC GATES'S OFFICE STUDY IMPACT ON NVN
MORALE IF THESE WERE AUTH.
3. (S) INITIAL IMPRESSION IS
UNCHANGED. SAM/AAA/MIG
ENVIRONMENT IS "EXTREMELY"
DANGEROUS, AND GOING AFTER PIECEMEAL
OR "SMALL POTATOES" TARGETS SEEMS
RIDICULOUS. MUST GO WHOLE HOG IF WE
ARE TO FORCE NVN OUT OF WAR. SECRET—
IMMEDIATE—JACKPOT

Buster personally carried the handwritten message to the
communications center adjacent to the command post.
When they'd transmitted it, he returned the only copy to his
office and burned the pages, as well as ten blank ones that
had been in the pad beneath them.

He sat back in his chair and heaved a long sigh. Command was a wearying job and needed no additional factors
to make it worse. He pulled the letter from Carolyn from his
middle drawer and placed it on the desktop to read once
again. It wasn't a big matter, just the fact that she'd learned
that their son had gotten himself into hot water at Columbia.
Not trouble so much as not applying himself and hanging
out with the wrong crowds, or at least that was what she'd
been told in a phone call from one of his instructors, who
was also a family acquaintance.

Mark was increasingly late for a number of classes and
often appeared for them unprepared and looking disheveled.
Buster snorted. Mark had always had a bit of the slob in
him. When he was a child his room had always looked as if
a tornado had just passed through.

Carolyn had called the campus and, after missing him
several times, had finally contacted Mark. He'd seemed penitent and said he'd clean up his act. She felt their son was
simply overwhelmed by the university scene. He was easily
influenced, and she worried that he might fall in with the
wrong crowd. She didn't mean for Buster to become concerned, because there really wasn't anything to worry about,
but it was nice to be able to share things with him, and she
knew he'd want to know.

Nope, Buster thought. She was wrong. All he wanted to

hear was how wonderful things were going at home, so he could concentrate on the considerable business at hand. Then he fussed at himself, for he knew the most important part of his life was bundled up in a five-three package he called Carrie and a gangling, grinning slob named Marcus. *God how he missed them.*

She finished the letter by telling him her parents were visiting next week and that her father said he was following every detail of the war. He'd told her over the phone that the whole thing would shortly be over with, now that Buster was there.

They were fishing buddies, her father and Buster, and the old man treated him like the son fate had cheated him out of. He boasted to his cohorts about Buster's achievements, and whenever Leska visited, he spent hours filling in the aging group of retired businessmen on the intricacies of the modern Air Force. He received letters at Takhli from people he didn't know—friends of Carolyn's parents—wishing him Godspeed and giving him advice. By helping to maintain Buster's morale, they felt they were doing their part to support the war effort.

One had written that he shouldn't listen to the liberal-controlled American press, because the country was behind their boys 100 percent.

Buster thought again about Carolyn's concern over their son and brushed it off. Mark was no better or worse than he'd been in his own youthful, hell-raising days.

2030L—Hanoi, DRV

Deputy Minister Li Binh

Li Binh arrived home weary, for it had been a long and frustrating day. After being let off at the entrance, she didn't wait for a servant to open the door, and once inside she ignored the fawning manservant who bobbed his head as he explained his slothfulness. She dismissed him and went to her settee. The girl-maid hurried in with tea. Li Binh simply accepted the tea and waved her away.

Dumb animal! she thought as she sipped and watched the girl flee. Most powerful males, she'd long realized, were dictated by their penises. Some lived for the satisfaction of the sex act, others for boasting about conquests. Remove their capability and they felt threatened, for they must constantly prove their manhood.

Her husband drew little real satisfaction from sexual acts, yet she'd known he'd have to prove his masculinity after his release from the hospital. Since he functioned best when the female was terrified or he was inflicting pain, Li Binh had thoughtfully added the young girl to the household staff. She certainly wanted no part of his experimenting. Their marriage bed had never been joyful, for neither of them felt coitus with the other was more than a rare necessity. The party and their careers had been important, not fumbling, half-hearted sex acts. And now, with his deformities . . . She shuddered at the thought.

Women, even powerful ones such as she, were different. It was seldom the satisfaction of their glands that drove them. More often they were compelled by warm thoughts, promises of satisfaction, sometimes even by the chase. Or so she'd believed until . . . Her mind clouded as she thought of her nephew Nguyen Wu, who had given her such pleasure. She missed their daily rendezvous. . . . She missed *him*.

Stop it! As she'd done many times before, she berated herself for her weakness. Her nephew preferred male companions. *Still* . . .

Xuan Nha entered from his room in the south wing, freshly bathed and smiling, a caricature with one arm and an eye patch. The flesh of his neck and lower half of his face, where the skin had been burned away, was pink and knotted with grisly scar tissue. He lurched and made pained expressions as he walked. *Hideous*, she decided for the hundredth time. She didn't rise, just examined him curiously and sipped hot tea. He took his seat gingerly, smiling like a fool.

"I heard you were praised today before Le Duc Tho," she said to massage his vanity.

He slapped his chair arm. "Tea," he rasped when the frightened maid scurried in. She noted the way he looked at the girl . . . like a victor. Finally, she thought, he'd succeeded.

"There is talk of reward for you, husband," Li Binh said quietly.

He pursed his lips. Before he'd been caught in the American bombing attack, Xuan had kept himself in strict control, seldom displaying emotions. He was like that again. Success and praise were rejuvenating him, she supposed.

"But there are those who say it is much too early for reward," she added. "They do not say it in my presence, of course, but I hear of such things."

He was looking at her.

"I am proud of your achievements," Li Binh said quietly.

The girl returned with the tea and, Li Binh noted again, regarded Xuan Nha fearfully, yet with an entirely new demeanor—the utterly vanquished. She watched her hurry out and wondered. Li Binh disposed of help when she felt they'd seen or heard too much. If sufficiently discreet, the girl and her family might last several months at the villa. But Xuan Nha had sadistic passions—which also jeopardized the girl's tenure. It would be interesting to see how long she remained alive. If he destroyed the girl and still displayed interest in rutting, Li Binh would provide another plaything. They were plentiful enough.

Xuan Nha broke into her thoughts by telling her of General Tho's visit, his talk about Quon, and his suggestion that the reeducation be ended. Xuan asked pointedly if the suggestion could have come from Le Duc Tho.

"Shall I mention this to the appropriate offices?" he asked.

Li Binh was quiet for a short pause, then said she'd relay General Tho's words. A flutter of emotion stirred in her breast.

Xuan pulled on reading glasses and began to pore over a report. She picked up papers of her own, but had trouble discerning the words, for warmer thoughts were in her mind. She decided to contrive a personal meeting between herself and Nguyen Wu . . . to tell him about the suggestion passed from Le Duc Tho.

The tingling sensation grew as she remembered other secret meetings with her nephew.

Saturday, November 4th, 1020 Local—Command Post

Colonel Buster Leska

The morning mission had been to a military barracks complex located just south and west of Hanoi. The pilots had liked the target, even though the area was heavily defended, because they'd be bombing enemy combat troops who were likely preparing to fight Americans in South Vietnam. But it hadn't been troops they'd found at the installation.

Bombs from the second airplane in the gaggle had hit one of the barracks buildings squarely and set off a tremendous explosion, lifting debris several hundred feet into the air. That explosion had set off another. The next flight, led by Captain DeVera, had bombed another part of the complex, and one of those buildings had gone up just as spectacularly.

Buster listened to the debriefings, then spoke with the intelligence officers preparing the message to be forwarded to higher headquarters. The pilots were exuberant about the mission's results, saying how they were in greater danger from the secondary explosions than from enemy gunfire. The intelligence officers were not as happy. Intell at Takhli, as everywhere, didn't like to make errors. If they briefed that the pilots would find troops at the barracks, they wanted them to find troops there. He got the impression they were still not totally convinced that there *weren't* troops at the complex, regardless of what the pilots *thought* they saw.

He was reading the synopsis put together by the intell major when Captain DeVera came over, sipping coffee and looking as if he wanted to say something.

"You got something, Manny?"

"Wondering if I could get into your office to see you for a few minutes later today, sir?"

"Is it important?" Buster had a busy schedule, an important meeting with the base commander and the civil engineer, a lunch date with his deputies, and in the afternoon a two-star was visiting from PACAF headquarters in Hawaii.

"I think so," said Manny.

"I'll be heading back to my office as soon as I'm done here. We can walk and talk."

Manny stepped back then as George Armaugh, the Deputy for Operations, came in and made a beeline for Leska.

Buster returned the draft report to the intell officer. "Beef it up. Make sure the headquarters pukes understand our guys hit a major ammo-storage site. You've gotta remember who you're talking to and spell it out that it was something damned big stored in there. Include the colors of the explosions and the height of the fireballs. That's so they can estimate the type and tonnage of explosives that went up."

"Yes, sir." The intelligence major went away wearing a forced, neutral expression.

Armaugh was peeved. "We've got a problem with sortie generation again. We have a big mission coming up this afternoon, forty birds on an alpha strike, and we don't even have enough flyable airplanes to put two spares on standby."

"Talk it over with Jerry." Colonel Jerry Trimble was Deputy for Maintenance, and increasingly the brunt of Armaugh's unhappiness.

"I already got his fucking excuses. Hell, he's not even sure he can give me the *forty* birds."

"I've heard from Jerry. You two have to quit squabbling, George."

"Goddammit, he's got to remember there's a war going on, and we . . ." Armaugh paused when he saw the stern look that invaded Buster's face. This was not the proper place for bickering among the senior staff.

"I've got to get back to the office," said Buster, motioning for George to follow.

"I'm going to have to send out a message saying we've gotta stand down from the mission because Trimble can't generate the sorties."

They went out the door into bright sunlight.

George was tight-jawed. "The airplanes we get are shitty half the time, and my guys have to bet their asses they can get them home. Dammit, the SAMs and triple-A ought to be enough. Instead, we've got to face a goddam . . ."

"George!"

Armaugh glared around as they began to walk, seeing only Manny DeVera, who came out and trailed a dozen paces behind them.

"Fly this afternoon's mission with what we've got, George. Just like we do every day."

"Well, dammit, it isn't right. We're flying combat up there, betting our asses, and we ought to be able to expect better. It's just downright shitty maintenance."

"You ever work in maintenance, George?"

"Jesus, no."

"Try putting yourself in their shoes. They work all night to get the birds ready. Then they get a big mission like this morning, with airplanes overstressed, some of 'em shot up, others needing routine maintenance, and they're pressed just trying to turn them around."

"Trimble blames everything on my pilots."

"With reason. Our pilots put the birds through abuse like nothing they've ever seen before. No airplanes, not even Thuds, can stand up under such stress. Every time they dodge a SAM, that's seven or eight sustained g's. Some of the guys pull seven g's coming off a target. They use afterburner a lot more than in peacetime, and fly at military power. We're aging the airplanes at ten or fifteen times the normal rate. Every morning we tear 'em up, then Jerry Trimble's people, who've half of them worked all night, try to put them together for an afternoon mission."

"That's just the way combat is."

"I know that. So does Jerry. He's a fighter jock. But it doesn't change the fact."

"They've got to keep up. My pilots have to."

"You may have pilots with big balls, George, but they don't work a *tenth* as hard as the maintenance people."

"Maintenance isn't facing the SAMs and . . ."

"Listen. I don't want to hear another word about how tough your pilots have it. They're paid to fly and fight. Your job is to see they do it. Jerry Trimble's people try to give you the tools to do it with. Normally they can, but then we get something like this, two big alpha strikes in a single day, and they have trouble keeping up."

"Then I'll have to send out a message telling higher headquarters we can't . . ."

Buster stopped cold and turned slowly to face Armaugh. "You're *not* sending out a message, George. You may talk it over with me, and if I agree that such a message should go out, *then* you can send it, but I'm *not* saying that, and I just told you something entirely different. I told you to have your pilots fly the mission with what they've got."

Armaugh stared back.

Buster softened his tone. "Go on back to work, George. You and your people are under a lot of strain. We've all got to keep doing the best we can."

After a long pause Armaugh's anger withered. "Yeah," he mumbled. The previous day the wing had lost two more pilots. George Armaugh was feeling the strain, but he was a good man, and Buster knew he'd come through.

George gave a quick salute and started to leave.

"How's Donovan holding up?" One of the downed pilots had come from Donovan's 354th squadron, and Buster had been with him when he'd been told about it. He'd become so angry that he'd developed a stutter, and his egotism level had become unbearable.

Armaugh seemed to be of a different mind. "Maybe I was wrong about him," he said. "He's doing a good job with his squadron."

"I get the feeling he's undergoing a personality change of some kind."

"We all do, Buster. Sometimes I have trouble sleeping nights after a bad one."

Buster nodded and watched him leave, still wondering about Yank Donovan.

"You need something?" George snapped at Manny DeVera, who still trailed along behind.

Buster called out, "I wanted to ask Manny about the ECM pod situation, George. He thinks we're having too many failures."

Armaugh gave him a "see, I told you maintenance was fucked up" look and headed back toward the command post.

As Manny hurried to join him, Leska glanced toward his office and noticed the base commander's blue sedan was already parked there. He hated to keep Mike Hough waiting again. He'd put the meeting off several times.

"I only have a couple of minutes," he said too brusquely. "I'll try to make it quick, sir."

Buster continued to walk as he listened.

Manny, leading the second flight to bomb the barracks complex, had delayed his roll-in so the first fireballs and smoke could drift some and he could get a better picture of what might be left to bomb, taking his four birds in a wide turn around the target area and dodging two groups of

SAMs as they ventured south of the city. They'd completed half the circle when he saw a building that hadn't been destroyed in the complex, and rolled in. After he'd dropped his bombs, he'd pulled off over Hanoi, and then, while he'd been very low, he'd seen something odd in the southern suburbs. The building his number three bombed contained ammo too, and when his bombs hit it, the explosion rocked Manny's bird. Getting the flight back together and joined up with the departing gaggle had taken the rest of his attention and skills.

At the debriefing Manny had held his tongue about what he'd seen, because it would be too obvious they'd ventured deep into the restricted zone during their recovery, and he sure as hell didn't want to tell that to the world.

Buster wasn't impressed with what DeVera reported. "There've always been trucks lining the streets on the south side of Hanoi, Manny. The convoys form up there and wait for nightfall. They know we can't bomb them while they're still in residential suburbs."

"Yes, sir, and I've seen them before, but *never* anything like this, Colonel. I saw two or three times as many trucks, carts, trailers, you name it, and they're all stacked high."

"Hard to see *that* much from the air."

"I've got good eyes and I was close to the ground. There were a large number of 'em right out in the open, but there was a lot of camouflage netting, and a bunch more were parked underneath. Down low like that you can see under it."

Leska looked evenly at him. "You were in the area we were told not to overfly?"

"There wasn't any way to avoid it, unless we'd bombed blind. There was a lot of smoke, and the direction we had to set up our dive gave us the only good visibility."

"Okay," Leska said, "now forget you told me."

"Yes, sir, but *before* I forget, they're also protecting that area like never before. They must've doubled the number of SAMs, we were bounced by MiGs, and there's a *hell* of lot more large-caliber triple-A."

Leska nodded. "Thanks for telling me, Manny."

"I thought you should know, sir." Manny saluted, then turned away toward his office.

Buster continued walking. He wondered if he should forward a JACKPOT message about Manny's discovery. He doubted that the convoys were really any different from normal, and the fact that the gomers had moved more defenses there wasn't unusual. The enemy often shifted SAMs and guns around.

He decided to take a look for himself.

CHAPTER NINE

Captain Manny DeVera

It was to be another strike at Phuc Yen, the large MiG base across the Red River, north of Hanoi. Lieutenant Colonel Yank Donovan was Scotch Force leader. Manny DeVera led Marlin, the second flight in the formation. Captain Animal Hamlin was his number three.

The only standing military structure on the big base was a large hangar at the northwest side of the runway. That was the target. Numerous guns had been noted in the prestrike photos a mile north of the hangar, so Manny had briefed his flight that those were to be avoided.

The navigation instrument needle swung about, showing they were passing over TACAN at Channel 97. Manny reached up and wiped a smudge off the "whiskey compass" with his glove. This was what they called the small instrument attached to the top of the canopy bow, because its small glass reservoir was filled with amber liquid. A magnetic compass floated freely in the reservoir. If everything else failed, the whiskey compass could provide a rough heading so you could head for home.

After crossing the "fence," which was what the pilots called the border of North Vietnam, Colonel Donovan told the force to "green 'em up" and "turn on the music": to set their armament switches and turn the ECM pod switches from STANDBY to ON. They flew eastward over the high green mountains at 20,000 feet, settling into proper spacing, separated by 1,000 to 1,500 feet within the sixteen-ship formation. A few miles ahead of them ranged the Wild Weasels, call sign Red Dog, to help shield them from SAMs and call out threats to the force. Flying above and slightly right of Scotch Force were four F-4 Phantoms from Ubon airbase, the MiG-CAP to help keep enemy interceptors off their back. Their call sign was Honda.

Manny heard a *brp-brp, brp-brp* sound, then a periodic *ticka-ticka* in his helmet earphones. He frowned and listened, and was not surprised when the Wild Weasel leader radioed and confirmed his discovery.

"Scotch Force, this is Red Dog," called the calm Wild Weasel leader. *"We're getting a lot of GCI activity. Be on the lookout for MiGs."*

The *ticka-ticka* sound heard over the headset each thirty seconds was made by a ground-control intercept radar called a Barlock. The *brp-brp, brp-brp* came from a height-finder radar. The enemy would know their altitude and position in the airspace. Not accurately enough to shoot them down with SAMs or guns—those systems had their own precision radars—but sufficiently close to send MiGs after them. The ECM pods did not jam the GCI radar frequencies.

It was not a fearful thing, knowing MiGs would be active, just another piece of knowledge so they'd understand what to expect. Forewarned, they could prepare for any confrontation. It was the unexpected that they disliked.

As they continued over the high mountains west of Hanoi, Scotch Force slowly descended through 18,000, then 15,000 feet. By the time they approached the Black River, they were flying at 12,000 feet. Ahead they could see the Red River Valley . . . flat as a plate, spotted with cities, checkerboarded with rice paddies. Thousands of small reservoirs, irrigation ditches, and streamlets glittered in the morning sun.

The force crossed the Red River twelve miles south of Yen Bai. Manny's mind began to chant its aggressive litany. *Remain calm—stay on the offensive—what's the best next move?*

"Check your spacing, Scotch Force," came Yank Donovan's terse radio call. He descended again, leading them lower yet, changing altitude so they'd not be predictable. Manny looked out at Animal Hamlin, off on his left wing, then to his right and the aircraft there. They looked good. His only criticism was that Yank Donovan was flying too slow for his liking. They were doing 480 knots, and Manny felt their minimum combat airspeed should be 550 to 600 when flying anywhere in pack six. He felt better when his aircraft's energy level was up.

He paused before making his radio call. Although relatively new at the combat game, Donovan was not the sort to take kindly to criticism. Manny waited a few seconds more, and when it became apparent they weren't accelerating, he pressed the transmit button.

"Scotch Force leader," he called. *"Marlin lead suggests we're flying too slow."*

Smatterings of flak popped harmlessly at their two o'clock, half a mile distant.

Scotch leader didn't answer Manny's call or respond by changing airspeed. Donovan was playing his own game, and since he was leading, they'd all dance to his tune.

Red Dog radioed from their vantage out in front of the force. Weather was fine for bombing . . . only a few clouds, and those were well east of the target area. The mission was a go.

"THIS IS BIG EYE. BANDITS AT BULLSEYE, TWO-EIGHT-ZERO FOR FIFTEEN. I REPEAT. BANDITS AT BULLSEYE, TWO-EIGHT-ZERO FOR FIFTEEN."

MiG-17's south of them. If they'd been MiG-21's, Big Eye would have called them *Red* Bandits. That was the new format.

"Honda flight's got a visual. Ten o'clock low for five. Engaging."

Manny glanced up and watched the F-4 MiG-CAP flight veer overhead, headed toward the bandits; then he peered carefully about the strike formation. Nothing except a few bursts of flak off to their left.

Donovan leveled as they approached 8,000 feet. They were out over the valley, headed toward the distant, shadow-cast mountains of Thud Ridge.

The Red Dog SAM-killers called a missile launch—targeted for the Wild Weasels, not the strike force. *"Valid SAM launch,"* Red Dog lead repeated. *"No threat to the force. Red Dogs, prepare to take it down."* The Wild Weasel leader spoke in a conversational tone, as if he were at breakfast asking for the salt, instead of preparing his flight to dodge a surface-to-air missile traveling at three times the speed of sound.

Manny looked, but could see neither the Weasels nor the SAMs. He let his eyes scan the area to their starboard, at the area just short of sprawling Hanoi, but he couldn't yet make out the big airfield. Very quickly they'd change course.

On cue the force swept around to their right, making their turns too slowly for Manny's liking. He mentally noted to brief the pilots to make turns abruptly, so they'd not lose as much of their jamming effectiveness while the aircraft was canted to the side, with the ECM pod's output shielded by the wing. So much to do.

Stay on the offensive, he reminded himself.

As the sixteen ships continued toward Phuc Yen, Red Dog made a reassuring radio call; the sky was now clear of SAMs. Honda flight, unable to catch the MiGs, returned to fly nearer the strike force.

Phuc Yen airfield was ahead and slightly left. Manny began a visual search for the targeted hangar, but they were still too far out.

Thirty-seven millimeter began to puff over the northern side of Hanoi. Popcorn flak. It formed in thick layers, white puffballs you had to fly through when you dived toward the target. The gomers threw a lot of the little stuff into the sky when you got anywhere close, as if there were endless supplies of artillery rounds.

Closer now. He could see the runway. *Stay on the offensive.*

Six rounds of big stuff, 85mm, blew in fiery balls that quickly darkened into towering gray blossoms. More and more flak burst in the sky as they approached Hanoi. The airfield became distinct, and Manny could make out the hangar, looking brazen and tough, standing alone amid the rubble of several others flattened in earlier raids.

Finally Donovan pushed up his throttle, and the force followed suit. Manny glanced at his airspeed as they accelerated through 500 knots. Better, but still not fast enough. He sucked a few breaths of oxygen, staring at the target, which was no longer so well-camouflaged. Most of the netting had been blown away in the furious bombing of the past several days.

Yank Donovan stroked into afterburner as he began his pull-up, and the rest of the force followed, noses lifted skyward as they climbed toward the perch. Now that the gomers knew their target, the flak intensified. The guns of Phuc Yen pounded staccato bursts of fire into the sky. Manny's mouth was set firmly; they'd started the maneuver too slowly and would have to stay in the stuff longer than necessary.

Too late to worry about it. Manny controlled a shudder as a flurry of rounds burst so close, he heard muffled thunder over the roar of the engine. He stared at the aircraft before him and watched as Donovan's four-ship leveled, then hesitated.

Hurry! Manny silently yelled. Donovan was delaying his roll-in. Finally Donovan, then the remainder of Scotch flight, turned sharply left and downward. They'd go after the many gun emplacements about the periphery of the airfield.

Manny immediately began his own leveling turn—they were at 13,000 feet—and cast a quick look back at the other flight members. He swiveled and eyed the target again, pulled in a breath, and turned up on his left wing. *Dammit!* Donovan's pause at the perch had thrown Manny out of the prebriefed position. He found himself attacking from the south rather than the west. He'd have to make a quick turn as soon as the bombs came off, to avoid the guns massed north of the airfield.

His mind was too cluttered! *Remain calm. Stay on the offensive.* He gave a hard shake of his head to clear it, settled the aircraft at forty-five degrees dive angle, and adjusted slightly to place the aiming pipper slightly above the hangar, which was rapidly growing in his vision.

Steady. Tracking. Good target picture. He released at 7,000 feet. *Yeah!* he exulted as he pressed the button and felt the bombs go. They'd be good, he decided. Either a hit or damned close.

He pulled the control stick slowly aft and to the right. Four g's—a nice, calm pullout. The flight ahead of him was climbing out in ragged unison.

Time to think about collecting his own chicks.

"Marlin lead's off the target to the right," he announced as his bird began to recover from the dive attack. He could see the flak clearer now that he was no longer tracking the target—so thick and heavy it rated an Oh-My-God. *Don't think about it. Stay calm. What's your next move?*

Bursts flashed harmlessly past, misses but close enough to make him feel vulnerable. He pulled harder to get away—realized he was being predictable in the constant turn and began to jink eastward. He glanced out to his right, toward Hanoi, and saw bright red bowling balls flashing through the sky—all seemingly directed at his airplane, as if he were some kind of magnet.

As he approached the southern extremity of Thud Ridge, Manny reversed left, to hug up beside its first high mountain.

"Valid SAM launch, Scotch Force. This is Red Dog lead. Valid launch!"

He eased off his turn and looked out sharply. Until they rejoined in the cooperative jamming offered by the pod formation, they were vulnerable to SAMs.

"Homing on us, Red. . . ." The transmission immediately shut off.

Manny soared a bit as he approached a hill, then quickly swung his head back around to stare out at the valley, still wondering if the SAM could be targeted for him.

Nothing in sight.

"Break, Red Dog four! Br—"

Someone was breathing heavy over the radio, holding down the transmit button.

"Red Dog four's hit!"

One of the Wild Weasel crews.

"Get out, four! Get out!"

The Weasel Thud must be burning. Manny did a tiny

dogleg right and left, so his flight could catch up. He consciously quelled an urge to breath harder. *Stay on the . . .*

Weeep, weeep, weeep. An emergency beeper was sounding its plaintive cry, followed by a second when the other Weasel crew member's chute opened.

Damn! Manny thought bleakly. Two men down.

As he turned back to face the mountain, Manny's airplane was staggered by a mighty jolt, then another, then a third! Each was accompanied by a tremendous explosion, deafening even in the sealed cockpit. The Thud reeled drunkenly, the controls instantly sluggish.

Oh, shit! *Calm yourself, dammit. Keep thinking of what you should do next.*

Gain altitude! was Manny's initial thought, and he instinctively hauled the stick back and checked that the throttle was full forward.

Smoke gathered low in the cockpit, and he could see light down there. The bird was hit, and he knew it was a mortal one. He forced himself to remain calm as he wondered how far west he could get if he stuck with the bird. He couldn't yet turn for home, for the ridge blocked his way, so he continued climbing as he flew northward.

Someone radioed that he had a visual on a SAM. Another voice said it was a burning aircraft. He listened to Animal Hamlin's New Jersey accent saying something about *Marlin lead* and . . . *bright fire.*

Manny's fire was burning so intensely, they'd mistaken him for a missile! He tried to respond, but heard no side tones to tell him the radio transmitter was operative.

Someone yelled for him to *get out,* as they'd done with the Wild Weasel a few seconds earlier.

All of those things happened almost instantaneously, but time had entered another dimension and dawdled unnaturally. Manny glanced toward his feet to watch the thick smoke curling there, then observed his gauges as the oil-pressure gauge went to zero.

No way to fly without oil pressure. *Stay calm. What's your next move?*

His UTILITY, P-1, and P-2 lights came on.

Can't fly far without hydraulics, either. Things were going to hell. *What's your next move?*

Weeep, weeep, weeep. A new beeper squealed.

"... *lead, Honda three's out of the airplane. I got one good chute in sight!*"

Another emergency beeper sounded. The Honda three front-seater.

The carnage wasn't yet complete.

"... *Honda four's hit!*"

"... *losing control of the ...*"

"... *get out, get out.*"

"... *dammit.*"

Two more beepers wailed, and the accumulation of sounds from the locator beacons drifted in and out of unison. Manny shut off emergency-guard frequency to eliminate the racket.

In a period of seconds, two F-4s had been downed. With the Wild Weasel crew already out, six men were floating earthward. A bad day for the good guys. None of those would be picked up, for the rescue force couldn't come in this far.

Steady your breathing. Keep thinking of what to do next. Manny's heart remained calm. He was determined to make it out as far as possible.

As soon as he could see over the ridgeline, he cranked the stick to the left. The bird responded ... falteringly, but he was turning. He settled on a westerly course of 285 degrees, which he reasoned was the fastest track between his position and the nearest mountain wilderness across the wide valley.

Climbing still ... more smoke boiling up from below. *Come on, baby,* he breathed. *We've got a long way to go.* He didn't wish to join the others below in their chutes, sure to be killed or captured. *Remain calm.*

He was past the ridge and over the flats, headed westerly at 690 knots, the Thud gamely struggling upward.

Can't get high enough, he decided, and continued the climb. He scanned his altimeter ... it was dead. He glanced at his airspeed gauge and found it inoperative. No inputs from the Pitot system, and he couldn't trust the rest of the instruments.

"... *left ten degrees,*" called Yank Donovan.

"... *you read, Marlin lead?*" Like the others, the first part of Animal Hamlin's transmission was also lost.

Manny turned the bird southward a bit, as Donovan had

directed, then again tried his radio—without luck. He couldn't transmit. Although the first words of transmissions were clipped, he could receive. His breathing remained calm, his thoughts lucid . . . as if he were an observer of the Titanic before it went belly up. He began a high-pitched laugh, but cut if off.

". . . *through sixteen thousand feet,*" he heard Animal explain in the cool voice. Yank Donovan asked something, and Animal replied he was coming up on Marlin lead's right side . . . that the airplane was burning and shredded. He said he could see right through the Thud's belly to the engine, as if it were a cut-away model. There was a big chunk torn out of the right wing, and three feet of the aft fuselage was missing.

"Keep flying baby," Manny urged his Thud. *Stay calm. Think of what you do next.*

". . . *keep your distance in case it blows,*" radioed Colonel Donovan.

Manny's eyes smarted and wept from the smoke. He leaned close to the canopy Plexiglas and saw an aircraft shape looming on his right. Animal Hamlin. The presence made him feel better. He leaned forward to check the situation indicator for his heading, but found that both electrical systems had shut down since his last look. He extended the ram air turbine for emergency power, but there was no change. He leaned well forward until he was close enough to see the needle on the whiskey compass, and corrected to 285 degrees, magnetic.

Another voice. ". . . *out, Marlin lead. You're burning!*"

He studiously ignored the advice. The farther he could make it to the west, the better his chance for rescue.

Animal's voice. ". . . *through twenty thousand feet, Marlin lead. You're burning on the right side of your bird. Dark smoke. I think oil from your ATM's feeding the fire. Make sure you've got the ATM shut down so it'll stop pumping oil.*"

Manny felt for the air turbine motor switch.

". . . *little better. Not burning quite so bright back there now.*" He owed Animal a drink for that advice.

Manny's feet were getting hotter. He looked to see if there were flames, but the smoke was too thick.

Animal's distinctive voice. ". . . *doin' good, Marlin lead.*

Awfully good. Turn ten degrees left again, though. You're in a slight bank and keep drifting north."

Manny fed in a slight correction ... what he thought to be ten degrees. Found himself starting to breath too rapidly and calmed it.

". . . out, Marlin lead!" someone yelled hoarsely.

Animal's cool voice returned. *". . . on the right side of your bird. Gotta start thinking about gettin' out, Manny. Coming up fast on the Red River, if that's what you been waiting for. Level off a bit now. You're in a slight climb again, and . . ."*

Hamlin didn't finish his sentence. Manny's radio had gone completely dead.

He couldn't see at all now, partly because of the smoke, mostly because his eyes were watering profusely. He blinked and leaned forward but couldn't see the whiskey compass.

Gotta get rid of the canopy, he decided, and had trouble finding the manual lever. He pulled. The metal bow was thrust up into the airstream, and the canopy disappeared. Manny had anticipated a flash fire and was clutching desperately on to the left ejection handle in case he had to immediately abandon ship ... but there was no flash fire and the smoke diminished. He blinked repeatedly to flush water from his eyes, wondering how tear ducts could carry so much liquid, then glanced over and saw that Animal's Thud was locked into position at his side. Hamlin gave him a nod and thumbs-up. It felt exhilarating to be able to see. He grinned and laughed into his mask as he returned the wave. Then he blinked some more and stared down over the side.

The Red River was directly before them, not more than a couple of miles distant. All he had to do was . . .

"Ungghhh!" he grunted, for the Thud pitched nose up into a steep climb. He stabbed with his left foot at the rudder, and the red-hot pedal fell against his leg, searing the skin and causing him to yell out in pain.

The damned rudder pedal had melted free! He tried to kick it away and felt his rubber boot sole grow sticky on contact.

He was fighting the stick as the bird soared, but little seemed to be working. He hung from his straps, now inverted, and the Thud did some kind of odd, twisting trick, and he was fluttering earthward in a spin.

There was absolutely no control!

Time to get out, he sagely decided. He had sufficient altitude for a clear ejection. He took a couple of seconds to position himself, as he'd practiced a thousand times in the simulator, then released the controls and grasped the ejection handle.

The Thud slowly righted itself and began a recovery arc, so he regrasped the control stick and felt a sluggish respond. Past the Red now. If he could only make it . . .

He groaned as the bird's nose pitched into a nine-g pull-up, which he'd thought impossible. This time he was tossed to one side when the aircraft reversed and began to flutter, only half flying, sinking earthward again.

"I got your number, baby," Manny coaxed, still panting from the g's.

He released the control stick.

No effect. The Thud continued to fall.

Dammit!

He grasped the control stick again. There was absolutely no response. *Remain calm.*

Manny fleetingly wondered if he was still beyond the river as he groped for the ejection handle, said a very quick prayer, pulled his heels back, sucked a shaky breath of oxygen, then pulled both ejection levers.

The explosive blast kicked him hard in the butt.

1440L—North of Bangkok, Thailand

Major Lucky Anderson

The gooney bird shimmied and whined throughout the take-off from Don Muang airport, as if it were the right of a lady of her age to act as she wished. C-47's had been designed and first built in the thirties and had been a mainstay of every conflict since. Other cargo birds, like C-119's, had been designed to replace her, but she was still flying while they'd mostly been relegated to boneyards or sold off to other countries. Goons were not pressurized—on this one Lucky could see daylight through gaps where the passenger door didn't fit properly—so they had to fly down low enough that the passengers or crew wouldn't need oxygen. As reliable and durable as a railroad pocket watch, gooney birds shuddered for no apparent reason, and you could see their wings articulating up and down, phenomena that scared the hell out of young jet-pilot passengers, but she'd complain and groan and keep flying, and get you there every time. In Thailand goons were used to shuttle passengers and low-priority cargo between the various bases.

Lucky was headed back. Returning to Takhli to finish his combat tour, and do it as a squadron commander. Not only that, when he'd been in Hawaii, he'd received a call from Flo, General Moss's spinster secretary, saying he was on the LC list. She'd said he owed her dinner, and Lucky had said "yes ma'am." One of Flo's favorites had been promoted, and she expected her due. Then she'd connected him with General Moss, who'd added his terse congratulations and said the promotion list wouldn't be released for a few days, "so act surprised when they tell you."

"Major?" A young brunette with shoulder-length hair, large blue eyes, rounded face, and pixie features sat beside him. She'd watched him curiously since seeing Linda embrace him at the airport. Her name was Penny Dwight, she'd told him after they'd been seated near the back of the C-47, and she was going to Takhli to be the wing commander's secretary. She didn't seem horrified as some women did when they saw his burns, simply took a long, critical look and acted as if it were normal for a guy to have no face to speak of.

She'd chattered a lot since they'd strapped into the aluminum bar and nylon-mesh seats that ran down each side of the old aircraft's interior. When she'd learned that Linda was his fiancée, she'd told him she'd once been engaged too, but she mentioned it no more and seemed to be suffering no trauma over whatever had happened. When she'd gotten the chance to come overseas, she said, she'd jumped at it. Lucky's first impression was that she was thrilled with the exotic assignment and seemed more than a bit naive and flighty. He wondered what she would become at Takhli. The place changed everyone who went there.

"You've been to Takhli," she said. "What's it like?" Her

voice was breathless, as if Takhli were some kind of exotic place like Bali or Tahiti.

"It's in the central Thailand savanna. Hot and dusty. Rains a lot in the summer months like everywhere over here, but between rains there's a lot of heat. Should be cooling off some now, and we'll have a few months of drier weather."

"I've always thought of Siam as being all jungle."

"Mostly farmland in the central portions. There's dense forest to the west, in the Kwai River area over toward Burma, and in the far east, near the Mekong River, and south, down in the panhandle all the way to Malaysia, but not in the central and northern parts of the country. Just grassy savanna and farmland."

"Good. I'm deathly afraid of snakes."

He started to tell her that there were plenty of big snakes around Takhli, that the words "Ta Khli" meant "place of the king cobra," but he stopped himself. She'd be the first American female assigned. If he scared her off, the guys would never forgive him.

She turned in her web seat, craning her neck to look out the window. Kind of pretty, Lucky thought, if she'd change her hair (the long hair didn't go well with her rounded face) and stop slouching. Of course, he was accustomed to the meticulous way Linda carried and groomed herself, and the comparison was unfair. Anyway, the guys at Takhli would finally have an American female presence. He wondered if it wasn't the doing of their new wing commander.

"We'll be landing in twenty-five minutes," announced the burly loadmaster as he made his way back through the passengers.

1444L—Route Pack Five, North Vietnam

Captain Manny DeVera

He was free-falling, tumbling earthward from 20,000 feet plus, wondering if the chute would open at 12,000 as advertised. The silence seemed loud since he'd left the roar of the engine. He could hear only a slight rushing sound outside the helmet.

Through the long free-fall he kept the oxygen mask in place—at altitude life-sustaining oxygen was force-fed from a small green cylinder at his side. A mechanical, chirping sound came from behind as a tiny motor activated and extracted the pin that bound the parachute together. A couple of seconds later he felt a tug as the chute deployed, then a harsher jerk, and he swung in a tremendous arc.

"Whooo-eee," Manny yelled. "Ride 'em, cowboy." During the next wide swing to his left he pulled on his right risers. The swinging motion slowed.

Now below 12,000 feet, he'd no longer require oxygen, so he tugged at the right side of his mask and pulled the bayonet connector free. The fresh air was delicious.

He moved his limbs. They were sore from flailing, but he'd not been going fast in the spin, and except for a throbbing, obviously dislocated left shoulder, he was intact. The shoulder hurt with a mounting intensity that was difficult to ignore—but he was alive, and that was something.

What's your next move?

Look around! He was indeed beyond the Red River, but only barely, descending toward a village in a crook of the wide stream. *Gotta slip the chute,* he decided.

First things first. The seat kit was hanging beneath him, and the raft was inflated and deployed on a long lanyard beneath that, like a bright-yellow banner saying, "Hey, guys, here's the Supersonic Wetback."

He had friends who'd successfully ejected from a Thud only to be crumped by the frigging seat pack when they hit the ground. Manny felt with his good right arm at one side of his butt, found the catch on the seat pack, and disconnected it. He reached around and—with more difficulty—found the second. The pack and raft dropped away.

Ignore the pain.

Another glance at the village far below. If he continued, he'd land smack in its middle.

He crawled up the risers a bit and tugged on a small red banner. Nylon cords slipped free, and panels at the rear of the chute became disconnected, reconfiguring it so the air would flow through and give him forward progress. Now the chute was steerable ... you could go left or right if you pulled down on those risers, and faster forward if you selected both front ones.... Not fast enough, though ... not

nearly enough. He estimated he'd still land in one of the
farmers' fields, short of the first densely foliated mountain
ridge.

He decided to add more slippage to the chute so he
could go faster. He crawled up the nylon straps again,
hooked his useless left arm in the vee, and this time pulled
very hard on the forward risers to increase the air flow out
the rear. The chute began to take him faster toward the
mountains. Maybe . . .

He needed even *more* distance—as much separation as
possible. He was pulling hard, but it was difficult with the
painful arm. Manny kicked up a leg, took a couple of stabs
at it, and succeeded in catching his left foot over the left
riser vee. He pulled down with the left leg and his right
arm. The chute billowed and flapped, but he was *really*
moving westward now, well past the first forested ridge and
headed toward a second. He looked back and saw the yellow raft fall to earth, taking a mighty bounce in a field beside the village.

He'd slipped a half mile, enough to help baffle pursuers,
but he wanted more.

Lower now, but not so low he couldn't continue to slip
the parachute. He tugged down harder with the good arm
and leg, until the chute flapped wildly and began to collapse, then he eased off just enough to refill it with air.

He sailed over a second ridgeline, which he'd estimated
was almost two miles from the village. There were no roads
or habitation he could see below him, but he didn't dare let
up, relentlessly applying the pressure on the risers and traveling ever westward.

He was much lower when he skimmed over a third,
lower ridge. A big swatch of what appeared to be elephant
grass was dead ahead. He decided to steer for it.

1458L—HQ Seventh Air Force, Tan Son Nhut Air Base, South Vietnam

Lieutenant General Richard J. Moss

Lieutenant Colonel Pearly Gates was standing before him, wearing a frown, when Flo buzzed. "Colonel Leska on line two, General."

Moss picked up. "Shoot, Buster."

"Sorry to bother you, sir, but I was just informed of something you should know about. Captain Manny DeVera just went down in North Vietnam. He's on the list."

"Pearly just came in to tell me. We don't have a location on him yet. How about you?"

"Not yet, sir."

"I just advised the control center that I want a maximum effort in there to get him out. They've got the rescue people alerted and on their way in."

"Thank you, sir."

Moss hung up, grim-faced.

"Perhaps we shouldn't allow the people we've got aboard the program to fly combat," Pearly offered.

Moss shook his head. "We need all the feedback we can get, so we can keep Gentleman Jim properly advised." He gave Pearly an unhappy look. "I've got a couple senators waiting for me to give 'em a rah-rah briefing on the air war. Don't hesitate to interrupt if you hear anything."

1504L—Takhli RTAFB, Thailand

Major Lucky Anderson

Halfway through the straight-in approach, with the gooney bird groaning and wheezing dramatically, the pilot announced that everyone should stay in place after they'd taxied in.

There was a ceremony of some sort being set up.

The goon touched down, then soared again before finally settling. The rear of the bird skittered as the tailwheel touched. The pilot turned off halfway down the runway. As he taxied past the endless rows of F-105 Thunderchiefs, Lucky found himself staring.

He loved the heavy fighters. Every airplane had its unique personality. In his mind the Thud was an iron lady who fiercely protected her pilots. She was rock steady, and you could make tiny corrections that were impossible in other fighters. Tough, she'd suffer terrible damage without complaint. He'd seen birds come home with missing vertical stabilizers and others with large portions of wings or aft sections shot away. Even when mortally hit, she'd try to get her pilots to safety before going down. She couldn't turn on a dime, but she was extremely fast at low altitudes, and if you wanted to get away from anything in the sky, all you had to do was stroke afterburner and angle the nose down. If she'd been human, she'd be a perfect mate for the warriors who flew her. She was big mama, and tried her damnedest to take care of her men.

The C-47 taxied up in front of base operations, and the left engine was shut down so the passengers could safely deplane. While the prop clattered to a stop, the rear passenger's door opened, and a tall, easygoing captain in a flight suit peered inside. He looked past Lucky and discovered his target. A grin grew on his face as he brushed unruly hair into place with his hand.

"Miss Dwight?"

The new secretary unbuckled, looking unsure, and made her way toward the door on still-shaky legs. Lucky was curious as to how she'd fare among the mob of horny fighter jocks, crew chiefs, and other womanless men at Takhli.

"I'm Captain Dusty Fields, ma'am. We have a little reception for you," the captain said, taking her hand to help her down.

There were throngs of men waiting in front of base operations. Penny Dwight emerged from the goon and stepped onto the tarmac, and looked startled when they began to cheer. Happy fighter pilots tossed flowers in her path as she walked onto a long red carpet. Crew chiefs and muscular load crews bowed in exaggerated poses. Burly line chiefs gawked.

Lucky pulled his sage-green hang-up bag from beneath the web seat.

The loadmaster was standing near the door, frowning at

the antics of the men outside. "Act like they've never seen a woman before," he said.

"She's the first round-eye to be stationed here," Lucky explained, watching the procession, which now included two happy noncoms holding umbrellas over her head to shield her from the sun. Lavish garlands of flowers were placed around her neck by grinning fighter jocks.

Lucky deplaned, glanced about to orient himself, then started across the ramp toward the 354th TFS, the squadron he'd been assigned to before he'd been shot down. A blue pickup pulled up beside him, and Colonel George Armaugh, the wing Deputy for Operations, nodded to him.

"Welcome back, Colonel."

Lucky shifted his bag to his left hand and saluted with his right. "Colonel?" He acted surprised at the rank, as General Moss had told him to do.

"You're on the LC list. Congratulations."

"Thank you, sir."

"Jump in and I'll drive you."

Lucky nodded toward the 354th squadron building, which was not far. "I'm just going over there."

"Things have changed. You're getting the 333rd squadron."

"Oh?"

"And the new wing commander wants to talk to you. You know Buster Leska?"

"Don't really know him, but we've met." Lucky placed his bag in the back of the pickup and crawled into the passenger's seat.

Armaugh drove slowly down the flight line. "We just got word that four birds went down on the alpha strike this afternoon. Two of 'em were ours."

Lucky grimaced.

"A Wild Weasel crew was shot down in pack six, with no chance of rescue, and a D-model made it out to the edge of pack five. Dunno if we can get him out either. It'll be close, according to how far he made it, I'd say."

"No position yet?"

"Somewhere near Yen Bai. That's all we know so far."

"That makes it doubtful. Who was it?"

"The Supersonic Wetback."

Lucky's jaw tightened. Manny DeVera had worked for him. He was a friend.

He stared bleakly out the window, then looked about. "I thought we were going to the wing commander's office."

"He's on his way to the command post, trying to find out more about the shoot-downs. He knew DeVera in Europe and thinks highly of him. One of the first things he did when he took over was name him to replace Max Foley as wing weapons officer."

"I'll be darned."

"Manny's doing a good job," Armaugh said. He drove out of the aircraft parking zone, crossed the street, and pulled to a stop before the command-post door. "I've gotta go out and monitor things while the birds recover. I'll talk to you later so you can tell me how it went with Colonel Leska, and I'll give you my pitch about what I expect from *my* squadron commanders."

Lucky pulled his bag out of the back, then deposited it at the guarded command-post entrance before he went inside to look for the wingco. He found the chalk-white-haired colonel sitting alone in his position at the rear of the command center, staring at the status boards.

Leska noticed him and waved him over. "Captain DeVera's down," he said evenly.

"I just heard." Lucky sat beside him, wondering at his level of concern. A lot of good fighter jocks were being shot down.

"They've got the rescue effort holding in there until the fighters make radio contact and get a positive position. Two Sandys and two choppers."

Lucky fished a fat cigar from his pocket and popped it into his mouth, a habit he'd acquired long before. He didn't smoke the things, just mouthed and chewed on them when he wanted to think hard on a subject.

Leska nodded at one of the operations sergeants in the front of the room. "He's got Sandy Control at Udorn on the line. No word about Manny's status so far." He turned to Lucky. "I guess you got to know the rescue folks pretty well yourself."

"Enough to have great respect for 'em. Manny went down near Yen Bai?"

"Just southwest from there. Yank Donovan's running the

rescue effort. He relayed word that they hadn't seen unfriendlies in the immediate area."

Donovan hadn't yet arrived at Takhli when he'd been shot down, but Lucky knew him. He was a superb pilot, but a difficult man to like. "Yank's good," he finally said.

Leska gave him a questioning look.

"Got an ego a mile wide." Lucky regretted the criticism as soon as the words were out, so he quickly added, "But he's good in the air."

They sat through five minutes of inactivity with no new word about the rescue.

"You're getting the 333rd squadron," Leska said idly.

"That's what Colonel Armaugh just told me. They're a good bunch of guys."

"I've been flying with them—watching over 'em while you were off in Hawaii and they were without a commander. That'll make 'em double happy to see you arrive."

"Thanks."

They sat quietly, waiting for word about the rescue attempt. And Lucky continued to wonder at the level of concern the wing commander was showing over one of his pilots.

1519L—Route Pack Five, North Vietnam

Captain Manny DeVera

He couldn't believe his eyes! It wasn't a field of nice, yielding elephant grass as he'd thought. Instead it was a big patch of the tallest bamboo Manny had ever seen, fifty or sixty feet high and each stalk up to eight inches in diameter. He held his legs tightly together as he dropped through their tops, and felt fortunate he wasn't skewered like a chunk of goat on a kabob spit.

The chute caught up on one of the things, and just as he started to relax, it slipped and let him fall to the ground, hard, where his right foot crumped and his butt slammed down so mightily onto his heel that he wanted to yell.

He paused for a hurtful, breathless second and *did* yell. "Jesus!" he bellowed. Then Manny remembered Sister Lucia's admonishments, as well as the deep shit he was

presently in. He quickly crossed himself and muttered how
sorry he was about speaking the name in vain. He sure as
hell didn't need to piss off the big guy.

As he switched off the emergency beeper and unlatched
from the parachute, he tried to peer about, but could see
only the thick bamboo stalks. Pain coursed through him
from the dislocated shoulder, fiery stinging from the injured tail—hurting so badly that he almost puked.

Nothing he could do about the ass-bone. *Gotta* do something about the shoulder. Manny knelt and dropped his arm
onto the ground, whimpering as it hit, then tried to grasp
the base of one of the smaller bamboo stalks. The hand was
numb and wouldn't function.

He found a vee of two shoots and wedged the hand
firmly, stepped down hard on it with his left boot, blew out
a breath, and very slowly stood, pulling hard.

Oh God! He continued pulling. The pain eased some as
the arm stretched, then the thing popped back into place
and he screamed in agony. After taking another apprehensive breath and tugging one last time, he staggered, and
stood stock-still, puffing. The arm still throbbed, but nothing
like before. Feeling began to return. He found he could flex
his fingers and move his hand.

Manny heard the drone of jets overhead and immediately
fumbled in a survival vest pocket for a hand-held radio. *You
didn't make it far enough,* his mind said soberly. *No way
they'll come in this far to pick you up.*

Then he remembered the other thing. He knew about
JACKPOT.

1537L—Command Post, Takhli RTAFB, Thailand

Colonel Buster Leska

Leska told Lucky Anderson he'd made lieutenant colonel.
"Pin 'em on before you go to your squadron."

"It's already effective?"

"Nope, not until the fifteenth, but I don't want a major
taking over one of my squadrons when there are fully eligible lieutenant colonels around. No use to hurt their morale
needlessly."

Lucky frowned. It wasn't right to wear the new rank before he was eligible.

"I decree it," Buster said. "You're an LC."

"Yes, sir."

Another long pause, then Buster looked about to ensure they were alone at the rear of the room and very quietly outlined the JACKPOT mission he'd been given by the CSAF, and how it would be designed to force the North Vietnamese from the war. He told him that he, Lucky, and Manny DeVera were the only ones on base who knew about it, or . . . he paused meaningfully . . . *were* to know about it. Anderson appeared impressed.

"The three of us are going to help out from here in the trenches. There's other key players being assigned and briefed at the other bases."

"Is General Moss aboard?"

"He's the critical team player over here. He consolidates and forwards the JACKPOT reports directly to General McManus. From there they go to the President."

Leska watched Anderson as the impact sank in, trying to get an initial impression of the man General Moss thought so highly of. He glanced at the aircraft status board, with Marlin lead circled in red. "That's why we're in here sweating about Manny being shot down," he said softly. "He's one of the few who knew about JACKPOT, and if he's capture . . . ?"

Lucky narrowed his eyes thoughtfully before shaking his head. "You don't have to worry about that part. Knowing what he does, Manny won't let them capture him."

1550L—Route Pack Five, North Vietnam

Captain Manny DeVera

He first contacted and spoke with Scotch Force leader, but it was Animal Hamlin who responded when Manny said, *"F-105 three-ship flight, you are passing overhead now."*

"Marlin three's gotcha, Marlin lead. You in that big patch of grass down there?"

"That's giant bamboo, three. Fifty, sixty feet high. Stuff's

*thick as hell and hard to get around in. Can't cut it with my
knife, so I'll have to squeeze through best I can."*

"*Marlin lead, this is Scotch Force leader. Sandys are on
their way.*" Donovan was talking about A-1Hs used to provide close support for rescue efforts. "*Give 'em ten minutes.
They want to get to a clearing, if possible, so they can bring
the chopper in.*"

"*Can't find a clearing.*" As Manny spoke into the radio, he
looked up at the sky, so he'd feel more as if he were speaking directly to Donovan. "*You see a clearing down here?*"

"*Hard to tell. Keep looking.*"

That was a lot of help, Manny grumbled, squeezing
through yet another unyielding thicket of stalks. He thought
of a briefing he'd received about highly poisonous bamboo
vipers. Periodically he'd stop and listen, and could hear absolutely nothing except the drone of jets high above. No
birds or chirrups from insects. *Nada.* Was that good or bad?
he wondered.

He pressed through a particularly tough group of bamboo stalks and crawled out the other side, then stood, staring
up and shaking his head in amazement.

"*Marlin lead, this is Sandy two-oner. How do you read,
babes?*"

Manny hastened with the radio. "*Marlin lead reads you
five by five, Sandy two-one,*" he responded, meaning he read
him loud and clear. "*I'm at the edge of a thicket of giant
bamboo, under some ferns.*"

"*Slow down your words, Marlin lead,*" said the A-1H pilot, and Manny realized he was spouting unintelligibly in his
elation—in his realization that rescuers might pick him up
after all.

He'd thought of the consequence, how he couldn't allow
himself to be captured.

Manny repeated his words slowly, listening as the sounds
of the nimble, propeller-driven A-1H came closer.

"*Ferns?*" Sandy 21 asked incredulously as it sank in.
"*You're under ferns?*"

"*Yeah. Big ferns. Really big.*" He didn't know how else to
describe them. Manny gawked up at a green canopy of out-
size, broadleaf plants that rose forty feet over his head. The
scene was eerie, as if he were a Lilliputian in an enchanted
forest glen.

"How's your physical condition, Marlin lead?"

"Kicked myself in the butt when I landed, but I can walk."

He hobbled through the wonder world, fighting his way past vines and furry bamboo that he knew not to touch because of their toxicity, before he found a tiny clearing—a small open space where the huge ferns didn't grow all the way to the branches of a towering teak tree.

He stared critically at the little patch of sky. *"I found a place I can see some blue,"* he told the Sandy driver. *"I can hear you, but I can't see you up there yet, Sandy."*

1616L—Command Post, Takhli RTAFB, Thailand

They waited for yet another nervous half hour, and Leska didn't talk anymore about JACKPOT. Periodically he'd give Lucky advice on how to handle his new command, or Lucky would ask about his policies, but they kept their minds tuned for word about the rescue effort.

A force of fighters recovered from a mission to pack two, and their call signs were erased from the combat board. The operational status of each airplane was confirmed and called in by maintenance, and a code was shown beside a list of assigned aircraft tail numbers. Code 1 meant it was clean. Code 2 meant it had discrepancies but was flyable. Code 3 was bad news.

Only the Res-CAP force remained on the combat board, with "Marlin 01" circled in red grease pencil. The downed Weasel bird, Red Dog four, had been lined through. At 1755 the ops sergeant raised a cautious hand. "A new status report's coming through on Marlin lead."

Leska grew still. Lucky stopped chewing his cigar. The ops sergeant looked tentative as he spoke on his phone. He turned. "The Sandys say Marlin lead reports he's banged up but okay."

"How long until the Jolly Greens get to him?"

"They're holding until the Sandys clear them into the area. There's a village four miles to the northeast they're checking out."

1625L—Route Pack Five, North Vietnam

Captain Manny DeVera

The Sandys had left him for a while to check for hostiles in the area. When they returned, they buzzed around a point well south of his position.

"*Sandy lead, you're too far south,*" Manny called.

"*Give us a long count on your radio so we can home on you, Marlin lead.*"

He slowly counted on the radio while the Sandy pilot used his radio direction finder. When the A-1H flew overhead, he stopped and said "*mark.*" After three passes they'd pinpointed him.

"*Jolly Greens are inbound,*" the Sandy driver announced in a monotone. "*They'll be here in eight or nine minutes.*" It was going very smoothly, Manny thought. Maybe it was all the saintly living he'd been doing lately.

Animal Hamlin came back into the area with the remnant of Marlin flight and asked Manny how things were going down there. His Jersey accent somehow lent a degree of normalcy to the situation. DeVera decided he owed Animal two drinks now, and told him so.

"*You're on,*" Animal said.

Yank Donovan came on the air, using an admonishing tone. "*Scotch Force, stay on the look-out for MiGs. That's the second call from Big Eye for this sector.*"

Manny scanned his tiny patch of blue sky with a worried look. MiGs? Would the choppers continue if there were MiGs in the area?

He heard the clopping of rotor blades in the distance— the most beautiful sound he could imagine. Then, "*Marlin lead, this is Jolly Green five-one. Get ready for a fast pickup.*"

"*Roger, Jolly Green,*" Manny quickly responded, hoping it would be so.

Sandy lead gave directions to Jolly Green, then rolled in and fired a marking rocket. "*He's three hundred meters north of my mark,*" said Sandy 21.

Suddenly Manny suffered from near heart failure as things began to fall apart.

Donovan called. *"This is Scotch Force leader. We've got four MiG-17's in sight east of us, not far beyond the river."*

Dammit, Manny's mind cried out. *Dammit to hell!*

"Jolly Green five-one, you hear that?" yelled the A-1H driver shrilly. *"MiGs in the area."*

The chopper pilot was quick to respond, his voice gruff and businesslike. *"You got your job, I got mine, fighters. Now keep 'em off my ass while I make this pickup."*

Manny was stunned at the chopper pilot's answer. His hopes soared yet again when he saw something hover into his patch of sky. *"Jolly Green, you're just south of my position."*

"Stand-by!" growled the chopper pilot in his terse voice. The Jolly reared and hovered, the wash from the big blades making the ferns and limbs of the tree wave to and fro.

"I'm fifty feet off to your right, in a little clearing," Manny tried to shout over the roar.

The chopper pilot hesitated for another long moment, then adjusted until he was directly overhead. The giant ferns whipped about wildly. A number of them flew to the ground.

"Yeah," Manny cried out, his voice lost in the great noise.

He saw the tree penetrator device lowering from a cable at the chopper's right door.

"Yeah!"

When it was a few feet overhead, someone grasped Manny's shoulder and he jumped mightily, again very near having heart failure.

"Get away from it!" thundered a deep voice.

"Oh, shit!"

"It's gotta touch the ground and bleed off the static electricity!" He was a huge black man, six four if he was an inch, and he swung the muzzle of his M-16 in an arc as he pulled DeVera back from the pickup device.

"Who the fuck are you?" Manny screamed.

"Santa Claus."

The device struck against the earth and gave off a bright spark.

"See! You can get fried, you touch those things before they contact the ground. Now go ahead and climb aboard."

Manny slowly comprehended that he was a paramedic,

one of the gutsy rescue guys they called PJs. He grasped the pickup device and tried to figure it out.

The black man grabbed him in one hand and the tree penetrator in the other, positioned Manny's legs over the lowered arms of the device, then crawled onto the opposite side and hugged Manny tightly. It all took no more than ten seconds. He stared up at the chopper and nodded vigorously.

The cable began to reel them quickly upward until they'd passed through the fairy-tale ferns. When they were level with the upper branches of surrounding teak trees, the paramedic bellowed for Manny to hang on—unnecessary advice, for he was grasping as tightly as he could.

The chopper rose and turned, then dipped its nose and charged westward toward safety.

The two of them trailed behind the big helicopter in the breeze, still thirty feet from its belly, thrashed by limber treetops. Manny held his death grip on the penetrator, and the big man held him in a grasp of steel. There was no way to fall off.

The chopper slowed just a bit, and they were reeled the rest of the way up and roughly pulled inside by two other guys.

"Keep that son of a bitch away from the door and don't let him get hurt!" yelled the pilot, in the same abrasive tone he'd heard on the radio. Later Manny learned that the crew had picked up two other pilots in the previous months. Both had died from wounds. They were overjoyed that they'd recovered a live one, and the pilot wanted to keep him that way.

The door gunner began to fire his machine gun at something on the ground as the chopper shuddered, now at max power, and picked up speed.

The huge PJ grabbed Manny, his face transformed and grinning from ear to ear. He planted a wet kiss on his cheek. "Gotcha!" he yelled exuberantly.

Manny began to laugh.

"Gotcha," the PJ repeated.

1637L—Command Post, Takhli RTAFB, Thailand

Colonel Buster Leska

The sergeant's voice was excited over the phone. "Marlin lead's been picked up and they're on their way out. No injuries to speak of. Captain DeVera says he's hungry and to have a drink waiting."

The Supersonic Wetback was okay.

Lucky Anderson pulled the soggy cigar from his mouth and looked at it distastefully, as if wondering how the unsightly thing had gotten there.

Leska felt energy reentering his body. "Where are they taking him?" he asked the sergeant.

"Direct to Nakhon Phanom," he replied.

Buster sighed audibly as he got to his feet. He waved at a major who'd joined the sergeant in the front of the room. "Have 'em fire up the base gooney bird and send it to NKP. I want DeVera back here ASAP."

"Yes, sir."

He turned to Lucky Anderson. "Get on over to the parachute shop and have your new rank sewn on. We've got work to do."

Anderson was smiling and nodding. They were bringing one home.

CHAPTER TEN

Monday, November 6th, 1520 Local—Route Pack Six, North Vietnam

Colonel Buster Leska

Before takeoff Buster had done two things to prepare for his private foray over Hanoi.

First, he'd ordered the photo shop to load the KA-71 70mm camera, mounted under the chin of his Thud, with film, and told the NCOIC that he'd want the stuff developed ASAP after landing. No, he didn't want interpretation of the film strips. Just send them over to his office when they'd been developed. After having more suggestions for support turned down, the NCOIC got the idea that Buster didn't want his people, or anyone else, looking at the film.

Second, he'd briefed his flight that he'd pull off the target straight ahead to make a brief tour of the countryside. He told the pilots to rejoin and begin their egress with the others, that he'd join them on their way out.

No, he wouldn't want a wingman. He'd be going low and fast and would be safe enough.

Buster didn't lie to his flight. He told them he wanted to take a solo close-up look at the Red River Valley because he felt he should know it like the back of his hand. He didn't tell them the examination would include the restricted southern suburbs of Hanoi. The pilots were curious and concerned, but didn't question his decision. It was appropriate that a commander would want to know as much as possible about his enemy.

It was an alpha strike. Thirty-two dive-bombers from Takhli, separated into two sixteen-ship formations. A four-ship Wild Weasel flight was assigned to fly with each formation, engaging any SAM sites that came on the air. F-4 Phantoms from Ubon would provide MiG-CAP. George Armaugh led Bear Force, Takhli's first sixteen-ship formation. Buster felt he'd need a few more sorties before taking on the mission-commander role. He was still in the learning phase.

Their target was the Gia Thuong storage complex, which consisted of four large warehouses, a rail siding, and a massive truck terminal on the eastern edge of Hanoi. General Moss had requested permission from the Joint Targeting Office at the Pentagon to strike the place as soon as he'd been shown the spectacular results from the "barracks" mission, wondering if they wouldn't find another buildup of munitions. Permission had been granted, which was surprising, because all such decisions had to be approved by the President and his circle of civilian advisors.

Two similar forces from Korat preceded them, and one of those would bomb Gia Thuong before they arrived. Bear Force would be second. Buster led the last four-ship flight, call sign Wolf, in that group. His rationale was the assumption that the North Viet defenses would be preoccupied with the strike force while he got his photos.

Their route led them across the Red River north of Yen Bai, then eastward, slowly descending as they flew across the valley. When they approached Thud Ridge at ten thousand feet, they turned southward and flew toward Hanoi. The fighters from Korat were in the target area by then, and when Buster momentarily switched to their strike frequency, he heard a loud profusion of chatter about SAM firings and flak, then awed voices talking about a fireball and tremendous explosion. He eyed the area ahead, but a towering cumulus cloud obscured the target.

The Korat birds finished bombing and started toward

their rejoin point to regroup their force. They sounded professional and a bit exuberant at the results.

The Takhli Wild Weasels, flying just in front of their formation, fired Shrike anti-radar missiles at SAM sites on the northern periphery of the city, but before Buster began to feel good about it, they announced that two other sites had fired missiles at the strike force.

"Stay in formation and keep the music going," George Armaugh radioed in a calm voice, *"unless you know a SAM's committed for your bird."*

It was a hard thing, knowing SAMs were coming up and continuing to fly straight and level, but like the others Buster gritted his teeth and did just that.

Three SAMs zipped cleanly, one by one, past the formation and blossomed in bright, orange-colored explosions 2,000 feet above them. He waited expectantly, but didn't see the second covey of missiles.

They were approaching the southern end of Thud Ridge, the Hanoi amoeba looming in the near distance before them, and could now see great columns of smoke from Korat's bombing. Armaugh began a slight climb to the perch, and the others followed, still in formation. A haze of artillery smoke covered much of the city, and a profusion of light-colored flak puffed above it in a thick layer. Here and there clumps of dark smudges bloomed from the bigger guns nearer their flight level. Buster noted artillery muzzle flashes sparkling on the ground beneath the haze, and indeed, most were coming from the far, southern side of the city.

George Armaugh made a curt radio call as he abruptly turned and dived toward the bright fires left by Korat's bombs. One by one the other aircraft followed.

When the twelfth ship was gone, it was Buster's turn.

He immediately turned his Thud up onto its left wing, turned sharply, then rolled inverted and pulled the nose down. As soon as he was established in the dive, he rolled upright and eased off on the throttle so he wouldn't go supersonic. The bird settled at forty-five degrees, and he fine-tuned the ailerons and rudder. The target area, now a profusion of smoke, tiny buildings, and ribbons of railroad track, erupted with more bomb detonations as he stared.

Another good hit—there was little of Gia Thuong left to destroy.

As he passed through 12,000 feet, a surface-to-air missile launched from a site half a mile beyond the target. Then another, and yet another.

Without hesitation he shallowed his attack, pulling harshly on the stick to level out some, jinked left and right again, again pushed over, and ... the smoke from the SAM firings was dead ahead. He concentrated on the center of the site, where the control van should be located.

"Wolf lead's attacking the missile site at our twelve o'clock," he announced. SAM batteries were fair game. The storage complex was already well bombed. The deadly SAM site needed attention.

"Wolf two, same."

"Wolf three's with you."

"Wolf four."

Flak began to track him, but the dark bursts were grouped low and to his left. He readjusted his flight path until the pipper was crawling toward the aim point. Smoke from the missile firings drifted in his direction, so he'd bomb a bit long to compensate for wind.

At 7,500 feet Buster pressed the pickle button and felt the aircraft grow lighter. He eased back on the stick, still thundering earthward but at a shallower attitude. He pushed the throttle forward and outboard into afterburner, no longer restricted by the poor aerodynamics of the bombs, and a few seconds later felt the kick in his seat as the burner lit.

The remainder of Wolf flight would turn right and climb to rejoin the rest of the force southwest of the target. He continued to descend, jinking straight ahead toward the coast, passing over the thousand streamlets of the Red River delta.

Nose twenty degrees down, going fast, 690 knots and accelerating, randomly jinking back and forth. He descended through 3,000 feet and continued down. Eased up some as he passed through 2,000, and more at 1,000. When he was low enough, 500 feet or less, he began a lazy turn to the right, back in the direction of Hanoi. He eased out of afterburner and dropped a couple of hundred feet lower yet, then rolled out on a westerly heading, racing across the lowlands in the direction he'd just come from.

He was doing 720 knots as he approached the southern part of the sprawling city. Low and supersonic. Too low to be seen on radar screens, too fast to be tracked by guns. By the time they heard the sonic boom, he'd be long gone—a very noisy blur. Ahead of him were hundreds of twinkles and flashes from guns, and he noted six different SAM launches in the course of a few seconds—formidable defenses now concentrating on Donovan's sixteen-ship strike force, which should be beginning their dive-bomb attacks.

Just before he recrossed the Red River, Buster manually switched on the camera, which would traverse from forward to rear and get fish-eye images of the earth beneath. Then he began a slight climb, reengaged afterburner, and kept the camera running as he leveled at a thousand feet.

This was the most dangerous part of the flight. He didn't jink, held the airplane straight and level, still going very fast—supersonic plus. They *might* have time to get off snapshots, but he'd surprise most of the gunners and was surely creating pain in more than a few eardrums.

He felt tiny aircraft shudders, imagined they were from flak bursting behind and about him, but didn't take his eyes from the flight path straight ahead. When there was no more city in front of the nose, he began to jink and again dropped down to hug the dirt, staying in afterburner.

Twenty seconds later he pulled out of the A/B detent and eased back on the throttle. He'd used a lot of jet petroleum on the ultra-high-speed pass—burned down to 6,000 pounds—so he'd have to conserve for the rest of the trip home. As he began his climb to clear the mountains west of the Red River Valley, Buster scanned the sky for Bear Force.

1814L

He was back at his desk in his office when the NCOIC of the photo lab delivered the film strips in a long envelope. "How'd they turn out?" he asked.

"We did as you said, sir. We didn't look."

"Thanks."

As soon as the sergeant departed, Buster pulled out the

long, four-inch-wide photo strips and spread them out on his desktop. It took five minutes of getting down close and staring before he got the knack of it, fifteen minutes before he fully realized what he had.

He couldn't tell if he'd hit the SAM site with his bombs, but it had been squarely before him when he'd released, and at debriefing, the other pilots of Wolf flight said it had been left a smoking ruin. He used a magnifying glass on the next strips, which he numbered one, two, and three with a black marker.

The first panoramic view showed the river and the south-eastern side of Hanoi. The film was fuzzy in places, but he found what he was looking for on that first one. Artillery pieces of all descriptions were clearly shown, hundreds, perhaps thousands of the things, some positions set into gutted homes and camouflaged by sheets of wicker, which had been pulled aside for action.

Everywhere he scanned, in every street and alley, there was a profusion of carts and motorized vehicles, and every one was heavily laden. The next two strips showed the same thing; trucks and vehicles of all descriptions loaded with mounds of supplies and weapons. There was a row of tanks, he counted thirty-four of the things, and those also were piled high.

He'd doubted Manny's version, but no more. The North Vietnamese were preparing for something big. Buster wondered if the headquarters people in Saigon were aware of what was happening. He'd seen no message traffic on the buildup.

He knew he must get the information to them, but what was the smartest route? He couldn't release the photos through normal channels unless he was willing to face punishment for what he'd done. It was obvious he'd purposefully taken the photos from low level, deep within the restricted area declared by the President of the United States.

Could he say, as Manny had, that he'd taken them while coming off the authorized target? Buster pondered that for a long moment before deciding it was unlikely he'd get away with it. If he released the photos through normal channels, they would probably go to the top, and there were men there who wouldn't flinch at sacrificing a mere colonel. His career would be jeopardized, and the importance of the message stated by the photos might be lost in the furor. He had too much left to accomplish to throw it all away without good reason.

Buster wanted to get the photo strips into the proper hands for closer study and analysis, but there appeared to be no easy way to do it. Should he ignore the film, perhaps burn the strips and act as if he'd never taken or seen them, then try to convince headquarters they needed to take low-level recce photos there themselves?

Send RF-4C Phantoms low level over Hanoi in the face of the defenses he now knew were there? One might make it through, as he'd done. It would be suicide for the rest.

What rationale could he use? *I've got this gut feeling something's going on there?*

You gotta be shitting me.

Buster drove to the O' Club and ate dinner. George Armaugh, also late to eat, joined him. George told him how it was dumb, the strike force going all the way to Hanoi like that and risking so many lives, and then finding that Korat had already taken out the target. They should've delayed and gotten the results before sending in Takhli. He began complaining about the shitty status of the airplanes they were getting and paused only when Jerry Trimble, the Deputy for Maintenance, came and sat with them and complained about the needless damage the pilots were doing to his airplanes. Then men were bickering when Buster stood abruptly and said he had something heavy on his mind and wanted to go think it over without listening to two grown men acting like five-year-olds. They were slack-jawed when he walked away.

He went into the stag bar, found it too crowded, then proceeded outside and to his trailer.

Maybe the generals in Saigon are aware of the buildup. What if they're not?

When he'd poured two fingers of Chivas Regal and was settled into his easy chair, he knew there was no way he could just forget about the photo strips.

He wondered if he shouldn't forward the photo strips as a part of the JACKPOT project. It didn't precisely fit in with what they were trying to do, but it might serve the purpose. *No. If someone gets hold of them and relates them to*

JACKPOT, the chief might lose the whole ball game because of the stupid, illegal photos.

He decided to take the film personally and immediately to Saigon, then remembered that a brigadier general and a covey of colonels were arriving the next morning from PACAF headquarters on yet another fact-finding mission.

He sipped his drink and wondered, then went outside and returned to the O' Club stag bar. As he'd expected he might, he found his man. Manny DeVera was standing beside Animal Hamlin, waving his arms and talking as Animal studiously picked a sad tune on his bright-orange guitar. As Buster approached, the Supersonic Wetback was regaling a group of fellow pilots about his shoot-down experience, describing how the rudder pedal had melted off before he'd ejected, using his fighter jock's prerogative to embellish a good story.

Buster interrupted and called him outside.

"Yes, sir?" Manny asked when Buster closed the door to the noisy bar.

"You got anything going tomorrow?"

"Just office work, sir. The flight surgeons say I'm supposed to cool it for a few days, 'cause of my shoulder and a bruise on my butt. No flying and no heavy duty. I tried to tell 'em I'm okay, but they say it's standard procedure."

"Can you sit okay?"

"Yes, sir. It hurts just the same if I'm standing or sitting. I'm taking APCs for the pain."

"Good. How about doing something for me?"

"You name it, sir." DeVera didn't hesitate. That's what Buster liked about the Supersonic Wetback. Once he made up his mind about something or someone, his loyalties were complete.

Buster told Manny to see him first thing in the morning. He had a package he wanted him to take to Saigon.

Tuesday, November 7th, 1100 Local—Saigon, Republic of Vietnam

Captain Manny DeVera

Colonel Leska had arranged for the midmorning T-39 flight, called Scatback, to take him from Takhli direct to Tan Son Nhut, but nothing coming back. He'd told him to get hops on military birds, and to take all the time he wanted. Manny was happy to get a few days away from Takhli, regardless of all the work to be accomplished in his new job. He'd never been to Saigon, and he was curious about the place.

After Manny delivered the package to General Moss's office, placing it in General Moss's hands as he'd promised, he'd called base ops and found that all the flights to Thailand were filled. He'd have to spend the night. He'd checked into the VOQ, gone to the gate, and taken a taxi for a tour of Saigon. The vehicle was an old, late-thirties-vintage Renault, and they rode with the windows down. It didn't look like rain.

A strange city, he decided as he gawked and the driver did his tour-guide bit. Vibrant and alive, and, except for multitudes of military vehicles and uniformed men, undefiled by the obscenities of war. The big streets, like Le Loi and Pasteur, were wide and nice in a very French colonial way. When he'd been stationed in Libya, he'd taken embassy flights to Morocco and had seen similar construction. Lots of white stucco and ornate, almost delicate, architecture. There the French had brought a bit of Paris to the African desert. Here the transplant was different, set into profusions of lush, tropical plants. The flower-sweet smells along Le Loi were almost masked by a heavy pall of exhaust fumes that permeated the air. The driver took him to John F. Kennedy Park, where he walked about putting-green lawns and examined a statue of President Jack, who had, following Ike's hesitation, pledged American support to the South Vietnamese.

He continued his tour, taking a late lunch of café au lait and crusty sweetbread on the veranda of the Caravelle Hotel, as he'd been advised to do by Lucky Anderson, who knew the city. There a small combo played quiet music, and he eyed the most strikingly beautiful girl, a Eurasian, he'd ever seen. She spoke French to her escort, a distinguished-looking man who remained very quiet. Manny imagined him to be a spook. Maybe a double agent who was walking some tightrope? Or ... how about an international jewel thief, with his beautiful mistress? Both of those fit well with the hotel's mysterious flavor. Then two obnoxious GIs brought their girlfriends in and raised hell with a snobby waiter, breaking the spell.

Back to the waiting taxi. The driver drove slowly past the presidential palace, to parks dedicated to past Vietnamese heros, before Manny finally told him to take him back to the base. The driver leered and suggested a trip down Tu Do Street, and Manny said, Why not? He'd heard of Saigon's infamous red-light district. It was a letdown, like boys' towns everywhere—GIs in and out of uniform, mixing with pretty but sullen whores. It could have been Reynosa or Nuevo Laredo, except the females were smaller. They were better dressed and obviously more streetwise than the farm girls in the Ta Khli boys' town, but he was willing to bet they fucked with the same wooden lack of enthusiasm.

The cabbie asked if he wanted to stop off at one of the bars.

Manny declined, but saw a yellow Kodak sign on the front of a store and told him to stop. Inside he found a smiling Chinese owner who reminded him of shop owners in Matamoros and Cuidad Juarez. They ignored prices shown on tags and haggled with straight faces. Manny started with a small 35mm, half-frame Olympus camera that he could carry in the cockpit and operate with one hand, thinking he might get a photo of a MiG or maybe a SAM explosion. After they agreed on a price, he asked to see a monocular. It was difficult to pick out targets on the ground through binoculars, but he'd heard it was much easier using one eye. He settled on a Nikon single-lens monocular, and a price. Finally he added a new Seiko Sportsmatic watch, since his previous one had been lost during the ejection, and haggled for a package deal. He spent a total of twenty minutes in the store and paid sixty bucks for everything. The store owner's eyes glittered when he received greenbacks instead of the colorful MPC script with Miss Americas printed in place of Presidents that U.S. servicemen were ordered to use under penalty of excommunication.

Back in the old Renault cab then, and the thing didn't want to start. When the cabbie began shouting, slapping the dash, and cursing, Manny decided he was getting to see the vehicle's final gasps. But he figured some French fighter jock had probably thought the same thing a dozen years earlier, because the ancient engine sputtered and caught, and the cabbie patted and soothed the dash in forgiveness.

"Back to the base," Manny said. He had seen enough.

They took a detour on the way, since the main streets were now blocked off for some visiting dignitary, and drove past shanties with woven rattan walls and mustard-colored tin roofs. The odors there were acrid sweet and more typical of the far east.

He had dinner at the Tan Son Nhut O' Club and *almost* picked up a nurse, a major visiting from the Philippines. She said her name was Marty, and asked if he knew a guy named Mal Stewart who'd been stationed at Takhli the previous year.

He told her he'd heard of him—that he'd been killed in action just before he'd arrived. She bit her lip and grew misty-eyed and wanted to know more. He told her what he knew, that the guy had been killed at the place they now called Termite Hill.

Marty was hefty, with legs that belonged on a Dallas Cowboy lineman and a florid face, but she was obviously horny and the only free woman in the bar. There'd been times Manny DeVera would've chatted up a reptile for a chance to clear his pipes, but he faithfully remembered his resolution about cooling it with round-eye women, who were the source of his problems. After three drinks he excused himself.

She wore a sad expression as he started toward his VOQ room alone.

Manny trudged out of the club, grumbling to himself that there was definitely something unnatural about self-restraint. He slowed and decided that the timing of resolutions should be more carefully considered. It had been a long while since he'd had a roll in the hay, and the nurse had intimated it was the same for her. He paused longer, argued his case to himself, and finally sighed as he went back into the bar.

When he motioned, Marty gave him a look of pleased triumph. No reason to be ridiculous about things, he told himself. In the morning, he'd get serious about the promise to quit his dealings with round-eye females until the combat tour was completed.

He grinned at the approaching nurse, who'd brought her purse and half-filled glass of gin.

"Whyncha come over to my room for a drink?" she asked demurely. "It's quieter there."

Thursday, November 9th, 1830 Local—Takhli RTAFB, Thailand

Tuesday's trip had ended up a nuisance, for he'd had trouble getting back to Takhli. After the session with the nurse, Manny had caught a C-130 going to Udorn Air Base, got another hop to Bangkok, then waited around Don Muang airport for four hours in vain. He'd spent Wednesday night in the transient barracks there, missed out on a cargo-filled C-130, and took the morning C-47 round-robin flight to Takhli. The short trip had taken him two full days.

After stopping by Colonel Leska's office to tell him the mission to Saigon was completed as ordered, he'd gone to his office and dug into the waiting paperwork.

The 354th squadron had suffered yet another combat loss, and in the early afternoon Lieutenant Colonel Yank Donovan dropped by his office to ask a few questions.

Manny was surprised that Donovan would do that, considering what had gone before. They hadn't spoken since his shoot-down, and Manny'd had trouble keeping his anger in check, wondering if Yank had learned anything about keeping up his airspeed. Yet while the atmosphere was difficult throughout the conversation, he'd felt that the squadron commander with the huge ego and darting eyes seemed interested in what he'd had to say.

The previous day a surface-to-air missile had shot down one of Donovan's pilots, and he wanted to know more about Soviet SAM systems, so Manny had described the SA-2 SAM system in detail. While Yank had listened, he'd not been all that attentive. Several times he'd interrupted and said yeah, he already knew this or that. When he'd finished, Donovan asked in a quieter voice if his squadron pilots were doing something wrong, since they'd been taking the brunt of the wing's recent losses.

Manny had said no, he hadn't noticed the 354th pilots doing anything different from the others. He'd been at Takhli for seven months, he'd told Donovan, and the losses seemed to go in cycles. First it would be one squadron, then another. It was just the 354th's turn.

Yank Donovan said the losses seemed awfully high. Manny told him they were down from a year ago, when fewer than 40 percent of the pilots were finishing their tours. He said it was something like 60 percent finishing now.

Why the improvement?

Because they'd learned a lot about Russian-built defensives, and no matter how much they disliked flying the gaggle, the ECM pod formations worked. SAM operators couldn't pick out individual aircraft on their radar scopes. Which allowed the Thuds to fly higher, out of most of the flak.

Maybe so, Yank had responded, but a SAM had come up and taken one of his airplanes out of the formation, so *something* wasn't right with what they were doing.

Manny had said that when it was apparent that a missile was committed toward a specific aircraft, they were to take evasive action in unison. He explained that maneuver.

Yank had said that was damned hard to judge when a missile was coming at you in particular, and Manny had to agree. He'd asked if the pods had been working properly. Yank had said no one had reported otherwise, but they seemed to malfunction too often. He'd added the last rancorously.

Before he'd left his office, Donovan had stonewalled his face and added a mumbled apology for his failure to follow his advice and push up the airspeed earlier, which *might* have contributed to Manny's shoot-down, and then *sort of* thanked him for not blaming him in front of the others. That small measure of humility hadn't come easily, but he'd gotten the words out.

Yank was egotistical to a fault, but in his unique way he'd tried to make things right. A real enigmatic jerk, was Yank Donovan. Then Manny began to think about the fact that a SAM had knocked down an aircraft that was supposedly in proper formation, and decided it had indeed likely been due to a faulty ECM pod. The formation should have maneuvered, but the jamming should've masked the bird.

He's spent three hours at the Electronic Countermeasures maintenance shop, learning more about jamming pods and how they worked. It was heady stuff, and by the time he broke for dinner, his mind was filled with explanations of jittered frequencies, complex scans and scan periods, pulse rates, and effective radiated power, which the ECM guys called "erps." The thing that stuck with him was the fact that when the maintenance troops brought the pods in for inspection, fewer than 50 percent worked entirely as advertised and only 70 percent provided enough erps to give adequate protection.

The pods were built by Hughes, and the company rep was a diligent, hardworking man who worried as much as anyone that the pods weren't performing well. He said one problem was that the pods' electrical components weren't withstanding the g-forces they had to endure. If a pilot pulled six g's on a pullout, the pod out on the wing experienced eight to twelve g's, sometimes more. The pod had its own ram air turbine, called a RAT, which was a small propeller that rotated and generated power, and that was also a weak link. It would be better, he said, if they could provide normal aircraft power to the pods and do away entirely with RATs.

Manny walked toward the club, trying to remember what he'd been told and thinking of solutions. The Hughes tech rep said the pilots at Korat were starting to fly with two ECM pods, replacing the AIM-9 Sidewinder missile on the right-wing adapter with a second pod.

Manny hated to see them lose a big part of their air-to-air fighting capability, but . . .

Up ahead he saw the wing commander's new secretary standing outside the club, talking with Dusty Fields. He'd seen her a couple of times in Leska's outer office and decided to find out more about her, but was always in too much of a hurry to chat. She wasn't a real beauty, more the kind you'd call cute or pixyish, he decided as he approached. But he liked the clash of dark hair, pale skin and blue eyes, as well as her trim figure. Which made him think of his last girlfriend, who'd had the way of grabbing her ankles and fucking him raw. He smiled just thinking about it.

If he was going to break his newest vow to have nothing further to do with round-eye women, it would take someone like his ex-girlfriend, Manny decided . . . or *maybe* Colonel Leska's secretary. He hadn't decided on the secretary—Dwight was her last name, he remembered. She carried herself poorly—slouched too much—and giggled often. That last habit was likely because she was the only American woman around, and the all-male presence made her nervous. But now she was smiling and seemed more relaxed. He decided to take another look.

"How you doing, Dusty?" he said, smiling at the girl but unable to recall her first name. He waited for Dusty to introduce them. Fields just eyed him suspiciously and moved protectively closer to the girl. Since she didn't move away, it was obvious Dusty had been using his charms and that some of it was working. The unsuspecting girl was being taken in by his glib and experienced tongue, and Manny wondered how he might set her straight about Dusty Fields.

"You two going inside for dinner?" he asked, continuing to eye the secretary. It was unfair, he thought, getting shot down the morning she'd arrived, and Fields jumping in and not waiting for him. As Manny's competitive spirit grew, she became better looking.

"We've eaten," said the girl without a first name, in a tone entirely different from the one he remembered in the office. She had a soft, melodic voice. Relaxed now, she didn't look half-bad.

Dusty didn't introduce them, just continued to look about as if Manny weren't there, as if he were waiting for something undesirable to leave so they could resume their talk. *The guy has no class,* Manny thought, *and* certainly *no sense of fair play.* Unable to think of a reason to hang around, he proceeded inside. Dusty had only one thing in mind. Disgusting, but the man was like that. They'd gone after the same women a few times in the past, each winning or losing about an equal number of times, but Manny felt his own lines were more honest.

He found an empty table in the dining room and thought about the fact that Dusty, a nice-looking guy with a pleasant face and a lanky body, *lulled* women with his schoolboy's grin and "aw shucks" demeanor. *Watch out for that clever snake, Miss No-Name Dwight,* he thought. Once she saw through Dusty's shallowness, perhaps he'd provide consolation. He paused at that idea. The Supersonic Wetback as consolation prize? No way. He decided to go after . . . whatever her name was . . . and beat out Dusty Fields, as he knew he could. Usually could, anyway. It would be interesting, as it always was when he and Fields competed.

Manny ordered a Salisbury steak with fried rice and asked the waitress to bring a fresh bottle of soy sauce. He used the stuff to add taste to the cardboard meals. As he waited, he thought more about the secretary and wished Dusty would fall down and bust something. Maybe break out with hives or pneumonia. She was increasingly appealing.

When the food arrived and he was about to pitch in, the girl and Dusty came through the entrance. Animal Hamlin was with them, toting his battered guitar case, and the three were laughing about something silver-tongued Dusty was saying. They angled toward the bar in back. He decided to pay a visit there after he'd eaten. Maybe sidle up beside them so he could at least learn the girl's first name. Perhaps show off some of his suaveness and show her what she was missing. No harm in that, he thought as he bit into the fried hamburger patty that tasted like a mixture of sawdust and soy sauce.

Half an hour later Manny went into the half-filled stag bar. The trio sat at a corner table. The girl listened to Dusty Fields tell a war tale while Animal plucked a tune and fooled with his guitar. Fields's hands moved vigorously over the table. Fighter jocks should be born with more hands, Manny had long thought, so they could describe their maneuvering better.

He noted that the fighter jocks in the crowd were more subdued than normal. The most-used adjective in the Thailand fighter community was "shit hot," which was spoken as one word and might be used in "that was a shit-hot mission" if a guy got a MiG or killed a tough target or destroyed a SAM site. Tonight the guys had modified the modifier for the sake of the lady in the bar. Some of the guys had flown a "sierra hotel" mission against the Bac Giang bridge up in pack six that day, for two spans had been dropped. The feeling about the round-eye female being in their stag bar was mixed—some of the guys liked to look over and see an American woman, while others felt that the sanctity of the male domain should be retained even in a dismal place like godforsaken Takhli.

Manny got a MiG-15 from Pak, the assistant barkeep. Jimmy, the head Thai bartender, was playing liar's dice with two new Wild Weasel pilots from the 354th squadron. He was obviously winning because periodically he'd squeal joyfully. Jimmy supplemented his income by gambling with the Americans, mostly with fresh arrivals because the old hands knew not to play with him. When Jimmy won, he took his due with relish—when he lost, he'd sulk until the pilots got intoxicated and gave his money back.

Manny was about to go over and join the group at the table, had even thought of a good entrance line, but then the girl stood and Dusty escorted her out the side door. Animal Hamlin watched them go, still seated and plucking notes on his orange guitar. *Damn,* Manny grumbled.

"How ya doing, Animal?" he asked as he approached.

Hamlin glowered. "I wish you guys'd call me Roger." He pronounced it *Rah-cher.* Animal waved at Jimmy, who was staring intently at the dice cup held by one of his antagonists. "Need a drink over here," he yelled. Jimmy didn't look up. Pak hurried over with a harried expression.

"I'll buy," said Manny. "I owe you for all the help when I got shot down."

"Damn right you do." Animal grinned as he ordered.

"Where'd Dusty and the girl go?" Manny asked in an innocent voice.

Animal picked a note, frowned, and adjusted. "Penny wanted to see a movie."

Manny filed away the secretary's name as he sipped his drink. He didn't want to appear to interested, but . . . "Dusty got something going with her yet?" he asked casually.

"She's nice," Animal said vaguely, adjusting again.

"They got something going?" he repeated.

"Dusty's keeping an eye out for her. Making sure the other fighter jocks don't try to take advantage or anything."

Which meant Fields was acting the big brother, the guy with the white hat. Manny mused. That was likely the best approach with her. He wondered if there was a way to out-good-guy Dusty. *Maybe,* he decided. In his new job, he had a built-in excuse to visit the wing commander's office more often than a squadron pilot like Dusty Fields.

Billy Bowes, C-Flight commander for the 354th Pig Squadron, came in and sidled over to the table. "Join you assholes?"

"I dunno," said Animal. "We're pretty particular. You wash off your war paint?"

Bowes was a Cherokee Indian from Oklahoma.

Billy noted that Jimmy was busy and waved to Pak. "Somebody's gotta keep you white-eyes straight. Win your wars for you, shit like that." He ordered a round for all three, which meant Manny had the one in his hand and two more stacked up.

They talked about how the missions were going, then about how Lucky Anderson, now Lieutenant Colonel Anderson, was doing with his squadron. Morale was soaring in the 333rd, Animal said, because of his leadership. Bowes grumbled and said he wished he could change squadrons. He'd advised everyone in the 354th to wait and see about the new commander—give him a chance. Now he'd made up his mind like the rest of them. He didn't trust Yank Donovan.

"How come?" asked Animal Hamlin as he picked out the first bar of "Wildwood Flower."

"He's an egotistical, narrow-minded, self-centered asshole, *that's* why."

"So what? So are all your friends."

Billy ignored the comment. "Anyone in the squadron takes out a target, Donovan acts like it was him that did it. He keeps saying *me*, *my*, and *I*, like he's the only one doing anything."

Manny finished a drink and started on the next. A pilot walked into the bar from outside, talking with a buddy, and forgot to remove his hat before one of the guys at the end of the bar vigorously rang the bell. "Shit!" cried the pilot, whipping off the hat. Too late. A bevy of catcalls erupted as he slunk to the end of the bar to buy a free round for the house.

Animal was still mired in the conversation about squadron commanders, crowing about what a sierra-hotel guy

Lucky Anderson was. How he'd elevated Dusty to become
B-Flight commander and himself as Dusty's assistant. Billy
was intently ignoring him, increasingly peeved because Animal had the better of the deal and he was stuck with Yank
Donovan.

Finally Billy had enough. "You guys can brownnose all
you want, but it doesn't—"

Animal quit picking the guitar and bristled. "Goddammit,
don't you say that!"

Arguments and scuffles were common in the Takhli bar,
but there were no real fights. Manny sipped his Scotch and
Drambuie and watched while they bickered. By the time
Manny had finished another MiG-15, his vision was blur-
ring. He grew tired of imagining how Dusty Fields was
making out with the secretary whose first name he'd again
forgotten, so he broke into their conversation.

"All I know," Manny interjected, "is that Donovan sure
was thick with Colonel Lyons."

Both of the others frowned, for that had nothing to do
with what they were talking about.

Animal was in an argumentative mood. "Donovan's a
good pilot. I saw him put his bombs on a target the other
day. Took out a truck park. Best bombs in the strike force."

Manny almost mentioned the lack of proper airspeed at
Phuc Yen that had helped him get shot down. He stopped as
he remembered today's *half* apology.

"So," concluded Animal Hamlin, "Colonel Donovan's a
little odd, but you can't argue with success. He's the best pilot in the wing."

"Bullshit," said Billy Bowes, draining his drink and waving
at Pak the bartender. Billy was good at placing his own bombs.
"I'd still rather work for Lucky Anderson," Bowes said.

Hamlin didn't argue that point. Manny was bored with
the subject. "You hear that Colonel Mack's on the full-bull
list that just came out?" he asked, his words slurred.

"Shit hot!" exclaimed Billy Bowes with a wide grin.

They talked about Mack MacLendon, who'd left Takhli a
couple of weeks earlier, then about the fact that he was
headed for the Pentagon, which was surely a waste of good
talent.

Animal hooted, "Let's have some music," to another pilot
from Lucky Anderson's 333rd Lancers squadron, and

strummed heartily. Several pilots gathered around Animal's table, and on cue they began to croon:

> *Oh, there once was a bird,*
> *No bigger than a turd,*
> *Sitting on a telephone pole. . . .*

By the time they'd finished the verse, others had joined and were also loudly singing.

> *Oh, he ruffled up his neck,*
> *And . . . shit about a peck,*
> *As he puckered up his little ass-hoooole. . . .*
> *Asshole, asshole, asshole, ass-hoooole . . .*
> *As he puckered up his little asshole.*

That was only the warm-up, and the group continued to grow in numbers. Although their harmony was dubious, they compensated with volume and serious intent. They sang the camel song, about the inscrutable sphinx—about Sammy Small and how he shouted "fuck 'em all!"—about how they loved their wives and ate their shit with wooden spoons—then they sang:

> *Beside a Laotian waterfall,*
> *One bright and sunny day,*
> *Beside his battered Thunderchief,*
> *A young pursuiter lay. . . .*

and went on about how the pilot wanted the crankshaft removed from his larynx, the gears from his brain, and so forth, and ended with:

> *Oh death where is thy sting-a-ling,*
> *Death where is thy sting,*
> *The bells of hell will ring-a-ling,*
> *For you but not for ME!*
>
> *Ohhhhhh!*
> *Ring-a-ling-a-ling-ling,*
> *Blow it out your ass,*
> *Ring-a-ling-a-ling-ling.*

Blow it out your ass.
    Better days are a-coming by and by!

They whooped and ordered more drinks, and made fun of a
new arrival who'd completed his first mission that day. A pilot's first five missions were flown in the lower packs, down
in the safer areas where he could learn a few ropes before
taking on the big boys up in pack six. Manny had suggested
that they increase it to ten flights and was formalizing the
combat introduction to make sure certain "training" blocks
were filled before the new guys "graduated" to pack six.

Damn, but there was a lot to do.

His thoughts returned to the girl named . . . oh yeah,
Penny! . . . and again he wondered how that cheating, no-
good Dusty Fields was faring. By then the somewhat plain
secretary had become downright pretty in Manny DeVera's
blurry mind.

CHAPTER ELEVEN

Lieutenant Colonel Pearly Gates

Pearly had been working relentlessly on the JACKPOT project for almost a month, but still felt he wasn't giving the job the justice it deserved. Part of the problem was the utter secrecy he had to exercise with every scribbled word. Sometimes he used his staff to get answers to questions, but whenever· he added specifics to the plan, he had to do it himself.

During his visits to Saigon, Colonel Wes Snider tried to help, but he was just too new to the combat operation to provide many of the required inputs. Snider was a tall, handsome man, who looked and acted professionally in everything he did. He had a ready smile and listened to people, and even the hard-core fighter jocks in the headquarters were getting to like him. As the Pentagon's B-52 Liaison officer, he worked with the SAC ADVON people there at Seventh Air Force and the bomber units at Anderson AFB in Guam, and U Tapao Air Base, south of Bangkok.

Snider was good with every phase of bomber utilization, from enroute tactics to bombing techniques to escape maneuvers, and held the trust of the B-52 community. They might question directives coming from tactical fighter jocks, but Snider was a dues-paid member of the "first team," as B-52 crew members liked to be called. When he was in Saigon, he worked on the plan with Pearly and sat in on the JACKPOT planning sessions with General Moss.

Snider had just returned from Offutt and had brought a copy of SAC's Linebacker Alpha, their Top Secret plan to bombard North Vietnam with B-52's, to Saigon. He'd carried it with the classification unmarked so he'd have no trouble transporting it, and told Pearly he'd sweated bullets every mile of the way, worrying it might somehow be lost and fall into the wrong hands.

They were in Pearly's office, going over the first draft of his OPlan.

Snider glanced through the pages. "This is a damned good start, Pearly—very complete, at least from the tactical end."

"I'm starting to blend in the Linebacker Alpha strategic side. It's slow work."

"How many pages so far?"

"Seventy-nine. When it's done, it'll be five times that big, and that's without addenda. I tend to be too wordy, but I don't dare leave anything out."

"You need a good wordsmith to help, someone who can write a technical paragraph in less than a thousand words." Snider leafed through the plan and set it down.

"We're going to have a big-time problem with that last annex," Pearly said. "Where are we going to get figures to let them know what it'll cost?"

"Forget 'em," Wes Snider suggested.

"Colonel Leska said they have to know what the bombing campaign's going to cost."

"That's the sort of thing you're going to have to leave to General McManus's people. They've got access to figures you don't. You'd just get bogged down. I'll tell them when I'm back there next week."

Since he didn't dare log the draft JACKPOT plan as an official document, Pearly handled the hand-printed pages as "classified notes" and marked the pages "Secret—Working

Papers." That allowed him to keep the folder unaccounted for and in his own safe.

Wes Snider eyed the package. "You got a title for it?"

"Just the JACKPOT OPlan."

"When you get your safe inspected, they're going to think you sure as hell keep a lot of working notes." Their safes were checked monthly.

"I've got all kinds of half-finished projects. Security inspectors look at 'em like they're written in Swahili."

Wes pointed at the document. "I think it's time to send what you've got, so the chief's people can see where you're heading."

"I agree."

"I also believe we should assign it a new nickname. Maybe just a number, but *something.*"

"How about Project X."

"How many Project X's you already got here?"

"About a dozen. Stuff the general wanted that didn't go anywhere."

"Then how about Draft Plan X-13. Sound innocuous enough?"

"Let's run it by General Moss."

"You ready?"

Their appointment was for 1345 hours. As Pearly stuffed the plan into its folder, he called out to his admin sergeant to see if the general was available. Sometimes Moss's other meetings ran long, and checking with his secretary was a good idea. The WAF told them the general would be ten minutes late.

"No harm in getting there early," Pearly told Wes.

Two women now worked in Plans and Programs: the sergeant who ran the admin functions, did the typing, and answered the telephones, and the new OIC of his Documentation section. Second Lieutenant Lucille Dortmeier waited just outside the door as he and Snider walked out. She was short and skinny and couldn't weigh a hundred pounds—a diminutive beanpole with flaming red hair, a profusion of freckles, and only a hint of breast.

"I need to speak with you, sir," she said to Pearly. She appeared upset.

"Go ahead, but I don't have much time."

She looked hesitantly at Wes Snider.

Pearly sighed. "C'mon in." He held the door for her and motioned for Wes to wait outside for him. "I'll just be a minute, Colonel."

"No sweat."

He shut the door. "Relax," he said, for she looked tense. Lucille Dortmeier had just arrived, fresh from admin school at Scott AFB, Illinois. Tan Son Nhut was her first assignment, and she took her commission and her job seriously. Beyond that he knew little about her. Since her arrival he'd been preoccupied with JACKPOT.

She remained at attention. He glanced at his watch.

"It's Master Sergeant Turner, sir," she finally said.

Turner had run the Documentation section and the five NCOs and airmen assigned there before Dortmeier's arrival. Pearly considered him to be good at his job, which was why he'd placed the green lieutenant in that office.

"What about him?" he asked.

"We've got differences in the way we run things. He resists everything I try to do."

"Such as?"

"The Top Secret vault, for instance. He insists that he *personally* inventory every document, every night. I feel the duty should be rotated between everyone working in the vault. I published a schedule, but he told the people there that regardless of what *any* schedule says, it's his responsibility and he'll continue making the checks until you tell him different."

Pearly sighed and glanced at his watch. "Look, Dortmeier. I've got important things to worry about, and I simply don't have time for this."

She opened her mouth to speak, then closed it. "I understand, sir," she finally mumbled.

"Sergeant Turner has eighteen years in the Air Force. Rely on him. Ask him questions. But for Christ's sake don't try to change everything he's got set up during your second week here."

Her face flushed brightly but she remained silent.

He walked to the door. "Come to see me in a few weeks, after you get your feet on the ground. If you still feel the same way, we'll call Turner in and the three of us will hash it over."

"Yes, sir."

He decided to add one of his philosophies. "When you get to a new assignment, Dortmeier, don't try to make changes until you know what's going on. Just keep your ears open and listen for a while."

"Sir, I studied . . ." She stopped herself, brows knit seriously. "Yes, sir," she said quietly.

Pearly left her standing in his office. He didn't notice the welling of moisture in her eyes, for his mind had returned to the upcoming meeting with the general.

They went into Moss's office together, an incongruous pair, Pearly thought sadly. Snider was perfectly groomed and, despite the heat, looked like a recruiting poster. Pearly knew he wasn't an attractive man with his wire beard, bulbous nose, and kinky hair that was impossible to comb into place. The hair was okay, because he wore it cropped short. He avoided heavy beard shadow by keeping a second razor at work and taking time to shave before lunch and dinner. Pearly dieted constantly, but regardless of how he starved, he remained a few pounds overweight. Now, although he'd carefully tucked it in before leaving his office, his shirt threatened to come out of one side of his pants. He sometimes wore elastic garters that connected the sides of his shirt to his socks, but they were uncomfortable and easy to forget when he dressed in the morning.

Wes Snider looked at ease as they waited for the general to finish his telephone conversation. Pearly felt self-conscious and carefully stuffed his shirt into his trousers.

Moss continued talking on the telephone as he waved them forward into chairs.

"I don't care if God himself gave you a direct order. I want 'em painted."

Pearly knew what the conversation was about. A few weeks earlier Moss had visited the Navy base at Subic Bay in the Philippines, and noticed something he liked about the place. Upon his return to Tan Son Nhut, he'd immediately called the base civil engineer and given him a task. During General Roman's visit two days earlier, one of his colonels questioned why the trees on base were whitewashed to a height of precisely five feet and surrounded by a neat circle of white stones. The base commander had taken the question as criticism, and this morning Pearly had noticed Vietnamese workers all over Tan Son Nhut, busily scrubbing paint off the trees.

General Moss obviously liked them white, and he was upset that the base commander had taken it upon himself to change things. "Right now," Moss was saying. "Today! No, I don't care about your goddam priorities. When I leave this headquarters at six o'clock, I want my trees looking proper, and I mean every *one* of 'em." He hung up, brooded for a moment about the conversation, then regarded Pearly. He still hadn't accepted Wes Snider into his circle of trusted staff officers, so he tended to ignore him.

Pearly placed the draft OPlan on his desk. "The JACKPOT draft OPlan, sir."

Wes Snider spoke up. "I feel we should rename the plan, sir, in case one of us has a slip of the tongue."

"Like what?" Moss growled, still grumpy about the trees.

"We came up with Project X-13."

Moss snorted. "I don't like it. Sounds like some kind of test airplane." He accepted few of Snider's suggestions.

"Yes, sir," Wes said.

The general thumbed through the pages, stopping periodically to scan.

"I also think we should send what we've got to General McManus, so he and his people can see what Colonel Gates is coming up with."

Moss didn't look up. "What do *you* think, Pearly?"

"I like the idea. And maybe they could send us anything they've got. Sort of level the playing field so we'll both be going the same direction."

Moss nodded abstractly as he read. "I'll let Gentleman Jim know this is coming and ask for whatever they've got." He frowned. "You show two more fighter wings and two more bomber wings from the States."

"As well as another carrier group."

"Not taking any chances, are we?"

"That's my initial estimate of what it'll take to accomplish the job in two to three weeks, bombing around the clock."

Moss read, "Initial attrition losses at four percent, dropping to one percent by the end of the sixth day."

"Unless they really conserve them, the enemy will start running out of missiles and artillery ammo on the fourth day.

If we prevent their resupply, we'll have little opposition by day eight."

Moss peered harder. "*These* figures seem high. Eighteen B-52's lost?"

"Yes, sir. I upgraded it from the SAC estimates."

"It's a more realistic number," Wes Snider agreed.

Moss grunted. "General Roman's going to shit when he sees that." Thus far Roman was not included in the planning, but at some date he would have to be.

"He'll realize it will take those kinds of losses if we go all out, sir," Pearly said. He'd briefed Roman on previous occasions about other plans.

Moss slowly replaced the top cover. "Run a copy. Then seal it and send it out in a classified embassy pouch. General McManus's eyes only."

Snider smiled. "I'll be traveling next week, sir. I can act as courier."

Pearly stood to retrieve the draft OPlan.

Moss regarded Wes Snider, who was also on his feet. "I'd feel better if we used the embassy run."

"Yes, sir."

"We've got a hell of a task. It's important to us." "Us" meaning the real people, the fighter pilots ... and Pearly Gates, whom he'd never accepted was *really* a navigator with 20/100 vision. He grouped him with his mafia fighter jocks. Snider was the outsider.

"Yes, sir," said Snider. "I believe it's important to America. We should have done something like this three years ago."

Moss stared, still measuring Snider. "Put your brain to work and think up a nickname for Pearly's OPlan. Since Gentleman Jim's trying to massage the President's ego, perhaps you can come up with something that'll make him know it's his baby."

It was Moss's way, to seize on ideas of subordinates and give them just enough twist to make them appear his own. Wes Snider knew the game. "I'll put thought to it right away," he said.

"Now if you don't mind, I'd like to talk to Pearly for a few minutes."

Snider quietly left the general with his more trusted advisor.

When the door closed, Moss reached into a lower desk drawer and pulled out a packet, then tossed it onto his desk. "Take a look at those."

Pearly pulled out three developed 70mm film strips, each numbered with felt-tip marker. He started with number one, peered hard, and nodded. He looked at the second, then the third with mounting excitement.

"Hanoi?"

"The southern suburbs."

"When were they taken, sir?"

"About a week and a half ago. On the sixth. I got 'em the next day."

"Looks like strike camera film."

Moss didn't respond. It was apparent that he didn't wish to discuss the film's origin.

Pearly examined them again. "It's the largest buildup we've seen to date. They're taking a big chance, piling so much into a single area."

"I'd like to bomb the hell out of 'em. That's why I wanted to talk to you."

"It would be impossible to get authorization, General. It's all residential area there."

"I thought Ho Chi Minh ordered the evacuation of civilians from Hanoi."

"More than a year ago. But that was for the northern *quartier* of Hanoi, not the suburbs."

Moss peered sadly at one of the photos. "So it's densely populated?"

Pearly didn't have to look again. He knew the area, even some of the street names. "Those were taken about five nautical miles south of the center of Hanoi," he said.

He walked to a large wall map of Vietnam and touched Hanoi, located in a large curl of the Red River. "The city's divided into three parts," he said. "Here in the core of Hanoi, the French called it the *quartier du nord,* you find the old villas, a couple of hotels for foreign visitors, the embassies, the Citadel or People's Army headquarters, an underground auxiliary headquarters they're still building, Ba Dinh Square, and most of the government administration buildings."

Moss stared at all the wonderful, however restricted, targets.

"Hanoi's sort of like downtown Saigon, with wide streets and old French buildings. To the north, around Ho Tay Lake and up along the river here, there's housing and slums. Right here, in fact, is where they're building the underground facility. We think they're going to move some of the headquarters facilities there, and MAC-V intell's asking the Joint Targeting Office at the Pentagon for permission to add it to our target list."

"Think they'll go for it?"

"It's a possibility. While they've never let us go after the targets in the city proper, they've turned us loose on overpasses, the Doumer bridge, and a power plant—all in that area around the northern suburbs."

"Go on."

"But here . . . *south* of the city core, there's huts built of thatch, like rice farmers live in, and narrow streets and alleyways. That's what we're looking at in the photo strips. There's more than two hundred thousand people living there."

Moss looked on grimly. "I'd *still* like to take out the supplies. It's like they're thumbing their noses at us. They're the ones putting their people in jeopardy."

"They know we're not *really* at war, sir."

A thoughtful moment passed. While their enemy was fighting all out, they most definitely were not. Finally Moss nodded toward the photo strips. "I mentioned to General Westmoreland that we had *reports* of massive supplies on their way south, including tanks. The supplies didn't surprise him, because they expected a buildup during the dry months. The mention of tanks got him excited, but not like you might expect. He said it's about damned time they brought in armor. MAC-V intell predicts a big spring offensive, probably somewhere in the delta or an all-out attack at our highlands bases. But the presence of tanks tells them the NVA just *might* be preparing to come out in the open and fight."

"I hope MAC-V knows what they're doing."

Moss snorted. "General Westy may be political and a showman, and he *sure* as hell doesn't understand air operations, but he knows as much about fighting a ground war as any man alive."

Pearly was surprised. Moss said few nice things about

Westmoreland. He often complained because Westy, like the SecDef, seemed enamored with big numbers and good press.

"His XO explained their attitude. The NVA and the Cong talk big and have a reputation for being tough, but they won't come out and fight to prove it. Once it becomes an open battle, he says our troops will kick the diddley out of 'em. He says Westy doesn't like the fact that he's continually asking for more troops ... I think probably because it's hurting him politically and he's got ideas of being another general-president like Ike. His XO said if the NVA come out to fight, it won't take half the people it will if they just keep sneaking around playing terrorist games. The Army'd love nothing more than an old-fashioned tank battle up in the highlands, and they're aching to prove the air-cavalry concept in a maneuvering fight."

"I hope they're right."

"That's *their* job, and they know what they're doing. One of *our* jobs is to interdict supplies, like we see in these photos. Problem is, like always, getting permission to *do* our job."

Pearly was back at Moss's desk, handling the photos. "Have you advised PACAF about the buildup?"

"Roman would want evidence, and if I sent him the photos, he'd start a witch-hunt to find out who took an armed aircraft into a restricted area. I called for recce flights up there, but one of the birds was shot down, and all the other one got was pictures of nets. The pilot who took these had to get right down in the dirt so the camera could see under the camouflage."

Pearly nodded.

"So what do we do about it all?"

Pearly stared at the lines of heavily laden vehicles, wishing he had an answer.

Five minutes later Lieutenant Colonel Pearly Gates returned to his office, his mind aswirl with thoughts of the massive buildup, of all the vehicles, including tanks, poised to come southward. He hoped to hell the Army could handle it. He knew the Air Force wouldn't get permission to bomb Hanoi.

He nodded and mumbled a greeting to Lieutenant Lucille Dortmeier and didn't notice the pained expression and anger in her eyes. He had bigger things to worry about.

1630L—VPA Headquarters, Hanoi, DRV

Colonel Xuan Nha

Mee pilots had been attacking bridges, airfields, and a variety of targets near both Hanoi and Haiphong, and Xuan Nha's VPAND had been preoccupied with trying to shoot down as many as possible with the few defenses they'd not moved south of Hanoi. It was increasingly difficult. They'd begun to shuffle defenses according to Xuan's intuitions, for more and more the targets were surprising ones that People's Army intelligence had not forecast.

At the urging of General Dung, Xuan had moved four SAM battalions, each equipped with three firing batteries complete with radars and missiles, south of Hanoi to protect the critical supplies gathered in the southern suburbs. At night long convoys would depart southward, but new ones gathered in their places, and there were many more to go. General Dung had ordered the mobilization of every available vehicle, motorized and otherwise, in the Democratic Republic that wasn't essential to the military. The idle defenses south of the city were frustrating for Xuan Nha, for the Mee bombing attacks were centered around north Hanoi, Haiphong, and the interconnecting bridges, and none were made on the well-hidden convoys.

Anyway, Li Binh had told him, the American politicians had made no indications that they might change their no-bombing-of-Hanoi policy.

After a long day of work that had begun well before sunrise, Xuan Nha trudged wearily down the hall and into a small conference room. He'd called for the staff meeting to discuss a matter that had pressed on his mind since he'd given up the 20,000 militiamen. The generals were again complaining about manpower shortages, and if nothing changed, he knew he'd be ordered to transfer even more.

It was no longer a problem he might have when General Luc recovered and questioned what had happened to his militia during his absence. Luc was slipping ever closer to death in his battle with stomach cancer. Now it was a different issue altogether, for when he replaced Luc as general of the VPAND, he didn't wish to inherit a weakened command. The militia was a key element of the Army of National Defense, and he wanted it to remain intact. He'd searched for a way to prove they were critical assets and keep them under his control. He thought he'd found it.

A major from the People's Army Air Force was in attendance, as were sixteen ranking staff officers and commanders of VPAND. Xuan nodded for Lieutenant Quang Hanh to close the door.

He opened with a description of an air-navigation station atop a mountain near the tiny Laotian community of Ban Sao Si, only a dozen kilometers from the border of the Democratic Republic. Mee pilots used it to position their aircraft before they entered the combat zone.

Since the station was viewed as only a pesky thing, the People's Army had mostly left it alone, focusing their energies on larger aspects of the war. Crusty old Colonel Trung, more than fifty years of age and a veteran of all the people's struggles in the current century, and who commanded VPAND antiaircraft and antishipping coastal artillery, had long disagreed and called for its elimination.

Trung was a warrior of older schools, who understood little about radars and missiles, who mistrusted airplanes and refused to ride in the things. But he'd hated the French and now despised the Americans, and knew that in war one did everything possible to make the enemy's life miserable. The existence of the Mee navigation site so close to their border became an issue for him, and he'd grumble about it to all who would listen. While unsophisticated, Trung knew the capabilities of artillery, and he favored bombarding the site into rubble. When told it was unreasonable to haul big guns over the tall mountains for such a small purpose, he'd argue to at least send a few capable troops with light howitzers.

Trung had been ignored during most of his arguments, but periodically someone would acquiesce and request that a force of Pathet Lao troops be diverted to overrun the mountaintop navigation station, which was protected only by a few dozen mountain tribesmen. The Pathet Lao expeditions had been meagerly manned and poorly equipped, for the Laotian communists had priorities of their own. Mee fighter aircraft had strafed, bombed, demoralized, and sometimes annihilated them, and the remnants of each group had eventually been recalled.

Now seemed a poor time to broach the subject, for the Pathet Lao were maneuvering forces throughout their country. Within the month they were to launch a massive series of attacks on Prince Souvanna Phouma's government troops in eastern Laos. They were entering a win-or-die situation, the most important drive of their struggle, and had little time for such diversions as a small navigation site on a mountaintop, which would be difficult to reach and impossible to hold.

Xuan Nha felt it was time for a new effort, using other resources.

He asked Colonel Trung to outline his rationale for wanting the navigation station eliminated, a topic the audience had heard from him many times. But they listened as Trung elaborated, for Xuan Nha nodded as if his words held sage wisdom.

When Trung finished, Xuan asked the major from the VPAAF to speak. The fighter pilot added fuel to Trung's argument by saying it had become more critical to the Mee pilots to have a final orientation before entering the combat arena, for they flew at higher altitudes than before and could not as easily see ground markings. It would be helpful to the VPAAF MiG pilots if the ground station was eliminated.

The pilot cast a quiet look at Xuan Nha, who gave him a subtle nod. Xuan voiced his thanks and the major departed. General Tho had agreed to provide a similar speech to the general staff, to gain their support for a modest expedition.

Xuan Nha spoke, outlining his plan.

The Commandant of Militia argued that his forces were stripped to the bone, that he already lacked sufficient manpower to patrol the coasts and borders of the Republic properly. If his finest militia troops were jeopardized by sending them to Laos—

Xuan interrupted. "Our *duty* is to protect the borders of the Republic—to keep them free of foreign threats. We know that a Mee site exists a few kilometers from our border, which the People's Air Force has just told us provides valuable support for their pilots. Do you doubt him?"

"Of course not, comrade Colonel, but the navigation station has been there a long—"

Again Xuan interrupted in his low, dangerous tone. "It is our *duty*."

The colonel judiciously grew silent.

Xuan Nha spoke again. Tomorrow he'd gain approval from the senior staff. He planned to show that the People's Militia was required and essential and must not be further dismantled.

The Commandant of Militia had one last question, a very good one. "Why will we be successful, when other forces have failed?"

Xuan Nha was ready. The generals would ask the same thing. He grew a small smile. "How did the Mee destroy the Pathet Lao expeditions?"

The commandant was hesitant. "By strafing and bombing them?"

Xuan nodded. "The Mee pilots flew very low and were able to see the Pathet Lao in the jungle surrounding the mountain. They *had* to fly down there so they could find the elusive targets. There were also friendly native villages throughout the area, which they had to avoid bombing. Then, *after* they located the hidden Pathet Lao, they dropped their munitions."

The commandant agreed.

"Another question. Why do they not fly low and slow over targets here in the Republic?"

"Because we would shoot them down with our artillery. But we will have very little artillery at the navigation station."

"Perhaps only a few small guns," Xuan Nha agreed.

"Then how," the colonel asked again, "will it be different this time?"

Xuan raised the eyebrow of his good eye and offered an indulgent smile. "I have received a shipment of new weapons that will stop the Mee pilots. Your militia will take them to Ban Sao Si, and when the Mee aircraft come to find us, your men will test the new weapons. If they work there, as I know they will, they will also work for our soldiers fighting in the South."

The militia commandant looked puzzled. "I thought we were to take no medium artillery?"

"The terrain will be difficult, so we will take only a few small, mobile guns, but that is not what I speak of. The new weapon is called 'Strela,' a Russian word meaning arrow."

He described Strela in detail. Finally he concluded. "The Mee navigation station at Ban Sao Si will offer a test to show how well they work. And our militia will be victorious."

1720L—Hanoi

Assistant Commissioner Nguyen Wu

Wu was remorseful as he slunk from Li Binh's villa and hurried toward the street.

Two hours earlier he'd been visited in his office by a discreet courier and handed a plain envelope. Inside, a note told him to appear immediately at the rear door to the villa so Li Binh could pass on information of importance. He'd canceled his final meeting of the day and hurried as never before, heart pounding wildly, praying to the fates that it would be . . . exactly what it had turned out to be. But he'd not considered the awful thing that had happened.

When he'd rapped cautiously at the villa door, he'd been immediately admitted by a very young, wide-eyed maid who ushered him to the north wing, then fled as if chased by demons.

He'd stood awkwardly at the door to Li Binh's bedroom, a place he'd once known well. After a moment she'd called him into the dimly lit room where she waited, a neutral look on her face. He was told simply to prepare himself, and it took a moment, seeing her languidly disrobing, before he'd understood. Nguyen Wu, feared instrument for the Commissioner of Death, had sunk to his knees and blubbered his happiness.

Li Binh had snapped at him and told him to hurry. She had a busy schedule. Yet he'd noticed the hungry look, one he'd recognized when things had been warmer between them.

He tried to please her as he'd done before, but it was an impossible task. There was no charade to act out, no way to fool her into believing he was overcome by her femininity, for she now knew of his preference for men. He'd spoken the same love words, and she'd allowed him to stroke her skinny and angular body, had even touched and fondled him in return . . . did she tremble? . . . but it was all for naught. After half an hour's efforts she'd sighed and told him to leave. She seemed unhappy, resigned, as if she'd proved something distasteful to herself.

His moment of opportunity was past. "It's been so long," he'd stammered in excuse, but by then she was half-dressed and intent on other thoughts. She'd related, almost offhandedly, that a high official was indicating a desire that Quon's reeducation be declared complete.

He'd hardly heard her words. When she repeated them, he'd sputtered that the release of important men such as Quon could come only from the Minister of Internal Affairs.

Li Binh said the official she spoke of was higher than Wu might imagine, that he could have the Minister of Internal Affairs crushed with a word. She'd advised him to handle the matter quickly, then motioned at the door and told him to leave as discreetly as he'd arrived.

As Nguyen Wu hurried past the iron gates into the quiet street and walked in the direction of his waiting utility vehicle, he was tormented. Was there now even a slight chance of redemption from his aunt? Her anger had been terrible when she'd learned about his sexual preferences. Now she'd given him another chance, and he'd failed miserably.

He cursed his body for being unable to respond. It was more than her being a woman. She was as imperious, as dangerous, and as sure of herself as any man. That fact had made it possible for him before. This time sheer fear of failure had turned his penis into a shriveled impossibility.

Next time I'll prepare better. I must make her squeal with pleasure.

He felt better until he had another thought. *Would there be a next time?* There must be! He would do anything, prove himself in any way, to return to the good graces of his beloved aunt.

Then he recalled the discussion about Quon, the once-famous fighter pilot. His aunt never spoke frivolously. The powerful person she'd spoke of was likely Le Duc Tho, whom he'd learned had arrived from the South. A tremor of apprehension coursed through him.

Nguyen Wu knew he must relay the message to the Commissioner of People's Safety.

Then he worried anew, for he'd visited horrors upon the ex–fighter pilot which far exceeded normal reeducation. Quon was still incarcerated in a miserable cell at the rear of the Commissioner's building, was still beaten thoroughly and often, was made to confess new sins daily. If he was to be released and reinstated too quickly, Quon would surely poison Wu's name with his powerful relative.

Only a few months before, Quon had arrogantly used his connections to have Nguyen Wu ignominiously removed from his position as Commandant of Rockets and Artillery and sent out on a fool's mission. But the man was arrogant no longer. He now answered his interrogator's questions humbly, and confessed readily. He divulged that his mother had been a common street whore, and that his dead son had been a traitor—admitted to every despicable act that rose in Wu's imagination. It had taken a long while, but Nguyen Wu was very good at his work, although he never soiled his own hands, of course. The ingredients to his formula were simple ones—degradation, starvation, and intense pain—and they'd all been used on Quon.

Now Nguyen Wu began to form a new plan, for he must reverse things. First he would convince Quon that he had studied the confessions and concluded that none of the things could possibly be true—that he'd have the interrogators chastised and removed from their posts. He had certainly meant him no harm and had only done his duty. He would examine his living conditions and demand more food and comfort for his *friend* Quon. Next he would plant the seed that *he* wished to become his savior, that *he* would try to engineer his freedom. It would take a little time, but it would surely work. Men in hopeless situations grasped at such threads.

Only then, when Quon realized that he was not to blame for his plight, would it be safe for Wu to advise his superiors that he should be released.

Life is so full of twists! Wu lamented, for he despised the famous fighter pilot and thoroughly enjoyed his torment.

CHAPTER TWELVE

Friday, November 17th, 0800 Local—Pacific Air Forces Headquarters, Hickam AFB, Hawaii

Colonel Tom Lyons

The headquarters was a collection of ugly, age-yellowed concrete buildings. Some fool had decided that the lessons of the disastrous air attack on December 7th, 1941 must not be forgotten, so the ugly marks of Japanese bullets had been left in the aging walls. *Stupid kids' games,* thought Tom Lyons as he strode through the entrance. What kind of idiot would want to be reminded of failure? He stopped at the security desk and gruffly asked for directions to CINCPACAF's office. General Roman's suite was on the top floor, he was told.

Tom said he was expected, and after the guard made a confirming telephone call, was told to go up. He chewed the sergeant's ass for taking too much of his valuable time before starting up the staircase, where he noted even more of the ancient bullet holes. *Ridiculous.*

Roman's secretary was thirtyish and not at all bad looking. She asked him to wait, explaining that the general had visitors from Washington.

"How long?" he snapped irritably. His wife had complained the previous evening about the fact that their household shipment hadn't yet arrived, and about the house not being nearly large enough for her things anyway. She wasn't accustomed to camping out, she'd sniffed. To an heiress who could write a personal check for a couple of the lesser Hawaiian islands, it might indeed be camping out. They'd find another house, he'd said, trying to soothe her.

They couldn't, Margaret Lingenfelter Lyons had wailed, because her daddy would be let down, and they simply *couldn't* do *that* to him. They'd have to make do. She just hoped it wouldn't be for *too* long.

It was one of her parents' several vacation homes, a 6,000-square-foot multilevel "cottage" built into the heights overlooking Diamond Head with a full-size kidney-shaped pool on the west lanai. Her father had lent it to them for the duration of Tom's assignment.

Margaret had been difficult since he'd shown up in New York two weeks earlier to break the news about the assignment. "High-strung," her father called it. She'd acted as if he were taking her to Borneo to live among savages. They'd partied every night for a week so she could say good-bye to her various acquaintances, and each function ended with her crying on yet another friend's shoulder about the cruelties of life and the stupidity of the Air Force. During one party her mother had taken her aside and told her first that she was exaggerating and finally that she was being downright tawdry. Margaret had shouted she *hated* her and hurried off sobbing to lock herself in her bedroom. Tom had tried to talk her out, but it had taken her father to cajole her into returning to her guests.

She'd gone along when he visited his parents in Cherry Hills, an upscale suburb of Denver. After their arrival she'd cried again, that time about his thoughtlessness in taking her to such a cold, windblown place, where she had trouble breathing the rarefied air of the mile-high city. She'd huddled in the big house, sipping warmed port and pouting while he'd visited with his parents. Margaret was impossible. If the two fathers didn't believe that the marriage was such an appropriate merger, Tom Lyons would have ended it long before. But both men had very pointedly expressed that view on several occasions, and it would be an exercise in poor judgment to go against either's wishes.

During the visit he'd summoned his courage and told his father about the poor efficiency rating he'd received at Takhli, and how he thought his records had been flagged at Military Personnel Center because a dolt three-star general named Moss had it in for him. His father hadn't reproached him. He'd simply made a telephone call in Tom's presence. It was not the first call he'd made in his son's behalf, for similar matters in the past had required similar intercession. When his father stepped back and said a matter was resolved, Tom knew it was so. This call had been to General Roman in Hawaii.

Thank God for his father, who'd spoken with Roman as if his four stars meant nothing. After he'd hung up, he told Tom his career would be salvaged. He'd added his advice. The keys to Joe Roman were the same as with most generals: ego and ambition. Roman wanted to become the next Air Force Chief of Staff. He'd sell his mother for the chance. Go to Honolulu, he'd told him, massage Roman's ego, and help him make chief of staff.

After Colorado, Tom was off to Hawaii with Margaret, to whom flying in first or any class meant hardship. She'd started complaining before they took off from Stapleton Field and had not yet stopped, although two days had now passed since they'd deplaned in Honolulu. Margaret made his life miserable. It had even been better, Tom told himself, when he'd been at Takhli flying combat. He'd conveniently forgotten about ordering his staff *never* to schedule him on tough missions and had told his parents, his children, and even Margaret, about his unflinching heroism in the face of the SAMs and MiGs he'd been briefed about but had never seen firsthand during his nine combat sorties in route pack one.

While his family cared little about such things, it made Tom feel better about himself, and he'd begun to elaborate, then *almost* to believe his own stories. He told them how he'd been the first pilot to hit the big bridge on the north side of Hanoi with his bombs. He said he doubted he'd be put in for a medal for it, because the wing commander had been jealous and had it in for him.

Now he sat waiting for General Roman, Commander in

Chief of Pacific Air Forces, covertly staring at the secretary's legs and wondering what it might take to fuck her, trying hard to forget about his wife back at the penthouse hotel suite.

The general's inner-office door opened and two men emerged, chuckling over some joke. Tom recognized the senior U.S. senator from South Carolina.

"You can go in now," the secretary said in her pleasant voice.

Tom rose and smoothed himself, glancing at her crossed legs. He saw her wedding band but didn't care. He was horny. Except for a single case of letting him crawl on just long enough to get his rocks off while she sniffed and complained, Margaret had had a constant backache or other excuse since he'd gone to New York for her.

A short, beefy man came to the office doorway and peered out. "Come in, Colonel." General Roman spoke in an unpleasant, growling tone. Lyons hesitantly followed him inside. He started to salute, but Roman made a curt head motion that told him it was unnecessary, and waved him toward a chair. "How's Ambassador Lyons these days?"

"Very well, General. I spent a few days with him on my way out."

"He telephoned last week. I told him we were looking forward to your arrival."

"He called? I didn't know."

Roman made a grimace, the kind of expression a baby made when it was gaseous. It was a moment before Tom realized it was his smile.

"We old workhorses stick together," Roman confided. "I first met the ambassador just after the big war, when I worked for Curt LeMay and we were trying to set up SAC. We needed government clout to give the bomber force proper emphasis, and your father was a great help. That's why I don't hesitate to take his calls."

"He speaks highly of you, sir." A lie. On the few occasions he'd spoken of them, his father had called Curtis LeMay a grandstanding idiot and Joe Roman a gross, ill-mannered, and incompetent fool. But, then, he thought poorly of all career military people.

"Well, I feel honored." Roman pushed a button, and his

growl deepened into a sort of snarl. "Bring us some coffee
in here."

"Yes, sir. Right away."

"Woman's dumb as a fucking wall," Roman said almost
pleasantly, leaning back in his chair to survey Lyons closer.
"Know what an automatic secretary is?"

She hurried in with a carafe of coffee and two mugs.

"No, sir," Lyons said, although he'd heard the joke a hundred times.

She poured into a blue cup with four large silver stars
about its circumference and set it at the general's elbow.

"Something you screw on your desk and it does your office work for you." Roman made his grimace-smile.

Lyons laughed, then glanced at the secretary.

"Would you care for cream or sugar, Colonel?" she asked
evenly, obviously accustomed to such talk.

"Both," Tom Lyons said, unable to resist a smirk. The
general knew how to keep a secretary in her appropriate
place. She poured, mixed with a small silver spoon, and
quickly departed. Roman watched her, then shook his head
and chuckled again at his joke.

Lyons broke the silence. "What position did you have in
mind for me, sir?"

"We'll get to that. First I wanted you to know that I
looked into a matter your father spoke about. That efficiency
rating Parker signed for you?"

"Oh?"

"It was shitty. I had it thrown out."

Lyons paused appropriately. "Thank you, sir."

"Also, there was a flag on your records at Randolph saying you were nonpromotable."

"I wonder who could have done that, sir. I've given every
assignment my best."

"Perhaps someone jealous of your family's money. It happens."

"It had to be something like that. I . . . I appreciate what
you've done, General."

"Or maybe it was because they thought you were caught
lying about the matter concerning Captain Manuel G.
DeVera."

Tom Lyons's heart plummeted. He'd expected the matter
to be forgotten after his father's telephone call.

General Roman was peering at his face with a cold expression. Tom Lyons swallowed, but couldn't move his eyes away. It was as if they'd been captured by the force of the man before him.

"I do not condone lying, Colonel. If you lie to me just once, I will not worry about giving you a bad efficiency rating or having a red flag put on your records. I will have you fucking court-martialed and summarily kicked out of the service. It will be as humiliating as I can make it, and be done so quickly your eyes will smart."

Oh God, Tom cried inwardly.

"Now, tell me. Did you lie to Parker about DeVera?"

Tom didn't want to answer. He wanted the matter to go away. "No, sir," he finally said in a low voice. "I . . ."

Roman nodded curtly, his eyes fixed.

Tom had stopped midsentence. Then other words gushed forth, as if of their own accord. "I will never lie to you sir. I am *not* a liar."

Roman leaned back in the big chair and gave his grimace. "I had the flag removed from your records. It's inconceivable to me that a son of Ambassador Lyons would lie to his fellow officers."

Tom forced a weak smile.

Roman pursed his lips thoughtfully. "One hand washes the other, Lyons," he said quietly. "Tell your father how I helped."

"Yes, sir. He'll remember this, sir."

Roman gave another brief grimace. "I don't mind doing someone a favor . . . if they're in the right and they're smart enough to return it."

Tom was nodding energetically. "My father was saying before I left how he felt you should be the next Chief of Staff."

"He said that?" Roman purred.

"Yes, sir."

"Well, I'll be damned." Roman's eyes still hadn't left his face. "I think it would be an honor if I were to be appointed as Cee SAF. And if I was, I'd have to bring along my most trusted people, wouldn't I?"

"Why, yes, sir."

"But, then, there're others who should be left behind."

"Sir?"

Roman spoke carefully, pausing every few words for effect. "Those who might get it in their head to lie to me or
make me look foolish. Like you told me you'd never do. I
appreciate that, Lyons. I demand loyalty from my staff, and
if one screwed up ... say he tried to fool me like they
thought you did at Takhli ... his ass would be gravy. I
wouldn't care if his daddy was a powerful politician with a
hot line to the President, I'd put him right down in the dirt
and leave him squirming."

Tom Lyons again felt like a child being chastised. It was
as if Roman would lull him, then push him back to the very
brink of a hot fire ...

Roman's voice softened. "So that's why I appreciate your
saying you wouldn't do any of those things."

... and then pull him out again. "You can trust me, sir,"
Tom said staunchly.

"Now let's talk about your position here at the headquarters. You'll be traveling—away from home a lot. That okay?"

"I don't mind, sir." Tom thought of his wife in the hotel
suite, and how periodically getting away from her would be
a blessing.

"Your *official* title will be vice commander of the inspector general team. Your *unofficial* duty will be to find out
what the fucking cowboys are trying to get away with in
South Vietnam and Thailand."

Lyons remembered how the fighter pilots at Takhli disliked "Bomber Joe" Roman and the way he called them
"fucking cowboys."

"You'll have priority travel orders, meaning you can go
anywhere, anytime, and bump almost anyone off a flight.
When you're out there, you'll be my eyes and ears in the
combat zone. I'll expect a phone call every day or two, between seven and eight hundred hours, Hawaii time."

"Yes, sir."

"I get reports from the unit commanders, Lyons. Statis-
tics and all. And I receive their bullshit excuses as to why
they don't want to comply with directives. I want the
straight word, from someone I can trust."

"You can rely on me, sir."

They spoke in more detail about what Roman expected
from him. After twenty minutes, during which time Roman's

eyes scarcely left Tom's face, he glanced at his watch, a time-honored signal that a general wished to terminate a meeting.

"How does the job sound to you, Lyons?" Roman asked.

"I feel honored that you place your trust in me, sir. It's only right that you know what's happening in the field, and it's a disgrace if the commanders aren't being straight with you."

"Do you have contacts out there you can work with, who'll tell you what's happening?"

He thought of the wing commander at Danang and Yank Donovan at Takhli. "A few," he said, thinking of pressures he would bring to bear on the two men. "I'll have to develop more."

Roman seemed pleased at his responses and changed subjects. "How did your family fare on the trip over?"

"We left the children at private boarding schools in New Hampshire until spring term's over. Only my wife accompanied me. She's at the hotel . . . resting."

"Senator Lingenfelter's daughter."

"Yes, sir." Twenty years before, Margaret's father had been appointed to fill a vacancy following the death of a New York senator. He'd served only two years and hadn't run for reelection, but he retained the title. Now primarily concerned with overseeing his extensive business interests, Wayland Lingenfelter also conducted fact-finding trips, met with foreign dignitaries, and chaired investigative panels for his old senate cohort, Lyndon Baines Johnson.

"I'd like you and your wife to be our guests at dinner tonight. That way you can meet some of my other staff." It was not a request.

Lyons didn't hesitate. "We'd be delighted, sir."

"Nineteen hundred hours at my quarters."

When Tom Lyons left Roman's office, he tried to think of a way to sweet-talk Margaret into attending. If she was stubborn about it, he'd go alone and make appropriate excuses. It wouldn't be the first time. She thought military people, especially generals, were boring.

He felt so good about the outcome of the meeting with General Roman that he stopped on his way out and said a few words to the secretary, letting her know he *might* be interested in taking her to lunch after he got settled.

He walked from the office and stepped down the hall

feeling better than he had in a long time. The job was better than he'd expected, with enough clout to make people take heed, and to ... he almost laughed aloud. Captain Spick DeVera wouldn't get out of it so clean the next time they tangled. He'd teach the lowborn idiot. And General Richard J. Moss might not be quite so quick to try to deep-six his career. This time they'd be dealing with the vice commander of the inspector general's office, Pacific Air Forces. He imagined Moss glad-handing and trying to get on his good side, and DeVera sniveling as he was summarily booted out of the Air Force. Those were only two, and there were so many others. He trotted down the stairs wearing a smile that kept growing. As his father had taught him at an early age, privileges are due the privileged.

Saturday, November 18th, 0730 Local—HQ Seventh Air Force, Tan Son Nhut AB, Saigon, South Vietnam

Lieutenant Colonel Pearly Gates

The third JACKPOT message from General McManus's office at the Pentagon was in.

```
SECRET—IMMEDIATE—JACKPOT
7 AF CC EYES ONLY—NO FURTHER DISSEM
DTG: 17/1900ZNOV67
TO: HQ 7 AF/CC, TAN SON NHUT AB, SVN
FM: CSAF/CC, HQ USAF, PENTAGON
SUBJECT: STATUS REPORT
1. (S) MET WITH J FOR 2ND TIME ON
16 NOV. HE IS LOOKING FOR ANSWERS
AND I BELIEVE IS "SOMEWHAT" RECEPTIVE,
HOWEVER CAUTIOUS. WHEN I MENTIONED
THE JACKPOT TIMETABLE OF "A TOTAL
OF THREE WEEKS" HE SEEMED
CONFUSED DUE TO CONFLICTING BRIEFINGS
BY SECDEF. THAT WAS BEFORE RECEIPT OF
YR DRAFT OPLAN. NEXT MEETING IS
SCHEDULED FOR ONE WEEK FM THIS
DATE AND I WILL USE SPECIFICS CONTAINED
IN THE PLAN.
```

2. (S) REVIEWED DRAFT OPLAN. THIS HQ
WILL USE IT AS MODEL FOR PROJECT, &
FORWARD INPUTS/CHANGES AS
NECESSARY. YR COMBAT ATTRITION FIGURES
APPEAR REALISTIC, BUT MAY POSE PROBLEM
IN SELLING. WILL ALSO NEED MORE
RATIONALE FOR SPECIFIC TGTS AND
ANTICIPATED COLLATERAL DAMAGE.
3. (S) RE. YR QUESTION. UNDERSTAND PILOT
RESTRICTIONS ADVERSELY IMPACT
COMBAT EFFECTIVENESS, BUT HAVE
THUS FAR MADE LITTLE PROGRESS IN
EFFORTS TO LIFT THEM. IF APPROPRIATE
I WILL MENTION TO J DURING NEXT
DISCUSSION, BUT SINCE MOST COME FM
J FOR POLITICAL PURPOSES AND I CANNOT
AFFORD TO DAMAGE RELATIONSHIP, IT MAY
NOT HAPPEN. J IS (A) CONVINCED HE'S
DOING "RIGHT THING" BY PROTECTING
CIVILIANS AND FOREIGN NATIONALS, (B)
IS IN CONSTANT PROPAGANDA BATTLE WITH
ANTIWAR GROUPS, AND (C) ENJOYS
CONTROL OVER "HIS" PILOTS.
4. (S) FYI, GEN ROMAN IS CURRENTLY
PROVIDING INPUTS DIRECTLY TO SECDEF
RE. YET ANOTHER BRIEFING TO J TO
SUGGEST TERMINATION OF BOMBING
NORTH OF 20TH PARALLEL. I DO NOT EXPECT
THAT EFFORT TO SUCCEED, BUT IT IS
INDICATIVE OF OPPOSITION WE FACE AS
THE JACKPOT PROJECT GOES FORWARD.
5. (S) SECDEF OFFICE HAS TOLD ONE AND
ALL ABT OUR FAILURE TO LOCATE MIGS AT
PHUC YEN. THIS TUNE WAS PICKED UP
BY HOSTILE PRESS, ANTIWAR GROUPS,
AND CONGRESSMEN. I HAVE COUNTERED
W/BRIEFINGS THAT LOSSES TO MIGS HAVE
DECREASED SINCE BOMBING PHUC YEN
AND OTHER AIRFIELDS, AS SHOWN IN YR
LAST JACKPOT MSG.
6. (U) KEEP UP THE GOOD WORK.
SECRET—IMMEDIATE—JACKPOT

"So what do you think?" General Moss asked when Pearly finished with the message and handed it to Colonel Wes Snider.

"He seems to like the draft OPlan."

"Oh, he'll make changes. Gentleman Jim's a perfectionist. But you're right, he liked what he saw."

Wes Snider finished reading the message and looked up, his eyes narrowed. "It's hard to believe what he says about General Roman."

"Do you still think we should bring Roman aboard?" Moss asked mischievously.

"Not if he's advocating limiting the bombing even more than it is now."

"Bomber Joe's not advocating anything, Snider. He's just betting his chips on the Secretary of Defense instead of Jim McManus."

"But why?" Snider was a model military man. A dictate of the system was that one remained loyal to one's superior officers.

"Because *someone* has to take over when McManus steps down, which will likely not be long. Gentleman Jim's had his heart attack, and he's not going to be reappointed in the spring shuffle. Roman's betting that the SecDef will be appreciative of his support and nominate him."

"But that's not right."

"May not be right, but it's a fact." Moss was observing Snider as if there was hope for him after all. "Have you come up with a nickname for the JACKPOT OPlan?"

"I've brought a few candidates, keeping in mind what you said about trying to make the President know it's his baby."

"And?"

"I had the idea that maybe we could use the L. B. initials. Like Lady Bird and Linda Bird are the same as Lyndon Baines. We could use Lady Bug, for instance, but I thought that was just *too* transparent."

"I'm listening."

"I looked up code words that aren't being used that start with the initials *L* and *B,* and came up with three or four dozen. Most were inappropriate, like Lazy and Bunion, so I tossed 'em out. I picked four combinations and feel you should make the choice, sir."

"Go ahead."

Wes read from a scrap of paper. "Linus Blanket, Lime Bucket, Lion Bait and . . . Line Backer."

Pearly did a doubletake. "Linebacker Alpha" was the name of the outdated OPlan Snider had brought from Offutt.

Richard J. Moss, who had played defensive back for the West Point class of '41, didn't have to think hard to come up with his choice, not realizing how very similar it was to the code name for the SAC bombardment plan.

"LINE BACKER JACKPOT," he muttered. "Got a nice ring to it."

Snider smiled happily, with good reason. The OPlan name would please Lyndon Baines Johnson, the Commander in Chief of Strategic Air Command, and General Moss as well. Three key, high-ranking, and powerful people would feel a personal stake whenever they heard mention of the code name. Wes Snider was confirmed in Pearly's mind as a canny staff officer.

Pearly walked back to his admin section, thinking hard about the JACKPOT message, the President of the United States, General McManus, and the LINE BACKER JACKPOT OPlan . . .

And ran squarely into Lieutenant Lucille Dortmeier as she emerged from the admin office. She went sprawling back into the room, clawing the air, and fell squarely on her butt. It might have been comical, but she squealed with indignance and pain.

"Oh, Jesus," he muttered, hurrying over to help her up, then watching her grimace and bite her lip. "Damn, I'm sorry."

"All right, sir." She avoided his offered hand, rolled over on all fours, struggled to her feet, and limped out without another word or look back.

Pearly stared after her, feeling like a bumbling fool.

The WAF admin sergeant immediately went back to her typing. Now something was wrong with her too, because she looked angry. Women banding together?

"Makes you feel dumb to do something like that," Pearly said lamely.

The admin staff sergeant struck a key particularly hard but continued typing, her mouth firmly set. Pearly paused for her comment, listened to the clickety click of the typewriter for an awkward moment, then went into his office.

A few minutes later he was going through the stack of correspondence in his in-basket when he came across Lieutenant Dortmeier's request for time off. She asked for a midweek day, the fifth of December, so she could be with her father, who would be visiting.

Visiting Saigon? Pearly absently wondered just who her father was as he wrote "approved" on the bottom of the page and placed it in his out-basket.

1735L—Fighter Tactics Branch, TFWC, Nellis AFB, Nevada

Major Benny Lewis

Benny had been busy since he'd been appointed to the JACKPOT program by the message from the CSAF. He'd gone to Strategic Air Command in Omaha twice, established contact with the four-star SAC commander, Colonel Wes Snider, and both project officers there, and gained their inputs on what they'd need from the tactical fighters for the strategic-bomber part of the all-out attack scenario. They spoke of F-4 MiG-CAP providing protection from interceptors, F-105 Wild Weasels keeping the SAM operators preoccupied, EB-66 ECM birds jamming the acquisition radars—and agreed to loan chaff dispensers and chaff bombs for fighters to use to mask the big bombers.

At the Armament Lab at Eglin AFB in northern Florida, he'd discussed new cluster bombs, as well as a very large antiradar missile being adapted from the Navy's shipboard Standard missile series. Both of those would be carried by F-105 Wild Weasels and could be available in four months' time if they were assigned appropriate R and D priority. A single call to a project officer at the Pentagon had made the priority happen.

Benny was amazed at the smooth way the JACKPOT people worked together, as well as the emphasis and clout they could garner for a request. They were all movers and shakers—and all were tired of treading water in Vietnam. They wanted to win.

Most of the time, though, was spent at his desk in the basement at Nellis AFB, improving the methodology of command-and-control, devising ways to mesh the timing and coordinate targets for around-the-clock attacks by hundreds of diverse aircraft in a relatively small area. Benny initiated a stream of three-way messages between himself, his contact at the National Military Command Center in the basement of the Pentagon, and Lieutenant Colonel Pearly Gates at Seventh Air Force.

He used the CSAF's program element number (PEN) for initial funding of Moods Diller's smart bomb project, then a quick reaction PEN for the upcoming combat test. The more he considered the anticipated large numbers of targets and the probable losses of aircraft, the more he became convinced that smart weapons might indeed make a difference. Instead of a force of thirty-two aircraft going after a single difficult target, with only a fifty-fifty chance of hitting it, the same number could conceivably go after sixteen targets and—if Moods's calculations were valid—destroy at least ten of them.

If they worked as advertised, smart bombs could increase effectiveness thirtyfold or more and sharply reduce peripheral damage. Benny, and even General White, were now in agreement with Moods that they could cut more corners and gain more mileage from an actual combat test than from so-called realistic tests on stateside weapons ranges. Once they showed the generals how they'd knocked out a real and dangerous target with a single bomb, there'd be no way to deny that the smart bombs worked.

Now, three weeks before the scheduled deployment for Moods Diller's Pave Dagger combat test, things looked to be on track. According to Moods the new transducer materials for the bomb kits and new lasers for the illuminators were working spectacularly.

"They're just what we'd needed!" Moods had exulted when he'd returned from his latest visit to the Texas team's laboratories. Then he'd gone into technical explanations that had given Benny another severe headache.

. . .

Lewis left the Center building and trudged to his car, his mind on the several projects he and his people worked on. Those were heavy enough, but as he opened the vehicle's door, he was reminded that his personal life had also become complex. There was yet another responsibility.

Three weeks earlier he'd met Julie Stewart as she'd deplaned from the San Francisco flight. She'd brought little Patty, the infant produced by the union between Julie and his backseater, and he'd grinned and made a general fool of himself. Then they'd waited in the McCarren terminal for another hour and met her mother when she arrived from her home in New Jersey.

Mom Wright had descended from the crowded Boeing jet as tight-jawed as the first time he'd seen her—which had been at Patty's birth six weeks earlier. When she'd gotten to the bottom of the stairs of the 707, she'd eyed him distastefully and thereafter simply ignored his presence.

She'd hugged Julie, brusquely taken the baby from him and looked her over carefully to ensure he'd done no damage, and spoke only with her daughter as Benny led the way to the baggage area. Once there Julie had interrupted her mother's conversation about how awful the trip had been long enough to tell Benny not to even *think* about lifting the luggage and had waved for a porter. While Benny led the procession out to his old Dodge sedan, Mom Wright harped about the heat and lack of humidity, and wondered about the baby's health in such an awful place. As Benny drove to the partially furnished apartment he'd rented for Julie, Mom Wright made her first pitch for her daughter to give up this foolishness and come to New Jersey, where she had a perfectly good house that would be a *much* more suitable place to rear a young lady like Patty.

There'd been constant discord in the weeks following Mom Wright's arrival. At first Benny had visited the apartment daily, just to be there—as he'd felt at first anyway—when Julie needed him.

Now he went there every second day, sometimes every third.

He loved Julie intensely—there was never a doubt that the short and well-endowed young woman was the one he wanted to share his life with—but he was fast tiring of the conversations Mom Wright conducted exclusively with her daughter and the way she'd wait for his arrival to come up with projects to take Julie's attention from him. She was conducting an obvious crusade to shield her daughter from him and was increasingly successful—not so much because Julie listened to her, but because Benny was growing weary of her intrusions.

Today Julie had called and asked him to drop over for dinner. "Seven sharp," she'd said in the husky voice she used when they spoke. He'd agreed, of course, although he'd not felt nearly as happy about it as he should have. But Benny would be there for her. He always was.

He drove to one of the squared-off wooden BOQ buildings—constructed in the early days of World War II in a semicircle about the periphery of the ramshackle Officers' Club—parked, and hurried upstairs to his room. There he showered, groomed, and strapped on the back brace, because hurrying up the stairs had created a new twinge. Next he pulled on chinos and a cotton shirt and, finally and most carefully, a pair of socks. The rest of dressing was not difficult, but bending down to pull on socks was an exercise in care. Once he'd been too quick about it and had spent the next two days in the hospital on the torture bed they kept for back patients.

Satisfied that he was presentable, and with an hour to spare, Benny walked to the club, turned left as he entered the door, and went into the stag bar.

Nellis Air Force Base was not only the largest fighter base in the free world, it was also a crossroads where fighter jocks from the corners of the earth gathered to conduct business. Weapons systems, some exotic, others mundane, were operationally tested. Fighter-tactics symposiums were convened to decide the future of tactical aviation. Top pilots from the various services and different countries of the free world were trained to be even better. Specially selected pilots attended Fighter Weapons Instructor Courses in F-100 Super Sabres, F-105 Thunderchiefs, and F-4 Phantoms. Just down the ramp from the FWIC buildings, pilots and electronic-warfare officers formed into Wild Weasel crews and trained, flying against electronic emitters that emulated enemy SAM and AAA radars. Pilots also came to Nellis to compete mercilessly for a variety of dive-bombing and gunnery trophies.

At all times there were two or three large-scale meetings ongoing, held on a variety of subjects. They said that if you dropped by the Nellis O' Club stag bar every Friday night for six months and stayed to watch the strippers imported from downtown Vegas, you'd likely see every fighter jock in the Air Force who was worth his salt. Strippers were the only females normally found in the stag bar, except for the occasional fun-seeking secretary or WAF officer who entered the forbidden ground to see what it was *really* like. Each was quickly ushered out and briefed on what they might expect, like being bitten on her buttocks by a snorting fighter pilot on all fours, or propositioned by a horde of guys with grins and wandering hands. Forewarned, they entered the male domain at their own peril. A number of truly adventuresome females persisted and even enjoyed it, for they could give as well as they received, and were remembered with awe and discussed in fighter circles throughout the free world.

The Nellis O' Club stag bar was the crossroads for fighter pilots. Tonight there was Lieutenant Colonel Sam Hall, up from Luke Air Force Base where he commanded an F-4 fighter training squadron, and when Benny entered the bar, the huge black pilot clapped him on the shoulder with enough weight to stagger a bull elephant. Then he did an *aw shit* when Benny crumpled. "Damn!" he roared, as he clutched him and kept him upright. "Forgot about the back."

Benny bit his lower lip for a moment, then grinned. "Buy me a drink and you're forgiven."

They shouted memories over the loud music and roar of the crowd, dodged a captain being chased by a sputtering major he'd just doused with a drink, and hoisted a couple of beers.

Sam filled him in on what was happening at Luke, and about their mutual friends who were coming there following Southeast Asia combat tours, to check out in F-4 Phantoms.

Benny said he'd read that Colonel Mack, who'd been their squadron commander at Takhli, had made the full colonel's list. Sam told him Mack was being sent to the Pentagon. They agreed that the place might finally get organized. Then Sam said that Colonel B. J. Parker had also been sent there, so they decided it might not be that easy a task for Mack after all.

Sam said he'd heard from Tiny Bechler, another squadron

mate from Takhli. He'd made captain and been sent to Hurlburt Field in Florida as an instructor in the forward air controller course. Benny told him that Max Foley had passed through a few weeks earlier, headed for an assignment at TAC headquarters in Virginia. Also, Pudge Holden and his bear, Sloppy Watson, had arrived at Nellis as instructors in the Wild Weasel course.

Wild Weasel backseaters were called bears. Speaking of them, Sam asked him about Julie Stewart, his backseater's widow. Benny told him she'd moved to Vegas, and he was going over to see her in half an hour or so. Sam said that was good—and regarded him with a slow grin.

"Nothing's going on, Sam," Benny said quickly, and a flutter grew in the pit of his gut.

"Well," said Sam Hall in his southern drawl, "that's too bad, Benny."

Benny was ten minutes late for dinner, and Mom Wright's lips were pursed tightly when he entered the apartment. Julie greeted him with her normal enthusiastic-but-careful hug.

"I just saw Sam Hall," Benny told her. "You remember Sam?"

"I never met him, but Mal Bear wrote about him in his letters. How's he doing?"

Benny started to tell her the news he'd learned.

"Julie," Mom Wright interrupted, with a sharp bite in her voice, "I think you'd better check on Patty. She'll need changing, since we're *already* so late for dinner."

"Sure, Mom," Julie said brightly, and Benny was left with stark, cold silence in the small living room.

After they'd eaten and were relaxing in the living room, Julie announced that she'd be returning to Pan Am, working out at McCarren Field. Benny tried to discuss it, and as usual, found himself frustrated. Every time he tried to bring up a subject, Mom Wright would interrupt with something else. Then the ladies went to the kitchen to clean up, leaving him with an after-dinner brandy in the living room. He tried to tiptoe into the bedroom to get a peek at the baby, but Mom Wright hurried in, her face pinched and stern, and closed the door. Patty needed her sleep, she said.

Thinking about yet another spoiled evening, Benny sat and sipped brandy and wondered if the hassle was worth it. So far in their three weeks, there'd scarcely been a moment alone with the woman he knew he loved, yet did not dare show it.

The ladies came in to join him, Mom Wright arguing vehemently against Julie's returning to work. It wasn't right that she do that to the baby—she wouldn't be around to help *forever,* Julie knew.

"There are nurseries, Mom."

"Yes, but . . ."

"What do *you* think about my going back to work, Benny?"

He started to say he thought it would be great, since she missed Pan Am so much, but Mom Wright interrupted and said that babies who were cast off into nurseries too early or too often developed problems.

Benny listened to her harangue as he finished his drink, then stood.

"You're leaving so early?" Julie asked, rising from the sofa.

"I told Sam Hall I'd be back and we'd talk some more," Benny fibbed. Sam had been on his way downtown to gamble away a few dollars and see the lights.

Mom Wright kept her seat and her stern expression.

"Good night, Mrs. Wright," he said, then smiled and nodded to Julie.

"I'll come out with you," Julie said.

Mom Wright frowned. "Don't be gone too—"

"Be right back, Mom," Julie said as she closed the door. She walked close at Benny's side down the sidewalk toward his car.

He started to open the door, but she touched his arm. He liked the feel of her hand. She kept it there, looking up at him under the dim glow of the street lamps. "You're so dear to me," she said.

"Ah . . . you too." He felt awkward. He wanted to hold her.

"Take care of yourself, Benny." She dropped her hand and started toward the house.

He was about to open the car door when he heard a small cry, and the sound of her returning. He'd turned halfway when she rushed into his arms, uttering a whimper. He held her. She raised her head and they kissed. Not a brotherly peck, but a long, deep, and very wet kiss.

They broke and she whispered something. He bent lower. "I love you," she repeated.

He blew a long breath and slowly nodded.

"Be patient," she said. Then she pulled his head down and they hungrily kissed again. It was the most demonstrative they'd been, and it felt natural and right. They stood there for five minutes of warm silence, but there were unspoken words between them. She nestled as close as she could, and he felt the warmth of her. When she finally went down the sidewalk, looking back with every second step, he got into the car and started it, then sat there for a long moment after she went inside.

He loved her with all his being. How long would it be? he wondered.

CHAPTER THIRTEEN

Saturday, November 25th, 2145L—Trailer 5B, Takhli RTAFB, Thailand

GS-7 Penny Dwight

Penny was thrilled with her assignment to Takhli. There was the distinct possibility that she was falling for a lanky guy with freckles, a shuck of brown hair that refused to stay in place, an easy smile that would melt a witch's heart, and a lopsided way of joking and making fun of situations that kept her laughing. She'd seen Dusty Fields every day since she'd gotten off the plane—when was it? Three weeks ago? Time was passing so quickly. He'd pressed himself on her daily, and she hadn't discouraged him.

Penny stood inside the door of the trailer, her back flat against the door, smiling and gazing at the interior of the trailer, thinking how close she'd come to inviting him in.

Stop kidding yourself, she thought. *You want him.* Something tried to tell her to go slower, to make sure before she charged ahead with a full-blown affair, but she tried to push it aside. She found herself doodling his name during slack times at work and had mentioned, in a letter to her parents, that she'd met a very nice guy.

She tried to envision Dusty as the settled-down father of their children—but it came out a bit garbled. *See,* said the distant something. *Maybe so,* she told the voice, *but he sure is fun.*

Dusty had wanted to come inside when he'd dropped her off at the trailer door . . . again. Each night she came closer to relenting, although she knew it was too early, that she must play coy for at least a little while longer—despite the fact that she'd changed her mind about the promise she'd made to herself that she would fastidiously maintain her innocence at Takhli.

Well . . . *almost* innocence. There'd been a fumbling time in the back of a family station wagon with a basketball player she'd adored in high school. He'd huffed and deftly broken through her barrier, and then finished and nervously zipped back up before she'd had time to decide if she liked it. And then there was the time, after she'd accepted an engagement ring from a charming, young, and inexperienced fellow civilian worker at Bolling Air Force Base, where she'd gotten her first government secretary job—when he'd convinced her he couldn't wait. She'd prepared carefully for that encounter—visited a doctor and had a diaphragm fitted, spent an afternoon making sure her bedroom was spotless, the music from her record player soothing, and the lighting just so—but the investments proved to be a waste. Two minutes after he'd entered her bedroom, her young fiancé had both of them half-disrobed, groped at her breasts for a few seconds of foreplay, then ejaculated prematurely over her abdomen. The second time, after he'd cajoled for the next two weeks, he'd played with her breasts a few seconds longer and made it down to her thighs before spouting his copious juice, groaning and blurting apologies. The third and final time, he'd erupted while he was still pulling off his trousers. After thinking things over, she'd decided the situation was regressing and judiciously called the relationship to a halt. So far her limited experience had taught her that men were a frantic, selfish gender who didn't—or couldn't—take nearly enough time with things.

Penny hoped it would be different with Dusty when they did it. She couldn't hold out much longer. If she got sopping wet one more time and again felt the tingling down to her toes so she could hardly feel them . . .

She went to the bathroom, where she pulled off her blouse and began to rinse away some of the dried perspiration with a washcloth. It was terribly hot and muggy outside, even though they called this the "cool" season. Thank God for air-conditioning. She couldn't imagine what it was like when pilots went out to fly. Dusty had told her that the heat rose to more than 130 unbearable degrees in the cockpits when they first lowered their canopies.

A flicker of apprehension about his safety ran through her, but she quickly blanked her mind about the dangerous combat missions he flew. Manny DeVera said their losses were way down from what they'd been a year ago, because they'd learned a lot about flying combat over North Vietnam since then. But no matter what he said, they were losing men. One had not returned just the day before—a captain they all seemed to like, and who Manny DeVera said had a wife and three children. Yet they'd just mentioned how he'd been a nice guy and went on about their business of preparing to fly again the next day. Penny shuddered and drove the thoughts from her mind.

Manny was the kind who gave off so much energy you could feel it when he came near, and he had buckets of charisma. If she wasn't so taken by Dusty Fields, she could imagine herself being drawn to the handsome pilot with the animal intensity, who could make a room come to life just by walking in. He'd been in her office that morning, in fact, leaning over her desk and joking, when a tall dark-haired lady had entered and given her a card showing she was the country coordinator for USOM/USAID. Her card read that she was GS-15 Linda M. Lopes.

"I'd like to see the wing comman—"

"You're Lieutenant Colonel Anderson's fiancé," Penny had blurted. Then she'd become embarrassed at her outburst and added in a more collected voice, "I saw you with him at the Bangkok airport."

The dark-haired lady had smiled. She was so well groomed and carried herself so regally that Penny was more than a little awed. She could be no more than five or six years older than Penny, and already a GS-15? She'd never met a woman who'd risen that high in the system.

Linda Lopes had paid a short visit to Colonel Leska, a courtesy call to tell him she'd be in the area for the next few days on USAID business. While she was inside the colonel's office, the chief master sergeant who ran admin at the wing commander's office came over to Penny and said to make sure the lady's usual trailer had been reserved.

A call to the billeting office revealed that trailer 9A was indeed clean, vacant, and as Miss Lopes had left it on her visit two months earlier.

Linda had stopped off at her desk again on her way out. "I'll be here for five days," she said in her businesslike tone, "and I'd appreciate it if you'd take any messages. I left this number at the embassy."

"You'll be at your trailer?" Penny had been unable to keep a trill of admiration from her voice. GS-15 Lopes had remained expressionless, as if she hadn't picked it up.

"In and out," she'd said. "I'll be working in the area, but I'll drop by there daily. Just have someone leave a note at my trailer and I'll get in contact with you."

She'd gone over and spoken a few words to Manny DeVera before she left. Penny felt she looked very sexy and quite mysterious. The enormity of what Penny was doing, that she was actually in ancient Siam, meeting people like GS-15 Linda Lopes, had thrilled her once more.

Manny DeVera had come back over to her desk, smiling. "So the Ice Maiden's here. That oughta make Lucky Anderson happy."

"Ice maiden?" Penny had asked, wrinkling her nose. It was a silly thing to call someone so sophisticated.

"That's the nickname the guys use. She's a good lady. How about dinner?" Manny had slipped the last sentence in very smoothly.

"Dusty and I are going downtown to do some shopping soon as I get off. It's Saturday and I only work half a day."

"Some other time?"

"Perhaps," Penny had lied to be polite. She'd already chosen, and there was no turning back, and certainly no playing around.

The previous night, when Dusty had walked her to her door and tried to talk his way inside, and after she'd firmly said no, they'd kissed and petted for ten minutes outside the dark trailer. Dusty had told her things like, "I never know if I'll make it back," and although she'd known it was a line he was using to get her into bed, she'd been affected. Penny

had hurried inside and cried to think about brave men like
Dusty facing death and perhaps never again sharing joy with
a woman. Tonight he'd not mentioned it when they'd kissed
at her door, although he'd pressed to come inside so they
could "talk and maybe relax some" together. It was a good
thing he hadn't brought up the fears, because if he had,
she'd surely have given in.

Why hadn't she relented and let him inside? Was she being *too* prudish? When would he stop pressing if she kept
putting him off ? Did she dare for *that* to happen? There
were too many questions for a woman to answer in a situation such as this.

When Dusty wasn't around, she confided in his friend
Roger, who was very talented with his music, and whom the
others inexplicably called Animal. Roger seemed very steady
and was happily married, and thus less dangerous. She'd
likely also confide in Manny DeVera, if he didn't have that
dangerous air about him that made warning bells go off.

Penny closed the bathroom door, then pulled off the rest
of her clothing and stuffed it into a laundry bag the maid
had left hanging on the door. It would be washed, lightly
starched, ironed, and placed on hangers in her closet or
folded in the dresser . . . all for a ridiculously low weekly
price. She turned to the mirror, peering critically as she examined herself. There were no wrinkles. She'd not yet
reached her twenty-fifth birthday and those horrors would
be a few years coming. She preened a bit and decided she
was acceptable. Her nose was too pointed, her mouth too
pixyish, her waist too long, her nipples too small, her left
breast larger than the right, and she had a deep dimple
above each buttock that was sure to embarrass her if she
ever stood naked before a man, but none of those were
overly distracting. She was no beauty, maybe, but she was
trim, had the proper equipment, and knew she was as ripe
and ready as a woman could get.

Shower time.

Penny adjusted the water flow to full blast, let it run until
it was steamy hot, stepped inside, and positioned herself so
the needles darted upon her breasts. Her breathing slowly
intensified. She gradually moved back until her buttocks
were against the cold metal of the stall and the water tingled

her tummy; then she arched and writhed a bit as the glow Dusty had left her with returned.

She languidly moved her hands down her body, making believe they were Dusty's. Her breaths came in low huffs now, but she was oblivious. Her fingers found her source and she moaned low. She began to work to finish the delicious feeling.

It took an effort not to cry out.

Dusty! she thought as she quickened. Then she thought of intense Manny and felt herself blush. She made a low grunting moan, followed by a series of mewing sounds that she tried to stifle.

Penny stopped, mouth wide, and held herself very still as the feeling slowly abated.

Oh, God, but she was ready!

Sunday, November 26th, 0700 Local—9 km Northeast of Channel 97 TACAN, Laos

Sergeant Black

The man called Sergeant Black was wearing jungle fatigues, with a single subdued E-6 rank on one collar and a floppy campaign hat on his head. A use-worn 7.62mm Automat Kalashnikov model-M folding-stock assault rifle rested at his side. He lay on a shale outcropping, binoculars fixed on the small clearing 200 yards distant.

One of his Hotdog team members was at his side, also staring at the clearing. He wore quite a different uniform, with baggy, olive-drab cotton pants, a matching shirt with sleeves half–rolled up, and tan canvas shoes. A wicker hat lay at his side. It was the field uniform of the North Viet Army as the Americans called it, or Viet People's Army, as they called themselves.

A dozen soldiers stood in the clearing, talking. One laughed and the sound carried. They obviously didn't anticipate observers.

"People's Militia," said the team member beside Sergeant Black derisively. The soldiers before them wore Ho Chi Minh sandals cut from truck tires, like the Cong in South Vietnam. Tennis shoes went to the regular People's Army.

Yet the soldiers Black observed looked purposeful and professional, not nearly as unkempt as other militia he'd seen. *What the hell are they doing in Laos?* he wondered.

He remained quiet. The seven men of the long-range recon detachment, code name Hotdog, had worked together for fifteen months. They were professionals and seldom spoke aloud or even used hand signals.

His six men didn't wear bogus uniforms. They'd deserted from the 321-B Division of the VPA, prepared to give their lives to rid the world of the Hanoi communists. After kidnapping a Special Forces sergeant and convincing the shaken soldier that they wished to turn themselves over to the Americans and no one else, they'd marched into an A-Team camp near the DMZ with wide grins and hands behind their heads. After intensive interrogations and a field test to prove their loyalty, they'd been joined by Sergeant Black. That was in violation of agreements with the South Viets, for defectors were to be turned over to them, for propaganda use in their "open arms" program. But Black, under the auspices of the new Delta Project and Command and Control–Central, headquartered at Nakhon Phanom in easternmost Thailand, was trying to prove a concept using North Viet defectors for long-range recon patrols into Laos (called Prairie Fire) and into North Vietnam (called Kit Cat). He'd found that the men of Hotdog could soldier as well as any Special Forces team he'd served with. Their skills had been proved on five forays into enemy territory, three into North Vietnam, one of those into the very heart of the country, in the heavily populated area west of Hanoi.

The Special Forces brass in Delta Project at Nha Trang, and CC-C at NKP, called them "Black's renegades," and he'd grown to like the name. He'd trained, lived, and fought with them, and they'd grown interdependent, as men who bet their asses on one another do. Black considered the rock-tough lieutenant, now out leading the remainder of the Hotdog team, as close a friend as he had. His name was Hoang Phrang, but everyone just called him "the lieutenant." He was a natural leader and the best soldier Black had ever seen operate in the bush.

Black was so impressed with his crew that he'd convinced the Special Forces brass at the Delta Project to try more small LRRP teams made up of SF leaders and NVA deserters. Other American-led indigenous teams had been formed, but none had been trusted sufficiently to routinely conduct sensitive Kit Cat or Prairie Fire patrols, as Hotdog did. One reason was that there were few team leaders with Black's unique qualifications, and of those, even fewer willing to bet their asses on a bunch of fucking deserters. So the indigenous teams were turned over to the South Viet Special Forces or given misinformation and dropped into North Vietnam areas where they'd be compromised and captured.

Such was the ridiculous war they fought. Hotdog was allowed to continue, but the team's days were numbered. The only thing that held them together was the fact that Black was highly regarded.

Three weeks earlier Black had been in Hawaii, visiting his family and recuperating from a wound left by a 12.7mm machine-gun round that had passed through his side. He'd been called to Fort Shafter for a quiet, closed ceremony. The four-star running U.S. Army Western Command had presented him with a fourth oak-leaf cluster to his Purple Heart and a Distinguished Service Cross, the second-highest medal the army gave out. Black had worn a sharp uniform for the presentation, with captain's bars on his shoulders and five rows of medals, jump wings, and a combat infantryman's badge on his chest. His plastic name tag had read DILLINGHAM, the same as an early-American missionary who'd dallied with a wahine convert. He also had Japanese, Portuguese, and a preponderance of native island blood. One branch of his ancestry traced back to Kamehameha I, the fierce warrior king who had consolidated the Hawaiian isles under his rule.

Black looked a bit Japanese, but he was too thick-chested. He had a Caucasian's nose, but his face was round, his eyes Oriental, and his hair as straight as a shock of black wheat. He was intense and intelligent, and had a thing for languages, down to picking up local nuances. He could speak French, German, Russian, and Japanese with authority. He also spoke Vietnamese with the crisp staccato rhythm of a northerner, and could get by in Thai, Montagnard, and most Hmong dialects.

Five days before, Hotdog had been flown from Nha Trang, where they'd received refresher training in LRRP ops by the superb Recondo instructors, back to the CC-C headquarters at Nakhon Phanom. There Black had received briefings on an easy recon patrol into northeast Laos, to pick up information on possible enemy movements. Ma tribesmen, distant relatives of both the Montagnards, who lived to their south, and Hmong, to their west, reported an advance guard of Viet soldiers moving into the area. MAC-SOG wanted to know who they were, and if they posed a threat to the CIA-operated air-navigation station installed on a mountaintop near the tiny village and deserted airfield called Ban Sao Si.

"Probably nothing to it," the lieutenant colonel who ran the headquarters C-Team had told Black. "The Pathet Lao are mobilizing to battalion strength all over Laos, and we're picking up a lot of NVA activity on the trails, so they've got bigger priorities than a two-bit nav station."

"Then why are we going in?" Black had asked.

"Because, one, the Ma tribe's been generally accurate in the past, two, the Air Force prima donnas want to keep Channel Ninety-seven on the air and get nervous when anyone threatens it, and three, after fucking off and getting soft in Hawaii, I figure you need an easy op to hone up on."

Black had wanted to take his Hotdog renegades with him on his R and R, but the same lieutenant colonel had rejected the idea. Like others, he wouldn't be at all surprised if the renegades decided to turn, or shed a tear if they were compromised and killed. But he was impressed with Black and the results he got on his ops, although he repeatedly cautioned him about the possibility of being captured and turned over by his own men.

Hotdog had been dropped in two nights before and quickly located their contact in the Ma village, to discuss the military force that was supposedly moving into the area.

The contact said four of the oddly uniformed soldiers had arrived and set up a radio in the tiny village of Ban Keng Long, and that a larger force was moving through the mountains toward them from the east. He hadn't been able to tell them how many soldiers were approaching, because the tribesmen had no concept of numbers beyond the mystical five, the numbers of fingers on a hand or toes on a foot. The Yards, which is what the Forces called Montagnards, were entrenched in Bronze Age mentalities, but they were downright sophisticated compared to tribes like the Ma, who lived in the hills and jungles to their north. The contact, who was also headman of his village, had pointed about himself with gestures that indicated there were quite a few soldiers coming through the mountains. That could mean ten, a hundred, or a thousand.

Black had rewarded him with a 500-round box of captured 7.62mm ammo, as well as a small bag of brass buttons he'd bought at a Nakhon Phanom market. The headman had graciously offered Black his two teenaged daughters for the night and grown embarrassed when he declined. The family's honor was salved when the stocky, bare-breasted maids were offered to his men, for the lieutenant had claimed one, and his men had taken turns with the other. By morning, when they'd prepared to move out, the father had been proud.

Hotdog was a horny crew, Black thought as he peered through the binoculars. He noted two new arrivals in the clearing. Both wore pith helmets with small dark-red stars at the front. One was older, with collar markings he couldn't discern. The other, much younger, carried a leather dispatch bag slung around his neck. A field-grade officer and his lieutenant?

He watched as the younger man gestured southward and the two discussed something. They reached agreement, formed the men in the clearing into trail formation, and came on, disappearing into a stand of trees. More soldiers appeared and followed in single file. They appeared as professional and sure as regular NVA. Black could hear the revving of engines in the distance. The roads were difficult, and the vehicles were obviously having trouble negotiating.

Black heard a slight sound to his right, the low clucking of a jungle bird. He edged back off the shale outcropping and watched as the remainder of Hotdog appeared. They'd been gone for two hours, since well before dawn.

The lieutenant nodded northward. "They are from the Army of National Defense," he whispered in a barely audible voice.

Black paused thoughtfully, his suspicions confirmed. VPAND People's Militia, never before seen outside the borders of North Vietnam. "How many?" he whispered in Viet.

"Don't know," came the answer. "At least two hundred, but I believe more. We saw utility vehicles and water buffalo hauling carts and five small artillery pieces. We couldn't get close because we are wearing the wrong uniforms."

"How many vehicles?"

"Four, but we could hear more."

Two hundred soldiers were a sizable force, thought Black, likely enough to overrun a small nav station defended by a handful of Yard tribesmen. If that was where they were going. It made sense, though, for there was little else of military value in the area, and this was not a normal route of passage.

Black gave the signal to move out. He planned to back off a kilometer or two, then contact the headquarters at NKP about the force they'd encountered and tell them it was headed toward the mesa with the nav station on top. An air strike would eliminate the threat if they attacked while the force was still enroute.

An hour later they'd strung the directional antenna of the HF single-sideband radio and connected the battery pack. Black made initial contact with Nakhon Phanom and gave the day's password. The response came from a man with a distinctive nasal voice that he easily recognized. His name was Larry, a sergeant he'd served with at an alpha detachment in the highlands, and Black felt pleased because it was someone he could work with. They'd developed their own distinctive way of communicating at the A-det—their own unique code words. Larry was also one of few at NKP who knew his real rank and that he was to be listened to.

"Buffalo Soldier, Hotdog counts minimum of two buckets of vee-pand militia on the move with utility vehicles and buffalo hauling horse pistols and supplies. Destination is likely Yankee two-one." He gave precise coordinates of the clearing through which they passed. *"Foliage cover's pretty sparse there, and they oughta make good targets."*

Yankee twenty-one was the CIA-operated nav station, so the headquarters was interested. Larry had him repeat his transmission, wary of the two "buckets," which meant 200, and he seemed perplexed that they were VPAND militia, who operated only inside North Vietnam.

Black confirmed. *"Minimum of two buckets, probably more. And they're confirmed as vee-pand militia, but they look damned professional. I've got bad vibes about 'em. I think they're gonna be tough unless you take 'em out right away."*

Larry asked if the guns were horse pistols, meaning howitzers, or air pistols, meaning antiaircraft guns.

"Horse pistols. No air pistols observed so far, but don't bank on it," he radioed. *"We're taking another look. You gonna give me an air strike on coordinates?"*

"Stand by, Hotdog. We're awfully busy. All kinds of hell's starting to break loose."

"I need an air strike, Buffalo Soldier."

"Stand by."

Shit. He waited. The lieutenant had left three men with a hand-held radio behind on the outcropping, to observe and count the militia force moving through the clearing. He had a feeling there were a lot more than they'd counted, and the lieutenant was seldom wrong.

Black also wanted to confirm the fact that there were no antiaircraft guns. It would make sense for a militia force of that size to bring along 14.5mm and 37mm guns, which were easy to haul and gave at least *some* protection against aircraft. They'd certainly be available to the VPAND, because that organization controlled air defenses inside North Vietnam.

The observers called in. They'd counted more than 300 militia troops passing through the clearing. A small number turned west toward Ban Sao Si, but the rest continued southward, toward the flat-top mountain where the nav station was located. They confirmed ten howitzers, fifteen supply carts, and a number of antiaircraft guns. Besides the six utility vehicles, there were also two tracked armored personnel carriers hauling closed trailers. Those, they said, were heavily guarded. New estimate: 332 soldiers.

After an hour had passed since his last contact, Black called Buffalo Soldier again, updated the numbers, and told them about the APCs hauling *something* they wanted to guard.

Buffalo Soldier had him repeat, then again told him to stand by.

"Hotdog requests air strike," he reminded Larry.

"I gotcha, Hotdog. Stand by."

"Every minute you wait, they're that much closer to Yankee two-one."

"Stand by, Hotdog. Be advised that Vientiane Control has a lot of requests today. The PDJ's hot. The papa-lima are raisin' hell over there." Meaning Pathet Lao troops were attacking in the Plains des Jars, and Black's request for air strikes had been outprioritized.

Black waited, thinking it had better not be *too* much longer or the airplanes would miss their chance to catch the militia in the open.

"Anything new from the men?" he asked the lieutenant in Viet.

The lieutenant shook his head.

"Bring them in."

The lieutenant relayed the order over his hand-held radio.

The single-sideband crackled. *"Hotdog, this is Buffalo Soldier."*

"Hotdog here."

"Proceed to Yankee one-zero."

"Where's my air strike, Buffalo Soldier?" The trees the militia were presently moving through were sparse, and they'd be easy targets. If they were able to travel five more kilometers, they'd be in the dense jungle surrounding the base of the mesa.

"Negative on air support for today, Hotdog. You're way down on a long list. When you get to Yankee one-zero, establish radio contact with Yankee two-one, then call me back."

Black huffed a single, angry breath. *"Message received. Hotdog's on the move."*

Larry responded with a beep-beep, meaning he understood.

Yankee ten was a prepared and provisioned location at the base of the steep-sided, flat-topped mountain. Black was not at all pleased with the directive to proceed there. At present they were free to move at will and set up where they thought best. When they got to Yankee ten, they'd be trapped between the mountain and the oncoming militia. He pointed at the single-sideband radio, and one of the men began to reel in the antenna while another disconnected the battery pack and snapped on the waterproof cover.

They'd move out as soon as the rest of the team arrived.

Monday, November 27th, 2045 Local—Trailer 12, Takhli
RTAFB, Thailand

Lieutenant Colonel Lucky Anderson

"That was a nice dinner, Colonel Anderson," said Linda as
he closed the door.

"Thank you, Miss Lopes," he replied as he unbuttoned
his shirt.

We're certainly getting domestic about things, he decided.

Don't fight it, his happy brain interjected, digesting the
scenery as Linda began removing her own top.

They'd gone off base to eat at a new establishment in Ta
Khli. Run by a canny restaurateur from Bangkok, the place
featured hot Thai dishes and Kobe steaks. While it was
known that their Kobe beef was actually water-buffalo meat
tenderized with various chemicals and energetic pounding,
the stuff was tasty, and you could cut it with a fork.

"I like your cutesy little vehicle," he told her. They'd
taken the white jeep provided by the USAID office in
Nakhon Sawan, the provincial capital not far northwest of
Takhli. "How come it's got *U-S-O-M* on the side?" he asked.

"Stands for U.S. Operational Mission. That's the USAID
branch for interaction with the locals in foreign countries, so
we can determine their needs."

"And pigs take off from short runways, right?" He knew
she was in the intelligence business—had been since she'd
graduated from Texas Women's University at age twenty-
two. No one climbed the General Scale ladder to GS-15 that
fast by handing out rice to villagers. He pulled off his socks
and placed them in the laundry bag.

"No kidding," she said with a deadpan face, watching as
he slipped out of his chino trousers. "We work with the locals on a lot of projects."

"But not all your projects have to do with giving away
food and blankets."

"Hey, fella. We're the good guys." Linda wouldn't discuss
details of her job. She was as closemouthed about her work
as he was about military secrets.

He couldn't help grinning. She was down to nothing on
top and wispy panties, showing off small but perfect breasts
and great curves. Linda was beautiful to him either with or

without clothes, but he preferred the latter. To hell with subtlety.

She eyed him and struck a lewd pose, stroking long fingers over her Venus mound, which was barely hidden by the bikini panties. "Like what you see, fella?"

"Uh . . . yes, ma'am." He started for her.

She held up her hands, frowned and shook her head. He stopped and watched her grind her pelvis like a stripper. "Feel vulnerable?" she asked.

"I would gladly give my soul for the privilege of fondling you, ma'am."

"That's what I wanted to hear. May fifteenth, in Big Spring, Texas, at the First Baptist Church, you will betroth your life to me. I'll wear white, of course, and you'll not make lewd comments about having made love to the virgin bride on four hundred and seven occasions. You'll wear your white mess-dress uniform with gobs of medals and look heroic."

"Jesus," he said, frowning. "That's only six months away."

"By then you'll have visited the burn center in San Antonio and begun your transformation back to your old, devilishly handsome self."

He glowered. "If I'd wanted to change my face, I'd have stayed at the center when I was there before."

"Yeah, but you've promised me, Paul Anderson."

"You traded sex for that promise, if I remember."

"Anything's fair in this game. A promise is a promise."

He sighed. "You're an insensitive woman."

"Maybe I should put on my clothes and go to my own trailer."

Dummy, cried his brain. He was getting hornier by the second, and it was showing.

"I mean it, Paul Anderson."

"If I agree to your terms, you'll stay and be a slave to my every disgusting desire?"

She eyed his protrusion with a wicked gleam. "I'll delight you beyond your wildest dreams."

"Maybe you should hear about some of my earthier night thoughts first."

"As long as they're about me, I'll allow them. Anyway, I doubt they come anywhere close to my own." She looked at him and grew the dreamy expression she acquired as she crossed the line from sanity to lust. Her voice hoarsened as she began wriggling out of the panties. "Take off your shorts."

He paused. "First I want you to tell me who's boss here."

"You're boss, now take off your damn shorts before I tear 'em off."

Half an hour later she huffed and nestled in the darkness. "God, we're great together."

She kept squirming until she was molded so closely to his side that a mite could not have crawled between them. Her knee was crooked over his leg and her hand caressed his spent maleness.

"You've been comparing?" he joked.

She was very quiet for a moment, then spoke seriously. "I've never been with another man."

"Just kidding."

"It's not funny to me, Paul. I was raised like that. My mother's the same way. We're one-man women."

"I know."

"I will never *be* with another man, Paul. I've got what I want. You'll never have to worry about that part of it."

He swallowed, embarrassed even in the dark.

"And if you're away from me somewhere and find another woman, just don't get serious, and don't let me know about it, okay?"

"I can't think of a reason to do that." He didn't like the way the conversation had turned, so he changed the subject. "Where are you going when you leave?"

"Takhli?"

"Yeah."

"I've got a couple more days here, then I leave for Nakhon Phanom."

"What're you doing at NKP?"

"Same as here."

"That doesn't give me a warm feeling."

He'd deduced that her tasks as head of USAID in Thailand included that of helping ensure the security of the bases. He *thought* she set up networks of locals, to keep an eye out for foreign agents infiltrating to spy on American military installations. He'd come to those conclusions by keeping track of where she went and some of the people she talked to. If he'd figured it out, he knew the same could be done by the enemy, and that made him worry all the more.

"Watch out for yourself, Linda. We hear more and more about Thai communist terrorists operating around the countryside."

"The CTs are vastly overrated. They hardly deserve the name, except in the far eastern part of the country."

"Like at NKP, where you're headed."

"Even there they're poorly organized. Anyway, I'll have a bodyguard along when I visit the villages."

"I'd feel better if you had a company of soldiers and went in a tank."

She laughed. "Now wouldn't that be cute? Here comes the lady who's here to help us . . . and all her infantry."

"Can't stop me from worrying."

"Good, I like that. I'll even try to call more often so you'll know I'm okay. But you're the one in danger, Paul, every time you fly. Even on those you call the easy ones. I see the loss reports. I'll rest a lot better when you've completed your hundred missions."

"I've got sixty-eight now. Just thirty-two to go. Anyway, now that I'm a squadron commander, bullets bounce off."

She didn't laugh. "Promise me that as soon as you get your hundred missions, you'll stop flying, even if you have to go back to the States before I do."

"Nope. We go back together. If that means I have to extend my tour, I'll do it."

"Hardhead. Now I'll have to transfer out early."

"Can you?"

"Richard said he'd arrange it. He knows about you and me."

"Richard?"

"Someone at the embassy."

"You work for him?"

She paused, and he knew she was considering her words. He'd obviously asked a sensitive question. "Sometimes," was all she said.

"I thought you were chief honcho at the USAID office."

"I am." She huffed a sigh. "Richard's Chief of Operations at the embassy."

"The guy you had the . . ." He'd almost said "affair," but stopped himself in time.

"Yeah, he's the one I went out with when you got so hardheaded and refused to see me or return my calls. Nothing happened, Paul, and it's over."

"If you work for him sometimes, I take it he's not *just* a diplomat."

"Time to change the subject, Paul."

"Hmmph."

"God, you have a nice body," she said, adjusting herself again. "We fit together nicely, sort of like a puzzle. I'm getting hot."

"Maybe you should move farther away."

"Not *that* kind of hot, silly. Juicy hot. Wall-clawing hot. Mmmmmm." She kissed his chest and began to move the hand that grasped him.

That one took longer, but it was the second act she'd always said was *her* time, and throughout she made guttural sounds of languid abandon.

Before they slept, she said she'd never been so happy.

CHAPTER FOURTEEN

Sergeant Black

They'd spent two days at Yankee ten, a tiny, reinforced cavern carved into a knoll near the only path leading up the oblong, steep-sided mountain. The bunker's entrance was hidden by thick jungle growth, and they had to wiggle their way in through a maze of vines. While he knew they were well hidden, it made Black nervous that the enemy was so close. More than a hundred militia had set up camp within half a kilometer of Yankee ten, and they constantly heard their voices.

The good news was that, while the North Viets had set up a three-man team with a 12.7mm heavy machine gun to watch the path, they hadn't yet attempted to send troops up the mountainside. Aside from a couple of shots fired from one of the howitzers, there was no offensive activity.

A cache of claymore mines and igniters had been stored at Yankee ten, for precisely the purpose they were being put to. Each night the Hotdogs had gone out and set up trip-wire booby traps at approaches they felt were most likely to be used when the militia started up the mountain. By the second night they'd run out of claymores, so three Hotdogs made a covert raid on a militia camp and stole a dozen satchel charges and a box of grenades, and they'd planted those too.

The radio antenna wire was properly strung over the top of the bunker, invisible to observers yet positioned so it was directional and the signal couldn't be picked up by Soviet monitoring stations in Hanoi.

Black had also inserted a fixed-frequency crystal into one of the VHF hand-held radios, and twice daily he spoke with the American up on top of the mesa. The guy took his time answering and spoke in a hesitant monotone, as if he weren't really interested. He said there was another American contractor and thirty-one Yards up there with him. Twelve were fighting men, the rest women and kids.

Jesus. Why the hell hadn't they moved the Montagnard noncombatants out when they'd first heard the NVA was on the way? Since the question was now more or less moot, with more than 300 enemy soldiers camped around the base of the mountain, he didn't ask. Black also wondered why the militia hadn't moved up the path. The CIA contractors had mined it in two strategic locations with high explosives, but the enemy should know nothing about those or the claymores the Hotdogs had set out.

While most of the Hotdog team thought militia were all lightweights, the lieutenant didn't share the opinion about this particular group, and he told the rest of them not to be lulled. While his men had been placing claymores, he'd gone out and watched and listened in on North Viet conversations. They were handpicked, and a large number, including all the officers, had combat experience with the old Viet Minh. They were waiting for something, excited about what they were about to do, and none of them were taking opium, which was supplied to NVA and Cong units to bolster courage before a battle. They'd brought few women along, so the men had to do most of their own chores. Discipline was good, he reported, and morale was high.

Not for long, Black thought happily, because he'd finally been promised air support.

He kept the volume on the single-sideband radio turned low and had to move close to the set when Buffalo Soldier called. It was his friend Larry. Two flights of tango thirty-fours were approaching their position.

Black could hear the distant drone of their reciprocal engines. T-34's, probably with Royal Laotian Air Force markings and piloted by American or Thai CIA contractors.

"Hotdog, suggest you button up and hunker down. They'll make a low pass or two, then start makin' crispy critters outa your vee-pand militia."

Which meant they'd come down low to spot the soldiers, then drop napalm. Black pressed the mike button twice. Message received.

The Yankee ten bunker was built on a slight knoll. They could see tree tops and little else, but none could resist the urge to watch. The engine noises grew louder. They spotted the first loose four-ship formation of propeller-driven aircraft a few kilometers to their west, turning toward them.

Yeah, he thought, and felt a small thrill.

A second flight appeared in the distance, flew closer, then settled into an orbit to wait their turn.

Two T-34's dropped lower and throttled back some as they approached.

Bam! Bam! Bam! Bam! Braaaa! Bam! Bam! Bam! Braaaaaa!

White puffs appeared in the sky near the low fliers. The prop-driven fighters began to twist and turn, but came on, ignoring the sparse 37mm burst and the few streams of tracers from 14.5mm and 12.7mm automatic weapons.

The two aircraft passed overhead, rocking their wings first to one side, then the other, to see better; then their engines roared louder and they began to climb. They'd obviously had a good look at the area, but Black was going to relay enemy positions via Buffalo Soldier anyway. Just to make sure. He lifted his mike and started to depress the switch.

A small streak of fire flashed through the sky, then another and another until four white plumes traced upward. One of the T-34's shuddered, and issued a stream of smoke.

What the hell! Black was still trying to comprehend what had happened when he saw the T-34 pitch nose-up and a shape drop away. A parachute blossomed. The T-34 tumbled to earth without dignity. A fireball erupted a couple of kilometers away where it crashed. A single, large cloud of oily black smoke drifted upward.

The chute was coming down much closer to them.

"Let's go," said Black, ready to retrieve the pilot.

The lieutenant raised a hand, watching the parachute. "Too many militia," he cautioned.

Black paused, agonized, then nodded agreement.

The figure dangling beneath the chute descended into the trees less than a kilometer distant. They heard loud shouts and several shots.

Sergeant Black got back onto the HF radio and told Buffalo Soldier about the aircraft being shot down.

"*Stand by,*" he was told. A few minutes later Larry came back on the air, keeping his calm. "*Could you tell what it was that got the tango three-four?*"

"*Rockets of some kind. Small, guided rockets. Only one out of four hit the aircraft.*"

He was staring out at the seven T-34's orbiting west of them. He wanted to speak directly to the pilots, but the aircraft didn't have HF, and his VHF hand-held radios were fixed on frequencies at the bottom of the band.

Black heard screams from the direction of the downed pilot. He recognized Thai words.

"*They've captured the pilot,*" he told Buffalo Soldier. "*Sounds like they're treating him pretty bad.*"

"*The other tango three-fours are going to RTB, Hotdog.*" Meaning they would return to their base.

"*We need the air support, Buffalo Soldier.*"

"*Not until they regroup and find out what it was that shot the bird down.*"

"*Whatever it was was pretty small, Buffalo Soldier. I figure if the T-34's release high, they'll be okay.*"

"*They're going to RTB, Hotdog.*"

"*Bullshit . . . we need 'em. The people up on top need 'em worse. I'll give coordinates of the vee-pand down here, and they can release high.*"

"*Sorry, Hotdog.*"

The engine sounds grew fainter.

Black was furious. "*Buffalo Soldier. Hotdog suggests you evacuate Yankee two-one.*"

"*Hotdog, I just got word from Papa Wolf. He wants you to*

*proceed on up to the top. We're gonna request some big-time
help to work over that area where you are now."*

Papa Wolf was the lieutenant colonel. He guessed that
the "big-time" help Larry spoke of meant Thuds or Phantoms, or even a B-52 strike. Black began to feel better, but
he was uneasy about going up the mountain, where they'd
be as trapped as the others there.

"Acknowledge, Hotdog," said Larry.

"Hotdog acknowledges." He paused. *"Tell Papa Wolf we
may not have much time unless you get us that air strike
ASAP."*

The voice on the other end changed. *"Papa Wolf here,
Hotdog. Go up and take a look at the situation. Will you have
to wait for darkness?"*

Black looked over at the lieutenant, who was listening intently. He shook his head.

"Negative," he told Papa Wolf.

*"Good. Give us a call after you get on top and take the
look. Buffalo Soldier out."*

Black saw that the lieutenant was already preparing the
men to move out, cleaning up the mess they'd made and
starting to tear down the HF radio.

He picked up the pretuned hand-held radio. *"Yankee
two-one, this is Yankee one-oh."*

He called for more than ten minutes before the guy on
top finally picked up.

"Yeah, go ahead." The voice sounded laconic and almost
sullen, which seemed odd after what Hotdog had just witnessed.

Black told him they'd be coming up the path, so to make
damn sure no one tried to blow them up. The guy didn't
sound happy about receiving visitors—but, then, he didn't
seem to be emotional about much of anything.

Fifteen minutes later they cautiously filtered out of the small
bunker, which was ripe from their accumulated odors. When
they were at the edge of the thicket, the lieutenant gave a
nod. Four Hotdogs moved quietly toward the soldiers manning the 12.7mm machine gun.

2130L—Trailer 5B, Takhli RTAFB, Thailand

GS-7 *Penny Dwight*

The time had come.

It was not a decision she made in the heat of one of their necking sessions, but while Dusty walked her from the O' Club to her trailer, as he'd done every night since she'd arrived. She'd known it before, when the men at the table began to talk about a pilot who'd been lost in a strafing pass. She'd regarded Dusty as he'd pursed his lips, listening to Billy Bowes describe the shoot-down, and she'd thought how tragic it would be if Dusty was never again to feel a woman's arms about him.

She'd wanted to reach out for him even then.

As they walked hand in hand to her trailer, she'd finished making up her mind to quit the waiting game. He deserved it. He'd put up with her delaying—she had put him off appropriately—and the diaphragm was securely in place.

When they arrived at the trailer, he paused, supposing they'd kiss like always, but she'd fished the key out of her purse on the walk over and purposefully continued up the steps to the door. Dusty cautiously followed. She unlocked the door and swung it open. Dusty didn't need to be asked. He stepped inside behind her, as if he'd done it before.

So confident, she thought.

"Welcome to my little home," she said, finding the lamp chain and switching it on. The overhead was too bright. He looked around—examined a set of paintings on silk she'd bought at the Ta Khli marketplace.

"I'd serve you a drink, but I don't keep anything here." She was increasingly apprehensive. Dusty still didn't speak. He nodded, almost abstractly. Penny felt a flutter in her breast. Was he even interested?

She motioned at the small table and chair. "Did you want to sit?"

He continued to examine the paintings. "Is that what you want to do?" Dusty's voice was lower than normal—thicker? Her heart began to pound, and she had trouble answering.

He smiled and came to her, and cupped her face lightly in his hands, looking intently, as if he could peer inside and examine her thoughts. She closed her eyes as he kissed her.

Not a soul-kiss, where a guy tried to push his tongue down your throat—just a long, pleasant one, the kind he could give her if they were in a room full of people. But it was nice—so nice that the heat grew in her—and somehow she knew it was going to be very different this time.

She was the one who sighed and pulled his head down with all her strength, as if she wanted to devour him. Dusty continued the kiss, and she wanted him to keep it up as long as she lived. His hands moved over her body—first over her back and she trembled—lower until he gently grasped her buttocks and sounds emerged from her throat that she couldn't control. She moved back slightly so he could run his hands over her breasts, then down, and she cried out as they neared . . . she could feel the moisture welling . . . he pressed lightly there.

It was not at all like the other times.

Dusty gently laid her on the bed . . . did he lift her?—she wasn't sure. She opened her eyes ever so slightly and caught a breath as he moved onto the bed, his face close, staring into her mind again and continuing to move his hands in ways she hoped would never cease.

He didn't ask if she was ready or what she wanted. Dusty knew. He was in total control. He spoke only with those wonderful hazel eyes, and her mind cried out *yes*. He moved away and began to remove his clothing, and as soon as she saw what he was doing, she also began to disrobe.

Could he hear her breathing like a freight train? Modesty left her. She didn't care if he thought her anxious. She felt no shame that she was suddenly so easy. She only wanted . . .

Dusty was pulling off his final vestige of clothing, also unembarrassed, still smiling. She looked, paused, and bit her lip when she took in the vision of his body, and then lower, to his erection. Oh, God, he was beautiful. He came to her and whispered endearments as he helped with her bra and panties, necessary because she was trembling and inexplicably weak.

He ran his hands over her again, lightly, and electricity passed from them into her bare skin. Penny couldn't focus her thoughts on his words, but they weren't the kind that needed response. He didn't hurry, seemed to have no urgency about him, but continued to caress and kiss and tell her of her freshness and beauty. He moved close, loomed over her. Looked at her eyes and kissed her forehead as she felt him enter, so slightly, then pause, then push gently.

It was maddening! She cried out, couldn't restrain herself from arching up, urging him farther into her. He kissed her again—another slow one like before—and pressed deeper. She began to tremble and cry. Suddenly there was an incredible tingling, a warmth more wonderful than any she had ever felt, spreading from her breasts to somewhere special and deep inside. There were animal sounds in the trailer—her own?—and she heard the crescendo growing, wavering as if from some distant source. He was moving, fully inserted, and began a slow, maddening rhythm.

Dusty-y-y! She clasped her arms around his shoulders, wanting to pull him entirely into her. Heat continued to build and she gasped at the sensation, then began to sob. He continued the rhythm, unheeding. She pulled at him with one clawed hand, pressed the other fist into her mouth as she cried out. He stiffened and groaned, and they strained together to make the union as tight as possible. Her crying ended, replaced by a shrill hiss.

Dusty slowly relaxed, then blew a long, shuddering breath. "It was good," he murmured.

She wanted to answer, "It was wonderful," but her voice failed.

They lay in place, hardly moving, and she felt contentment she'd never before experienced. She stroked his chest with a light touch. Was this love—when you could share so completely?

Penny found her voice. "I want you to teach me," she whispered. She knew there were things men liked from women, things her friends never talked about directly when they spoke about men, and she desperately wanted to please him. "Tell me what you like."

"I liked what we just did."

"I want you to be happy, Dusty."

"I am."

She almost told him she loved him, but stopped herself. She didn't know that and certainly didn't want to frighten him away. He was a devout bachelor, Roger Hamlin had warned, and she knew not to make him feel threatened.

"There's one thing," he said softly. He explained, and she

whispered she'd try, but he'd have to guide her. A wave of apprehension swept over her, and she wondered if she could really do it, whether she wouldn't get sick to her stomach . . . and what he'd think of her afterward.

A few minutes later, when their breathing was calmer and she could feel that he was stirring inside her, she took a breath of resolve, wriggled free when he rolled onto his back, and did not delay, lest she became so embarrassed it would be impossible. She kissed his chest, lingered there, then traced lower with her tongue. She felt shy as she continued, but he whispered instructions and she complied.

In the next minutes Penny learned more about pleasing a man than she'd ever imagined in her nightly showers. She became increasingly intrigued as she worked, wielding fingers, tongue, and mouth with increasing skill. He panted louder, whispering endearments and encouragement. She labored tirelessly, relentlessly, and grew increasingly excited as she discovered that sexual gratification came not only from physical contact, but also from the responses of a mate.

Penny was surprised when Dusty—who she'd felt would be the one to teach her—became so aroused that he whimpered and thrashed, grew taut as a bow. Just as he'd done with her, she now controlled his pleasure. She learned to bring him to the edge of a precipice, to back off and let the ecstasy dwindle, then to subtly build the fire once more.

Some instinct told her it was time. She again built him slowly and this time continued as he began to moan, quiver, and tense. It came as no surprise when his liquid flowed. She tasted him, then drew back and finished with her hand, unembarrassed, staring happily in the dim lamplight at her accomplishment.

Dusty quietly stroked her hair as she cleaned him with a towel she'd left under the pillow . . . in case. "God, that was great," he whispered.

Did he think she was through with him?

She bent and began again, although he grunted, "No more." She was gentle, for he'd become sensitive—but she had no intention of stopping until she learned more. Dusty whispered more urgently for her to stop. She paused, lifted her eyes, and tried to focus on his face, then returned to her gentle labor. There was so much to learn—and she was thoroughly enjoying . . .

Control?

She continued to please him despite his weakening protests. A few minutes later he pulled her up and they made love.

When Dusty left the trailer, saying he had to get up early to fly, he promised to drop by her office after he landed. There was a new tone in his voice, an intimacy.

"Don't tell anyone about . . . ," she'd started to whisper, but he was gone. It was a thing with her, that others might think her promiscuous. Old memories.

Penny lay still for a while, thinking about the evening. She smiled, spread her arms, and stretched deliciously, feeling incredibly wise and utterly fulfilled. She stood on wobbly legs and endured a wave of light-headedness, then went into the bathroom to shower. As she adjusted the water flow, the thrill rushed through her again, as if he were there. Tomorrow night she'd learn even more about men, and Captain Dusty Fields in particular.

Did she love him? she wondered. Penny thought so, but it didn't matter. Whatever it was they shared, she wanted to continue. Before she saw him tomorrow night, she planned to have her hair cut; Dusty had hinted she'd look great in a pageboy style—and watch her posture; Dusty said he was worried about her back, because she slumped too much. A gentle way of telling her. She wanted to please him. She smiled again, thinking she'd certainly shown him that.

2355L—BRL TACAN, Laos

Sergeant Black

The trek to the top had taken more than an hour. The path had been relatively steep at the bottom, but quickly narrowed and became so vertical, they'd had to climb on all fours. After a kilometer the terrain abruptly flattened, and they'd passed a grassy area with a tattered wind sock—an airstrip to enable short-takeoff-and-landing (STOL) aircraft to bring in supplies. Beyond the small airstrip the path widened, but quickly became steep once more.

Twice the Hotdog soldier on point had stopped abruptly, and Black had stepped forward and made a loud query in Yard language. After a shrill response they'd continued, both times past stretches of road with sheer drop-offs, then past quiet Montagnards with faces of stone. Those were obviously the positions where explosives had been planted.

They'd found the top of the mountain to be relatively flat, as Black had been briefed. Farthest south and lowest on the mesa top was the small Montagnard settlement, a thatch hut and four old olive-drab squad tents, where scrawny chickens pecked hopefully in the dirt and skinny dogs cringed and bared teeth at the newcomers. Things hadn't looked right. The children had been too quiet, the faces of the bare-breasted Yard women too stoic. Several men had examined them without smiles.

They know what's gathering below, was Black's thought.

The highest point was near the opposite, northern end of the oblong mesa, and the air-nav station antenna and boxlike building were there. Immediately south of the TACAN, on a slight slope, were two small prefab buildings. Not far from them was a tremendous trash heap, a stack of barrels, and a generator shack with a two-banger diesel engine chugging noisily inside. Large electrical leads were strung to the TACAN, smaller ones to the buildings.

The first prefab he'd checked was stacked high with boxes of provisions. In the second, along with a malfunctioning and constantly whining air conditioner, Black had found an American. He'd stood unsteadily beside a table littered with paperback books, cans full of smashed-out cigarettes, and dirty dishes. His mouth sagged as he returned Black's stare.

He was fat, with a scraggly beard, wore only thongs, undershorts, and a bulging, dirty T-shirt, and looked to be in tune with the total mess of the place. When Black had stepped farther inside, a naked Yard woman sat up on the lone cot, stared and blinked for a moment, then halfheartedly reached onto the floor for her wrapabout skirt.

"Hiya," the droopy-eyed contractor had said, and shoved out his hand. "M'name's Buddy Canepa." The room smelled of booze and stank of another sharp order that Black recognized.

Canepa's eyes had been bloodshot, his breath rotten, and he'd been so stoned that he couldn't function.

Black had reached over and stubbed out the joint burning in the ashtray, and Canepa's eyes followed his movements as if he were observing, but was neither surprised nor in sync with reality. He'd frowned when Black screwed the top onto an opened bottle of Jack Daniel's.

They'd arrived on the mesa at 1355 hours. At 1405 Black had entered the man's shack. By 1410 he'd cleared the room of booze and given a sack of marijuana to the lieutenant for disposal. At 1440 he'd had the battery connected and the antenna strung, and was on the radio speaking with Larry at Buffalo Soldier, and was about to tell him what he'd found when a second American hobbled painfully into the room, held upright by a Yard tribesman. The Yard had deposited him into a nearby chair.

"Stand by for a few minutes, Buffalo Soldier," he'd told Larry.

This guy was small and wiry, and had an olive-drab bandage wrapped around his bare midriff. He'd regarded Black bleakly. "So they sent you anyway," he'd said. "I told 'em to keep you and your men down below, so you could tell us what's going on down there."

"Who're you?" Black had asked.

"Just call me Jones. I'd've met you when you arrived, but I was busy running a check on the TACAN equipment."

He'd groaned a bit as he moved to a more comfortable sitting position.

Black had nodded at his wound. "What happened?"

"Yesterday morning the bad guys let off a couple of artillery rounds, just to set up their range, I guess. First damned round went off about twenty yards away and I got hit by shrapnel."

He'd been pasty-faced and did not look well at all.

"Bad?"

Jones had drawn a painful breath. "Think they got a lung. Gets messy when I cough."

"You in charge here?"

"Yeah." He'd grimaced with pain. "Been here for the past year, off and on."

Black had nodded at Buddy Canepa. "Him?"

"They sent him to take over when I leave next month.

Dumb shit's been half-drunk since he arrived, and when they started shelling, he jumped the rest of the way in the bottle." Jones had grunted with another pain, then spoke sharply to the woman in her language. She'd hurried out of the shack. "Silly shit's promised her half the world, and she believes him."

Canepa had stumbled to the side of the room and tried to pull on a pair of filthy walking shorts. Black eyed him as he lurched around, one leg in the shorts, trying to remain upright. "You let him get away with all this shit? Smokin' dope and acting like Lord Jim?"

When Buddy Canepa had succeeded with the walking shorts, he regarded Black, waving a screw-on cap in his unsteady hand. "Where's my bottle?"

"We get some jewels sometimes." Jones had eyed Canepa with great distaste. "Hope the dumb fuck drinks himself to death. I let Vientiane know he's a loser, but he's supposed to be good with the equipment, so they wanted me to try him for another week. Now he's stuck here with the rest of us."

Black had looked around the disheveled room. "Where do *you* live?"

"Out at the other end of the Yard village. I gave him the shack here so he could monitor for radio calls and stay out of my way."

"How are the Yards?"

Jones had grown increasing weak, and his voice was dwindling. "Good. They're tough and ready to fight. Vientiane shoulda pulled the women off the hill, though." He'd described the locations of things on the mountaintop: the TACAN, the Yard village, a small munitions bunker, and the maintenance-and-supply building.

"You're lucky you made it up the mountain in one piece," Jones had added after a long grimace. "Canepa almost forgot to tell me you called. The Yards would've blown the road, and you with it, if I hadn't told 'em about you coming up."

"Any way we can get off the hill without using the road?"

Black had to wait a long while as Jones endured a series of coughing spasms that released bright blood onto his hands. "Don't think so," he'd finally said. "There was a path on the north side, but I had the Yards blow it."

Black had sent the lieutenant and another Hotdog to investigate.

"I'd better call in to Buffalo Soldier," he'd told Jones, who motioned weakly to the Yard tribesman to take him back outside. This time it took two of them to support him.

As he spoke on the radio, Black had found himself increasingly upset, first at Larry, then at Papa Wolf, who'd tried to calm him.

"Either get us the air strike or start thinking about getting us out of here," Black had urged. *"I don't feel good about holding this place."*

Papa Wolf said they had their hands full of emergency requests, most of them nearer home base. The big offensive they'd expected for the past month was under way. Vientiane Control had responsibility for protecting the nav site, knew they had a badly wounded man there, and had promised relief.

Black sighed as he ceased his transmission, wondering how long they had.

Vientiane Control was run by contractors who coordinated other contractors' Pilatus, T-34, C-130, C-123, and helo aircraft, but seldom with the U.S. Air Force, whom Black desperately wanted to become involved.

Shortly after Black had signed off, the lieutenant had come in and told him he'd posted men with radios at strategic points overlooking the jungle. He said there was movement. More militia were arriving, as many as they'd seen and counted before.

That meant there were 600 men below. Black had gotten back onto the radio and told that to Larry at Buffalo Soldier. *"Put Papa Wolf back on,"* he'd said.

When the lieutenant colonel had come back on, Black repeated what he'd told Larry. *"We gotta get air support in here ASAP, sir. There's a battalion of militia down there."*

"We're working on it, Hotdog. We got lots of business right now, and there's the area-of-responsibility problem with Vientiane. I'm working it with MAC-SOG, but they're swamped."

"The Viets were likely just waiting for the reinforcements, and now they're here. If they're not going to send air strikes, Vientiane better think of evacuating."

"We've already relayed that suggestion."

"What about the big-time support you promised?" Black had reminded him.

"There's the coordination problems with Vientiane, Hotdog, and then there's the thing about losing the tango three-four." They'd signed off on that discouraging note.

Black had gone out and found Canepa sweet-talking the Yard woman. "Get your ass back in there and contact Vientiane Control," he'd told him. "Tell 'em to pull us out of here ASAP."

Canepa had mumbled his agreement, so Black left for another look at the perimeter.

When darkness had fallen, Sergeant Black's mood wasn't improved. The lieutenant had reported that the second trail down the mountain, the one Jones had ordered blown, was now a sheer drop-off. Black had told him to set up more booby traps around the perimeter using seismic mines they'd found stored in the ammo bunker near the Yard village, and gathered the Yards together to tell them to keep the kids away from the mines.

He'd asked how they were organized to fight if the Viets made it up the mountainside.

Each man had his assigned task, and they were equipped with M-16's, but Black knew it would be a hopeless drill to try to fight off that many soldiers. It hadn't helped his disposition when Buddy Canepa emerged from the shack long enough to cajole the Yard woman into going inside.

It had been a shitty day followed by a shittier evening, Black thought. When he checked on Jones, he found him resting fitfully, his breathing ragged and uneven. Two Yard men were hunkered nearby, regarding Jones closely with their stoic expressions. A death watch.

Black left them, wondering what he was into. A while later things grew intolerable when Black was walking around in the dark, and lights came on inside the shack. He stormed in to find Canepa on his feet, yawning and stretching. He'd put on a pair of cleaner Bermuda shorts.

"Turn off the fucking lights!"

Canepa gave him a puzzled look. "Why?"

"Jesus! Turn off the fucking light so the fucking Viets won't shoot your fucking ass off with the fucking howitzers they've got at the bottom of the fucking mountain."

Canepa shrugged, still floating. "They can't see us. We're too far from the sides."

Black didn't bother to point out that the militia would have men posted on surrounding mountains to watch them. He motioned at the woman, then the door. "Go," he told her in Yard. "Go back to your people and do not come back here."

She showed no emotion as she departed.

"Hey!" shouted Canepa. "Where you going?"

Black closed the door behind her and turned an exasperated eye on the contractor. "There's six hundred North Viets down below and they're going to skinny up this mountain, Canepa. Then they're going to kill everything that's up here, and that includes you."

Canepa's voice was confident. "They'll take me out before that happens."

"They?"

"Jones told me that's in the site instructions. We call for evacuation and they come get us."

"Did you see the NVA shoot down the fucking T-34 this morning? The pilot worked for the same people you do. They can't get in here."

Buddy Canepa trembled noticeably. "Jones said they're sending me home next week."

Black sighed. It was hard to get through to him. "This place isn't going to *be* here in another week. It *may* not be here in another couple of hours."

"They'll get me out," the contractor nodded, reassuring himself.

Black went over and, one by one, began to turn off lights.

"Anyway," Canepa said in the gloom, "you're here now, aren't you?"

Black wondered where they'd dug up this character, who was fast eroding his already mediocre image of CIA contractors. He left a single hooded lamp burning at the desk. "Okay, what kind of comm gear you got?"

Buddy Canepa's brow furrowed. "Ask Jones."

"Jones is dying, for crap's sake. I don't think he can even talk anymore."

Canepa bit his lip and his eyes walled.

"Now . . . what kind of radios have you got?"

Canepa pointed out the Handie-Talkie he'd spoken to

Black on, then a set up on the desk beside Black's directional rig. "That's preset to Vientiane Control. We check in once a day, or when we've got an emergency." It was an expensive Hallicrafter civilian model. The thing was turned off, for Christ's sake. Black switched it on and let it warm up.

"Did you call Vientiane like I told you?"

Canepa hedged, and Black knew he had not. "Before he got hurt, Jones told Vientiane to get us out. They said to sit tight, that they'd send in fighters to knock out the troops."

"Did Jones talk to 'em today?"

Buddy's face grew troubled as he tried to remember. "I guess he told me to," he finally mumbled. "After you said you were coming up the mountain, I guess I figured you'd take over that kind of thing."

"Well Mr. Canepa, we are in deep shit. If there's any way to get our asses out of here, you better think of it."

Canepa sat at the desk. "I'll give Vientiane a call."

Vientiane was quick to respond. *"Roger, Yankee two-one, we've been trying to contact you all day."*

Canepa scratched his chest, glanced at Black, and managed something about the radio being fucked up.

"Are you okay?"

"You better come and get me out." His voice was plaintive.

"Is Hotdog on site?"

"Yeah," Canepa said.

There was a pause before Vientiane Control came back on. *"We're going to try for another air strike tomorrow, but it's looking iffy."*

Black thought about that, then pushed Buddy Canepa aside and took the mike. *"This is Hotdog leader. We need air now. Right now."*

"No way we can do anything tonight. Tomorrow's the earliest. This whole country's coming unglued, Hotdog."

"You gonna give us something worthwhile, or use tango three-fours again."

Vientiane Control's voice was sad. *"You'll get what we can spare, Hotdog. We've got priorities. You're not the only ones in trouble, and the pilots are concerned about the rockets."*

"How about some fast movers? Those were dinky little

rockets. They couldn't reach a fast mover, if he was to release up high." Black didn't think so anyway.

"You're talking to the wrong people if you want fast movers. It's going to be hard to get anyone to go back after what happened there this morning, but we'll try."

Black was increasingly exasperated. *"Ask the fast movers, for crap's sake."*

A pause. *"They're out of our channel of authority, Hotdog. And don't try calling 'em on the UHF."*

Black turned to Canepa. "You've got a UHF radio?" he said.

Canepa frowned. "Maybe. There's more radios. I told the woman to put 'em in the storage shed."

Black spoke to Vientiane. *"This is Hotdog. You'd better start evacuating these people."*

"We're waiting for authority to . . . stand by." Vientiane gave them another long pause. *"Hotdog, I just got authority to pull you. Problem is it won't be until late tomorrow. Think you can hold out until then?"*

"We can hold out until the North Viets down below get serious, no longer."

"Give us a call in the morning."

"If we're still here." Black signed off, cursed a bit, then grabbed a flashlight off the table, stomped angrily to the door, and went outside.

The lieutenant joined him as he rummaged through the mess in the storage shed, looking for the UHF radio. "We found a way down," the lieutenant said in Viet. "Down the west side."

"That just means there's another way for the militia to get up here," Black growled.

"I don't think so. It is so steep we will have to use ropes. We can go down but not up."

"Are the Viets guarding it?"

"There is a communications platoon at the bottom. We must be very quiet."

"Keep planting the mines. Put them as far down the slopes as you can."

"Mebbe beddah we leaf dis place, bruddah." The lieutenant switched to the island pidgin Black had taught them in frivolous moments.

"Just get the booby traps set up. We've got to hold the

Viets off as long as we can. They are going to try to get everyone out of here tomorrow evening."

He found a hand-held UHF radio in a box marked, Pork & Beans. He tested it, then began a search for extra batteries. *Fuck Vientiane.* He'd made up his mind to contact the next group of fighters that passed overhead. If he could get Air Force fast movers to give him a strike on the Viets, it would be safer for the contractors to bring in a STOL cargo plane to get everyone out.

"Mebbe we beddah leaf, bruddah." The lieutenant, like most Viets, North and South, didn't give a damn about Montagnards. "Mebbe too lade, we waid 'round."

Black found the batteries. A box of six. "Maybe," he agreed. "Now go finish with the booby traps."

CHAPTER FIFTEEN

Wednesday, November 29th, 0600 Local—Over Laos

Lieutenant Colonel Yank Donovan

The strike was to be a straightforward one, directly across the heart of the Red River Valley to the big storage area at Gia Thuong, where three weeks earlier Korat had bombed and caused tremendous secondary explosions. Reconnaissance photos showed renewed activity there.

Yank thought it was stupid to think the gomers would put their eggs back in the same basket. They'd find nothing at Gia Thuong. Yet when his squadron was tasked to provide pilots and aircraft for the effort, Yank had placed himself on the schedule to lead the effort.

They'd be going to downtown Hanoi, and it would be another dangerous one. He was mission commander, Bear Force leader, and his flight would be first on target. They were the chopper flight, their task to release CBU-24 cluster bombs on gun emplacements and suppress the flak for the others who followed.

Lieutenant Smith was flying on Yank's wing. Bear three was Captain Fields, a flight commander from Lucky Anderson's 333rd squadron. Captain Hamlin flew on Dusty's wing. They were all steady and experienced combat pilots. It was a good group, Donovan thought. He could concentrate his concerns on the remainder of the formation.

The air refueling went as planned, without delays caused by an anxious pilot or overeager boom operator. The aircraft all seemed to be in good enough condition, so he sent home the two airborne spares that tagged along as far as the tanker.

Good so far.

The flight leg from tanker drop-off toward the Channel 97 TACAN was quiet. The pilots mulled over their individual beliefs, the religious said their prayers, and everyone mentally went through their emergency procedures in case something went wrong.

Yank Donovan's mind was busy with other things— twinges of worry that he tried to relegate to the back of his consciousness. Not about his own abilities or safety, of course. Those were handled by his experienced and orderly approach to flying. Yet apprehension was gathering in the pit of his stomach like a heavy lump of clay.

It concerned others; the men in his squadron, the pilots in the strike force he was leading. The feeling was uncharacteristic for Yank, who wasn't accustomed to giving much of a damn about anyone. He tried very hard to mask it from others. It was confusing enough to himself, and hadn't been helped by the telephone call from Colonel Tom Lyons the previous evening.

.

He'd learned his detachment—not to worry about others— as a boy in Chicago. His pa had been a burly, pleasant construction worker who'd immigrated from Ireland as a young man and was so proud of his new country he'd been given the nickname "Yank" by his Irish friends. When his son was born, he immediately changed it to Big Yank, and the baby—Little Yank, of course. From his earliest memories Big Yank had been a union man, and sometime enforcer of his local's rules. In Chicago it wasn't whether a job would be accomplished using men from the steelworkers union—they all were; it was whether they'd use the right local.

His mother had been beautiful, and Big Yank squired her to night clubs with pride and a glare for any man who looked too long. She talked about that after he was gone, how Big Yank was loving and protective and how they'd dance until early morning. It was on one of those evenings that his father had faced off against too goons who'd tried to harass him for working a job they felt was reserved for their local. He was used to such badgering and held his peace until they made the mistake of calling his wife a slut. He'd put both of them in the hospital, one with a broken arm and concussion, the other with crushed ribs. Big Yank was tough as a ball-peen hammer, but he was killed the next week on the job, falling seventeen stories in the cab of a poorly secured overhead crane. The family was left with a hefty stack of bills and a few thousand dollars of union insurance. His mother was distraught.

Yank's mother might have been flawlessly beautiful and perfect in many ways, but she wasn't trained to make a living in the big world. When the last family members had left after the funeral, she'd brooded and hardly left the apartment for more than a month. Several times twelve-year-old Yank had told her not to worry, that he'd get a job and make enough money so she and his four-year-old sister wouldn't have to worry. She'd say that was sweet of him and then cry and drink more gin.

Finally she started to go out, leaving Yank to watch over his sister for several hours each night. At first his mother had seemed nervous about it, but as the months passed, she reverted to her smiling, happy, and loving self. Then she began to stay out all night, not returning until Yank was about to leave for school. On Saturdays and Sundays she often wouldn't show up until noon. She'd also developed a new self-confidence that he'd never before seen in her. There was no more worrying about money. They moved into an upscale town home, where his mother spent a lot of time in her bedroom on the phone.

Yank had asked no questions. He earned good grades at school and was popular among his classmates, including the prettiest girls.

One blustery day when Yank was fifteen years old, his mother didn't return home until much later than normal, and when she did, there were reporters waiting. She called him to her and quietly told him he must be very strong, because people were going to say bad things about her.

A page-three *Tribune* article told how Shaleen Donovan, aka O'Brien, was operating one of the most successful call-girl rings in Chicago's recent history, sanctioned and protected by unnamed union officials with links to organized crime.

Yank's shame was overpowering. His girlfriend dropped him like a hot rock. Bullies at school made snide remarks, and there was relentless snickering behind his back. His sister often came home early from grade school crying, because older girls made fun of her and boys would corner her, pull up her dress and ask if she was a whore like her mother.

They were sent to private schools—his sister to a local parochial school, which brooked no nonsense among the students; Yank to a military preparatory academy in Colorado, which he'd selected because of those offered, it was farthest from Chicago—and from the source of his shame.

His mother was obviously doing well at her chosen trade once more, for she'd moved into an even larger town home, one complete with a full-time nanny to watch over his sister. Yank visited very seldom. He kept to himself at the academy and, when pressed, told other student-cadets that his parents were dead. When his mother visited, he said she was his aunt.

Before he'd been smashed to pulp, Big Yank had told him to always learn something from life's experiences, good and bad. During his teen years Yank discovered a few big ones.

He had an innate understanding of logic. Mathematics and physics were easy, for they entailed numerical solutions and comprehensible laws. English and the social studies were boring and mundane subjects to endure, but he had no trouble developing thorough understandings of chemistry, calculus, and electronics. At age seventeen his application was accepted to attend the University of Colorado at Boulder. It was there that he became interested in the world of flight, for the many and complex laws governing that wonder of nature intrigued him more than any other field. He joined the Air Force ROTC program. All the while the money continued coming in from Chicago, dutifully sent by the woman he described as his aunt, and whom he'd asked please not to visit.

It was during his second year at Colorado that he'd met

Tom Lyons, a senior who he later found had been suspended from Princeton for cheating. Tom was from an old, filthy-rich, and respectable Denver family, and after a few weeks at Boulder, he inexplicably tried to befriend Donovan. Yank remained a loner and did not reciprocate.

Lyons said he needed help on an upcoming test. The subject was structural physics, which was incomprehensible to him and a snap for Donovan. When Yank declined, Lyons hadn't seemed angry. Two days later Yank went to his dorm room to find a plain envelope with his name printed on the outside. It contained a typed article to be provided to the campus newspaper, about an undergraduate student whose mother was one of the most infamous madams in the Midwest. Names were omitted from the note.

Yank helped with the tutoring, and somehow got Lyons through his finals. When they parted, he'd felt it was unlikely he'd ever see Tom again, and rested easier. During his final two years Yank successfully maintained anonymity.

He'd learned something that time too.

Upon graduation he'd gone into the Air Force as a second lieutenant and forevermore severed his ties with Chicago. Preflight training had been a drag, but soon after Yank reported to Laredo AFB for flight school, he'd discovered what he'd been put upon earth for. He'd excelled at both academics and flying. Flight skills were the great equalizers. Little mattered to the instructors except how well you could interpret instruments and control a mass of aluminum, wire, and Plexiglas through the proper airspace. He'd nursed the propeller-driven trainers about the sky with skill, soaking up every tidbit of knowledge the instructors had to offer. A natural, they'd called him. He'd graduated at the top of his class of forty-nine pilots in 1953, during the final days of the Korean War. Before he reported to his next assignment, to upgrade into jets, the war had wound down to a militarily unsatisfying stalemate.

Yank's personal world had been dramatically changed when he'd pinned on the sliver wings. He'd been transformed into a professional, whose potential was bounded only by his abilities. Yet he couldn't change his basic being and did not try to shake off the mantle of suspicion and selfishness that had armored him.

He'd vigorously set about securing his niche, flying

F-94's, then F-89 Scorpions, and finally F-102 Deuces for
Air Defense Command, all with excellence. In 1961, as a
captain, he'd won the prestigious William Tell Trophy,
ADC's intercept profile and missile marksmanship competition, held at Tyndall Air Force Base in Florida. That same
year he'd taken a wife.

It was decreed by the Air Force that to rise in rank one
must have a spouse, and that she must be socially acceptable. At age twenty-eight he'd carefully selected, then easily
won, a quiet, rather plain southern girl, mindful of her place
and content to remain in the background. From the first
their household revolved about Yank's career. There were no
children. He treated her well enough, but refused to share
privacies, such as the manner of the death of his parents.

The Air Force approved his application to return to the
University of Colorado to earn his master of science degree
in aeronautical engineering, and upon graduation Yank upgraded into F-105's. The change of missions, from firing
missiles at incoming Russian bombers to dropping bombs,
came easy for him, and he'd quickly become known as a superb dive-bomber and gunnery master. After an operational
tour at Yokota, Japan, he'd returned to McConnell AFB in
Kansas to introduce other pilots to the Thud. By then he
was sure that he was the best.

Yank prided himself on needing no one, relying solely on
his wiles and abilities to succeed within the system. He suffered a few friendships with subordinates who were awed by
his flying achievements, and with selected senior officers
who could help him win promotions. He avoided association
with colleagues who were in competition. He remained a
loner.

Upon his arrival at Takhli, the ghosts returned to Yank's
life, for one of the first men he met was Tom Lyons, who
greeted him as if they'd been college buddies.

Lyons hadn't mentioned the ghosts then, but during the
previous evening's telephone conversation he'd made a
poorly veiled reference—how difficult it was to make rank
these days, how the slightest scandal could ruin a man's career. He'd said that since he was now on the I.G. team, he'd
expect word about any screwups Yank saw at Takhli, and
gave him his phone number at Hickam. He said he'd be
traveling often to the combat zone and would stay in touch.

• • •

That conversation had been troubling Yank.

Neither could he reconcile his growing inner turmoil as the strike force proceeded toward the Hanoi target and the danger waiting there. They were not far from the Channel 97 TACAN, and the North Vietnamese border lay just beyond. He found it hard to believe he was worrying about others—the men of his squadron, the pilots in this strike force who relied on his leadership. Yet he'd done just that since watching Captain Ron Wilshire smack into the ground. Then there'd been others, and he'd learned how easily lives were snuffed out. Young men, good men, bastards, snivelers, weaklings, or heroes—little of that seemed to matter. It was as if a roulette wheel turned and their time arrived.

He'd seen men die. One in pilot training school at Laredo when a student had come in on his solo flight and become spatially disoriented on landing, and another on the McConnell gunnery range when a pilot had flown too low on a strafe pass and hit the ground. But those he'd rationalized by knowing the pilots had fucked up and more or less killed themselves. These seemed different—and had less to do with flying skill than with beating the odds.

Like two weeks before, when one of his pilots had been flying in the pod formation and the SAM had selected him to kill. An unlucky spin of the wheel. Another letter to write to a wife, that one twenty years old and five months pregnant. The young pilot had been especially nervous the previous evening. Did he somehow know it was his turn? He'd come to that conclusion.

He looked out and scanned the pilots in the closest airplanes. If his theory was right, they'd all come home today. The members of Bear flight had been jovial the previous night and businesslike during the early-morning briefing. None had appeared uptight.

Since coming up with his theory that the guys who were sad the night before were the ones who bought the farm the next day, he'd been watching the young pilots closer—to either prove or to dispel the notion. Dusty Fields had been the most cheerful of the lot at the mission briefing. Yank liked the brash, yet soft-spoken young captain from Lucky Anderson's squadron, and the previous night had watched

him lift a few beers with his guitar-playing buddy until the
wing commander's secretary arrived.

*"Airplanes approaching Channel Ninety-seven TACAN,
this is Hotdog,"* came a scratchy call over the emergency
guard channel.

Yank frowned, wondering who could be calling and
whether he should answer.

*"This is Hotdog, Air Force. We're in dire need of air sup-
port down here."*

"Hotdog, this is Bear Force leader," Yank finally replied.
"What's your location?"

*"Hotdog is at Channel Ninety-seven. Request fast-mover
air support. We're estimating more than six hundred North
Viets on the southern and eastern sides of the mountain."*

Yank wondered again. *"You working with an airborne
FAC, Hotdog?"* Yank was referring to a forward air controller
in a spotter airplane, like an O-1 Birddog, to point out targets and manage the strike.

*"Negative, Bear leader. We had tango thirty-fours in here
yesterday, but one of 'em had a problem with a North Viet
guided rocket, so I doubt they'd send us an airborne FAC.
We sure as hell need air support, though. Got a bunch of
good targets down here."*

"You say you've got SAMs in the area?" Yank asked incredulously.

*"Dunno what they are, but one of 'em knocked down a
T-34. I don't think they'll be a problem, as long as you release
high. Looked like it was a short-range missile."*

"Stand by, Hotdog."

Donovan switched to enroute frequency, puzzled by the
call. *"This is Bear Force leader,"* he announced. *"Anyone
know anything about someone with the call sign Hotdog in
this area?"*

He was answered by silence.

The bearing needle swung about as the formation passed
over Channel 97. Donovan led the force into an orbit
around the TACAN, then called that he was going off frequency and dialed in the airborne command post controlling
the area.

"Cricket, this is Bear Force leader," he called.

Cricket responded.

"You know anything about someone called Hotdog down at Channel Ninety-seven TACAN?"

Cricket told him to stand by. Thirty seconds later Cricket said they had no idea who he could be talking about. *"That's not a known radio call sign, Bear Force leader."*

"What's the call sign of the people manning Channel Ninety-seven?" he asked. He would talk to the proper guys and find out what was going on.

Cricket couldn't answer his question. *"Suggest you proceed with your mission, Bear."*

"Sounds like an American voice," Yank argued, *"and he says they're in trouble."*

"Perhaps you should contact Red Crown," replied Cricket.

Cricket was supposed to handle the area they were presently in. Red Crown was the shipborne command post responsible for alpha strikes into pack six.

Yank thought hard, then released a pent breath. *"Bear lead requests that you find out who Hotdog is, Cricket."*

Cricket came back on the air, the voice more sure than before. *"Bear, Cricket has been advised by Red Crown that you should ignore the radio call and proceed with your mission."*

"Cricket, is this Hotdog an American?"

"Cricket is out."

Yank muttered some choice words about the Cricket controller as he switched back to the enroute frequency. Before he could check in, Hotdog called and again requested air support.

"We were ordered to continue with our mission, Hotdog," Yank radioed. *"I'll give you a call on our way out. In the meanwhile, try to get in touch with a FAC or someone and convince 'em you're real."*

"Never mind, Bear leader." Hotdog's voice sounded weary. *"Hotdog's out."*

Yank rolled out on their preplanned easterly heading, shepherding his force toward the target. As he visually checked the big formation over, Yank wondered what the hell the call had been about. He had a nagging suspicion that Hotdog was indeed real, and in trouble. He decided to check it out further when he got back on the ground at Takhli, and scribbled a note to himself.

They entered North Vietnamese airspace.

"This is Bear Force leader. Green 'em up and check your music's in standby."

One by one his flight, then the other flights in the sixteen-ship formation, checked in and told him they were ready to fight, and that their ECM switches were in the ready position.

A couple of minutes later, when they were over the high green-clad mountains of North Vietnam, he began a very slow descent and called for the force to turn their music on. Static from the jamming pods made the RHAW receivers hiss, and their CRTs half fill with electronic grass. Yank turned the RHAW audio down and checked the green light on the lower right panel, showing that his ECM pod was indeed operating.

The Wild Weasels, call sign Kingfish, were ranging a few miles in front of the strike force and called a SAM site near the Red River. *"Be on the lookout when you go by, Bear Force,"* radioed Kingfish lead.

Yank clicked the radio button twice, giving him a "yes" answer. He liked to maintain as much radio silence as possible.

As they crossed the Red, Captain Dusty Fields called a SAM launch from their ten o'clock position.

"Check that your music's on and hold your positions," Yank cautioned.

He found the missiles visually and watched as the first stage boosters dropped away, leaving fiery trails as they fell to earth. The SAMs, now smaller and more agile, began to sprint toward them.

The missiles didn't seem to be guiding on any particular aircraft. He relaxed a bit as the SAMs passed their altitude half a mile distant and continued upward.

The sprawling city of Hanoi grew in the distance. The target area lay just beyond. His flight was to take out the guns with cluster bombs, eliminate part of the threat so the others could gain some respite from the heavy flak as they bombed.

Big Eye airborne radar announced red bandits at 270 degrees for fifteen miles of Bullseye. That was in their area, but no one could see the MiG-21's.

Another trio of SAMs were launched, those from one

o'clock, not far from the target area. Flak puffed in dark smudges over the big city. It would intensify as they dived toward the target. Yank Donovan's pulse quickened slightly as they approached ever closer. They were at the initial point. He pulled on the stick and led the force into their climb to roll-in altitude—the perch. At 12,000 feet he abruptly turned, rolled inverted, found the target area visually, and tucked the stick into his lap. When he rolled back upright, the aircraft had settled at fifty degrees dive angle, and he began to jink. He eyeballed, squinted, saw the target clearly before him.

The largest building was still only half standing, down on one side from the previous bombing, but a number of specks moved about on the ground. Vehicles or large animals, he presumed. He bunted the bird, flattening his dive some so he could aim beyond the target. Muzzle flashes blinked frantically there. He steadied the aircraft and ceased maneuvering, preparing to release. The sight picture came together. At 6,000 feet he pickled the CBUs, felt the aircraft lighten, and pulled off target to his left. He started to jink in slow, random moves, never harshly, like a ballerina dancing erratically and saying, *You can't catch me.*

They'd rejoin six miles north of the target. That was the way he'd briefed it.

"*Pull out! Jesus!*" he heard on the radio. No call sign, just the words.

He looked back. Flak bursts blossomed. Big stuff, fifty-seven and eighty-five—and a lot of it. Two birds were off the target, trailing not far behind. He searched the area, but couldn't yet see the fourth. The flak diminished as he passed over the foothills of Thud Ridge, and he began making lazy S-turns so it would be easier for his flight to catch up.

The rest of the strike force was bombing now, hardly speaking on the radio. Good radio discipline, he thought—just as he'd demanded at the mission briefing.

The Wild Weasel flight called a SAM launch from the southern side of Hanoi. They were not coming for him. Big Eye called bandits again, but though he looked, he couldn't see them.

As he continued to S-turn and jink toward the rejoin point, a Thud pulled up on first one, then the other side of his aircraft. He felt a tremor of apprehension. Yank held his tongue and waited for a few more seconds, then looked back for the fourth flight member. There were only the more distant birds of the strike force.

"*Bear flight, check in,*" he finally barked over radio.

"*Bear two.*"

"*Bear four.*"

Where was Captain Fields? "*Anyone got a visual on Bear three?*" he asked.

"*Bear Four saw him go down in the target area.*" There was a catch in Captain Hamlin's voice. "*I think it was an eighty-five round that got him. Big explosion.*"

Yank Donovan suddenly felt like puking. He tried to speak into the mask. No words emerged. He took a deep breath. "*Was there a chute?*" he finally croaked.

"*He took a direct hit. He didn't get out.*"

1310L—355th TFW Headquarters, Takhli RTAFB, Thailand

Colonel Buster Leska

Buster was a few minutes late for the Wednesday-afternoon staff meeting. He'd spent the time trying to console Penny Dwight, had met her with the news when she'd returned from a noontime appointment at an off-base Thai hair salon. She'd come into the outer office smiling, showing off her new hairdo, and he'd taken her to one side and told her about Dusty, because he'd seen them together and thought things were likely getting thick between them. She'd tried to cope bravely for a while, then had lost it. She'd held her eyes tightly closed and begun to shake her head and sob. He'd sent her to her trailer to grieve in private. The admin chief master sergeant had volunteered to drive her.

When Leska finally entered the conference room, the others stood to attention. "Be seated," he said, and brusquely sat at the head of the long table.

The colonels were at the main table, squadron commanders and lesser staff in folding chairs assembled to his right.

Buster was not in a good mood. For one thing, the constant bickering between his deputies for operations and maintenance was continuing to get on his nerves. He'd had to jump on Jerry Trimble's case for yelling at George Armaugh and berating him on the flight line in front of several crew chiefs. If the situation went on much longer, it could come to blows between the two colonels. He was fast losing patience with them both.

For another thing, he'd received word from Carolyn that his son, Mark, was going to be booted out of Columbia if he didn't raise his grade-point average. The poor grades, according to their faculty friend, were because he spent most of his time running around with a group of long-haired and generally undesirable characters instead of studying. Carolyn wanted Buster's advice. Perhaps the situation was even worse, she'd said, for there were growing reports of LSD use on campus, and with the friends he kept . . .

Carolyn was beside herself with worry.

General Moss wanted another input for JACKPOT.

George Armaugh demanded that maintenance be improved, so they could meet their operational taskings from headquarters.

Jerry Trimble demanded that operations slack off on their unreasonable demands, which were destroying morale among his overworked crew chiefs.

His secretary and chief of admin were temporarily gone, and he had an urgent message to get out to PACAF headquarters.

And he had to keep all of those things from clouding his judgment.

"You guys ready to start?" he growled to the assembled group.

Lieutenant Colonel Lucky Anderson stood up from his seat at the side of the room. "I was just talking with Yank here, and he's got a damned interesting story, Colonel."

"Go ahead."

Donovan spoke in a terse voice about a radio conversation with someone called Hotdog when the strike force had approached the Channel TACAN that morning.

"Who the hell's Hotdog?" asked Colonel Armaugh.

"Got me." Donovan was acting more than a little morose. He'd lost a pilot in his flight, Penny's boyfriend, and it was obviously eating at him.

The conversation continued for a bit, including the unlikely remark from Hotdog that a T-34 had been shot down

by a small guided rocket. Buster shrugged. "If no one knows
if the call was real, let's move on to another subject."

Lucky Anderson took his feet again. "Colonel, I think
I've got some answers, but it's pretty sensitive. And listening
to Yank, I think it's important we try to get them help
ASAP."

"How sensitive is it?"

"Could we speak in private?" Anderson looked concerned.

"After the briefing."

"Yes, sir."

"Okay, let's get the show on the road." Buster didn't like
long staff meetings.

They started with an aircraft-status report from maintenance. George Armaugh began to complain, bringing a
quick put-down from Buster. Next operations gave a rundown of the previous week's combat sorties, and Buster had
to glare at Jerry Trimble to keep him silent. The Deputy for
Logistics gave a report about the resupply efforts and added
that they were processing a request from Captain DeVera
for a large number of additional ECM pods. When he asked
for more rationale, Buster said this was not the place and
told him to have his experts help Manny with the request.
He said he'd approved it, and that should be enough clout
for the colonel to get off his duff.

The meeting went quickly, because they realized the old
man was in a bad mood. Which made Buster wonder if he
shouldn't be bitchy more often, so he could keep the
meetings shorter and to the point. When the others had left,
Buster motioned to Anderson. Lucky followed him to his office and closed the door, obviously serious about the secrecy
of the Hotdog matter.

"So who was it that called Yank Donovan?" Buster asked,
anxious to get it over with.

"The only Hotdog I know about's an Army long-range recon patrol. A very special team."

"Special how?"

"I promised not to discuss them. Let me put it this way,
Colonel. They saved my ass."

"When you were shot down?"

Lucky Anderson stared at him for a moment, then gave

a tiny nod of his head. It was apparent he wasn't about to tell more.

"So how do you interpret this radio contact?"

"I know the team leader. He wouldn't have called unless they were in deep shit."

"So why isn't the Army requesting air support?"

"I can't say, but the guy running Hotdog wouldn't do this unless the situation was tense."

"Special Forces?"

"Yes, sir. I can't tell you more. I'm not even sure I know much more."

"Damn!" Buster muttered. There was too much pressing on him. He blew a breath. "Well, let's go over to the command post and call MAC-SOG on the scrambler phone. Surely they'll tell us if their people are in trouble."

It took fifteen minutes to get hold of MAC-SOG headquarters at Nha Trang, then five more before Buster was put through to someone who might know of such things. Finally a full bull answered who said, very pointedly, that there was no such thing as a Hotdog team assigned to Surveillance and Observation Group in Vietnam.

"What about in Laos?"

"It's against U.S. policy for Americans to operate in Laos."

When Buster repeated what his mission commander had heard on the radio, and asked if a T-34 might have been shot down near Channel 97, the colonel said he knew nothing about a downed aircraft.

When Buster hung up and relayed what had been said, Lucky Anderson's mouth became a taut line. "That's pure bullshit, Colonel. They're just not telling us."

Buster nodded to the command-post tech to shut down the secure telephone console. "Well, there's nothing we can do about it, if they don't want to help their own people."

He had other things to worry about.

1550L—Trailer 5B, Takhli RTAFB, Thailand

GS-7 Penny Dwight

Penny was devastated. The admin chief had delivered her to the trailer and asked if she'd wanted him to stay, but she'd wailed "no," and shut herself inside.

They'd told her there was no hope that Dusty had survived.

After long, shuddering bouts of tears, she would collect herself. Then she'd remember his grin or the way he'd move his hands to try to put his impossibly unruly hair back in place, and start crying again. Finally she held her head and sat quietly, letting the misery consume her. She hardly heard the knocking at the door, and then almost didn't answer.

Roger Hamlin was there. "Just came by to see how you're doing," he said. She let him in and they sat at the table, avoiding each other's eyes and remaining quiet for a long while.

"I hate this war," she whispered miserably.

"You gotta keep living, Penny."

She shook her head sadly.

"That's something you learn, Penny. Some of the people here have to give their lives. It's their job to face that possibility, and they do it for whatever reason makes 'em tick. And when they're gone, the others have to keep living."

She sniffed, looked at the ceiling, and shook her head. "I don't ever want to feel that callous about it, Roger. Last night Dusty and I shared . . ." Prudence stopped her when she realized what she'd been about to say.

"This morning Dusty told me you were very . . . special," Roger said quietly.

She looked up sharply. "Did he say anything else?"

"No. Just that you . . ." He swallowed, and his eyes became misty.

Penny wondered just what Dusty had told him. If he'd let on what she'd done, she would just *die*. She wanted to feel ashamed. Dusty had been Roger's best friend, and here he was trying to build her spirits, yet . . .

They'd been quiet for a long while when Roger came around and knelt beside her and held his arm lightly over her shoulder. Penny huddled there. She pulled a tissue from a box on the table and blew her nose.

"Your hair looks nice," Roger said.

She'd had it trimmed in a pageboy cut, so it would frame her rounded face. "I did it for Dusty," she said forlornly.

"You gonna be okay?"

She eyed him glumly, then nodded.

"I've gotta go to the squadron for a meeting."

She thought before saying quietly, "Don't tell the others what Dusty said about us last night, okay?"

"He just said you were special . . . not like other girls he'd met."

A burden left her. "I just don't want any . . . ah . . . stories started. It's bad enough as it is."

"I understand. You take care?"

She pulled in a ragged breath and nodded.

He patted her on the shoulder and stood.

"Thank you for coming by, Roger."

"You want me to check back later? Maybe escort you over to the club? One of the Weasel pilots plays a mean banjo, and we're going to get together for some tunes after dinner. Music helps take my mind off things. Maybe it'll help you too."

She started to say no, then reconsidered. Roger was happily married and safe.

"I'll drop by about six." He paused. "I'm sure gonna miss him," Roger said as he left.

After a bit she got up and scrubbed her face with a washcloth, pleased that Dusty hadn't said anything about what they'd done. She knew that men sometimes talked about an easy conquest, as if they were showing off a trophy or something.

She shuddered at the thought. That had been about the worst thing that could happen to a girl in Seymour, Indiana, where she'd been raised. After the single, unsatisfying time in the backseat with the high-school basketball player, the guys had looked at her and treated her entirely differently. A girlfriend had learned that he'd spread it around that he'd "banged her cherry so far back, she'd be using it for a taillight," and also that she'd been a lousy lay. Penny had been utterly mortified. As soon as she'd graduated, she'd left town—moved as far from Seymour as possible, to Maryland, where she'd lived with an elderly, widowed aunt until she found work. Then there had been her fiancé at Andrews, who'd let their co-workers believe they were sleeping together, acting as if he were a real stud.

The fact that Dusty had not talked made her feel even warmer toward his memory. Another flood of sadness swept over her. "I *hate* this damned war," she whispered again.

A little later she wondered if it could have been anything she'd done that had caused Dusty to be lost. Whether he'd been tired from their lovemaking. Whether she'd somehow robbed him of his alertness, or if he'd been distracted by thoughts of her. The ideas were disturbing.

1645L—Channel 97 TACAN Station, Laos

Sergeant Black

The militia soldiers were quiet down below. They could afford to wait—he could not. First he'd been turned down by the fast movers he'd contacted on the UHF radio; then Vientiane Control had told them there'd be no air strikes today. Their only hope was to be evacuated, which Vientiane reassured him would be done. The controller wouldn't say how or precisely when.

Black had trouble with that because, one, he didn't see how they could safely get a cargo plane into the site, and two, he didn't trust Vientiane Control. When he'd tried Buffalo Soldier, there'd been no more advice. Larry said they'd again urged Vientiane Control to extract them. Buffalo Soldier had no authority over air assets in northern Laos, and combat ground operations were verboten there.

Papa Wolf had come on the air once and said if the evacuation failed, to somehow get out of the immediate area on foot and give them a call so they could put a rescue effort together.

Great advice, with 600 soldiers down below eager for blood.

Papa Wolf signed off by chiding him for using the UHF. He'd been chastised by MAC-SOG because Black's team had called on an unauthorized frequency for illegal air support.

The Hotdog team members were idle. They'd spent the night placing the mines, so he'd told them to rest so they'd be able to help with the evacuation tonight.

Lying bastard, he told himself. He still didn't believe Vientiane Control was serious about getting them out.

Black was restless, so he walked through the Yard village and talked to the people there, joking with the kids and admonishing them to stay close to home and not wander off.

Buddy Canepa came over to complain. He said he'd gone to the supply shack and found the cases of booze had been stolen. Black told him he'd had them removed.

"It was private property," Canepa tried. "Just give me one bottle and we'll forget it."

"Get fucked," Black said cheerfully.

"How's Jones?" Buddy Canepa finally asked.

"He died this morning."

They heard an explosion from below, and Black walked toward the precipice in that direction.

"What the hell was that?" Canepa asked.

"Booby trap," said Black. "Amazing the shit you hear when you're sober."

He continued to the side and looked down. There was a second explosion. The Hotdogs were good with booby traps.

He heard the sounds of a chopper and looked around until he saw it. Coming from the east, the direction of North Vietnam. A speck at first, then it grew. The chopper flew directly over the militia soldiers, so he supposed it was North Vietnamese.

It kept coming, directly toward the mountain top. Black unslung his AKM, staring as the thing grew closer. It didn't look like the helicopters he knew were in North Vietnam, but . . .

He aimed, then heard a Yard yell something to him. *A friendly?* He lowered his weapon.

A stream of 12.7 fire reached up from below, and the chopper began to take wild evasive action. It was a small one with a bubble canopy, and it passed over Black, swung about, and settled in a cloud of blowing stones and debris. He watched closely, still handling the AK. The rotors clopped to a halt, and a grinning pilot unstrapped and stepped out. He wore jeans, a checkered shirt, and an Orioles baseball cap.

"Whoo-ee," he yelled exuberantly. "Fooled 'em that time."

Black went closer. "What the fuck are you doing here?"

"S'posed to take out three Amer'kins." The pilot peered. "You one of 'em?"

"How about the rest of my men?"

The chopper pilot frowned. "They Amer'kins?"

"What about noncombatants? The Yard women and children."

The pilot glanced at the Montagnard village. "Got me, Jocko. Maybe they're sending someone else for 'em, but I'm here for three Amer'kins. That's all I can haul, and all I was sent for. I get a ten thou bonus for each of you folks I deliver alive to Luang Prabang."

Buddy Canepa hurried up, smiling. "Let's get going," he said. "I'll pack a couple of bags."

"No bags," said the pilot. "She's a two-people bird, and she'll be strainin' to get up with the four of us. Anyway, we gotta wait for dark. No way I can do that act twice and get away with it."

"Jones is dead," grumbled Canepa. "That gives us more room."

The pilot grimaced. "I get half pay for bringing 'em out dead. Maybe we should take the body." He pondered for a bit before rejecting the idea.

"I oughta be able to take just one bag," complained Buddy Canepa.

The lieutenant walked up, and the pilot did a bug-eye act when he noted the NVA uniform. It had happened before with other unsuspecting Americans. The lieutenant enjoyed his moment and tried to look menacing.

"He's tame," Black said, looking with disgust at the tiny helicopter.

The pilot didn't appear convinced.

An explosion sounded from below as a booby trap was set off.

Black knew it was no use to call Vientiane, but he wondered if Buffalo Soldier knew the score, so he returned to the hut.

Larry wasn't manning the radio. *"Papa Wolf advises that you take the chopper,"* a new, belligerent voice told him.

"I've got my detachment here, and there's nineteen

*women and kids, and they send a two-man chopper? That's
bullshit, Buffalo Soldier. Let me talk to Papa Wolf."*

The man on the other end sounded impatient. *"I repeat.
Your orders are to take the chopper. Acknowledge, Hotdog."*

Black sighed angrily. *"We've got a bad frequency or something, Buffalo Soldier. Can't hear you worth a shit. Hotdog is
out."*

The voice turned angrier. *"Hotdog, be advised . . ."*

Black left the hut and stalked to the chopper, where the
pilot was switching between talking with Canepa and carefully eyeing the glowering lieutenant.

The lieutenant kept up his menacing appearance as he
came over and quietly spoke to Black. "The militia are
grouping at the bottom of the mountain. Two places." He indicated the main trail and then due south, the gentlest of
the steep slopes.

The sun was drooping into the mountainous horizon.

"Won't be long now until it's dark," called the pilot. "I
figure we oughta wait until after midnight before we take
off." He pulled a bedroll from the chopper and placed it
next to a skid, then stretched out and used it for a headrest.

Black left them and went to the Montagnard tent village,
where he carefully looked about until he'd found his candidates.

1830L—O' Club Dining Room, Takhli RTAFB, Thailand

Lieutenant Colonel Lucky Anderson

"How'd it go today?" he asked Linda after the waitress
brought their menus.

"Fine. Is that the girl the men call No Hab?" she asked.
He chuckled. "Yeah."

"She's cute."

"She's a farm girl from a little village east of here, across
the Phraya River. Some of the girls from over there migrated
here when the base opened." He saw no use to add that the
majority had become hookers downtown—No Hab had
been given the job in the dining room because a Thai officer
stationed on the other side of the base was a distant relative.

"There's some dense jungle across the river," Linda said knowingly.

"The last bastion of the Bengal tiger. They still hunt them using elephants, beaters, the whole shebang."

"Sounds like something out of Kipling."

"The Kwai River's there. I came back from a mission with a little extra fuel one time and went over to take a look at the bridge built by British POW labor. The one in the movie."

"I loved Alec Guinness in that." Linda frowned. "I thought the bridge was blown up. That's what they showed in the movie."

"Then they rebuilt it, because it's still there. It looks out of place. Big steel structure like you'd find in Europe or the States, but it's out in the middle of the jungle."

No Hab returned, poised her pencil over her pad, and raised an eyebrow as she imagined waitresses did in the States. The fact that she could read and write only a few necessary numbers wasn't nearly as important as the image.

"We'll both have Salisbury steak," Lucky told her, which was number four on the menu.

She pursed her lips and scribbled furiously. At the end of the meaningless scrawl she put down 4—4.

"Watcha wan on de side?" she asked.

"Potatoes?"

"No hab po-ta-to."

They ordered salad, for No Hab confided, after much prodding, that a shipment of lettuce had arrived.

No Hab nodded seriously, then left.

"She's in love," Lucky said. "An airman in my squadron asked to marry her, and she said"—he tried to grin like No Hab—"ho-kay."

Linda looked after the girl. "So she'll be going to the States?"

"Maybe. Thais don't take marriage as seriously as most Americans. You want to get married, you find a Buddhist priest and say I marry you. You want to be free, you go back to him and the marriage is annulled."

Linda grimaced. "I've heard about that."

"Which means she'll live with the airman while he's here, but when he goes home next year, she may decide to stay in Thailand."

"That's *terrible*."

"Not to their way of thinking. I tried to explain all that to the airman, but he was so lovestruck, he didn't understand what I was trying to tell him."

She made a face at him. "After we get hitched, I'm going to make sure you never get anywhere *near* a Buddhist priest."

The salads arrived. The lettuce had obviously been exposed to heat somewhere on its long route, for it was wilted and soggy, a shapeless, greenish blob smothered with the mixture of catsup and mayonnaise that served as dressing.

"You're leaving in the morning?" he asked, eyeing the ugly salad.

"Yes."

Yank Donovan walked past and Lucky said hi, but the man didn't respond.

"That was rude of him," Linda said.

"Yank's down today. Sometimes it's difficult not to take the war personally. You've got to grow a thick skin. Yank's having trouble with that."

"I've seen you awfully despondent when you lost a friend."

"Yeah, but I continue to function. Yank's letting it get to him *bad*. I think he relates losses to his personal capabilities, which he's never doubted for a moment."

Linda picked at her salad, her nose wrinkled like a little girl's, and he thought again how fortunate he was to have her.

"How long will you be at NKP?" he asked.

"Two weeks. There's a lot to be accomplished."

He didn't like the thought of her running around an area where the Thai CT operated. Then he recalled the conversation with Donovan about the radio calls from Hotdog. "While you're there, look up a fellow named Sergeant Black for me, would you?"

She took out a pen and paper and scribbled a note to herself. "He's a sergeant?"

"Claims he's an E-6. I don't know what to believe, but I owe him a lot."

She cocked her head inquisitively. "Something to do with when you were shot down?"

"Something," he said. He'd promised Black that he'd

keep his secrets. "Look him up and ask about the CT situation in the NKP area. He'll know."

"Where would I find him?"

"He's attached to a Special Forces unit there. I think he called it his C-Team headquarters. Something like that. He may be in the field when you get there."

"I know a little about the unit. Why would this man be so knowledgeable, Paul? I get very thorough briefings about CT activities."

He tried another bite of salad and pushed it away, using the time to phrase his words. "He knows a lot about spook stuff," he finally said. "He may even know about your operation."

"Handing out foodstuff and shovels to natives?"

"Humor me, okay? Look him up."

"I will if you'll tell me more about how you were shot down and what you did on the ground all that time." Linda had wanted to find out from the first. She claimed it was her right to know everything that made him tick, his being her personal property and all.

He stared. She was the most trustworthy person he'd ever met, but he'd promised. . . .

She was serious. "Just give me an abbreviated, no-secrets account, Paul."

He thought a while longer before nodding. "It'll have to wait until we get to the trailer."

"I understand."

"I can't tell you about Sergeant Black's involvement, but there's other parts I'll share."

Dinner arrived, the hamburger burned to crisp blackness.

No Hab beamed. "En-choy!" she said happily before rushing off.

Thursday, November 30th, 0200 Local—Channel 97
TACAN Station, Laos

Sergeant Black

Buddy Canepa had worried because Black ignored the periodic calls from Buffalo Soldier. He'd also ignored calls from Vientiane Control, and that concerned Canepa even more.

"What if they need to tell me something?" Canepa whined. As he'd continued to sober up, he'd become concerned.

"Talk to 'em when you get to Luang Prabang," Black had told him, but he wouldn't let him answer the calls.

During the night five more booby traps had been heard exploding on the slopes below. Another sounded, from the south, and this time Canepa jumped.

The pilot came into the hut, yawning. "I think they've started up the mountain," he said.

"They've been coming up for the past six hours," Black replied.

"Are they close?" asked the pilot.

"Not yet."

"How do you—"

They heard a whoofing sound; then an explosion rocked the building. The militia had begun shelling with their howitzers.

"*Now* they're close," said Black. A round struck at the far northern end of the mountain top, near the TACAN. "They'll try to soften the place up before they attack."

The pilot peered out the door. "We better go. They might get lucky and hit the chopper."

They went out. "See you guys in a minute," said Black, and walked into the darkness toward the Yard village.

They were ready. He greeted the mother as she lifted her head and listened to another whoofing sound. A phosphorous round hit and made a spectacle near the TACAN.

"This way," he said, and she followed.

A tremendous explosion sounded from below. The uppermost pathway had been blown by the Yards. The militia would be delayed a little longer there.

Another round struck and splayed bright white tendrils.

"Hurry it up," the pilot urged from the helo cockpit.

The chopper's engine coughed and caught, and the rotor blades began to churn.

Black took the first kid's hand and stepped under the blades, opened the door, and deposited him in the seat beside Canepa.

"Hey!" bellowed the pilot.

"Be right back."

He made the trip two more times, and each time the pilot yelled that he couldn't do that. Black wedged the last two kids between the seats.

"Get them out of here!" screeched the pilot.

Black walked around the helicopter and leaned in the half-opened window to the pilot.

"I'm gonna walk out of here," he yelled.

"Goddammit, you can't . . ."

Black pressed the muzzle of the AKM against the pilot's throat. "When I get to Luang Prabang, I'm gonna call on you. If I hear anything bad's happened to these kids, I'm going to cut off your balls and feed 'em to you."

"Jesus," the pilot muttered, his head held as far back as he could get it.

Another artillery round exploded, this one closer.

"Understood?"

"Yeah."

One of the kids, a three-year old girl, cried out for her mother.

"Now get the fuck outa here." Black backed away from the chopper. The pilot waited for another moment to collect himself. Then the engine surged and the blades clacked noisily.

The chopper rose, dipped, and disappeared toward the northwest.

Black held his breath, watching and listening as the helicopter's sounds receded.

Two blinding plumes traced through the sky. The chopper exploded and trailed fire as it plunged earthward. The militia had not been fooled a second time. They'd been waiting with their guided rockets.

The mother watched in numbed silence long after there was only darkness. So did Black. The children had been the healthiest he'd found in the tent village. He was not sorry.

Their deaths had been merciful compared to what the others faced.

Finally he started back toward the prefab building. As he went inside, a round fell near the trash dump. Flying cans and bottles clattered against the sides of the hut. He aimed and fired two 7.62 rounds into the contractor's radio, then bent down to the HF set Hotdog had brought and called for Buffalo Soldier.

This time Larry answered. *"Hotdog, we've got help on the way. A dragon ship."* Puff the Magic Dragon was an AC-47, a gooney bird with infrared sensors and a Gatling gun mounted at the door.

"What's the ETA, Buffalo Soldier?"

"Two hours, fifteen."

Black noted that the shelling had stopped. *"Too late."* A booby trap went off at the southern perimeter, beyond the Yard tent village. *"They're here."*

He kept the mike button held down so Larry could hear the automatic-weapons fire.

"How about the contractors?" Larry asked.

"One died this morning of his wounds. The other was killed in the chopper when they tried to get out. The militia got 'em with the rockets, same as with the tango thirty-four."

"Good thing you didn't go along, huh?"

Black started to tell him about the Yard kids, but held his tongue. It would serve no good purpose.

"How about you guys? Any way out?"

"Dunno. Have Puff take out this mountaintop when he arrives. None of the good guys will be around by then, and I do not like the place."

Larry gave him two beeps.

Black stepped back and fired two rounds into that radio, too.

A burst of auto-weapons fire thumped through the walls of the hut, and he crouched and ran to the door, opened it, and sprawled forward into the dirt. A firefight picked up tempo near the Yard village, AK-47's and M-16's fired on full automatic. A piercing scream from a woman. A child wailed fearfully.

He heard a slight sound beside him and swung the AKM muzzle around.

"C'mon bruddah. Le's ged gone fum heah."

A Yard voice yelled angrily and was answered by a profusion of gunfire. Black hesitated, then followed the lieutenant.

0615L—Green Anchor Air Refueling Route

Lieutenant Colonel Lucky Anderson

The KC-135 Stratotanker flew its elongated orbit and nourished the F-105 fighters that clung to the long appendage hanging below and aft. A flying gas station, the guys called it. Papa tanker, they also called it, because of the needle prick that was jabbed into the fighter's open receptacle. Sometimes when he was feeling feisty, the Supersonic Wetback would radio, "Take it easy with that big thing, sweetie, but it's soooo nice," when the boom operator connected.

Other tankers, those that trailed hoses with baskets on their ends, were called Mama tankers, because you inserted a probe into the basket and pressed forward until it latched there. That was when Manny DeVera would say, "This won't hurt much, sweetie, and it's guaranteed to prevent acne."

On this early-morning mission DeVera wasn't along, and the fighter jocks who hooked up just said the normal stuff like, "Go single pump," to remind the boomer that the Thud's fuel tanks were fragile and could burst from overpressure if the boomer used dual pumps.

"*Thanks for the gas,*" Lucky radioed as the last member of his flight disconnected and sluggishly joined back on his wing.

He took a moment to look about at the beauty of the morning, one of those times when the sky was multishaded with blues and golds and the earth below was shrouded in darkness.

Nice, he thought. *Really nice.*

The tanker went into a slow left turn, leaving them, for they were past the Laotian border.

"*Scotch flight, go en-route frequency,*" he called.

"*Scotch two.*"

"*Three.*"

"*Scotch four.*"

He switched to the preset frequency shown on the flight-data card, waited a couple of more seconds after the radio stopped tuning, then called Scotch flight to make sure everyone was on freq. They were.

"Push 'em up, Scotch flight." That one didn't require a response. The others kept up as he eased the throttle forward and the big jet accelerated until the ground speed readout showed 420 knots. He would not be so precise about the airspeed, but they'd finally been briefed that there really was trouble going on at the Channel 97 TACAN and didn't know if it would still be on the air. The briefers hadn't mentioned Hotdog or people in danger.

Flying at 420 knots meant they were traveling at seven nautical miles per minute, making it easier when they estimated their positions. Since Lucky had also computed the figures on the flight plan based on a ground speed of 420, if he flew the appropriate heading for the amount of time shown on the card, he'd be at the next turnpoint at the proper time.

As long as Channel 97 was operational, they didn't need precise navigation until they'd passed it, because the TACAN instrument in the aircraft would read out its range and bearing. If it was lost, it would make things more difficult.

Today's missions were against shitty targets, truck parks in pack five, which had made his decision easier. If Hotdog called for help again, he planned to ask Black a couple of questions to establish his authenticity, then give him whatever fire support he required.

When they were seventy miles away, according to his Doppler navigator, he switched his TACAN to 9-7, and watched and waited as the needle rotated around the face of the instrument.

No lock-on.

He settled back in his seat and continued on course. Perhaps when they drew closer? They should be in range, dammit. He tried tapping on the glass face of the instrument.

Nothing.

Fifty miles out. Still zippo . . . nothing at all.

"Scotch flight, this is lead. Any of you guys getting anything on your TACANs?"

They all reported in the negative.

At thirty miles he switched to guard frequency, 243.0,

and made his call. *"Hotdog, this is Scotch. I repeat, Hotdog, this is Scotch. How do you read me? Over."*

Lucky waited quietly. There was no response.

He called again. This time the shipborne command post answered, also on guard frequency. *"Scotch, this is Red Crown, repeat your last transmission."*

Shit, he said to himself. He started to switch to Red Crown's normal frequency.

"Scotch lead? Scotch three's got ground smoke at twelve o'clock."

Dark wisps streamered from a mesa surrounded by dense jungle. The TACAN's fuel supply?

"Roger, three," Lucky responded, feeling downbeat. Too late to save the TACAN. He wondered how Hotdog was faring. He decided they were likely already back at NKP, having a cold beer and cursing fighter jocks for not helping.

"Scotch force, let's join into formation," he radioed, and began to slow down so the other flights could catch up and get into position.

The flights were relatively quick about it, since they'd anticipated the loss of the TACAN. As soon as they were in a semblance of the proper formation, Lucky decided they'd further refine their relative positions while enroute.

"Scotch force, push 'em up and green 'em up," Lucky radioed. Time to throttle to 540 knots, the combat en-route airspeed he preferred in pack five, and prepared the weapons stations.

After settling on the new speed and checking that everything was right with his bird, Lucky continued monitoring for a call from Hotdog until they were well out of radio range.

CHAPTER SIXTEEN

Saturday, December 2nd, 0850 Local—Fighter Tactics Branch, TFWC, Nellis AFB, Nevada

Major Benny Lewis

It had been envisioned that there would be two centers of activity for the JACKPOT project: Saigon, where the plan would take raw form using inputs from the combat units, and Washington, where the plan would be polished and General McManus would convince the President to authorize it. A third hub developed at Nellis Air Force Base, where Major General Gordon White's analysts and project officers had an equally critical role—to determine appropriate weapons for the aircraft that would participate in LINE BACKER JACKPOT, and specify the best possible tactics for their use. The stream of JACKPOT messages between the three centers was consistent and heavy.

At Nellis only White and Lewis were cleared for JACKPOT and knew what the activity was about, but their inputs became invaluable. General White initiated a high-priority study project that examined a major, conventional, round-the-clock bombing effort by joint strategic/tactical air forces. He used numbers and types of aircraft contained in the draft

LINE BACKER JACKPOT OPlan forwarded from Saigon, and specified a target area in the western USSR with terrain and defenses similar to Hanoi's. He relayed the results to Colonel Mack MacLendon, who'd been appointed to Buster Leska's old position in the office of the CSAF.

Major Lewis was occupied with nuts-and-bolts aspects, getting the project gurus at Strategic and Tactical Air Commands to agree how they should mesh air refueling, ingress and egress procedures before, during, and after a bomber strike. His office ran flight tests using F-4 Phantoms to dispense chaff in massive, twenty-by-one-hundred-mile corridors that could shield B-52's flying at high altitude. He also stayed up to speed on the Pave Dagger project, for he was increasingly convinced that Moods Diller's smart bombs would make a difference.

The date of the Pave Dagger combat test was fast approaching, and Moods and his group were frantic with activity. They'd shipped thirty new Mk-84 2,000-pound bombs to Danang. The three laser pods selected for the test were flown and calibrated on the Nellis range daily. Forty bomb-guidance kits were at the Nellis weapons shop, undergoing grueling bench checks.

There were, as always, last-minute problems. Although the lasers and bomb kits were much better than before, they still needed tweaking. One task was to determine the constant error rate of the bombs, so they could correct for it. Volumes of drop-test data were reduced to meaningful information. It appeared that only a modest pitch-down bias would have to be introduced into the electronic circuitry, but that correction was critical, since it would make the difference between a direct hit and a near miss.

Another problem developed with two of the three zot machines, the target illuminators that were now mounted in pods, which would be hung under the right wings of the Phantoms. After fifteen minutes of power-on operation, the rear-cockpit circuit breaker would sometimes pop out, taking the entire system off-line. The only fix was to wait ten minutes, reset the breakers, then turn the system back on for another fifteen minutes of operation. The senior Texas team engineer finally traced the problem to the illuminator pod's power supply and sent in a panic order for new, better-cooled black boxes.

A final challenge was to perfect the servo mechanism that used electrical impulses from the seeker head to move the bomb fins. That one was solved when Moods used a servo drive from an AGM-45 radar-seeking missile and found it was easily adapted to the smart bombs.

All of those things were believed to be fixed, but no one was sure, and there was no time to conduct further bomb-drop tests on the Nellis ranges prior to departure. Those would have to be done in the combat test after they were in place at Danang.

Moods and crew didn't have time to tinker. Deployment was scheduled for Monday, December 11th, six days hence, when a Strategic Air Command KC-135 tanker would be flown in from March Air Force Base, in Southern California. Moods' GIB, or "guy in back," which was what they called the pilot systems officers (the PSOs were also sometimes called "pizzos") manning the rear cockpits of F-4 Phantoms, would be in charge of a five-man weapons maintenance team of NCOs who would load the bomb kits and pods into the cargo bay of a KC-135 tanker, then look after them on the trip across the Pacific.

Moods would depart a day earlier, as he was scheduled for a Monday-morning presentation at Hickam AFB in Hawaii. PACAF headquarters had asked to be briefed about the combat test to be held in their theater of operations, and though the tests had been approved and coordinated by the Pentagon requirements division, that step was deemed prudent. The SAC tanker would stop and pick up Moods at Hickam after his briefing, and transport him to Danang with the highly classified equipment and the military team. Eight engineers from the Texas contractor team would travel by civil airliner to Saigon and catch a hop to Danang.

Moods was convinced that all combat test objectives could be accomplished in thirty days of intensive flying and evaluations. He'd scheduled the team's return to Nellis for January 15th.

Benny Lewis talked all of that over with Diller, sipping coffee and deciphering the man's machine-gun bursts of speech. He knew something was definitely wrong, for he was beginning to understand Moods, even when he was excitable and his words and phrases ran together. Sometimes he even caught himself answering Moods in the same way.

If there were two of Moods, they could get them excited
and use them for sensitive radio traffic, as the Army had
done with Navajo Indians during World War II, and the
Russians would be scratching their heads and tearing their
hair out trying to decode their messages.

"What's Pam think of you being gone for a month?"
Benny asked during a pause.

Moods darkened. "Doesn't like it." Pam was a rawboned
captain nurse at the Nellis hospital. They were a couple, and
Moods spent his nights at her condo. Pam was talking about
marriage, and Moods was thinking up fewer reasons why
they shouldn't.

As Moods brooded, Benny wondered about his own situation. Julie's mother had become a permanent fixture at her
apartment. The last time he'd asked when she might be
heading home to New Jersey, Julie had taken a breath and
said, "Well, she *is* a great help with the baby," which they
both knew was no answer at all.

-ci15Julie was back at work with Pan Am, coordinating
flight attendant schedules at the operations desk. She felt
useful when working, but was on a guilt trip about not
spending enough time with Patty. Their relationship was unchanged. After his visits to her apartment, now every third
or fourth night, Julie would follow him to his car and they'd
talk and kiss, and she'd tell him she loved him and to please
be patient.

Benny Lewis was indeed a patient man, but he sometimes wondered if things were really going to develop beyond what they had.

**Tuesday, December 5th, 1300 Local—Seventh AF
Headquarters, Tan Son Nhut AB, Saigon, South Vietnam**

Lieutenant Colonel Pearly Gates

Wes Snider was off to U Tapao to talk with B-52 aircrews,
so only Pearly had been summoned into General Moss's office to discuss the JACKPOT project. Moss handed him the
latest message from General McManus.

Paragraph one concerned McManus's latest discussion
with the President and was informative:

1. (S) MET WITH J ON 26 NOV. HE WAS IN
PENSIVE MOOD. SAID HE WAS GETTING
PRESSURE FM SECDEF AND OTHERS TO
UNILATERALLY CEASE BOMBING AS SIGN
OF GOOD FAITH TO NVN, & FM CONGRESS
TO EITHER PURSUE THE WAR MORE
VIGOROUSLY OR GET OUT. HE FELT IT WD
BE DISGRACEFUL TO "THROW IN THE
TOWEL" LIKE SOME "2 BIT COWARD." I
ADVISED THAT A LARGE-SCALE COMMUNIST
SPRING OFFENSIVE IS ANTICIPATED, AND
IT MIGHT BE GOOD TO LAUNCH JACKPOT
BEFOREHAND. I ALSO SAID, AS U SUGGESTED,
THAT WEATHER WILL BE MOST APPROPRIATE
DURING DEC TO APR FOR A BOMBING
CAMPAIGN. J IS "VERY" CONCERNED
THAT THE NVA WILL ACHIEVE A DIEN BIEN
PHU–TYPE VICTORY—FEELS THE PRESS IS
WAITING FOR ANY SMALL NVN SUCCESS,
WHICH THEY WILL BUILD INTO
SOMETHING BIGGER—HE SEEMS
INCREASINGLY INTERESTED IN OUR PLAN
& REEMPHASIZED IMPORTANCE OF
SECRECY. HE SAID IF THE WRONG
PEOPLE LEARN ABT IT, IT WILL MAKE THINGS
IMPOSSIBLE. HE ALSO REVEALED THAT HE
WAS HAPPY THAT <u>SECDEF WD SHORTLY
BE LEAVING CABINET,</u> AND HE'D BE
ABLE TO APPT "HIS OWN MAN." SAID IT WD
BE BEST TO WAIT FOR NEW SECDEF TO COME
ABOARD BEFORE MOVING ON JACKPOT.

The underlining had been General Moss's doing. He disliked the Secretary of Defense intensely and called him the
Edsel mechanic.

2. (C) SPECULATING ABT NEW SECDEF
(RUMORS ARE MANY) IS NEWEST PENTAGON
GAME. WHITE HSE SOURCE SAYS J
FAVORS ONE OF THE FOLLOWING: SEN.
WAYLAND LINGENFELTER, CLARK CLIFFORD,
ONE OF BUNDY BROTHERS, OR AVERELL

HARRIMAN. IN MY JUDGMENT CLIFFORD
IS TOO BUREAUCRATIC, LINGENFELTER
TOO CAUTIOUS, HARRIMAN TOO
POLITICAL, MCGEORGE BUNDY TOO
MERCURIAL. BILL BUNDY IS SMARTEST OF
THE BUNCH & MOST LIKELY TO
AGGRESSIVELY PURSUE "SUCCESSFUL
AND EARLY" END TO THE WAR. HOPE HE
MAKES IT.

Paragraph three concerned changes McManus wanted to
make to the plan, to establish a special communications
node from Saigon's to the Pentagon's basement command
center. He'd placed his newest JACKPOT member, Colonel
MacLendon, in charge of that effort.

Paragraph four was somewhat encouraging:

4. (S) UNLESS/UNTIL WE GAIN APPROVAL
ON LINE BACKER JACKPOT DO NOT EXPECT
MAJOR CHANGES, I.E.: TO STRIKE
"IMPORTANT" TARGETS. J CONTINUES TO
SELECT/APPROVE TGTS WITH GREAT
CAUTION AT PVT MEETINGS (STILL NO
MILITARY ALLOWED). HOWEVER, I WILL
SEEK A "MODEST" ESCALATION AND
LIFTING OF RESTRICTIONS DURING NEXT
MEETING, TO PROVE AIR POWER CAN BE
EFFECTIVE IF PROPERLY USED. THE
"PROOF" WILL BE AMT OF SCREAMING
FROM NVN PROPAGANDA TO STOP BOMBING.

For a while they discussed the message, as well as the fact
that Pearly had now finished with the first draft of the LINE
BACKER JACKPOT OPlan.

"Go ahead and send it," Moss said, eyeing the nine
pounds of paper before him.

"Yes, sir." A weight was lifted from Pearly's shoulders.

"Anything else?"

"The Channel Ninety-seven TACAN station. I'm getting
requests from the Thailand wing commanders that we do
something about a replacement. They all say the same thing.
It's important to the pilots on their way into pack six, so

they can form up properly and have a positive departure and recovery point. Not only that, General. Wes Snider and I agree that it's essential we put in a ground station called an MSQ-2, to help the B-52's bomb when they start going north on the JACKPOT missions."

Moss nodded wearily. "Snider briefed me about the MSQ-2 thing. I guess we need it. How does that tie in with Channel Ninety-seven?"

"The location at the mesa is optimum for both pieces of equipment. We need that mountain back, sir. I'd suggest a B-52 strike if there weren't all the friendly villages in the area."

"The Air Force doesn't own the place, Pearly. The spooks do."

"I know, sir, but can't we talk to them about it? Maybe encourage them?"

"I have. The Smith Brothers aren't at all interested in hurrying back into a place that's swarming with that many North Vietnamese."

The CIA was collectively called the Smith Brothers, because so many agents introduced themselves as either Mr. Smith or Mr. Jones.

"We'll need it for LINE BACKER JACKPOT, sir," Pearly said stubbornly.

Moss sighed. "I'll approach MAC-V and tell them the problem. Westy's still in the States drumming up support for more troops, but his vice is holding just as many useless meetings."

"How about MAC-SOG, sir?"

Moss's brow furrowed. Surveillance and Observation Group, which reported directly to Westmoreland, contained all unconventional warfare elements. Special Forces, SEALs, Marine recon forces, and the CIA's contractor and pacification elements, were all amalgamated, however loosely, under MAC-SOG. So were the Air Force's Special Operations units, which contained C-130's, C-123's, helicopters, and other USAF aircraft and aircrews. Moss felt that he, as the senior U.S. Air Force officer in Southeast Asia, should control Air Force assets, not some grunt general wearing a French lady's cap.

"We'll see," he finally said. He looked at his watch.

Pearly started to rise to his feet.

"Wait for a few minutes more," Moss said. "I've set up a meeting with an old friend. We were classmates at West Point and went to pilot school together. That was back when we were full of piss and vinegar. You may have heard of him, because somehow the ham-fist ended up with nineteen kills in the Pacific."

Pearly was impressed. "Is he still in the service, sir?"

"Retired two years ago as a major general. Now he's a vice president at Lockheed, building airplanes and making too much money."

"What's his name?"

"Wild Bill Dortmeier."

Pearly Gates immediately realized just who Lieutenant Lucille Dortmeier's father was, whom she'd gotten the day off to see. Just one of the most famous fighter pilots alive.

"His son Willie flew Thuds out of Takhli. Went down in pack six, fate unknown."

"I remember, sir." Why the hell hadn't he connected it? It had been a sad day for General Moss when Lieutenant Willie Dortmeier, son of a close friend, had been shot down.

"I just learned that his daughter's here, working for you. Is that right?"

Pearly nodded. "Yes, sir."

"Little Lucy's like family. Used to call me Uncle Rich. Why the hell didn't you tell me?"

"I didn't put two and two together," Pearly said sheepishly, "and she never told me."

"Christ, Pearly, it's only one of the most famous names in the Air Force." He shook his head. "Anyway, stick around and tell her father how she's doing."

A male voice broke in on Flo's intercom. "I hear there's a free drink around here someplace."

Moss stalked to the door, opened it, and shouted, "It's your turn to buy, you has-been ham-fist."

"Bullshit, you'll *always* owe me, Rich."

They were shaking hands energetically, grinning wide. Moss led his friend inside. Dortmeier, gray-haired and looking distinguished in a white linen suit, frowned at Pearly Gates. "Am I interrupting?"

"Not at all. We were just finishing and I felt you might want to meet Lucy's boss."

"You're Lieutenant Colonel Gates?"

"Yes, sir," said Pearly.

"Lucy wrote just after she got here, about you and your branch. Talked like you walked on water, and was thrilled to be put right in as OIC of a section."

Moss shook his head. "Hell, Bill, I'd have placed her here in the command section if I'd known she was here."

"No way for you to know. She's like her brother Willie— won't let anyone help her career. Says she's got to make it on her own. Told me to butt out, and damn near in those terms."

"Where's Little Lucy now?"

"Won't let me call her that anymore, so you better not either. She's waiting down by the entrance. Wants to show me Saigon. Only took the one day off, because she says she doesn't want to take more time off than that."

Moss looked at his old friend soberly. "Why'd she come into the Air Force, Bill? Last I heard she'd finished her bachelor's degree and was doing whiz-bang work on becoming a lawyer."

"She and Willie were close. The day we heard he'd been shot down, there wasn't any more time for law school. She came into the Air Force on the proviso she'd be stationed here."

"Hell, the Air Force needs good lawyers. I can . . ."

"Don't even *think* of helping. She didn't even want me to mention her when we talked. When I tell her I talked to her boss as well, she's gonna crap."

Pearly picked up the LINE BACKER JACKPOT OPlan off the general's desk and prepared to leave the two friends with their discussion.

Wild Bill Dortmeier turned to him. "How's she doing in her job, Colonel Gates?"

"She's very conscientious, sir."

"Well she's certainly closemouthed about it. That first letter, all she could do was talk about her job and what a great boss you were. She hasn't mentioned her work since, and when I try to talk about it, she just says she can't and changes the subject."

Pearly's face reddened with shame at the way he'd treated the man's daughter. He hedged. "We work with a great deal of classified material, sir."

Moss took the heat off. "What the hell's this 'official' trip of yours about, Bill?"

Dortmeier grinned. "I'm like Lucy. Can't talk about it."

"Hell, I'm boss here. If it has to do with airplanes, I own 'em."

"Not all the airplanes, you don't. I'm visiting Special Operations and agency people. If you'll remember, Lockheed builds C-130's and U-2's. I'm in charge of special-ops programs at the plant."

Richard Moss flushed. "Dammit, I ought to—"

Dortmeier laughed. "I *thought* that'd make you happy."

"I'll leave now, if that's all, sir," said Gates.

"One last thing, Pearly. Have we heard any more word on the status of General Dortmeier's son?"

"Nothing new, sir. First there was intelligence that he'd been captured by the NVA, then nothing. He's not listed on any of the POW reports released by Hanoi." He left the room quickly, not wanting to answer questions about Second Lieutenant Lucille Dortmeier and the way he'd reacted when she came to him for help, or how he'd knocked her sprawling on her butt.

If he'd only known . . . , but he realized that it made no difference who her father was. She was a young officer working for him, had come to him with a problem, and he'd brushed her off because he was busy with "other things." Sometimes it was too easy to think the Air Force consisted of hardware like airplanes, and even plans like the one he was carrying. But that wasn't true, and he knew it. It consisted of people, and the rest were just tools they used to get their jobs done. When you lost sight of that, you became just another second-rate guy who'd been promoted beyond the level he deserved.

He decided it was time to amend matters between himself and Lucy Dortmeier.

2100L—O' Club Stag Bar, Takhli RTAFB, Thailand

Captain Manny DeVera

Penny Dwight hadn't spoken more than a dozen words to him since Dusty Fields had been killed six days earlier, and

Manny had been so busy recently that he'd not had a chance to press his case. Now he stared over at the table she shared with Animal Hamlin and thought he'd better get on with it, because she'd likely be snapped up again if he waited too long.

Penny's new pageboy cut accentuated her face and features much more nicely, and she seemed to be carrying herself better, as if she was proud of what she had. She should be proud. She was wearing a fancy gabardine flight suit, which Dusty had talked her into ordering from a Bangkok tailor. Manny decided she'd sent in precise measurements, because Penny's assets were well displayed. It was candy-pink, with red valentine hearts on the shoulders instead of rank. Patches from all three fighter squadrons were sewn in place across the back. On one shoulder was an arrowhead patch with the distinctive silhouette of an F-105 in its center. On the other was a black patch, with RED RIVER VALLEY FIGHTER PILOTS ASS'N printed at the bottom in bright yellow. The River Rats had been formed the previous summer, when pilots from Takhli, Korat, Ubon, and Udorn had gotten together for a "tactics" conference, which ended up with some good cross talk between F-105 and F-4 units, as well as a lot of hell-raising. To become a member, you had to fly across the Red River into the Hanoi area. For the secretary, someone had obviously decided that the rules should be bent.

A number of the River Rats had ordered the special "party suits" in their squadron colors, but none were nearly as spectacularly filled as Penny Dwight's. Yep, he decided. It was definitely time to file a claim, while there was only good ol' sober-sided Animal Hamlin with her. She'd been seeing a lot of him since Dusty's death.

Manny frowned and wondered if Hamlin might himself be moving in. He quickly pushed the idea aside. Animal was happily married and very badly wanted to change his image, as well as the nickname. Yet there was something in the way Animal looked at her from time to time, then quickly pulled his gaze away.

He's probably just wishing, Manny decided. Dusty had told him Penny was a nice girl, that propriety was big with her. It was likely as he'd thought; she was seeing Hamlin because he was a straight arrow. Yet Manny had seen stranger things than a nice girl falling for a married guy after an innocent beginning. It was time to move before something like that happened. He paused. She *was* prettier now, with the haircut and new bearing, but he wondered if some of that was because she was the only act in town.

Maybe. He collected his MiG-15 drink, his cigarettes—he was smoking a few again—and crossed the noisy room to their table. Both looked up as he approached. "Mind if I join you? Getting lonely over at the bar," he said.

They pushed around the small table and made room as he pulled up a chair.

"I like your party suit," Manny joked with an ogling leer.

"Thank you," she said, almost demurely.

"She didn't want to wear it, but I told her it would help cheer everyone up," Animal said.

"I dunno about everyone," said Manny with a grin, "but I know one guy who appreciates it."

She smiled halfheartedly.

"You guys look like you're running low. Buy you a drink?" Manny asked.

Penny shook her head. "I've gotta go. Big day tomorrow. We've got another PACAF inspection team coming in, and I have to get Colonel Leska's instructions out to the units." She didn't seem to be giggling as much as before, and her conversations were more than one-liners. Penny Dwight was definitely blossoming.

"You can't leave this soon," Manny said woefully.

She stood, and Manny followed suit. Animal Hamlin started to scramble to his own feet, but she gave him a small shake of her head, and he immediately settled. Which made Manny wonder again.

"Walk you to your trailer?" he asked.

She gave him the half smile. "Thank you anyway." She headed for the door with no further word.

Manny settled beside Animal Hamlin. "Well, hell." They watched her leave. "How about you, Animal? You want a drink?"

"I wish you guys'd call me Roger." He was fumbling with his guitar case.

"Who's that?"

"That's my name, dammit."

"Too hard. Animal's easy to remember, and nobody'd

know who I was talking about if I called you Rotchur or whatever you said."

Animal shook his head sadly. He had the guitar out of the case and was examining it. "I'd better restring this thing pretty soon."

"How's Penny holding up?"

"She's coming around."

"Only person she'll talk to is you. How come?"

Animal shrugged. "Good sense, I guess." He picked a few notes.

"I thought it was maybe, you being happily married and all, she thought you were safe."

Animal Hamlin nodded vaguely. "I suppose."

"You oughta put in a good word for me, Animal. Tell her I'm a good guy."

Hamlin gave him a sideward look. "Compared with what?" he joked.

Pak, the assistant bartender, was making the rounds, so Manny called him over and ordered two drinks.

When Pak returned to the bar, Manny shook his head. "Something's been bothering me, Animal. That's a good guitar, right?"

"Damn good," said Animal as he strummed some brisk chords. "It's a Gibson."

"Then how come you spray-painted it bright orange?"

"Had it stolen just after I got here. Air cops found it on a Thai when he tried to take it out the gate. Since I painted it orange, I can leave it anywhere and no one tries to steal it."

"The thing sure is ugly like that," Manny agreed.

One of the 357th Wild Weasel pilots was coming across the room. He wore a black handlebar mustache and was carrying a drink and a use-worn banjo. "Music time!" he hollered to Animal Hamlin in his Tennessee twang.

CHAPTER
SEVENTEEN

Wednesday, December 6th, 1500 Local—VPA Head-quarters, Hanoi, DRV

Colonel Xuan Nha

The generals continued to meet daily to engineer the victory demanded by the Enlightened One, and with each meeting the bickering in the room grew more strident. The subject was still where and how to stage the great victory over American ground forces.

General Tran Do, deputy commander of communist forces in the South, had been unable to attend the Hanoi meeting because of ongoing battles in the South. With Le Duc Tho away his hands were full, for the Viet Cong irregulars were difficult to control in the best of times. Even so, he'd sent voluminous pages of a plan he'd put together, his suggestion for a bold spring offensive.

Colonel Van Tra, commandant of combined Communist forces in the Delta and Saigon regions, had come in Tran Do's place to present his grand plan, and from his first day he'd seemed appalled at the continuous dissension and bickering. The attendees listened to Tran Do's plan, but it only seemed to fuel arguments, centered about every phase of the operation. Where would they hold the battle? How would they move men and supplies with appropriate stealth? How much of both were required? Should they include Viet Cong irregular troops in the important phases? Who should lead? Who should be second in command? Which troops should be held in reserve, and where? Was the timing—just after the Tet holiday truce—truly appropriate?

Today General Giap listened quietly to the bickering, letting it go on and on, although he'd indicated they must soon reach decisions. Periodically during an argument one of them would look to him for arbitration, but he'd just look on as if interested but not willing to interfere. When they spoke of Mee air intervention, however, he finally motioned a hand. The tone and volume of the arguments abated, but not enough. "Quiet," he uttered, and it became so.

"General Dung has just told me of a victory. A small battle, but a victorious one." He indicated that Van Tien Dung should provide details.

Puzzled looks prevailed. Ten days before, four crack People's Army regiments had been soundly defeated at Dak To, ground up with terrible losses after a twenty-day battle by a *lesser* number of American soldiers. Each day the estimates of communist casualties from the bitter fighting at Dak To grew. Certainly no victory had been reported to the group.

Dung's answer was a surprising one. "Colonel Xuan Nha sent an expeditionary force of militia to our western border to eliminate an enemy base there. . . ." Dung outlined what had happened at Ban Sao Si, changing the poorly defended navigation station to a stronghold, describing mountain tribesmen as enemy soldiers, expanding even the inflated estimates of destroyed Mee aircraft provided by the exuberant Commandant of Militia.

Xuan beamed his pleasure. This was the highest compliment he could be paid, to be extolled by his country's top two generals. The Enlightened One might be the supreme leader, but to a military man like Xuan Nha, praise from either of the nation's warrior leaders was a grand reward. This time it came from both! As Dung continued, it became apparent he would use the achievement at Ban Sao Si as a stepping stone to another subject. "Colonel Nha used a new

weapon to protect his men from air attacks." Dung nodded
for Xuan to provide details.

Xuan began to describe the shoulder-fired Strela missile,
but from his first words of infrared, solid propellant, intercept trajectories, and so forth, the generals' attentions
flagged. As he began discussing firing strategies, some
gained their feet to stretch wearily. He added a comment
about Strela being the answer to their requests for antiaircraft weapons in the South and said he'd send a group of his
men there to operate them. By then no one listened, so he
concluded.

Without pause the men went back to bickering over
where the attacks should be staged. General Tran Do's plan
was again detailed to the group by Colonel Van Tra, calling
for a strong attack on Saigon to paralyze the Mee and their
puppet army, while other forces simultaneously staged massive attacks upon Mee and ARVN bases throughout the
Mekong Delta and the central highlands. Yet others would
isolate, then take and hold Hué and Quang Tri. A few griz-
zled veterans raised eyebrows and relayed, for the hundredth time, their conviction that the plan was too
decentralized, that the various, widespread battles would be
too difficult to control.

General Dung argued for a quite different battle. He said
it must be held at a location they could easily resupply. His
staff officers had identified that place to be Khe Sanh, where
mountains surrounded a Mee base very near both the borders of the Democratic Republic and Cambodia. The terrain
was sufficiently similar to that of Dien Bien Phu to warrant
strong consideration.

Yet another general, this one on General Giap's own staff,
argued for multiple attacks throughout the South, much like
General Tran Do's plan, but those would be mere diversions
while massive numbers of troops poured directly across the
demilitarized zone, to march in a great tide down the coastal
highways, taking one city after another.

Xuan Nha listened as the generals argued, wondering
why they weren't interested in the Strela. But he'd had trouble convincing them of the need for other sophisticated
weapons and knew he shouldn't be surprised. Colonel Van
Tra, the arrival from Saigon, remained aghast at the petty
bickering. *Welcome to Hanoi politics,* Xuan Nha thought,

where political connivery is more important than accomplishments. He remained jubilant that the success at Ban Sao Si had been used as an example by Giap and Dung, for with those words of praise his position at the head of the VPAND was secured.

He thought the words "General Xuan Nha," and liked the sound.

Thursday, December 7th, 0645 Local—O' Club Dining Room, Takhli RTAFB, Thailand

Colonel Buster Leska

"G'mooning, Kunnel," said the waitress.

"Good morning," Buster answered brightly as he walked toward the reserved table at the rear of the room. He felt good this morning, *damn* good. He took his seat, accepted the typed menu, and pulled out his reading glasses, as if it were really necessary to examine the bill of fare.

B. J. Parker had done it differently. Every morning he'd demanded poached eggs on toast and bacon. Fresh eggs. Crisp bacon. The club officer had known that, and while the kitchen might run out of the various ingredients for other breakfasts, they'd kept enough on hand for the wing commander. B.J. had joked about it, saying it gave the pilots something to bitch about, which was a healthy tradition, and he'd continue to have a breakfast his aging stomach could digest.

When Buster had been a buck captain, he'd watched wing commanders get preferential treatment, and he remembered his resentment. Buster had the same menu as the rest of his officers. But regardless of how he demanded that he receive the same service as others, the club officer made sure his menu was freshly typed and easy to read, and that the chair at the head of his table was sturdy—unlike many of the others that wobbled precariously as the officers sat.

The three fighter-squadron commanders came into the entrance, talking with one another. Buster motioned and caught Lucky's eye, then waved them over. It was seldom all three were available at the same time.

They'd attended an 0600 intell meeting at the command post, the hottest topics being the loss of the Channel 97 TACAN, the buildup of supplies being funneled into the Ho Chi Minh Trail, and the fact that they were being sent out to bomb even fewer good targets. Increasingly the pilots were sent to patches of jungle that were suspected of sheltering truck parks, and when they bombed them, they most often got no secondary explosions or other feedback to show if anything had been down there. They were starting to call themselves "monkey killers," a nickname previously reserved for bomber crews.

As the three lieutenant colonels made their way down the length of the room, Buster evaluated them, as he often did his critical staff officers.

Obie Zeigler had turned out surprisingly well. His tendency to be overcautious was giving way, and he'd made some *almost* bold decisions for his 357th squadron.

Lucky Anderson was as capable as Moss had predicted. Maybe as good a combat commander as Mack MacLendon. His 333rd squadron ran so smoothly and got such fine results that Leska spent little time worrying about it. Anderson was a born leader, and his men would do about anything for him short of assassinating the Pope. Maybe that too.

Then there was Donovan, whom he'd insisted on putting into the job. Buster hated to be wrong. He was, though. He'd thought Yank would build a squadron of prima donnas like himself. Instead Yank was increasingly withdrawn, and Buster knew it was related to combat losses. His men disliked him, for Yank was not a lovable type at the best of times, and he seemed even more self-centered. The 354th squadron continued to function well, because they had a strong ops officer and good flight commanders. Yank spent so much of his time second-guessing wing ops and nitpicking the way they were flying combat that he was beginning to miss staff meetings, and Buster was tough on commanders who couldn't spare time to keep themselves informed.

The three lieutenant colonels arrived, muttered their "g'mornings," and sat.

Zeigler cast an appreciative eye at the door. "Look at that." The deputies for maintenance and logistics had entered, ushering newly arrived secretaries. Both were sharp looking. The younger one wore a miniskirt so short it was awe inspiring even to Buster's middle-aged eyes.

"Now *that's* worth fighting for," Obie Zeigler said with a grin.

After a minute of talking about the merits of having round-eye female secretaries rather than burly admin sergeants, they watched as Manny DeVera and Animal Hamlin came in, Manny opening doors and rushing about to seat Buster's secretary. Penny Dwight was looking better than she had since her boyfriend had been killed more than a week earlier. *The young,* Buster observed to himself, *are resilient.*

Obie put it another way. "That gal does not let moss grow twixt her toes."

"Yeah," growled Yank. "Her *big* toes." It was the kind of statement the old Yank Donovan would have made, and made Buster wonder if he wasn't finally reverting.

"Manny's doing a great job as weapons officer, Colonel," Obie Zeigler said.

Buster nodded in agreement. "He's a good man."

Even Yank agreed. "The ECM pods are working better since he started working the problem."

Obie pursued it. "He's flying the tough ones and setting an example. The Supersonic Wetback briefs something, then he goes out and shows the guys how to do it."

Lucky Anderson spoke up. "Manny's got moxie you don't often find in a captain."

"About time you said something," said Obie. "You've been as talkative as wallpaper."

Anderson tried to ignore his friend's comment. Zeigler nudged Donovan. "Man's in love—only time he's human's when the Ice Maiden's around."

"I've never liked that nickname," Lucky complained.

"Hell, we all like her, Lucky. She's one sharp lady." Zeigler nodded to the others. "I was at Sembach in fifty-nine, when Lucky and the Ice Maiden first met. They made all the wives'-club gossip columns . . . went around giving each other secret looks like they were a couple teenagers." He turned back to Lucky. "Where's Linda, anyway? Back in Bangkok?"

Lucky was embarrassed by the attention given his private

life. "She's making the rounds of the bases. I'm expecting a phone call tonight from NKP."

"I'm surprised you two never tied the knot."

Anderson mumbled something. "What was that?" asked Donovan, leaning toward him.

Lucky's voice remained hardly audible. "We get married in May. I'll be done before then, and she's going to get an early transfer. Middle of May in Big Spring, Texas. You're all invited."

"Hot damn!" Zeigler grinned. "Gentlemen, we're witnessing the end of a long and pleasant friendship."

"Congratulations," Buster said. "I'll expect a free drink at the stag bar tonight."

"I didn't want to announce it on a loudspeaker," Lucky grumbled.

Obie Zeigler raised his voice to a near shout. "HELL, LUCKY, WE WON'T TELL ANYONE THAT YOU'RE MARRYING LINDA IN MAY AT BIG SPRING, TEXAS!"

Buster chuckled as Anderson looked frantically about. While it was often difficult to define the expression on the badly burned face, Lucky was obviously mortified.

"Yayyyyy!" hollered a group of grinning captains. "Shit hot!" shouted a lieutenant. Manny DeVera hurried over and energetically pumped Lucky's hand. "That's great! Congratulations!"

Anderson stood, grimacing as others lined up. "Thanks, Obie," he snarled.

"Don't mention it," Zeigler said heartily as the line continued to grow.

Leska took it all in wryly.

During the hubbub Yank Donovan leaned toward Buster with a look more troubled than normal. "I got a phone call from Tom Lyons yesterday, Colonel. He's the new deputy commander of the PACAF inspector–general team."

Leska hardly heard. He certainly didn't care much about the subject. "So?"

Donovan opened his mouth to say more, then stopped himself. "Just thought you'd want to know," he finally muttered.

Buster smiled at the hard time the guys were giving Lucky Anderson. A captain asked if the marriage to the USAID lady meant she'd start handing out shovels to the pilots. Animal Hamlin said hell no, it meant the 333rd had to start dropping rice on the North Vietnamese.

1425L—South of BRL TACAN, Laos

Sergeant Black

It was their eighth day since skinnying down the western precipice. Only six of their seven had gathered at the base of the vertical path. One Hotdog was missing. Two of the surviving renegades were wounded, one with a head wound where a bullet had shattered his jaw, the other with a fractured leg suffered after a thirty-foot fall down the mountainside.

For the first two days they'd holed up in one of the thousand limestone caves that honeycombed the western side of the mountain, quietly because a group of militia were camped close by. The lieutenant had covertly pulled his bayonet knife, to ensure silence if the pain became too much for either of the injured men to bear. Thankfully, he'd not had to use it. On the third day the militia camp had been left with only six men in attendance. The four healthy Hotdogs had taken care of them, their gunfire muffled by Phantoms bombing the mountain. During that attack the militia had fired several guided rockets, but as Black had forecast, the Phantoms were too high and flying too fast for them. The first night, when the AC-47 had dropped down to fire its guns, it had intermittently released flares to decoy the heat-seeking rockets away from the aged aircraft. The dragon ship went unharmed, although several rockets had been fired at them too.

If they'd only done that before the militia came up the mountain, Black had commiserated, but he'd dismissed the thought; it was a *what if,* and he didn't have time to clutter his mind with those.

After killing the six soldiers, they'd set and splintered the one Hotdog's injured leg, unbound and forced soft food through the other's shattered jaw, then set out walking southward, past the militia gathered about the mountain. It proved to be slow going. After five days of travel, Black estimated they'd come less than forty klicks. The Hotdog with the injured leg slowed them some, but the one with the wounded jaw had grown delirious, and they'd had to lead and sometimes carry him.

They had maps spread and were trying to plan their route. They were 500 kilometers north of their home base at Nakhon Phanom, with no way to contact Buffalo Soldier. Since they couldn't lug the thing down the mountainside, Black had destroyed the HF radio, leaving only the hand-held VHFs with their very short range. To their east was North Vietnam, and to the west concentrations of enemy troops. They couldn't travel to the southwest, for the Plains des Jars, thick with Pathet Lao guerrillas, lay in that direction. Travel southward was equally dangerous. Before leaving NKP, Black had seen estimates of 70,000 Pathet Lao, gathering into battalion strengths throughout the panhandle.

The lieutenant suggested that they walk southeast to Muang Hiam, where Royal Laotian government forces manned an often-besieged outpost on the eastern rim of the Plains des Jars. Before they'd left NKP, Black had heard Muang Hiam was about to be engaged by a Pathet Lao force, but he went along with the idea, for he had nothing better to offer. They made three more kilometers before the Hotdog with the shattered jaw collapsed. They placed him in a cool spot and forced water down him, but he became unconscious. Half an hour later they heard a long, low moan, and the lieutenant gripped his hand while he thrashed. He finally stiffened, relaxed, and died.

The group sat about and talked about their dead comrade's exploits, how he'd been a faithful friend and a good soldier. The lieutenant said he'd come from a village near the coastal city of Cam Pha, where his father had been a fisherman.

"When we go to Ha Wa Eee," said Nguyen, the youngest of the group and also the dreamer, "we will *all* be fishermen."

They talked about the missing man and spoke well of him too. The Hotdog with the broken leg said he hoped he'd been killed, because if he'd been captured and it was found that he'd deserted to fight for the Mee, his fate would be severe.

"Yes," said the lieutenant in a soft voice. "We must not be captured."

They nodded and were silent for a while. They all had their individual reasons for despising the Hanoi regime. The lieutenant's case was not uncommon. He'd returned from officers' training to find that his thirteen-year-old sister had been taken while his parents had been tending their fields. A neighbor had whispered that a passing sergeant had seen her outside their house and led her away toward the nearby training camp. When his parents had hurried there, she'd already been sent with a company of soldiers going south to battle. They'd been given two small sacks of rice and told that the girl would be well treated. They should be proud she'd been chosen to serve her country. The lieutenant hadn't told his parents what the NVA did with the young girls commandeered from the countryside, or that they did not remain young after a few months of tending to the soldiers' needs—preparing their meals, serving as unit whore, and bearing huge loads of camp goods on the daily marches. He had nightmares about the treatment he knew she was receiving. If she was lucky, she'd died of disease or childbirth on the trail while carrying a fifty-kilo pack through the jungle.

Young Nguyen sighed. "I will be very happy when we go to Ha Wa Eee. When will that be, Sarge Brack?"

"Be patient." Black had promised to help get them to the Hawaiian Islands. People there were tolerant of the various races, he'd told them. They'd fit right in. He believed that. Nguyen asked him to describe Ha Wa Eee again, and Black spent an hour talking about his home. Their home too, once he got things moving properly. They remained spellbound as he described it.

When he finally grew silent, the lieutenant said in island pidgin, "Mebbe we bettuh sleep, bruddahs."

Early the next morning they crossed a well-traveled road. After talking it over, Black and the lieutenant left the injured man attended by the two others beside the muddy Hong Neun River while they slipped into Houa Muang, a small walled city a couple of kilometers distant. There they spoke to several people who didn't seem to think it odd that an NVA officer and an American sergeant were together. They were accustomed to seeing soldiers of many descriptions, and it made little difference what uniforms they wore.

The two returned with bad news. The outpost at Muang

Hiam, where they were headed, had been abandoned to foreigners, likely NVA, for a man had gestured at the lieutenant's uniform. Others like them were thick in the area, especially to the south where they were heading.

They talked the situation over again. The lieutenant shook his head grimly. "They are everywhere before us."

"And behind us," Sergeant Black offered, studying the map. He thought of something, nodded to himself, then traced with a finger. "We could go down the Hong Neun."

The lieutenant frowned. "That is into Vietnam," he said.

Black moved the finger. "Remember this place?" A year earlier, on their first recon into North Vietnam, they'd manned an observation post on a branch of the Ho Chi Minh trail.

The lieutenant's eyes narrowed.

"We need a long-range radio. We left one in the cache there."

The lieutenant lifted his head and stared thoughtfully at the muddy river. "Will the battery pack still be charged after so long?"

"I can think of no other way."

"We will need a boat," the lieutenant said.

CHAPTER EIGHTEEN

Monday, December 11th, 0755 Local—PACAF Headquarters, Hickam AFB, Hawaii

Colonel Tom Lyons

Tom had been at the headquarters for only three weeks, but he'd already made a trip to Saigon to look into problem areas General Roman felt were important. After hard questioning, mostly using threats of courts-martial on young enlisted men, he'd found that the people at Seventh Air Force had been withholding information, and Bomber Joe had been able to make corrections that forced the "fucking cowboys" to toe the line.

That morning Lyons had arrived at his office to find a note on his desk. Roman wanted to see him at eight o'clock, following his morning intell briefing.

Lyons stepped into the general's outer office and regarded the brunette secretary. Good legs, superb ass, and passable tits. Definitely worth expending effort on.

Since learning that the general shared confidences with Tom, her attitude toward him had improved. She treasured her position as the general's executive secretary and was careful to treat Roman's inner staff better than others. She was also impressed with Lyon's family and their old money. He'd taken her to lunch the previous week, and she'd hung on to his words about life among the privileged—hardly able to take a bite of her meal, she'd listened so hard. She was "in the bag," as his father once said about a woman he'd been eyeing. Meaning she'd be a sure thing.

Her husband should pose no problem. He might even be the key to push her into the sack.

"Colonel Lyons," she greeted from behind her desk, smiling as if pleased to see him.

He used his haughty look. Her kind expected to be treated like furniture. "Is the general available?" he asked.

"He's finished with the morning briefing and will be off the telephone shortly. Coffee, sir?"

He gave her a brief nod.

She hurried to the urn, carefully poured a cup, and dutifully brought it to him.

After ten minutes, when he'd finished the coffee and periodically eyed the brunette as she typed, she purred that the general was ready to receive him. In the bag.

He went inside quietly, as he'd learned to do, and stood waiting for the general to motion him forward. It was somewhat of a charade, for a couple of follow-up phone calls after their initial conversation had served to change things solidly in Tom's favor. His father, along with his powerful father-in-law, had let it be known through third parties that they *might* be willing to back Roman in his bid to replace General McManus as CSAF. The rotation would come in the spring, unless McManus had another problem with his heart and it happened sooner. Since word of the two powerful men's support had been leaked, Roman had treated Tom with increased respect.

Roman beckoned from his massive desk. "Got something for you to chew on, Lyons."

"Yes, sir?"

The general sat back in his chair and mused for a moment, the corners of his mouth turned downward as if he'd tasted something unpleasant. "Concerns Jim McManus, the Cee SAF. Seems the old fart's up to some connivery."

"Oh?"

"He paid a couple of visits to the White House. At least

two, maybe more. Very quietly, like he didn't want anyone to know."

"What was the subject, sir?" Lyons asked.

"That's the part that pisses me off. The report of the visits came from a fellow in the SecDef's office, but he didn't know what they talked about. There's some typical Pentagon whispers, but they're just farting in the wind."

Bomber Joe abruptly stood and walked to the window to look out upon Pearl Harbor. He stared for a moment, then nodded at the scene. "Twenty-six years ago Jap torpedo planes flew right down that channel out there, Lyons. Took out our battleship navy. I feel like the men who were betrayed back then. McManus is working some kind of surprise, and I don't like it one bit."

Tom Lyons held his tongue.

"You haven't heard anything from your . . . ah . . . relatives about this?"

"Sir, if I had, you'd have been the first to know."

"McManus is pulling something slick, Lyons, and I want to know what it is."

"I'll see if I can find out, sir."

"You do that. Maybe"—he hesitated, phrasing carefully—"your father-in-law could fill you in. He talks with Johnson."

"Yes, sir, but it's unlikely he'd tell me about their conversations." Senator Lingenfelter was indeed a confidant of the President, but Tom knew it would be difficult to gain hard information. His wife's father had agreed to help with the rumor that he *might* support Roman for CSAF, but that had been a simple matter, and he could always change his mind. Betraying a confidence of the President was something quite different. He was consistently closemouthed about such things.

"Have you heard of something called JACKPOT?" Roman asked quietly.

"What is it, sir?"

Roman worked his jaw angrily, then abruptly shook his head. "Dunno. Something McManus's plans people are working on. They may have changed the name, because as far as I can find out from my contacts, that code name hasn't been reserved. I think it might be what the Cee SAF's seeing the President about. That fucking cowboy Moss may have something to do with it."

Lyons was surprised. "General Moss?"

"Yeah. I get feedback from the same Pentagon source that Jim McManus and Moss are exchanging love letters that may have something to do with this JACKPOT thing. He couldn't find out anything more specific."

"But General Moss is your subordinate."

"The bastard's going behind my back, and it's probably not the first time. I'd've replaced him a long time ago, but he's got powerful supporters, and it appears McManus is among 'em."

The intercom buzzed and Roman gruffly answered, and dictated something to the secretary in a terse voice.

As Roman talked, Tom Lyons thought about Lieutenant General Richard Moss, who several months earlier had booted him out of his headquarters and sent him to Takhli, where his latest problems had begun. If there was a way for Tom to get even, he'd not hesitate.

Roman slammed the phone down. "Woman needs a good fucking," he muttered.

Tom had entertained the same idea.

"JACKPOT." Roman repeated the word a couple more times.

"Perhaps I should go to back to Saigon and nose around the headquarters there."

"Yeah. You do that. But first go out to the bases where you have contacts and see if they're sending Moss backup data. Try to check into any back-channel message traffic. Find out what this fucking JACKPOT thing is and get the information to me ASAP."

"I'll give it my best, sir."

"Before you go, see if Senator Lingenfelter can find out anything, okay?"

Tom hesitated. "I'll try."

Roman stalked to his desk, still brooding. He glared suddenly. "It's got something to do with the war. You can bank on it."

Tom mused.

"Lyons, I'll let you in on something else."

"Yes, sir?"

"If and when I get the Cee SAF job, I plan to suggest that we stop all bombing of North Vietnam that doesn't directly support our ground forces. It's counterproductive.

Read the strategic-bombing survey conducted after World War II, and you'll learn that bombing a population does not end wars. The Luftwaffe tried it with England, and it just strengthened British resolve. Same thing happened in Berlin. That's what we're doing with North Vietnam. Every time we send a bunch of fighters up north to drop bombs and one of the things misses and hits a farmer's house, we piss off more people and make them band together that much closer."

That made sense to Lyons. He remembered hearing about the postwar survey when he'd attended the Air War College.

"If we'd hit the right targets, or if we were determined enough to nuke the bastards, it would be different. *That* would put an end to the thing. But we won't, so we should stop doing this halfway shit."

Tom remained attentive.

"I wonder if McManus is suggesting something like that, stopping the bombing." Roman pursed his lips thoughtfully.

The general looked at Tom sharply and gave the grimace-smile. "Moss doesn't like you, Lyons. It was him that had the flag put on your records saying you were nonpromotable."

"Oh?" Tom fidgeted uneasily, although he'd guessed that.

Roman chuckled. "You ever think of what'll happen if McManus keeps making points with the President, him being buddies with Moss? What you going to do if Moss or one of his cronies gets the Cee SAF job when McManus steps down? How long do you think you'd last?"

Lyons stared, a knot growing in his stomach. *Could that happen?* he wondered.

"So you see, we've both got an interest in finding out what's going on with this JACKPOT thing. You . . . and me. If I get the top-dog position, you'll come along with me, and that means a star. If someone like Moss gets it, I'll retire, and you might as well go fishing with me."

At the mention of wearing a star, Tom Lyons grew more intent. He became determined to find out everything possible about JACKPOT. He even wondered if there was a way to get the information from his father-in-law. As General Roman continued, Lyons's mind was busy, thinking of how a star on his shoulder would make so much that he'd endured worthwhile. While the general's mood continued to darken, his own improved considerably.

As he left the inner office, the secretary was leaning over a file cabinet, sorting through a drawer. Tom stared at her nicely rounded ass for a moment, then approached closer, remembering what his father liked to say, that "privileges are due the privileged." Fucking her would certainly be one of those. He'd been screwing a couple of call girls lately, because Margaret was indisposed more than she was available to him, and he looked forward to something fresher, and with more challenge—like the general's ambitious secretary.

He cleared his throat.

She turned, then smiled as she took her seat at the desk. "Yes, sir?"

He dropped his voice. "This evening after I get off, I'll drop by the Hale Koa downstairs bar. Maybe I could see you there. Buy you a drink and talk things over."

She furrowed her brow. "I don't think . . ."

Tom Lyons didn't appreciate hesitation from women of lower class. "Seven o'clock," he said in a more authoritative voice.

She grew flustered. "I mean . . . your wife, colonel. You're married."

He shrugged and gave her a smile. "So are you." Her husband was a civilian who worked on the transient aircraft flight line. He'd been a GS-8 for five years now, and his supervisor said he'd likely remain in that grade for another three. Tom had made it a point to find out.

She looked troubled.

Dumb bitch. He didn't hesitate to apply leverage. "I believe your husband's eligible for promotion this cycle."

She stared. "I think so."

Of course she knew. She also knew that his bosses would be attentive to the Deputy IG for PACAF. A word to his supervisor, and perhaps another to the lieutenant colonel *he* worked for, would undoubtedly make a difference in the priority list submitted to the promotion board.

"Maybe I can help." Lyons arched an eyebrow. "We'll talk about it over a drink."

Her eyes remained evasive, but he knew she was thinking about it. Her words emerged in a small whisper. "I don't think it would be advisable for us to be seen in a bar together."

He glowered, wondering if he'd made a mistake about the level of her ambition.

"Someone might talk." She looked about for listeners and deftly licked at her lower lip. "You know how rumors get started."

He understood and felt relieved. She was still in the bag. "You're right." He fished a key out of his pocket—the one to a Hale Koa guest quarters used by visiting dignitaries. "Room six-oh-four. Seven o'clock. Don't bother to change." He left, glancing back only once. She was at her desk, examining the key with an amused look, then putting it into her purse.

In the bag. Another notch on the old musket. The fleeting thought that she'd been awfully easy to convince passed through his mind, but he dismissed it.

Lyons smiled to himself as he walked down the hall toward the stairs. He had a briefing on his morning schedule. Some guy from Nellis Air Force Base pitching some pie-in-the-sky idea called Pave Dagger, which was some kind of homing bomb. He hoped it would be a short presentation, because he planned to drop by the Hale Koa for an early lunch, then go up to the guest suite and make sure the bar was properly stocked and the room ready.

She was the kind who'd be impressed with horse-piss champagne, anything chilled in an ice bucket with a white towel draped over it.

Yeah. Fuck her for a couple of nights running to put himself in a proper mood before he left for Saigon. If she performed well, he might even put in the good word for her husband.

Maybe not. It would be enough to give the silly bitch a few hours of his time. Keep dangling the promotion carrot in case he wanted more of her. Young and up-and-coming. On his way to wearing stars. Old moneyed family. Hell, she should be grateful he asked her.

1000L—XOO Briefing Room, PACAF HQ

Captain Moods Diller

The classified pitch was to a group of twenty staff officers, most of them majors and captains from ops and requirements. There was also a full bull from the IG shop.

Moods kept it light, simplifying the complex Pave Dagger concept to basic and understandable elements. He also worked hard to keep his speech from reverting to rapid-fire mode, which some found difficult to understand.

As the briefing continued past eleven o'clock, the colonel from the inspector-general team began to peer at his watch and frown.

Moods asked if anyone had questions about the illuminator pod, which he'd just described.

"Why Danang?" the colonel from the IG team barked unpleasantly.

Moods blinked, caught unawares. "I . . . uh . . . they have the assets we need for the test."

The colonel's frown deepened.

Had Moods said something wrong? He elaborated. "We had to choose one of the F-4 units, because we use Phantoms to carry the illuminator pods. Danang's the biggest F-4 base in the theater and has a large maintenance setup. Then there's the—"

The colonel snorted impatiently. "Whose stupid idea is this anyway?"

Moods stared, first at the colonel, then at the image of the pod on the screen. "Ahhh. It was first thought up-by-a-group-of . . ." He realized he was rushing his words, so he took a breath and slowed his speech. ". . . engineers out in—"

The colonel waved his hand. "We don't have time for shit like this at our combat units. If you didn't know, there's a war going on, *Captain*." He spat out the rank as if it were a dirty word.

"The test . . . ah . . . the combat test has been approved by the Pentagon requirements directorate, and—"

"Why didn't you ask us first?"

"Colonel?"

"You've got trouble speaking clearly—perhaps you can't

hear either. I said"—he pronounced his words distinctly—"why ... didn't ... you ... ask ... us ... first? It's a simple question, *Captain*. Why didn't you have the common courtesy to request permission from the major command where you wanted to hold your test? Is that too much to ask?"

"I ... uh ... coordinated with Seventh Air Force headquarters in Saigon, and I thought ... with the Pentagon Requirements Division telling us to proceed—"

"Ahhh," said the colonel, removing a pen from his pocket. "Who at Seventh Air Force approved the request?"

"You see, the Requirements Division—"

"That's at the Pentagon, *Captain*. Now, specifically whom did you speak with at Seventh?"

Moods blurted the only name he remembered. "Lieutenant Colonel Gates?"

The colonel wrote the name down. "Thank you. Now I would appreciate it if you held up this ridiculous test of yours until we find out—"

"Colonel Lyons?" A major from the ops-requirements branch interrupted.

The IG colonel regarded him morosely for daring to intrude.

"We knew about the test, sir. Both from Nellis and Seventh Air Force, and we received the message about the test from the Pentagon two weeks ago. The Deputy for Operations approved it."

Lyons was momentarily silenced. Since the PACAF DO was a major general, Moods felt the colonel's argument was over. He was wrong.

"Don't you think I knew that, Major!" Lyons suddenly snarled.

The major drew back.

"Of course I did, and I also know the paperwork was improperly staffed and coordinated before it went forward to the general."

The major blinked incredulously. "I personally briefed the general, and—"

"Who's your superior officer, major?"

"Lieutenant Colonel Brown, sir, and I believe you'll find—"

"Have Brown report to me"—he glanced at his watch—"first thing in the morning."

"Sir?"

Lyons stood and turned his glare back upon Moods. "We'll see about your dumb-shit project, *Captain*."

He stalked out.

The room was very quiet.

"Who was that?" Moods finally asked.

The major shook his head, his look troubled. "He's new. Name's Lyons, and he's the Deputy I.G." He sighed. "Our two-star Deputy for Operations was just reassigned, and we're waiting on his replacement . . . and he knows it."

A captain from ops spoke up. "The guys at the IG shop tell us Lyons is a good man to avoid. He's got a shitty memory about everything except people he dislikes, and from what they say, it's easy to get on the list."

Moods thought about that for a moment, then continued his Pave Dagger briefing where he'd left off.

He was wrapping things up with a final question-and-answer period when a sergeant came in. The aircraft commander of a KC-135 had just phoned. The aircraft had been refueled and they were waiting out on the ramp for him. Takeoff was scheduled in thirty-five minutes.

Moods Diller was not unhappy to leave the headquarters.

1225L—Near Nakhon Phanom, Thailand

GS-15 Linda Lopes

There were three in the white USOM jeep: Peter Johnston, who was her field man in the Nakhon Phanom area, a driver-interpreter-bodyguard named Pham, who was Peter's employee, and herself. The men occupied the front seats, with Pham's CAR-15 assault rifle resting between them, and she was alone in the back. They rode with the canvas top up to shield them from the hot sun, but the side panels had been removed for air circulation, and dust billowed inside and threatened to clog their nostrils whenever Pham drove too slowly.

They'd just left a small village and were stopped at a crossroads, discussing whether they should continue to the next town or return to the air base for lunch and a shower in Linda's trailer.

"We'll leave the decision to you," said Peter. "You're the lady."

As well as your boss, she thought archly. Peter was a bit of a brownnoser and tended to fawn. If he worked for Paul Anderson, he'd probably get his ass chewed daily. Peter was not so fortunate, for he worked for Linda, and her way was much simpler. If a subordinate screwed up, she'd patiently tell him his error and advise him to improve. She'd do that a total of three times, and then she'd quietly get rid of him. Peter Johnston had recently made his third and final error. She was the Ice Maiden and had a reputation to uphold in the fiefdom dominated by males.

"Let's eat," she decided. Pham put the jeep into gear and turned right, onto the river road leading toward the American base just north of the city of Nakhon Phanom. "Naked Fanny," the Americans there called both the town and the base.

It had been another frustrating morning. The villagers were nice enough, if a bit withdrawn, but she hadn't liked the man Peter had selected to act as their local contact in the network. It wasn't that the man had done anything wrong, but rather his habit of staring away haughtily when she asked a question.

Peter said the others in the village looked up to the man, but Linda felt it was something else. Fear? And why should they fear the man? He wasn't the headman. That was an ancient, semi-senile codger who'd led the village since he'd been appointed more than twenty years before.

"I don't like your selection," she told Peter as the driver picked up speed on the wide dirt path called the river road, because it paralleled the Mekong River. As they went faster, less dust poured inside. She used the respite to clench her eyes and mop her face with a handkerchief.

"The contact?" Johnston frowned.

"I didn't like the way he refused to look me in the eye."

Johnston chuckled. "The Thais here aren't used to seeing a woman in charge. He was probably worrying about losing face because he was even *talking* to you."

Linda had experienced that and knew how to cope with it, but she had the feeling this was something different. "It was more than that," she said.

Peter grinned. "You're the boss. You don't like him, I'll pick another contact."

"Do that. I've got to get back to Bangkok in the morning. Richard called and left word we've got a group of congressmen coming in, and they want a briefing on the grain-distribution program."

Richard was not only the Chief of Operations for the Bangkok embassy, but also head of State Department intelligence for Burma, Laos, Cambodia, and Thailand. South Vietnam eluded his grasp, for that effort was closely orchestrated by Ambassador Bunker, who preferred to use the CIA for his purposes. Since the agency was so preoccupied with military ops in Southeast Asia, she felt the covert intelligence effort in South Vietnam was in the dark ages compared to theirs. Richard was damned good at his job.

So was she. When Linda briefed the congressman tomorrow about their successes in their USAID projects, improving their image and making the Thais think well of Americans, she wouldn't be lying. Too bad she couldn't brief them on the other efforts that took up the majority of her time. Of the eight major U.S. military installations in Thailand, six were protected by secretive networks of local informants. The Thai Army had used their information to chase down four North Viet agents, two with radios still in their possession, and they were hot on the tracks of a fifth. They'd also broken up two cells of local communist terrorists who were using the national telephone system to report information about American operations, and intercepted a courier from another. All of that had been due to information Linda gleaned from her networks.

But she'd not had that kind of success at NKP. CTs crossed the river from Laos almost freely and escaped there when they required sanctuary. While Laos was ostensibly neutral, Prince Souvanna Phouma's government walked a tightrope between two rampaging lions. They accepted U.S. military and financial aid to help fight off Pathet Lao guerrillas, but not so much or so overtly that they'd be seen as U.S. allies, like Thailand and South Vietnam. They spoke in friendly terms with the Russians, North Vietnamese, and Chinese, but not so friendly as to anger the United States. They were enemies of neither capitalism nor communism. When Khmer Rouge from Cambodia or Thai CTs crossed into Laos, they did so at peace as long as they didn't make trouble for government forces.

Recently, the tempo of the battles raging between Laotian and Pathet Lao forces throughout the central and southern parts of the country had increased dramatically, and coordination with the Americans had all but evaporated, which made her job at NKP difficult.

Linda desperately wanted to establish a useful network of observers in the villages around the base. The CT were reporting on base operations, which included some very sensitive missions, directly to the people who ran the communist effort throughout Southeast Asia, the Lao Dong party and Viet People's Army in Hanoi. Thus far the people Peter Johnston had recruited in the villages had given them little information. Which made her question Johnston's ability and was the reason for the extended visit.

What she'd seen had not been reassuring, and she'd come to a decision. When she returned next week, she'd bring Johnston's replacement. She liked the pleasant-natured, redheaded man, but he just wasn't holding up his end of the board.

They drove through a small village along the river road, past stilted shanties and piers with long, narrow boats, then past a fish-merchant establishment, with its large drying racks and the pervasive, pungent odors of sun-cured fish.

The driver nodded ahead at the thick trees where the road reentered the jungle. A roadside marker read: Nakhon Phanom 14 km. "Mebbe nod long now," the driver said.

Johnston laughed. "You hungry, Pham?"

"Berry, berry."

That was Pham's unique way of saying "Yeah, I'm hungry as a horse," and also, "It is indeed a beautiful sunset," or even, "That Woman's awfully pretty." You'd ask him any question and if he agreed, he'd say "Berry, berry." Linda had first thought he meant "very, very," but when she'd asked, he'd frowned and shook his head. "Berry, berry," he'd repeated, as if that was what he'd said, and what he'd meant. Pham had been an English instructor at a Nakhon Phanom school when Johnston had hired him.

Your lack of hiring skills are another nail in your coffin, Peter, she was thinking as Pham slowed down and negotiated a turn in the road. They emerged in a small clearing, and he continued going slowly, for there was another sharp turn just ahead.

It happened too quickly for her to comprehend. Her first realization that something was wrong came when the vehicle skidded and teetered, but there was also the loud staccato sound of automatic-weapons fire, a brief shriek from one of the men in the front seat, and the force of being hurled sideward. Although her seat belt was fastened, Linda's head careened off the back of Peter's seat, then was jolted sideways as the jeep rose onto its two left wheels.

The jeep skidded and slowly toppled, as if they were in stop-frame action in a movie. As the vehicle continued, sliding on its side, the canvas top was torn away.

"Ummphh!" she grunted when the jeep came to a rest, still on its side.

It became very quiet. Then she heard a low groan, and the word "Jesus" sobbed by Peter Johnston. Linda moved and grunted painfully because the seat belt was cutting her in two. She fumbled with it and saw that Peter was doing the same thing in front.

Peter succeeded in freeing himself first and slid down onto Pham.

"Get the rifle," she hissed with effort. The belt was cutting off her wind.

Her own seat belt finally came loose, and she fell into the dirt of the roadway, resting there for a moment to collect her wits. She carried a small-caliber pistol in her shoulder bag, but she couldn't find the bag and wondered if it hadn't been thrown out. She ignored the metallic taste of a nosebleed and the thumping pain behind her right eye as she felt around her.

"Oh, Jesus!" Peter cried out. "He's dead." Peter Johnston rose to his feet staring down in revulsion, then staggered away from the jeep. It was his last screwup. The loud, staccato burst was short, and he immediately wilted.

Linda heard sounds from behind the overturned vehicle, and her mind raced.

Blood was still gushing from her nose and covering her blouse. She tended to bleed profusely when anything rapped her anywhere *near* her nose.

Think of something!

She heard the noises again, of humans moving with caution.

Play dead!

She smeared bright-red from her nosebleed onto her blouse, then went limp and closed her eyes, drooped her jaw, and generally tried to appear lifeless.

Closer sounds now.

A foot prodded at her side, and a voice muttered an order in Thai. She heard their grunts and sounds then as they searched one of her companions.

She prayed that someone would come along the road.

Pop! The sound of a small-caliber pistol.

More chatter from the men. A low laugh.

Pop! The pistol sounded again. She suppressed a shudder as she wondered.

Someone came close then and knelt beside her. She felt something metallic being pressed against the base of her neck, and suddenly she knew!

BOOK II

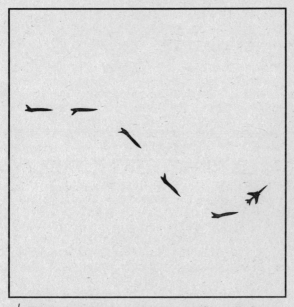

√ **Six** [spoken "check six"] [fighter-pilot jargon, circa 1966] < words used to warn another pilot to observe his rear quadrant closely for enemy aircraft—*Informal* phr. cautioning others to watch out for themselves, remain wary of sneak attack.

CHAPTER NINETEEN

Tuesday, December 12th, 1500 Local—VPA Headquarters, Hanoi, DRV

Colonel Xuan Nha

It was Giap's day of decision. The meetings and bitter arguments had gone on for more than a month, but this afternoon he entered the meeting room with a brooding countenance and did not respond to greetings. His mind was weighted, and he wanted no distraction.

Vo Nguyen Giap took his seat before them and spoke very slowly. "This is my decision after listening to you for so many days." He stared out at the group gravely, taking his time, and Xuan Nha knew he was attending a momentous point in the great War of Unification. General Giap, with his great sense of the historical, would finally outline his road map for victory.

"Honorable Le Duc Tho, messages from commanders in the South, and Colonel Tran Van Tra here, have told us that if given the proper encouragement, the people in the South will join us in a massive uprising. We must make that happen."

His voice cracked with brittleness. A sign of aging? Of weariness of war?

"General Tran Do sent a detailed plan from his headquarters saying we should attack relentlessly, massively, in a dozen vulnerable locations. Good. An ambitious plan. It shall be done. Colonel Tran Van Tra traveled many dangerous kilometers and tells us that if he is provided with appropriate resources, he will be able to take Saigon, if only for a short while, which will create disorder within the puppet government. I agree. He shall be provided with the resources and it shall be done. General Dung says that the American Dien Bien Phu should be at Khe Sanh, since it is near both the borders of the Democratic Republic and Cambodia, and we can easily mass and group our soldiers and supplies. Good. I agree. We shall attack there. My own staff says that we should capture and hold their provincial capitals. I agree. We shall attack and take them and hold them.

"It shall be in *all* of those places, and the fight will be made by *all* of our forces, including *all* regular and irregular units in the South. There shall be no idle reserves. The battles will be widespread and quickly grow to include the people, the angry civilians who will rise up to join us and fight. You shall all have your wishes. You shall all provide your victories."

The audience was stunned by the outrageous scope of the plan.

"Each of our commanders in the South must do as Xuan Nha has done at Ban Sao Si . . . win a single, modest victory, take and hold a single area . . . but that will mean many victories, that we control many places . . . and the result will be like ten Dien Bien Phus!"

The room remained hushed. Expressions varied from apprehension to smiles of wonder.

Giap looked at Le Duc Tho, who had quietly slipped into the room and surely knew about his decision. "With your concurrence I shall name General Tran Do to coordinate the attacks according to the plan he has submitted."

"A wise choice," said Le Duc Tho. Xuan peered at the powerful man, thinking he'd likely asked for that selection. If things went wrong, Tran Do would be blamed. If they went well, Le Duc Tho would claim credit, for Tran Do was his deputy.

"We shall attack relentlessly," said Giap, "and all of the South shall be set aflame." He turned to Colonel Tran Van Tra, who had traveled so far for the meetings. "Surely you have had enough of talking."

Van Tra readily agreed.

"We will provide you with men, artillery, supplies. Take Saigon . . . offer it to the Enlightened One."

"I will leave immediately."

Giap studied General Dung, then pursed his lips. "Send your force to the hills about Khe Sanh as you wanted, and begin your attacks ten days before Tran Do's battles begin. Engage and destroy the Mee forces there. If they are persistent, as they've proved to be in the past, hold and paralyze them. We will tell the world that we are about to win a great battle, and while the Mee worry about Khe Sanh, we shall be moving units and massing supplies."

Dung agreed, though characteristically hesitant to do so.

Giap asked the group to continue to meet for a while longer, for now they must agree upon the timing of the hundred great battles that would mark the beginning of the end of the great War of Unification. Without further word he left them.

The meeting continued, but at 1530 Xuan Nha slipped out to gain a report about the Mee air attacks of the day, and how his forces had done with them. Quang Hanh waited in an outer office. His report was a good one; no targets had been bombed in the Hanoi or Haiphong areas. The Mee pilots had sent two waves of aircraft to Vinh and attacked the dock areas. Except for several reconnaissance flights, there was little else to report.

Xuan dismissed the lieutenant, wondering if the Mee were not also up to something momentous. When he turned to go back into the meeting, he found General Tho before him.

"It is a glorious day," said Xuan Nha.

General Tho was not there to speak about Giap's decision. "More than a month has passed since we last talked about Quon," he said.

Xuan Nha remained silent.

"Did you speak of the matter with your wife's nephew?" he asked.

"I passed the message," Xuan said, wishing he'd followed

up. He'd *assumed* that Li Binh had spoken to Nguyen Wu. Surely she'd not forgotten such an important request. He decided that it must be Wu who was dragging his feet for some reason or other.

"Le Duc Tho will depart soon," said the general, eyeing him. "The matter is to be concluded. Quon's reeducation must be completed before my uncle leaves. Quon's assistance to me is important in these turbulent times." General Tho had relied heavily upon Quon since the very formulation of the VPAAF.

"I will relay the message once more," said Xuan Nha.

"Your wife is a capable and valuable asset to the Republic," said the VPAAF general in a slow and deliberate tone. "My uncle does not wish to bring discredit to her nephew, but . . ."

He left the remainder of the sentence unspoken as he returned to the meeting.

Xuan stood silently, angry that Nguyen Wu hadn't released Quon. He would speak with Li Binh again. If Le Duc Tho's anger was unleashed, they both had much to lose.

1545L—Seventh AF Headquarters, Tan Son Nhut AB, Saigon, South Vietnam

Lieutenant Colonel Pearly Gates

Twice Pearly had met with Second Lieutenant Lucille Dortmeier and asked her if there was still a problem in her section between herself and Master Sergeant Turner. Both times she'd remained at attention, regardless of what he'd said about relaxing, and barked out *No Sir!* like a cadet in training.

This time he was determined to get through to her.

She reported to his office, not saluting only because he'd made it clear they had to maintain a working relationship, but standing stiffly nonetheless.

"Ease up," he tried. "Relax."

She didn't respond, but simply stood with her eyes locked straight forward.

He sighed and shook his head. "You're not making things easier, Lieutenant."

"Am I doing my job properly, sir, or do you have a criticism?"

As impertinent as it sounded, it was the first time she'd reacted.

"Let's call it criticism. You aren't doing your job."

She flinched.

"You come to work, sit in your office like a robot, and go home at the end of the day."

She finally moved her eyes to look at him.

"Remember when you first came to see me about your problem with Turner? That's the way I expect lieutenants to act. Eager to bite off more than they can chew."

She waited for a moment, then spoke slowly. "Sir, you made it quite clear that I was making waves, and you didn't have time for my childish complaint. You were correct. I looked closer and found that Sergeant Turner is doing an excellent job running the section. Any actions I take would be superficial, perhaps even detrimental. I feel it's in the best interest of the Documentation section to stay out of the way . . . sir."

"Did I say your complaint was childish?"

"That was my impression, sir."

"You feel unnecessary?"

"That too. Yes, sir."

"Why didn't you tell me that when I tried to talk with you last time, or the time before?"

"You mean just after you found out who my father was? I do not want special treatment because of my father or what he once did . . . sir."

"Or your brother and what he did?"

She opened her mouth to speak, then closed it and swallowed. She spoke in a softer voice. "The fact that my brother was shot down should not give me any special privilege."

Pearly huffed a sigh.

"I would like to transfer out of Plans and Programs, sir."

He thought about it for a moment. "Nope," he finally said. "I figure any officer that's as hardheaded as you has a place in my branch."

"Sir?" She gave him a slightly startled look.

"See, I'm hardheaded too. First I'm going to keep you here until I get through to you that I am not God. I make mistakes right up there with the best of 'em, but normally

I'm too hardheaded to see it, and if I do, I'm too hard-headed to admit it. Then I'm going to show you how you can use your own hardheadedness to advantage, because I've been through the mill and know the lumps you have to take when you've got the affliction."

A smile quivered at her lips.

Pearly leaned back in his chair. "Will you *please* relax? You make me nervous standing there like that, like I'm sup-posed to be swearing you in or something. Hell, Dortmeier, I damn near flunked out of ROTC because I questioned why we had to march and stand at attention so much. I thought the Air Force was about flying, not doing eyes rights in front of reviewing stands. I remained hardheaded about that until I got my ass chewed enough to see the light."

Lucille Dortmeier relaxed.

"Now, please sit down."

She did.

"Is Turner still giving you a hard time?"

"No, sir. Like I told you, he's very good at his job."

"And the section runs well."

"Exasperatingly well. I'm really not needed there."

"Good," he said. "I've got something else in mind for you."

The diminutive, skinny redhead grew a puckish look. "Something requiring a spoiled hardhead?"

"Something requiring someone who can write as well as you do."

Pearly saw the general at 1600 hours, to show him the re-sults of the morning air attacks. There'd been no missions to pack six and no losses. A four-ship Wild Weasel flight had bombed a SAM site west of Vinh, in northern pack two, and a strike flight had found and bombed a string of barges on the nearby Ca River.

Moss told Pearly he'd received a short JACKPOT mes-sage from General McManus, telling him he'd meet with the President again the next day. He wanted to know if they had any new inputs from the field that should be discussed. Pearly could think of none. Moss said he'd send another message to encourage the chief to ask for the lifting of restrictions.

Before he left General Moss's office, Pearly asked permission to bring another person aboard the JACKPOT program. Not to meet with them and talk about strategy or policy, but to help Pearly fine-tune the LINE BACKER JACKPOT OPlan.

The general readily agreed. He'd known Little Lucy Dortmeier since she was a pup, he said, and trusted her implicitly. He said he'd add her name to the access list and would so advise General McManus.

1640L—Wing Commander's Office, Takhli RTAFB, Thailand

GS-7 *Penny Dwight*

Two weeks had now passed since Dusty Fields's death, and the heavy weight of sorrow was being lifted from Penny's shoulders. Although she'd said she'd never forget him, it was increasingly difficult to remember his face or the mannerisms that had so permeated her mind. Now she often thought of another man, who was pressing his suit.

Manny DeVera had just gone into Colonel Leska's office to talk business, and she thought again how nice he was, and how the feeling of danger in his presence had become something she found herself anticipating. As she'd grown to know him, she'd found him a gentleman, sort of a pussycat, really, yet *very* masculine. Roger Hamlin was like a brother, and she could share privacies, like how she missed the feminine luxuries she'd taken for granted back in the States. With Manny it was different. They bantered and joked in an entirely different way, and she was driven to impress him, while with Roger she felt no such urge.

Roger was like family. Manny was another thing altogether, and although he likely didn't know, she was increasingly hooked. If Dusty hadn't captured her attention so quickly, it could easily have been Manny DeVera back then, and the time wouldn't have been wasted, and the tragedy of Dusty Fields's death wouldn't have consumed her.

In the two weeks since Dusty's death, Penny had matured—had changed in some intangible way that she knew was for the better. She'd grown new confidence, worried more about herself, paid attention to her looks, and was conscious about the way she carried herself. Dusty Fields had done that for her, had made her realize she could be pretty if she wanted to be and acted that way. As a result, the men at the base, even the colonels who came into the office, were reacting differently to her. With her newfound confidence came another benefit; she was also calmer and better at her job. Penny sat at her desk, sorting through the day's correspondence and glancing periodically at the colonel's door. Manny DeVera had certainly noticed the new Penny. He was even more attentive and was pursuing her with increasing vigor.

She would start going out with him—without Roger as chaperon—just as Manny wanted her to do. Since she'd made that decision in her trailer the previous night, she'd realized that the same danger flag that had once frightened her was now drawing her, like a mesmerized moth, to his bright flame. Some flame! Penny smiled. She was impatient, but knew she couldn't rush things. People might think she'd not mourned sufficiently over Dusty.

Manny was quick-witted and intelligent, intensely handsome, and had the kind of physique that her girlfriends in the States discussed with rolling gaga eyes.

There lurked, in the back of her mind, the possibility of losing him to combat. Penny wouldn't be able to handle another emotional impact like that. But he was most definitely the one. The timing though, was important and had to be just right—because she also knew it wouldn't take Manny long at all to talk his way inside her trailer.

Penny began to establish a timetable for Manny DeVera. Some might think her calculating. Her mother would call her wise and tell her to wait even longer. But Penny felt another week or two would be just about right. Then no one could call her uncaring or callous about Dusty.

Penny studied her desk calendar, placing her pencil on a series of dates that had been tentatively set by Colonel Leska. She nodded happily to herself. When the Christmas bombing halt was ordered by the President, she planned to tell Manny DeVera they would start going out together—alone. Then, after a few evenings, she'd offer him a Yuletide present that neither he nor she would soon forget.

She felt giddy, and the sensual, tingling sensation grew.

She pulled on her reins, as she'd recently learned to do. For ten more days it must remain a threesome, with good old trustworthy and safe Roger there between them. The new way Manny looked at her when she caught him unawares told her he'd wait.

Manny emerged from the colonel's office and walked toward her desk. Penny observed how he moved with athletic grace.

He gave her his easy smile. "Dinner downtown tonight?"

Penny hesitated, feeling his electricity but determined not to let him know. "Roger says a USO group's coming to the club. A trio from Australia singing Aussie folk songs. He thinks we ought to go."

"Sounds okay," Manny said, not particularly enthusiastically. "See you tonight."

She stared at his muscular back as he walked toward the door. The man was positively sexy. She tried to imagine how Manny would be in bed. Her cheeks flushed hotly. Other memories of Dusty Fields had faded, but not the thoughts of that wonderful night when she'd come alive.

Penny almost changed the timetable.

CHAPTER TWENTY

Thursday, December 14th, 0700 Local—Route Pack Six, North Vietnam

Colonel Buster Leska

Since the loss of the Channel 97 TACAN, the strike force had changed their method of operation. Instead of rendez-vousing at the nav station near the border, they now formed into the big formation, although loosely, soon after dropping off the tanker. They flew that way across the huge, grassy plain of central Laos, then tightened up as they approached the tall mountains of westernmost North Vietnam.

They'd done so that morning, as the early sun illuminated more and more of the earth below. Then onward, a two-ship element of Wild Weasels roving on either side and slightly forward, each carrying four CBU-29 cluster bombs and two AGM-45 Shrike radar-seeking missiles. Today a second sixteen-ship formation followed five miles behind, and aft of them was yet another flight of Weasels. The first big formation had crossed the border at 18,000 feet, the second at 21,000, and now both gradually descended. The 32 F-105D strike birds carried a total of 192 M-117 750-pound bombs, an explosive force equivalent to a small nuclear device. More than a mile above the Thuds, two flights of F-4D Phantom MiG-CAPs, each loaded with a gun pod, four AIM-7 radar-beam-rider Sparrows, and two AIM-9 heat-seeking Sidewinders flew in modified fluid-four formations.

Together they were called a composite strike force, and such a powerful armada had seldom been seen in the history of tactical air warfare. Yet there were problems that plagued them. To launch from their individual bases, meet with the tankers and refuel, drop everyone off with full tanks, properly join and form up, proceed precisely along a planned route, and arrive at the target area at the directed time over target was a triumph of planning and execution.

The fact that the TACAN was no longer available made it all more difficult.

Any of a thousand potential errors had been compensated for by the existence of the navigation site, for you could always pause there to wait for tardy members of the formation, call in airborne spares if any of the strike-force birds had problems, precisely set up formation spacing, and take a deep breath before plunging into the maelstrom.

When the TACAN needle swung as you passed overhead, you knew you were at a specific point on the face of the earth. It was reassuring, like a last friendly face—for when you left it, you knew the world before you would be hostile, and when you returned to it, you gave an inward sigh of relief, because somehow it meant you were back with the good guys. It didn't matter that Laos was a hotbed of military activity. The Pathet Lao guerrillas below weren't shooting at them with SAMs and MiGs and heavy AAA, as they found around Haiphong, Thai Nguyen . . . and especially Hanoi, where they were headed.

Buster wondered about his repeated requests that the TACAN station be reinstalled.

They crossed the big Red, ECM pods on, looking diligently for SAMs and MiGs, and continued toward the distant shadow of Thud Ridge. Their target was the Yen Vien rail yard on the northeastern side of Hanoi—again. Seventh Air Force had reported the largest concentrations of supplies ever, freshly arrived at Haiphong harbor and somehow transported to Hanoi despite downed bridges and daily surveillance for barges on the rivers.

Everyone now knew about the massive resupply efforts

moving toward South Vietnam. They were finding and bombing more supply concentrations at the transshipment points around Hanoi, such as Yen Vien, and were interdicting more convoys on the jungle trails, but they were still restricted from going to the source—the streets of south Hanoi, where the real buildups could be found—and the supplies steadily, inexorably, made their way south.

Barracuda, the Wild Weasels ranging before them, called two separate missile launches as they crossed over the valley. Both groups of three missiles missed by a considerable margin.

The ECM shop was doing better at maintaining the pods—the failure rate was much lower, like one in seven or eight—due to emphasis, added technicians, and better support by the manufacturer. On every other Thud they'd removed the second Sidewinder and replaced them with another ECM pod, so the added jamming made the formations work even better. They'd not lost a single aircraft in the pod formation to a SAM since they'd made the improvements. Each missile that missed meant more kudos for Manny DeVera's astute work.

As they passed over Thud Ridge, Buster swung the formation southward. The aircraft turned in sharp, crisp movements, so they'd quickly be wings level again, for they radiated jamming power at the earth more efficiently when flying straight ahead.

Another missile launch, this one from Thai Nguyen, but Barracuda flight announced they were not guiding on the strike force and immediately went on the attack.

They reached the initial point, and Buster went into his climb, followed by the other birds of the force. Flak over Hanoi was thick, as always. Buster looked about the airspace sharply as he climbed, gaining a last impression of the situation, then approached his perched altitude and immediately rolled in on the target.

The rail yard and makeshift warehouses were glutted with supplies waiting to be moved into Hanoi. Three fiery explosions erupted and flung dark clouds of debris skyward.

They were forced to turn away from the target toward the east, because it was verboten to fly over Hanoi proper. The pilots knew the rules. So did the Hanoi gunners, and they concentrated their artillery fire there. One aircraft was lost, and two more heavily damaged as they came off the target on their predictable paths.

Takhli RTAFB

After he'd debriefed, Buster found he had a respite before his next scheduled meeting. He returned to his quarters, retrieved a soda from the fridge, and relaxed in the comfortable easy chair he'd placed near the window of the trailer.

He sipped at the soda before picking up the latest letter from Carolyn. She'd visited Marcus at Columbia and mentioned the rumors that drugs were prevalent on campus and how she was concerned, since he looked as scraggly as the drugged-out hippies they saw on television.

Mark had told her not to worry. Before he'd left for Thailand, Buster had sat down with him and told him a few facts, one of them being that if he ever used, even experimented with, drugs, including marijuana, he'd be forever banned from military flying. Although he might have fallen off on his grades, drunk too much beer, and hung around with some of the wrong crowd, Mark said he still wanted, more than anything, to fly.

Thank God for that talk, Carolyn had written. Mark had pledged to change his image, even get his hair cut a *little* shorter. He'd said she would see the changes when he arrived home for the three-week Christmas break.

Quit worrying, Mom, he'd said.

Which was like telling the Mississippi to dry up. He was their only child.

Buster left the trailer and trudged toward the club for an early lunch, thinking about his family, how he missed them and how badly Mark was in need of a heavy, fatherly hand right now.

Lieutenant Colonel Lucky Anderson hailed him, saluted, and joined on his left side.

"How're things going?" Buster asked. Anderson seemed a bit hangdog. The previous evening he'd complained that his fiancée hadn't called for the past four days.

"Women!" Anderson muttered.

"Still no call, huh?"

"I'd chew her ass out if she didn't outrank me," Anderson quipped.

"You talk with Yank Donovan this morning?"

"I saw him."

"How's he taking the loss?" The guy who'd been shot down was from the 354th squadron.

"Same as he took the others. Bitching about the restrictions that make us predictable for the gomer gunners. Acting like someone's picking on him personally."

"Maybe I'm losing it too," Buster said. "I get the same feeling sometimes."

0900L—Danang AB, South Vietnam

Captain Moods Diller

Moods looked up at the sign over the front door of the wooden shack that read, Pave Dagger HQ. A crude stiletto had been painted above the letters.

"Whaddaya think?" he asked the overweight head engineer for the Texas team.

"I think we're gonna have the lab set up and ready by tomorrow, and have three laser pods ready for you to fly in about three days. You better get us some birds to prepare."

"Th' sign," Moods said in his exuberant tone. He pointed. "Whaddaya thinka th' sign?"

The contractor cocked his head critically. "It's uneven. Who did it?"

Moods showed him the black paint on his hands.

"You? Well then, that's different. I didn't want to hurt anyone's sensitivities. It's lopsided and downright ugly, Moods."

The men of the Pave Dagger test team, military and civilian, got along well and joked incessantly. They knew they were doing something important, even if others didn't.

"You guys thought the government was gonna pay you for coming over here, didncha?" Moods retorted.

"It's a beautiful sign, Moods. It should be hung in the Louvre."

"Did you say loo or Louvre?"

"It would be inspiring in either place. It's got a kind of
. . . charm?"

"You're learning."

The engineer peered around. "They didn't do you any favors, putting us out here at the end of the runway."

"I told 'em in the message we needed isolation. I guess
you can call it that." They were a hundred yards from the
noisy runway, close to the south perimeter on the U.S. Marine grunt side of the base. Nearby was a collection of decrepit squad tents, kept for overflow new guys the jarheads
might get in. Marines at Danang did not live nearly as well
as either the Army or, especially, the Air Force.

"We're too far from the avionics and weapons shops,
Moods," the engineer complained. "Hell, they're more than
a mile away. They'll either have to move us or give us better
transportation to run back and forth."

Moods nodded at an aging brown pickup with faded government markings stenciled on the side. "They lent us that."

"That's a piece of crap." The engineer eyed the vehicle
and sighed. "I'll get the company to bring in a pickup and
maybe a van."

"I was hoping you'd get your cheap company to spring
for something since we're about to make 'em rich."

"How'd your morning meeting with the wing commander
go?"

Moods frowned. The 366th TFW commander had not
seemed overjoyed with either him or his project being on
his base. He'd not been responsive when Moods asked
about the two F-4Ds which were supposed to be assigned to
Pave Dagger for field modification.

"I dunno," Moods answered truthfully.

"Maybe you oughta ask for a better location and a building with more room."

"Can't hurt tryin'."

Moods drove to the business side of the base and found
the communications center adjacent to the command post.
He'd hand-carried a typed Secret message he wanted to
send to Benny Lewis at Nellis, telling him they were in
place, the equipment had made the trip intact, and they'd
be ready to fly in three to four days. The comm-center
sergeant refused to send it.

Why?

Because his detachment wasn't one of the units authorized to send message traffic.

Moods showed his temporary-duty orders.

TDY orders didn't mean he had access to the comm center. No, not even if they showed he had a Top Secret clearance.

How could he get on the authorized list?

That would have to come from the wing commander's office.

Moods drove to wing headquarters and asked the wingco's secretary if he could please be added to the authorized list at the comm center. She said those were handled by the adjutant, but after a half-hour wait, the major adjutant gave him a song and slow shuffle, telling him he couldn't be authorized since his was neither an official unit nor an authorized tenant of the wing.

He waited another half hour to see the wing commander.

The 366th wing commander, who had a solemn, yet nervous air and wore the same unfriendly look he'd displayed at 0600 that morning, received him warily. He told Moods that this being a special case, he'd allow Moods to send his messages out of his own office. Since he was bending the rules, he said he'd personally have to examine every piece of incoming correspondence they received and approve anything they wanted to send out.

Moods blew an exasperated breath, gritted his teeth, and showed him the simple two-paragraph message, which the wing commander read closely, then signed out. He told Moods to drop it off with his secretary—that it would be sent out in the next batch.

Moods didn't waste his time by asking for the team to be moved to a better location.

It was an ignominious beginning for the Pave Dagger test project.

1400L—Seventh Air Force Headquarters, Saigon

Lieutenant Colonel Pearly Gates

"You're doing good work," Pearly told Lieutenant Lucy Dortmeier, examining her changes to section four of OPlan LINE BACKER JACKPOT.

They were in his private office. She spent most of her time there, working at a small desk he'd had brought in, because they felt the plan shouldn't leave the room unless it was to be taken to Moss for approval, or a copy sent to the Pentagon JACKPOT team. They'd told others in Plans and Programs they were working on a project for General Moss, something to do with changing the ways the units reported mission results, which in fact was one of Pearly's ongoing efforts.

In the three days since he'd briefed her on the project, Lucy had displayed amazing efficiency. She'd impressed him with her eye for detail, her thoroughness, and the amount of work she could cram into a twelve-hour day. She'd learned to research and prepare briefs in law school. Her handling of English was superb, and she'd gleefully eliminated Pearly's militarese gobbledygook, clarifying four of the plan's twelve sections into plain language. That alone had reduced the bulk of the plan by thirty pages. She said she'd have the rest done within another week.

He'd had to explain little. She knew the difference between "sorties" and "missions," about "sortie" generation and "turn-around times," that a "Flight" on the ground was a subunit of a squadron, and a "flight" in the air was a group of aircraft. She knew "MiG-CAP" flights were MiG-killers, and "Wild Weasel" flights were SAM-killers, that "flak suppression" flights were AAA-killers, and "strike" flights were target killers, and that "Res-CAP" were fighters that located and then protected a downed pilot until rescue helicopters arrived. She'd learned most of those things in her years as an Air Force family member and picked up the rest in her few weeks at the headquarters.

She smiled at Pearly's compliment. "You don't mind my changes?"

"My God no," he said. "I tend to make things twice as long as they should be."

"You're just very thorough, Colonel. It's a lot easier for someone like me to condense what you've written than it would be to actually know and write it all."

She also knew how to exercise diplomacy around bosses.

•   •   •

At 1500 hours Pearly and Colonel Wes Snider met with General Moss to learn the latest news concerning JACKPOT and the LINE BACKER OPlan.

Moss was in a jovial mood and included Wes Snider in his smile.

He told them he'd just received their eighth message from the Chief of Staff, telling about his latest meeting with J.

"He said the President likes the LINE BACKER JACK-POT name. He picked up on the initials right away."

"Maybe we *should* have called it Lady Bug," quipped Wes Snider. "Then we'd have Lady Bird on our side too."

"L.B.J.'s upset about the lack of movement in the war and told McManus he's tired of waiting for the North Vietnamese to start talking turkey. Gentleman Jim realized that meant he was getting more interested in JACKPOT, so he jumped right in and presented the request for removing the restrictions on our pilots and going after better targets."

Moss leaned forward and told them in a more hushed voice that there was to be a group of new targets released within the hour. The same message would bring an easing of restrictions. It wouldn't be nearly as much as they wanted, but it would be a start.

They talked for another half hour, for it appeared as if they were about to see the first sign of acceptance of the project they'd worked so hard on. When the message center called that the classified TWX was in, Moss had a copy brought directly upstairs.

Pearly got back to his office at 1900 hours, following a session at the Tactical Air Control Center, where he'd briefed the on-duty fighter-plans officer about what the general wanted transmitted to the units. The WAF admin sergeant had left for the day, but Lieutenant Dortmeier was still working doggedly on the OPlan.

She looked up, half glasses perched on her nose. "You look happy."

"*Very* happy," Pearly said. "We were tossed a crumb, and we're so starved we love it."

She furrowed her brow, then went back to work with red and green pens.

Pearly had a thought. "You ... uh ... got a date or anything tonight, Lieutenant?"

She peered up at him. "No."

He immediately got cold feet. "Just wondering," he mumbled, and acted as if he were searching through his in-basket. She was still staring, and he knew he was red-faced. "Guess I'll be going, unless you need something from me," he said.

"No, sir. I'm done for the day myself. The words are starting to blur together." She changed her glasses and blinked. She wore half glasses for close-up work—large, horn-rimmed ones for long range. She was almost as near-sighted as Pearly, her glasses nearly as thick.

"Going to the club for dinner?" he asked, trying to build courage again.

She nodded.

"Maybe I'll see you there," he finally said, and started for the door.

"Wait up, Colonel," she said. "I'll walk over with you." When she'd secured the OPlan in the safe and he'd locked the office, both the inner and outer doors, they went downstairs and checked out at the security desk.

Both remained silent as they walked toward the club. It was quite dark, with a sliver moon and bright stars. Insects were setting up a chatter. A bird squealed, another answered.

"It's sure a nice night," said Lucy Dortmeier.

"Unh-huh." Pearly had never married and seldom dated, blaming that fact on his dedication to work. He was okay around casual female acquaintances or women at work, but grew awkward when around them socially. Like now.

During the past couple of days he'd begun to view Lucille Dortmeier less as a fellow officer and more as a woman. She was small, skinny, feminine, stubborn, and very intelligent, and somehow all that appealed to him. The fact that she was appealing made him nervous.

They walked on quietly. Back in the office he'd wanted to say to her, *I feel like celebrating. Would you be kind enough to allow me to take you to the club for dinner? Maybe a steak, with a bottle of wine?* Those were the words that had formed in his mind, but he'd screwed it up. Now he felt coarse next to her petiteness.

They arrived at the entrance to the O' Club, and she waited as he opened the door. He started to ask if she'd like a drink before dinner, then wondered how he could word it without it sounding like a come-on. "I'm ... uh ... going into the bar."

She nodded pleasantly, hesitated for a short pause, then started toward the dining room. "See you tomorrow, Colonel."

He went into the lounge, still feeling awkward. Wes Snider was there, seated at a table near a corner and talking with two pretty civilian secretaries. He waved Pearly over.

"Let me buy you a drink. You're working too late." Wes introduced everyone.

Pearly had a couple of drinks with them, listening with half an ear, responding on cue, thinking about the work he had stacked up for the next morning. When he went into the dining room, Lieutenant Dortmeier had already left.

Friday, December 15th, 1000 Local—Wing Commander's Conference Room, Takhli RTAFB, Thailand

Lieutenant Colonel Lucky Anderson

The key operations staff, including squadron commanders, had been summoned. The staff was in place, waiting for the wingco, when Penny Dwight came in and told Lucky he had a telephone call.

Buster Leska was coming out of his office as Lucky went by. Leska nodded and watched as he picked up the telephone at Penny's desk, then proceeded into the conference room. Leska didn't delay staff meetings for a single attendee.

"Hello," Lucky said into the receiver.

"My name's Richard, from the Bangkok embassy."

"Linda's spoken of you." It was the guy she'd once dated.

She'd also said he was her "sometimes" boss, Anderson remembered.

"Just wondering if you've heard from her in the last couple of days. I've—ah—got something to pass on to her."

"She called from NKP Sunday night," he said, "but not since."

"Yeah? Well if you hear from her again, please ask her to call me." He gave a number.

"Something to do with work?" Lucky asked as he jotted down the information.

"Yes. It's important. Thanks." The connection was terminated.

Lucky stared at Richard's telephone number for a moment, wondering if he should worry. He decided not to. Linda sometimes disappeared for a few days, then emerged without explanation, saying she'd been working with locals, determining quotas and that sort of thing.

He slipped quietly back into the conference room, where Buster Leska had the floor.

"What's it about?" Lucky whispered to Yank Donovan.

Yank sourly nodded toward Leska, meaning he should listen up.

"Every wing commander over here's forwarded requests to lighten up on the restrictions. Two that especially stuck in our craws were the large buffer zone with China, and the no-fly circle around Hanoi. As you know, that last one severely limits our tactical options when we go up to bomb a target near Hanoi. The enemy knows we've got to turn in a certain direction to avoid the restricted area, and he knows we've got to fly around it when we're coming in or going out."

Buster let that soak in for a bit. He'd accurately voiced what the rest of them grumbled about in the bar. "Well, gentlemen, someone up there listened. As of now there's no longer a no-fly restriction around Hanoi, and the no-fly rule has been lifted for the buffer zone."

There were smiles around the room.

"Does that mean we can start striking the previously released targets in there?" Colonel Armaugh asked. It was a logical question. Once a target outside the restricted areas had been selected by the President, Seventh Air Force planners had the option of attacking them again.

"Let's take one gift at a time," said Leska. "We'll still need executive authority to bomb targets in either place."

"Yeah, but do you see a chance of that happening?" the DO persevered.

Buster Leska paused thoughtfully, then nodded his head. "Yes."

"Wonder why the President's changing his mind. Think we'll start getting better targets?"

Lucky knew that the wing commander had gone as far as he dared and watched him ponder his response.

"Who knows what makes politicians tick?" Leska finally said. "But, yes, I believe this is the first step. I think he's about to let us go ahead and win this damn two-bit war."

CHAPTER TWENTY-ONE

Sunday, December 17th 0715 Local—O' Club Dining Room, Takhli RTAFB

Captain Manny DeVera

It was a nonflying day for him, he'd finished with his most critical business at the weapons office, and it was Sunday. He knew it was Sunday because the *Bangkok World* newspapers they'd just brought in from the early flight from Don Muang were in color. On other days they were black-and-white. The other reason he knew was that Penny Dwight had announced to her two favorite male friends the previous evening that she was going to sleep in, and for them not to dare disturb her for breakfast.

Animal Hamlin went to the counter and bought a paper, then returned to their table. "You want the funnies or the front page?" he asked Manny.

"The front page."

Animal separated the newspaper and passed it over. A few seconds later Hamlin was sipping coffee and chuckling over Li'l Abner. "I get a kick out of the shmoos," he said in his Jersey accent. "Sure as hell could use a few around here."

Manny agreed. Schmoos tasted like pork chops when they were fried. He'd give a lot for a meal of pork chops and fresh eggs, instead of the reconstituted, once-dehydrated potatoes, limp and greasy bacon, and reconstituted, once-powdered eggs he was eating.

He picked at his breakfast while reading about a concert the king of Thailand had attended. A British orchestra was touring Asia. Next an article on a guy named Thompson, who was an American ex-patriot who'd become a multimillionaire in the Thai silk business, and how he'd recently been kidnapped. Next about a USAID executive who'd been ambushed and was feared kidnapped by communist terrorists.

He reread that final one, written by a reporter in Muang Sakhon Nakhon, in far eastern Thailand. Yesterday the police from nearby Nakhon Phanom had located a vehicle in the jungle north of the city. They'd also found the bodies of two men. The executive was missing. None of the names had yet been released by the police, but one of the dead men was identified as a Thai, the other an American, and both worked at the Nakhon Phanom USAID office. The article went on to describe the CTs as being increasingly active in that area, and warned the people there to be vigilant and contact the provincial police before traveling in remote areas.

Manny looked about the dining room until he found Lucky Anderson eating breakfast at the wing commander's table, deep in conversation with Buster Leska and Colonel Trimble, the Deputy for Maintenance. He thought about the newspaper article, then went over to their table and waited until Trimble paused and looked up.

"You got something, Captain DeVera?" He was obviously unhappy with the interruption.

Manny regarded Lucky. "Something here I thought you might be interested in," he said. "You talk to the Ice—" He stopped himself, remembering that Anderson didn't like the nickname. "You talk to Miss Lopes recently?"

"Why?"

"Article here's about USAID people. I remembered she runs the agency and thought you'd be interested. Looks like one of her top people was kidnapped and—"

"Let me see that." Lucky took the paper and carefully

read the article, then abruptly got to his feet and left the room.

"What does it say in the article?" Buster Leska asked.

"A USAID vehicle was shot up over near NKP by commie terrorists. Two men were killed and some executive was kidnapped."

Colonel Trimble looked concerned. "Lucky said she hasn't called in a few days and he was getting worried."

"You don't think it could be *her*, do you?" Manny thought of Lucky Anderson as he would a big brother.

"We'll find out more when he gets back," said Leska. "Have a seat, Manny."

Colonel Trimble grinned at him. "You still interfering with things over in my ECM shop?"

"Yes, sir."

"Good." He looked at Buster. "Captain DeVera not only tells 'em what he wants, he spends time trying to help. The technicians think he's great."

"They've raised the OR rate on the pods sixty percent by making the right changes," Manny said. "Now we've got a few more pods in, too."

Buster nodded. "I like the way you're hanging two pods on some of the birds."

"We haven't lost a single bird that had two pods aboard to a SAM," said Colonel Trimble.

"Then we need to get more of the things and load two on all the Thuds," Buster said.

Manny shook his head. "There aren't many more of these old ones that use a RAT for power. There's plenty of the new kind that take aircraft power, but we're not wired for 'em. Unless we can get the assembly line reopened or get our birds rewired, this is all we'll get."

"Meaning we'd better preserve what we've got," said Trimble.

Lucky appeared at the opposite end of the room, head down and looking as if he'd been walked on. "I called the embassy," he breathed as soon as he reached the table. "It was Linda."

Manny felt himself blanching. "Jesus," he said, staring at Lucky.

"I've gotta go to NKP."

Buster observed him evenly. "You'd just get in the way. Why not leave it to the guys who know what they're doing?"

Lucky's voice trembled with emotion. "You're saying I can't go?"

"No. I'm just telling you we need you here, and it's unlikely you'll be able to do anything for her there."

"I can take the eleven o'clock round-robin to NKP."

Buster sighed. "Cut orders putting your ops officer in charge until you get back."

"Yes, sir. How long have I got?"

"Use your judgment. Soon as you realize you're getting nowhere, head on back."

Lucky nodded curtly and left.

"Jesus," repeated Manny, thinking of his friend's anguish. Then he thought about the Ice Maiden. "Jesus."

1045L—Takhli Base Operations

Major Lucky Anderson

Lucky stared numbly as the round-robin gooney bird dropped onto the end of the runway. A dull, persistent ache gnawed in his chest, and horrors kept buzzing about inside his head, making it difficult to think clearly. He kept going over his phone call to Linda's office in the Bangkok embassy. All the people there could tell him was what was already in the newspaper article. Then they'd connected him with a familiar male voice that sounded entirely too collected.

Linda was missing, the voice said evenly.

Was she alive?

They didn't know.

Had the embassy been contacted about a ransom?

Not so far.

Who had taken her?

They had no idea.

"She's my fiancée," he'd pleaded with the voice. "I've got to know what's happening!"

If he didn't realize that, the voice on the telephone had said quietly, they wouldn't be talking. Linda's name hadn't been released to the press.

"Who am I talking to?" he'd demanded.

"This is Richard. We spoke once before, remember?"

"I'm going to NKP to find out what's going on," he'd told him.

"I'd rather you didn't, Colonel."

"I've got to."

"Do what you must. We hear anything, we'll contact you." Richard had then terminated the conversation.

As he watched the gooney bird taxi off the runway, Lucky realized that Buster Leska had likely been right. He wouldn't even know where to start when he got to Nakhon Phanom. He had friends there. One worked in Igloo White, a secretive project to set up eavesdropping sensors on the Ho Chi Minh Trail. Another was a pilot he'd been stationed with when he'd flown F-100's, who was now ops officer of the O-1 Birddog squadron. While it was unlikely he'd be any help in his search for Linda, at least he'd be able to cadge a bed and maybe be introduced to the right people.

He remembered another friend at NKP. *Yeah,* he thought as he started walking toward the gooney bird, which was coming to a halt, brakes squealing like a thousand-pound rat. Sergeant Black might be able to help.

Monday, December 18th, 0800 Local—HQ Seventh Air Force, Tan Son Nhut AB

Lieutenant Colonel Pearly Gates

Pearly's Plans and Programs (Out-Country) branch at the headquarters was concerned only with ROLLING THUNDER, the air war over North Vietnam, and was made up of two sections, Documentation and Combat Programs. The first kept track of classified material. The second consisted of three officers, two NCOs, and five airmen. Two of the officers were fighter pilots, one from Thuds, the other from Phantoms. The third was an airborne command post radar controller.

Combat Programs ensured that headquarters' plans accurately reflected friendly and enemy capabilities, and that the units knew what was required of them by the various and voluminous directives. In effect Combat Programs told the units what, when and how to fight in North Vietnam and interfaced with the Tactical Air Control Center, which sent air tasking orders out to the flying units.

Two other officers were attached to the headquarters and worked closely with Plans and Programs (Out-Country). When he was present, Colonel Snider represented Strategic Air Command assets, the B-52's and KC-135 units that rotated in and out of the theater. A major from the Ninetieth Special Operations Wing, which was the property of Military Assistance Command–Surveillance and Observations Group, was assigned as the MAC-SOG liaison officer. He was a C-130 Hercules pilot and had been sent to Saigon from Nha Trang, headquarters for the Army's Special Forces, as well as the Air Force's Special Operations.

The Special Ops major had the unlikely name of Friday Wells. He disliked both the headquarters assignment and the city of Saigon, and was not hesitant to tell anyone who listened that he was the best damned Herky pilot in the Air Force and was being grossly misused.

There were jokes about Herkys and Herky people in the theater. A number of fighter jocks changed the name of their ungainly aircraft to "turkeys," called their pilots "turkey drivers," and made jokes like, "It's hard to soar with the eagles when you're in the company of turkeys."

The six of them, Pearly, his three Combat Programs officers, Wes Snider, and Friday Wells, met that Monday morning to share recent developments.

When Friday's turn came, he said the tempo of the war in Laos was still escalating, and the good guys, the Royal Laotian Army, were not faring well. Pathet Lao troops had gathered in battalion strengths throughout much of the country and were attacking government-held outposts. He also told them a long-range recon patrol had confirmed that it had been Russian-built SA-7s—shoulder-fired, infrared missiles—that had driven off slow-flying, propeller-driven airplanes before they'd overrun the Channel 97 TACAN station.

He added that another source had confirmed that SA-7's were being brought into South Vietnam, along with a small group of trained operators. So, he said, the others had better start thinking of placing flare dispensers on their aircraft as they were doing with their Special Ops birds. The SA-7, he said, was unsophisticated and easily decoyed by brightly burning flares.

One of the fighter pilots said he wasn't concerned about Thuds or F-4's, because they could release their bombs higher and fly faster than the SA-7's limited speed and effective range could cope with. Forward air controller birds, like O-1's, didn't have much of a heat signature and weren't considered good targets either, if they kept turning. The most endangered aircraft were A-1H Sandies, helicopters, cargo birds, and airliners, and they'd been alerted to change their flight and approach patterns to avoid overflying enemy-held areas at vulnerable altitudes.

Wes Snider said the B-52's flew too high for the SA-7's, that the little missiles would run out of fuel between 5,000 and 6,000 feet altitude, and the BUFs flew above 30,000.

After more discussion about heat signatures of various aircraft, Pearly brought up the TACAN again and asked Friday what it would take to get the CIA, or *someone*, to set up another nav station at Channel 97. The Thuds and Phantoms flying into North Vietnam needed it.

MAC-SOG's working on a solution to get the site back, was all Friday would tell him.

After an hour the meeting broke up and Pearly checked in at his office. The admin sergeant had a couple of new messages. She said Buster Leska had called from Takhli and asked if Pearly had information concerning the ambush of USAID officials near NKP. He said the missing woman was Lucky Anderson's fiancée. Which made Pearly groan. Anderson had paid his dues when he'd been shot down and set a record for the number of days on the ground before being rescued. Now this. Life wasn't playing fair with the badly scarred LC. He decided to corner Friday and request information from his spook contacts at MAC-SOG. He'd also have to pass on the info to the general, because Moss thought very highly of Anderson.

The second request was from Flo. General Moss wanted him to appear with Wes Snider at ten o'clock for a short meeting.

Pearly went into his inner office and nodded absently to Lucy Dortmeier, still thinking about Lucky Anderson.

"I'm done cleaning up section nine," she said with a sat-isfied smile. "Only three to go. You want to look over my work?"

"Wait'll I find out something." Pearly dialed Friday's number and asked his question.

"I can tell you right now, Pearly. No one knows anything. USOM, that's another name for USAID, has been screaming about it and now the State Department's in the act, raising hell with us about not alerting them about the extent of the terrorist problem in that area, which is a bunch of bullshit because they knew. Just a minute." He paused. "Something was just placed on my desk." He paused again. "I'm coming up to your office. See you in a minute, okay?"

While he waited, Pearly filled Lucille Dortmeier in on Lucky Anderson and Linda Lopes.

"That's terrible," she said, her face reflecting genuine sympathy. Lucy had come to the war theater with a purpose: to find out more about her brother who'd been shot down eleven months earlier and be close by when he was re-leased. But she had no illusions about the awful treatment the POWs were receiving from their captors. If Linda Lopes was alive, she was likely being treated no better.

Friday came into the office, wearing short-sleeved cam-ouflage jungle fatigues with blackout rank and wings. Those and an Aussie hat were his uniform, and no headquarters puke could tell him differently. He took a seat, brandishing a document with a red "Secret" cover.

"Couple things in here I couldn't say on the phone," he said. "This GS-15 lady has a Top Secret SI clearance and possesses specific knowledge they *definitely* don't want the bad guys getting their hands on. They're giving the matter a high priority."

"Getting her back, you mean?"

Friday shrugged. "What I mean is they do *not* want the info getting out. *Period.* If they can rescue her, so much the better."

"You mean they'd eliminate her if that was the only way?"

"I don't think you headquarters guys listen. There's a high priority, a *double-A* priority, on the effort to contain her information. That's all."

Pearly nodded as if he understood.

"One more thing. The woman's code name's Clipper, same as the operation they've set up to investigate and do damage control."

"Operation Clipper?"

"Just Clipper. She's Clipper, and so's the effort. That's sensitive, and I don't think you're supposed to know."

"Thanks, Friday."

"No sweat. I'm taking off now. Heading over to Nha Trang to fly a couple of sorties so I can keep my hand in. Need anything, call the duty desk at the detachment."

"If you hear anything more about Clipper, let me know."

"Will do." Friday huffed as he rose from the chair, rendered a sloppy salute, and left.

"He's certainly not very military." Dortmeier frowned.

"Special Ops people are a bit different," Pearly agreed.

At ten Pearly accompanied Wes Snider into the general's office.

Moss didn't deal with niceties. As soon as the door closed, he said he'd received a call from General McManus on his scrambler telephone the previous night. "Three days from now the President's traveling to Australia to attend Prime Minister Holt's funeral, then he's coming to the combat theater for a couple days. Beat the drums, tell the guys they're doing a great job, all that."

Pearly frowned. "Isn't that dangerous for the President, sir?"

"Won't be when they get through securing the areas he's going to visit. They're not announcing his schedule. Won't until he's gone. Know another reason he's coming?"

"JACKPOT?" breathed Wes Snider.

"He wants a firsthand look at things, and he told General McManus he wants to get the word about the LINE BACKER JACKPOT OPlan right from the horse's mouth. He asked him who the horse was over here. I'll fly a leg of the flight on Air Force One and talk to him one on one."

"With L.B.J.?" Pearly asked incredulously.

"You haven't had your Pentagon tour yet, Pearly. Once you do, you'll get over being excited about meeting Presidents."

"That's for sure," agreed Wes Snider. "Every other week

they're trying to get you to go over and be window dressing for somebody's visit. Stand around the Rose Garden or back lawn and look pretty and don't tell civilians what kind of dinks are running their country."

Moss chuckled. "That's not bad. I thought you bomber pukes liked that sort of bullshit."

"I'd rather have a tooth pulled than go to another White House function."

"You meet Johnson? I was stationed there before he was elected."

"L.B.J. wasn't bad," reflected Snider. "He'd come around and talk to the guys in uniform if he had time, tell them he knew it was a pile of horseshit, having to show up. But then none of us heard him telling our bosses to stop sending us."

"Anything I should know about him?"

"He was in the Navy Reserve before World War II—likes to tell how he volunteered for active duty five minutes after he heard about the attack on Pearl Harbor."

"I heard he was an ex-swabbie," said Moss.

"He's not as obnoxiously pro-Navy as some. He spent his war tour flying around the Pacific for Roosevelt and served at MacArthur's headquarters in Australia. He still speaks highly of him. MacArthur presented Johnson with a Silver Star after he survived a hairy flight in a navy bomber, with Zeros using them for target practice."

"Well, at least he knows what war's like."

"He gave his medal away last summer," Wes said. "Pinned it on a captain from Takhli who'd shot down two MiGs. There were a number of people at the Pentagon who thought he was okay, but *none* of us trusted his cabinet or advisors, especially those left over from the Kennedy years. We felt if he'd get rid of the lot of 'em and start listening to the professionals, guys like Rusk at State and at least a few of the generals on the JCS, he'd be a pretty good wartime president."

Moss looked at his watch, then back to the two men. "I want you both thinking about what I should say to convince L.B.J. to proceed with LINE BACKER JACKPOT. We'll talk again tomorrow."

Before they left, Pearly asked if the general had heard about Lucky Anderson's fiancée. He had not, so Pearly told him what he knew.

General Moss grew a face of stone. "Keep me posted," he said quietly.

As Pearly was leaving, he heard him mutter, "Goddam, fucking, no-good war!"

1400L—Hanoi, DRV

Assistant Commissioner Nguyen Wu

The three People's magistrates sat, wordlessly watching him. They'd called him from his office without providing reasons, and he'd been led to the People's Court at Ba Dinh square by men from his own commission, the ones he sent to gather citizens named to be reeducated.

The chief magistrate finally asked his first question. *Why had Wu not responded to their order for the immediate release of Air Regiment Commandant Quon?*

He'd received the order only the previous morning, he blurted in a trembling voice, and—

Comrade Quon should have been released immediately. The matter had been passed to them by an important government figure.

Wu grew numbed.

Air Regiment Commandant Quon, hero of the People's Democratic Republic, had been judged reformed and reliable. Did the assistant commissioner have argument with the judgment of the People's Court?

Wu agreed totally with the court's decision, fawning, telling them he'd attend to the matter immediately. Quon would be released and taken to his home as soon as he returned to the ministry building.

They stared at him without emotion. He was dismissed.

As he fled from the People's Court, Nguyen Wu was distraught. He'd wanted to speak to the Commissioner about it, had wanted to expedite the matter since his aunt's first warning, but Quon wasn't ready. He'd not responded to Wu's shift to kindness, had ignored his whispers that he was working to obtain his release. He'd simply stared without expression at Wu, as he might at an insect, and did not even act grateful that the beatings had stopped.

Wu had grown to despise him even more.

Other men in Quon's position would have groveled for the kindness he'd offered. Had someone spoken to him? Told him that his father-in-law was intervening? It seemed impossible, for the prisoners—the *reeducation trainees*—were kept isolated.

Now the matter had been taken from Nguyen Wu's hands. Quon would not be released when Wu felt he should, but now . . . *immediately* . . . and he wasn't ready at all!

Wu's misery was compounded by the fact that he'd not yet been reconciled with his powerful and beloved aunt. He wondered if there was any possible way he could repair the terrible rift that had grown between them. He must find a way. Another tryst, where he would give her the pleasures he still had to offer?

But there remained the problem of Quon, of turning the man loose before he understood that Nguyen Wu was not responsible for the horrors that had been visited upon him.

Reeducation Trainee Quon

The time had arrived for his release, which he'd known would come since his first day. That knowledge was the difference between Quon and the other trainees. He'd known there would be an end to the beatings, a stop to the confessional lies dragged from his tormented soul.

That it was about to happen had become apparent the moment Nguyen Wu had shifted tactics. When Wu had demanded loudly before the guards that Quon be moved from the tiny cell to a larger one—when he'd whispered that he was working to have him released—when he'd inquired about his health, and Quon was visited by a physician—when he'd asked about the food, and food became palatable. But more than anything, when the beatings had stopped, Quon had known he was about to be freed, because if it were up to Nguyen Wu, they would continue. Even as he'd spoken of mercy, malevolence had glittered from Wu's eyes.

As soon as he'd realized it would soon end, he'd no longer cooperated with the worthless dog. He'd simply stared at Wu and refused to answer his simplest questions. As his body and mind were restored by nourishment, he was increasingly tortured by memories of confessing to terrible things about himself and his family.

Wu was again in his room, speaking to him in low tones, but he was both nervous and anxious, and Quon knew the time had arrived.

"I have just come from the People's Court," Wu started, "where I persuaded them . . ."

Quon slowly stood, staring as Wu mouthed more meaningless words.

A guard brought a uniform, the one he'd worn the day he'd been picked up at Phuc Yen by Wu and his secret policemen. Even as he disrobed, dropping the hated striped pajamas onto the floor, Wu continued to babble and Quon to stare.

"I spoke many times in your behalf. You must realize that I held no personal part in this, comrade Quon. One must do his duty. I know that you are an excellent patriot to the—"

"Yes. A man must do his duty," Quon interrupted in monotone.

Wu swallowed, then nodded vigorously.

"Please provide me with a vehicle and driver," Quon said quietly as he pulled on his uniform. "If necessary I will walk, but—"

"I will be happy to *personally* take you, comrade Quon."

"I would not be so presumptuous," Quon replied in a caustic tone.

"I do not mind. In fact—"

"The vehicle?"

"As you wish. I just want you to realize that—"

"I hear your words. Now I am anxious to go."

They both stared. A tic formed at Nguyen Wu's jaw.

CHAPTER
TWENTY-TWO

Thursday, December 21st, 1500 Local—Command Post, Danang Air Base, South Vietnam

Captain Moods Diller

The test team had been in place at Danang for a week, and all the pods and bomb kits had been checked and tuned on the bench in the ramshackle Pave Dagger building. Moods and his backseat pilot were impatient to fly. Everyone and everything were ready to test, but the two promised aircraft had not yet been made available.

Moods had inquired at the Deputy for Maintenance's office and been told that the release of the two aircraft hadn't yet been approved by the wing commander. When Moods had gone to see the wing commander, twice he'd been left waiting in the outer office as others paraded by, and he was told the commander was busy. Finally, on his third attempt in as many days, he'd gotten in and was advised by the wingco that there were other, higher priorities. The North Vietnamese Army was still attacking at Dak To, and they were providing close air support to save American lives. It was difficult, close-in work, and they needed every available aircraft.

Great, Moods had told him. The Pave Dagger smart bombs could be used. They could pinpoint-bomb targets that would take a dozen or more normal sorties to hit.

The wingco said he wasn't going to experiment when the lives of American ground troops were at stake.

Moods had written a message to Benny back at Nellis, pleading for him to somehow gain leverage and support for his tests. He'd submitted it to the wing commander's secretary, but didn't receive a memo-for-the-record back, showing it had been sent. When he queried, she'd said it was still on the wingco's desk for signature.

At their next meeting the wing commander had told Moods that he couldn't give him the two birds because not only were they still pounding the NVA in the hills around Dak To, they were also trying to stop the supplies that were pouring into South Vietnam at a rate unparalleled since the beginning of the war.

When Moods again offered their services, the wing commander had said he didn't have the time or the inclination to experiment, that Moods's people would just have to settle back and wait until they got a handle on the interdiction problem. The fact that they'd not had a handle on the interdiction problem for the past three years wasn't lost on Moods.

He'd wearily asked about another matter. They'd sent thirty 2000-pound bombs to Danang, specifically earmarked for the Pave Dagger project. The munitions people could find only twelve of those. He wondered what might have happened to the others.

The wingco shrugged and told him to ask the Deputy for Logistics.

Finally, Moods had asked to get the classified message back that he'd wanted to send to Nellis. He said he wanted to reword it.

The wing commander found and returned his message.

When Moods asked, all the Deputy for Logistics could tell him was that the bombs had been delivered to the Chief of Munitions, and showed him the shipping document.

Moods tore up the old message and wrote a new, longer one, addressed to Benny Lewis's Fighter Tactics branch. He filled it with gobbledygook phrases and made it sound as if everything was humming along fine, except there were combat priorities they had to honor. In a middle paragraph he said that he'd require the immediate support of Second Lieutenant G. S. White, and requested that he be briefed on the Titanic Project.

The only White assigned to the Fighter Weapons Center at Nellis was Major General Gordon S. White. Until Moods had written the message, there'd been no Titanic Project, but he felt his Pave Dagger test was headed in the same direction as the British luxury ship when it played chicken with an iceberg.

The wing commander did not pick up on that. The message was sent as written.

1740L—Nakhon Phanom Air Base, Thailand

Lieutenant Colonel Lucky Anderson

It was Lucky's fourth discouraging day at NKP, and so far he'd repeatedly run into dead ends as he tried to find out about the ambush and Linda's circumstances.

When he'd gone to the Special Forces compound gate the first day, the guards checked a roster and said they had no Sergeant Black listed, and that he'd need authorization to enter the place. He said he was from Takhli and tried to explain the purpose of his visit. When the sergeant on duty asked for his travel orders, he said they were being forwarded, but that wasn't good enough. Lucky didn't pursue the matter; if Black wasn't there, he could serve no purpose by nosing around the Special Forces camp.

He'd gone to the Air Force security police, and they'd acted as if they knew nothing about the USAID incident beyond what they'd read in the newspapers. Maybe he should talk with the police in town, they said. Just take a Thai bus from the main gate. So he'd traveled into the city of Nakhon Phanom and found no one at the police station who could speak enough English to answer his questions. When he'd repeatedly said "USAID," one officer had brightened and given him directions to that office. The place was manned by a lone Thai secretary who spoke only rudimentary English. She kept wringing her hands and repeating that Mistah Jah-stone was gone. When he asked about Miss

Lopes, she said that she was also gone. He'd hung around for a while, hoping an American might show up, but none did.

He'd returned to the base and tried the security police again, and a major begrudgingly told him he might try the Thai provincial police. Maybe it was their show, he said. Their headquarters was in Sakhon Nakhon, sixty-five miles west on the national highway. Lots of potholes, he said. So Lucky went to the motor pool to check out a vehicle, and a harried sergeant said he was fresh out, but they'd likely have one for him the next morning. Could he show his orders, please? By then he'd had orders made up and forwarded from Takhli, so he showed them.

"You're next on the list, Colonel. Tomorrow morning I'll have you a pickup."

He felt exasperated and miserable as he trudged from the motor pool back toward the room in the officers' hootch his friend in Birddogs had provided. Four days, and all he'd drawn were blanks. Lucky knew he was getting an official runaround from damn near everyone, but could think of no way to force the issue. He thought about calling General Moss for leverage. It was the sort of thing he never did, running to the brass for help—but it was for Linda, and there was nothing he'd not do to retrieve her from harm.

He was wondering about calling Moss as he stopped off at a small, crowded base snack bar and ordered a hamburger and fries. The cheerful female cook plopped the precooked things onto his tray and added a Coke.

"I see you made LC," said a quiet voice behind him in the line. "Congratulations."

It was Sergeant Black, wearing a civilian bush outfit.

"I've been looking for you," Lucky said.

"We just got in." Black nodded to the Asian behind him in the line, who also wore civvies. Lucky recognized him as the lieutenant on Hotdog team. Both men looked tired.

"We need to talk," Lucky said. He picked a table in a corner. Most of the people in the snack bar were Army Special Forces, with their cocky attitudes and disdain of outsiders, which included anyone who hadn't earned a beret. His officer's rank gave him little special consideration.

Black and the lieutenant joined him. When they'd deposited their trays on the table, Lucky shook their hands. "You're a hard man to locate, Black."

"When we arrived, I was told you were looking," Black said. "I also heard there was a lady asking about me a few days ago, using your name."

"She's why I'm here." Lucky explained the relationship, then what he knew about the terrorist attack and how he'd been running into dead ends.

Black listened closely, without expression, and the lieutenant also tried to follow his words. A couple of times Black would halt Anderson and explain to the lieutenant in Vietnamese. The Hotdogs weren't good with English, Lucky remembered.

"So that's where I am now," Lucky finished. "Smack up against another dead end."

They ate for a while in silence. Lucky's burger had the taste of rancid soy sauce.

"Is there any way you can help?" he finally asked.

"I doubt it. Sounds like a CT operation. Besides advising the Thai army, we don't get involved in domestic counterterrorist ops."

"I need your help, Sarge."

"I'll see what information I can get. Probably not a lot, but I'll try."

"I appreciate it."

Black nodded and went back to his hamburgers. He ate two of the greasy things, with a side of rice, a beer, and a slice of dried-out apple pie.

"How's your team doing?" Lucky asked.

Black guzzled beer for a bit, pondering the question. "Streamlined," he finally answered. "We lost two men last time out."

"Sorry about that."

"Yeah." Black bobbed his head thoughtfully. "Good people. They'll be hard to replace."

"Did you make a radio call up around Channel Ninety-seven TACAN a few weeks back?"

Black stared at him for a moment, then took another sip of beer. "Maybe."

"The mission commander you talked to was a guy named Donovan. He wanted to help, but the airborne command post denied permission."

Black shook his head. "Let's talk about it in private some-time, okay?"

"Sure."

"Where you staying, Colonel?"

Lucky gave him the location and phone number of the hootch.

"I'll be in touch." Black stood, and the lieutenant followed him to his feet. "We've gotta be going. Nice to see you again, sir."

1800L—Hanoi, DRV

Colonel Xuan Nha

The visit was a short one, and not pleasant. Xuan had decided to call on Quon as soon as he'd heard he'd been released. He wanted to find if Quon was angry, whether he somehow blamed him for not gaining his release quickly enough. He also wished to judge the man's condition and mental state, for it was likely they'd be working together again. Xuan Nha's radars, rocket forces, antiaircraft and anti-shipping artillery—all worked closely with the People's Army Air Force, and Quon was likely to be an important figure again in the VPAAF.

While they'd not been close, they'd enjoyed a relationship founded upon mutual respect. Xuan felt that Quon was surely one of the most dedicated warriors in the Democratic Republic, which had likely made the arrest and reeducation all that more difficult for the country's most renowned fighter-pilot commandant. They'd also shared a distrust for Nguyen Wu, who had now caused both men great grief. In Xuan's mind that matter must remain unspoken, even though he'd heard Wu had been stripped of his power.

While Quon's home wasn't as grand as Xuan Nha and Li Binh's villa, it was nonetheless much larger and more private than those of other officers of his position. Quon's wife showed him in and said that he'd been resting and would join them shortly. She was a quiet one, but did her best to entertain Xuan before the fighter pilot made his entrance.

Xuan Nha hid his shock as they exchanged greetings, for Quon had aged twenty years in the course of the three months since he'd last seen him. He walked oddly—in a slight stoop, with arms held immobile at his sides as if they were useless appendages.

Quon examined him as well. "You have healed a great deal since we last spoke," he said quietly.

Xuan shrugged. "Do you mind if I sit?"

"Of course not."

"I can stand for longer periods now," Xuan Nha said proudly as they both took seats on the wicker chairs adorning the small parlor.

Quon's wife brought tea in small ceramic cups, and they sipped the hot, bitter liquid.

"You have returned home to the villa," Quon said. It was not a question.

"That part of my life is returning."

Quon didn't have to tell him that his own life was difficult, that he was having trouble readjusting to normalcy. He still had a prisoner's pallor, and a nervous, suspicious air about him.

"General Tho visited," Quon said. "He speaks highly of your advice to save the aircraft."

"He is kind."

They spoke of the weather, and how Hanoi had been unusually cool and dry recently.

"Good flying weather for your pilots," Xuan Nha said.

Quon nodded. "I do not know if I will fly again." He'd added the last without prompting.

Quon had enjoyed piloting fighters, and the glory that had gone with it. In his twenty-four years of combat flying he'd shot down a total of fifteen aircraft—seven German fighters and bombers when he'd flown with the Free French in Russia in the forties, eight American fighter aircraft in the ongoing conflict. Those were the numbers Quon cited. The party newspaper credited him with many more. He'd been extolled as a Hero of the People, revered by the pilots under his command.

"We have missed your expertise, Quon. When will you return to work?"

"I go to Phuc Yen tomorrow to survey the damage and the salvage operation. Then I will travel north to observe the operation at dispersal bases in southern China. When I return to Hanoi next week, I will resume my position as air regiment commandant."

"It will be difficult with your forces deployed."

"Such things change. We always knew, you and I, that the Mee would eventually bomb Phuc Yen. My headquarters will now move to Gia Lam. There are too many civilian aircraft for the Americans to attack there. . . ." Quon's voice trailed off.

Xuan Nha watched his compatriot closely as he drifted into some reverie.

Quon suddenly blinked his eyes and looked about, as if surprised he was still in the room.

Xuan sipped his tea, which was growing cool.

Quon spoke in a low voice. "How is your situation at home, Xuan Nha?"

Was it a general question? Xuan Nha believed not. He considered his response.

"Is Nguyen Wu still shaming you?"

Xuan was startled. He opened his mouth to speak, then slowly closed it. "Li Binh and I are . . . friends," he finally explained, his voice low.

"When Nguyen Wu worked for you and plotted to place you in disfavor with the party, it was not right. It is also not right for him to shame you by rutting with your wife."

Xuan felt uneasy. "Perhaps we should speak of other matters," he said in his pained rasp.

"I learned much about Nguyen Wu. We were not friends, and I expected to be treated badly, but he did other things. His men had me write a confession that my revered mother was a common prostitute, and another that my son was . . . a traitor." Quon's voice caught.

"I must go."

"Stay for another moment, Xuan Nha. I have something to tell you."

Xuan did not want to hear. He despised and distrusted political matters, and regardless of what he might think of them, discussions of Li Binh or Nguyen Wu entailed high-level politics.

Quon nodded. "My son was dear to me, Xuan Nha. I wish I had shown him that before he was killed by the Mee."

"Yes," said Xuan. "You once told me." He knew he must

not tell Quon that Nguyen Wu had engineered the killing of his son. Quon was bitter enough.

Quon sighed. "But you cannot know how I feel, for you have no son. I am a warrior like you. I have risked my life many times for the party and the Democratic Republic, and I will do it again. But I was not a good father. It is difficult to do both well, and I did not. When my son was killed, I was consumed by grief. Now I am consumed by shame, for I was forced to call my son a coward and traitor. I do not forgive. I do not forgive myself—and I do not forgive Nguyen Wu."

Xuan wished desperately that he'd not come to Quon's home.

"Perhaps with time . . ." he began, but Quon shook his head.

"I will never forget. Neither should you."

"Mine was . . . different."

"While you were in the hospital, your wife's nephew rutted with her in your own bed. I told you it was happening, remember? I told you because you were a fellow warrior and what was happening was not right."

Xuan Nha forced out a breath.

"Did you know that he boasted to all of Hanoi about making you the fool?"

Xuan bowed his head. He'd known.

"Do you forgive him, Xuan Nha?"

"She threw him out," Xuan croaked painfully.

"She invited him back into your bed one day last month, Xuan Nha, while you were working at your office."

"Nguyen Wu?" Surely it could not be true.

"I have resources, Xuan Nha. People who observe and speak to me. I have been briefed very thoroughly since I came home."

He kept his tongue.

"So you see, we both have shame to bear."

"I must go."

"One last thing. My son was greatly cherished by his grandfather, Le Duc Tho."

Xuan Nha hesitated. "Did you tell him about the confessions about his grandson?"

Quon shrugged, then winced from the pain in his warped shoulders. "Le Duc Tho knows many things," he said hoarsely. "If Li Binh were not so useful, he would have destroyed them both. She still shields her nephew from harm. Le Duc Tho has passed on his displeasure to the Commissioner of People's Safety, so Wu will be discredited, but it is not enough. Where do your loyalties lie, Xuan Nha?"

Xuan reflected for a moment. "I have no powerful father-in-law, Quon. I have only my own wiles, and as a military man they are not many."

Quon looked at him. "Someday, my friend, you will be called upon to take a stand."

1945L—Ta Khli Village, Thailand

GS-7 *Penny Dwight*

The threesome was downtown, eating sumptuous steaks at the new restaurant, sipping Singha beer and talking about inconsequential gossip. Penny finished her meal last and regarded the two pilots, who were deep in a discussion about Buster Leska and how he'd recently turned in the staff sedan driven by the previous commander and replaced it with a pickup.

"Why'd he do it?" Roger Hamlin asked.

"Because he wants every jock here to know he doesn't accept special privileges."

"Driving a pickup won't change anything. A commander ought to have a staff car."

"You think he's not different from other commanders?" Manny asked.

"He's okay," Roger admitted.

Manny leaned forward. "Guess what his *latest* change is?"

Roger didn't have to respond. Manny was in his talkative mood.

"Colonel's are no longer mission commanders."

"Huh?" Roger looked puzzled.

"Colonel Leska announced it this morning in our ops staff meeting. He started out by saying that he was no longer going to lead missions, because his reflexes aren't what they once were, and the guys need the very best out in front sizing up the situation and making decisions."

"I'll be damned."

"Yeah. Here's a guy who killed six MiGs, a real hero, and he's big enough to admit he's no longer the pilot some of the young guys are."

Roger was drinking more than normal, but he wasn't so intoxicated he didn't realize the importance of what was being said.

"Then Colonel Leska read off a new list of authorized mission leaders, and not a single full colonel was on it."

"How about Lucky Anderson?"

"All three squadron commanders made the list, but *most* of 'em on there were majors."

"I'll be damned," Roger Hamlin repeated. Then he raised an eyebrow. "How about you?"

Manny nodded. "I'm there, soon as I get my checkout."

Roger shook his head in wonder that a captain could be a mission commander.

Penny waved at a waiter. "I'd like coffee," she said. She was tipsy and becoming sleepy.

"You sure?" Manny asked. "The stuff they serve for coffee's pretty awful."

"I want something," she said. She was feeling the drinks. Penny had a low tolerance for alcohol. Tonight, though, she felt like celebrating.

Manny ordered hot tea for her and himself, and Roger asked for another Singha beer. Penny liked the way Manny took charge of a situation, as he'd done with the coffee—not overbearing about it, but very sure of himself. *He's the one,* she thought, observing him, intensely happy that they'd have to wait no longer. The bombing halt hadn't yet been announced, but she'd decided to stick with the schedule on her desk calendar—which she'd underlined about a hundred times. Tomorrow when Manny asked her out, as he did almost every day, Penny would tell him yes. Christmas night she'd offer her present.

Penny thought about him often, awoke each morning with him on her mind and went to bed wishing he were with her. *If he just wasn't flying the combat missions,* she thought.

Penny observed Manny as he spoke animatedly with Roger. His shoulders were wide and his chest powerful. She looked at his hands. They looked strong, but she was sure

they could be gentle. In idle times she sometimes day-
dreamed about him, as she'd once done over . . . She tried
to pull her thoughts back to the dinner, but was drawn back
to the night with Dusty, and how wonderful it had been.

He was killed the next morning, a nasty thought interrupted. *A coincidence,* her mind replied. She'd convinced
herself of that, but the thought sometimes recurred.

She observed Manny once more, and the tingling sensation returned to warm her. She drew a sharp breath, and
when both men paused and turned to her, she smiled and
acted as if there were nothing amiss. Roger gave her a
knowing grin, because she'd told him about some of her
feelings. When the men returned to their talking, the sensuous feeling quickly returned.

During the bus ride back to the base, Penny remained
quiet, scarcely listening as the two young pilots spoke about
some colonel they disliked who was visiting the base.
Manny said he'd seen him coming out of the medical clinic
with a worried look, and he was going to talk to Doc Rogers
about it. He hoped the son of a bitch—excuse me, Penny—
had something terminal.

She failed to get the colonel's name.

During a quiet period she pulled her eyes from Manny
long enough to observe Roger. He'd had too much to drink.
Penny was also tipsy, even after the hot tea. Manny held his
drinks much better than either of them, she decided happily.
Roger appeared increasingly sad and withdrawn as he stared
out the window at the darkness.

"Something wrong?" she asked him.

Roger shrugged. "Just thinking of Christmas," he said.
"How I'll be here, and my family's back in the States."

Penny felt for him. Roger adored his family, was always
quick to whip out pictures of his wife and toddler son.

"How 'bout a drink at the club when we get back?"
Roger asked, brightening. "I'll play a few tunes and pull myself out of this blue mood."

"Maybe one." Manny said he had to go to the comm center, because they were expecting a message from the States.
The Christmas cease fire message, Penny thought through
the thickening haze brought on by the alcohol.

"How 'bout you, Pen?" Roger asked. He looked tense.
She wanted to go straight to her room, feeling tipsy as she

was, but sometimes she could cheer Roger up when others couldn't.

"Okay," Penny said, then impulsively leaned over and kissed his cheek. "That's for worrying about your family like you do."

When she'd told Roger about her feelings regarding Manny, he'd approved, with the reservation that she watch after herself. Manny was like Dusty Fields, he said. A confirmed bachelor. Tonight she just might even have one more drink, to celebrate her new beginning. Show Roger support in his troubled time and have a last little fling before claiming her man, and finding out more about the guy who called himself the Supersonic Wetback.

Takhli Officers' Club

Colonel Tom Lyons

Tom wasn't happy. He'd been on base all day and had largely been ignored, despite his position on the IG team. He'd dropped in on Yank Donovan in the morning, and even received a cool reception there. The guy he was relying on to give him the scoop about what the people at Takhli were up to, how they might be cheating or sending information to Seventh Air Force about something called JACKPOT, had been nonresponsive when he'd quizzed him about what was *really* going on. When Tom had intimated that he could bring up certain unsavory facts about his background that were sure to ruin a squadron commander's career, Donovan had stared at him rudely, and Tom realized he was wasting his time, as he'd done at Ubon and Udorn.

It was not a great day for Lyons, and it was made worse by the visit to the Takhli clinic, and the flight surgeon who'd given him embarrassing advice and medication for his drippy dick.

General Roman's secretary hadn't been at all what he'd expected. After a lusty and uninhibited encounter in the hotel room, he'd grown suspicious and made some phone calls, and found that her husband had booted her out a month earlier for screwing around with every senior officer who'd give her a tumble. The bitch, he now railed inwardly, hadn't told him that one of her encounters had passed on a juicy dose of the clap.

He planned to proceed to Korat the next morning, which would complete his tour of the Thailand bases. Then he'd return to South Vietnam, visit Seventh Air Force Headquarters and a few of the bases there with unannounced, impromptu inspections. Thus far he'd heard nothing at all regarding the JACKPOT project, and hadn't even been able to dig up new dirt on how the "fucking cowboys"—he liked Roman's term—were cheating in the combat theater.

He finished with the typically lousy meal they served at the Takhli club, and sipped at a cup of lukewarm coffee the stupid Thai waitress had been slow in bringing. It was enough to make a more common man turn to drink, he thought.

He watched as Captain Manny DeVera opened the door for a young woman and an obviously intoxicated fellow carrying an old guitar case. He remembered the girl from his visit to the wing commander's office.

He despised DeVera, had done so since they'd met several years earlier and he'd refused to cooperate when Lyons's ass had been on the line in an accident investigation. He'd tried to get even when he found him here at Takhli, but his efforts had backfired. Shouldn't let spicks in the Air Force, he grumbled to himself, and they *sure* as hell shouldn't let them become officers.

A few minutes later he watched DeVera come back into the dining room and make his way toward the door. Their eyes locked, and the swarthy captain let a smile grow on his face. Impudent bastard, Lyons thought. A few months before, there'd been an incident over a female, here at Takhli. When he'd tried to teach the Peace Corps bitch a lesson about how she shouldn't fuck around, the Spick had jumped him—from his blind side, of course—and had refused to stop pounding on him until he'd promised never to do it again. It had been a demeaning and outrageous experience. Hatred smoldered hot within Tom Lyons's chest.

After paying, Tom decided on an after-dinner drink before retiring to his guest trailer. As he entered the gentleman's bar, he heard music and glanced left, toward the small stage. The young, intoxicated man he'd seen earlier was hunched over a gaudy orange guitar, chording a tune in rough harmony with a fellow who picked wildly at a banjo.

"Yeah!" a captain yelled as the crowd of a dozen clapped in cadence.

Primitive, he thought. Tom was about to pass through to the stag bar when he noticed the secretary sitting alone at a nearby table, sipping cognac and staring at the musicians.

He surveyed the girl closely as he ordered a gin and tonic from the bar, then approached her with a smile. "Mind if I have a seat?" he asked. She observed him with a tipsy expression, but her eyes brightened as she noted his colonel's rank. "Sure," she said, slurring the word. The ladies felt safe around senior officers.

Tom Lyons introduced himself pleasantly and learned that her name was Penny. He regarded the musicians seated on the edge of the small stage, surrounded by a small but growing crowd. They began a lively song, this one about the Doumer Bridge.

"They're very good," he lied. He thought they were atrocious.

She took a swallow of cognac and peered at the stage, but had difficulty focusing.

"Your boyfriend?" he asked, indicating the guitar player.

"Nope," she said. She gave him a secretive look. "Do you know Captain Manny DeVera?"

"The captain and I go back a long way," he said smoothly.

She sipped the last of her drink, making a face at the taste. "I've been celebrating," she slurred. She giggled and leaned forward conspiratorially. "I'm in love."

"How about something tastier?" he asked, giving her his friendliest smile.

"I better be goin'," she said. "Gettin' awful sleepy."

"Don't worry, I'll make sure you get to your trailer safe and sound." Tom went to the bar and ordered a double Black Russian—vodka and Kahlúa—and took it to the table.

"Try that," Tom said, placing the drink before her and wondering at his fortune. Maybe things weren't so bad after all.

Twenty minutes later, as the guitar player was beginning a sad ballad, he led the girl toward the entrance.

She had trouble remembering her trailer number. When

she finally did, he had to support her most of the way there, then fish through her purse to find her key.

GS-7 Penny Dwight

A rushing, gurgling sound filtered through Penny's stupor. The toilet? She groaned and turned, then awoke just enough to notice a light coming from her bathroom doorway.

"Nggghh," she grunted, for a savage headache throbbed relentlessly. She closed her eyes to shut out the light, her head pounding so wildly she felt nauseous. Penny heard water sounds and slowly became alert. *Who?* she wondered, but nothing in her memory was registering.

"You finally awake?" The voice sounded disgusted.

Penny blinked and peered. A man's shape was silhouetted in the bathroom doorway, looking down on her. He wore no clothing, and Penny realized that she was sprawled across her rumpled bed and also naked. The top sheet and blanket had been pulled onto the floor.

"Manny," she tried hopefully. The man moved closer and uttered a small laugh.

Penny pulled back, placing an arm over her breasts. "Who are you?" she asked.

"I'm the guy who just fucked your brains out."

She was sore down there, and very confused.

He knelt closer. She tried to move away, but he grasped her arm and held her firmly in place. "My name's Tom Lyons. I want you to tell that to DeVera. Tell him Colonel Tom Lyons fucked his girl."

Penny was so frightened she scarcely dared to breathe. "Please go," she said in a thick, quavering voice.

"You invited me, don't you remember? You invited me in and asked me to fuck you."

She shook her head, knowing she wouldn't do that regardless of how much she'd drunk.

"I've had better pieces of ass. You just laid there acting like you wanted to puke."

Her breasts were sore. Had he done that too? "Please leave," she tried.

"Not yet. This time I want you to remember, so you can tell the spick."

His words weren't registering in her muddled brain.

"Will you remember?"

"Yes. Now please go."

He pulled her protective arm away with one hand and roughly felt her breasts, first one, then the other, making them hurt. She tried to twist away. "Go away!"

He slapped her face—she recoiled in surprise.

"Keep your voice down," he hissed, kneading her breasts harshly. Each time he squeezed, fiery pain shot through her like a jolt of electricity.

"Oh, God. *Please* go."

"Not yet." His breath was coming faster and he was becoming excited.

"Stop!" Penny cried.

He issued an angry, guttural sound as she tried to pull away again, then grasped an arm tightly about her, holding her in place as he continued to knead her breasts.

"Stop!" she wailed, hoping someone might hear.

He slapped her more violently. "Quiet."

"Please," she sobbed.

She sucked a breath as the hand moved to her abdomen.

"Please." She gasped as he shoved fingers into her. She was wet, but not from arousal. Her eyes had adjusted, and as he knelt lower, she could see his erection. As he continued delving into her crotch with the rough hand, she moaned.

"Like that, huh?"

"It hurts!"

He lowered himself and pushed, missed, then roughly shoved her legs apart and tried again. She grunted with surprise as he entered, again as he shoved deep.

"Stop!" she squealed with outrage.

He made guttural sounds as he frantically worked in and out.

"Oh Godddd!" she cried desperately, trying to push him off as the tempo continued to increase. He tensed and strained, pressing deep, then muttered a loud, grunting sound. He collapsed on her, blowing out a long, contented final sigh.

Penny endured his weight helplessly, her thoughts confused and desperate, head pounding violently with the awful headache.

"Better that time," he muttered. He was still inserted, and she could feel that part of him begin to relax too.

"Get . . . off," she said, her breath slow to return.

He slowly pulled his head up and stared at her, his face crinkling into an ugly smile.

She remained silent as shame replaced outrage.

"You'll remember that one," he said proudly.

"Yes," she huffed unevenly. "Now *please* get off."

The colonel pushed himself up and got to his feet, laughing low as he began to retrieve his clothing, neatly stacked on top of the table. "Tell the spick I left a present for him."

She didn't comprehend, just wanted him to leave.

"Don't get ideas about crying rape or anything," he said. "I've got four guys from the IG team along who're going to be telling everyone how you begged me for it."

His words penetrated. The alcoholic haze was still with her, but she knew she didn't want him spreading word that she was a tramp, like the basketball player had so long ago. "Please don't let them do that," she pleaded.

"Promise to tell the spick?"

"Don't let anyone talk about me." Her head was pounding unmercifully.

"DeVera, dammit! Tell him every juicy detail, or I'll stay and fuck you again!"

"Yes, sir," she quickly whispered. "I'll tell him."

He began to hum a tune, obviously pleased. Penny stood on wobbly legs, stumbled once, took a couple of deep breaths, then pushed by him and into the bathroom. She closed and locked the door behind her, shaking violently, feeling numbed. Thoughts were difficult. She found and loaded her white douche bulb with water and solution. It was difficult to do, because she couldn't stop her hands from shaking.

She squatted, inserted, squeezed. The water was startlingly cold. Penny repeated the act.

In the other room the trailer door slammed. Penny felt her gorge rising and quickly turned, knelt, and grasped the bowl to vomit. She remained locked in the bathroom for a long while. As she continued to grow sober, she wished she could die. The self-confidence she'd developed in the past weeks had left her. She was unsure and felt dirty and terribly afraid.

Friday, December 22nd, 1515 Local—Fighter Tactics Branch, TFWC, Nellis AFB, Nevada

Major Benny Lewis

The second message from Moods Diller was spread before him and was just as confusing as the first he'd received. Again there was the reference to Lieutenant White, which obviously meant Major General White, and a second puzzling mention of Project Titanic.

Which indicated that the Pave Dagger test was in deep trouble and Moods needed high-level support . . . but why didn't he just come out and say what he meant?

General White was away, gone to Matamordas Island, Texas, ostensibly to observe a live weapons release by B-52's, but secretively meeting with an SAC general officer about JACKPOT. When LINE BACKER JACKPOT kicked off, Strategic Air Command wanted to send ten three-ship cells in trail up to Hanoi, and Gordie White wanted to talk them into using more diverse tactics. So far it had been a hard sell. The SAC general said his B-52's had such great electronic jamming power they wouldn't have to worry about SAMs. JACKPOT being so secretive, it was impossible to bring the argument into the open with normal classified message traffic. Also, General McManus had great faith in the ops staff at SAC headquarters.

So with General White off on business and intending to remain away for the next couple of weeks, Benny had no one he could turn to with gritty questions, especially those concerning JACKPOT and the ongoing Pave Dagger combat tests. He wanted to fire off a message to Moods, telling him to clarify the issue, but warning bells told him Moods was being deliberately vague with his gobbledygook messages. Something was definitely wrong at Danang.

He checked his calendar and decided to move up his visit to the war theater, previously scheduled for the following month. There was little holding him at Nellis. He was caught up with his JACKPOT tasks, and even the mundane parts of his normal work.

The situation with Julie was as unclear as Moods's message. She was busy with her work at Pan Am, and with her mother still present, they got together less and less. Now usually only on Friday nights for dinner, and always at her apartment. They still kissed soulfully when he went to his car to leave, and still mouthed the word "love," but her mother was now coming between them even more forcefully, and he increasingly found himself blaming Julie. Whenever he approached the problem, she'd artfully sidestep the issue and say she *couldn't* just tell her mother to leave.

She'd also repeat that she loved him dearly, but Benny was beginning to doubt even that. Maybe a period of separation would be good for them both, he told himself.

When he called Julie and told her he'd be traveling to Southeast Asia, her voice trembled with concern. Did he really have to go? she asked. When he'd convinced her it was necessary, and calmed her concerns that he might be in danger, she said she wanted to see him.

There was a catch of resignation in her voice when she said she loved him, and for him to remember that every waking hour. He told her it would be more than a week before he left. On New Year's Day, he said. He'd see her for dinner tonight at the apartment, he reminded her.

"I want us to plan an evening alone, with just the two of us," she said.

She'd said that before, though, and it hadn't materialized. Except for an infrequent lunch, there'd always been little Patty and Julie's mother. Benny Lewis hung up after the conversation confused, feeling the same, empty ache he experienced whenever they spoke.

CHAPTER
TWENTY-THREE

Saturday, December 23rd, 0825 Local—354th TFS, Takhli
RTAFB, Thailand

Colonel Buster Leska

Periodically Buster liked to visit the fighter squadrons to see
how things were progressing and talk to the squadron commanders. Today was Yank Donovan's turn in the barrel, and
they sat in the 354th squadron commander's office.

Donovan's losses were no higher or lower than those of
the other squadrons, but the subject seemed to permeate his
mind. He was telling Buster how he'd lost another pilot, this
one down in pack two, bombing the Ho Chi Minh Trail.

"It should have been an easy mission," he was grumbling.

"Sometimes," Buster told him, "the gomers just get in a
lucky shot. A golden beebee."

Over the past two months Yank had gradually lost enthusiasm, although not his confidence. He'd seen some of his
finest young pilots die while facing impossible odds in pack
six, and others shot down as they bombed invisible targets
they felt were the result of frustration on intelligence's part
about not being able to find enemy supplies under the
dense jungle canopy.

Buster might have been more understanding if the same problem wasn't faced by the entire wing, as well as all the other Thailand units. Yank Donovan had changed, some for the better perhaps, because for the first time he was recognizing others in his selfish world, but his disposition was not improved. This morning he wore his usual sour expression and seemed even moodier than usual.

Buster glanced at his watch. "I've got an airplane to catch," he said. He was going to Korat, where President Johnson was scheduled to deliver a speech to the troops. Moss had sent a classified message telling his wing commanders to attend.

When he rose, Donovan followed. "I've got something I've gotta tell you, Colonel."

"I'll be back tomorrow afternoon."

Donovan frowned as they went out the squadron's front door and walked toward a blue pickup with a WING COMMANDER placard and an eagle on front. There was no driver.

"I'll ride along," Yank mumbled.

He's made up his mind and has to talk, Buster thought, wishing he had more time.

When they were seated, Donovan turned to him. "Colonel Lyons visited the squadron a couple of days ago."

That was no revelation. "He and his people visited *all* the squadrons, Yank. He said he was on a tour of the bases, looking at our ops routines."

"He's called me at least twice a week since he got the IG job."

"Oh?" That was interesting.

"Keeps wanting to know anything we're doing contrary to PACAF rules." He looked at Buster squarely. "I went along at first, Colonel. I told him things he wanted to hear, like how some of the guys weren't honoring the restrictions as well as they could've."

Buster thought about that. It explained why he periodically received angry messages from PACAF headquarters mentioning specific names and incidents. They'd been minor transgressions, blown out of proportion.

He started the pickup's engine, thinking about what Yank was saying.

"I want you to know I've stopped telling him anything.

Lyons is just out to get himself promoted by sucking on the blood of others."

"That's pretty strong."

Donovan's voice was even. "You've been decent to me, Colonel. Most of the pilots here are doing their damnedest, and it's not easy with all the bullshit we have to put up with. I couldn't keep on shooting them in the back like that. Lyons is out to get you and everyone else here."

Buster remained silent as he drove toward base operations, where the gooney bird waited.

"This last time he wanted to know about something called JACKPOT," Donovan said.

Buster fought to keep his face passive. "Go on."

"He kept prodding to see if I knew anything about it."

"Did he tell you what it was?"

"Something General Moss is trying to hide from General Roman. Lyons wants to find out what it's about."

Buster parked in his space in front of base operations. "Did you tell him anything?"

"I didn't know what he was talking about. I'd never heard of anything called 'JACKPOT'."

Buster worked to keep concern from his expression.

Yank squinted out at the flight line. "Anyway, don't worry about me telling Lyons anything in the future. I doubt anyone else here will talk with him either. He's not well liked."

"Was he making any progress, finding out about this . . . JACKPOT?"

"I have no idea." Yank Donovan wouldn't meet his eyes. Admitting error had been difficult and demeaning for his vast ego, but he looked happier.

"Do something for me, Yank."

"Yes, sir?"

"Whenever he calls, find out what he's after and let me know, okay?"

Yank grew taut. "I really don't want to speak to him again."

"You owe me that much, Yank."

Donovan mused for a moment, then huffed a breath and nodded.

Buster left it at that. As he walked toward the gooney bird, his mind boiled with activity. General Moss would be at Korat to attend the President's speech, but he doubted he'd get a chance to speak with him alone. He'd have to wait to inform him about General Roman's queries after he returned to Takhli and Moss to Saigon.

What would happen if Roman found out about JACK-POT? Would he somehow scuttle the project, as General McManus had feared?

As he stepped inside the gooney bird and made his way to a seat, Buster became increasingly paranoid and began to wonder if the discussion with Yank Donovan hadn't been contrived by Lyons to get his reaction.

0900L—Nakhon Phanom RTAB, Thailand

Sergeant Black

The lieutenant colonel had called him into his office for a private meeting at 0600 hours, to give him an early Christmas present.

"I'm pulling you off Hotdog," he'd said.

Black had felt it might be coming after the loss of two of the two men. "How about the matter we discussed last week, sir?"

"There's no possible way to get them American citizenship."

"I promised 'em, sir."

"It was a promise you can't keep."

"I see, sir." But Black hadn't really understood. Hotdog had given as much as was humanly possible to help Americans, so hadn't they earned it?

"They should rightly be turned over to the South Viets."

"Not *rightly*, sir. That isn't *right* at all."

The lieutenant colonel who went by the call sign Papa Wolf had sighed. "You're a hardheaded fellow. Makes me wonder why they sent the major's list down with your name on it. You made it two years early. It's not me taking Hotdog away from you, it's the U.S. Army."

Black had been astounded.

Papa Wolf had stood to shake his hand. "Congratulations. Your date of rank will be in mid-March."

For more than a year, even in private, others had called him Sergeant or Black. It would feel strange to show up for work as an officer, wearing a different name tag. But, then, he'd be a different person. Black was the enigmatic tough guy who ran around in the bush with his bunch of renegades. Major John Dillingham would be just another field-grade puke.

"Then I can keep Hotdog until then?" Black had asked.

"I'm taking Hotdog off the active list as of today."

"But why, sir?"

"Because you're the only *living* man I've got in my group who's been put in for a second Distinguished Service Cross, and I'd like to keep you that way."

Black had paused only a heartbeat before shaking his head. "I refuse the promotion and the medal, Colonel."

Papa Wolf had immediately become upset. "That would be a *foolish* mistake."

Black had drawn a deep breath. "If it takes it, I'll get out of the Army and lobby as a civilian to get Hotdog what they deserve."

They'd eyed one another for a long while. After a full minute Papa Wolf had spoken. "I'll need a new XO in April. I'd like to pick you, but you'd have to take the promotion."

Operations officer was the second most coveted job at the headquarters. Only the command position was better, and that was debatable. Under normal circumstances Black would have salivated for the job, but he'd held his tongue.

"Let's say I kept you on with Hotdog until March. No more drops into hostile territory and no hazardous patrols. Would you volunteer for the XO slot?"

"As of this second, sir."

"Which means you'll accept the promotion and the medal?"

"As long as you let me work to get Hotdog their citizenship, yes sir."

"Only until mid-March. Anyway, the embassies will tell you the same thing they told me."

"I've got to try, sir."

"Yeah." The lieutenant colonel had stared. "If you tell anyone we had this conversation, I will remove your balls and joyfully roast them."

"Yes, sir."

Papa Wolf had suddenly chuckled, and somehow Black

knew he'd been had, that the lieutenant colonel had expected him to rebel. "Get the hell out of here, *Sergeant*."

It was natural that when Black drove to the O-1 pilots' hootch in an M-151 jeep, his mind was on his team. It took effort to bring himself back to his task. He, as well as the three healthy members of Hotdog who lounged in the backseat of the open vehicle, wore civilian clothing. M-16's were wrapped in a blanket under the rear seat, and they wore sidearms under their shirts.

Lieutenant Colonel Anderson was waiting in front, also wearing civvies as he'd been asked to do. Black pulled up, waited as he crawled into the front passenger's seat, then immediately put the jeep into gear and departed for the gate. Twenty-five minutes later they pulled to a stop on a back road, in a small clearing surrounded by jungle, and the three in back jumped out and deployed around the vehicle with their M-16's.

Black pointed. "The Mekong River's past the trees there, Colonel. Maybe two hundred meters from here. The vehicle, a white jeep with USOM stenciled in large black letters on the side, was coming down this road with two men in front and your lady in back. Five bad guys were in those trees. The vehicle was just about there"—he jabbed his finger—"going very slow, when they shot the driver. Took him out with bursts from one or two AK-47's. Five shots hit the vehicle, two hit him, and the vehicle flipped on its side . . . right there." He indicated the edge of the road. "The white guy crawled out of the vehicle on the far side, and they shot him. Either then or later they finished the two men with a single round in the head, using a small-caliber pistol. Then they pushed the vehicle back on its wheels, rolled it into the bush there, and covered it with branches."

"What about Linda?" Anderson's voice croaked. He was understandably shaken.

"They found the shooters' and her footprints leading away."

"Which direction?"

"Back into the bush. And from there?" He shrugged. "No one knows for sure."

"Maybe to the river?"

"I believe so. The USAID people had just visited a village farther down the road and were probably headed to the base. It happened about oh-twelve-thirty. There's a lot of boats in the area, but around noon the river traffic slows down because of the heat. I think they took her across. No one saw them, but when it comes to CTs, a lot of people around here get amnesia. I think they took her across and maybe handed her over to their Pathet Lao buddies."

"But they could've just taken her into the jungle somewhere."

"Could be."

"Who's looking for her?"

"Every Thai law-enforcement agency and military outfit in the area. The Thai Army's in charge of the search. They sent a full colonel to take over the investigation. The State Department's got the heat turned up in Bangkok, and they're demanding complete secrecy. That's why no one'll talk to you about it. And no one likely will, unless they're told different."

"How about our people? Are we doing anything?"

"It's not our country. Much as we might want to, we can't go charging around interrogating their people."

"How about unofficially?"

"Even unofficially they're our allies, and we've got no jurisdiction. Our people at NKP worked with the locals on the initial investigations, but when they kept coming up with blanks, they stood back and scratched their heads like everyone else. They've got a lot of pull with the officials here, but no one seems to have answers."

"So it was probably Thai CTs, but we don't know, and it could be they've taken her across the river and handed her over to the Pathet Lao guerrillas, but we don't know that either." Anderson shook his head. "Sure seems to be a lot we don't know."

Black sympathized, but he felt there was something he had to tell him. "Come with me, Colonel."

They walked to the place where the USOM vehicle had come to rest on its side, and he pointed at the ground. "When they examined the vehicle, there was blood inside, and also on the ground. It was your lady's blood type, so we know she was hurt. Possibly hit by the burst that killed the driver."

Anderson stared intently at the ground—now covered with boot prints and marks of bare feet—as if searching for her there. The Hotdog lieutenant joined them, and he looked there too.

After a long pause Black continued in a soft voice. "She's very likely dead from the injury. Neither the CTs nor the Pathet Lao—if they got her across the river, which I think is where they went—are big on first aid and prevention. When they're left unattended, wounds get infected fast here in the tropics."

"What makes you think they crossed the river?"

"I'll show you." Black went back to the jeep and retrieved the last M-16, motioned to the lieutenant with a hand signal, then for Anderson to follow. One Hotdog remained with the jeep. The lieutenant and the other Hotdog went into the thicket where the CTs had set up the ambush, and Black led the major after them. He pointed out the firing positions, then plunged on. After pushing their way through for a few yards, they found themselves on a narrow, well-beaten path. Five minutes later they were at the bank of a wide river the color of burnt orange.

The Mekong was empress of southern Indochina, just as the Hong Song ruled in the North. But the Hong Song, or Red River, was a streamlet compared to the Mekong. The empress of the South began her twisting trek in China's vast Qinghai Province, north of the high mountains of Tibet and very near the source of the Yangtze, the great river of China. She'd already flowed for more than a thousand miles when she came into sight of the Red River headlands, where they paralleled one another for a few miles until separated by a high mountain range. There the Red River turned and entered North Vietnam, nurturing the farmlands of the Hong Valley and the important cities of Hanoi, Haiphong, and Nam Dinh. The Mekong had another thousand miles to go. She became the border between Burma and Laos, then Laos and Thailand, then ran the length of Cambodia, and finally across the southern extreme of South Vietnam to splinter the land into a vast, rich delta. Her silt replenished soils, her waters provided irrigation, and her surface supported transportation for people of six nations.

The four men stopped at her bank and stared out at the murky water. A long boat was passing a few meters off shore, sculled by a lean, ageless man who very carefully did not see them.

"Someone's been pulling boats up on the bank and hiding them in the brush there," Black said, pointing. "Two-to-one odds we know who the someone is."

Anderson walked to the hiding place and examined marks where something had been dragged across the earth.

"I believe they'd crossed the river the previous night in two small boats, then set up the ambush where they did because they could get away so quickly."

"Did they know who they were shooting at?"

Black pondered that one for a moment. "They'd probably heard about Americans in the white jeep asking questions in the villages and were told they passed here. From what I've been told, your lady was asking questions about *them* and paying people to tell her about *their* movements. That likely got their interest."

"Do they know she's important?"

"They do now. The press has told everyone who could read."

"If they know, they might treat her better."

Black nodded. "That's a possibility, *if* she's still alive. If she is, they're probably trying to get information. Later they might decide to use her for propaganda or trading material."

"What kind of information could they be after? She's USAID, remember."

Black didn't answer. From the questions she'd been asking, he knew she'd been doing a lot more than passing out food to villagers. The CT, and certainly Pathet Lao officers, would be smart enough to deduce the same.

Anderson was looking across the river, the expression indeterminable on his badly scarred face. Again Black noted the lieutenant watching Anderson closely. A thorough warrior himself, the lieutenant said he felt a kinship with Kunnel Lokee Anduhson. Now he shared his grief.

"Is anyone searching across the river?" Lucky asked.

"Patrols into Laos have to be approved by MAC-V, and the reason has to be a damned good one. But we've got our sources there, and so far we haven't heard a peep of information regarding your lady. Until we do, there's not the slightest chance for a patrol."

"I agree with you, Black. I think they took her over there. Now it's a matter of raising the priority to get her back."

"The effort to find her has a double-A priority, which is as high as I've seen. You're not supposed to know that. Her code name's Clipper. You're not supposed to know that either."

"Clipper," repeated Anderson.

"Yeah."

"Fuck the rules, Sarge. Take me across and let's get her out."

"It wouldn't do any good, unless we knew where to look. Let the intell people do their thing, Colonel. Once they find something, you can damn well bet, with that kind of priority, they'll act on the information."

Anderson shook his head helplessly.

"I'll keep nosing around. If I find anything more, I'll let you know."

"I appreciate the help, Black."

"You should return to Takhli."

"I'm thinking about it. But, God! I wish there was something I could do. I feel so fucking *helpless*."

"War's shitty."

"Yeah." He stared out at the river for a bit longer, then released a pent-up breath and turned to Black. "They're moving me out of the hootch. General Moss talked to the wing commander yesterday, so he knows about me now, and they're moving me into a VIP trailer. I think they said number four. If you find out anything, you can reach me there."

Black motioned to his men, and they headed back toward the jeep. Throughout the walk the lieutenant continued to observe Lucky Anderson. His concern was genuine. He knew how the communists treated prisoners. Black wondered if he was thinking about his youngest sister, taken to serve an NVA unit in the jungle.

1050L—Korat RTAFB, Thailand

Lieutenant General Richard J. Moss

The President had flown from Canberra, Australia, directly to Korat. The speech he was giving to the gathered officers and airmen was full of rah-rah stuff about how they were fighting for democracy, and how they were going to beat up on the North Vietnamese until they ended their aggression against the peace-loving people of . . .

It would have been a great show for the VFW back in Podunkville. The problem here was that most of the audience knew that the guy in front of them was the only one who could turn them loose to win, and thus far he had refused. Still, he was their commander in chief, so the guys listened and wanted to believe, and gave him a good response.

After five minutes of it Moss motioned to his driver, and they slipped off to his vehicle. He was taken directly to base operations, where he sent the driver on.

Air Force One, the sleek blue-and-white Boeing 707, was parked on the ramp in front of base ops, and he walked toward it. The aircraft commander, a full bull, was doing a walk-around inspection of the big aircraft, followed closely by two sharply dressed enlisted men. They brought their own crew chiefs along.

Moss ignored the security policemen who were eyeing him and hailed a plainclothed Secret Service agent, as he'd been told to do. "I'm General Moss," he said, although he was wearing a silver-tan uniform with three stars on the collar and his name tag above his right pocket.

It wasn't enough. He was asked for his identification card. The agent checked the photo and information on the plasticized card, examined the contents of his briefcase, then nodded to the security policemen and led him aboard. Inside, he motioned at a seat in the forward cabin.

"The President will be along in about half an hour," he said.

Moss nodded absently and started to lean over to look out the pressure-glass window.

"The President doesn't want your presence known, General. Please stay away from the window."

"Sure," he said, and pulled back.

"We'll fly from here directly to Cam Ranh. When we get there, the President and his staff will get off, then you'll wait for half an hour and deplane."

"It's your show." He watched the agent leave.

A steward wearing a white uniform with no visible rank

came through. "Anything I can get you while you're waiting, General?"

"No, thanks." He frowned. "Are you military?"

"Tech sergeant in the Air Force, sir. Stationed at Andrews."

Moss looked about at the rich surroundings, wondering. "How many military advisors did he bring along?"

"Only the flight crew and stewards are military. There's Senator Wayland Lingenfelter and a few others, and his press secretary."

The pilot and crew came aboard, talking together as they went into the forward cabin.

"Twenty minutes until the big man gets here," said the steward.

1155L—Base Operations, Korat RTAFB

Colonel Tom Lyons

The Band of the Pacific struck up "Ruffles and Flourishes," then "Hail to the Chief," and the President of the United States went up the boarding ramp, turned and waved, then disappeared inside. Last on, first off, according to protocol. Tom watched as the engines were started. No one emerged before the door was secured and the ramp was pulled away. That meant Moss was still inside and obviously would remain there for a least the next leg of the flight. Tom had monitored him from his position at the front of the crowd listening to the President's speech. He'd seen him leave and followed, and watched as he'd been escorted aboard the aircraft.

What's Moss doing aboard the President's airplane? Something to do with JACKPOT?

He wondered if there was any way to find out from his father-in-law, who was also aboard, traveling with L.B.J. as friend and advisor. Likely not. Not only was Lingenfelter closemouthed when it came to political business, he'd never been fond of Lyons. Tom was tolerated, so long as he treated Lingenfelter's daughter as royally as her father thought she was due.

Then he knew the answer. Margaret was the darling of

the senator's eye. He'd tell her things he would reveal to no
other. All Tom had to do was get her to ask the right question . . . convince her it was in her interest as well as his
own. A smile grew at the thought of reporting that information to General Roman, and the reward the general had
promised for his trusted staff.

And that was the key to Margaret! All he had to do was
dangle the promise of a move to the Pentagon. She loved
living in Washington, D.C., near her parents—the social
scene, mixing with the powerful movers and shakers. She
would ask her father the question.

And Tom Lyons would have his star.

1900L—Base Operations, Tan Son Nhut Air Base, Saigon, South Vietnam

Lieutenant Colonel Pearly Gates

General Moss appeared contemplative as he stepped down
the ladder of the T-39 Sabreliner and walked toward his
waiting staff car. Pearly and Moss's driver saluted as he approached. Moss motioned for Pearly to join him in the vehicle, and they crawled in back.

When they were seated, Pearly opened his mouth to
speak, but Moss curtly shook his head and ordered the
driver to take them to the headquarters. He was troubled,
Pearly could tell.

They remained quiet until they were inside Moss's inner
office, and even then as the general went to the cabinet beside his desk and pulled out two whiskey glasses. He
opened a small refrigerator and fished out ice. The cubes
made a clinking sound as he added two to each glass.

"You drink Scotch too, I believe?"

"Yes, sir."

Moss poured from a crystal decanter, eyeballed, then
poured again. He handed Pearly his drink. When Pearly was
about to thank him, he turned, walked to the large wall map
of the combat theater, and stared.

"We're in deep shit," he muttered.

"Sir?"

"America." Moss took a drink and slowly shook his head.

Pearly frowned. "I take it he didn't buy our argument."

"I didn't argue much. Sometimes it was like we had two discussions going at the same time. Johnson wasn't what I expected. He's in so far over his head, he's about to drown."

Pearly remained silent.

"He opened by trying to describe the situation in the States. About the rioting on the campuses and demonstrations in the streets. Now and then he'd stop and stare, and change the subject to his ranch in Texas. Things are simpler there, and he'd love nothing more than to forget 'all this shit,' like he called it, just go there and let the . . . his words now . . . 'let the bastards get what they deserve.' "

"What bastards?"

"Who knows? The rioters? Congress? The communists? Not us. He said every time he hears another soldier's been killed, he gets sick to his stomach and wants to puke. It hurts him, he said, and he meant it. All that 'Hey, hey, L.B.J., how many kids did you kill today' stuff is getting to him. He said he wants to do the right thing, but he's catching hell from every side, no matter which way he turns."

"Did you get to talk about LINE BACKER JACKPOT?"

Moss nodded. "I talked. When I told him the OPlan was designed to force the North Vietnamese to withdraw from the fight, he just stared back at me and asked, 'But what if it pulls the Chinese into the war?' "

"We thought he'd bring that up."

"Some of his advisors tell him it's a possibility."

"The Chinese are in the middle of an internal revolution and have too many troubles at home to attack *anyone* right now."

"I told him that. Tried to explain the 'cultural revolution' you described in your brief. He got glassy-eyed, like a bored kid in a history class."

Pearly took a drink of the general's whiskey. It was a very smooth single-malt.

"Then he says if winning's all that easy, how come he wasn't told before McManus came sneaking over to see him? I said it *won't* be easy. That we'd need a buildup of forces, two more wings of fighters and a couple more B-52 wings. Another carrier group of A-6's and F-4's.

"L.B.J. just shook his head then and said, 'That's all you guys want to do, bring in more troops and airplanes. How much can this two-bit, shit-pot place hold?' Then he says, 'What if the Russkies step in?' "

Pearly nodded. They'd anticipated that one too.

"So I went over my brief on how they're too far away and don't have enough ships or naval air to challenge us, and he says, 'They could threaten us right in the U.S., especially if we strip away our defenses.' "

Pearly shook his head. "They wouldn't start World War III over a warm-water port, which is all they'd really get out of it if the bad guys won."

"I told him that, so next he brought up Korea. He says, 'What if they start a second front in Korea? We can't fight two wars over here.' I told him if North Korea thought they had a chance, they'd attack in the next five minutes. They don't, and they know it. South Korea could probably kick their ass by themselves."

"He sounds worried."

"He's troubled. Nervous as a cat and doesn't trust anything he hears. Next he asked me if I was sure we could force the North Vietnamese out of the South if we just bombed them. I told him I was, if we did it smart and tough. We'd keep pounding them day and night until they cried uncle, and how we felt that would take about two weeks. He perked up then, because he liked the idea of them yelling uncle."

"Me too," Pearly said.

"But then he frowned and said he was worried about collateral damage to civilians and innocents who got in the way. He said, 'Your bombs aren't that selective, General. If we do it, a lot of people are going to be killed, and the peaceniks are going to make my life miserable.' I said if we *don't* do it, a lot more people are going to be killed before it's over."

"Did he buy that?"

"Like I said, he's in way over his head, afraid to make a decision because he's scared it'll be wrong. I've seen commanders get like that in combat. They get weary of sending men out to die. That's when you've got to pull them out of the fight and replace them."

"It's difficult, sending men out to die."

"Sure it is. That's why we get four years of bullshit training at West Point, to teach us how to use our resources, which includes humans. Even then it's hard. Some can do it, others can't. Maybe Johnson *was* a naval officer in World War II, but he never had to make that kind of hard decision, and he's not trained for it. That's why he pukes every time he hears he's responsible for another man's death. He can't just call in his top generals and tell them, 'Here's the resources you get and here's the national objectives—now go out and make them happen,' because assholes like the Edsel mechanic keep telling him he can't trust the military. He's an elected politician, for Christ's sake, and he listens to the people, but he only hears the loudest voices. The press, the liberal congressmen and anarchists in the streets, all say we're a bunch of jerks who want to napalm babies. He might not trust them, but he gets confused and doesn't know who he *can* trust."

Moss took a long swig of his drink, and Pearly thought he was about to throw the glass across the room.

"Then there's no chance for JACKPOT?"

Moss signed. "Yeah. I think we've won, Pearly. I think he's going to turn us loose."

Pearly was amazed at the switch.

"First I heard all the arguments against it. Then, when we were in the approach to land at Cam Ranh Bay, he turned and looked me in the eye. He thanked me for meeting with him, and I thought that was it, but then he said, 'When we do this thing, I'll want you in charge, Moss.' I told him I was a three-star reporting to a four-star in Hawaii, and he shook his head. 'You planned it,' he said, 'and you'll be in charge.' "

"That's great, General."

When Pearly left, Moss was still brooding. He'd said he'd get a JACKPOT message out to McManus right away, but he had not yet started writing it. There was something about it all he didn't like, something that made him uneasy and worried for his country.

2030L

Pearly stuck his head into Lieutenant Dortmeier's new office. "You're still working?"

She was busying about the place, putting things in order. She'd been assigned the room only late that afternoon and was pleased to get out of the corner nook in Pearly's office. "How did *The Meeting* go?"

The Meeting had been on their minds constantly since they'd learned that L.B.J. would talk with Moss.

"Let's walk over to the club and I'll tell you," Pearly said.

"Done. I needed something to pry me out of this place."

They both knew she'd waited anxiously for news of what had transpired.

"And," Pearly mustered courage, "I'll buy supper."

"If you're buying, it must have gone well," was all Lucy Dortmeier said as she retrieved her cap and purse, which made Pearly feel rather silly about the way he'd been so hesitant to ask her.

Sunday, December 24th, 2100 Local—VIP Trailer Four, Nakhon Phanom RTAB, Thailand

Sergeant Black

Black had taken Lucky Anderson to dinner in Nakhon Phanom city, because it was Christmas eve and seemed the thing to do for the troubled pilot. The lieutenant had accompanied them, but afterward dropped out, saying he had to check on his men. Two were Catholic and felt melancholy on Christ's birthday. He was inebriated, as were Black and Anderson.

In his VIP trailer Lucky poured yet another drink for the two of them. "The lieutenant's a nice guy," he said. "Hard to understand him, though."

"He's speaking a mix of Viet, English, and island pidgin, so it's no wonder. He's getting better, though." Black took the glass from Anderson and told him about his losing attempts to get the Hotdogs to the States. "You know anyone who might be able to help?"

"I'll get you a name from the USAID people. I call the embassy almost every day to see if they've heard anything new about Linda."

For a while they were both quiet, sipping their drinks and contemplating. Anderson finally asked what had happened at the TACAN station when Black had called for fighter support.

"I got my ass chewed for that radio call," Black said, feeling a trace of bitterness, and also the growing numbness of intoxication. "We're supposed to go through proper channels. I was in shit up to my neck, or I wouldn't have tried it, but they didn't buy my excuse."

"Why?"

"Got me. Interservice rivalry, I guess. You guys are the junior service and all that horseshit, and they think it's disgraceful to ask for support unless it's something worked out between our asshole generals and your asshole generals."

"What was going on? All we heard was that the TACAN station was overrun by NVA."

Black brooded for a moment, then shook his head sadly. "Can't talk about our ops."

"But you *were* in trouble."

"I lost two men there." He almost told him about the Montagnard noncombatants, but stopped himself. Anderson had his own troubles.

"I didn't know you guys carried UHF radios. I didn't think there was any way you could talk to us." Lucky took their glasses to the fridge, dropped in more ice cubes, and refilled them with raw whiskey. He swayed a bit on his way back.

"Normally there isn't," Black said, "but they had a UHF up there."

"And the brass got upset about you making the call?"

"It's against their rules."

"Stupid rules."

"Yes, sir. Stupid."

Anderson brooded. "I thought we were the ones with the dumb fucking restrictions. I guess they've got different dumb ones for all of us." He shook his head sadly. "Makes you wonder, doesn't it?"

"Sometimes I ignore the *most* stupid ones. I've gotta."

Lucky became thoughtful. "What kind of radios do you carry?"

Black paused before responding. "VHF FM hand-helds." He saw no reason to mention the special-purpose HF packs.

"Can you tune them?"

"Nope. They're preset to our op frequencies."

Anderson pulled a small notepad from his shirt pocket

and retrieved a pen. "Give me one of the frequencies. One you don't use very often."

Black hesitated. The operational radio frequencies were highly classified and closely held.

"I've got a good reason."

"One-oh-six point four."

Anderson wrote it down. "You get in trouble next time, and you see Thuds flying in the area, give us a call on that frequency."

"You've got VHF?"

"We've got a VHF instrument landing system in the Thud. We can receive audio, but we can't talk. I'll spread the word to fly with it preset to one-oh-six point four. Next time you get in deep shit, we'll be able to help. What's a good code word?"

"I'm not sure this is a good idea, Colonel."

"Bullshit. Give me a code word. I'd want to know if it was you or some gomer talking. You're from Hawaii, right? How about ... Tiny Bubbles?"

Black snorted, feeling the alcohol and slurring his words. "That's for haole tourists. Ever'one from the islands hates the fuckin' song."

"How about 'aloha'? "

That was better. "Okay."

"Just say, 'F-105's, this is Hotdog. Aloha.' I don't give a diddley shit *what* the rules are, you say that to us, you'll get support."

"I don't think we'll have to use it. We won't be going on any more—" Black stopped himself. He'd said too much.

"Even better if you don't need our help, but I'll spread the word anyway." He pronounced it 'shpread,' and his eyes looked watery.

Black nodded gravely.

Anderson sat back in his chair. "I'll be going back to Takhli tomorrow. Might as well, because I'm getting no-where here. I talked to the provost marshal today, and from what he said, you know more about it than he does."

"An' tha's not much."

Anderson gave a distressed shake of his head. "Sure makes me feel helpless. Wish you could have met Linda, Black. She's one hell of a woman." Lucky was slurring his words.

"They showed us her official photo. Nice-looking lady."

"Yeah." Anderson grew quiet.

"I'll give you a call if I hear something."

"There's nothing new you're not telling me, is there?"

Black started to tell him the latest intell. That Clipper's cover had been utterly blown by her own man trying to recruit a new agent. Before her arrival the local USAID representative had told the man, in the presence of others, how she had intelligence networks set up at other bases, and that the woman was *very* important. The new recruit was himself a suspected CT, operating out of the last village they'd visited, and he'd disappeared after the attack.

But Black did not say that.

"No, sir," he said. "It's as if she dropped off the face of the earth." That part was true.

"You think they'll kill her?"

"I dunno." It was also true that Black's toes were growing numb. They did that when he'd drunk too much. He took another sip of whiskey, enjoying the glow. "I'm glad you're going back, Colonel. This isn't your kind of ball game."

Lucky Anderson stared into space for a long moment, then dropped his head into his arms, consumed with grief, a condition that was not helped by the booze.

Black left quietly. He was determined to help if at all possible, but sincerely doubted he could. The night air felt cool on his face. He took a few deep breaths before walking to the jeep.

CHAPTER
TWENTY-FOUR

**Monday, December 25th, 1855 Local—O' Club Stag Bar,
Takhli RTAFB, Thailand**

Captain Manny DeVera

Christmas day was not a joyous one for most of the men at
Takhli, and was helped little by the fact that there was a
two-day bombing pause imposed by the President. Most of
the pilots preferred to continue flying, racking up counters
toward the magic one hundred missions, rather than sit
around thinking sad thoughts about being so far from their
families.

Manny was listening to Animal Hamlin complain about
how much he missed his wife and son, and how the tape his
wife had sent had been demagnetized and garbled in the
mail system. When he played it, it sounded like a barnyard
full of strange animals.

Manny's mood was made no better by the puzzling situation with Penny Dwight. He'd thought their relationship
was fast developing, a fact confirmed by Animal between fits
of nostalgia about last Christmas, which he'd spent with his
family.

"She told me she really likes you," Animal told him, "and

for me not to feel bad when she starts going out alone with you. She's hooked. You treat her good, okay?"

"She's a nice girl," Manny answered, realizing that was precisely what Dusty and Animal had called her. Penny might not be the woman of his dreams, but he liked her well enough, and she was posing a definite challenge by being so hardheaded about refusing to see him. Going to bed with him was another matter, but not even to talk with him was a real blow to his pride. He'd been encouraged by Roger's revelation, yet the secretary had stayed in her trailer for the past three days, saying she was sick. The one time he'd seen her, in the dining room the previous evening, she'd been alone and asked to remain that way when he and Animal had tried to join her. She'd kept her eyes averted, had eaten quickly, and immediately returned to her trailer.

"She's avoiding me," Manny groused for the dozenth time.

"She's sick. You notice how pale she was? And how she's not taking care of herself?"

He'd noticed. "Wonder what's wrong."

"I asked Doc, and he says she's probably got the flu—maybe a stomach problem. He said she ought to go over to the clinic to see him."

"Think we should drop by her trailer and try to cheer her up?"

"I tried. She wouldn't answer the door."

Something, Manny thought, was definitely wrong. He decided to find the source of her problem.

1945L—Trailer 5B

GS-7 *Penny Dwight*

"Please go away," Penny said to the door.

The knocking sounded again. "It's Manny. We gotta talk."

"Go away."

The knocking continued.

She went into the bathroom and washed her face, determined to ignore the insistent sound. Penny had washed a lot since the shameful night. She showered several times daily, but there was a stench in her nostrils that refused to leave, and regardless of how she cleaned herself inside and out, she felt dirty. Now she was beginning to itch.

"Penny," she heard, "my knuckles are getting raw. You want me to go around with bloody paws?" He knocked on the metal door again, saying, "Ouch! Ouch! Ouch!"

"Go away, Manny DeVera."

"Not until we've talked."

He knocked again, this time with a distinct tempo.

"You like that one? It's called 'Unchained Melody.' It was our prom theme song back in high school. I've got a lot of 'em."

"Just go *away*."

He rapped again, at a faster tempo. "That one's 'Blue Suede Shoes.' Remember? You were pretty young when it came out, but my bunch really liked it."

"Manny. Please go."

"Not until we've talked."

"No!"

"Why?"

"Because . . ." Penny drew a breath and blurted the truth. "I'm afraid."

There was a small pause. "You're afraid of me?" The voice sounded incredulous. "Hell, Penny, I'd roll around out here in the dirt, if you wanted. Why would you be afraid of me?"

She tried another tack. "I'm sick. I don't feel good."

"Then you need to talk with the docs. Roger checked, and they say you haven't been by."

"Go away."

Manny paused, then spoke in a lower voice. "I like you, Miss Penny Dwight. I like you a lot."

She suddenly and without reason began to cry.

"Please don't," Manny said mournfully.

She couldn't stop.

"Okay. I'll go," said Manny, resignation heavy in his voice.

Penny heard the creak as he stepped off the stoop, and felt even worse. She'd promised to tell him. The colonel had said he would spread the story, so Manny would find out anyway. She felt the deadened numbness of resignation as she cracked the door.

"I've got something to tell you first," she said in a mono-tone.

Tuesday, December 26th, 1025 Local—Weapons Office

Captain Manny DeVera

In all his life Manny DeVera had never known such outrage as he'd felt when Penny had detailed the encounter with Colonel Lyons. Not even when he'd been charged with trumped-up false accusations.

Once she'd begun, Penny hadn't been able to stop from baring her shame and guilt. She'd poured it out without being prompted, all of it, from the sex to the threats and the promise Lyons had forced from her to tell DeVera, and he'd listened with pained ears. When her agony had been at its worst, Manny had tried to reach out for her, but Penny had drawn away with a look so frightened he'd wanted to cry.

He'd repeated what he'd said before—that he liked her—he liked her a lot. She'd immediately begun to bawl, but that time she didn't cringe when he'd put his arm about her shoulders, so he'd held her and soothed her until she'd finally stopped crying.

"He said he wanted you to know what he'd done," Penny had told him, and Manny'd felt awful, knowing it had been his fault that Lyons had picked her out. Lyons despised him and had taken it out on her. It had taken an hour of repeating what he felt for her, going much further than he'd intended, before Penny relaxed enough for him to feel good about leaving her alone.

She'd asked him what to do, and he'd told her to push it out of her mind and leave the rest to him. He'd told her that he'd make sure nothing like that would ever happen again.

She'd clutched him then, and he'd held her for a while longer.

Manny DeVera, confirmed bachelor, had made a commitment, and he meant to keep it. As he'd sat there, holding and comforting Penny, he forgot about any previous reservations, and she became pretty and pure—despoiled by a true villain.

When he'd finally left her trailer, he'd dropped by the

club to check on any rumors the IG inspectors might have
started, as Lyons had told Penny they would. There were
none the pilots he'd spoken with knew about. The IG team
had departed the following morning, and no one could remember any words spread by or about Lyons.

He'd dropped by and told that to Penny, so she would
stop worrying, and returned to his room at the Ponderosa for
the night. Before he'd gotten to sleep, which was difficult
enough, he'd thought of something else. The fact that he'd
seen Lyons emerge from the medical clinic with a frown,
and that he'd told Penny he'd left a present for the spick.

This morning he'd dropped by the clinic, and his flight-
surgeon friend had told him something normally held in
confidence, for Doc Rogers disliked Tom Lyons as thoroughly as the others at Takhli who knew him.

Lyons had . . . an infection.

Manny had played a what-if game with him then, like
what if, the night after he'd been checked by Rogers, Lyons
had gotten a girl drunk and taken advantage of her, and
hadn't told her about the infection?

"What girl?" the Doc had immediately asked, his face
stone rigid.

"Could she catch this . . . infection . . . from him?"

"Anyone he came into sexual contact with would get it.
He was in a most infectious period, and I told him that.
What's the girl's name?"

"You'll keep it confidential?"

"As best I can."

He'd told him it was Penny Dwight.

The doc had exploded in anger. Lyons had an advanced
case of gonorrhea, he'd said, the hardy strain the guys called
killer clap. He told Manny to send her over immediately.

Manny had dropped by Penny's trailer, and this time
she'd not hesitated to let him in. She was dressed and ready
to go to work.

It was one of the hardest things Manny had ever done,
but he'd told her what the Doc had said. Penny had taken
it in without tears. She'd just quietly thanked him, and he'd
left.

He doodled angrily on the desktop, thinking about it all
for the hundredth time, then rose and pulled on his Aussie-
style go-to-hell hat. It was time for the weekly staff meeting.

When he entered the wing commander's office, he was surprised to find Penny back at work. She glanced up, but studiously ignored him as well as the colonels and lieutenant colonels into the small conference room. She was, he noticed, slumping again, as she had when she'd first arrived at Takhli.

He bent over her desk and whispered, "Did you see Doc Rogers?" She nodded, still slumped and not looking at him.

As he went into the meeting, he glanced back and caught her peeking. She returned her attention to a piece of correspondence, her expression wistful. Tom Lyons's face loomed in Manny's inner vision as he went to the side of the conference room for non-colonels.

Buster Leska strode in and waved them into their seats. They began to discuss aircraft status, the numbers of sorties they anticipated during the next week, and how the partial lifting of restrictions was helping them use proper tactics.

Manny DeVera's mind was elsewhere—trying to think of a way to even things between himself and Colonel Tom Lyons. It had been rape, but Manny knew there'd be no way to make the charge stick. Lyons was too slick for that, and all it would likely do was make Penny look bad . . . as if she were an alcoholic pushover. The man didn't deserve to live.

Lucky Anderson was there, quiet, unsmiling, and looking haggard. After his return from NKP the previous day, he'd told Manny there was no new word about Linda Lopes. Manny sympathized. Lucky's problems stemmed from communist terrorists, his own from a colonel in his own service. He wondered which was despised most.

1215L—Ministry for External Affairs, Hanoi, DRV

Deputy Minister Li Binh

The day before, word had been passed from Li Binh's sources confirming that an American civilian had been captured and was being held by the Pathet Lao. Western newspapers claimed the American female was an official in the foreign-assistance apparatus of the American embassy in

Bangkok, but Li Binh's sources revealed that she was also an intelligence agent.

Li Binh had immediately seized on the possibility that it might be beneficial if her nephew was the one to draw truth from the woman. Nguyen Wu remained in disfavor for angering Le Duc Tho. He'd been relieved of duty and would soon be discharged completely from his post. If he was to regain any degree of stature with the Lao Dong's Central Committee, of which she was a member, he must prove himself in some spectacular way. It was awkward to have a family member so poorly regarded by the group. Li Binh hated nothing more than embarrassment.

She'd demanded that the woman be brought to Hanoi for interrogation, but the Pathet Lao were hedging. They wanted her for themselves. It wasn't surprising. Li Binh had realized from the first that the American woman was a prize and would not be easily given up.

She bounced a pencil on the desktop, thinking of alternatives, and then of her nephew. Her mind wandered to her hideous husband. The situation at the villa was tolerable, for they'd come to a comfortable impasse. Both knew there would never again be a true husband-and-wife relationship, yet there were quiet times during which they would talk—boast of achievements and speak of government figures without worrying about consequences. Such times were valuable.

There was another need in Li Binh, growing as it periodically did, which hadn't been satisfied the last time she'd allowed her nephew access to her body. But once Nguyen Wu had pleased her greatly, and she increasingly found herself thinking of those secret encounters.

It would be troublesome to take another lover. And if the man boasted, as males were often wont to do, it would be difficult. She was certain that wouldn't happen with her nephew. He was appropriately terrified by what she'd done the previous time he'd shown lack of discretion. Li Binh had also grown realistic in another line of reasoning. Regardless of his fondness for rugged males for sex, he'd been responsive to her needs—certainly more so than the halfhearted and fumbling Xuan Nha had been, even at his best.

After she decided the best way to give Nguyen Wu access to the Mee spy, he must be carefully instructed on what was needed, to make sure he knew of the consequence of failure. She made up her mind abruptly. She'd meet with Nguyen Wu—privately of course—and brief him. The most secretive place she could think of was still the villa. Only the servants were there in the daytime, and they understood that a loose tongue meant quick and merciless death.

And at the villa they could ... Li Binh hastily penned a note, sealed it, and called in a clerk. She gave him succinct delivery instructions, and when he left, she felt a giddiness and sudden lilting of spirit.

Even as she felt the rush of excitement, her organized mind asked about a solution to the problem of the female spy. If she could not have the woman brought to Hanoi for interrogation, she would convince the Pathet Lao leaders to allow interrogation on their soil. All that remained would be to agree upon a proper location. And, of course, Nguyen Wu must prepare to travel.

Li Binh wrote a note of instruction to a field agent in Laos, examined it, and added a few words before sending it out. She then hurried from her office with uncharacteristic urgency.

1900L

Colonel Xuan Nha

Xuan had only to point with his finger for the young maid to do his bidding. He indicated the opened door, and she rushed to close it.

"Here," he muttered as he sat heavily on the side of the bed, and the girl hurried to help him disrobe. She started with his low boots, pulling them from his feet with effort and placing them carefully nearby.

"What happened today?"

She answered immediately, for she'd learned the painful alternative. "They met, Colonel master. Nguyen Wu came to the villa and went to the mistress's room."

Xuan suppressed emotion. He'd done that when he'd heard about his wife's philandering during his long hospitalization. He'd used his wiles to put an end to the meetings

with her nephew, and until his discussion with Quon, he
had believed the secretive meetings had stopped.

He pushed himself up, and the girl deftly pulled off his
trousers.

"Did you listen to them?"

"As you told me, Colonel master. I could not hear all the
words, but there were some."

"Did they . . . fornicate?"

"Yes, Colonel master. Twice. The mistress was very loud.
You could hear her everywhere in the house." She nodded
seriously in the silence as she folded his trousers neatly and
placed them on the upright clothing stand with his shirt.

"Her words?" he finally rasped when the girl returned to
his side.

"She was crying out in her joy. It was not like the last
time. There were no—"

He grasped the girl's face with his powerful hand. "When
they were not fornicating," he demanded. "What did they
say?"

The girl sputtered in fear, then swallowed mightily as he
relaxed his hold just a little. Her face was distorted when
she spoke, her eyes wide and the words hardly audible.
"They talked about a Mee woman spy who is somewhere in
Laos, Colonel master." She was trembling with terror, as
Xuan preferred when he was questioning.

"What else was said?"

When the young girl was slow responding, he shook her,
squeezing her face so tightly that his fingernails drew blood
where they dug into flesh. She made small sounds, but did
not cry out, for Xuan had taught her to endure stoically. He
relaxed his grip.

Garbled words gushed forth. "That was all, Colonel master. When Nguyen Wu departed, he left quickly, but he was
smiling as if he was very happy."

"And then?"

"The mistress also left. She seemed pleased too, Colonel
master."

Quon had been right, Xuan thought. He'd indeed been
shamed. It was not over. As his rage grew, he felt in need of
some sort of release. Sexual, perhaps?

"Remove your clothing," he croaked, and the girl hastened, dropping them about her feet, all the while trembling

in his grasp. He observed her small body with half interest. The girl was unique in that he'd seldom, other than with Li Binh, of course, fucked a woman more than once. He was growing stronger, he decided, staring at the face held tautly in his clawed hand. There was great strength in that hand. Since the other had been amputated, he'd exercised it relentlessly.

Perhaps it was not only sex he wanted. The maid knew far too much. With simple questioning, Li Binh could discover what he'd learned. He pondered killing her, wondering idly if he simply squeezed hard enough, he could do that. Pop her skull, as he might a roach's.

Likely not, but then . . . He sat on the bed, looking with renewed interest at the naked girl's terrified expression as he began to squeeze. For the next ten minutes awful, shrill sounds echoed loudly inside the room, even though the girl's mouth was partially muffled by his palm.

He stared at her face as he continued the pressure—transforming what he saw—imagining Nguyen Wu there, and grasping harder yet, using every ounce of fervor and power—grunting aloud as tendons in his arm bulged with the effort.

When he finally relaxed his grip, he was puffing hard, chest heaving from the exertion.

The screams continued. He'd not been able to crush her small skull in the grasp, but she'd surely have a headache for a long while.

"Quiet!" he rasped.

Her sounds reduced to painful whimpers.

"Never speak of what you tell me," he ordered. "Not to anyone."

"Never, Colonel master!" she cried from bloodied lips beneath his fingers.

He grunted brusquely, then released his hold and examined the girl. Bloody flaps of flesh hung loosely at the sides of her face, and an ear was half-torn away. Her nose had been broken and mashed almost flat, and her right eye was weeping yellow viscous fluid where a finger had gouged it. She'd be sightless in the eye, he decided, like himself.

He became aware that he had an erection.

"Now!" he barked, and had to slap her and repeat himself to gain her proper attention before she scrambled onto him, lifted and fumbled to insert him, all the while moaning from the excruciating pain. Perhaps he'd not kill her right away, he decided as the girl began to rise and fall energetically. She was too unsightly to continue in the house, where others might see her, so he'd have her work in the garage area.

Perhaps the lieutenant might wish to use her. Xuan Nha prided himself on being good to his men.

CHAPTER
TWENTY-FIVE

Friday, December 29th, 0050 Local—Northeast of Nakhon Phanom Air Base

Sergeant Black

"It is quiet," said the lieutenant, staring out and across the river. The night was moonless and dark.

There were three of them. Black, the lieutenant, and the senior sergeant. Together they pushed the long, narrow boat into the water, and Black held on to it as the other two climbed in. When they were in position, the lieutenant clucked his tongue twice, and Black shoved them off, then watched as the dark shape was swallowed by the night.

Sergeant Black watched for thirty long minutes, until he saw the blink-blink-blink of a dimmed flashlight from the other side.

They'd made it across and secreted the boat with no hitches.

He watched for another moment before making his way back toward the roadway and the jeep he'd left there.

.   .   .

Black was relieved when Lieutenant Colonel Lucky Anderson returned to his base. He genuinely liked the pilot, but he'd only been in the way. Black had continued to check with intell about the high-priority Clipper affair, and as if it had been Anderson's presence holding things up, they'd gotten their first news of Clipper's fate two days after he'd left. That was the same day that all hell broke loose in southern Laos. The Pathet Lao, backed by NVA regulars, had selected the day after Christmas to attack there as they'd done in the north.

Although the assaults had been anticipated, the Special Forces headquarters camp at NKP had become frantic with activity. A-detachments were alerted and recon teams diverted or deployed. Every available human resource was either put to immediate use or placed on standby status. Except Hotdog, of course, for Black had made his devil's agreement with the lieutenant colonel that he'd not be placed in jeopardy.

When two different indigent sources reported that Clipper was alive across the river, seen in first one, then in another, Pathet Lao camp, the news was lost in the noise of the battles and guerrilla movements in Laos. Only Black had seemed interested that she'd been reported in two different camps, meaning she'd been moved at least once. It likely also meant she was expected to survive. The P-L traveled light. If she was badly wounded, they'd have killed her and tossed her body into the Mekong. The report on the AA-priority Clipper matter was also important to the lieutenant colonel commanding the headquarters C-Team, but with everything else happening, it was no time to request a cross-river expedition. There were simply too many P-L and NVA units running wild in the southern Laotian panhandle. Clipper would have to wait. Intell was told to continue monitoring and to pinpoint her location.

Black had gone to the old man and argued that it was the perfect time for Hotdog to try to rescue her. With all the NVA over there, they'd blend in. It was the sort of thing they were best at.

He'd been reminded, one, of his agreement not to place himself in a hazardous situation, and two, that the lieutenant colonel code-named Papa Wolf and his staff had more important things to worry about just now.

After three days Black had run out of patience. If they waited longer, Clipper might be moved. Once transported to northern Laos or Hanoi, she'd be irretrievable. Since he'd made his agreement not to go on recons, he sent the lieutenant and the senior sergeant. Their mission was to find the woman and, if it was a simple matter, to bring her back.

They were to return within seven days. Period.

He reached the road, made a single birdcall, and heard it echoed. A dim flashlight was switched on, illuminating the side of the jeep. Black emerged from the bush and walked to the vehicle. The other two Hotdogs quietly crawled inside with him.

"They gave the signal," he said in Viet. The others were quiet as he started the engine and drove toward the base.

Black wondered if he should notify Colonel Anderson, to tell him Clipper was alive. He decided against it. It would be better when he had more definite news. Perhaps, if the lieutenant was successful, Clipper could call him herself.

0655L—Route Pack Six, North Vietnam

Captain Manny DeVera

The foul mood that festered in Manny because of what had happened to Penny didn't evaporate when he flew combat, and he had difficulty concentrating on the mission. Her transformation in his mind was completed—by being the target of Lyons's contempt for him, every flaw had disappeared. Where she'd been acceptably attractive, she became beautiful. He'd forgotten that her conversations were sometimes silly, that her depth was sometimes questionable. She was the maiden ravaged by the beast, and the beast had done it to attack Manny. DeVera hated Lyons so intensely that his stomach boiled with it.

Today they flew to the auxiliary MiG bases. Most of their recent missions had been to the lower packs, trying to find and destroy convoys on their way south, so they weren't as keen as they should have been. That fact was made apparent by all the radio chatter, as leads barked for their flights to get into and stay in proper position, called out SAMs and AAA that weren't a threat, and twice misidentified their Phantom MiG-CAP flight as MiG-21's.

It was Manny's third time as mission commander, but his first to lead a strike formation to pack six. That should have made him more alert, perhaps more conservative, but he had trouble erasing the image of Colonel Tom Lyons from his mind.

He was leading the sixteen-ship effort to bomb Kep airfield, northeast of Hanoi, out in the wide, featureless expanse the pilots called "the flats." The pilots disliked flying there. If you were shot down, there was no chance of being rescued. And when you bombed, you had to recover into the ECM pod formation quickly, for without terrain features there was nowhere to hide.

As mission commander Manny was first to soar up to the perch, then to roll in and dive-bomb the target.

The flak looked to be only moderate, which came as a pleasant surprise.

He was halfway through the dive maneuver, about to release his six bombs, when someone called MiGs *"west of the target."*

Manny kept his eyes glued on the runway, got the proper sight picture, and pickled off the bombs. He recovered smoothly, pulling four g's, and began to jink out to the north as they'd briefed the rejoin, before he began looking around for the MiGs.

Nothing but blue sky and a few puff clouds. No flak. He S-turned so the force could catch up easier.

An excited radio call erupted. *"Bear Force Leader, you got a MiG at your eight—"*

Bright flashes zipped past his canopy.

Manny yelled something unintelligible as he kicked the rudder pedal and wrenched the stick to turn into the MiG. He swiveled his head right and saw . . . nothing. He whipped it the other way and saw the nose of a MiG-17 emitting brilliant staccato flashes.

He'd screwed up by believing the radio call, had turned away rather than into him. The hail of big, 30mm rounds were reaching out from Manny's left five o'clock. He felt the big bird shudder.

He'd already pushed the nose over and selected afterburner, and was jinking wildly, trying to screw up the MiG driver's aim point—not giving him an easy tracking solution. Manny was yelling at himself, wondering what the hell was wrong with the afterburner, when the thing finally lit and his bird was hurled forward.

There was nothing in the sky that could keep up with a Thud in a dive with burner lit, and a couple of seconds later there were no more bright streaks passing his canopy. But those were very long seconds, and he'd taken another hit. Manny continued to fly fast, but nudged the aircraft into a gentle westward arc. When he was certain there was no longer a threat, he pulled the throttle out of the A/B detent and continued the turn as he decelerated. His wingman, who'd tried to come to his aid, joined up.

There was no firelight—no telelites showing inoperative systems. Number two looked him over for battle damage and found a few large holes in his vertical stabilizer. Nothing major. Manny assumed his bird was okay.

They rejoined the force, *his* force, west of Thud Ridge. There were two SAM launches but no close calls on the way outbound.

All the way out, even when they were joining on the tanker, he thought of nothing but what the force should do next, and how they would do it. *Keep calm—stay on the offensive—think of the next move.* Just as Lucky Anderson had taught him to do.

Only when they'd passed over the Laotian border, headed west toward the orbiting tankers, did he allow himself to return to other thoughts, and the first ones were not charitable toward himself.

Fool! he berated himself for allowing the MiG to sneak up as it had. He thought of other things he'd done wrong. He'd let himself become preoccupied with things not involving the mission and had not paid proper attention. Manny DeVera swore that he'd never again allow himself to think of anything other than the mission at hand when he was flying combat.

He also pledged to handle the matter with Tom Lyons as expeditiously as possible, so he'd no longer be plagued by thoughts of what the no-good bastard had done . . . through Penny Dwight . . . to him.

Sunday, December 31st, 2320 Local—Desert Inn, Las Vegas, Nevada

Major Benny Lewis

They were alone, having a nice evening to themselves. The first time they'd done that.

Ever since he'd told Julie he was leaving on New Year's Day for the trip to Southeast Asia, she'd called daily. Just to ask how he was and talk, she said. The evening had been her idea. She'd made dinner reservations at the small French restaurant a block off Main, told him how she'd dress—hinting that she'd love to see him in coat and tie—asked his preferences, and preselected the menu.

The meal had been superb. She'd done the impossible; after they finished with the liqueurs, she led the way to the Desert Inn, to the top-floor lounge, where a table was reserved and waiting.

The President would have had difficulty getting a reservation there. When he asked how she'd done it, she just lifted an eyebrow and smiled. He'd tried to order drinks, but the waitress ignored him and brought them a single glass of white wine.

"Forty minutes until Mr. 1968 comes marching in," Julie announced.

She wore a strapless black party dress made of material that shimmered with every move, accentuating her spectacular figure. Her long dark hair fell in natural waves. And, Benny was thinking, she had the brownest eyes and the warmest, most winsome smile he could remember seeing. *Hopeless,* he told himself, thinking of the way he'd been attracted since the first time he'd laid eyes on her. It was not something definable, but even then, when he'd not known he was in love, he'd felt a warmth and easiness around her that he'd felt with no one else.

Julie made a face in the subdued light. "You're staring at my nose."

"What?" he said, jolted from his thoughts.

"You're thinking my nose is too big, aren't you?"

He laughed. "Not what I was thinking at all."

She rolled her eyes and threw up her hands. "Here I

work my buns off to get this hunk of a guy out alone, ply him with booze, and he looks at my worst feature."

"Honest, I was—"

Julie leaned forward, giving him a mock glare. "Do I stare at your dimples, even though they're cute and I know you're bashful about having 'em? Do I?"

He grinned. She was acting like her old self, the lovable side of her he'd scarcely noticed since her mother had arrived.

"Okay, wise guy, you finished with your wine?"

"You ready for another?"

"Nope, but I'm ready to leave."

"We just got here."

"One drink's enough."

"They'll have the big celebration at midnight and we'll miss it."

"That's why I want to get out of here." She stood and waved at the busy waitress, who gave her a smile and nod in response.

"I'd better pay," he said.

"All taken care of. We girls stick together." She began to slither through the crowd.

She slowed, then stopped and turned to him, held out her arms.

"Just one dance," she said.

The band was playing "Stardust."

"Nice," Julie said in her whiskey voice as she nestled against him. They moved together without working at it. They continued until the band finished.

Julie gave him the mysterious smile and pulled his hand. "C'mon, hunk." He followed. She pulled him straight ahead, toward a group of revelers waiting for an elevator.

"You want to go home?" Benny asked incredulously.

"Something I want you to see," she murmured, and he saw the same imps in her eyes he'd noticed during dinner. They crowded into the elevator car, where Benny wedged himself between Julie and the wildest drunk.

At the second stop, the fifth floor, Julie tugged and he followed her out.

"This way," she said cheerfully, pulling him along down the corridor. She looked at numbers on doors, stopped, fished a key from her purse, and grinned. Her eyes were sparkling, her voice husky. "You do the honors."

He gave her a quizzical look. Julie opened her mouth to speak, then swallowed and hesitated. "Hope it's okay with you," she said. She suddenly didn't seem quite as sure of herself.

The room had two large beds. A bottle of champagne was nestled in an ice stand near the balcony. Benny was astounded—almost said something stupid, like, "Well, I'll be damned," but didn't.

When he shut the door, she came close. "With you leaving tomorrow and all, I thought we should celebrate privately."

"Yeah," he finally managed, wondering if he sounded as dumbstruck as he felt.

Julie kicked off her shoes and padded to the ice bucket, then turned and frowned. "I want this night to be perfect. Smile, damn you, Benny Lewis."

He gave her a chuckle, but he was nervous and was sure it sounded contrived. "You've gotta put up with me being a little overwhelmed, Julie."

"Surprised you?"

He nodded.

"Surprised myself too. After I decided what I wanted to do, I didn't know if I'd have the courage to carry through with it. When I told Mom—"

"You told your mother about this?"

"My God, no. She'd have apoplectic fits if she knew I'd gotten us a room for the night and plotted to get you here. But I did tell her we were going to be very late and not to worry, and she gave me a lecture like I was a teenager about to jump on a motorcycle with a Hell's Angel."

"She's . . . unique."

"You've been patient."

There's been no alternative, he thought. Benny chided himself for being mean.

"Champagne?"

When he'd opened and poured, they went onto the small balcony. They were on the back side and looked out over the city and the dark mountains beyond. He placed his arm about her shoulders and felt protective. Julie snuggled and sighed contentedly.

It was going to be as perfect as it could possibly be, he thought.

At midnight there came a swell of noise. They kissed, and he felt more sure.

"I love you, Julie."

"God, I hope so. I'm crazy about you."

When they went inside a few minutes later, he took pains to appear calm. He'd looked forward to making love to Julie for so long, with such fervor, that it was difficult. He went about switching off lights until there was only one, shining dimly in the corner farthest from the bed. It was all perfect.

They disrobed, standing close, in such silence that the sound of their breathing seemed loud. Julie was first to shed the last of her clothing, and his breath became harsher. Her breasts were even larger than he'd imagined, curving in perfect half-moons, so full and firm that the perky nipples looked upward. Her tiny waist flared into hips she complained were matronly, but which suited her voluptuousness. She'd shaved her pubic hair into a small, neat patch of darkness, and emanated a pleasant, mixed odor of light perfume and musk. He observed her silently, wanting to tell her how beautiful he found her, but held his tongue for fear he'd spoil the moment.

She gave a nervous little laugh, came close, and lifted a hand to his chest. "You really do have a wonderful body," she said in the low whiskey voice. "Is your back—"

"Don't worry about my back," he said. "I feel great."

She held her arms lightly about him. They kissed, explored a bit with gentle hands, then crawled into bed and nestled. He became aware that she was trembling. *Stay calm*, he told himself.

"I adore you, Benny Lewis," Julie whispered. She wrapped her arms around him and held him as closely as she possibly could. They kissed more ardently. He stroked her wonderful body until she cried out, and he could restrain himself no longer.

The lovemaking had been heated and frantic, for he'd shown absolutely none of the calmness he'd intended. He tried to tell himself that was because it had been so long, because he'd looked forward to their lovemaking so avidly. He'd never before been that way with another woman and felt ashamed that he'd been inconsiderate.

They were both quiet now, lying side by side. As the minutes passed, Benny felt increasingly awkward. Julie passed a gentle hand over his chest.

He turned to her, admonishing himself to be gentler and more in control as he caressed and slid his hands about her secret places. Small sounds issued from her throat. *That's better*, he said to himself. She began to tremble and breathe faster. He'd rolled over her and was about to enter, this time determined to satisfy her before thinking of himself.

Julie groaned, arched, and called a name. Mal-Bear. Her dead husband.

Benny stopped cold and felt an icy shiver course through him. He pulled away as she realized her mistake and tried to apologize. He said that was okay, don't worry about it, but the words had been uttered and the moment lost.

He couldn't shake the vision of the man who had been his best friend. He wanted to stroke her face, but something held his hand.

They tried it once more. Mal Stewart's specter looked on from a corner of the room, his presence strong.

"Is your back hurting you?" she asked when he finally pulled away.

Benny muttered an excuse about having so much on his mind. The trip, he said. His back was fine. They continued to pet and stroke.

She told him to just rest, then nuzzled her head on his arm.

He hadn't really lied. He *had* been working relentlessly, trying to tie up the loose ends of LINE BACKER JACK-POT before his departure, putting in twelve- and fifteen-hour days ... worrying about the success of Pave Dagger ... concerned about Julie and the baby, but frustrated by her mother's nagging presence.

Weariness washed over him like an ocean wave. The ghost in the corner stirred. Benny came fully awake, hesi-tantly looked there, and saw only the outline of a chair and the curtains shimmering at the opened doorway to the bal-cony. He listened to Julie's even breathing, decided she was asleep, then adjusted himself and her head on his arm.

He tried to sleep, but was plagued by the agonizing

memory that haunted him . . . of a helicopter rescuing him, but not his best friend. Mal Bear Stewart had died saving his life. Julie's husband. Grief and guilt consumed him. It was a while before he could sleep.

He drifted very slowly toward the surface. An involuntary low moan came not from his throat but from his soul.

"Go back to sleep," a husky voice whispered. His arm was moist where she'd been crying.

0900L

When Benny awoke, the telephone was ringing insistently. He was alone, and his back was pinging with small spasms from the previous night's exertion.

Julie's cheerful voice on the phone told him it was time to get up and called him a sleepyhead.

He asked where she was.

"Home." She said she couldn't talk right then. He supposed her mother was nearby.

Benny looked at the clock and scrambled upright. "Gotta go!" he mumbled.

"Take care of yourself," Julie said.

"Bye!" He didn't hear her say she loved him. In fact, as he showered quickly and threw on his clothes as adroitly as his back would allow, he was still troubled and unsure. He wondered if she'd still be in Las Vegas when he returned from the trip.

2000L—O' Club Stag Bar, Takhli RTAFB, Thailand

Lieutenant Colonel Lucky Anderson

Lucky sat at the end of the bar, nursing a drink he didn't want. Two of his squadron pilots tried to talk to him, but he was in a private and unsocial mood, so they drifted away. He fixed his attention on Manny DeVera, who sat at a table at the far end of the room talking to Captain Rogers, one of the flight surgeons. The doc seemed argumentative about something Manny was saying.

Captain Hamlin, one of the better pilots in Lucky's 333rd squadron, came in with Buster Leska's secretary. Doc Rogers and Manny DeVera got to their feet to greet them. After a few words the doc left for the bar.

Lucky observed idly, not truly interested. Other than Linda, very little interested him now. The Supersonic Wetback began a story, waving his arms and speaking loudly, and Lucky noted that the girl's eyes were pinned to his face. She watched Manny as if he were some kind of sage telling great truths.

Animal Hamlin's laughter was loud when Manny came to the end of his tale. The three stood, and DeVera put his arm protectively around the girl. The two slipped out the side door, and Hamlin watched for a moment, then made his way over to a group of squadron-mates.

Lucky pulled his attention back to his glass and the melting ice cubes. There'd been absolutely no word about Linda. Not from Black, or Richard at the embassy, or from anyone in the cop shop at NKP. Not from anyone. Soon after his return he'd gone through the pictures he had of her, stared at each one, and remembered each good time. He wondered if he'd treated her well enough—if he'd told her how dear she was to him often enough. He knew he wasn't good at expressing such things.

He'd put the photos away very carefully, and hope had coursed through him. Seeing the image of her animated face had done that. No one that vibrant could be dead.

Lucky had taken the photos out and gone through the same drill the next night, then the next. They renewed his faith and refreshed his mind's picture of her.

He pushed the glass away and stood. Time to go to the trailer. He had to fly in the morning, an easy counter to pack two to look for trucks in the mountain passes and barges on the Ca River. They'd been getting easier ones lately. But regardless of where they were going, the four o'clock get-up call would come early, and he wanted to be fresh and ready. Lucky wended his way through the crowd of noisy fighter jocks to the side door. Not many spoke to him, for they knew his new moods. He ignored pleasantries as often as he answered them.

Tonight he'd take a look at photos Linda had given him of herself as a child. He especially liked the one of a thirteen-year-old gawky kid with a shy expression. He'd joked with her about being all knees and elbows. She'd told him that was the year she'd discovered there was some kind of wonderful difference between boys and girls, and she'd so badly wanted to be beautiful. She'd been taller than the boys in her class, and that was why she was hunched over in the photo. She said she'd spent the year walking around like that, trying to think of a way to shrink.

He wondered where she was.

Lucky passed the Supersonic Wetback and his girlfriend. Manny was pointing at the sky, explaining the different stars. They'd been taught the prominent ones in pilot training so they could use them for reference when they flew at night. He remembered pointing them out to Linda, and his surprise when he found she knew more about them than he did.

He arrived at his trailer and went inside.

Captain Manny DeVera

Manny went back into the stag bar and looked about. Doc Rogers was pushing away from the bar, preparing to leave.

"Walk out with you?" Manny asked.

Rogers gave him a frown as they fell into step. "The answer's still no, Manny."

"I'm not asking for much, Doc."

"You're asking me to do something illegal."

"Don't you guys sometimes send medical-exam sheets out . . . like if you catch something after a patient's left the area, so they'll know what they've got? I phoned a lady friend at PACAF, and she gave me his address. All you've got to do is mail it."

"No way, Manny. We forward to the medical facility nearest the patient, never to a home."

They exited through the front door, and the doc headed for his trailer. Manny called after him, "You want him to get away with what he did?"

Doc Rogers stopped, turned, and looked at him for a long while.

"We've gotta stop him, Doc. Teach him he can't get away with it."

Rogers sighed. "I'll make a copy of the consultation form, and you can stop by and pick it up tomorrow. But Manny, if anyone asks, I'll tell 'em I don't know a damn thing about it."

"Thanks, Doc." Manny returned to the bar to have one more drink and think about the next step in his program of retribution.

CHAPTER
TWENTY-SIX

Thursday, January 4th, 1968, 1100 Local—Ban Si Muang, Laos

GS-15 Linda Lopes

The heat was stifling in the thatch hut, but she could endure it. She could withstand anything they tried to do to her!

Be tough! she told herself for the hundredth time.

The band of men who'd ambushed the jeep and taken her across the river had vanished after handing her over to another group of armed ragtags. Then she'd been dragged from one camp to the next for two weeks, furtively and always at night. Pathet Lao, she was sure. They'd mistreated her some, kicking her when she'd stumbled and yelling at her in angry words she hadn't understood, but they'd fed and watered her enough to get by and took her to urinate and defecate when she had to go. The worst part of those first days had been the fear of the unknown as she'd wondered about her fate. Then something new had happened; she'd been marched down the rutted dirt roads in broad daylight. Past gawking farmers and townspeople, her captors yelling to them, pointing at her and joking.

At first it had been puzzling why they'd become so brazen. Then it became obvious that they were in control in the area. Most of the people they passed were expressionless. Some seemed sad when she was marched past. A few joked with her captors and made obscene gestures.

Her latest jail was a bamboo cage built into one side of a single-roomed thatch hut. Not so small that she couldn't stand and take two steps in any direction, but restrictive enough to activate claustrophobic tendencies. They kept a guard with her day and night, who sometimes watched the cage but more often stared off in daydreaming sessions.

Her treatment, she'd decided in those first days, would be dictated by whether they suspected what her job entailed. If they did not, she'd likely continue to be treated well enough, perhaps be kept for a while and then released in some sort of trade, or in a grand humanitarian gesture. Perhaps turned over to an American peace group. Linda could think of no advantage for them to keep her, as long as they didn't suspect she also worked for State Department intelligence, setting up the networks around the bases. It was unlikely they'd know, she reasoned. Most Americans didn't know about the organization.

So far there was no indication that they knew. No one had questioned her. None of the Pathet Lao spoke English. The ones she'd met, even those she believed were the leaders at this latest camp, were a backward group—not nearly as sophisticated as she'd imagined them to be.

More than anything, she wished they'd give her a change of clothing. Nothing fancy, just something that didn't smell so ripe. Her sandals had been taken the first night, and she'd been left barefoot. For three and a half weeks she'd lived in the filthy sailcloth trousers and blood-stiffened linen blouse she'd worn on the jeep trip.

Her reverie was broken when a man came into the room, then came closer and stared. This one was somehow different from the others. He spoke tersely to the guard, who quickly responded and became nervous. An officer? He appeared too young to have much rank, but the guard was now beside the cage trying to appear alert. The officer went to the door and beckoned, and when a new person came in and approached the cage, Linda's heart plummeted.

It was the man from the village who'd refused to meet

her eyes when she'd asked her questions. The man Peter Johnston had wanted to recruit.

Oh damn! She tried to recall how much they'd told him. The young officer and the man from the village spoke at length, and again it was apparent who was in charge. The officer carried the conversation. The CT answered when spoken to.

"I sink you an' me mus' tawk, Muss Lo-pees." The words startled her. His English was not terrible. "I am Lootna Boun Pouva, an' I spen' two ye-ah in Eng-lun. I awso spen' two ye-ah in Mosk-va. I be da one you tell you see-creets."

He nodded, and the guard began to unlash the cage door.

Phase one begins, she thought grimly, working to remain calm. She wouldn't allow herself to give in. *Express surprise and play innocent. Say nothing at all.* Not yet, anyway.

When the door was opened, she was beckoned forth.

The guard tied her spread-eagled to the side of the cage, facing out. It began with a quiet beating, using a bamboo stick. She'd never known the stuff could be that hard—or that a methodical thrashing of her stomach, ribs, and arms could be that painful. The officer gave instructions and the guard administered the blows. He didn't even use all his strength, but after the fifth time the bamboo stick landed, she groaned aloud from the pain, and after the twentieth she began to cry out sharply each time it struck her flesh. The blows continued until she was shrieking and begging for them to stop.

When the blows ceased and her sounds had abated to moans, the officer asked her name.

She told him.

Whom had she spoken to in the villages around Nakhon Phanom?

She'd passed out food and implements to the headmen at several villages.

He said he was growing impatient.

The next whipping took twenty minutes, and her stomach and chest felt as if they were raw and turning to mush. Each time the bamboo struck, she howled at the awful pain.

Another questioning.

Don't say anything. Say nothing. Don't say anything. Don't answer.

She tried remaining utterly quiet that time, and the next, and the next . . .

"We mus' tawk more," the officer finally said in a pleasant tone. He barked instructions in Lao and left. Linda was untied and shoved back into the cage. She hurt everywhere.

She huddled in a corner, the pain so intense that she ignored the swarms of flies that buzzed about her and walked on her face and in her hair.

How long can I last? she wondered. They were onto her role in intelligence, but how much did they really know? She couldn't tell them. She mustn't. But again she asked herself how long she could endure, because it was only the beginning and was sure to get worse.

A while later the officer returned, this time with visitors. She recognized the cotton field uniforms of the North Vietnamese Army. One wore junior officer's markings. The other was older and tough looking. The Pathet Lao officer gestured at her. He kicked dramatically at the side of the cage, and she cried out and cringed. He laughed, and the Vietnamese joined in.

They were leaving when the NVA officer held up a hand and walked back in, very close to the cage. His expression wasn't cruel. She would remember that he had soft eyes.

Hardly moving his lips, he whispered four low words, stared for a split second longer, then turned and spoke to the Pathet Lao officer in a belligerent voice.

The door closed and Linda was left alone with the guard.

She sat upright on the floor, the pain in her abdomen and ribs intense.

Nod ver' long now, the NVA lieutenant had whispered, and she wondered what he could possibly have meant.

1400L—HQ Seventh Air Force, Tan Son Nhut Air Base, Saigon

Major Benny Lewis

Flo, the general's spinster secretary, had filled Benny in on the local headquarters gossip by the time Moss called out that he'd see him. It was Benny's courtesy call. Before he visited the various units, it was proper protocol to stop in at the headquarters. Normally he'd see a colonel in operations, but in this case General Moss had demanded that he stop by. Benny had worked for him at Nellis before they'd been sent to the war zone.

Moss was at his desk. Lieutenant Colonel Pearly Gates stood before a large wall map of North Vietnam.

Moss smiled. "Good to see you, Benny." They shook hands warmly.

"You're looking well, sir." The general was sun-bronzed and the picture of health. He played a relentless game of tennis, Benny remembered, and most often won.

"I am, I am. How about you? How's the back?" The last time Benny had visited, he'd had a bad time of it. The plane ride over had been awful, and he'd wrenched something coming up the stairs to the general's office. Moss had brought in a flight surgeon to medicate him, and when he'd left, it had been via a med-evac bird. Thus far, this time was very different.

"I feel fine. Flew over first-class. Pampered and slept like a baby all the way, sir."

Moss pointed a finger. "You watch that back. Tennis, that's the therapy. I still play three games a day, minimum, and I've got the stamina of a twenty-year-old. Bring it up with your flight surgeon. Soon as he clears you, get yourself down to the courts and start practicing." Moss grinned. "Then come back over here and I'll whip your young ass just like I have every time we've played."

Benny laughed.

Moss said, "We were discussing how the Jackpot operation's going to look by the fourth day, when it's in full swing. We're all cleared here. Go ahead, Pearly."

Gates pointed to targets on the wall chart and told about forces and timing. The strikes would be massive and continuous, day and night, with little respite between waves of striking combat aircraft.

"What about defenses?" Benny asked.

"By day four they'll start running out of missiles and large artillery ammo. By the sixth day they'll be depleted of SAMs. That's using our latest estimates of their stockpiles."

Benny settled into the chair Moss had indicated. "I've got a ringer to toss in the game."

Pearly turned and frowned. "Something I didn't consider?"

"You're using big formations of fighters. How about our smart bombs?"

Pearly's jaw tightened. He'd already been stung once, when he'd banked on using smart bombs on a campaign to eliminate the enemy's bridges, and they'd not been ready. "Are they operational?"

"They will be as soon as we complete the combat testing."

General Moss's eyebrows grew knitted. "Smart bombs," he muttered uncertainly.

Pearly clarified. "That's the Pave Dagger project at Danang."

"I remember *something* about it."

"Moods Diller's in place with a group of technicians and civilian engineers," Benny said.

Moss sighed. "Oh, yes. Homing bombs." He shook his head in a mild show of disgust.

Benny spoke up. "They were getting a CEP of thirty feet on the Nellis ranges." "CEP" stood for "circular error probability," or average miss distance. "Moods is using two-thousand-pounders now, and he's shooting for a zero CEP."

"The Nellis ranges aren't combat," Moss cautioned. "Not the same at all."

"I've watched them impact and seen the films, General. They worked, and now they've improved them even more. But you're right, sir, it's different here. That's why they're in the combat theater with the test, where they've got real targets in a hostile environment."

Pearly remained dubious. "Will they be ready in time?"

"When do you figure LINE BACKER JACKPOT will kick off?"

"Four weeks after we get the nod from the President. It'll take that long to get the forces and weapons in place."

"Is he close? I get the idea we simply don't have a firm handle on a date."

"I spoke with the President a couple weeks ago," said Moss. "I believe it will be another month, maybe two, before he's ready to give us a green light."

Benny Lewis nodded. "The tests will be completed. I'll

see to it." He didn't want to tell them quite yet about Moods's problems.

"How about availability?" Pearly asked. "I'd imagine the kits are pretty complex."

"We'll have to make it a quick-reaction order. Another problem will be training the pilots."

"And you think they'll work?"

"If only *half* of the bombs guide properly, that means we still can take out as many targets with twenty-four modified birds as we can with two hundred strike aircraft."

Moss was skeptical, and he said so.

"When they brief the test results, you'll be impressed, sir. I was the biggest doubter of all until I saw the steady improvements for myself. Moods is really onto something."

"Is that why you're here early? You weren't scheduled to show up for another few weeks."

It was time to tell him. "I received some strange messages from Moods, indicating he was having problems getting the test started. Then I got a letter. From what he said, the wing commander's a roadblock. He refuses to cooperate and won't even let Moods send classified documents off base. I came early so I could look into it."

"I've got one of my best commanders at the 366th," Moss said. "He wouldn't hold up your tests unless he's got good reason."

"I don't know about the rest of his problems, but if he can't send out secret information, Moods is in a bind, sir. The entire Pave Dagger project's highly classified."

"I trust my commander. You want me to give him a call?"

"I'd appreciate it if you'd let me find out what's going on first, sir. Perhaps Moods is doing something wrong. Maybe it's just a case of rubbing the CO the wrong way."

"Yeah. Go check it out." From his tone Benny knew it was going to be a hard sell. When Moss trusted one of his men, he did so implicitly. Fortunately, Benny was also one of that group.

"When I'm done at Danang, I'd like to visit the other fighter bases, to talk tactics with the JACKPOT project officers. Is that okay with you, sir?"

Moss nodded, but Lewis could tell by his hesitation that there was something on his mind.

"Anything you'd like me to be looking for?"

"There's a colonel from the PACAF IG going around to the bases. We think General Roman's gotten wind of the OPlan, and this guy's snooping around, trying to find out more. If you run into him, back off. He's carrying weight from Roman and likes to throw it around."

"What's his name?"

"Tom Lyons. A bonafide asshole with political influence."

Benny's face clouded. "I've met him." When Benny had traveled to Takhli on his last trip, Lyons had accused him of trying to have his backseater declared dead so he could take Julie to bed. It was the closest Benny had come to murdering someone.

"When are you leaving for Danang?"

"I'll take the base shuttle first thing in the morning. One other thing, sir. Who's your LINE BACKER JACKPOT project officer at Danang?"

"The wing commander."

1945L—Tan Son Nhut Officers' Club

Second Lieutenant Lucy Dortmeier

Colonel Gates finished his meal and sat back. "Care for an after-dinner drink?"

Lucy begged off. "Not tonight, Colonel. I'm bushed, and I want to get out of these shoes and relax. Rain check?"

"Sure," he said, but Lucy could tell he was let down. He enjoyed having someone to talk with and confide in as much as she. Following the long days of work, they went to the club for dinner often, except on the rare nights she dated a captain from the intelligence shop.

"Why don't you come over to my room?" she asked on a whim. "I keep a bottle of Grand Marnier handy." He'd introduced her to the delightful after-dinner drink.

He brightened. "Sure you don't mind?"

"I'd enjoy the company."

They left the club and walked toward the company-grade bachelor officer's quarters, where she had a room on the second floor.

"What did you think of Major Lewis?" he asked.

"We talked about my brother. He knew him at Takhli."

"Benny was shot down too. Twice, in fact."

"He didn't tell me about that."

"Broke his back in the second ejection."

They entered the BOQ, and she led the way upstairs and down the hall to her room. He followed her in, leaving the door open. Colonel Gates was always correct, the epitome of a gentleman.

She poured them both half a glass of liqueur, handed his over, then sat and pulled off the ugly oxford work shoes they issued women in the Air Force.

"That feels wonderful," she said, wriggling her toes.

He sat on the bed and looked around. The room looked sterile, for Lucy refused to decorate.

"Welcome to the Dortmeier hovel, Colonel."

"We're off duty. Call me Pearly, like everyone else."

She gave him an arch expression. "Only if you call me Lucy."

"Little Lucy?"

"General Moss must've told you. I was the runt of the litter and hated the nickname."

"Still?"

"Just Lucy if you don't mind." She wondered. She'd not minded at all when the Colonel . . . no, Pearly . . . had said it. She decided that he had a nice smile, and that he should use it more often. He was a serious man. Some of the enlisted men called him Colonel Grumpy.

They spoke for more than an hour, drank two more liqueurs, and Lucy forgot about being tired. When he finally left, she wished he'd stayed longer.

She decided to tell the intell captain to take a hike. Perhaps she could get Colonel . . . Pearly, darn it . . . to take her to a base movie now and then.

2100L—Nakhon Phanom RTAB, Thailand

Sergeant Black

The lieutenant and the senior sergeant had returned. He'd picked them up at the landing spot an hour earlier. Clipper wasn't with them, but the lieutenant wanted to return immediately with the rest of the Hotdogs to pull her out. He wanted to so badly that Black worried that he might take action on his own. He'd seldom seen the lieutenant so upset.

They were mistreating her, he'd said, and grew stony-faced when he spoke about the beating they'd administered before his arrival.

After debriefing him Black went directly to the lieutenant colonel, who, with communist attacks flaring across southern Laos, was working long hours. Papa Wolf had dark circles under his eyes and wore a tired expression when Black came into his office.

"I need a few minutes, Colonel."

"Shut the door," he said wearily.

Black did so. "We've located Clipper, sir."

The lieutenant colonel frowned, then brightened. "The USAID woman?"

"Yes, sir."

"Where?" He didn't ask how Black had gained his information.

"She's in a P-T headquarters camp outside of Ban Si Muang." P-T meant Pathet Lao guerrillas.

"Show me."

Black fingered the town of Ban Si Muang on a wall map. "Not far at all, sir. It should be a snap to go in and take her out."

The lieutenant colonel grunted. "How many men there?"

"Ninety-two total, mostly couriers and headquarters people. Only twenty, maybe twenty-five, would be any kind of help in a fight."

Papa Wolf pursed his lips. "Where are they holding her?"

"In a hut toward the rear of the camp. One guard inside, no one on patrol outside."

"What's her condition?"

"No obvious bad injuries. Her face is a little cut up, likely from the vehicle overturning. She's also hurting from the beatings."

"Shit," muttered the lieutenant colonel.

"They're using bamboo clubs. They've just started to interrogate, and so far she isn't cooperating."

"Good." The lieutenant colonel wrote down notes. "How reliable is your information?"

"Type 2-C," meaning it was highly reliable, made by a U.S.-trained foreign national.

"Time of observation?"

"Eight hours ago."

That note was added. "I'll pass it on." He looked back at his paperwork.

"Can we get authorization for a raid, sir?"

"I'll send the sighting info out in the morning status report. Problem might be, with all the other crap that's going on, getting the resources to put something together."

"They may not keep her there long, sir. I think we should move quickly."

"I realize that, but *nothing* moves quickly with MAC-V, and that's who it'll take to authorize a cross-border operation."

Black blew out a breath. "I'd like to take Hotdog over tomorrow night, sir."

"You say there's ninety guerrillas there? They'd have your renegades for lunch, Black. Then we'd be trying to get both you *and* the woman out."

"With all the NVA around the countryside, we could walk right into the camp, just like . . ." He'd started to say *just like my men did.* The lieutenant had told him he'd almost tried to get the woman out, even when it had been only himself and the sergeant. With all five of them using NVA bully tactics with the Pathet Lao, he felt there was a very good chance. If that didn't work, they could create a diversion and use force. He was scornful of Pathet Lao capabilities and doubted they'd put up much of a fight.

The lieutenant colonel didn't allow him to present the lieutenant's logic. "We'll wait for proper authorization and use an appropriate force. And remember our deal, Black. You don't go on recon patrols that might place you in jeopardy."

"Yes, sir." *Dammit!*

"Thanks for the intelligence. Now get on out of here while I finish the status report."

Black exited the office, feeling shitty and hoping to hell MAC-V responded more quickly than they normally did.

A letter had arrived from Lucky Anderson that morning, asking about Linda Lopes and giving him the name of an embassy official to contact about sponsoring the Hotdog renegades for American citizenship.

Before going to bed, Black penned two letters. One to

the embassy official in Bangkok identifying himself, outlining what he wanted, and asking for guidance. The other was to Lieutenant Colonel Paul Anderson, telling him that there was reason to believe that the lady in question was alive. He didn't elaborate.

CHAPTER
TWENTY-SEVEN

Friday, January 5th, 1100 Local—Pave Dagger Test Headquarters, Danang Air Base, South Vietnam

Major Benny Lewis

The situation was worse than expected. Moods said they were now down to four of the specially designated Mk-84 bombs in the munitions bunkers on the opposite end of the runway. They'd been disappearing, and no one would tell him where they were going. Probably being used on routine combat missions, he said, which was a bloody shame. Those had been carefully selected for weight and balance for the Pave Dagger test. Now, except for the four, they'd have to use whatever bombs they could get their hands on.

Benny looked about the inside of the small, cramped, and decrepit building, then motioned his head toward the door leading to the ramp. "Where do they park your test birds?"

The overweight senior engineer from the Texas team's company snorted, and Moods told him they still hadn't been assigned aircraft. "We're at zero, Benny. Zee-*row*. They keep telling us there's no airplanes available. Higher priorities, they say."

Lewis grimaced. "Hell, I thought a 1-A was as high as they got."

"Exigencies of combat, I'm told."

"And the wing commander won't let you send messages?"

"Not without a hassle and until he's read and corrected every word. We think he's intercepting 'em too. We were supposed to receive new bias voltage settings from Texas, but they've never arrived."

"Is it just the wing commander, or are you getting flak from everyone?"

"One word from him, and the bullshit will stop, Benny. It's all coming from the top."

"I'll go talk to the man."

The delay was a short one. The secretary told him to go on in as soon as the colonel was off the phone. Lewis motioned for Moods to wait in the outer office.

Benny reported in, telling the colonel he was the fighter-tactics branch chief from Nellis, here to observe the progress of the Pave Dagger combat tests.

"How're they doing?" the wingco asked. Benny could hardly believe his ears.

He was careful to keep his voice even. "From what I've seen, sir, the entire project is on hold. The project officer believes someone's deliberately holding things up."

The colonel's expression turned nasty. "What do you mean, *deliberately*, Major?"

"All he's trying to do is follow orders. He was directed to come here and run a very classified, very high-priority test."

The wing commander frowned. "Whose priority?"

"Headquarters Air Force, priority 1-A, sir. That was included in the initial messages to PACAF and puts it at an equal with nonessential combat missions. From what I was briefed yesterday by General Moss, the 366th wing's had few of those since the battle at Dak To."

"You saw the general?"

"Yes, sir. He asked me to pass on his greetings."

The wing commander pursed his lips thoughtfully.

"We really need to move with these test sorties, Colonel."

"Why the rush?"

Benny glanced at the closed door, drew a short breath, then plunged on. "The Pave Dagger laser-guided bombs are to be used in LINE BACKER JACKPOT."

Ten minutes later Benny left the colonel's office with a pledge of support and authorization to send and receive classified messages. On his way out he picked up Moods, who was studying a wall photo of the commander in chief as if Lyndon Johnson's bulldog smile held something interesting. As they exited the outer office, Moods kept his head turned toward the wall, avoiding a full colonel with a haughty air, who was waiting to see the wing commander. Benny recognized the man, but he was more interested in Moods's odd behavior.

When they were outside, walking toward the decrepit pickup, Moods looked back. "That guy in there's the one who gave me all the heartburn when I tried to brief the project at PACAF."

Benny was thinking about a run-in he'd once had with the colonel, as well as General Moss's advice. "His name's Tom Lyons. Watch out for him and stay out of his way."

"You don't have to tell me," said Moods.

"Let's get some lunch, then we'll go back and hopefully get some work done."

"How did your meeting go?"

"I got his pledge of support for the project."

"I'll believe it when I see them taxi over a couple of test birds."

As they drove to the club, Benny decided that if the delays continued, he'd try to get the tests moved. There were other F-4 locations.

A giant of a man, wearing fatigues with subdued captain's rank and a weathered Aussie hat, sauntered along the sidewalk. Benny took a second look and told Moods to pull over to the side.

"Captain!" Benny shouted in a mock angry voice. "Get your raggedy ass over here."

The huge captain looked up, a snarl growing on his face. Then the look froze and slowly changed to a wide grin.

"Well?" Benny yelled.

"I'll be double gah-dammed."

The behemoth hurried over, reached through the open window—which made Moods Diller cringe—and began to pump Lewis's hand. "Benny!" The giant shook his massive head.

"Where you headed, Tiny?"

"Th' club for lunch. Jesus, but you look good. How's the back?"

"Fine, but I can't convince the flight surgeon. I'm still grounded." Benny half turned. A small spasm shivered through his back, and he let out an involuntary grunt. He didn't think the others had noticed. He drew a breath. "Moods, this is Tiny Bechler, who's as fine a lieutenant wingman as they ever made."

Tiny beamed. "Made captain a couple months back. Now I'm a hell of a lot smarter."

"Talking about smart, meet Moods Diller. He's so smart he's gonna buy us drinks tonight."

"No way," Bechler roared. "I'm buying. You saved my ass one time too many to forget."

"What the hell are you doing here? I talked to Sam Hall a couple of months back, and he said you were in Florida."

Tiny nodded. "Stationed at Hurlburt Field, just outa Fort Walton Beach. I teach in the forward air controller course there. Really progressing. I went from bein' a single-seat fighter pilot to a schoolmarm."

Benny chuckled. "Why are you here?"

"We put together a road show. I'm on temporary duty over here to crosstalk with the airborne and ground FACs, making sure they've got the latest word."

"Just you?"

"Naw. I've got a ROMAD with me." ROMAD was the acronym for radio operator, maintainer, and driver. "He knows more about radios than Marconi did. We've already been to Bien Hoa. Couple more weeks we'll go over to NKP and talk with the O-1 Birddog drivers."

"Let's have lunch."

"Damn right."

Moods drove into the club parking lot. "That guy's big as a house," he said, looking back.

"Tiny likes to act dumb and grouchy. Sort of his trademark. But he's got his act together. An Air Force Academy grad who loves to fly."

"I sure as hell wouldn't want him mad at me."

"That's not an unintelligent thought, Moods."

The three men joined up at the club entrance, where Tiny rendered Benny a stiff and very proper salute. He did that with men he admired, which numbered few.

They took a seat in the dining room and talked like lost cousins.

"I made some friends here I'll introduce you to tonight," said Tiny. "Marine fighter jocks flying old F-4Bs. Good guys. I'm teachin' 'em some of our songs, and they're trying to get me to quit the sissy Air Force and join the Marines."

Moods tapped Benny's arm to gain his attention. "Guess who?"

Two colonels walked through to the elevated area at the side of the dining room and were seated at the table reserved for the wing commander.

1215L—Danang Officers' Open Mess

Colonel Tom Lyons

Lyons sat across from the commander of the 366th TFW. The friendship went back to pre–Air Force, even precollege days, to when they'd both attended an exclusive middle school in Golden, Colorado. His friend's family more or less owned the city of Milwaukee, but Lyons's family money was real, had been passed down and nurtured for four generations, while his friend's family's money was newly earned from land development and food distribution. They were nouveau riche who craved old-money respect.

The caste system was entrenched at the exclusive middle school, and his friend had been flattered when Tom singled him out. Over the years Tom had taken him along to a few family holiday gatherings, and his friend still spoke about the people he'd met, which included Rockefellers, Kennedys, and DuPonts as well as past and present Presidents of the United States.

Though apparently troubled, his friend remained appropriately respectful.

"You told me the Pave Dagger test was low priority," he said.

"General Roman thinks it's a waste of time and sure as hell doesn't want it interfering with combat sorties." It was a lie. Roman hadn't been briefed on the project.

"It's got good priority at Air Force level," the wing commander said.

"So . . . they're wrong."

"I can't go against the Pentagon, Tom."

"You don't work for the Pentagon. You work for PACAF."

"I work for General Moss at Seventh Air Force. *He* works for your general at PACAF."

Lyons raised an eyebrow. "You got a problem?"

"The test manager from Nellis dropped by my office asking questions. He'd coordinated the visit with General Moss. I can't ignore it, Tom."

"I see." Lyons didn't speak his real mind. If he had, he would've spoken in a sharper tone. But things weren't going well. He had bigger concerns than a pie-in-the-sky project from Nellis, namely trying to find out more about JACKPOT.

"I can't hold up their message traffic any longer, either. This Lewis guy's going to report back to General Moss, and I can catch shit for it."

"Do what you think's best," Lyons said. "You want to give away two airplanes so they can play silly games, go ahead. I was just looking out for your interests when I made my suggestions."

His friend hurried to smooth things. "I'm appreciative, Tom, and I'm a team player, but I can't refuse to support them any longer."

"Just make sure they don't interfere with your primary mission. General Roman wouldn't like that one bit." Tom was tired of the subject. He was also tired of batting zeros at every base he visited whenever he tried to learn about JACKPOT. He hoped his friend could provide answers.

A smiling Vietnamese waitress arrived to take their orders. The food at the DOOM club, which was what everyone called the Danang Officer's Open Mess, was infinitely better than the slop Tom had suffered in Thailand.

When the waitress had departed, he decided on a direct approach. "You know about a project called JACKPOT?"

His friend was drinking iced tea and almost strangled. He gave Tom a sideward glance before shaking his head. "Never heard of it," he said in a strained voice.

Liar, Tom thought. He could hardly suppress his excitement.

Tuesday, January 9th, 1225 Local—Arming Area, Takhli RTAFB

Captain Manny DeVera

Manny sat at the end of the runway in his Thud, canopy opened, watching with interest as each pilot taxied onto the runway and took off. He was *sitting spare*, which meant he was the ground spare and would take off only if another aircraft had a problem and couldn't go. The F-105's were hardy and had few maintenance glitches, so ground spares were seldom used.

The afternoon force was going back to pack two to look for truck convoys, barges, water buffalo, horses, bicycles—or any of the other conveyances known to be hauling supplies through the mountain passes into Laos, where they'd turn southward. If they'd been fragged to fly into pack six, they would launch airborne spares to tag along until the refueling was completed. There could be no holes in the formation for a pack-six mission. In the lower packs that was not nearly as important, for the majority of defenses there were visually fired artillery.

First Manny had observed the Wild Weasel flight, four two-seat F-105Fs. Next had come the first two F-105D strike flights, and they'd taken off without a hitch. Snake flight, which was the third and last strike flight, was led by Animal Hamlin.

As Animal took the active runway, Manny settled his head back against the rest, thinking it was shitty to come this far, make all the preparations, and not fly. He'd done the flight planning, attended all the briefings, put on the flying gear, all of it, and now he'd taxi back, shut down the engine, and return to his office to sift through paperwork. *Shitty,* he thought, and sipped water from a tube to avoid dehydration. The crew chiefs made sure the bottles behind the headrest of the ejection seats were full and the water was ice cold for their pilots.

Manny wished someone in Snake flight would abort. He enjoyed flying with Hamlin, who was adventuresome in the air. He'd get right down amongst 'em and try to root out the convoys, and had more success at it than most. He was a good guy—a loyal friend and a leader in the air.

Animal checked his engine at full throttle. The tower cleared Snake flight for takeoff.

"Bite 'em in the ass," Manny said as Animal engaged burner, released brakes, and his Thud began to roll. He watched for and saw the brightening of the jet's exhaust plume as water was sprayed into the engine to give additional thrust. It was unusually hot, and with their full loads, the Thuds needed all the power they could get.

Animal's F-105 passed the 2,000-foot marker, and Manny thought he was going a bit slow. Probably the angle he was observing from, he decided. At three, then 4,000 feet down the runway, Animal's jet still seemed slow.

Manny sat up straighter and stared. Five thousand feet and the nose should be rotating.

Damn, Manny thought. He was beginning to worry in earnest.

The nose finally began to rise. Manny sighed with relief. He'd likely . . .

"*Snake lead, abort!*" someone yelled over the radio.

Animal was too far down the runway for that. "*Negative, Snake lead!*" Manny radioed.

But Hamlin had reacted to the first call. The drag chute deployed and the bird's nose immediately dropped.

"Shit!" Manny wailed. The Thud rolled on and on, yawing wildly as Hamlin tried to brake, then disappeared off the far end of the runway, spewing dust and angling sharply to the left. There was a deep ditch there.

A fireball erupted.

Just the fuel. No bomb explosions, Manny thought.

He stared, pulled in a breath, then lowered his canopy as he pressed the radio button. "*Tower, ground spare will assume Snake lead.*"

A short pause followed.

"Roger, ground spare," answered the tower operator. *"You're cleared onto the active."*

Manny taxied around the remainder of Snake flight and pulled into position.

"Snake lead is number one for takeoff," Manny radioed. He pushed his throttle forward to check the engine at full military power.

"Ah roger, Snake lead. Altimeter is three-zero-one-point-niner. Wind is calm. You are cleared for takeoff."

1320L—355th TFW Commander's Office, Takhli

GS-7 Penny Dwight

She'd heard sirens and Klaxons, heard the clop-clop of the emergency helicopter rushing back and forth, so she'd known something was happening. The voices she'd heard over the colonel's radio had sounded professional and calm. Colonel Leska had hurried out to the crash site.

When he returned half an hour later, he told the office admin crew that the pilot was Captain Roger Hamlin. Penny felt no hysteria this time. She was utterly numbed.

"Is he . . . ?" she asked.

"He was killed." Leska said he knew they were friends. He was sorry about it, he said, and waited for her reaction. She just nodded, stared out the window for a long moment, then resumed typing. Her fingers were unsure, so she had to be very careful not to make a mistake.

"Do you want to go to lunch or anything?"

"No, thank you," she replied. She had to finish the report.

Colonel Trimble came in to brief Leska about the increasingly critical aircraft situation, after losing *another* bird. He appeared upset as he went into the wing commander's office.

Five minutes later there was Colonel Armaugh, who also appeared to be angry, and when he joined the other two in Leska's office, voices could be heard through the door. Armaugh said maintenance had given his pilot a shitty bird.

He was talking loudly, and Colonel Trimble answered in an even louder voice that Armaugh's goddam pilots didn't check properly for engine decay. Why the hell couldn't he have them . . .

Colonel Leska emerged, leaving the other two shouting inside his office. He scribbled two notes and handed them to her. "Please capitalize everything," he said in his neutral tone.

Penny rolled the report out of the carriage, then typed what he'd given her. He read them over and nodded. "Thank you, Penny." He remained calm as he went back into the noisy room.

The shouting match quieted. When the voices resumed, they'd became subdued.

"You can't do this," Colonel Armaugh said loudly, but the anger was replaced by a different emotion.

"I just did, George," Colonel Leska answered.

When the deputies for operations and maintenance emerged from the Wing Commander's office, they both appeared to be in shock.

1650L

It was late, almost time to get off work for the day, when Manny DeVera came by to see her . . . as she'd known he would.

"You heard about Roger?" he asked grimly.

She nodded.

"Let's go downtown. Go somewhere and do *something*," he said.

She regarded him closely. Manny looked sad, but where was the awful remorse you felt when a friend was killed? Horribly killed. Burned and mutilated. He'd called Roger Hamlin a close friend, just as he'd said Dusty had been, yet there was no real mourning. Even worse, where were her own tears? Had she become as callous as they were?

"I don't want to see you anymore," she said.

His brow furrowed. "What?"

She shook her head.

"I don't understand."

"I just don't want to see you anymore."

Manny turned to frown, then released a sad sigh and left.

A tear blurred Penny's vision. She squinted her eyes and willed it away. Manny would be next, she knew.

Thursday, January 11th, 1400 Local—Honolulu, Hawaii

Colonel Tom Lyons

The taxi pulled up in front of the large hillside home, and the native-islander cabbie turned and gave him a grin. "Need some help with the bags?"

"Of course," he responded icily. The man was a fool, but Tom's spirits refused to become dampened by a simple aborigine. He'd returned from the difficult mission General Roman had given him with complete success. In the morning he'd brief the four-star on the details of what he'd learned about the cockamamy plan they were concocting at Saigon. His friend at Danang had, after a great deal of badgering, told him what he knew. Tom had telephoned the general immediately with an outline of what he had, but he'd saved the juicier tidbits for later . . . for tomorrow morning's face-to-face when he'd brief him on the rest of it.

His friend at Danang had said he didn't know many of the real details, but that was okay. He would embellish it, to make Lieutenant General Moss look just as silly as he really was. The fools actually thought if they continued bombing, with different targets and a few more aircraft, the enemy would roll over and kick their feet in the air.

Outside the taxi, Tom looked up at the clouds that roiled over the mountains to the north, then stretched wearily and watched as the cabbie pulled the two heavy bags from the trunk. "Up there," he said, pointing at the entrance at the top of the steep concrete stairway.

"No way," said the cabbie. He dropped Tom's Cartier soft luggage beside him.

Tom glared. "You want a tip, don't you?" The cabbie gave him a stare.

Lyons angrily paid him precisely what had been shown on the meter.

"Another buck more, asshole," growled the Hawaiian.

"The sign there says fifty cents a bag. Come to think of it, make it two dollars. I put 'em in the trunk too."

"Sue me," Tom said, and started to turn away when a vise grip squeezed his arm. Lyons gave a yelp and tried to pull away.

"Two more dollars, asshole." The grip tightened until it threatened circulation.

Lyons quickly pulled out his money clip and peeled off a five. "Have you got change?" he asked tremulously.

The cabbie took the five and crawled into the taxi. "Sue me," he said before taking off.

Tom was so relieved the Hawaiian was gone that he forgot to get his license number so he could turn him in. He struggled as he lugged the heavy bags up the stairs to the entrance. He'd bought a few things for his wife in Saigon. She liked surprises. Then he'd tell her he no longer needed information from her father, as he'd begged her on the telephone the previous week.

He'd learned what Moss's conversation with Lyndon Johnson had been about and would not need inputs from Senator Lingenfelter. The thought gave him extra strength as he pulled his bags up the final steps. When no one answered the doorbell, Tom tried to let himself in with the key. It didn't work.

He leaned close and called out, "Margaret?" When he received no response, Tom peered through the glass beside the door. The furniture was cloaked with dustcovers as they'd been when he and Margaret had first arrived—as if the vacation house wasn't in use.

"What the hell's going on?" Tom grumbled angrily to himself. His wife seldom left home. She'd normally be on her fifth vodka tonic by now. Margaret was eccentric and spoiled, but he'd not expected her to act *this* strange.

He walked around and through the gate of the rear garden fence. The swimming pool caught his eye as he approached the rear door, and he stopped and stared. There was a profusion of clothing and furniture, some floating, most of it sunk to the bottom. Uniforms, suits, tuxedos, shoes, underwear, an antique bureau—all of it his own. The leather easy chair he treasured and the huge French desk from his study rested on their sides at the shallow end. He hurried closer and ... *Christ!* ... his new handcrafted persimmon golf clubs lay directly beneath him. *Who the hell could have done this!* His immediate thought was of vandals. He staggered toward the white wrought-iron patio furniture, knowing he had to take a seat and calm himself.

There must be a rational answer.

A paper was weighted on the crystal-topped table. A note from Margaret?

It was a copy of an official form, filled with typing. He peered closer, read the words. "Takhli Medical Dispensary," was typed into the FACILITY block. In the NAME block was "Thomas F. Lyons, Colonel, USAF." Under DIAGNOSED ILL-NESS OR COMPLAINT was ...

Jesus! His hand began to tremble.

Beneath the form was a short note, scribbled in Margaret's distinctive, childlike scrawl.

Tom,
I am leaving you forever. Do not telephone or try to follow. Father is as angry as I am, and has told me he will personally shoot you if you approach me or bother me in any way. If I have contracted your disease, he says he will do so regardless. You may gather your clothing and belongings—they are all where you see them now—and immediately depart. You are not welcome in my father's vacation home. Do not attempt to go inside, because the security company has been directed to turn you over to authorities for breaking and entering. I despise you, and always have. May you rot in hell.

Margaret Anne Lingenfelter

Tom moved into the Royal Hawaiian Hotel that afternoon and arranged for his clothing and personal goods to be removed from the pool. When he called home, his mother said his father was down with a cold and accepting no calls; her hesitant tone told him different.

When he went to dinner that evening, Tom Lyons was despondent. For the first time in his life he was on his own.

He was thankful that his military career was intact, and after dinner he went up to his room and worked hard on the presentation for General Roman.

The next morning the general's secretary regarded him coolly, almost angrily, as if she'd not been the cause of his awful predicament. He did not speak to her beyond the minimum words required to gain entrance to the general's office.

The audience with the general began well enough, although there was none of the near camaraderie of before. It was obvious that the general had learned of Margaret's departure, for he did not open as he usually did by mentioning her or Senator Lingenfelter's name.

Lyons told him about JACKPOT, a half-baked and poorly thought-out plan to change targeting from bridges and such to concentrate on the populated areas of North Vietnam. He embellished, saying that hotels and prominent downtown buildings as well as military and industrial targets in the center of the city would be targeted. The general looked on incredulously.

"What aircraft would be used?" the general asked.

Lyons hadn't been told those details, so he winged it. "Fighters only," he said.

"Well that part's good," Roman sighed. "The fucking cowboys would be the only ones to get egg plastered on their faces."

"They're also planning to use the Pave Dagger bombs they're testing at Danang Air Base."

"What the fuck is Pave Dagger?" the general growled.

"It's a new sort of munition that ... uh ... gives off bright light." He couldn't recall details of the briefing he'd sat in on, just remembered it had been Buck Rogers bullshit and there was some new kind of source of illumination.

"Light?"

"To blind the enemy," Tom said in a more positive voice, trying to remember.

"For crap's sake, are we dealing with a bunch of loonies?"

"You might say that, sir," Tom said happily.

The general soon glanced at his watch and dismissed

both Tom Lyons and any worries he had regarding JACK-POT, for the idea was so ludicrous it posed no threat to his ambitions. Just as soon as he was named Cee SAF, he said he'd scrap the plan so it could not be seized upon to reflect poorly on the Air Force.

CHAPTER
TWENTY-EIGHT

Tuesday, January 16th, 0655 Local—Over Eastern Laos

Lieutenant Colonel Lucky Anderson

The air refueling had gone well enough. Their next challenge was to rendezvous at the North Vietnamese border so they could join in the big ECM pod formation. Without the TACAN nav station, the task was more difficult.

Going from the air refueling area to the join-up point, the four-ship flights were to fly eastward in a loose semblance of the sixteen-ship formation, but they'd fucked it up. Whisky flight, supposed to be the third in the formation, dropped off their tanker a few minutes later than the others and hurried to catch up. They sped toward the join-up point, and since there was no TACAN to home on, Whisky lead used his Doppler navigator system for direction while he studied target photos. Half an hour later number three in that flight called that he thought they were north of course, and after Whisky lead checked his compass against the flight plan and looked about vainly for landmarks, he agreed.

Lucky, who was mission commander, heard the chatter on the radio. By then he and the fourteen other aircraft, including the two airborne spares, had arrived at the Laotian–

North Vietnamese border and were entering a left-hand orbit to wait for them.

"*Whisky lead,*" he radioed, "*this is Scotch Force leader. State your position.*"

"*Roger, Scotch, stand by.*"

Dammit, Lucky grumbled. It was obvious that Whisky lead had no idea where he was.

After a couple of minutes, he radioed again, speaking slowly. "*Whisky lead, Scotch Force leader will continue to transmit on radio. I want you to home on my radio signal. Short count follows: one-two-three-four-five-four-three-two-one. Scotch out.*"

Military aircraft have a direction-finding position on their radios, which allows pilots to home on radio transmissions.

"*Roger, Scotch Force leader. Whisky lead shows you at our four o'clock position. We must've somehow got ahead of you.*"

"*We're waiting for you, Whisky,*" Lucky radioed, increasingly irritated as he continued to lead the other aircraft in the orbit. Lucky did not like surprises—not at all. He'd briefed the mission carefully and liked things to go as planned.

"*Scotch, Whisky still doesn't have you in sight. Could you—ah—give me another countdown?*"

He could see them clearly, for Christ's sake. "*Whisky flight, I've got you in sight,*" Lucky radioed impatiently. "*We're at your ten o'clock position, five miles out, at our briefed altitude.*"

Another long pause.

"*Whisky four's got them in sight,*" announced an enthusiastic lieutenant. "*Nine o'clock and slightly high.*"

"*We're turning to port, Whiskys,*" radioed their lead.

Lucky watched as the four aircraft turned and climbed toward them, wondering how much fuel they'd wasted. He called the F-4 MiG-CAP and the F-105F Wild Weasel flights, both of which were orbiting a few miles inside North Vietnam, and told them they were adjusting their TOT by seven minutes.

When Whisky flight was within a couple of miles, Lucky led the way out of the orbit, and the flights began to join into a single sixteen-ship formation.

He asked for a status check. Since all aircraft were fit, he

sent the airborne spares home. Whisky flight was still joining up as they approached the high mountain range marking
their entry into North Vietnam.

"This is Scotch leader. Green 'em up and push 'em up," he
announced. *"Check your music on, and set up proper spacing."* He set his own weapons panel switches, adjusted his
throttle full forward, then backed it off a bit, and switched
his ECM switch from STANDBY to ON.

The strike force, now roaring along at 590 knots, began to
jockey positions until they were flying as close to the man-
dated 1,500 feet and forty-five degree separation as they
could eyeball. Manny DeVera had persistently worked with
the pilots, and they were getting damned good at it, Lucky
decided.

It had been an ignominious start, and Lucky hoped the
gremlins would get themselves ironed out before they
crossed the Red River. *No more surprises!* he grumbled.

The world beneath them was exposed in a bright glow
from the morning sun. The rolling hills and occasional steep
mountains were heavily forested—teak trees, reaching up
150 feet above the jungle floor. A few miles to their right
were bleak, wind-shaped limestone formations called karsts,
which appeared like desolate spires and castles. Ahead in
the distance was the great valley formed by the Hong Song,
the Riviere Rouge, or the Red River, according to your
tongue.

When you approached the Red from the west, you entered a new world. On the ground you went from Stone Age
to Bronze Age cultures. From their height the multitudes of
rice paddies made the valley look like a crazy quilt of tiny
checks, interspersed with ribbons of water, villages, and
sprawling cities.

The hissing static on Lucky's radar warning receiver
grew a couple of spikes, and the AAA light stopped blinking
and became steady. He was centered in the beams of two
Firecans, the van-mounted dish radars that fed targeting information to batteries of antiaircraft guns. Then the beams
swept on by, for the strobes disappeared and the light went
back to blinking, now just picking up background radiation
from their ECM pods.

Today, at least against AAA radars, the pods were doing
their work.

"THIS IS MOTEL. RED BANDITS AT BULLSEYE, THREE-ONE-ZERO FOR TWELVE. I REPEAT. THIS IS MOTEL. RED BANDITS AT BULLSEYE, THREE-ONE-ZERO FOR TWELVE."

The powerful over-the-horizon radar at Udorn had announced that Red Bandits—MiG-21's—were flying twelve miles northwest of Hanoi. Lucky scanned the sky ahead but couldn't see them.

"This is Scotch Force leader," he radioed. *"Keep your eyes out for the MiGs."* No response was required as they crossed over the Red River and continued east, slowly descending.

"Scotch Force, this is Red Dog lead. We've got an active SAM just west of Phuc Yen and two more in the target area." The Wild Weasels were making their first call. There would be many more, for the strike force would bomb the small bridge spanning the Canales des Rapides, located immediately north of Hanoi.

Lucky acknowledged the Weasel radio call.

"Whisky three has two bogeys in sight at our three o'clock, low, traveling west!"

Anderson craned his neck, then saw them. He immediately called the Phantom MiG-CAP. *"Trigger, this is Scotch lead. We've got two MiG-21's passing south of us, and they'll likely try to set up for a stern attack. You got 'em in sight?"*

"Negative, Scotch. Trigger three, drop back and take a look."

"Scotch leader, this is Whisky lead. The MiGs are starting to turn."

"Hang in there, Whisky." Lucky had his eye on the MiGs, which had misjudged and begun their turns too late. By the time they rolled out, they'd be miles behind.

"They're turning on us, Scotch!" The voice was shaken and filled with adrenaline.

Lucky kept his voice even. *"They screwed up their intercept, Whisky. They're overshooting."*

"Whisky lead's jettisoning and taking evasive action!" Meaning that the Thud driver was dumping his bombs and fuel tanks, putting his nose down, and going into afterburner.

"Negative, Whisky lead!" Lucky said sternly.

Silence answered him.

"Trigger three's got the MiGs in sight. We'll take a high-

angle Sparrow shot, then come around at 'em." The F-4 pilot's voice was straining as he pulled g-forces.

"Trigger four has 'em turning north."

"I got 'em. I got 'em. Fox one ... no splash."

The Phantom drivers chased the MiGs northward, firing more missiles but missing.

"Whiskys, this is Scotch Force leader, check in," radioed Lucky.

"Whisky three."

"Whisky four."

A short pause, then a hesitant and penitent voice. *"This is Whisky lead. I'm a couple miles south of the formation, rejoining."*

"Whisky two, same."

"You still got your bombs, Whisky lead?"

"Negative. I jettisoned. The MiGs were coming in on us, Scotch."

"We'll talk about it when we get on the ground," Lucky replied evenly, keeping anger from his tone. They were abeam the MiG base at Phuc Yen. He peered ahead, beyond Thud Ridge, at the Red River, then at the streamlet branching off from it. *"Scotch Force leader's got the target in sight."*

The fourteen aircraft with weapons still aboard released on the target. Scotch flight carried cluster bomblet units, and decimated AAA guns and gunners both north and south of the stream. The ten other aircraft dropped their twenty 3,000-pound bombs. One of those struck the bridge's southern approach, and another partially knocked down the adjacent span. Eighteen bombs missed, although some were close and likely did some structural damage.

Whisky lead and his wingman orbited north of the target, dodged a threesome of SAMs, and waited to rejoin the safety of the strike force on its outbound journey.

When they'd crossed back over the Red, then the Black, rivers, Lucky decided they were safe enough, so he pressurized his cockpit and released the right catch of his oxygen mask, letting it dangle to one side as he thought about what he'd do after they'd landed.

He had only a couple of minor write-ups on his aircraft to tell the maintenance people about, and there was nothing unique about the mission, so the intelligence and mission debriefings would be short. And finally, he would take the captain flying Whisky lead aside and give him a butt-reaming he wouldn't forget.

Brief 'em as you planned 'em. Fly 'em as you briefed 'em.

Good words for a fighter jock who wanted to grow a bit older.

The captain was on his twelfth mission, still getting his feet on the ground, and this was his first time to pack six, flying in place of Captain Hamlin. He'd survive the ass-chewing, and if he listened hard, he might even survive the remainder of his combat tour.

Lucky relatched his mask and called Red Crown, then gave the "Successful" code word and a snapshot description of defenses in the target area. When Red Crown acknowledged, he switched back to mission frequency, checked in, unfastened the mask for comfort again, and went back to scanning the sky for MiGs.

Lucky Anderson was smiling to himself. He'd enjoyed the flight more than others in the recent past. He was like Phoenix rising from the ashes, and there'd been no way to get him upset for long in the past couple of days. The short letter from Sergeant Black was already dog-eared and barely legible, because Lucky unfolded it and reread it about a hundred times a day.

Linda was alive.

1400L—355th TFW Commander's Office, Takhli RTAFB, Thailand

Colonel Buster Leska

The atmosphere in the command section had become more peaceful now that the constant bickering between Colonels Armaugh and Trimble had ceased. The silence was golden.

George Armaugh no longer argued violently that his pilots received dogshit airplanes. He no longer had operational pilots assigned to him.

Jerry Trimble no longer complained that the pilots were wrecking his birds and overworking his mechanics, for he had no airplanes or maintenance men assigned to him.

The solution had been an easy one, and Buster wondered

why he hadn't thought of it earlier. First he'd done his
homework by asking Seventh Air Force to approve his action. General Moss had howled with laughter and told him
to report back on how it went. Then, the very next time the
two colonels had charged into his office with their complaints, he'd let them carry on for a while, then handed each
a signed note.

To Armaugh:

> BY ORDER OF THE COMMANDER, 355TH TFW:
> EFFECTIVE IMMEDIATELY, YOU ARE
> RELIEVED AS DEPUTY COMMANDER FOR
> OPERATIONS, AND WILL ASSUME THE
> POSITION OF DEPUTY COMMANDER FOR
> MAINTENANCE. OFFICIAL ORDERS WILL
> FOLLOW.

To Trimble:

> BY ORDER OF THE COMMANDER, 355TH TFW:
> EFFECTIVE IMMEDIATELY, YOU ARE
> RELIEVED AS DEPUTY COMMANDER FOR
> MAINTENANCE, AND WILL ASSUME THE
> POSITION OF DEPUTY COMMANDER FOR
> OPERATIONS. OFFICIAL ORDERS WILL
> FOLLOW.

The two men's positions had been reversed. Both were
scrambling to come up to speed in their new job, and the
peace and silence at the staff meetings was conducive to
getting much more accomplished. They were good men, and
would quickly discover just how difficult the other's position
had been. Armaugh would develop an appreciation of how
hard maintenance had to work to keep the birds flying.
Trimble would learn to bear the losses of pilots flying combat.

Buster felt very wise.

Lucky Anderson had just left his office after telling him
about the screwup in today's mission, and Buster included
his concerns in the message he'd been preparing. He reread
the words he'd carefully printed for transmission and decided they were proper.

SECRET—JACKPOT
7 AF CC EYES ONLY—NO FURTHER DISSEM
DTG: 16/0700ZJAN68
TO: HQ 7 AF/CC, TAN SON NHUT AB, SVN
FM: 355 TFW/CC, TAKHLI RTAFB, THAI
SUBJECT: JACKPOT INPUTS
1. (C) PARTIAL LIFTING OF RESTRICTIONS
HAS BEEN BENEFICIAL. WE LOOK
FORWARD TO FURTHER CHANGES, AS
REQUESTED.
2. (S) LOSS OF CHANNEL 97 TACAN HAS
AFFECTED THIS WING'S COMBAT
EFFECTIVENESS. IT WOULD BE ESPECIALLY
DESIRABLE TO HAVE IT BACK ON THE AIR
PRIOR TO INITIATION OF LARGE-SCALE
ACTIVITIES, SUCH AS ENVISIONED IN
OPLAN.
3. (S) FYI, LT COL DONOVAN RECEIVED TWO
(2) MORE PHONE CALLS FM COL LYONS
RE. JACKPOT, & REPORTED SAME TO ME.
1ST CALL FM DANANG, 2ND FM PACAF HQ.
LYONS INDICATED HE KNOWS MORE THAN
PREVIOUSLY, BUT DIDN'T EXPLAIN.
SECRET—JACKPOT

**Saturday, January 20th, 1330 Local—Pave Dagger Test
Headquarters, Danang Air Base, South Vietnam**

Major Benny Lewis

The Danang wing commander had become easier to deal
with following their discussion, but he still was not truly responsive. When they received the two F-4's for field modification and use on the test, which was a full week after he'd
seen him, it was the final straw. Both were hangar queens,
nonflyable until hundreds of hours of major maintenance
could be performed, and then the birds would have to be
scheduled for test flights and certified ready.

Benny had told Moods to have his men and the Texas
team continue to tune and peak the seekers and bomb kits,

and to stand by until he returned. Then he'd departed on a base shuttle flight. That had been five days earlier.

Now, half an hour after his return to Danang, he had Moods gather the entire bunch in the too-small, decrepit building near the end of the runway. Benny sipped a cold beer as they assembled. He'd missed breakfast and lunch and needed something to fill him.

"You guys ready to go to work?" he asked when the last men had arrived.

Moods's backseat PSO piped up. "Neither of the test birds is ready to fly."

"Forget about 'em."

"Sir, we can't modify them until they've been—"

"I said forget 'em. They can have their trash back."

"Sir?"

"I made three stops after I left here. First was in Saigon, where I told General Moss about the horseshit going on here."

There were smiles.

"Second I went to Ubon, over in northeast Thailand, and spoke to the wing commander. He liked what I told him about your smart bombs—thinks they might be the hottest thing since Sherman partied in Atlanta. He's sick and tired of the Thud wings telling him they can outbomb his Phantoms all to hell and wants to teach 'em a lesson."

"Can't agree more," said Moods's PSO, an avid F-4 proponent.

"Then I went back to Seventh Air Force and General Moss approved the move."

"We're moving?" Moods asked.

"Tomorrow afternoon they're sending us two C-130's, and we'll haul everything to Ubon. Think you can get everything boxed up and ready by then?"

"Why the big rush?" complained the Texas team lead engineer. "We've done nothing but sit on our asses for the past month."

"That's over. I want you to get moved and complete the test ASAP."

"Something hot coming up?" asked the pilot GIB, much happier.

"Maybe. Let's prove these things work, so the company can crank up the assembly line."

"Yes *sir*," said the lead Texas-team engineer. He was smiling broadly now.

"How about bombs?" the backseater asked.

"They'll have thirty picked out and ready for you. The best they can find."

More smiles.

"Another thing. I want tighter security this time. Don't tell anyone here where we're going. I want us to load up and be out of here before anyone realizes it. When we land at Ubon, I want you to move in and set up shop as quickly as possible. And don't put up any signs or anything announcing you're Pave Dagger."

The men began to talk among themselves. Happy chatter. They were finally going to see progress.

Benny drove the battered old pickup back to base operations, where he had a late lunch at the snack bar—the same greasy burger and fries and watery soda pop found at all such places. Hunger did not improve their taste.

When he'd told Moss about watching the 366th commander and Tom Lyons sitting together and confabbing like brothers, the general had at first been angry with Benny, then had turned quiet, then reflective. He'd said he'd call the wing commander in and find out if he'd given anything away. When Benny dropped back by after visiting Ubon, Moss hadn't shared what he'd learned, but he'd authorized the move to Ubon and told him to watch their security.

As he finished the last of the greasy fries, he felt another twinge in his back. He tried hard to relax it until the spasm passed. The shaking and shuddering of the C-130's he'd taken on two of the flight legs had not been nearly as gentle on his ailing backbone as the commercial airliners. Still, he'd made the flights and suffered no real, lasting pain, so he knew he was healing. After taking a single muscle-relaxant pill and three or four aspirins, he was able to sleep just fine.

On his way out of the snack bar, Lewis saw Tiny Bechler standing with a lanky staff sergeant and a stack of bags and boxes in front of base ops.

"Going somewhere?" he asked.

"Yeah." Tiny introduced him to his ROMAD. "We're headed over to Nakhon Phanom. Talk to the O-1 Birddog pilots and teach 'em the ropes."

Benny laughed. The Birddog pilots at NKP nurtured rep-

utations as the best airborne forward air controllers in the
free world.

"Take care of yourself, Tiny."

"Will do. You heading back to the States soon?"

"Soon enough."

Benny drove back to the shack at the end of the runway.
He'd decided to stay with the test for a while longer. He
could think of no compelling reason to return to Nellis.
More and more he'd been thinking that his relationship with
Julie had come to a turning point . . . and was headed for
nowhere in particular. Several times he'd started to write
her as he'd promised, but something would clutch at his
hand and the words wouldn't come. Each time he'd think of
the night they'd spent together, the awkwardness and the
boorish way he'd treated her—the anguish he'd felt over the
memory of her dead husband—and he'd put off writing for
yet another day.

Benny missed Julie and still wanted her more than any
woman he'd met in his life, but the more he thought about
things and the way they'd become, the more he realized
she'd be better off free of him. Perhaps her mother was
right. He wondered if Julie would be there when he returned, or if she'd be in New Jersey, setting up a new life.
By not writing, he knew he was encouraging her to go, yet
he was increasingly at peace with himself about the decision.

1840L—O' Club Dining Room, Takhli RTAFB, Thailand

GS-7 Penny Dwight

The short major had freckles, a head of the reddest hair
she'd ever seen, and light-blue eyes. His name was Rudy,
like the reindeer, he liked to say, which he thought was a
great joke. When he'd asked her out the first time, she'd
turned him down. The next time she'd done the same. This
time she'd thought it over, asked herself *why not*, and accepted.

He was very nice, well mannered, and thought she was
beautiful. He was also a supply officer, and as a nonpilot he
didn't fly. She didn't find Rudy exciting and wasn't particu-

larly drawn to him, but he wasn't going to be shot down in flames and threaten her sanity. He was also able to feel sorrow for others. He'd told her about his best friend at his previous base, and how he'd developed a heart condition. He said he worried a lot about his friend, and she noticed moisture welling in his eyes. He was normal and vulnerable, Penny told herself, and not at all like the fighter pilots.

Rudy was ten years older than Penny, but she felt she'd recently matured a great deal herself. For the past three months she'd lived in a far different, emotional, and violent world, and she knew she could never be the same again.

Penny was changed from the wide-eyed girl who'd arrived at Takhli, enamored with exotic Siam, captivated and cowed by the bold, adventuresome young pilots. It had been like a dream, as if she'd been dragged at a maddening pace through scenes from a bad movie. The smoke-filled bar with pilots singing the obscene songs of their odd fraternity. Heights of passion she'd not dreamed possible in an evening she'd never forget. Her lover killed. The awful night when the colonel had used her like a whore. Lovable Roger, with his gaudy guitar, now gone forever. She'd never believed she could become like the pilots, numbed and callous and taking death in stride as if it were part of the dues and not an awful, terrible thing . . . but she had. The evening following Roger Hamlin's death, she'd hardly cried. She'd grieved, but there'd been no sobbing, none of the heart-wrenching emotion she'd felt when Dusty had been lost—when she'd been normal. Death was a part of a fighter pilot's life. Roger had played his role, and more would go as he had. It was all a part of the movie—of a game they played. They didn't mourn one another.

Penny was determined to rekindle human charity within herself.

She'd not believed that her heart-thumping infatuation over Manny DeVera could end, but something had certainly changed, and abruptly so. It was a part of her journey to normalcy. She was distancing her life from theirs, fearful of what they'd done to her and of what might happen if she didn't move away. So she'd agreed to go out with Rudy— dinner at the club followed by a visit to the on-base Thai market. She'd never go out with Manny DeVera, or again wear the silly party suit to the club and act as if she were one of their insane cult.

They ordered steaks, and the waitress made a big deal about "hab punkin pie."

"Perhaps later," Rudy told her in his correct tone.

"Mebbe no hab punkin pie latah," she warned.

He ordered pie with their steaks, and Penny smiled.

Manny DeVera came into the dining room with Smitty Smith, and they took a seat nearby. Manny tried to catch her eye, but Penny ignored him and very deliberately reached over to touch the major's hand. The redhead jumped a bit, then showed a nervous smile.

"Have you been here long?" she asked Rudy, making small talk.

"Only a month. I'm still getting my feet on the ground." He leaned forward and his eyes came alive. "You wouldn't believe the volume we work with, and the items are so diverse that manual accounting and reordering methods are becoming useless." He went on to tell her about an automated inventory/reordering system they were installing, and how the keypunch operation would vastly improve their lives.

She stared and nodded and tried to give his speech full attention, quelling the urge to look over at the other table to see what Manny was doing.

She certainly did not miss him. She refused to. He was a part of the madness.

Captain Manny DeVera

"Forget her, Manny," said Smitty. "You're gonna blow your reputation."

"She won't even look at me," DeVera lamented. He was sure he felt more emotion for Penny Dwight than he had for any other woman, yet none of his magic seemed to work with her.

Smitty grinned. "You seen Colonel Armaugh's secretary? Now *there's* a foxy female, and she still hasn't gone out with any of the guys. Bazooms like watermelons. You oughta lay on the old Supersonic Wetback charm."

"I've gotta deal going with myself. No round-eyes until I

finish my tour. I get in trouble every time I chase round-eye women."

"Then what're you doing worrying about who Penny's out with?" Smitty looked cherubic, more like a teenager than a combat-hardened fighter jock.

"That's different," Manny said, then adroitly changed the subject. "How're you doing with the Thai base commander's daughter?"

Smith grew quiet. Everyone knew about his on-again, off-again relationship with the stunningly pretty Thai commander's numbah-one daughter by his numbah-two wife. Every two weeks, around payday, the girl would become reenamored. She'd telephone him at the Ponderosa and simper about how she missed him. They'd date once, then she'd insist that he take her shopping in Nakhon Sawan or the downtown Thai marketplace, where she'd blow his money in yet another spending frenzy. As far as they knew, she remained virginal, and Smitty was poor as a church mouse.

"You gonna get any of that girl?" Manny asked mischievously.

"She'll be worth the wait." Smitty didn't sound sure of himself. He was getting smarter, putting aside enough to make weekly trips downtown to the Takhli Villa, where sympathetic whores vied to relieve his anxieties. He was popular at the Villa. Whenever he entered the place, half the girls became dreamy-eyed and ignored business. Several had done the unthinkable and offered themselves at reduced prices for the cute *Lootna Smitty.*

"Forget the Thai colonel's daughter," Manny advised. "Go downtown and run for mayor. The girls'd vote you into office."

"Same as you oughta forget about Penny," countered Smitty.

Manny looked over at her table and forlornly shook his head. "What the hell does she see in him?" He sincerely didn't understand how she could ignore him for a *supply* officer.

"Maybe he's a nice guy." Smitty took a bite of hamburger steak, frowned, and doused more ketchup on it. "You better eat or it's gonna get cold."

"So what. Tastes the same either way."

Smitty grinned. "That's like you used to say about women. Turn 'em upside down, and they're all the same."

Manny continued to stare at Penny, who was listening intently to the redheaded major. She was not the same as other women he'd met—not at all.

Monday, January 22nd, 1000 Local—CC-C, Nakhon Phanom RTAB, Thailand

Sergeant Black

The commander had summoned him to his office. Black appeared there alone, as usual, and carefully closed the door.

Papa Wolf was in better spirits than the last time he'd seen him, which meant to Black either that the situation in Laos was becoming manageable, which was doubtful, or that they'd received orders to mount an operation.

It was the latter. "How's your team, Black?"

"They're healed and ready to fight, sir."

"Can you handle a routine patrol?"

"We're still at reduced numbers, but yes, sir. We're ready."

"We've been *tentatively* tasked to assist in an air operation, which I can't go into details on at this time. We'll need to insert a recon patrol to observe from the ground. Since it's a critical op and we're low on personnel, I'm going to use Hotdog to augment and back up."

Black was instantly happy. His deal not to participate in missions had been like a ballerina agreeing not to dance.

Papa Wolf glared at him. "Get that smirk off your face."

"It's a smile. Certainly not a smirk, sir."

The lieutenant colonel nodded at the wall map. "We'll drop you in separately, just in case, and you'll join the primary team at a base-camp observation post."

"Who's the primary team?"

"Banjo. They'll be in charge. Hotdog's only being used because of your ... ah ... unique qualifications for enemy recon."

"Banjo's good." Black wondered if they'd be returning to the mountaintop TACAN station. He hoped so. They'd left unfinished business there.

"When do we go, sir?"

"Ten days to two weeks. MAC-V's given tentative tasking to MAC-SOG, but we're still awaiting approval. The XO will brief you on specifics as the time gets closer. Let's say ... four days from now." The lieutenant colonel was giving him an odd fish-eye look.

Black wondered why he was being told this by the old man; normally he'd be alerted and briefed by the XO, not the commander. And why only general details? They were usually given specifics as early as possible so they could plan their activity down to a gnat's ass.

"Make *sure* your team's prepared, Black." The fish-eye again.

"Of course, sir." He saluted and started to leave.

Papa Wolf's next words held him up. "Regarding the Clipper operation you've been asking about? Your jet-jockey friend's fiancée?"

Black slowly turned back.

"I'm about to tell you something I'll deny ever mentioning. Understand, Black?"

"Yes, sir."

"They're through hesitating at MAC-V. They're about to do something about her, even though the priority's been reduced."

"It's about time we did something, sir. It's been three weeks since we discovered her location. That seems like a hell of a long hesitation."

"Big wheels move in mysterious and ponderous ways, Black, especially at MAC-V. But they've received a new HUMINT report that her physical condition is deteriorating. According to the source, she still hasn't told them what she knows, but she's likely about to break."

Black agreed. Few humans could long withstand continuous beatings. "Then they're finally going in after her?"

"They're not interested in mounting a ground operation with large numbers of enemy troops in that area. They're looking for an easier solution." He sat back in his chair and fixed Black with the odd gaze. "This coming Wednesday, that's two days from now, they're flying two dragon ships over from Nha Trang. Wednesday night they'll take out the camp at Ban Si Muang with Gatling guns."

"And the woman with it?"

"Most specifically the woman."

"Jesus!"

"She simply knows too much."

"Are they sure she's still there?"

"She was four days ago. That's when the last sighting was made."

"She's one hell of a brave lady, Colonel."

"Yeah. She's no pushover."

"It's not right, what they're going to do."

"No." He stared again. "It's not right at all."

"Our deal's off now, isn't it, sir?"

"Our agreement that you aren't to be placed in jeopardy?"

"Yes, sir."

"Since I'm sending you on the recon patrol, I suppose you might say that." He paused. "But it doesn't mean you should do anything foolhardy."

"Of course not, sir."

"Before you get your briefing from the XO, you might want to give your team a couple of days to ... ah ... prepare for the operation. Some kind of exercise that I'll leave to your judgment." The fish-eye again. Now Black understood.

"I'll do that, sir."

"Watch after yourself, Black."

"Yes, sir."

Black left the lieutenant colonel's office with an ominous feeling. They had only two days before the gunships arrived. Although it would be without official backing, Papa Wolf knew precisely where he'd take Hotdog for their premission exercise.

Black drove to the snack bar, the same place he'd met Lucky Anderson, and ordered two burgers and white rice from the happy Thai waitress. He held off on the usual beer. They'd have only a single day for planning, and there could be no trial runs. Tomorrow night they'd cross the Mekong.

As he ate, he considered the night river crossing, then the hike to Ban Si Muang. By the time he finished, he'd decided they would don the NVA uniforms before crossing the river and try to remain out of sight until they arrived at the guerrilla headquarters camp.

From the snack bar he went to the obscure compound at

the rear of the camp where the Hotdog recon team was billeted . . . to begin nailing down details of the Clipper op.

He found the lieutenant in his quarters. "Let us find a
private place," Black said in impeccable Hanoi Vietnamese.

The lieutenant smiled in anticipation. They'd been idle
too long. "The woman?" he asked tentatively. He'd asked
several times about her. His mind had been troubled by
Lucky Anderson's grief and what he'd seen in the Pathet
Lao camp.

"Yes," Black answered. "We are going to bring her out."

CHAPTER
TWENTY-NINE

Wednesday, January 24th, 0030 Local—Ban Si Muang, Southern Laos

Sergeant Black

The Pathet Lao headquarters camp was located immediately west of Ban Si Muang, a town at the base of a low, stark hill that jutted rudely upward from the jungle. More than a thousand years before, an enormous figure had been carved into the stone of the hill's western face. The rock had quickly become covered by vegetation, and merchant caravans going through the area carried tales about the "Green Buddha of Ban Si Muang." Although the ancient figure grew weatherworn and featureless, the village attracted small numbers of curious Buddhist priests. In 1907 Ban Si Muang was given a single short paragraph in *Le Monde's Travelers Guide to Indochina,* which attracted numbers of adventuresome European tourists and swelled the numbers of local merchants and vendors. A small hotel was built. Just as proclaimed in the tour book, the villagers were gentle and delightfully shy. The last European tourists had left thirty years ago. When the Pathet Lao guerrillas arrived to set up a small headquarters camp, they'd felt it their duty to promote

communistic atheism and chased away the Buddhist priests.
Those last departures had occurred only six weeks earlier.

The Viet People's Army lieutenant and his four men had
entered the village quite openly in the early afternoon. Then
they'd arrogantly taken hot bread and several ripe mangoes
from a small market and refused to pay, telling the merchant
he should be glad they didn't take more.

A Pathet Lao foot patrol had warily approached, and the
lieutenant had sent the senior sergeant forth to tell them
their truck had broken down several kilometers to the east.
They'd need transportation to go back to retrieve it in the
morning. A short argument had broken out when the Pathet
Lao leader demanded to see their papers, and two of the
Hotdogs joked that AK-47's were all they needed. The
leader had literally screamed in anger. The lieutenant had
raised his own voice and calmed things by showing travel
authorization. The patrol leader couldn't read Viet, but he'd
seemed mollified. The lieutenant had then drawn him aside
for a private talk.

After reaching an agreement, the lieutenant had called
for only the senior sergeant to accompany him. He'd ordered the three others, Black included, to wait in the village
while he and the sergeant accompanied the patrol to their
headquarters camp.

It was an alternative to the strategy they'd worked out,
and the lieutenant had switched to it without explanation.
The original plan called for them to enter the camp together
and demand the woman be turned over. They had hastily
forged documents with the authorizing signature of a senior
Pathet Lao official. As Black had watched the lieutenant and
his sergeant stride toward the camp, he'd known there'd
been a reason for the change. But as minutes and then hours
crawled by and the three of them trudged impatiently about
the dirt-poor village, he'd begun to worry and couldn't keep
his mind from pondering a few *what-ifs*. At 1600 hours he'd
sent a third Hotdog to the Pathet Lao camp, following the
dictates of yet another alternative plan. When they *still*
didn't emerge, he fretted even more.

The previous day Black had forwarded his second letter to the Bangkok embassy, to request political and humanitarian asylum for the members of Hotdog. That was, the
immigration official had written, the best vehicle for such

an unorthodox request. Black hoped the renegades survived long enough to allow the bureaucracy to run its course.

At 1840 hours, when the villagers had begun to withdraw into their stilted thatch houses for the night, Black and the remaining Hotdog had left the village and walked out the road to the south. After a hundred meters they'd stepped off the road and slipped through the jungle for half a kilometer to a prearranged rendezvous point.

There Black had stopped and worried anew about allowing the team to split up. Several times he and the Hotdog checked their weapons. At 0130, if there was still no contact, they'd slip into the camp, locate the Hotdogs, set off claymore mines, rescue Clipper, and withdraw in the confusion. That final alternative was mostly desperation, in the event deception failed.

It was after midnight when they heard the lieutenant's low birdcall, answered, and watched the three men slip into the tiny clearing.

"The woman is gone," the lieutenant whispered. "We had to wait for the interrogator I met on our last trip. He delivered her to a night convoy on a roadway east of us."

"When?"

"He took her yesterday and delivered her to the convoy leader late this morning. He was angry, because he felt the woman was weakening and about to talk."

"Where is she being taken?"

"North. That was all they would tell him."

Black blew a single long breath. So close!

"Were they suspicious of you?" he finally asked.

"They remembered us from the time before. They're frightened of the Viet People's Army. The Lao know who to look up to."

"Go on."

"I told them Hanoi had ordered me to check on the Mee woman as we went by Ban Si Muang. The camp commandant was anxious for us to leave. When Nguyen came to tell us you had gotten a radio call that our truck was repaired and on the way, the commandant was so relieved he began to laugh out loud. When I continued waiting, he kept asking if we should not hurry in case the truck might miss us. After the interrogator arrived and I questioned him, they were too joyous about our departure to be suspicious."

"Good," Black said.

"I do not feel good about this, Sarge Brack," said the lieutenant. "I do not belive we will hear about the woman again."

"There is nothing more we can do. Prepare to leave."

"I need to rest for a moment," young Nguyen complained, still huffing. "We ran all the way here."

"You are soft," said the senior sergeant. The others liked to joke that Nguyen was a slothful youth.

The lieutenant remained sad. "If we had come just two days earlier, we would have her."

At least, thought Black, Clipper won't be here when the gunships come to destroy the camp. "Let us return to the river," he said.

"In file," the senior sergeant ordered gruffly.

As they formed, then set off in the quick-shuffle gait that People's Army soldiers were trained to use, Black forced himself to shift his mind from the woman's plight to the training he needed to instill in Hotdog. Regardless of failure, the exercise had gone well, but he wanted them in better physical condition when they deployed on the recon patrol in two weeks. It would likely be their last one together.

1000L—Hanoi, DRV

Deputy Minister Li Binh

They'd met often in the past weeks, and Nguyen Wu performed his task with a newfound authority that drove her to the brink of madness. She glowed from his attentions.

Her nephew lay on his back, spent from exertion.

"The Laotians insist on keeping the Mee spy," she told him.

"Have they . . ." He waited to catch his breath before continuing. "Have they finally . . . agreed upon a location?"

"I insisted on a specific place, nephew. I do not want you in danger."

"Thank you, beloved aunt. May I ask where?"

"A village called Ban Sao Si. It is in Laos, very near the

border, and Xuan Nha assures me it is heavily defended. You will be taken there in a helicopter."

Nguyen Wu looked troubled. Helicopter travel was dangerous with all the American fighter aircraft about.

"Do not be concerned," Li Binh said soothingly. She felt very protective of her loving nephew. "The Mee will have other things to concern them."

"When shall I depart?" He stroked her thigh, much more sure of himself than he'd been. At first she'd been troubled by his subtle changes—now she was grateful.

"In one week. The woman will not arrive there until then, and you will be safe traveling." She smiled as she thought of the reason. The Mee would indeed be very busy. Then she sobered. "You must succeed, nephew. You must strip her mind of all secrets."

"I will not fail." He continued to move his fingers on her skin.

Li Binh trembled deliciously at his soft touch. She'd also changed. A few weeks earlier she would never have shown such weakness, but back then he'd not yet shown her his new talents.

"Will the Mee woman be under my control, beloved aunt?"

"The Lao insist on having their own man there to watch, and demand that he be in charge of her safety. They have their own purposes when you are done with her."

"That might make my task more difficult. I work best when I can use my own methods."

He traced light fingers through the sparse hairs of her mound. She drew a sharp breath when the butterfly found her clitoris and lingered.

Li Binh arched her back, closing her eyes and allowing the exquisite sensation to grow. Her nephew had wonderful, tapered fingers, and other ways that delighted her as much.

She felt his warm breath on the down of her leg, then as he moved higher. She shuddered as his tongue traced a path on her abdomen.

"Now!"

"Not yet, beloved aunt," came the impudent whisper, and he continued to move the tongue in an ever larger circle.

"Please," she whimpered in a new voice.

He dared to ignore her, continued with tongue and fingers. They moved in unison, lightly, like the wings of . . .

"A butterfly," he whispered. "Do you love it, beloved aunt?"

"Don't stop!"

"Never," he whispered, and the tongue moved subtly, flickered repeatedly, maddeningly.

She arched, reached down and caressed his head, and encouraged him to continue. Then she groaned, trembling and thrashing with the grandness of it, pressing his face to her vagina with all her strength.

The tongue darted into her.

She screamed.

The orgasms continued for ten long and wonderful minutes.

She collapsed onto her back, breathing heavily, drained as never before.

He was also huffing, and telling her of his devotion.

She did not doubt him. As she rose and began to dress, still trembling, Li Binh vowed to keep her nephew from harm . . . forever.

"Beloved aunt," he muttered, and she could tell that he was about to ask for something. He did that now that he'd become bolder.

"Yes?"

"The Commissioner has ordered another man to assume my duties. I am an assistant commissioner in name only now, and soon they will take even that."

"I know. It is a time for patience."

"They do not even care if I report to work. It is very humiliating."

"That is why you must not fail with the Mee spy woman. Return with her secrets and things will change. That will prove to the Lao Dong party how valuable you are. Perhaps . . . you will no longer be only an *assistant* commissioner."

Her nephew smiled despite himself.

"Return with her secrets, my nephew."

"And if she proves difficult? What if the Lao who watch over her do not allow me to get her information?"

"If they interfere too much, send word to me. I have ways to change it."

1500L—Weapons Office, Takhli RTAFB

Colonel Buster Leska

There was a three-hour pause in Buster's schedule, and he took advantage of the respite. He'd received a letter from Carolyn and another from her father, which he would take to his trailer to read in privacy.

In her recent correspondence things had been going well at home, so since there was no urgency, he wanted to linger over and savor her words. Carolyn was good at lifting his spirits.

Before going to the trailer he'd walked across to the operations building to see Jerry Trimble, to ask about things in general and see how he was coping with the change of jobs. Buster liked to do that periodically, pop in on his key people and hold informal court, learn their problems and challenges and try to view things from their eyes. But Jerry was out at one of his fighter squadrons, likely doing the same thing.

Before leaving ops Buster stopped at Manny DeVera's weapons office and looked in. The Supersonic Wetback had been despondent lately, was having problems with his social life since Penny Dwight had decided to forsake all connections with fighter jocks.

Like now. Manny was at his desk, brooding and hardly aware of his surroundings.

"You busy?" Buster asked.

DeVera was quick to gain his feet. "No, sir."

Buster shut the door behind himself and took a seat alongside Manny's desk. "How're things going?"

Manny sat back down, nodding. "We got in twelve new ECM pods this morning from the States. That oughta help."

Buster pointed at a wall map. "We may start flying a few close air-support sorties in South Vietnam. Our units there are getting overwhelmed by all the immediate taskings."

Manny looked at the map. "Oh?"

He should be more interested, Buster thought. "The NVA started attacking in mass at a place called Khe Sanh four days ago, and it's kind of touch and go. We were just alerted that we may have to help the F-4's and F-100's."

"Our guys can handle it. We'll need more snake-eyes though." Snake-eyes were 500-pound bombs with retarding fins that popped out as they were released, giving them high drag, which immediately slowed them down. They could be released lower and closer to the target, and thus were more accurate.

"Check on that with munitions, would you?"

"Yes, sir."

Buster leaned back and regarded him. "You seem awfully down at the mouth."

Manny tried to smile. "Nothing important, Colonel."

Buster knew the cause—his own secretary. "Let me give you a bit of advice from an old pro, Manny. Very few women are cut out to share our kind of life."

Manny nodded, looking miserable.

"It's asking a lot to expect them to put up with our bull-shit. We're a unique group. We fly high-tech killing machines and judge each other by how effectively we destroy things. Not only can we kill the enemy without remorse, we can send friends out to die, and then do it tomorrow and the day after that. In the process we lose some sensitivity."

Manny looked troubled. "I don't believe we're animals."

"Nope, just a bunch of guys who find ourselves in life-or-death situations a lot more often than most. In wartime we find ourselves facing those situations on a daily basis."

Manny's lips were pursed.

"And we shield ourselves from the emotions involved in killing and dying, right?"

"Yes, sir."

"How about a decent woman, whose basic instincts are to nurture life? How do you think she's going to accept our special little pact with death and our flip-flops between duty and social life?"

DeVera frowned.

"We don't *want* them to accept it. We don't want them asking how many gomers we killed today, or how close we came to smacking into the ground. We try to shield them, so they'll never know that sometimes we get so scared we want to puke."

Manny observed him with a pensive look.

"Some women can handle it, most can't." Buster stopped, thinking of his own words, about Carolyn and how grateful he was to have her as his life's partner, but how he couldn't really share all of himself.

"I get your point, boss. It takes a good woman to understand, right?"

"You've got to sift through a *lot* of good ones until you find one who's not going to fold when things get tough."

"What about Penny? You don't think she's right?"

Buster got to his feet, shaking his head. "Who knows, Manny? I just thought you should know where she's coming from. She's a decent girl and she's been through a lot. She's had to do a lot of growing up in a short time. You can see the difference. Penny's a different person from when she got here."

"Yeah," Manny muttered.

"And if you haven't figured it out, females are different." *That* was his point.

After the sermon Buster went by the class-six store, where booze and soft drinks were sold. He purchased several packs of soda and carried them to his trailer, put some in the refrigerator and the remainder in a cabinet.

He then placed the two letters on the dinette table and eyed them as he popped the lid on an orange soda.

Buster had called home on Christmas day and enjoyed brief conversations with Carolyn and Mark, who'd spent a portion of his school break there.

In her earlier letters, Carolyn had written that Christmas with Mark had been a delightful time, made better by the fact that he appeared normal, and not at all like the horrible dope-head she'd envisioned he was becoming. He'd even gotten a haircut of sorts, although it would still be too long for Buster's liking, and had dressed in clean jeans and tie-dyed T-shirts. She'd told Buster how she'd tried to fatten him up, for their son was becoming skinny to a fault.

Mark had developed a passion for the Beatles, she'd written, and she was beginning to come around. Their music wasn't all that bad, she said, although she didn't really understand what their latest hit, "Strawberry Fields, Forever," was really about, and she still preferred their old Frank Sinatra and Perry Como records.

"Me too, Carrie," Buster said to her unopened letter.

When Carolyn wanted to put him in a proper mood, she'd pull on a sexy black nightgown, put on some soft Sinatra; then her eyes would go soft and he'd begin snorting like a bull. He guzzled soda pop. He remembered Carolyn smiling the secret way she did when they'd just finished, whispering how happy and in love she was.

God, but he was horny.

He envied the young studs who visited the ladies in Ta Khli village to lighten their loads. He'd done that during his first combat tour in Korea, before he'd returned and married Carolyn. On his second tour he'd abstained. Except in his mind a few times, he'd never cheated on her, even though trysts with ladies of the evening weren't generally regarded so much as cheating, but rather a physical necessity. While broad-minded toward others, Buster had never been able to really differentiate or rationalize the act for himself. Cheating was cheating.

Fighter pilots, especially those who were presentable or on their way up through the system, seldom had to search for opportunities to take women to bed. Females of varying degrees of beauty, wealth, and even chastity, were vulnerable. For some it was the way the men lived in constant danger. With others the attraction wasn't definable. The devoutly pacifist wife of their church's pastor had once whispered to Buster that she was available. The normally shy daughter of a local politician had been caught *en flagrante* in the bachelor officers' quarters of an East Coast fighter base. She'd knocked on doors at random and offered, then provided, oral and vaginal sex to more than a dozen junior-officer pilots. Those were not unique incidents. Women were readily available to them.

Buster Leska didn't partake. He preferred to remember the Sinatra songs and Carrie in her glazed-eye moods. He loved her as intensely now as he had when they'd married.

Time for his prize. He had another hour to savor the letters.

The best, he decided, should come last. Buster opened the one from her father.

It was short and direct. He was advised to come home immediately. Carolyn needed his help with Marcus.

Shit! Buster immediately tore open the second letter. It was neatly typed on Carolyn's personalized light-blue stationery.

January 16th

Dear Buster,

   I hate to trouble you with family
problems when you already face such
great challenges, but I simply cannot keep
the truth from you any longer and I must have
your advice.

   I am beside myself with worry and pray
daily for strength to continue.

   While I didn't lie in my previous letters about
Mark's appearance and his promises to
improve, you should also know that he had
been placed on probation by the end of last
semester. He failed to attend most classes or
to turn in the required papers, and
received incompletes or failures in four of
his five courses.

   I was notified last week that he was being
suspended for disrupting two classes he
wasn't signed for. Mark and several others
showed up shouting that the instructors were
"warmongers" and splattered chicken blood
on them and the podium.

   The school demanded that he depart the
campus immediately.

   This news came from a new, quite
unsympathetic counselor. When I tried to
telephone Mark, his roommate evaded my
questions and would only tell me he was gone.
I've since been advised that the roommate
was also suspended.

   I immediately prepared to travel to New
York to locate Mark and bring him home, but
was then called by the NY police. Mark has
been identified as a participant involved
in the burning of a campus police car.
When they went to his dorm room, some of
his clothing had been taken and he was gone,
and the police are demanding to know his
present location.

Page 2.

I did not know where he was, of course,
and was beside myself with worry. I still am.

Mark finally called last night, Buster. He
sounded quite intoxicated and refused to
tell me where he was calling from. He just
kept saying he was okay and not to worry.
He said the campus police were fascist pigs
and other things which weren't at all like
him. When I told him you'd be worried sick,
he said he could no longer call you father,
for you'd been lied to so much that you'd
become a part of the system. Then he said
good-bye, that he had a bus to catch.

What do I do, Buster? I telephoned my
parents, but father just says to have you
come back to straighten things out, that
it's not all my burden to shoulder.

I realize that you can't do that, and I probably
shouldn't even write this letter, but I have
no one else to turn to who will understand.
I don't dare leave the house for fear I'll miss
a call from Mark, or from a hospital telling
me he's sick or has been hurt.

I have been through other crises, and
know you think I am strong, but I am beginning
to doubt everything. I love you dearly, and
miss you so much that I cry constantly.
I've never felt more helpless.

Forever yours,

Your Carrie

Buster reread the letter twice more. Then he took a deep
breath and picked up the phone. He told the command-post
sergeant to place an immediate call to the Pentagon operator
and have them patch through to his home telephone.

Friday, January 26th, 0720 Local—Nakhon Phanom Air Base, Thailand

Black and Captain Torgeson, leader of the seven-man Banjo LRRP team, were seated alone before the briefers, who were detailing specifics for the op.

The area of interest was the mountaintop TACAN station at Yankee 21, as Black had hoped. The first speaker was the major, XO of the C-Team headquarters unit for Command and Control–Central, who gave the mission objectives and overview.

It was improbable that they'd get choppers to use on the op. Although the major didn't explain, Black knew things were frantic on the NVA supply routes, and there was a tremendous effort underway to intercept and slow the traffic. Every available LRRP team was being used as trail-watch teams or to place detection sensors, which meant the HH-3's were busy.

"Special Ops C-130?" the Banjo leader asked hopefully.

"More likely by a contractor C-123."

"Air America?"

"Probably Air South or one of the others."

That news was not so good. Air Force Special Ops, Air America, and Bird and Son crews were generally very good. Most of the others, although also under op control of MAC-SOG, were regarded as CIA "Sunday help" and not always deemed reliable.

The major's pointer tapped on a rugged mountain immediately north of the village of Ban Sao Si. "Yankee five-four will be the observation post and base camp. The Viets are also using the mountain, but high-altitude recce photos show them farther down, with a good path leading down to the village but poor access to the top. I doubt they send patrols up there, but you'll have to set up as if they do.

"Banjo will be dropped in here, twenty-two kilometers northeast of the observation post. After they're inserted, Hotdog will be dropped in twenty klicks due north of the O-P. You can both take up to eight hours to get into position." The XO gave detailed instructions on how to proceed to Yankee 54 by the most surreptitious routes from the two DZs, then the routines, signals, and passwords to be used for join-up.

The S-2 intell officer took over. He gave times of radio transmissions, more code words, cache sites, and suspected enemy troop locations. The dirt strip at Ban Sao Si had been cleared and improved, and was being used by occasional light aircraft and helicopters from Hanoi. That was one place they wanted examined in detail. They also wanted to know specifically where the SA-7 Strela missiles and 37mm antiaircraft guns were located, and about all troop concentrations. They estimated there were 500 Viet militia remaining, but weren't at all sure because of the dense jungle canopy south and east of the flattop mountain.

They were shown all known farm villages and locations where Ma tribesmen had set up hunting and foraging camps.

"That's a major concern," said the intell captain. "If it was just the Viets, the Air Force would bring in their heavies and bomb the shit out of the place. But there are as many as five thousand civilians scattered through the area. Before the zoomies arrive, they've got to know which locations to avoid just as well as where to bomb."

Air Force? Black raised a hand for attention. "I thought Vientiane Control had operational control of the area."

The XO stepped forward to answer. "Not for this one. The Air Force is going to bring in their best, and enough of it to make sure the job gets done. They want the nav site back and told Vientiane to butt out. General Moss at Seventh Air Force raised hell with MAC-SOG and told them he doesn't want an Air America contract T-34 anywhere near the place until his fighters have pacified it. He didn't even want us in there. MAC-V stepped in and there's been a compromise."

Captain Torgeson frowned. "If the Air Force wants to handle the air effort, why can't we get an Air Force bird to drop us in?" He, like Black, did not trust all of the CIA contractors.

"Like I said, it's a compromise. It's not really a joint op, because there's clear dividing lines. MAC-SOG handles the surveil, which means we send you guys in. After you've taken a close look, we call up the Air Force and tell 'em it's their game. They come in and lay on the bombs. We take over again—sanitize the mountain, and leave a detachment there as nursemaids. Then they bring in new nav equipment and an installation team. Clear lines of authority and responsibility."

"So what if we get in trouble up there?" Captain Torgeson asked.

"The Air Force is putting fighters on one-hour cockpit alert at Ubon Air Base."

"We can't talk to 'em on our radios."

"Your team will carry a UHF portable radio. They're also putting an airborne forward air controller on alert at a Lima site up north of here. Same people who'll be coordinating the bombing. You can talk to the O-1 pilots on button B of your VHF hand-held."

Sergeant Black was pleased. This time it looked as if they'd get the air support required.

The XO nodded to the S-2 intell briefer, who resumed where he'd left off. "Ban Sao Si is a farm village, with several hundred noncombatants. The people there probably don't get along very well with the Viets, since they've bickered for the past thousand years or so, but they're outgunned all to hell. Just a couple hundred yards away from the village, adjacent to the airstrip, there are new structures we know to be militia targets. We believe it's the same throughout the area. Good guys and bad guys almost side by side. That will be job one, to pinpoint everything."

As the end of the briefing approached, the XO stood before them again.

"Banjo will drop in one hour before Hotdog. Two hours later the team leaders will make initial radio contact. Keep it abbreviated. A max of seven hours later, you'll join hands at Yankee five-four. Black will run the surveillance effort, and Captain Torgeson the comm and housekeeping."

"I thought I was in charge of the patrol," Torgeson complained. He was a new captain, a West Point graduate, and after the patrol was finished, was in line to command a twelve-man A-Team, the most coveted job for a Special Forces company-grade officer. He had reservations about going out with the renegades, and—as far as he knew—Black was an E-6 NCO.

The XO raised his palms, as if it were beyond his control. "That's the way the old man wants it, okay? Black's got the surveillance, you've got the communications, housekeeping, and any required firepower."

Torgeson still did not look happy about it.

"Don't worry," Black said smoothly. "My guys'll stay out of your hair."

Captain Torgeson, however reluctantly, agreed.

1100L—Pave Dagger Test Headquarters, Ubon RTAFB

Captain Moods Diller

Moods stood before the group of Pave Dagger civilian engineers and enlisted technicians and the two F-4 aircrews borrowed from the host wing. He could still feel the marks left by his tight-fitting oxygen mask, as well as the tension of flight, although they'd shut down engines more than an hour earlier. It had been their third test mission.

In both the first and second flights the designator pod had developed problems, for the circuitry hadn't taken well to the high humidity of Southeast Asia. The Texas team had repotted everything and recharged the black boxes with super-dry nitrogen. That had robbed them of three days, and time had become their number-one enemy.

Major Benny Lewis came in and gave a nod and wave of his hand to get on with the briefing. He'd been called out of the room for a phone call, and they'd been waiting for him.

Moods plunged ahead. "We went out with three birds. I was flying with the illuminator pod, and both of the other F-4Ds were carrying Mark 84 Pave Dagger bombs."

Moods turned and pointed to the target photos—two small wooden bridges, a river pier, and a coastal dock area, all in route pack two—blown up to many times their original size.

"Those're the culprits-we-went-after. Biggest problem was-locatin' th'-dam-thing."

The F-4 aircrews from across the field looked at one another in consternation.

"Better slow down, Moods," Lewis told him. "I don't think they've been around you long enough to understand you when you're excited and talking about your toys."

Moods took a breath and nodded, then slowed down his speech to what seemed a snail's crawl. "The small bridge in this photo was our first target. After we arrived, I set up a right-hand orbit at 6,000 feet, and my GIB turned on the illuminator. Soon as he was slewed and fixed on the target he called 'mark,' and the first shooter activated the first bomb, entered a thirty-degree dive attack, got a lock-on light, then released bomb number one."

The pilot of the second shooter aircraft approached the photo of target number one and drew in a large X just to the right of the target. He pointed. "My GIB took movie footage of the sequence, and the film's still being developed. But I watched it all the way down. Everything looked right on until just before impact, then the bomb's path flattened and it hit just a little long."

"What happened to the bridge?" asked a technician.

"A two-thousand-pound bomb hitting that close? Blew it all to hell."

There were several cheers.

Moods shook his head. "Not good enough, guys. Thirty feet isn't what we're after."

He nodded at the photos. "We went on to the second target, a couple of miles downstream, and did the same thing there. We illuminated, and they released bomb number two."

The pilot who'd marked the first impact walked to the second photo and examined it.

The Pave Dagger people watched pensively.

The pilot cocked his head and dragged out his words dramatically. "I think it hit about . . ."

He grinned and made a neat X at the center of the bridge.

". . . there."

The room erupted in cheers and good-natured banter.

Moods waited until they'd quieted. "Same thing happened with the other two bombs. One near miss and one direct hit."

The borrowed pilots shook their heads in amazement. "Fan-damn-tastic!" said a GIB.

"We've got to find the problem with the two misses," Mood said, frowning and peering out at the room.

"We'll find the problem," said the pudgy senior Texas-team engineer.

"Some problem," muttered the F-4 GIB. "Best damn bombs I've ever seen."

Benny Lewis appeared pleased. Moods walked over to him.

"Not a bad start," Benny said. "Congratulations."

"I want ninety percent hits. *Then* I'll feel good about it."

"You've got twenty-six bombs to go, Moods."

"Yeah."

"You better hurry up and get more test missions in," Benny told him. "There's a holiday bombing pause coming up in four days. That's what the phone call was about."

Moods was puzzled. "What holiday?"

"It's called Tet. Sort of like our Christmas. Washington, the South Vietnamese government, and Hanoi all agree. No ground action or bombing missions for a week."

CHAPTER THIRTY

Tuesday, January 30th, 0545 Local—Tan Son Nhut Air Base, South Vietnam

Lieutenant Colonel Pearly Gates

The blaring Klaxon horns woke him first. Then, through the thick fog of deep slumber, Pearly realized the shouting and rushing of personnel, and even the distant reverberations and whooshing sounds were not a part of his dream.

A voice shouted over a loudspeaker to take cover.

Pearly rolled out of bed and shook his head, then groggily began pulling on a fresh shirt and a pair of trousers.

Whooosh. Whump-whump-whump.

His mind registered then, and he grabbed a pair of boots and slipped them on as he pulled the door open. People were rushing down the hall.

The full impact hit him . . . they were under attack . . . the sounds were incoming rockets and artillery. His heart pumped wildly—he felt giddy with excitement and fear.

The pistol! Pearly went back inside, pulled on a drawer, and grabbed the issue .38 Special revolver. He hurried out and down the hallway, joining the mob, bootlaces flapping, gun belt slung over his shoulder.

"Where the hell's our shelter?" someone new shouted.

"Downstairs and out the south entrance! There's a bunker!"

"Go! Go! Go!"

Whump-whump-whump-whump. Much louder. The building rattled ominously.

"What the fuck?"

"Jesus!"

Pearly was hotfooting it with the others toward the south end of the building, heart still thumping, urging the guys in front of him to move faster when he remembered . . .

She said she slept like the dead. A bigger fear crawled into his stomach. He broke off at the next exit and began to take the stairs three and four at a time. The loose right boot crumpled and he sprawled, yelled hoarsely, fell hard against a wall before he steadied himself. Pain shot through his right ankle.

He hobbled on, wincing with each step but not delaying.

Sirens and another Klaxon horn joined the initial hubbub. *Whump-whump-whump.* Distant again. The lights in the stairwell flickered on and off.

Out the door into the morning gloom, then to his right. He lurched along faster, past the end of the field-grade officers' BOQ.

A voice yelled for him to get into a fucking shelter. He ignored it and continued, heart pounding wildly. He'd talked with her until midnight, sipping Grand Marnier and sharing small thoughts. Today was supposed to be an easy one, with the Tet truce and suspension of all bombing. And she'd said she slept like . . .

A tremendous boom resonated, and he could see dark smoke billow beyond he next BOQ building. *Jesus it was close!*

He saw a line of people crowding into a sandbagged bunker and slowed. She'd more likely be in the next one, but he paused at the bunker entrance and yelled her name.

"Come on inside, dammit!" someone bellowed.

"Lieutenant Dortmeier!" he called again.

A distant explosion sounded like rumbling thunder.

"Get out of the way!" someone yelled.

No response from Lucy.

Pearly stepped back, and three guys pushed past him

into the bunker. Ignoring the bolts of fiery pain that shot
through the ankle, he hobbled on past the length of her
building and to the next bunker. A captain stood just inside
its mouth with his M-16 ready, looking scared. He peered
hard at Gates before deciding he wasn't a Cong. Pearly
shoved by him and bellowed her name.

"Here!"

A shape came from the black depths of the bunker. "Colonel?"

"Yeah," said Pearly, huffing with the exertion. "You okay?"

"Yes, sir." She was fully clothed and not nearly as disheveled as he was.

Pearly took a painful step, and she told a captain to move
over for her colonel, then asked him to sit down. He did.
When the pressure left the ankle, it felt wonderful.

"Sprained the damned thing," he told her.

Another series of explosions.

She knelt before him, pulled off the loose boot, and gingerly felt his ankle. "It's swollen twice its normal size."

Pearly slowly regained his wind, then released a long
breath and stared at the entrance. "Gotta go."

"That's crazy," she said. "We're under attack, Colonel."

"It's a major one," he agreed. "Never been in one this
big." He didn't want to go back outside.

"I thought we were in some kinda truce," someone
nearby said.

"Tell that to the Cong," someone else answered.

"Lace up the boot, would you?" Pearly asked Lucy.

She slipped the boot over the swollen ankle and began to
gingerly pull on the laces. "Where are you going?"

"Tactical Air Control Center. They'll be busy as hell if
this thing's big as I think. MAC-V's been picking up enemy
movement all around the country, but they thought the attacks would come later." He grunted at the pressure on the
ankle. "Lace it tighter."

She did, and he grimaced as dull pain pulsed with his
heartbeat.

He blew a couple of breaths. "Yeah, like that."

Whooosh. Whump-whump-whump. Pearly felt the earth
shake.

She tied the knot and began to secure the other boot.
"I'm coming along," she said.

"I don't think so. They're only supposed to have key staff there. Anyway, I don't want you out in the open."

"I'm coming," Lucy said stubbornly. "I'll help you walk."

Fifteen minutes after they left the bunker, they approached another, much larger underground facility. The snout of an M-60 .30-caliber machine gun protruded from sandbags piled about the entrance. The steel-helmeted security-police weapons crew eyed them warily as they approached in the sparse light. Another SP waved them forward.

Inside the TACC Pearly hobbled toward the fighter-duty station, where General Moss was speaking to a captain and his full-bull chief of staff.

Moss spotted him. "Where the hell have you been?"

"Had to check on Lucy to make sure she was okay."

"Yeah," Moss muttered as if that were a good excuse, then turned back to his conversation.

Pearly interrupted. "They're holding her at the door. She's not on the access list."

Moss turned to his chief of staff. "Straighten that out. Tell 'em to let her in."

"Yes, sir," the colonel said, and went toward the entrance.

"How big is it, General?" Pearly asked.

"Danang, Bien Hoa, and Cam Ranh are reporting artillery attacks, but we don't know how bad off they are. Lots of confusion. MAC-V command center's too busy to answer, so when things calm down, we'll send runners." MAC-V was also located on Tan Son Nhut, not far distant.

"I'd better call the Thailand bases and have 'em load out and prepare to back up the in-country fighters, sir."

"Yeah, you do that."

"More status reports coming in from the units, General," said the captain.

Pearly left them and went to his emergency station, where he took his seat and pulled a telephone closer. He opened the reference notebook he kept at the position and started to go over munitions stored at the various bases.

Lucy Dortmeier came over and sat beside him. "How can I help, sir?"

"Just sit there, watch, and learn," he said. Pearly nodded out toward the large room, with the multiple Plexiglas status boards and maps. Emergency action officers were continuing to arrive, but they knew their duties, and the place looked less and less like a center of confusion.

"This is where they run the air war," Pearly told her.

At one status board the air bases under attack were being listed. Five were shown, then a sixth. "We're going to be busy," said Pearly.

He telephoned the command post at the first Thailand base on his list.

1500L—Command Post, Ubon RTAFB, Thailand

Major Benny Lewis

The Ubon Command and Control Center was crowded with key personnel, who listened raptly as each new report came out of Saigon.

The varying accounts were confusing, the best analysis offered in a running dialogue by an intelligence officer, a lieutenant who seemed able to put it all together in some perspective. NVA and Viet Cong were attacking ARVN and U.S. Forces bases throughout South Vietnam, but the majority of enemy successes were being reported in the provincial capitals. *Every* provincial capital. They were already calling it the Tet offensive, for it was the first day of the Buddhist holiday season.

Benny pushed his way through to the forefront of the room, then paused as the wing commander was briefed on the status of his F-4's. He had forty-four Phantoms airborne, on their way to and from targets in South Vietnam. New targets were being called in over nonsecure lines, as happens only with emergency tasking.

A break came in the activity.

"Colonel?" Benny asked.

The wing commander nodded in recognition.

"I'd like to offer our support, sir. We can give you accuracy on the tough targets."

The wingco grunted. "Couldn't do that, Lewis, even if we wanted to. You're not listed in the tasking orders coming out of Saigon, and neither are your munitions."

"Yes, sir, I know. I was wondering if you could get us added to the ATOs."

"Everything's immediate tasking right now. If Seventh tells us to use you, we will, but I don't have time to screw with the system. We'd just confuse things worse than they are."

A duty officer yelled out that Seventh was asking for a diversion of two flights of fighters. An airborne FAC had multiple targets near Hue. Tanks.

Perfect for the smart bombs, Benny thought. They could pinpoint-bomb the tanks and stop them cold. "Sir—" Benny began, but the wing commander waved him away.

"Dammit," Benny muttered. There had to be some way to get Pave Dagger included in the ATO.

He went to the rear of the room, found a free telephone, and tried to raise the TACC in Saigon. With the emergency situation the duty officers were discussing classified subjects in the clear. He'd have to do the same. The scrambler phone was in constant use.

He tried to get through a total of thirteen times, but was repeatedly cut off. Finally the TACC answered.

Benny asked to speak with Lieutenant Colonel Gates. Another wait.

Pearly came onto the phone, speaking crisply. "Gates here."

"This is Major Lewis, Pearly. Benny Lewis."

"Shoot."

"We've got twenty smart bombs ready to go, Pearly, and we can build ten more. Give us a tasking. We can bomb their eyes out."

"I'm too damned busy to even think about you guys right now. We've got people in deep shit all over the country. I'll get in touch when this is over."

Benny rushed his words. "We can help, Colonel. Give us a couple tough ones and—"

The line was dead.

Lewis hung up, disgusted.

The intell lieutenant was relaying new information. The U.S. embassy in Saigon had been attacked by Viet Cong, and they were inside the building. MAC-V reported that ARVN ground forces had been pushed out of Hué, Quang Tri, and Dalat. Fighting was also heavy in the delta.

"We've gotta launch two more flights of Fox fours," announced a duty officer. "Waterboy control's saying they've got new targets."

Benny listened a while longer, then left the command post and drove to the Pave Dagger building, where the team was busily preparing for action.

He told them to slow down their efforts. Their modified birds were to be used to drop regular munitions by unit pilots.

"I offered our services," he told them resignedly, "but we were turned down."

Moods looked bleak.

"How's it going in South Vietnam?" asked the senior Texas-team engineer.

"The good guys are getting stung. NVA and Viet Cong attacking everywhere."

CHAPTER
THIRTY-ONE

Wednesday, January 31st, 0915 Local—Western Mountains, DRV

Assistant Commissioner Nguyen Wu

As the big Russian helicopter churned westward over the high mountains, Wu felt not in the least threatened. Just as his beloved aunt had promised, the Mee had bigger concerns than a single helicopter. The news of the attacks was exhilarating; for the second day brave communist forces were challenging the Americans and the Saigon puppet army throughout South Vietnam. Hanoi radio announcers exulted that the people of the South were rising up to fight shoulder to shoulder with the heroic liberators of the People's Army, determined to throw out the hated Mee invaders and defeat their traitorous lackeys.

The enemy was on the defensive. While Saigon teetered on the brink, provincial capitals throughout the country had fallen to the Viet People's Army and their Popular Front Liberation Army allies. In each city, traitors were being executed and provisional governments established.

A glorious time for the Democratic Republic! A time of vindication for Nguyen Wu as well, he thought happily. His trip was secret, and only a handful knew what he was about. After he broke the Mee woman and returned with her information, he'd bring yet another victory for his country. Like victorious commanders in the South, he'd be extolled by Lao Dong party elders.

His beloved aunt had provided this chance for redemption, and he'd not fail her. He had absolutely no doubt that the Mee woman would break and tell her secrets. He was a master at such things.

As the flight droned on, Nguyen observed his strange new staff. No longer in favor at the Ministry of Internal Affairs, he'd been forced to search elsewhere for people, but no one had wanted to cooperate with the disgraced assistant commissioner. Li Binh had helped finally, asking her husband if Nguyen Wu could "borrow" a few of his officers.

Xuan Nha had told her he too was pressed by shortages of personnel. There was talk of a retaliatory invasion by the Mee, he'd said, and if that happened, his militia would be the front line of defense. He'd finally offered these two, who were all he would spare.

Wu had felt he'd been cheated by the selection of the men. After questioning them at some length, he'd confirmed that Xuan Nha had done him no favors.

One was a bureaucratic administrative officer, a major who'd been relieved of his duties due to incompetence. The major would record the details of their mission—according to Nguyen Wu's interpretations, of course—and document what the woman said when she began to tell her secrets. He'd told him to write down everything. Now the man sat near the helicopter door, clutching his courier bag of pens and notepads as a combat soldier might his rifle.

The other man was a grotesquely fat and ill-mannered sergeant who had blubbered with gratitude when offered the new option. He'd raped and murdered two peasant women in Haiphong who had scorned his advances. A third woman he'd attacked had lived to identify him, and he'd been on his way to join a People's Army convict battalion, to be used as a beast of burden, carrying great loads of dangerous munitions southward on the trails. Little food was wasted on the convicts, for as soon as they reached the war zone, they were plied with opium, strapped with explosives, and pushed toward enemy positions. The obese sergeant had been selected because he spoke English.

Beyond his duties as an interpreter, Wu had at first thought the piglike sergeant to be useless, but after reconsideration he wondered. He'd undoubtedly be loyal to the man who'd saved him from certain death, and his proclivity for violence might be . . . useful. There would be no change to Wu's formula for obtaining confessions: degradation, starvation, and intense pain. He doubted the sergeant would hesitate at any of those treatments on the Mee woman.

After a miserable hour of flight they passed over the final high mountain chain of Vietnam, and the terrain quickly gave way to the green foothills of easternmost Laos. Nguyen moved up between the two pilots and stared ahead.

The tiny village of Ban Sao Si was nestled in a valley between two foliage-clad mountains. The one on their right was tall, but not special. The other, south of the village, was dramatic, flat-topped and sheer on all sides, with deep ravines gouged into limestone by aeons of water runoff. This was the mountain where Xuan Nha's militia had relentlessly shot down Mee aircraft before scaling the steep cliffs and overrunning the enemy force.

Wu noted the scorched earth and pockmarks left by artillery rounds and enemy bombs. The place of the militia's glorious victory, which would likely bring Xuan Nha another promotion. His own victory would take place in the tiny village in the mountain's shadow, and his reward would be as great as Xuan Nha's. His beloved aunt would see to it.

The helicopter landed at one side of the earthen airstrip. The rotor blades were still clattering to a stop when Nguyen Wu stepped out the door and surveyed the area.

There were two newly constructed wooden buildings nearby, a thatch village beyond.

The fat sergeant huffed up behind him, groaning under the weight of both of their bags.

The major joined them and stared about with wide eyes. He'd never been this far from the Hanoi headquarters, and had certainly never seen a rude encampment like the one before them.

Militia soldiers wandered aimlessly about the open area.

"Poor discipline," Nguyen Wu muttered. He began to think of how he should upbraid the senior officers, then remembered that he could no longer do that. His superiors were searching for excuses to rid themselves of him, delayed only by Li Binh's periodic interference. He no longer carried a letter of authority, describing limitless power over civilians and demanding cooperation by military commanders. There was only a note provided by Xuan Nha at his aunt's encouragement, stating that Nguyen Wu was to be provided sustenance and the means to accomplish his task.

His reduced authority was made apparent when he went to the headquarters building to meet with the camp commandant and was summarily shuffled off to an unsmiling captain, who acted as if he had more important duties than being nursemaid to an obscure Hanoi bureaucrat and his obviously inept staff. They were shown an unkempt office in the second building by the captain, who then pointed out locations of air-raid shelters, feeding and latrine facilities, and a nearby vacant area where they could set up camp. A gang of impressed local laborers would be available to build a sleeping hut and whatever else they might require.

The major, still staring at the sandbagged bunkers, nervously asked about the air raids he'd mentioned. The captain said there'd been a few since their victory over the Americans, but none here. He motioned at the stark, flat-topped mountain with a look of satisfaction.

After the captain left, Nguyen Wu looked over the open area, then turned to the two men. "Have the workers construct three huts. Two for sleeping, and another for interrogation." The major dutifully wrote down Nguyen's order.

Wu motioned at the building housing their office. "Have them build a table at one side of the room, and a small cage in the corner for the woman," he told the sergeant.

The obese sergeant looked about as the major scribbled. "At once!" Wu barked.

The sergeant waddled away, wheezing with the effort.

"Now," Nguyen Wu said to the major, "we await the woman's arrival."

1100L—VPA Headquarters, Hanoi, DRV

Colonel Xuan Nha

Massive ground battles were continuing on schedule throughout the South. Since the Mee were using all their aircraft to avert disaster there, the Democratic Republic was free of air attack.

Only for the present, Xuan Nha reminded himself. The Mee would soon come north in angry response, and his rocket-and-artillery forces must be prepared to greet them. He'd sent messages to battalion and area commanders, exhorting them to use the respite to prepare.

But other matters also nibbled at Xuan Nha's mind. No one any longer questioned that Xuan Nha would be named as successor to General Luc. His position within the power structure was entrenched, more secure than ever before. He was not at all a political man, but he knew the time had come to deal with enemies.

There was an ambitious colonel within the Army of National Defense who was senior to Xuan Nha—the Commandant of Militia, who had too often questioned Xuan Nha's decisions. His supporter within the general staff was General Luc, who hovered at death's door. Xuan Nha signed an order relieving the colonel of his Hanoi position and reassigning him to a newly created important post guarding the southern borders and beaches from invasion. The colonel's headquarters would be established at Dong Hoi, a few kilometers from their southern border. Xuan Nha ordered that the reassignment be featured in *Nham Dan,* the official newspaper of the Lao Dong party.

The colonel and his headquarters would certainly become targets for assassination teams sent to vulnerable areas of the Democratic Republic by the Saigon government. He'd be kept busy surviving, and that far from Hanoi he'd present no further arguments to Xuan Nha's directives.

Then there was Nguyen Wu, who had foolishly continued to shame him by meeting with his wife in his own household. Quon had told him he must take a stand, and he knew it was so. This matter must be handled with discretion, for he didn't dare to confront Li Binh's authority openly. Yet the time seemed appropriate, with Wu so far from the sanctuary of Hanoi.

He wrote a note to Quon by hand, explaining that the source of their "mutual shame," whom he would subsequently call an "official," had been helicoptered to Ban Sao Si that morning. He told what he knew of Wu's mission, to interrogate a Mee woman held by the Pathet Lao, and that he didn't yet know when he was to return.

The courier took the sealed note to Gia Lam airfield, where Quon had set up his new offices. He returned with a simple response from the fighter-pilot commandant, asking that he be kept abreast of the "official's" schedule.

1850L—O' Club Dining Room

GS-7 Penny Dwight

Rudy sat across from her, avidly rambling on about what he'd heard of the events in South Vietnam. The Tet offensive was on everyone's lips at the base.

They'd finished dinner and were killing time before heading to the base theater to catch the seven o'clock movie, which starred Elvis Presley. Forget the story line, Penny loved just watching Elvis. She remembered thinking that Manny DeVera had the same ultrasexy smile.

As he droned on, Penny grew increasingly bored with Rudy's conversation. She knew what was happening with the offensive, because she had access to classified messages and reports that he did not. Like the fact that a team of VC had taken over the bottom floors of a wing of the U.S. embassy in Saigon, trapping a number of government workers above them. American paratroopers had been landed by helicopter on the roof of the massive building, saving the terrified bureaucrats and wiping out the enemy suicide squad. She also knew that fighting was fierce in some areas of Saigon, as it was in the various provincial capitals. The pressure on the American bases was fast being relieved by air strikes and artillery, followed by mop-up action by ground forces, but fighting in most of the country was being borne by the ARVN, and American commanders had their fingers crossed that they'd fight.

But she let Rudy continue to tell her his version of what was happening, and tried to show interest in his analysis that the communists were now so entrenched that it would take a million or more American troops to dislodge them. And that, Rudy said, would create a logistical nightmare. Did she realize how much effort it took to maintain just a thousand new men in a combat zone? How many tons of food, fatigues, and razor blades? How many . . .

Manny DeVera came into the dining room, escorting a blond wearing a miniskirt and an utterly tasteless sleeveless blouse—the Deputy for Maintenance's secretary, whom Penny hadn't previously seen out with a man. She looked back at Rudy and nodded agreeably as he made some point about the mountains of jungle boots, shorts and socks it took to . . . Her eyes moved to the table where Manny pulled the chair out for the blond.

She knew Manny had put in a ten-hour day, then flown twice that afternoon to South Vietnam. Squadron pilots were flying two and three sorties daily to augment the in-country fighters trying to relieve the pressure on beleaguered American and allied soldiers. Penny wondered if Rudy knew the difference between in-country and out-country forces, or even between a sortie and a mission.

She scarcely heard as Rudy changed subjects. Her eyes narrowed as she examined Colonel Armaugh's secretary . . . pretty enough, if somewhat common . . . and if you overlooked the fact that she dressed and acted teenagerish. Manny looked tired and drawn sitting beside her, as if he could go to sleep there at the table; but the girl gushed and laughed as if he should have nothing else on his mind but her prattling.

"Would you believe that, Pen?" Rudy was saying, now also staring at the other table. "He actually believes my men can order something with no justification and not even a stock or part number. Of course he's not trained in logistics, but you'd think a little of it would rub off."

"Who?" she asked.

Rudy frowned, as if she should know. "The guy I'm talking about, Pen. Your old friend Captain DeVera there. He wants the world, and he wants it right now." Rudy hmphed. "He's got a hell of a lot to learn about supply."

"What did he ask for?"

"You're not *listening*, Pen." He sang the word chidingly. "DeVera came in demanding we expedite an order for new electronic test equipment for the avionics and ECM shops, and raised so much hell that my men had to call me for help. Like I told him, we have higher priorities, and anyway, the funds would come out of the DM's account, so an expedite order would have to be authorized by one of *their* account managers, preferably by the colonel himself, and presented by one of *his* people." There was something irritating about the tone of Rudy's voice.

"Manny's just trying to help the maintenance people," Penny tried to explain. "He says they've been ignored far too long. They really like him, and they—"

"So what does that have to do with proper ordering procedures?" Rudy was frowning, perhaps with reason. Penny had told him early on that she wanted absolutely nothing more to do with Manny DeVera. "Anyway . . ." Rudy glanced at her reproachfully, as if he'd been interrupted. "I told Captain DeVera to come back when he's read the directives and knows what he's talking about, and *never* to raise his voice to my people again." He nodded with a hint of triumph, and Penny found herself wanting to defend Manny.

"You might regret that, Rudy."

"And just *why* might I regret it?" Rudy snapped. "I'm right. DeVera's wrong. He was even borderline insubordinate. I did him a favor by making it a simple chewing out. Next time . . ." Rudy nodded knowingly, as if next time he'd fix DeVera good.

"Manny's trying hard to get things done, and the colonels all know it and support him."

"What in the world does *that* have to do with proper ordering procedures?" He was growing increasingly exasperated.

"Nothing." She looked at the twosome again. The girl had her hand on Manny's arm and was leaning close, talking low. She giggled at something he said, as if she'd known him forever and they were . . . lovers? Penny's ears began to burn. She suddenly felt *very* irritated.

Rudy looked at his watch and gave his mouth a final swipe with his napkin. "We'd better get outa here, Pen. The movie starts in ten minutes."

"I'm not going." The swiftness of the decision surprised her.

His brow furrowed. "I thought you wanted to see it."

"Why don't you go alone?" Penny abruptly stood, pawed through her purse, then picked out three dollars and dropped the money on the table. "That should cover my dinner," she said.

"What did I do?" Rudy asked incredulously.

"You will never have an earthly idea," she said . . . as if *she* did . . . and left him with his mouth drooping.

"Pen?" he called out. Rudy used the pet name because he said it was also a female swan, and she was just as graceful and beautiful. She thought it was silly.

Penny marched resolutely toward the door, wondering why she was being such a snippy bitch. She decided. Men are utter fools, and that's reason enough. Then she stopped, turned, and without thinking further, went directly to the table where Manny DeVera sat with the blond.

The girl was talking, but Manny looked up. "Hi, Penny," he said.

"You are impossible!" she said in an outraged voice.

He looked as puzzled as Rudy.

Penny turned on her heel and stalked out the door, so incensed that tears formed in her eyes.

CHAPTER
THIRTY-TWO

**Monday, February 5th, 0945 Local—Near Quang Tri,
South Vietnam**

Captain Manny DeVera

"Ford zero-one, this is Waterboy," the airborne command
post finally responded.

Manny noted their distance and bearing from the Danang
TACAN before he pressed the throttle-mounted transmit
button. *"Roger, Waterboy. Ford is holding hands with Dodge
in orbit at two zero miles northwest of Delta Alpha Golf.
We've got eight fox one-oh-fives with five-zero minutes of
fuel, loaded with snake-eyes and twenty mike-mike."*

*"Waterboy copies Ford and Dodge flights—eight nickels
carrying full fuel, snakes, and twenty mike-mike. Stand by."*

"Ford and Dodge are standing by."

After a few seconds Waterboy came back on the air. *"Ford
zero-oner, we've got immediate targets. Descend to flight
level zero-fiver-zero and establish orbit at three-two-fiver at
seventy-five miles of Delta Alpha Golf. Contact Patches five-
one bravo on frequency three-two-three-point-six for instructions."*

"Ford lead copies." Manny read back the frequency and

coordinates, then led the eight fighters into a rapid descent, flying northward past Hué toward the new position a few miles offshore from the coastal city of Quang Tri. They set up a right-hand orbit at 5,000 feet, as directed. Manny called the O-1 airborne FAC, call sign Patches five-one bravo, on the new frequency, while he eyeballed dark plumes of smoke rising over the sprawling provincial capital.

"*Ford lead, this is Patches five-one bravo. Confirm you're carrying snakes.*"

Manny told the FAC pilot that six Mk-82 snake-eye bombs were loaded on each bird.

"*Ah roger, Ford lead. I've got you in sight. Turn and fly heading of two-seven-zero.*"

As they approached, Patches five-one bravo directed the Thuds into a racetrack orbit north of the city. Manny spotted the light aircraft flying very low, immediately northwest of them, and told the FAC he had him in sight.

"*We're receiving automatic weapons ground fire in the area, Ford. No big stuff. I've got targets. There's about fifteen tanks in four different groups just off the north-south coastal road.*"

Manny rogered. They'd been prebriefed that tanks had been seen in the area.

"*Keep your eye on me, Ford lead. I'm gonna mark.*" The O-1 wheeled, leveled, dived, and fired a single white phosphorus rocket.

"*Ford zero-one's got your mark in sight,*" Manny radioed.

"*There's three PT-76 light tanks moving south, about three hundred meters north of the mark,*" the Birddog pilot said.

Manny saw dust trails on the road. "*Got 'em, five-one bravo.*"

"*I'll want you to release north to south. Avoid the houses adjacent to the road.*"

"*Roger, north to south.*" Manny extended farther around the arc, keeping an eye on the rising dust.

"*Take 'em out, Fords, but conserve your munitions, because I've got more of 'em for you.*"

"*Ford flight,*" Manny radioed, "*we'll drop two bombs each on the first pass.*" He checked that his switches were properly set for twenty-degree dive bomb and to release in pairs, then turned and nosed over. It would be close-up work, calling for pinpoint accuracy.

The dust plumes grew in the combining glass as he closed—eyes fixed on the targets—flying much lower and slower here than they did over North Vietnam.

He pickled. In the last seconds, as he began pulling up and away, he saw that the tanks had veered off the roadway. A not-so-near miss.

Manny pulled up sharply and went around, jaw tight, watching the bombs released by the second, then the third Thud. The tanks were frantically weaving and turning. Eight aircraft released snake-eyes in pairs. As the bombs dropped away, large fins popped out and slowed their flight . . . and all of them missed. On the second try Dodge two scored a direct hit on a tank. On their third and final release, Manny hit another. When he looked back, it lay on its side next to the road, a streamer of black smoke marking the kill.

Patches five-one bravo called for more flights of fighters, then authorized the Thuds to try their guns while the others were inbound.

Ford and Dodge flights made strafing passes on a second threesome of tanks the FAC pointed out, spewing hails of twenty-millimeter rounds. One tank was stopped dead.

"Good work," the FAC pilot told them as they departed and were replaced by two flights of F-100's. Patches five-one bravo sounded as weary as Manny felt.

"Bullshit," DeVera muttered to himself. Out of fifteen tanks they'd destroyed only two and damaged one.

Before they went off frequency, they heard the FAC tell the F-100's to hold in their orbit, because he no longer had the tanks in sight. He was going to drop down to take a closer look.

"Damn!" Manny said as he switched to their enroute frequency.

Twelve light tanks were still headed into a rendezvous with American and allied soldiers.

1035L—Tactical Air Control Center, Tan Son Nhut Air Base, Saigon, South Vietnam

Lieutenant Colonel Pearly Gates

In the past six days Pearly had spent one thirty-six- and two twenty-four-hour tours in the TACC, and he was tired and irritable, which made the captains and lieutenants attentive whenever "Colonel Grumpy" approached.

The attack on Tan Son Nhut had been dealt with. Shells were no longer landing on the air base, and the runways were open for business. Except for Khe Sanh and a couple of smaller fire bases and outposts in the highlands, NVA and Viet Cong attacks on American positions had been blunted. But there would certainly be more to come, and Pearly wasn't at all happy with the way everything was going.

Fifteen light tanks, PT-76's, the best the Russians had to offer, had been located by an airborne FAC, hurrying brazenly down the coastal highway from the north. Seven flights of fighters, including F-105's, F-4's and F-100's, had been called in to destroy them as they approached Quang Tri. They'd been elusive, darting off roads, behind buildings, and into thickets of trees. It was frustrating that only five had been destroyed and two damaged.

Several more PT-76's had been reported at various locations in the central highlands, five of them not far from Khe Sanh. Were they the same ones? Where were the damn things headed? Those were questions the duty officers tried to resolve for MAC-V, where action officers were hoping for an open confrontation as soon as the city fighting calmed down.

The TACC fighter duty officer had alerted all flying command posts and airborne FAC units, just as the MAC-V command center had alerted their own units and recon patrols, to remain on the lookout for the tanks.

They wanted to know where they were. Pearly wanted to resolve how they'd destroy the damn things once they located them again. He sat with the two pilots, a major and a captain, from his plans and programs branch, trying to come up with answers.

"We're *going* to find the damn things," he said resolutely, "and when we do, this time I want 'em taken out."

"It's not like they're lined up in a big battle formation," explained one of the pilots, "like in World War II. They're in small groups, and these guys are fast. Every time we think we've got 'em cornered, they disappear and pop up somewhere else."

"We found them in the open the one time, and more than half still got away," Pearly grumbled.

"Should've got 'em with guns," the quieter pilot said, "but our guys were loaded with the wrong ammo. High-explosive incendiary instead of armor-piercing incendiary rounds."

"Had the right bombs loaded, though," said the more gregarious major. "Snake-eyes are damned accurate."

"But most of them missed," Pearly reminded him.

"Going after small, fast targets like that, they did well to take out the ones they did."

Pearly remembered something. He motioned to the senior pilot. "Call Major Lewis at Ubon and ask him about their Pave Dagger bombs. See what he says about taking out maneuvering tanks."

The major looked dubious. Neither he nor the other pilot had been overly impressed by the Buck Rogers smart bomb briefings.

"Not next week, dammit," Pearly growled, and the major quickly gained his feet.

"Tell the Ubon command post to call Lewis over so you can talk to him on the secure phone." Things had calmed down enough that they were back to using proper security procedures.

"Will do." The major didn't look as if his heart was in it. They were all tired.

Pearly glanced at his watch and decided to get out of the TACC for a hot meal rather than open yet another C-Ration container. They had hundreds of the things, cardboard boxes full of them, but the best selections, like Salisbury steaks and franks and beans, had disappeared early.

Pearly felt his chin with its two-day wiry stubble and decided to drop by his room for a shave and hot shower. It felt good just thinking about it.

He telephoned the office and waited to be connected with Lucy Dortmeier.

"How about meeting me for lunch at the club in about an

hour? You can fill me in on what's been happening at the office."

"Eleven-thirty, sir?" Her voice was upbeat and professional. With the other officers serving in the TACC, Lucy had been left in charge at the office.

"Sounds good." He hung up, feeling better after hearing his voice. He stood and stretched, shuddered with the effort, happy to be leaving the place that smelled like a locker room at halftime.

The pilot returned. "I spoke with Major Lewis."

"That was quick."

"He was in the command post, filling in for one of the action officers. They're putting in long hours there too."

"What did he say about their smart bombs?"

"Says they should work great on tanks. Told me they've dropped ten of the things so far and have a fifteen-foot CEP."

"What do you think?"

The major mused for a moment, then looked up with bloodshot eyes. "Fifteen feet's a damn impressive average miss distance. A two-thousand-pound bomb going off that close to a tank should blow the thing all to hell. But from what he's saying, they're getting sixty percent direct hits and that's better yet. I'd say we ought to give 'em a chance."

Pearly nodded slowly, still reluctant to be trying something new in the middle of a fight. "Let's talk about it more when I get back from lunch."

"How about if I call Major Lewis back so his people can bolt a few more bombs together and stand by?"

"Can't do any harm, I suppose." Pearly limped gingerly toward the door. His ankle still hurt like hell.

1250L—355th TFW Commander's Office, Takhli RTAFB, Thailand

Captain Manny DeVera

He'd spent half the night working with munitions people, crashed, and slept hard for a couple of hours, then been awakened at four-fifteen for the first mission briefing. He was bone-weary following his second sortie of the morning, but the wing commander had wanted to talk as soon as he'd landed.

Manny was shaky—so damned tired his fingernails ached. He planned to fly once more, then head to the Ponderosa and collapse.

Colonel Leska called him directly into his office, where he and Colonel Trimble were working on a schedule for the next day.

"Another max effort in the morning, Manny," said the Deputy for Operations. "This time we're heading to Mu Gia pass. F-100 Misty pilots are reporting so many convoys stacked up there, there's traffic jams." Mistys were fast-mover forward air controllers, used in areas too dangerous for O-1 Birddogs, like some of the mountain passes of the Ho Chi Minh Trail.

"The guys are pretty beat from all the flying," Manny said, examining the names. He had to squint. He was too tired to see straight.

They worked on the schedule for half an hour before everyone was happy. Manny's new boss, Colonel Trimble, seemed more secure in his ops job. It had been a while coming, after being so abruptly shuffled over from maintenance.

Buster Leska shooed them out. "I'll talk to George Armaugh for his inputs. We've been working his people awfully heavy the last few days."

As they left the office, Trimble wore a look of satisfaction from the colonel's last statement. It might have been humorous if Manny didn't feel so damnably tired.

"Captain DeVera?" The voice was low.

Manny stopped and looked at Penny Dwight, peering at him over her typing.

He approached and she gave a small smile. "Tired?"

He shrugged. She looked nice.

"Too tired for dinner tonight?"

"Of course not," he said without hesitation.

Her voice remained even. "Drop by my trailer about sevenish?"

"Sure."

"It's been a while since we talked, Manny."

"Too long," he said, trying to keep elation from his tone. He left the wing headquarters building feeling better, even dredging up a spring to his step. Smitty had been right about taking out the blond secretary. Jealousy had done its thing with Penny Dwight.

He saluted a major, grinning his greeting, and the guy looked at him as if he were crazy.

But Manny DeVera had come to a new revelation about himself. For the first time in his life, he felt he might be in love. There was very little that could make him unhappy.

Colonel Buster Leska

Manny looked bad, he thought. He'd had puffy bags under red-rimmed eyes, and Buster had noticed that his hand trembled. He'd been that tired himself a few times in Korea, flying quick turn-around missions. He jotted a note to send his weapons officer on a good R and R when the emergency flying gave them sufficient slack. Right now he needed him.

While he waited for the Deputy for Maintenance to report, Buster reread the letter that had just arrived from Carolyn, and his heart ached once more.

Not for Mark so much now, for he was beginning to resign himself to the fact that their relationship was on the verge of destruction. He worried some about his son, but the majority of his waking hours were spent in concern for Carolyn, who bore the world on her slender shoulders.

He was a warrior. He'd dedicated his life to flying and fighting when called upon. As commander of an F-105 wing, he was responsible for men and machines that could, if appropriately directed, unleash awesome destructive power. Carolyn had signed up too, but she'd done nothing to deserve the turmoil she was now having to endure.

Mark had called her again. She'd tried to use reason, to cajole him into returning home. She'd exhausted every argument while he'd railed against the establishment and said they were out to destroy him and his beliefs.

When she'd asked about the talk he'd had with Buster, and his desire to become a pilot, Mark had scornfully replied that he no longer wished to be a baby-killer like his father. He'd told her not to worry about him, and when she said that was impossible—he was her son and only child—he'd told her that he was doing what he had to. She'd written that he'd had a catch in his voice as he hurried to hang up.

Please call, Carolyn pleaded to Buster in the letter. She needed very badly to hear his voice. Each day she drifted deeper into depression. She'd feared for Buster's safety from the moment he'd left her, and now, with Mark gone too, everything seemed magnified.

She said she prayed daily for Buster's continued welfare . . . and that he'd call.

But there was no way to place a call to the States with everything happening. All telephone lines were blocked to everything but official calls, and even those were most often interrupted by higher-priority traffic.

With all the recent frantic activity—he'd been flying early every morning, then returning to work through the day and long into the night—he treasured every moment of rest, and fell asleep the minute he hit the bed.

He started to reread the letter, then stopped himself and dropped it into a drawer.

There were too many tasks before him. Too many men who depended upon him for guidance.

A single knock sounded on the door, and George Armaugh stepped into the office. "You wanted to see me?"

"Yeah, George. Have a seat."

In the past few days Armaugh and his maintenance people had worked dog hours to keep the airplanes prepared to fly, and weariness was reflected in his eyes.

"We've got another big mission in the morning," Buster said.

1400L—Ban Sao Si, Laos

GS-15 Linda Lopes

The long, dusty trip from the Pathet Lao camp had been hard on her, yet provided a respite for her battered chest and abdomen. Throughout the ride she'd remained bound and blindfolded, sliding about the bed of a small truck at the feet of half a dozen soldiers. Aside from being occasionally used as a footrest, having her knees and elbows scraped raw and bloody and becoming bruised from head to toe, she'd been treated moderately well.

They'd hurried, driving at night and even during some of the daylight hours. She'd once been briefed that the communists moved their convoys so cautiously it took several months for them to travel the meandering routes from Hanoi to South Vietnam. This journey took only thirteen days, and although she didn't know the route, she knew they'd come a considerable distance.

When they arrived at the destination, the voices spoke in a different tongue. Linda was led from the truck, staggering and reeling on unsure legs, and deposited onto a hard dirt floor. When the blindfold was removed and she was unbound, she found herself in a small office with chairs, a table, and a small, four-by-four bamboo structure.

An obese man wearing a North Vietnamese uniform regarded her. Rolls of fat stretched the fabric of his uniform, and his face was badly pitted. He motioned the soldiers outside, then pushed her toward the cage. She crawled in and he secured the door, still examining her with narrowed eyes. He grew a pensive look, shifted his weight, and released a long blast of gas. Sergeant Gross, she named him.

An older officer came in, eyed her briefly, then sat at the table. He moved papers about nervously, scribbled notes, and stared at them.

Sergeant Gross asked something in a low voice, and the officer nodded.

Another man entered and both became alert. Sergeant Gross stiffened respectfully and Paper-Shuffler bolted to his feet. Someone important? The newcomer was tall for an Asian, extremely thin, and had delicately sculptured features. He wore no rank on his uniform, but appeared extraordinarily neat. There was a strange, flat cast to his eyes as he stared at her. He wrinkled his nose in distaste, an almost effeminate expression, and spoke in a high, lilting voice. Sergeant Gross waddled purposefully from the room.

Thin Man joined Paper-Shuffler and they spoke. Paper-Shuffler nodded vigorously and scribbled new words on a pad. There was no doubt who was in charge.

Linda tried to gain an impression as to whether Thin Man would be compassionate or mean, but she could get no sense of what he was like. When he observed her, as he periodically did as he dictated to Paper-Shuffler, there was a complete lack of expression. It was as if she were a sack of rice, she decided.

Sergeant Gross came back in, unfastened the cage door, swung it open, and gestured.

Linda crawled out, then stood on shaky legs as he tied a rope around her neck and tugged it so taut she gagged.

Oh God! They were going to hang her! She clawed wildly at the noose.

Sergeant Gross gave the rope another jerk and led her to the door. Linda followed obediently, still gagging. Outside, her eyes were blinded by the brilliant afternoon sun. When she faltered, she felt a harder tug, and stumbled after the sergeant, grasping at the rope and trying to loosen it.

They'd emerged from the rearmost of two wooden structures, into a clearing where a few dozen soldiers moved languidly about in the midday heat.

Sergeant Gross stopped at an edge of the clearing. Two soldiers brought buckets of water and deposited them beside her.

"Take off your clothes," Sergeant Gross said in a low voice. The sound of English coming from his pudgy lips was unsettling.

Linda hesitated.

He gave the rope a tug. She choked, stumbled, and began to disrobe.

She wore no bra—had discarded it after the first bamboo-rod beating because her breasts had been so bruised and swollen she couldn't endure the confinement. When only her panties remained, Sergeant Gross gestured again. His insistence on full nudity was surprising, for she'd found the Lao guerrillas to be somewhat shy. This one was different. His eyes were alternately fixed on her breasts and crotch, and his breath caught in anticipation.

She awkwardly stepped out of the filthy underpants. The sergeant barked shrill orders, eyes lingering on her nudity, and a man gathered her clothing and hurried away.

Sergeant Gross reached forward and pushed down on her head, and when she hesitated, he did it again. She slowly squatted, looking about as gawking soldiers began to gather.

Gross spouted words to the men with the buckets. First

one, then the other poured water over her head. She sputtered and blew, but it felt wonderful.

"Wash," Sergeant Gross grunted.

She moved her hands over herself.

More water cascaded over her head, and she continued to rub away grime

"Stand," he said, staring again. Muttering and laughter came from the gathered soldiers. It was unlikely any had seen a nude Caucasian woman. They came closer, curious, talking and tittering among themselves.

One reached out and boldly grasped a breast.

Linda pulled away, glowering.

Laughter.

A man in dark clothing pushed his way through the gathering and spoke sharply to Sergeant Gross. He had a sorrowful look about him. The two men talked, then Sergeant Gross chattered at the gathered men, who moved farther back but continued to stare. He also worked angrily with the noose about her neck, shoving her fingers aside and grasping at the knot. She sucked grateful gasps of air as he brusquely pulled the loop over her head.

They waited in place, Sad Man growing increasingly impatient. Five more minutes passed before the man returned with her clothing. They were twisted together, as Asian women do when they wash a garment.

Linda pulled them on, shuddering as the cool fabric embraced her skin.

Sergeant Gross grunted and motioned, then marched her back to the office, where Paper-Shuffler still sat with poised pen. The meticulous Thin Man smiled as Sad Man stepped inside. The two spoke together, and Thin Man's smile quickly disappeared, replaced by an expression of disgust. Finally he motioned deftly toward Sergeant Gross and took a seat to observe.

Sergeant Gross approached her, sweating profusely.

"We know you," he said. "You spy for Mee pigs." He gestured grandly at Thin Man. "The assistan' commissioner is ver' busy man in Hanoi. He nod have time for waiding. You mus' talk and tell truth." Though his voice rose and fell in improper inflections, Sergeant Gross's English was acceptable, and his pronunciation quite good.

Then, with a suddenness she hadn't anticipated, he swept his pudgy hand round in an arc and backhanded her.

She stumbled against the small cage, blood spouting from her nose.

Sad Man yelled at Sergeant Gross as Linda held her hands to her face. Blood dribbled freely through her fingers. Nausea welled. The cartilage was surely broken, for the pain was intense.

Sad Man spoke angrily to Thin Man, who looked even more disgusted.

Sergeant Gross nodded at Thin Man's new instructions, faced her, and brusquely began to ask questions.

We know you travel to the American bases and have spies working there. What are the names of your agents?

We know you work for the CIA in Bangkok. Who are your bosses?

We know you also work for the CIA in Saigon. Name all the agents there.

We know you . . .

She remained silent. It was not as if Sergeant Gross really wanted answers, only to show her what they knew and reveal questions they wanted answered. He paused for only a short time between each, letting it soak in.

They thought she was with the CIA and knew a lot more than anyone in her position would know about their operations.

"I am not with the CIA," she said after a moment of silence. "I work for the USAID office in Bangkok and do not know any agents or spies. We are a humanitarian agency."

Neither Sergeant Gross nor the others were listening. He'd walked to the table and was lifting a three-foot length of bamboo, which he showed to Sad Man. Linda's heart tumbled.

Sad Man examined, then hesitantly nodded.

Sergeant Gross came back to her and waited, smiling. She could tell that he was looking forward to his task.

She waited for it to begin.

Thin Man regained his feet, approached her, and examined her without expression. He turned to Sad Man and said something. Sad Man replied and Thin Man clenched his teeth angrily, then bolted from the room, trailing words over his shoulder.

Sergeant Gross sighed unhappily as he put away the length of bamboo, and motioned brusquely to her. He pushed her out the doorway, Sad Man following closely behind. She was herded across the open yard to a thatch hut, where Sergeant Gross grasped her by the nape of the neck and roughly shoved her inside. Sad Man was shouting at him as he secured the door.

The dark interior of her new home was featureless, with a ratty-looking sleeping mat, bowl, and cup on one end. Behind the mat was a small wooden bucket—a traditional Laotian chamber pot.

Linda sat quietly, eyes still watering from the bolts of pain that shot from her nose. She made herself think—digest what had happened and evaluate the people she'd just met.

Something was going on between Thin Man and Sad Man, some sort of struggle she didn't understand. She prayed Sad Man would win. Thin Man and Sergeant Gross scared the hell out of her.

That evening Linda was given only half the meager rations she'd received before. She didn't care, because the broken nose hurt so terribly. She remained nauseous and could hardly hold down even that small amount.

1940L—O' Club Dining Room, Takhli RTAFB, Thailand

GS-7 *Penny Dwight*

Manny had picked her up precisely at seven and tried to maintain a light and upbeat conversation, but throughout the meal she'd uttered but a few words. Penny knew what she had to do and refused to be deterred. It would be difficult enough without allowing him to distract her, which she knew was a possibility regardless of her resolve.

She had trouble quelling the urge to reach out and comfort him. Since he'd met her at the trailer, he'd tried to hide his intense weariness, but there was little chance of it, with the baggy eyes and the slow way he was talking, which wasn't at all normal for him. He'd aged a dozen years from all the work the colonels were laying on him in addition to his normal hard efforts and flying once or twice a day.

Manny seemed increasingly puzzled by her silence.

Penny looked about the crowded dining room. It was not the place for intimate discussion. She returned her gaze to his face and felt the old quiver of reckless emotion. This was the man she wanted. Certainly not Rudy, although he'd make someone a suitable mate. Perhaps the silly blond she'd seen with Manny.

For the dozenth time Manny mentioned how nice she looked. She had been taking care of herself, watching her appearance more closely, since making up her mind about Manny DeVera. She'd been slipping some before, but Rudy hadn't seemed to care.

"Could we go somewhere more private?" she asked quietly.

"You bet," Manny said with a grin.

She impulsively reached across to touch his face. "Your eyes look so tired."

He shrugged and her heart did a two-step.

They got up and Manny paid. They went outside and were immediately bathed by the humid warmth. She led the way to the pool, in front and to one side of the club's entrance, and sat on a chaise longue.

Manny stood before her, looking awkward.

She spoke quietly. "Sit down, please. I've got something I have to tell you."

The chair squeaked a slight protest as he sat beside her, and he released a small grunt of weariness.

A shout, followed by laughter, came from the side entrance that led into the stag bar.

She took a deep breath. "I love you, Manny DeVera."

He leaned to kiss her, but she turned away.

"Not until we talk."

Manny waited.

"Do you love me?"

He was quiet.

"I've got to know. It's very important."

His voice was low. "I think so. I've never felt this way."

Penny nodded. "Me either. I was engaged once, but the feeling wasn't anything like I've got for you. I came close to loving Dusty. I think I could have, if we'd had longer."

Manny remained quiet. She appreciated his thoughtfulness.

"But I love you desperately, Manny."

He exhaled slowly. Happiness or fatigue? she wondered.

"I want to make love to you. I want to have your children. I want everything you're willing to offer."

"Maybe we should—"

"Please," she interrupted, "I've got to say this, Manny, and it's very difficult." She'd practiced her speech carefully and knew she must not be sidetracked.

He waited for her to continue.

"I'd be good for you, Manny. I'd be there whenever you wanted, and I'd promise to never look at another man as long as I live. We'd be right for one another. I know we would."

Although he said nothing, somehow, in the silent communication that only people in love can share, she knew he agreed.

"I want you to myself. I don't ever want to see you with another woman again, like the other night."

"Nothing happened. I just took her to dinner and for a drink after."

"Do you love me?" she asked again.

"Yes." He said it with little hesitation.

"You can have me, Manny. Tonight and every night of my life from now on."

He placed his arm around her shoulders, and she didn't pull away.

"But you'll have to promise me something. Just one thing."

He gently pulled her closer, raised a hand to trace her cheek. She noticed how it was trembling from his weariness. "You name it," he whispered in his deep voice.

"That you'll stop flying combat."

CHAPTER THIRTY-THREE

Thursday, February 8th 0520 Local—VOQ, Ubon RTAFB, Thailand

Major Benny Lewis

The orderly had awakened him five minutes before and said he was to go to the command center. "You've got a classified call, sir. I'll drive you."

Benny scrambled into the same jungle fatigues he'd pulled off the previous evening. As he gingerly pulled on his socks, then the canvas-sided boots, he remembered and pounded a few times on the wall. Moods and his GIB occupied the adjacent room in the visiting officers' quarters.

"Yeah?" came Moods's muffled response.

"I've gotta go over and take a classified call at the command post. You better get hold of the shooter crew and prepare to launch."

"Yeah!"

"Head on down to the squadron. I'll be there soon as I get off the phone. If it's a false alarm, we'll go to the club for breakfast."

Two F-4's, one with the illuminator pod and the other loaded with two Pave Dagger Mk-84's, had been loaded and kept ready for quick launch in the event they received tasking from the Seventh Air Force Tactical Air Control Center.

Ten minutes later Benny burst into the command post and hurried over to the scrambler-phone console.

An airman dialed through, connected with a similar scrambler unit at Seventh Air Force, and handed him the receiver.

"Benny, this is Pearly Gates. Over." The voice sounded as if it came from an echo chamber, and was accompanied by a periodic squeal. Only one person could speak at a time, so you had to tell the other when you were finished.

"You got a target for us? Over."

"The shit hit the fan at an outpost near Khe Sanh last night. The NVA overran a place called Lang Vei. Over."

"The tanks? Over."

"Nine or ten of the damned things. More than three hundred friendlies KIA'ed, some of them Americans. We lost track of the tanks again, but they can't have gone far. We're sending up three O-1 FAC birds and a C-47 with heat sensors to find them. I want your guys to try to take 'em out. How many bombs you got loaded up? Over."

"One shooter. Two bombs. Over."

"We need more. You got more bombs bolted together? Over."

"Sure do. Over."

"Have 'em load three more aircraft. Over."

0925L—Near Quang Tri, South Vietnam

Captain Moods Diller

They'd loaded the additional shooters, giving them a total of eight modified Mk-84 2,000-pound bombs. Moods led Pilgrim, a five-ship flight of F-4D Phantoms. They were leaving the initial orbit, heading west, following Waterboy's directions.

The O-1 FAC called. *"Patches zero-two echo has you in sight, Pilgrim. Turn right ten degrees and I'll be five, six miles off your nose."*

"Pilgrim lead has you at our one o'clock, Patches zero-two echo. Confirm you're over the small stream flying south."

"That's me, Pilgrim. Continue to let down to five thousand feet."

"Pilgrim flight's descending to flight level zero-five-zero."

"I've got six tanks in sight down here, trying to hide in a thicket of trees. Watch for my mark, Pilgrim. I'm shootin' willy petes."

Moods kept his eyes glued as the tiny propeller aircraft turned sharply and dived toward a small stand of trees which covered perhaps half an acre. There was a flash. Two white phosphorus rockets splayed tendrils when they struck side by side at the near edge of the trees. *"Pilgrim lead's got two willy pete marks in sight, Patches echo."*

"That's the thicket, Pilgrim lead. Four tanks on the south side, two more somewhere near the middle. You're cleared to drop."

Moods went into a slight bank, flying an arc around the copse of trees. He directed the two shooters to set up an oblong racetrack orbit, then advised the O-1 to stand clear because of the large size of the bombs and their blast effect.

"I'm looking . . . I'm looking," the pilot in the rear cockpit muttered over intercom. He was viewing the world through a video camera with several levels of magnification. First he'd get the big picture, then slowly zoom in.

"I've got the trees now. Going to times ten. Yeah . . . yeah."

"You got the tanks?"

"Just trees. All looks the same in there."

Moods thought about it, then radioed for the first shooter to turn inbound and head directly for them. They were still evaluating different drop tactics, but this one seemed to work best with multiple shooters.

"Turn on the zot," he told the backseater over intercom, eyeballing the trees.

"I don't have 'em yet, Moods."

"We're gonna drop one right in the middle of the thicket."

"Zot's on." The laser was activated, casting its pinpoint of brilliant light.

He depressed the radio button. *"You'll be releasing one bomb on this pass, Pilgrim two, at about eight thousand feet slant range from the target area."*

He could see the F-4 shooter bunt slightly over. This

time he'd told them to try dropping at just ten degrees nose-down. If that worked, next time they might even try releasing when they were flying straight and level. The idea was to get the bomb seeker in view of the target, so the steering mechanism could take over.

"Pilgrim two's got a lock-on light."

Moods made the call for Pilgrim two to release the weapon, holding his right turn as steady as possible to make his backseater's job easier.

He could see the weapon release. As the aircraft pulled up, he followed the bomb on its trajectory.

"I think I can see one of 'em now, Moods!" cried the backseater.

"Keep the illuminator going."

"I'm slewing to the target."

"Don't move it much, dammit."

"I'm on it!"

"You think it's a tank?"

"It's something man-made. The foliage looks different."

The bomb made a smooth correction, falling now at a steeper angle.

"The bomb's guiding," Moods muttered.

The bomb exploded in the midst of the trees. Its concussive wave blew the trees outward like ripples after a pebble was dropped into a pond. Pebble hell—a big damn rock!

A small secondary explosion—followed by a thick streamer of black smoke.

"You got something in there, Pilgrim lead!" radioed the excited FAC.

Moods continued flying the arc around the copse of trees. He could feel the excitement growing.

"It was a tank all right!" yelled the GIB. "I can see it now."

"Pilgrim two," Moods radioed. *"Turn back inbound now. You'll be releasing bomb number two."*

"I can see motion in the thicket, Moods."

"Track whatever it is," said Moods. "We don't want any of 'em getting away."

"One of 'em's out of the trees now," said the GIB. "He's running."

"Zot him."

"Illuminator's on!"

When Pilgrim flight left the position fifteen minutes later, five tanks were burning brightly. The FAC felt the other PT-76 had also been destroyed in the thicket. He told them he'd never seen anything like the kind of accuracy they'd shown.

Moods was numb with elation. The bombs were like his children, and he was very proud of them.

1125L—Command Post, Ubon RTAFB, Thailand

Major Benny Lewis

The scrambler phone was working.

"They got five, maybe all six, Pearly. Over."

"I got a call from the FAC. He's dancing a jig. Good work, Benny. Over."

"The credit goes to Moods and his guys. Over."

"Buy 'em a drink. Tell 'em it's on me. Over."

"Make sure the word gets out, Pearly. Over."

"Will do. I'll inform higher headquarters ASAP. Over."

"You gonna send us some more work? The guys are raring for another chance to show their stuff. Over."

A short pause followed. "I would've told you before, if it hadn't been for all the Tet bullshit. We got a message from the PACAF IG questioning your Pave Dagger project. Someone there wants to shut down your test. They also sent a query to the Pentagon. Over."

"They can't do that! Not now. Jesus, we just gave 'em a success. Over."

"Let's low-key it for a couple of days while I get the word about the tanks out. I'll try to arrange something new for you. Maybe give Moods a target that'll help convince everyone. How does he feel about flying up in pack six? Over."

"That's what it's all about. Pave Dagger's designed to take out tough targets so we don't have to send half the Air Force after 'em. Over."

"Let me see what I can come up with. We'll probably be going back up north in a few days. In the meantime, tell the guys they did good work. Over."

"Will do. Over." But a large part of Benny's elation had evaporated. Someone was trying to kill the Pave Dagger project.

Tuesday, February 13th, 0745 Local—HQ Seventh Air Force, Tan Son Nhut Air Base Saigon, South Vietnam

Lieutenant Colonel Pearly Gates

The briefers from intelligence gathered their charts and quietly left the general's office.

Pearly mused on what they'd been told. The Tet offensive had presented the grandest gamble and the most thorough whipping for the North Vietnamese thus far in the war. They'd gambled all their chips and failed. With their backs pressed to the wall, the Army of the Republic of Vietnam was fighting like furies, soundly drubbing the NVA in almost every confrontation. The NVA were losing thousands of their best soldiers. Entire crack units were being decimated, and not a single provincial capital remained in their hands. Although fighting remained fierce in some sectors, there was little doubt as to the outcome. Even the infiltrators who'd slipped into Saigon were being relentlessly hunted down.

South Vietnamese Buddhist leaders who had sympathized with Hanoi's goals were outraged that the armistice had been broken to defile the Tet celebration of life. Rather than rise up and take arms with the NVA, they looked on somberly, sometimes even mouthing support for the ARVN.

From the viewpoint of every major military headquarters, the Tet offensive was a solid victory for democracy. The only glitch was the press. Reporters rushed avidly about the city, interviewing every "official" and "qualified" source, meaning paper pushers and dissidents, who would agree to make a statement. If the words jived with their stories of gloom and doom, they'd send it out. When exuberant American or ARVN commanders told about kicking VC ass or humiliating entire NVA units, their stories were downplayed and often shelved. Self-serving articles and broadcasts from Hanoi were quoted in faithful detail. According to the press agencies, the Tet offensive showed the vulnerability of the allies and new tenacity by the communists.

Both General Westmoreland and President Johnson had issued upbeat statements very early in the confrontations, describing the heroic stand of allied troops. Antiwar activists called their words establishment propaganda, regurgitated Hanoi's assessments, and gleefully spouted that it was the beginning of the end for American adventurism in Southeast Asia.

Pearly wondered what he'd believe if he was a Kansas farmer or a housewife in New Jersey. It was troubling.

But General Moss was happy this morning, had been cheerful since calling Pearly into his office to sit in on the briefing. "We've got a new JACKPOT message," the General said when the door closed behind the last briefer.

He held it up and read: "In the wake of Tet, approval for LINE BACKER JACKPOT now seems assured. J is increasingly resolved to win the war as quickly and efficiently as possible."

Moss wore a thoughtful expression as he scanned the message further.

"Does he have any idea when it may happen?" Pearly asked.

"No, but I've got a feeling it's close. Gentleman Jim says the incoming Secretary of Defense is reluctant about further escalations, so Johnson's toying with the idea of briefing him on the project, showing him there's a way to win."

Pearly nodded. "I think it's time to start briefing a lot of top people."

Moss raised an eyebrow. "Like who?"

Pearly took a breath. "General Roman, for one."

Moss's lips became a taut line.

"The people at PACAF could give us a lot of good input to help finish the OPlan."

"Gentleman Jim doesn't trust him, Pearly. Neither do I."

"General Roman may approach things differently than we do, but no one can question his patriotism. I think if he was made part of a plan to win, he'd go for it."

"He's going around the system—straight past the Chief of Staff to the SecDef."

"He was going directly to the *old* Secretary of Defense. I wonder if he's got a line into his replacement."

Moss snorted. "Roman's half politician. I'll bet he's sending messages right now."

"Then by convincing him, perhaps we could get a positive word through him to the new SecDef."

"Dumb idea, Pearly. Forget it."

"General, he knows something's afoot. He sent Colonel Lyons out looking for answers, and from what Colonel Leska reported, just *maybe* he's found some."

"Then if what you're saying about his sense of patriotism is true, he'll go along."

"Not if Lyons is giving him the wrong word. A lot of truth can get garbled when you're dealing with third parties. I don't trust Lyons. I think he'd present his reports in the most self-serving way possible."

Moss grew reflective. After the visit by Benny Lewis, when Benny told him about the cozy relationship between Tom Lyons and the wing commander from Danang, Moss had called in the commander and questioned him at length. He'd said that he and Lyons had discussed only the results of his informal inspection, but Pearly knew the general still wondered.

"Just an idea, sir," said Pearly. He'd planted the seed. Anything further would be up to Moss and McManus.

1000L—355th TFW Commander's Office, Takhli RTAFB, Thailand

Captain Manny DeVera

Colonel Leska had called him in to talk business—to ask how well prepared the pilots were to go back to pack six, for they'd been alerted that a large-scale strike would be ordered the next day. Throughout Manny had tried not to show his fatigue as well as the utter glumness he'd felt over the past week, during which time Penny had not spoken to him once. The previous evening Penny had gone to the club and even joked around with a few of the guys in the bar, which she'd not done since Animal Hamlin's death. But when Manny had approached her, she'd just given him a wistful stare, then said to another of the guys that she had to go to her trailer.

How the hell do you feel good when you know what you want, and you want it so badly that you'd die for it, but you can't make it happen because it would destroy your manhood?

Penny's demand was unfair and unreasonable. There was no way he could quit flying combat—just drop his life and back out on his friends. He'd gone around the entire week feeling as if his stomach were stuffed in his throat. No matter how hard he tried, Manny couldn't forget Penny and her demand. He wanted her—wanted to live his life with her as she'd said. He couldn't remember feeling so intensely about a woman before. He couldn't sleep at night thinking about it, and that just added to his being do damnably tired.

The talk with Leska was over, yet Manny remained seated.

"You've look troubled the past few days," the colonel said.

Manny wanted to talk about his dilemma with someone whose judgment he respected and trusted, but he didn't know how to begin. He was also so very tired that he didn't trust his own thoughts on the thorny subject.

"You got a problem, Manny?" Leska prodded.

He decided on the "good friend" routine. "A buddy of mine needs advise, sir, and I'm having trouble giving it. Could I run it by you?"

"Shoot."

"He's in a bind right now, and I'm trying to tell him what to do. It sort of relates to what we talked about in my office that time. About how a guy has to choose his lady carefully, so she's right for him?"

Leska nodded.

"Anyway, this guy's found a perfect lady. She's pretty and they can talk without even speaking . . . know what I mean?"

"The poor bastard's in love."

"More than he's ever thought he might be. I mean, he's had his share of women, but this time he's hooked. He can hardly think, he's so hooked."

"It gets like that sometimes."

"You ever feel that way, Colonel?"

Buster Leska nodded. "I've been there. Is this friend of yours one of our combat pilots?"

"Yes, sir."

"Then it's a damned dangerous time for him to be getting emotionally involved."

"This lady's awfully worried about him. She gets sick every time he flies."

"I see."

"She loves him too," Manny added quickly.

"If she really feels that way, she knows a man has to do what he must."

"What if she asks him to—"

The wing commander's radio erupted with noise. Colonel Jerry Trimble's voice. *"Eagle one, this is Eagle three. We've got a bird in trouble. Started losing hydraulic pressure on his way to the tanker. He'll be landing back here in ten."*

Leska lurched to his feet and reached for his flight cap as he raised the radio. *"Eagle one's on my way."* The wing commander was halfway out the door and hurrying.

As Manny went through the outer office, he glanced at Penny Dwight. She regarded him somberly, following him closely with her large blue eyes. He went on outside, the lump still heavy in his throat.

Colonel Buster Leska

The talk with Manny was forgotten as Buster watched and listened to the unfolding drama from his pickup near the approach end of the runway.

Lieutenant Colonel Yank Donovan had noted the problem early and had reacted immediately, turning homeward as the Thud he was flying lost both the primary hydraulic system and the AC generator.

He'd slowed down, extended his ram air turbine, and done all the right things, but the Thud flew poorly with only the smattering of hydraulics supplied by the standby utility system.

Yank diverted to the jettison area and punched off his bombs, then entered a long, straight-in approach. He radioed that he thought his gear were all down—that he felt it—but was getting no indications.

Then Donovan lost his radio.

The Supervisor of Flying radioed several times—in the blind, for they didn't know if Donovan was receiving—for him to lower his tail hook in case he had to take the far end barrier. With loss of hydraulics, there could be only one application of brakes, and it was unlikely the Thud would be able to stop on its own. Donovan's wingman, who was glued to his side and giving hand signals, also relayed the instructions.

Buster watched for the ailing bird to appear in the northern sky; finally he saw two dark specks with wings.

Donovan's wingman radioed that they'd be continuing with the approach. Donovan had signaled that he'd land on the first pass.

A cable was stretched across the runway, lifted, and supported by donuts so the Thud's lowered arresting gear—or tailhook, as the Navy called it—could catch on and bring the bird to a halt, before going off the end. Unlike Navy birds, the Thud's tailhook was not strong enough to endure an approach-end engagement.

On the plus side, Yank Donovan was a superb pilot who had a much better chance than would a less experienced one. On the minus side, the wingman reported that the Thud looked to be only marginally controllable.

The specks grew larger as the two birds closed on the runway, flying in close formation. Just before Donovan touched down, the second Thud would pull up and away.

The tower operator radioed to other aircraft in the area that the runway was temporarily closed due to an emergency in progress. Buster found himself holding his breath in anticipation and forced himself to breath normally.

The crippled Thud dipped erratically toward the ground, and Buster couldn't help gritting his teeth and sucking a breath. The bird slowly pulled back up into position.

Closer now. He'd jettisoned the bombs, but kept the two wing-mounted, 450-gallon fuel tanks. If the gear collapsed, the big tanks would act as a cushion.

The tailhook was lowered. The descent looked good. The landing gear appeared okay, but there was no way to be sure they were locked into position.

The main gear kissed the concrete as the bird touched down at the 1,000 foot marker—the gear held as Yank deployed the drag chute then held down on the brakes—the aircraft slowed—suddenly the Thud veered toward a side of the runway—slewed more and created a shower of sparks from the right drop tank as the bird dropped onto its right side and went off the runway. After plowing up fifty feet of dirt, the airplane came to a halt, kneeling to the right, resting on the collapsed fuel tank. Then the left main gear very slowly folded, and the bird was cocked back, sitting on nosegear, two misshapen wing fuel tanks, and the aft fuselage.

Firetrucks rushed alongside. Men in asbestos suits hurried into positions around the aircraft. The rescue chopper hovered low overhead. One truck began to spray a mist of water over the bird to cool it, while two others gushed fire-retardant foam onto the tanks and the trail of fuel the Thud's fuel tanks had left in their paths.

A fireman hurried up the angled left wing, slipped once in the foam, and knelt beside the cockpit. He peered in, then turned and gave a terse hand signal.

"Pilot's alive," came the radio call from the fire truck.

Buster drove closer as the canopy was opened. He parked near one of the fire trucks and waited.

Yank was a bit slow emerging, so the rescue fireman encouraged him, and he came out abruptly, yelling hoarsely. Rescue people were taught to get the pilot out as quickly as possible. The best way to help him along was to place hard thumbs under both armpits and gouge upwards. It was painful, but if the pilot was conscious, it worked.

Buster laughed, listening to Yank Donovan's bellows of outrage as he hurried past the rescue man and scrambled, half sliding, down the wing.

"Over here," Buster called out.

Donovan walked to the pickup, glaring back at the firemen, smelling of the pungent odors of fuel and chemical foam.

"Just doing his job," Buster said cheerfully.

"Wish he'd do it less vigorously," Yank said, dolefully rubbing his armpits.

"You did good work up there."

"Almost lost it on final."

"I saw."

They watched as a maintenance crew arrived and a chief master sergeant began to yell at his men, then at the emergency crews, to tell them to back away from the damn thing because he had to bring the cherry picker over, move it, and fix it.

Other aircraft were holding and waiting to land. The tower estimated the first ones could begin their letdown in twenty minutes.

"Jump in," Buster told his squadron commander. "I'll give you a ride."

He liked happy endings to emergencies.

After he'd deposited Yank at his squadron, Buster returned to his office. With his morning meetings canceled due to the emergency, he had an hour to himself.

He'd gotten through to Carolyn on the phone again that morning. Things remained disturbing at home; their son was still swallowed up somewhere by the counterculture. While they both knew that the war was splitting families across America, it was difficult to believe it was happening to *them*. Neither could accept it, but they had no alternative.

A notice had arrived in the mail, reclassifying Marcus's draft status and ordering him to report for a preinduction physical. Carolyn told him that quietly, and Buster knew she was numbed by it all. She was not only fearful that their son had become lost to them, but also by the alternative, that he might return and be sent off to fight in an increasingly thankless war.

There'd been yet another call from Marcus two days earlier, and he'd sounded even more sure that he was doing the right thing. Buster had tried to tell her that Mark had made his choice and was legally responsible for his decisions. They had to let go. While the course of action was painful, he knew it was the only one he'd be able to live with. With his wife it was not nearly so black-and-white.

Carrie, he'd wanted to say. *America's been sending our youth out to fight for democracy for almost two hundred years. I love Mark dearly, but I can't agree that it is the right of every individual to judge the right and wrong of a particular conflict after the shooting's begun. Then it comes down to supporting your fellow citizens ... today just as it has in every other war.*

He had, of course, said none of that. He often found it hard to comprehend, himself.

He'd been dismayed when Carolyn said something. Perhaps it was more the gist of all her words, rather than the single announcement. But he perceived that she was being torn . . . forced to choose between husband and son.

Is it really so wrong, she asked, *that our son doesn't want to kill?*

Her voice had been sad, but he'd discerned that she was withdrawing somehow—pulling away from him—drawn by her intense love for the child she'd borne.

CHAPTER
THIRTY-FOUR

Thursday, February 15th, 0045 Local—Over Northeastern, Laos

Sergeant Black

"You guys ready back here?" asked the contractor load-master.

"Yeah," Black told him, gritting his teeth and telling himself *never again*. He intensely disliked this kind of flying, and even more so when he was uncomfortable with the air-crew's ability.

"You get the go code from Buffalo Soldier yet?" he asked.

"We were having trouble with our HF radio last time I checked. I'll ask again." The loadmaster went forward to the flight-crew compartment.

They'd spent the past two and a half hours in an Air South C-123, the smaller, two-engined look-alike of the C-130 Hercules. The C-123, not nearly as reliable or capable as its bigger brother, continuously shuddered and shook. It was deafeningly noisy, and this one's right engine periodically belched blue flame from its exhaust.

Flying with Air Force's Special Ops people was scary because they liked to get down low and skim the treetops in the pitch-black of night. The same was true of major CIA contractors like Bird and Son. But they were pros, and Black believed they knew what they were doing. This Air South pilot flew a lot higher, and while Black wasn't as worried about smacking into the side of a mountain, the bird's flight path was not nearly as stealthy. That fact was compounded by the belief among Special Forces teams that some of the smaller contractors' crews knew where they were only when they could see the ground. At night they'd sometimes give you a jump light when they *thought* they were in the *vicinity* of the drop zone. That was a generalization, and perhaps without merit, but it didn't make Black feel any better.

To make matters worse, they'd be jumping under an almost full moon, so if they were dropped near a village, even with their dark chutes there was the possibility of being seen. Black wished to hell they'd used a chopper to transport them, so he could look over the pilot's shoulder and make sure of where they were. Or that they'd been dropped in by a Special Ops crew. But since no helicopters or SOF or Air America or Bird and Son aircraft were available, here they were.

The loadmaster came out of the crew compartment and started back toward him.

The first recon team, code name Banjo, was to have jumped in an hour earlier and immediately radio in their success code. Buffalo Soldier was to advise Vientiane Control, who would relay word to the C-123 crew. Hotdog was to jump only after the first team was inserted and moving out toward the observation post at Yankee 54.

Black hoped they'd get the go-ahead. He didn't want to remain in the shuddering C-123 longer than was absolutely necessary.

The loadmaster knelt close so he could shout over the roar of the noisy engines. "The navigator still can't get the fuckin' HF radio to work. Aircraft commander says it's up to you. He don't wanna go any farther if it's an abort."

Shit! Black glanced at Hotdog, then back to the loadmaster. "How long until we're there?"

"We're fifty miles out."

"Dammit, how long?"

"Maybe fifteen minutes."

Black looked at the Hotdogs again. They were honed and ready. But without a go code . . . "Have they heard from the other aircraft? I mean, was the other team even dropped?"

The contractor's brows knit. He obviously hadn't asked.

"Fuck!" Black shrugged out of the parachute harness and went forward, lurching with the wild motions of the aircraft.

The copilot knew no more than the crew chief. "The damn HF radio quit on us. We've got no way of talking to Vientiane without it."

"How about the other airplane? Can you find out if the other team jumped?"

"We're supposed to stay off the VHF."

"It's important."

"We're probably out of radio range."

"It's *damned* important."

The captain nodded to the copilot, who spoke into his mike, trying to raise the other C-123. On his third attempt, he raised an answer and spoke a few words, then turned back toward the captain and nodded. Banjo had made their jump.

"Well?" asked the aircraft captain.

Black considered odds. Banjo was a hotshot recon team with good men and several insertions behind them. It was unlikely they'd have problems. He hated to screw up an op because of a fucked-up HF radio.

"We'll jump," he finally said. "You just make damned sure you drop us out at the DZ."

The aircraft captain glared angrily. "You do your job and don't worry about ours, okay, Sarge? You got a problem with that, we'll abort right now."

The navigator leaned toward them from his console and shouted, "I've got us twenty-three nautical miles out. We'll be at the DZ in about eight or nine minutes."

About? Black shook his head grimly as he started back.

Black checked his equipment again as he buckled into the chute, then sat staring at the loadmaster, who was speaking with the flight crew on intercom. He turned to Black and nodded at the flickering red light on the jump console.

The Hotdogs rose to their feet, lined up and hooked up, and shuffled toward the rear of the bird. The lieutenant was first, Black last, the other two sandwiched in between. The loadmaster eyeballed them without checking them over, speaking into his headset mike.

As a motor whined and the cargo ramp started to drop, Black looked at the jump lights. He liked Hotdog to go out fast, one right after the next, so they'd have minimum separation.

The ramp was down and air churned about the wide exit.

They waited expectantly.

Green light.

0127L

Hotdog was assembled in a small clearing on an elevation with a view in all directions. Black held a small flashlight as he and the lieutenant knelt over a chart and compass to pinpoint their position, which appeared not at all like their designated DZ.

He looked out at the moonlit shape of the mountain they'd skinnied down two and a half months earlier, and read the bearing, then mentally adjusted for compass variation. One-four-oh degrees to the mountain. He drew a pencil line on the map, turned and went through the same procedure for a peak to the west, then another to the east. When he'd finished, he stared at the result. They were somewhere within the small triangle made by the three lines. The lieutenant placed a finger on a knoll, and Black grunted his agreement. They were twenty-odd kilometers southwest of their designated drop area, only seven kilometers west of the enemy-held airstrip at Ban Sao Si and four kilometers east of a smaller village.

He didn't have time for the curse he wanted to mouth about the CIA's hired help. There was a likelihood the enemy had heard the aircraft. There was also a distinct possibility that their chutes had been seen emerging from the noisy, too-high C-123.

Black studied the map to fix features in his mind, then refolded and put it away. Without further contemplation he rose and motioned northeastward.

They'd travel a bit before burying harnesses and chutes, continue directly to Yankee 54, and join up with Banjo on the mountain looming behind Ban Sao Si. It would be a quicker trek than anticipated, for they were much closer than planned. It would also be more dangerous. They were definitely in Indian country.

After half an hour he estimated they'd come two kilometers, so they stopped at a mountain stream, cut a single panel out of each parachute, and buried the remainder. Not much farther along their beeline route, the Hotdog on point held them up and led them around the perimeter of an encampment of soldiers. They began to climb. This mountain was not nearly as steep as the one at Yankee 21, but the foliage was dense. At 0345 hours they cautiously approached the lookout post three fourths of the way up the mountain, and Black waited while the Hotdogs searched for unfriendlies, and for Banjo.

As anticipated, being so early, they found no one. They were alone at Yankee 54.

The lieutenant told Black in a disgusted tone that the militia soldiers they'd passed had been sloppy and inattentive.

"I like my enemies sloppy and inattentive," Black responded in Viet. He was burrowing a cubbyhole in the underbrush at one side of the clearing and lining it with his parachute panel to keep out insects. Finally satisfied, he sat back and looked at the lieutenant in the moonlight.

"Banjo team should be coming in. Tell the men to be alert."

"They know."

"It is good to be back at work," Black said without thinking, then wondered about his sanity at making the comment.

The lieutenant understood. "Yes," he said, searching about the periphery of the clearing for a sleeping place of his own, "but it will be better when we get to Ha Wa Eee."

A week earlier, after the failed mission to rescue the woman, the lieutenant had confided that he was tired of war. Black thought about that as he crept into his hole, pulled his People's Army issue rucksack into position, then tucked the nylon parachute and mosquito netting into place. He lowered his head onto the rucksack, cleared his mind, and a moment later was asleep.

A hiss awoke him, and it took a moment to gain his bearings. It was late, already 0640, and the small mountain clearing was bathed in the glow of morning sunlight. Black fussed at himself for being drowsy as he eased upright. He heard sounds of a helicopter in the near distance.

He nodded his appreciation to the Hotdog who'd awakened him, then carefully emerged from his hidden sleeping place.

There was no sign of Banjo team. The lieutenant was perched cross-legged on a rock at the top of the small clearing, looking through binoculars. He continued his observation for a moment longer, until the sounds of the chopper blades stopped, then raised an eyebrow at Black.

Black took the binoculars, adjusted fingerwheels, and stared at the large, six-bladed helicopter resting at one side of the narrow dirt strip below. Men were walking about it, pointing and shouting instructions as a swarm of others pushed it closer to the trees and covered it with netting. He could also see the outline of a small propeller-driven observation plane nestled into the foliage.

"An officer got off the helicopter with a courier bag," the lieutenant said.

Black studied the grass strip closely, then the group of thatch huts beyond. Ban Sao Si. Two large newly-constructed wooden buildings had been built between the village and the runway. The militia's headquarters?

"Any sign of Banjo?" he asked.

"No."

They were in a good position. The village, now bustling with activity, was only four kilometers away. The mesa that had once born the TACAN station was eight kilometers beyond Ban Sao Si, its top slightly below their position, and he could observe movement there too.

He lowered the glasses. "The HF radio?"

The lieutenant pointed. "While you slept, we set it up in the trees there."

Black glanced at the lieutenant and noted a mischievous look. "Get ready to send a patrol to check our perimeter."

The lieutenant nonchalantly motioned northward. "Nothing behind this mountain. The nearest soldiers are at *their* observation post four hundred meters below us. Typical militia. Twelve men and three women, and they are not alert. One of the women is old and ugly, the others . . ." He shrugged, as if to say "so-so." "There are animal trails there,

there, and there, all leading down the mountain. No one below is watching them. We are watching all three." He cocked his head thoughtfully. "There may be a small problem."

"What is that?"

"I think they know about us. Ten minutes ago they sent a company of men toward the drop zone." He pointed again. "You can see them through the binoculars."

Black looked until he saw men-specks walking on a dusty road, double-file but bunched up and looking more like a mob than a formation.

"These are poorly trained and very unprofessional," said the lieutenant. "Not the same kind of soldiers we saw here before. They will not be able to find us."

"Good work," Black muttered as he started for the radio, to make their initial call to Buffalo Soldier.

"Perhaps you should sleep late more often, Sarge Brack," grinned the lieutenant.

Wise guy. He found the radio, examined and rearranged the antenna, then hooked up the battery pack and double-checked the power level and reflected signal ratio. He stared at his wristwatch until it was time.

Buffalo Soldier immediately responded to his call.

"Hotdog is at Yankee five-four," he told Larry on the other end.

"Roger. Any problems?"

"There's no sign of Banjo."

"We know. You'll be alone there, Hotdog. Anything else?"

He thought about the fucked-up insertion location and the fact that the militia were deploying toward their DZ, but answered, *"Negative on the problems."*

"Is your position secure?"

"Affirmative, Buffalo Soldier. Position is secure."

"How's the view?"

"We've got a good line of sight with all objectives."

"How about Yankee two-one?"

"We've got good L-O-S. There's movement up there. No estimate on numbers yet."

"Yankee oh-three?" Meaning the dirt strip.

"Good L-O-S. There's one Sunday Hag and one Sunday Oscar Alpha down there now." Meaning there was a Soviet chopper and an observation aircraft on the dirt strip below.

"Yankee oh-four?"

The village. *"We've got it in sight. What's all this for?"*

"Stand by, Hotdog."

Black waited.

After a moment Larry came back on the air. *"How quickly can you get the numbers and locations, Hotdog? Minimum."*

Before leaving NKP, they'd told him he'd have ten days to look around and pinpoint everything. *"Five days?"* he tried.

Another wait. *"Hotdog, try to complete it in three. Break-break. Expect an incoming papa package of two at fourteen hundred hours, location Yankee seven-zero."*

Although they considered the directional, low-frequency HF signal-sideband radio secure, he was to add twelve hours to anything spoken by Buffalo Soldier. Which meant that at 0200 hours tomorrow morning someone would be dropped in at . . . he mentally went over the locations . . . a point nine klicks behind and north of the mountain.

"Roger, Buffalo Soldier. Yankee seven-oh at fourteen hundred hours."

After he signed off, Black wondered if whoever they dropped in might shed some light on the changes Buffalo Soldier had referred to. He felt a nagging dread. It was seldom good practice to alter things in the middle of an operation. He also wondered what had happened to Banjo. They'd been in charge of communications and had been carrying the UHF radio, and thus were the only ones who could talk with the fighters. Then he remembered the airborne FACs, and the fact that the radios in the O-1's would be set to monitor channel B on their hand-helds.

They'd have to make do with what they had.

1235L—Pave Dagger Test Headquarters, Ubon RTAFB, Thailand

Major Benny Lewis

The air tasking order for the following day had been received from Saigon, and the tasks for the Phantom wing at Ubon had been fragmented out. They'd be a part of a medium-sized bombing effort to strike targets in the Hanoi area.

The morning frag order for Ubon was to bomb new construction at the Phuc Yen MiG base that had been photographed by recce birds.

There was a special amendment to the air tasking order sent from Saigon. The one Benny and Moods had been awaiting. Two F-4Ds, coded PD-1 and PD-2, were tasked to bomb the small but critical railroad bridge over the Canales des Rapides.

The first Pave Dagger would be the illuminator bird, flown by Moods Diller and his GIB. Pave Dagger number two would be the shooter, one of the volunteer F-4 crews Moods had been working with—only one aircraft dropping bombs on a difficult target, which would normally require dozens of sorties.

Benny sat with Moods at his desk in a corner of the open room, pointing out the weakest parts of the bridge structure. He also observed his friend's reactions.

"Except for a flight of Weasels, you're going to be all alone over the target," he said.

Moods was engrossed with the photo.

"Wild Weasels from Korat will work over the area and keep the SAMs preoccupied during your time over target. They'll try to give you a three-minute window to locate the bridge and drop the two bombs. That's not giving you much time to get the job done."

Moods nodded almost abstractedly. He pointed at the middle span. "We'll take it down here," he said.

1400L—Ban Sao Si, Laos

GS-15 Linda Lopes

Ten days had passed since her arrival at the North Vietnamese camp, and they'd been odd ones. She was treated with disdain by the North Vietnamese, bullied like an animal, but the bamboo-stick beatings were administered halfheartedly, as if they didn't really expect answers.

Her broken nose had been the worst part. She spent hours holding it firmly in place with her fingers trying to straighten it. It was not only vanity. When it healed, she wanted to be able to breathe through the thing, a task which was impossible while it remained swollen. On the sixth day it was still terribly sore, but for the first time she was able to draw in a small flow of air. She became hopeful, and each night continued to hold it rigidly between her fingers. A small, tender knot of gristle had formed at each side of the bridge.

"You're tough," she kept telling herself, as she'd done at the Pathet Lao camps, and the self-exhortations worked. She also thought of Paul Anderson a lot, and as the feeling of intense love for him bolstered her, she concentrated on what he'd told her about his own brief period of captivity by the North Vietnamese.

Each time she was interrogated, the Sad Man, whom she had pegged as a Pathet Lao official, looked on quietly. He was obviously in charge of her treatment, a fact that the Viets liked not a bit. Sergeant Gross continued to go through the motions, reiterating the same questions, slapping the length of bamboo against her chest, stomach, legs, and arms, but there was no conviction to it. The Thin Man, whom she feared most, seldom watched the questioning, and when he did so, he appeared uninterested.

The beatings were administered in the hut, and there came to be a sort of ritual about them. Sergeant Gross would stand outside while a soldier unfastened the door. Then he would step in and eye her with his hungry look for a moment before motioning. She would go to a bamboo rack, where the soldier would tie her, and the sergeant would begin, barking a question, then striking her with the stick, always under the watchful eye of the Sad Man. Twice more the sergeant had led her outside to be bathed, and the soldiers gathered to stare and joke about her nakedness. The sergeant seemed to enjoy those times most of all.

She heard the familiar commotion at the door and stood, waiting fearfully as she had for each of the other sessions, muttering, "You're tough," over and over in a low voice.

The door opened, and Sergeant Gross stepped inside and stared with his narrowed eyes. This time he had a length of rope with a noose tied at one end, as he'd had that first day, and a smile danced about his pig's feature as he shoved it toward her.

She took it and frowned. *Where was the Sad Man?*

"Pud id on!" Sergeant Gross demanded, and abruptly kicked her leg. Linda gave a small shriek as she fell back, clutching her shin.

She slipped the loop about her neck.

Sergeant Gross watched with glittering eyes. He snapped his fingers and held out his hand.

Linda handed over the leash end of the rope.

Thin Man came in then, also smiling. He said something to Sergeant Gross and laughed in his high, reedy voice.

"The assistan' commissioner wan' you know you be-rong to him. T'ings haf change. You be-rong to him"—he smiled meanly—"an' to me."

Where was the Sad Man? she wondered again.

Assistant Commissioner Nguyen Wu

The woman stood dumbly as he examined his trophy. She was nude, because he'd ordered her to remove her clothing.

Early that morning a courier had arrived on a helicopter, carrying official missives for Nguyen Wu, the Viet militia commanding officer and the Laotian watchdog official.

The commander was told that all militia personnel were to comply with Assistant Commissioner Wu's every wish, under penalty of summary execution. The order was signed by Colonel Xuan Nha.

Nguyen's beloved aunt had also worked her magic with the Laotians. The message for the Pathet Lao watchdog was that the Mee woman was turned over to the assistant commissioner until he'd retrieved her secrets. It bore the authority of a high official of the Lao communist party.

The Pathet Lao nurtured some ridiculous idea about trading her to the Americans. They could do so, but Wu doubted if anyone would want what he left for them.

Nguyen Wu didn't hate the woman . . . did not have any feelings for her except his natural antagonism toward that sex. She was a tool to provide answers that would return him to favor with the party. He would impress his beloved aunt as never before. He had absolutely no doubt that the Mee woman would talk.

He walked slowly about her and eyed his subject. She

was tall and very correct in her bearing. Although she was a captive without hope, she'd not been stripped of her pride.

Ridiculous.

The Pathet Lao had tried to beat answers out of her and had gotten nowhere. That meant she had resolve. The silly, backward guerrillas had been impressed that she'd resisted so staunchly, for they'd been told that Americans were soft and nonenduring.

Nguyen Wu held no such regard for her. She was an animal to be broken. He'd learned how to do that. Degradation, starvation, and intense pain. First he would remove the pride, even the sense of humanity. He would dissolve all vestiges of civilization until left with a shell that would respond without hesitation.

He spoke instructions to a soldier and the man hurried out.

"Do you want to rut with her first?" he asked the Sergeant. The fat and ill-mannered man had been like a dog in heat since he'd first seen the woman.

The sergeant swallowed and attempted to suppress his anticipation. "If you wish, I will try, comrade, even though she is large and ugly."

"I do not want you to be gentle."

The sergeant's eyes glittered happily.

The soldier came back inside with a chair. Nguyen eyed the woman for another moment, then motioned for it to be placed back near the wall.

He sat.

"First perhaps a small beating," he said.

"I did not bring the bamboo, comrade." The sergeant was breathing harder now, a fact that was not lost on the woman, who watched him suspiciously.

She knows, thought Wu. He wondered what she was thinking.

"Use your fists and feet," he said.

Wu turned to the soldier who had retrieved the chair. "Gather twenty men who have been without women and who would like to fuck the Mee."

The sergeant struck the woman on the side of her head with his hand. She staggered and grunted.

"Get on with it," Wu said to the sergeant, then settled back with a bored expression to watch.

He'd picked his man well. The sergeant spent twenty full minutes kicking and beating the woman with his fists until she was cowering on the dirt floor, fresh blood pouring from her nostrils.

The sergeant motioned to several of the soldier's who'd gathered in anticipation at the door. They came in and held her down as the sergeant fumbled with his trousers with shaking fingers.

"She is a whore," Wu said to the soldiers. "Treat her like one."

They felt her breasts and one who was holding a leg thrust fingers into her and laughed loudly when she groaned.

The obese sergeant shoved the soldiers hand aside and knelt between the woman's legs, said something in a thick voice to her, then grasped hard on a breast and held himself with the other. He pushed harshly into her, and immediately began to rut. The outside world was quickly gone for the ill-mannered fat man who had trouble attracting the most desperate of the camp's prostitutes.

Wu looked on with interest. Women didn't excite him, but this particular incident was unique. The sergeant continued to labor vigorously, making high, piglike sounds from his opened mouth as he lurched and jerked. Wu peered at the woman's face. She squinted her eyes tightly, her face expressionless, head jolting with each of the sergeant's thrusts. Periodically she would cry out when the sergeant squeezed especially harshly or hit her with a fist.

The sergeant groaned, grasping harder yet on the woman's breast as he stiffened. He half rose, grimaced, and grunted loudly as he strained. The woman squirmed and tried vainly to escape. After a short, puffing pause, the sergeant began to pump anew, using more cautious strokes, breathing through his mouth.

When it was apparent that he was going to repeat the act, Wu spoke tersely. "Let the next man have her!" He had to raise his voice and repeat himself to gain the sergeant's attention. Wu motioned brusquely at the next man in line.

"When the others are finished, you can have her again," said Nguyen Wu to the sergeant.

Nguyen Wu watched as three more men toiled over the Mee woman. He went outside finally, bored with the woman's thrashing and dwindling shouts of outrage, and walked about the compound yard. The attitude of all who saw him was quite different from what it had been before. Men whispered and scattered at his approach. He was again a man to be reckoned with. And very soon all of his powers would be fully restored.

BOOK III

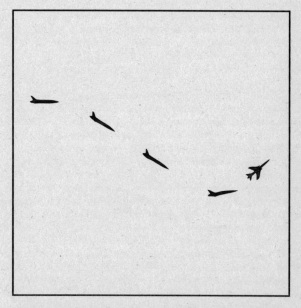

tan•go u•ni•form [military jargon, circa 1968] < phonetic alphabet acronym for "tits up"—*Informal. adj.* describing something which has failed, is dead, done for.

CHAPTER
THIRTY-FIVE

Friday, February 16th, 0200 Local—Location Y-70, Northeast Laos

Sergeant Black

Black and three Hotdogs waited at the DZ for the "packages" Buffalo Soldier had mentioned. Yankee 70 was an indistinguishable part of an uninhabited valley north of Ban Sao Si, covered to head height with elephant grass. The slope there was gentle, a good place for a drop.

Precisely on time Black heard the low, steady drone of aircraft engines from the west. He held out a powerful hooded flashlight and waited, remembering that the night's code was alpha. A dark shape loomed in the western sky, skimmed over the mountain, and dropped lower as it continued toward them.

Short-long, short-long, short-long, he signaled. The C-130 passed overhead, then the left wing drooped and it turned toward the north.

Two dark chutes blossomed, the dangling humans swinging in wide arcs . . . a precise low-altitude drop. Black aimed the flashlight at them, blinked several more dit-dahs, and scrambled toward the first impact point a hundred yards distant.

He hurried, then slowed when he heard rustling sounds of human movement. "Baltimore," he called in a low voice.

"Oriole," came a gruff response. There was more noise, subtle sounds of the man struggling out of his parachute. Black stepped in beside him and watched as he finished shedding the harness, then as he rolled up the nylon parachute. He was very large, six four or five, he estimated.

"Bring your chute," he whispered.

The man jumped. "Shit, I didn't see you there."

Black led him toward the other "package." As they came close, he repeated the password and again got the proper response. They found the second man hunkered down, examining something. While the two conferred in whispers, Black took both chutes and cut a panel from each with his knife.

"You Sergeant Black?" asked the big man.

"That's me." He finished, sheathed the bayonet knife, and rolled up the panels. "These are good to curl up in when you sleep. Help keep the bugs out."

"Captain Bechler," the guy said, kneeling beside the other guy and peering at something on the ground. "I'm your FAC."

"Forward air controller? I thought they were going to use an airborne FAC."

"Tell you about it later. This is Staff Sergeant Young, my ROMAD."

"Hope to hell the thing's okay," Young lamented. He looked up at them. "Radio was on a ten-foot tether, and it hit awfully hard."

Black looked closer. It was too dark to see more than a boxlike shape.

"It's our backup UHF," said Young, "so we can talk to the aircraft. The primary went tits up before we dropped. You got a ground-to-air radio?"

"No."

A Hotdog slipped in beside them, and Bechler did a double take. Black motioned toward the remnants of the two chutes, and the Hotdog disappeared to bury them at a discreet location.

"Looked like a fuckin' gomer," muttered Bechler.

"He used to be one."

"I hate fuckin' gomers."

"That one may save your butt if things start going to hell. You two ready to move out?"

Captain Bechler got to his feet, grumbling about gomers being assholes, then asked, "How far we got to go?"

"Nine klicks."

The big man stuck out his hand. "They call me Tiny. You?"

Black shook the massive paw. "Sergeant Black."

"First name?"

"Sergeant."

Tiny Bechler chuckled. "You some kinda spook?"

"Something like that."

The radio operator hefted the radio and adjusted carrying straps over his shoulders. Captain Bechler did the same with a bulky pack.

"While we're walking," Black instructed, "remain quiet and follow my lead. We'll try to stay well clear of the Viet camps, but they'll have patrols out."

"You're boss, Sarge."

A moment later the Hotdogs were assembled and positioned. Black motioned to the lieutenant, then beckoned for Bechler and Young to follow.

0500L

The trek back to Yankee 54, although uneventful, took two and a half hours. During that time neither Air Force man uttered a word. They were both in good physical condition, certainly better than Black had expected.

Black looked on as the lieutenant helped the Air Force men burrow sleeping niches into the jungle, making sure their positions couldn't be observed by someone walking through the clearing. Then he and Bechler left Sergeant Young tinkering over his radio in the dark and quietly walked to the rock at the top of the clearing. There Black told him what he could expect to see the next morning.

"Lots of targets," said the big captain. "I'm gonna enjoy this."

"How about the airborne FAC they were going to use?"

"An O-1 Birddog got hit by an SA-7 missile three days

ago near Mu Gia Pass, and the brass at Seventh Air Force
are nervous about sending 'em up here until they get flare
dispensers."

"So they sent a ground team."

"Yeah. And here we are. Been a couple years since I got
my five jumps at Benning." He shook his massive head. "I
didn't like that low-level jump one bit."

"They tell you what happened to Banjo?"

"Your button colonel at NKP said they were dropped way
off to the west somewhere and landed smack in the middle
of a bunch of gomers."

"Jesus."

"They lost a man. He said they'd've lost more, but the
gomers were surprised as hell when these guys started landing right on their camp."

Black's anger toward the contractor aircrews intensified.

"They were going to use the same people to drop us, but
your colonel said bullshit and raised enough hell to get it
changed. Had a Special Ops C-130 flown over from Nha
Trang."

"Are they bringing in another recon team?"

"He said you'll have to work it alone. Said they stirred
things up enough as it is, and he doesn't want to chance another insertion."

Black wasn't unhappy. Hotdog did best when they operated independently.

"When're you gonna talk with Buffalo Soldier next?"
Bechler asked.

"Oh-seven-hundred. I'll let 'em know you made it okay."

"Ask 'em to drop in another PRC radio, in case this one's
not repairable."

"You got any other way to talk to the airplanes?"

Bechler heaved a sigh. "I carry a couple hand-held survival radios just in case, but I've had 'em awhile, and that
one's got better range and endurance."

"If they won't chance another recon team drop, the colonel might hesitate at that too."

"Damn it, we've—"

"Keep your voice low. Sound travels in the night when
it's quiet like this."

"Sorry," Bechler whispered contritely.

"Why the hurry-up all of a sudden?" Black asked. "I was

supposed to have ten days, then this morning they told me I've only got three days to look around."

"Messages from God and the Pentagon came in saying they want the TACAN back on the air ASAP. They wanted to drop in another FAC, but he was off somewhere on R and R and the rest of 'em were busy on other projects. I happened to be here on temporary duty, so they asked if I'd like this little diversion."

"Where are you from?"

"Hurlburt Field in northern Florida."

"You're a fighter pilot?"

"You've gotta be to become a FAC. Six months ago I was flying Thuds out of Takhli, looking down on this place."

They spoke about other things for a few minutes; then Black remembered Lieutenant Colonel Anderson was stationed at Takhli and asked if he knew him.

"Lucky's a good man. Sure is shitty, what I heard about his lady being kidnapped."

"Yeah." Black decided he liked the moose-sized captain.

Tiny Bechler nodded at the moonlit scene below. "Maybe we can even the score some for him. Soon as we get another radio and you've got things pinpointed, we'll call up the good guys and then the fun begins."

0658L—Route Pack Six, North Vietnam

Lieutenant Colonel Lucky Anderson

It would be the second time they'd bombed in pack six in the past two days, and Lucky had volunteered to lead both efforts.

Angrily. For Linda.

He knew never to allow personal emotions to cloud judgment in combat and made sure he didn't place the others in unnecessary danger, but each time he pressed the pickle button and the bombs fell away, he prayed the weapons were doing the maximum damage.

Lucky despised the enemy . . . but he also despaired at the fact that the war was being allowed to continue. He wanted to hurt the North Vietnamese so badly that they'd stop fighting. Perhaps then there'd be word about Linda—

about all his friends who'd been shot down and captured. He thought about JACKPOT—the plan to end the war through relentless bombardment. Such a thing would work. It seemed ridiculous that it hadn't been done two years earlier.

As the sixteen-ship formation flew abeam the curl in the Red River to their north, Lucky checked his altitude. They were slowly descending, passing through 8,000 feet just as he'd planned it.

Takhli's target was the auxiliary airfield at Hoa Lac, west of Hanoi. The enemy had been actively repairing all of their air bases.

The formation loosened, anticipating the climb to dive-bomb altitude.

He could see the target runway at their one o'clock. It wouldn't be long now.

Captain Manny DeVera

Manny was in his dive. The sight picture was not great—the half-constructed building was too far left. He jogged the stick a bit to correct, then pickled before he was really ready.

Damn! The bombs would be lousy, he knew. Probably impact a couple hundred feet off target. A burst of flak erupted close by, shaking the aircraft. He twisted and jinked toward his left, pulling too hard and letting off a bit to compensate—wondering why the hell he couldn't get his act together. He knew the answer.

Keep your mind busy with essentials, like what you're going to do next. All of that was easy and just fine when your thoughts were sound.

So goddamn tired! The Thud shook again from a near miss, and he felt a sudden jolt of numbing fear. He'd experienced them before, but he'd learned how to master them, and—

More dark bursts appeared ahead, and Manny pulled the stick harder. The sick feeling intensified and grew in his chest, and he could not quell it. He panicked, began breathing fiercely and shaking uncontrollably as he pushed the throttle against the afterburner stop.

He was still in burner, climbing and looking back as he

raced westward, when he swung his head forward and saw two aircraft dead ahead—and dodged hard left to avoid them.

He dimly heard the angry radio call over guard channel, complaining about a Thud that had damn near rammed one of the Phantoms.

Captain Moods Diller

Moods hadn't seen the Thud that almost ended his mission and ruined his day until the last second. It had come up from below, at his two o'clock, and flashed past in full afterburner, climbing through his altitude like a scalded ape.

Lark two-two yelled over the radio that the Thud had damned near rammed them.

Things were tense enough without that. Moods was more nervous than he'd been in a long while, since the last time he'd been to Hanoi, more than a year earlier. There was nothing as nerve-racking as flying in pack six.

Lark flight, which consisted only of Moods and his wingman, were flying slightly right and behind the Ubon F-4 formation, hiding in the jamming noise created by their ECM pods.

At least, Moods thought, the weather was good.

They were halfway across the valley now. Thud Ridge loomed in the near distance, Hanoi sprawled to their right. Flying at 8,000 feet.

The captain in his backseat checked the illuminator pod again. This was the third time. It was operating okay, he announced. Then, "We're two minutes from the target."

Moods ignored his chatter. He could read the clock. They were both nervous as cats, and not only about the AAA and SAMs they'd surely find. If things went right, it would prove everything they'd been working on for the past ten months. If they screwed up—or the illuminator quit—or the bomb guidance circuitry failed—or if they . . . *Stop it!*

The sixteen-ship formation of F-4Ds began to climb, setting up to dive-bomb Phuc Yen.

Moods and his wingman continued straight ahead, toward their own destinies. Past the southern extremity of Thud Ridge. A SAM radar signal grew out of the fuzz of the jamming noise on his RHAW scope, and Moods knew they were being tracked.

"Baron lead's got SAM activity at your two o'clock, Lark." Baron was the call sign of the Wild Weasels sent to keep the enemy occupied while they dropped the Pave Dagger bombs.

Moods saw the F-105 Weasel flight ahead, turning starboard toward Hanoi. He searched the ground, followed the course of the big river eastward, saw the division where the Canales des Rapides veered from the main channel of the Red River.

The SAM signal seemed to grow more persistent. Both the SAM and ACTIVITY lights glowed brightly on the warning receiver—which on the F-4D worked properly only half the time.

"Baron lead is Shotgun!" Meaning the Weasel had launched a radar-seeking missile.

The SAM and ACTIVITY lights went out as the SAM radar went off the air.

Moods kept his eyes glued on the small dark line crossing the Canales des Rapides. *"Target is at one o'clock, eight miles,"* he announced over radio for the benefit of both his wingman and backseater. *"Lark two-two, extend,"* he called in a too-dry voice.

"Lark two-two," acknowledged the wingman. He would drop back, swing out far to the right as he climbed, then turn back inbound toward the target, and set up for his dive bomb.

Ten seconds slowly crawled by.

"Target's in sight," the GIB said over intercom. "I'm magnifying. Going to times ten."

For the hot action in pack six, they'd modified the tactics they'd used in lower-threat areas. This time there'd be little room or time for error.

"Damn thing won't stabilize!" cried the GIB.

They were fast approaching the target.

"Keep trying," Moods said over intercom.

The backseater was using hot mike, meaning the intercom was activated at all times, and Moods could hear the loud, grating rasp of his breathing.

"I'm turning," said Moods, beginning his orbit around the bridge far below.

"I've got the target again! Shit. The image is dancing all over the place, Moods!"

"Use less magnification," Moods said, "and try again."

"Yeah."

"*Lark two-two is approaching the release point.*"

"*Do not drop, two-two,*" Moods radioed. "*Set up again.*"

"*Lark two-two.*" The shooter sounded concerned, which was understandable considering he had to pull up, go back around and try again while flying in the most dangerous area on earth.

"I'm back to times five," the GIB muttered.

Another missile site's radar signal danced on the RHAW receiver, a bright-green finger pointing to the four o'clock quadrant of the small cathode ray tube.

"*Lark two-one, this is Baron lead—we're showing SAM activity on you again.*"

A shrill tone squealed in his earphones.

"*Lark, you've got a valid launch.*"

The GIB spoke in a happier tone. "I've got the target. Good picture."

Moods gritted his teeth. He was watching the strobe grow on the radar warning scope, and at the same time looking out for the missiles. "Turn on the illuminator," he told the GIB.

"*Lark two-two's approaching release zone,*" called the shooter, "*beginning my dive.*"

"I've got the zot turned on, holding on target," said the GIB.

"*Lark two-two, drop one,*" Moods radioed. He held the aircraft very steady, looking for the surface-to-air missile, praying it wasn't guiding—and if it was, that he'd see it in time to dodge it.

"The illuminator's on the center of the bridge," the GIB said.

1114L—Pave Dagger Test Headquarters, Ubon RTAFB, Thailand

Major Benny Lewis

Lewis pushed his way through the door, carrying a cardboard box.

The crowd was jammed into the lab room, where Moods Diller and his pilot GIB were regaling the technicians and engineers with the gritty details of the mission.

Moods pointed at the backseater. "He kept trying to get a stable picture, but the magnification was just too much."

"Soon as I backed off a bit, everything settled down."

The senior Texas-team engineer was frowning. "We'll try gyro-stabilizing the pod. In the meanwhile we should either change the videcon, or get an increased pixel count on the video monitor."

"Enough talk about pixels and that crap!" Benny yelled to the group.

"You got something, Major?" asked the GIB.

"People at Seventh Air Force called," Benny said. "They just got a look at the BDA film. The bomb damage assessment interpreter confirms what you guys saw. The middle span's down."

"Yeah!" shouted an exuberant tech sergeant.

"General Moss passed along his congratulations."

"Maybe they'll *all* start listening closer now."

"When do we get our next good target?" Moods Diller asked. "We got the last twelve bomb kits peaked and ready."

"Soon enough. Don't be so anxious."

"Gimme another bridge," said the pilot GIB.

"The regs say you can only fly one pack-six sortie a day. No more flying today."

"Yeah. Maybe one of those is enough," said the GIB. "But tomorrow . . ."

Benny pointed at the cardboard box. "That's champagne, and there's another case in the back of the pickup."

The loud tech sergeant hurried toward the door. "You oughta know better than to leave it out there, Major. The Thais steal anything that's not tied down."

A grinning airman first class ripped the lid off the first box.

"Now," crowed the GIB, "we'll start *really* proving our stuff."

The airman started passing out magnums of champagne.

The GIB wasn't through. "These smart bombs are so accurate we could take out Ho Chi Minh's private crapper."

"No use to get personal," joked the pudgy lead engineer. "They might retaliate."

"The battle of the shitters?"

"Damn war's getting serious."

1305L—VPA Headquarters, Hanoi, DRV

Colonel Xuan Nha

The room was occupied by only a handful of the military leaders who normally attended the meetings. Giap and Dung sat at the forefront of the room, the lesser commanders in the rows of chairs behind.

A People's Army intelligence major was providing a candid briefing of the status of the war, and the effects of the widespread attacks in the South.

Two entire People's Army divisions had been decimated to the point that they would have to be reconstituted from the bottom up. Losses included three of their most capable general officers. The People's Liberation Front had suffered even worse. Whole regions were leaderless. Only in the Song Mekong Delta had they made lasting inroads.

It was all most disturbing. There'd been the initial flush of victory as their forces attacked throughout the South, but within two days they'd begun to suffer defeat after bitter defeat.

A second briefer moved to the front of the room, smiling childishly at General Giap. He bowed solicitously, obviously uneasy that he'd been selected to present the next topic.

The worst situation that might happen.

If . . . the puppet Saigon Army now moved quickly and decisively to solidify their victories, responding with the same vigor they'd shown during the past three weeks . . .

If . . . the American Army mounted a counterattack at Khe Sanh, as was expected, and broke the siege that was beginning to falter there . . .

If . . . the American air forces brought in even more air-craft and began an around-the-clock bombardment of the Hanoi and Haiphong areas . . .

General Dung interrupted, wondering what made the in-telligence briefer think such a thing was even remotely pos-sible.

A colonel stood and warily approached the front of the room, careful to keep his eyes diverted from both Generals Giap and Dung. He cleared his throat testily and spoke in a high voice. "There is a new intelligence input from the So-viets, who intercepted an American colonel's telephone call from Saigon. There is a project called 'Zhack-pot,' which calls for a buildup of Mee air power, followed by a relentless bombing campaign."

Was such a thing possible? Mee politicians had never shown such resolve in the past.

"We believe it is only a plan now. But there was also ref-erence to a December meeting between the general in Sai-gon believed to be writing the plan, and President Riddin Jah-soh."

There followed a deep silence around the room. No one dared to utter their long-held fear that such a bombardment might actually take place. The aging leaders of the Demo-cratic Republic would surely pull back the military forces—agree to anything to ensure the fragile infrastructure of the nation, and all their achievements of the past twenty years, was not destroyed.

"There is also another development. We have heard of new weapons carried by Mee fighter aircraft, with such great accuracy that a single bomb will destroy the most heavily defended, difficult target. We believe that was how the Mee did such heavy damage to the Canales bridge this morning. There was only one bomb, released from very high, yet the weapon struck precisely in the middle of the bridge's central span."

General Dung turned to Xuan Nha, by far the most tech-nically minded member of the general staff. Xuan gave him a small, private nod, confirming that had indeed happened.

The intelligence colonel continued. "The Mee have al-ways avoided bombing Hanoi proper, for fear they will kill civilians and foreign visitors. If they have such an accurate weapon, and decide to use them here in Hanoi . . ."

Visions of the selective destruction of city power stations and warehouses—of Ho Chi Minh's residence—of the People's Army headquarters buildings situated beside civilian housing—even of truck convoys forming in the streets—immediately came to mind.

General Giap spoke for the first time during the briefing. "This cannot be allowed to happen," he said quietly.

Grave looks darted across the room.

Giap turned to his aide. "Call the Minister for External Affairs"—he paused thoughtfully—"and Deputy Minister Li Binh. Tell them we have a matter of urgency to discuss."

Half an hour later the intelligence colonel presented the same disastrous scenario to the two senior members of the Ministry of External Affairs.

The minister shook his head gravely, but was not quick to provide a solution.

Li Binh wore a neutral expression, seated at the minister's right hand. She waited dutifully until she was called upon by a look from the minister.

Her voice was matter-of-fact. "I received the briefing from the Russians about this *Zhack-pot* plan," she said, "and my office has begun to react. We have sent message to several groups in the United States, trying to find out more. They will also begin to spread fears there that the President is considering expanding the war, which would surely bring disaster for the Mee."

Giap brooded. "Will it work?"

"The Americans are at the very beginning of an election to choose their new political leaders. This includes their President. Their politicians are most vulnerable to criticism just now."

Giap fluttered an impatient hand. "Continue."

"For the past three weeks Western newspapers have printed reports about our massive attacks throughout the South—how we have met our objectives in all areas—how the corrupt Saigon puppets are on the brink of falling. Critics within the American government are calling for explanations from their military. Americans are demonstrating. It is becoming as it was when we did the same thing in Paris in 1953. There the French listened to us and distrusted their political leaders. Now the same is happening in America. Where are the Western newspapers receiving their information?" Li Binh smiled. "We write it for them in my Office of Truth. Their news agencies cannot get enough of our truth."

Giap mused thoughtfully.

"We will do the same thing with this *Zhack-pot* plan as we did with their plan to bring more American soldiers to the South. We will discover their secrets and then provide them to the press. Western newspapers delight in embarrassing their politicians."

Giap spoke a simple sentence. "This plan cannot be allowed, comrade Madam Binh."

Li Binh nodded firmly. "It will not."

1615L—Pave Dagger Test Headquarters, Ubon RTAFB, Thailand

Major Benny Lewis

The others were gone, some of them tipsy from alcohol, all of them inebriated with success.

Before he'd left with the others, Moods had cornered Benny and told him he'd received a letter from his live-in girlfriend, Pam, who'd run into Julie Stewart while shopping at the base exchange. Julie was worried because she'd not heard from Benny. When Pam told her he was okay, she'd been relieved.

"You oughta write her," Moods had told him.

So here he was, sitting at the small desk and staring at the piece of paper before him like some kind of robot, trying to decide what to write.

He'd penned an introduction of sorts, apologizing for not having written before, and asking about the baby, little Patty, and her mother. And Julie herself, of course.

But as he wrote, he felt odd. He'd written other letters to loved ones—those when he'd been flying combat during the most dangerous time of the war—to his wife and kids.

He'd found that his wife had been cheating on him almost from the time of his departure.

That heartache was past, but not the reluctance to share

his inner thoughts. His ex-wife had stung him very thoroughly and destroyed something he'd felt was inviolable.

With Julie, of course, his feelings were entirely different. He felt comfortable in her presence, enjoyed just being around her and laughing at her corny jokes, liked just to sit and watch her do things sometimes.

Then, the only time they'd been intimate, he'd utterly blown the whole thing. He'd felt he was violating a trust between himself and his friend who had married her.

The same thing was happening now. It was as if he were writing to another man's wife.

He's dead, dammit. She's free!

And then he knew what it was—what it had been when he'd made love to her and felt the chilling presence. He was happy she was free. Did that mean he was also happy that his best friend had been killed?

That's absurd!

The outrageous question remained with him, and he couldn't make it go away. He forced a tortured breath, wondering what he should write. Julie was worrying, Moods had said.

An airman first class came through the outer door, looking around and carrying a red-covered message.

"Major Lewis?"

"Yes."

The airman said he was from the comm distribution center and had him sign for a classified message.

Benny waited until the courier had departed to open the cover. There was no one else to share it with, since the others had departed for the NCO and Officers' Open Messes to continue their celebration.

SECRET—IMMEDIATE
DTG: 15/1400ZFEB68
FM: CINCPACAF/IG, HICKAM AFB, HI
TO: HQ 7 AF/CC/DO/DP, TAN SON NHUT
AB, SVN
8 TFW/CC/DO, UBON AB, THAI
PAVE DAGGER OPNS/UBON AB, THAI
INFO: HQ USAF AF XO/IG, WASH D.C.
TFWC/CC NELLIS AFB, NV

SUBJECT: COMBAT TEST ACTIVITY/PAVE
DAGGER
REF 1: (S) HQ USAF/XO MSG DTD
10/0800ZJUL66, PARA 2B AUTHORIZES
TERMINATION OF INESSENTIAL ACTIVITIES
WHICH THIS HQ DEEMS MAY INTERFERE WITH
COMBAT OPERATIONS. REF 2: (U) 15 FEB
68 TELECON CINCPACAF IG CV TO USAF
XOO CONFIRMED PACAF AUTHORITY.
1. (S) PACAF/IG INCIDENTAL INSPECTION
REPORT, DTD 14 NOV 67, FINDS THAT
PROJECT PAVE DAGGER TESTS ARE
CREATING COMBAT AIRCRAFT SCHEDULING
PROBLEMS, AND ARE JEOPARDIZING
CRITICAL ASSETS.
2. (S) FOR 8TFW/CC: TERMINATE ALL
SUPPORT FOR SUBJECT TEST PROGRAM.
MK-84 BOMBS DESIGNATED FOR TEST WILL
BE DEMODIFIED AND RETURNED TO
GENERAL WEAPONS UTILIZATION. PAVE
DAGGER ILLUMINATOR PODS AND TEST
EQUIPMENT WILL BE RETURNED TO POINT
OF ORIGIN VIA PRI-5 SFC SHIPMENT.
3. (S) FOR 8TFW/DO: FORWARD COPIES
OF ALL PAVE DAGGER MESSAGE TRAFFIC
AND TEST DATA TO THIS HQ, ATTN. PACAF/IG,
FOR DETERMINATION OF POSSIBLE
VIOLATION OF SECURITY PROCEDURES
AND PRUDENT SAFETY PRACTICES.
4. (C) FOR TFWC/CC: REQUEST YOU RECALL
PAVE DAGGER TEST PERSONNEL
TRAVELING WITHIN THE PACIFIC AREA
OF OPERATIONS NLT 28 FEB 68. FUTURE
DEPLOYMENTS MUST BE AUTH BY
CINCPACAF/XO.
SECRET—IMMEDIATE

The message was so ridiculous that at first Benny wondered
if it might be a joke. After reading it twice more, Benny replaced the red cover and put the message into the safe.

The telephone rang. It was the Ubon wing commander,
asking if he'd received his copy.

He said he had.

What the hell was going on?

Benny said, quite truthfully, that he had no earthly idea. He said he planned to fly to Saigon to discuss the matter with General Moss.

The wingco said he thought that was a good idea.

For the next ten minutes Benny tried to think of a way to lessen the shock for the Pave Dagger team. He decided to wait until the next morning, after they'd celebrated their success.

He secured the safe and left, leaving the unfinished letter on the desktop.

Ban Sao Si, Laos

GS-15 Linda Lopes

The degradations had been complete. When they'd forced her the first day—so many men, she'd not tried to count them—she'd lost the last vestige of her will to live. When it was over, when the last man had used her, and the soldiers and even Thin Man had left, Sergeant Gross had taken her a second time, then had stood above where she lay curled and silent on the dirt floor. He'd spoken slowly, told her she was a whore and should become accustomed to pleasing men. He'd demanded that she look at him, and she'd painfully done so. Then he'd pulled out his familiar stubby penis and urinated on her, moving the yellow stream up and down her body. He'd left, laughing.

Linda had slept, awakened to the stench of semen and urine, and had searched for something to kill herself with. They'd taken the rope. There was nothing else. There had been no food that night, only a single cup of water.

The next morning Sergeant Gross returned with two soldiers, had her remove the semen-encrusted, ragged clothing she'd somehow struggled into, and they took her outside and dumped water over her. After that they returned her to the hut, and the sergeant shooed the others out. He offered her a tiny bowl of rice, and she salivated for it. He told her how she was to earn it, then beat her with his fists and mounted her from the rear.

When the sergeant had finished he puffed for a bit and said she'd earned her new name. *Whore,* he called her, and made Linda repeat the word aloud.

She ate greedily. It hadn't mattered how she'd gotten the food. As soon as she'd finished the bowl, the sergeant tossed her the noose and led her, still nude and stumbling from weakness, into Thin Man's office.

She was pushed into the cage. Paper-Shuffler seemed embarrassed as he went on about his business and ignored her presence. An hour passed before Thin Man came into the office, closely followed by Sergeant Gross, who carried a greasy paper packet.

Thin Man went to his desk and sat, then turned to eye her. It was a neutral look, as he might give to an inanimate object.

Sergeant Gross spoke to Thin Man in Viet, and she understood only the word "whore."

Thin Man tried the sound of it, looking at her as he spoke the word. The sergeant cuffed her and told her to answer to her name, so the next time Thin Man uttered the word, she responded.

Sergeant Gross asked a question about the cell of confidential informants she'd established near Korat Air Base. Linda remained quiet and stock-still. The sergeant unfolded the packet and displayed rice laced with dark chunks of meat.

"Do you wan', whore?"

"Yes," Linda breathed.

"Rike before, you mus' earn it."

She didn't speak, just eyed the food and took in the rich aroma.

Sergeant Gross asked her again about the cell of agents at Korat. She licked her lips but didn't answer.

Thin Man spoke again, and she was taken out and returned to the hut, where another line of bantering, curious soldiers waited.

Linda wasn't able to count them that time either as they mounted her, one after the next. When the last one was done, she was washed down and returned to Thin Man's office. Then Sergeant Gross beat her relentlessly with the length of bamboo.

She'd thought herself drained of all energy and caring,

but Linda screamed her agony until there was no sound left in her. It wasn't at all like before. Sergeant Gross used all of his strength and knew precisely where to concentrate his blows. Her breasts, her face, and her feet. He continued even after she had no more screams in her—even after her teeth were broken and her nose moved about on her face as if it were made of liquid—even after her breasts felt like boils, and the soles of her feet were on fire.

When he asked his questions that time, she answered, and Paper-Shuffler diligently wrote down each of Sergeant Gross's interpretations. The questions and answers continued for a long while, until she was drained of knowledge about the intelligence community. Names, locations, everything she knew—went onto Paper-Shuffler's notepad.

She'd broken, but the fact didn't seem important, only that the awful beatings had stopped. There was food afterward, but only a tiny portion.

She was not returned to the hut, but deposited in the small cage and left there. She came to sleep, urinate, and defecate as she crouched animal-like. A small trench was dug into the dirt floor. Soldiers came in the morning and afternoon to dump buckets of water over her and flush outside the urine, feces, and the acrid smells of her.

Sunday, February 18th, 0850L

How long ago had that been? How many days? How many beatings, questions, and responses? How many times had the sergeant come into the office in the night and dragged her from the cage to use her in whatever way he wished?

There was no more left in her to give for her country. She prayed only for death.

There was never enough food. Linda was scarecrow thin, and her thoughts were seldom lucid. She could scarcely distinguish between fantasy and reality, but somehow through the fog of her existence she remembered something Paul had told her.

The Viets were fearful of insanity, and treated mad people with caution.

It was daytime. Paper-Shuffler and Sergeant Gross were working. She uttered a low howl and cast unfocused eyes about the room. They looked at her oddly, but she didn't care, just continued the low howling sounds.

When they questioned her that day, she didn't respond, simply continued to howl in the low and mournful way. Sergeant Gross beat her violently, and she screamed just as she always did, but when he asked his questions, she reverted to the low howls and blank stares.

Thin Man gave a direction. She was shoved back into the tiny bamboo cell, and a bowl of food was brought and placed near her. With the mightiest of efforts, she ignored the bowl.

Thin Man spoke again, his eyes narrowed, his face wearing a look of concern. Sergeant Gross pulled her from the cage and again offered the food. She ignored it. He pushed rice into her mouth and recoiled as he watched it falling from the sides of her mouth.

Thin Man had to speak sharply to get Sergeant Gross to continue, for he was suddenly very wary and seemed frightened of her.

After another effort Linda swallowed a small bit of food.

Thin Man looked pleased. Sergeant Gross fed her more. He asked her a question, and she responded with the low howl and vacant stare. Thin Man gave quiet instructions. Sergeant Gross guided her back into the cage, and they left her alone.

Linda Lopes felt a tiny flutter of gratification.

Madness. Feigning it had been easy, for she was close to that border, and at least part of it was real. *How much?* she wondered vaguely, and how long would her tiny victory last?

CHAPTER
THIRTY-SIX

Monday, February 19th 0700 Local—Y-54, Northeastern Laos

Sergeant Black

The moose-sized FAC was lying flat on the rock outcropping, peering across at the mesa hilltop through a tripod-mounted spotting scope. Black watched him shift his view down toward the end of the dirt runway, then to other locations where the lieutenant and his men reported antiaircraft defenses and encampments of between 800 and 900 troops. He seemed to be very thorough in his examinations, referring to notes he'd made on a compact clipboard.

Two UHF survival radios were at his side on the rock. The PRC radio hadn't survived the jump, and although Air South had air-dropped another the previous night, God only knew where it had landed. Black was guessing some Laotian farmer was likely using it to dam up a rice paddy. Sergeant Young stood off to one side, frowning and feeling useless without the PRC to nurture. He was skeptical that the survival-radio batteries would last long enough to direct the strikes. Buffalo Soldier had relayed TOTs for twelve flights

of fighters, and the numbers were growing. That meant
they'd need to make a lot of transmissions.

Captain Bechler told the radio operator they'd operate
with what they had, and if that meant using semaphore
flags, they'd do it. The runway and the mesa would be obvious and fair game, but the fighters would first be directed
to destroy the various air defenses and troop concentrations
hidden in the jungle, and told precisely how to avoid the
concentrations of civilians in Ban Sao Si and several smaller
jungle villages. They had to have an FAC direct their fire if
they were to be effective. If they bombed blind, they'd kill
innocents and lay waste to a lot of empty jungle.

The first time over target was scheduled at 0720 hours.
The scene below remained quiet when they heard the first
distant rumblings of aircraft.

"Thuds," Bechler said.

Black guessed Tiny's ears must be tuned for the sounds
of the various jet engines, as his were for different weapons
fire. He followed Bechler's gaze and surveyed the western
sky.

The hand-held radio sputtered with noise. *"Bongo, this is
Viper zero-one, transmitting in the blind."*

Bechler smiled and raised the small radio to his lips. *"Viper flight, this is Bongo, your FAC on this fine morning, and
I've got targets for you, buddy."*

0719L—Over Channel 97, Northeastern Laos

Lieutenant Colonel Lucky Anderson

"Bongo, Viper lead reads you three by three," Lucky answered, which meant he could hear the FAC's radio only
marginally well. Five by five was optimum in both loudness
and clarity. Anything below a three was considered definitely substandard and difficult to decipher.

"Ah roger, Viper lead. Give me your particulars."

*"Viper flight is four Fox one-oh-fives, carrying CBU-24's
and full twenty mike-mike. I've got three more flights of
Thuds behind me with hard bombs, and we'll stick around
for the next forty-five minutes."*

"Ah roger. Expect SA-7's, thirty-seven-millimeter guns,

and small arms fire. Hold your flight above flight level zero-five-zero, and keep your Mach up until we've made the area hospitable."

Lucky's flight was to take out the defenses with their cluster bombs and guns, then hang around while the other Thuds attacked, ready to take out more defenses should they threaten.

"We'll use your CBUs first this morning, Viper lead." Bongo described a knoll halfway between the mesa and the village of Ban Sao Si, then an area near the end of the dirt strip, where the SA-7 shoulder-fired infrared guided missiles were positioned.

Lucky winged over to lead the first attack, at thirty degrees dive angle, on the position nearest the mesa. He selected to drop a single CBU-24 and settled the aircraft very precisely. He was passing through 7,000 feet when a Thud driver announced that a missile had been fired from the location beside the runway.

They'd been briefed that intelligence didn't believe the SA-7's would be able to keep up with a fast-mover aircraft like the Thud. Lucky continued his dive and released at 5,000 feet. Two more SA-7's were called out. None of them came close. The cluster bomblets hit where he'd intended, sparkling brightly as they exploded.

The FAC confirmed it. *"Good hit, Viper lead. Viper two, put another CBU a hundred yards north of lead's."*

"Viper two." The wingman was already in his delivery dive.

As the remainder of the flight dropped their bomblets on the small knoll, four more infrared missiles were fired from the dirt strip . . . and all missed. Viper three, Manny DeVera, released early and pulled up wildly when a missile launch was called, but that one came nowhere close either.

"Yeah!" exulted the FAC. *"Now let's take out the rest of the defenses, Vipers."*

Each of the four aircraft dropped a single CBU-24 on the area near the end of the runway where the SA-7's had been launched. Again DeVera's cluster bombs were off target, and Lucky wondered. The Supersonic Wetback was a better marksman than that. Then something happened that made him forget all about Manny.

As the last Thud pulled off target, Lucky noted muzzle flashes from the ground and called them out to the FAC.

"*That's a concentration of thirty-seven-millimeter guns, Viper, . . . they're too . . . the village for your CBUs. How . . . a strafing pass?*"

"*Your radio's breaking up, Bongo. Understand a strafe pass on the guns?*"

"*Affirmative, . . . lead.*"

Lucky dipped toward the guns. Normally they'd slow down and strafe at ten- or twenty-degree dive angles, but he maintained the thirty degrees in case they hadn't taken out all the SA-7's. The muzzle flashes continued as he flew toward them, and red baseballs flashed past his cockpit. The M-61 Gatling gun growled and spat out 400 rounds of fury in a single burst.

After the second bird had strafed, there were no more flashes from that location. Number three noted another cluster of guns, and he and the Viper four took those out. The enemy was down to small arms. The Vipers tested the defenses by flying lower, appearing more vulnerable. There were no more missile firings or 37mm.

"*. . . work, Vipers. Now . . . in the . . . flights.*"

"*You're breaking up badly, Bongo. Understand you're ready for the other Thuds to come in?*"

"*. . . the hard . . .*"

"*Bongo, this is Viper lead. Your transmissions are breaking up and unreadable.*"

A slight pause.

"*This is Bongo. How's this radio, Viper lead?*" The transmission was weak but readable.

"*I'm reading you three by three again, Bongo.*"

"*This is my second and last radio, Viper, and I'm going to conserve the battery by limiting my transmissions.*"

"*Understand, Bongo. I'll relay that word to the next birds.*"

Lucky called in the next flights of Thuds, then held Viper flight up at 8,000 feet, as briefed. The F-105 pilots dropped napalm and 500-pound bombs in pairs on concentrations of soldiers camped in four different areas around the mesa. There was no more antiaircraft fire.

After the third flight of Thuds finished their attacks, and Bear Force arrived on the scene, Viper flight was relieved.

Yank Donovan checked in and brusquely said he'd take control. By then Bongo's transmissions on the new radio had grown very weak, and he was transmitting only essential information.

Lucky told Yank about the FAC's failing radio and advised him to limit his conversations with the FAC.

Lieutenant Colonel Yank Donovan

Anderson was right about the FAC's radio. The damned thing was hardly readable, and with each transmission it grew weaker. *You'd think the dumb shits would plan ahead better than that.*

After the first flight had dropped napalm on a small troop concentration, the second was preparing to strafe two wooden buildings beside the small dirt strip. There, Bongo said, they had to exercise care, for there were noncombatant civilians very close by.

"... *from west to east and* ... *take out* ..."

"*This is Bear Force leader. Say again, Bongo,*" Donovan growled angrily.

"*I said* ..."

Dammit! "*Repeat your transmission, Bongo.*"

A low hissing sound, then silence.

0820L—Ban Sao Si, Laos

Assistant Commissioner Nguyen Wu

Nguyen Wu huddled at the dark, far end of the sandbagged shelter, beside the trembling admin major. The fat sergeant was curled into a fetal position nearby and refused to move.

So far the Mee had not bombed here, but they surely would. The lieutenant who was nearest the mouth of the shelter had just come from another encampment, and he said the airplanes had been eerily accurate. It was as if they knew precisely where each bunker and ammunition supply was located.

Wu's own breath came in shallow wheezes, and he could not remember being so frightened, yet he remained coherent, which was beyond the capabilities of his two men.

Where were the shoulder-fired missiles they'd been told would protect them? For more than an hour the aircraft had bombed and fired their guns in the area, and there was no longer the reassuring sounds of antiaircraft fire. Not even rifle fire.

So close, his mind kept whispering. He had the Mee woman's information. As soon as she regained a glimmer of sanity, there were a few more answers to be obtained, but he did not think many. He certainly had enough to impress his superiors in Hanoi.

He reached out and pulled at the leather courier's pouch the cowering major clutched to himself. In it was the notebook containing the woman's confessions.

"Give it to me," he demanded.

The major resisted, holding the pouch tightly to his body, as if it somehow protected him.

"Give it to me!"

The major heard, but Nguyen Wu had to pry his fingers loose. He pulled the pouch away, thinking of what it contained.

His redemption.

Suddenly he realized there'd been no sounds of bombing for the past several minutes. Had the Thunder planes gone? The lieutenant near the doorway peered outside and announced that there were still many fighters circling above, but none were attacking.

Strange.

A thought glimmered, then slowly took form. Several small trucks and weapons carriers were parked just beyond the runway. If the aircraft delayed longer, he might be able to escape!

He went cautiously toward the opening, was blinded by the brightness for a moment, then squinted up at the airplane specks.

"Why have they stopped?" he wondered aloud.

The lieutenant shook his head.

Nguyen Wu made up his mind. "Come with me," he shouted back to the dark shapes of his two cowering men. Neither the major nor the sergeant responded.

"I will have you shot," he shouted. "Come here!"

There were whimpers from the major, but no signs of movement. Both men were frightened into lumps of stone.

"Where are you going?" the lieutenant whispered anxiously. Even in the danger of the moment his voice held respect, for the officers had been briefed of his renewed importance.

Wu eyed him. "Can you drive a truck?" he said.

The lieutenant's eyes glittered in comprehension. He stared up at the sky with some suspicion. "The airplanes will return to bomb."

"Let us hurry," Wu ordered, and hesitantly moved out of the door. The lieutenant followed.

Nguyen Wu heard the sound of a truck's engine. Someone else had the same idea. "Get a truck and bring it to the building there," he ordered the lieutenant. "Use your weapon if anyone tries to stop you."

The lieutenant hurried toward the camouflaged vehicle park as Nguyen continued toward his office. The hideous and filthy Mee woman might have more answers to provide. When he arrived in Hanoi with her, no one could doubt his worthiness.

As he hurried, he looked toward the eastward road and noticed how it disappeared into the jungle. If the Mee Thunder planes delayed only a little longer . . .

Sergeant Black

Sergeant Young vainly tried switching batteries between the two survival radios, but it didn't help. Captain Tiny Bechler sat, staring helplessly, first at the targets below, then back up at the fighters. His primary conversation became *goddam no-good radios* and *fucking gomers down there.*

A stake-bed truck revved its engine near one of the wooden headquarters buildings below and fled eastward down the dusty road, where it was quickly swallowed by the dark jungle which lay in that direction. Another vehicle stirred. Antlike figures scurried around it and began to load.

The fighters hadn't yet been directed toward the headquarters compound. It was to have been next. Afterward, if there were survivors, the Hotdogs were to take a few prisoners there.

"Some of the bastards are getting away!" Bechler turned and raged at Black. "How come your asshole Army bosses don't give *you* fucking radios you can talk with the goddam airplanes on. This is pure *bullshit!*"

Black was equally upset by the turn of events. "Why didn't you remember to put fresh batteries in your backup radios? And as far as that goes, why don't your airplanes have VHF—" That was when Black remembered the conversation with Lucky Anderson in the trailer at NKP.

"Goddammit, Black—"

"Shut up for a minute," Sergeant Black snapped, trying to remember.

Bechler glared, then blew out a helpless sigh. "Fuck!" he bellowed. Another truck was preparing to leave the compound.

Black went to the lieutenant and spoke in an urgent tone. The lieutenant barked an order, and one of the men hurried up with a hand-held VHF squad radio. Black stared at the thing and tried to recall the conversation with Anderson. He'd given him a VHF frequency, and they'd come up with a code word. He'd drunk too much that evening, but he vaguely remembered something about a Hawaiian word.

He switched to preset frequency D, 109.5 megacycles, then stared out at the F-105's orbiting south of the mesa mountain. *"F-105's, this is Hotdog. Tiny Bubbles. No, make that Aloha, F-105's. Aloha!"*

"What the hell are you doing?" Bechler growled. "They don't have a fucking VHF radio."

Black repeated his radio call a couple of times, watching the fighters. Nothing. He switched the radio wafer switch to E, 106.4. *"F-105's, this is Hotdog. Aloha."* He repeated the call twice more as the fighters continued in their orbit.

He was about to switch to F frequency when he heard the FAC mutter, "What the hell?"

The flight of Thuds had turned toward them, and the lead bird was waggling its wings.

Black watched and began to smile. "Colonel Anderson told me they'd be able to hear, but not talk to us."

Bechler brightened. "The goddamn ILS. Why the fuck didn't I think of that?"

"He said they'd fly with their systems turned on when they were around here. We've got plenty of batteries for these."

The flight of F-105's came back overhead, and again the leader waggled his wings.

"Give me that thing," said Bechler in an exultant tone, and Black handed the radio over.

"*Wildcat flight this is Bongo. If you read me, turn right.*"

The flight of F-105's made an immediate right turn.

"*Wildcat, I'm going to have you strafe two wooden buildings at the edge of the village. There's a truck loading up there that I want you to get, too. Be aware that there are noncombatants in the village itself, so make sure you . . .*"

0841L—Over Channel 97, Northeastern Laos

Lieutenant Colonel Yank Donovan

"*F-105's, this is Hotdog. Aloha.*" The transmission was clear, and for a moment Yank thought it came over the radio. But when he adjusted the radio volume, the sound didn't change.

He'd flown with the ILS switched on ever since he heard Hotdog the previous time and was told by Anderson that it was indeed an American he'd heard.

Yank ordered the other pilots to turn on their ILS so they could hear too, then had Wildcat flight turn and fly toward the valley.

The FAC, Bongo, picked up his litany and directed Wildcat to strafe a couple of buildings near the dirt strip very carefully, because of the village just beyond.

Wildcat used their Gatling guns, carefully as the FAC directed, to shoot the compound to pieces, blow up two trucks that were trying to get away, and destroy several other vehicles parked under camouflage. Next they revisited the various troop locations in the valley with Gatling guns, bombs, and napalm. After half an hour of it, a force of F-4's showed up. Yank told them he'd keep a couple of F-105's in the area to relay the FAC's words and direct their fire, because the Phantoms had no instrument-landing-system equipment.

Yank had cycled out to the air refueling tanker and was back on the scene, relaying the FAC's directions, when the second and final F-4 force prepared to depart. The valley had been sterilized of air defenses, and the FAC said he saw no green uniforms moving about any of the encampments.

As Yank prepared to follow them from the area, a camouflaged C-47 approached from the south, banked and orbited around the mesa, and began to chew up the mountaintop with Gatling guns and cannon. Puff the Magic Dragon was on the scene.

He departed, knowing he was leaving the place in capable hands.

1125L—Y-54, Northeastern Laos

Sergeant Black

The spectacle was nearing completion. In the distance the final flights of fighters were forming up to return to their bases. Those were F-4 Phantoms. Black had counted a total of twelve different call signs, which meant that fifty-odd fighters had pounced on the area. Add the C-47 gunship that was still beating up the mountaintop, and it accounted for a lot of munitions dumped onto the area in the course of the four hours.

Half an hour earlier, in the midst of the final furious action, the lieutenant and two of his men had slipped down the main trail leading toward the village to take prisoners, officers if possible. They were in little danger. The fighters had pounded and strafed all moving things into oblivion, directed by Captain Bechler's magnified vision and calm instructions. Cluster bomblets, high explosive bombs, napalm, and 20mm cannon fire had been rained furiously upon the militia surrounding the mesa.

Black had witnessed the aftermath of a B-52 attack in the iron triangle—choppered in only minutes after the bombers had finished. He'd seen wily Cong and hardened NVA soldiers wandering dumbly about, weapons abandoned, mouths agape, and blood trickling from their ears, uncaring if they lived or died. The destruction below appeared similar to what he'd seen, if more selective. Areas of the lush valley forest had been flattened by concussive waves from bombs. The Soviet-built observation plane still issued a tiny streamer of smoke from where it lay gutted and burned. The compound had been riddled with 20mm gunfire. The only sounds they'd heard during the final hour of bombing had been occasional distant shrieks of agony and abject terror.

The lieutenant called from below on his hand-held radio. They'd crossed the dirt strip and were outside Ban Sao Si village and had met no opposition, no one who wondered who they were or why they were there. The final survivors were fleeing.

"Are there any potential prisoners?"

The lieutenant paused. "We can take our pick," he finally answered.

They decided on four men they found near the village, still whimpering and cringing in a bomb shelter. Three were officers, the other a sergeant, and all looked to be unharmed, although they were crying like babies. Hotdog quickly stripped them of weapons and marched them forth. They arrived back at the small clearing near the mountaintop at 1255 hours, and Black looked them over.

The men were still in shock, not caring that Black wore an American uniform, likely not even realizing what it was. All four had pissed in their pants, and the smell of urine was strong. The two lesser officers had brought their leather pouches as the lieutenant had directed, and when Black barked instructions, they surrendered them. The sergeant was obscenely fat, with a pocked face and eyes that were wide with terror. He'd periodically babble words of gratitude and obeisance until the lieutenant would again tell him to be quiet.

Captain Bechler came down from his rock to examine them, his eyes glittering. "So these are the bad guys."

"Yeah. That one's a major. Those two are couriers. The ugly bastard there's a sergeant."

"I think they are all intelligence people from the headquarters down there," said the lieutenant in Viet.

"Find out," said Black.

"Are we going to take them back with us?" Bechler asked.

The lieutenant swaggered up to the major, leaned forward like an angry drill sergeant, and began barking questions.

"Maybe," Black told Bechler, listening to the responses.

The two sublieutenants worked in intelligence. The soft major and the fat sergeant worked for a bureaucrat, an assistant commissioner of some sort from Hanoi. All were members of the Army of National Defense militia.

"Take them away and question them," he told the lieutenant, who was leaning forward and glaring meanly at the cowering major.

Two Hotdogs took the prisoners off to continue the interrogation.

"They gonna kill 'em?" Captain Bechler asked cheerfully.

"I don't like killing anyone unless they need it," said Black, "like if they're shooting at me."

"Maybe you don't, but how about those guys doing the questioning?"

"They generally feel the same. But then maybe we will have to kill them. Now they've seen us, we can't let 'em go back to their people. If the brass doesn't send transport to take 'em back . . ." He shrugged.

2015L—Trailer 5B, Takhli RTAFB, Thailand

Captain Manny DeVera

Manny approached the trailer awkwardly, feeling so screwed up inside he might puke. He'd been like that for hours—gone around in a fog for the last . . . how many days? Today had been the final telling. They'd flown to the old Channel 97 TACAN location and kicked hell out of things there, facing only light air defenses.

He'd led the second element of Lucky Anderson's flight, and when the enemy fired a couple of dinky little SA-7 rockets at him, he'd become so rattled that he'd released his CBUs off target and pulled up sharply, even though the missiles came nowhere near him.

His entire outlook had become screwed up. After mastering his fears before, even being shot down and doing all the right things, he was afraid to fly combat.

Big, tough warrior?

Fucking coward!

He'd wanted to go to Buster Leska again, to come out with it and ask his advice, but he'd balked. He revered the colonel, sort of as he would have his father had he known him. The wing commander was the finest leader of men he'd ever known, with the proper mix of authority and fighter pilot to lead a bunch like the Takhli hot chargers. But Manny was no longer a hot charger. He'd been scared shitless recently when he flew, even when the threat was nothing at all like it would be when they returned to pack six.

Fucking coward.

And when he did go back to pack six . . . He shuddered, felt boxed in—so confused that he didn't know where to turn except to the trailer, where he was standing and staring stupidly at the number on the door. He knocked finally, heard a stirring inside, wanted to turn and walk away.

The door cracked.

"I need to talk," he said in a low, weary voice.

She swung the door wider, and he glanced around before entering.

He didn't tell her of his cowardice—he simply couldn't make himself do it. But he agreed to her terms. It wasn't nearly as difficult as he'd thought it would be. He told her he'd no longer fly to pack six or on dangerous missions, but only on the easiest, least-threatening missions. No one, he said, was likely to know the difference. As weapons officer he could beg off the big missions by telling the schedulers he had other work to do.

Was that enough? he asked. She whispered that she was happier than she'd ever been.

They made love, and although it was their first time, it was as if they'd known one another all their lives. It was a gentle coupling, and he tried to be considerate, for she said she was inexperienced. When they finished, she whispered for him to stay in her, and held her body very still as she traced his face with loving fingers. A short while later they began to move together, as if it had been mutually planned, and worked in quiet unison.

Sometime in the next few hours, the sick feeling of fear left him.

He rose silently at three in the morning, pulled on his clothing, and departed while she was still asleep. As he walked the half mile to the Ponderosa, Manny refused to think of anything except the woman who had vowed to love him and remain by his side forever. The time with her had been relaxing, as if he'd been drugged.

It had been so much easier to make the promise than he'd imagined.

Great weariness suddenly swept over and through him, and he staggered drunkenly as he walked. He stopped and retched up dinner, then began to cry as he continued walking.

CHAPTER THIRTY-SEVEN

Sergeant Black

This time when the Hotdog sentry hissed, Black came instantly alert. After a glance at his watch's luminous dial, he wondered. He'd left instructions not to be awakened until four.

"The lieutenant would like to talk," he was told.

Black rolled out of the parachute panel and stretched to limber himself, then followed the Hotdog toward the rock outcropping. The lieutenant was there, smoking a cupped cigarette and staring down at the moonlit landscape of the valley. Black approached him and paused for him to speak.

"Something one of the prisoners said bothered me, and I could not sleep," said the lieutenant, "so I went back to question him more."

Black suppressed a yawn. It would be better if they were rested in the morning. Buffalo Soldier wanted them to trek to the mesa and report the status of things there. The Air Force was pressing to reestablish the TACAN station just as soon as they knew all enemy troops in the area had been neutralized.

"The major says the woman was in Ban Sao Si."

Black came instantly awake. "What woman?" he asked.

"Come ask for yourself."

They went into the brush and down a path for twenty meters, where a Hotdog sat guard on the four prisoners, who were securely bound with parachute cord.

The lieutenant turned on his flashlight, illuminating the major's face. "Tell him," he ordered.

The militia major licked his lips nervously. "An American woman was held at the headquarters compound."

Black's heart raced. "What does she look like?"

"Dark hair. Very tall and so thin she looks like a stick-woman. She was a prisoner of the Pathet Lao, but they gave her to the assistant commissioner to question."

Clipper! "Who is this assistant commissioner?" he asked.

"He is from the Commissioner of Death's office in Hanoi. He was very cruel to her, and she became crazy. No one even wanted to fuck her anymore."

"What do you mean?"

"The assistant commissioner wanted all the men to fuck her. Some of them did, but then she was crazy and no one wanted to go near her."

Black's mind became so swelled with outrage that he had trouble speaking the next words. "Did she answer his questions?"

The major had sensed his fury and became too frightened to continue.

"Answer him," snapped the lieutenant, "or I will cut your throat very slowly."

The militia major opened his mouth, but it took a moment before coherent words emerged. "She told him . . . many secrets before . . . she was crazy."

"Is she alive?"

"I do not know. He was starving her. Perhaps she is dead from that. Perhaps she was killed by the airplanes. Perhaps"—he swallowed—"the assistant commissioner killed her. He left our bunker when the bombing stopped for a while, and did not return."

The lieutenant had become so angry his voice trembled. "How many men forced her?"

The major winced, expecting a blow. "Many," he finally

whispered. His eyes darted. "The sergeant can tell you." The major looked toward his right, where the other prisoners were bound. "The sergeant helped the assistant commissioner get men to fuck her."

The lieutenant's flashlight moved to the fat sergeant with the pocked face. "You," he said. The sergeant moaned with fear, unable to bring himself to answer.

The lieutenant slipped his bayonet knife from its sheath and jabbed it an inch into the man's soft stomach. The sergeant screamed.

"Quiet!"

The sergeant's voice subsided to whimpers.

"Is she still there?" he asked. The man spouted words.

"Speak slowly."

The sergeant stared at the knife in his midsection, blubbering. His words were punctuated with sobs. "I think she is there."

"Tell me where." The lieutenant withdrew the blade a bit.

The sergeant's words came in a rush. "In a cage in the assistant commissioner's office." The office was in the second wooden building in the headquarters compound. He told how she smelled badly, lying in her own waste. How she howled like an animal and was crazy."

"God," Black breathed.

The lieutenant asked the sergeant if he'd fucked her, then how many times, and the man was stupid enough to answer. When the lieutenant twisted the knife, he admitted other things he'd visited upon the woman.

Black disliked torture and forbade his men to engage in it. But this time he didn't interfere as the lieutenant pressed the razor-sharp knife ever deeper. The lieutenant was driven. Other soldiers had taken his young sister. He'd spoken often and wistfully about the woman code-named Clipper, whom they'd come so close to rescuing.

The sergeant looked down at the blade as it continued in, holding his breath as if afraid that if he moved, something would come out.

The lieutenant held the knife fully into the sergeant's flabby stomach. "Remember what you did to the woman," he whispered to him.

"Unghhh."

"Remember as you leave this world." The lieutenant pulled the razor-edged blade upward, slicing cleanly, then slowly pulled out the blade and wiped it on the sergeant's shirt. He watched the man frown hideously with the sure knowledge that he was dying.

The obese sergeant turned with a questioning look, then stared back down as his guts began to slither forth.

Sergeant Black rose to shaky feet. "Have the men prepare to leave," he mumbled numbly. He wasn't at all sure he wanted to find what was left of her.

An hour passed before they'd finished breaking camp and formed up to descend the mountain.

Captain Bechler whispered something to Black.

"What did you say?" Black asked.

"Where are the prisoners?"

"They're not coming," Black said. He brusquely motioned for the men to move out.

0618L—Ban Sao Si, Laos

They'd left the FAC and radio operator with a Hotdog, hidden in a thicket so the others could search for Clipper. As far as Black could tell, there were no living militia in the valley except for a number of badly wounded who'd dragged themselves into shade or to water to die. All who'd been able to walk had fled to the east, back toward North Vietnam. Ma tribesmen had arrived and were joining the Lao villagers in stripping dead and dying Viets of weapons and possessions.

When Hotdog reached the headquarters compound, light was filtering over the mountain. Even before they entered the buildings, it was apparent they would not find the woman alive. Both wooden buildings were rent by gaping bullet holes. The northern side of one had collapsed. The second structure was standing, but barely.

They went inside that one and pushed around fallen timbers. There were no sounds of life. Two men had been caught in an office, cringing together in a corner as their bodies had been shot to pieces. Black steeled himself before continuing toward the back, prepared to face the worst.

The lieutenant called from a room. He'd found the correct office, for in its corner there was an empty cage. The lieutenant stared at the foul-smelling thing with hard eyes.

"She is gone," Black said quietly in Viet.

The lieutenant dropped to his haunches and continued to stare at the cage. He pointed to small bits of human feces on the floor. His finger was shaking.

"She is gone," Black repeated. The lieutenant did not hear. He was obsessed, as if the woman were a reincarnation of his young sister, taken to service the unit of NVA soldiers.

They went outside and began to look through the rubble about the buildings for sign of the woman. Throughout their search the lieutenant remained tense, his eyes burning fervently. He was more disturbed than Black could remember him, even when he'd lost his men.

When they'd searched the area thoroughly, including the two bunkers, and still found no sign of her, the lieutenant resolutely disappeared in the direction of the village. Black looked about the building for a while longer before following.

0730L—Weapons Office, Takhli RTAFB, Thailand

Captain Manny DeVera

He couldn't shake the awful tiredness, nor the sick feeling. While the time spent with Penny had been a respite, afterward he'd gotten very little sleep, and even that had been troubled.

The words on the pages of the documents before him were meaningless, and Manny couldn't bring himself to assign them importance.

Like a weapons-utilization report showing the pilots were using too many rounds of HEI ammunition, as opposed to more plentiful API rounds. Or that a shipment of AGM-45A Shrike missiles would be delayed because the ship carrying them was held up in mid-Pacific with engine problems. Or a test report from Nellis showing that level bomb releases, dropping on cue from something called an MSQ-2—hadn't he read about something like that being installed somewhere here?—were getting 850 feet circular error probability at seventy-five nautical miles from the site.

None of that seemed important. Half an hour earlier he'd taken himself off the afternoon flying schedule, although the force was only going to pack two to bomb near Vinh. But there were two SAM sites known to be in the Vinh area, and he'd promised not to fly into danger. The 333rd squadron scheduler had thought nothing of the change. It had been as easy as making the promise the previous evening.

He'd tried not to, but throughout the night, as he'd lain in his bed at the Ponderosa, his mind had kept returning to the vow he'd made, both for Penny Dwight and to quell the awful, consuming fear. Not flying the tough missions was a way to cope with both dilemmas—or was it somehow just one? It didn't matter.

He thought of the emotion he shared with Penny. Not intense. More like a quiet seaside where you could sit and watch the waves and tide and know they'd be there doing the same thing tomorrow and a thousand years hence.

Fatigue washed about inside him, as it had been doing for the past week. He wondered if Leska would discover his secret changes in scheduling. The man was tuned to his surroundings and knew his men well. Manny remembered the trust the wing commander had shown—still showed—in him.

Was he really letting anyone down? Yesterday he'd decided he was not. Then why did the sick feeling keep periodically rising into his throat?

0809L—Ban Sao Si, Laos

Although the FAC had tried to minimize the damage to Ban Sao Si, several of the thatch huts had been destroyed by gunfire, and there were continuous wailing sounds of women in mourning. Black moved quietly along the dirt street, his weapon at the ready, for there was the distinct possibility that soldiers were hiding in the village.

He held up in front of the fifth thatch house. From inside he could hear the lieutenant's angry voice, speaking in Lao.

After a bit the lieutenant came out with an elderly and thoroughly frightened man. "He knows what they did with her," he said.

The man nodded energetically. "I saw them take her."

Black frowned.

"The crazy stick-woman," he said, nodding again. "Yesterday the bombs stopped for a while, and they put her in the back of a small truck and pushed away others who wanted to go with them. When they left, there was only the driver, the important man from Hanoi, and the crazy stick-woman. They drove away very fast. Others shouted for the driver to stop, but he did not."

"Which way did they go?" Black asked wearily, but he knew.

The old man pointed to the road going east. North Vietnam was not far in that direction. Perhaps two days of driving through the rugged terrain.

"So close," Black muttered. "We were so fucking close again."

"It is a very poor road," said the lieutenant. "We can follow and catch them."

Black mulled it over. The weapons carrier could speed for only a couple of klicks until the road entered the mountains; then it would have to slow to a crawl. There was a possibility that they might catch up with them, since the vehicle would have to remain on the twisting road. But of course there were also many fleeing soldiers in that direction, and pursuit might be dangerous.

The decision was too heavy. "Let's go back to the others and set up the radio," he told the lieutenant.

Twenty minutes later he was connected with Buffalo Soldier.

Larry asked what had delayed his scheduled radio call.

"We've learned that Clipper was being held in Ban Sao Si before the air strike," Black told him. *"You'd better get the old man on the radio."*

After a couple of minutes Papa Wolf's voice responded, and Black explained the situation.

"You say Clipper's broken?"

"*Roger. She went through a lot of bad shit first, though. I'd like to go after her.*"

Papa Wolf paused before responding in a heavy voice. "*Negative, Hotdog. Get on up to the top of the mountain and give us the report I asked for.*"

"*I can tell you now, sir. There's nothing and no one up there. The North Viets who weren't killed have all run.*"

"*Let's stick to the game plan, Hotdog. We've got choppers holding until you report it's clear.*"

Black sighed, knowing there was no recourse short of mutiny. "*I'll give you a call from on top.*"

"*Papa Wolf out.*"

"What was all that about?" Captain Bechler asked. "Who's the woman you were talking about?"

Black felt sadder than he had in a long while. "A very brave lady," he answered.

As the Hotdogs busied themselves with tearing down the radio, Black thought of a final, desperate possibility and called the lieutenant over.

"Send a man to the Ma village," he told him. It was only seven klicks to the southeast. "Have him tell the headman about the woman, and that we will reward them for any information they give us."

The lieutenant nodded. "I will go myself." The intensity remained in his gaze.

"Send someone else."

The lieutenant took a moment to answer. "No," he said quietly. "I will go."

Black returned his stare.

"I must."

Black started to argue, but knew it would do no good. "Meet us on the mountaintop. They want to take us out by helicopter before dark."

The lieutenant nodded, then looked over at his men, a tic exercising a small muscle in his jaw. He turned eastward without further word and set out in a quick gait.

1635L—Channel 97, Laos

Sergeant Black

At 1500 hours, after Black had reported the mountaintop devoid of soldiers, three big CH-46 helicopters had landed and disgorged a twelve-man Special Forces A-Detachment and fifteen combat engineers. They would ensure the mountain was secured and prepared for the mobile TACAN, which was to be flown in the following day with Air Force technicians and another piece of equipment called an MSQ-2, which was even more sensitive.

The Hotdogs, the FAC, and the ROMAD all watched as the men went about their business, waiting for the lieutenant's return. As the time for their scheduled 1700 departure drew near, Black became increasingly concerned.

When the first lieutenant pilot of one of the choppers came over and told them to load their equipment for the trip to NKP, Black told him he still had a man out there who was supposed to go with them.

"Hell, Sarge," the pilot said, "we're gonna have so much air traffic through here the next few days, it's gonna look like O'Hare International. He can catch a ride when he gets here."

Captain Bechler came over and pointed a huge finger at the lieutenant. "He says to wait, you fucking wait." The chopper pilot looked up at Bechler, who was the approximate size of two men, with warranted concern.

"It's okay," Black said, peering out at the Hotdog team who waited near the top of the roadway that led up the side of the mountain. "He's right. The lieutenant can catch a ride when he gets here. I'm just concerned that one of these guys will decide to shoot him and claim a kill. The only clothes he's got with him's the NVA uniform he was wearing."

Bechler looked unhappily at the roadway. "I like the little bastard, even if he does look like a fucking gomer. He's got balls."

Black went to find the captain who commanded the A-Detachment. He located him near the old Montagnard village site, where he was setting up business in a squad tent while his men stacked sandbags and prepared a perimeter.

"I've got a man still out there," Black told him.

"One of your renegades?" he asked sourly.

Black knew the captain only vaguely. He was new to the combat theater, but already very opinionated. "One of my men," he repeated wearily.

"Long as he doesn't look hostile when he shows up, we probably won't shoot him."

"Don't." Black pinned him with a cold look.

The captain returned it. "Where'd he go, Sergeant? Off chasing pussy? You oughta control those renegades of yours better."

Black bristled. For the past few hours he'd been thinking about how, this being his last recon op with Hotdog, there was no longer a need for the charade he'd kept up for the past fifteen months. "I know you didn't have a way of knowing this, but I'm a captain. I make major next month, and I'm being assigned as your XO. If you fuck up and shoot my man, I promise you I'll get even. You got that, captain?"

The A-Detachment commander gaped at him with disbelief.

"Call Buffalo Soldier and verify it with Papa Wolf. In fact, I'd like you to do that, so there won't be any misunderstanding."

"I will."

"And when you're through, I want you to brief everyone on your team that if anyone shoots my man, I'm going to have *your* balls."

Black stared for a moment longer, then left the tent and walked toward the waiting chopper.

The other Hotdogs still stood at the roadway, looking increasingly worried. The recon team had always worked together, and more than anyone, even Black, the lieutenant was their leader.

Black motioned for them to join him.

The senior sergeant came alone and spoke in Viet. "I think we should go for him. We know the way to the Ma village."

Black shook his head. "He is not there."

The sergeant looked perplexed.

"Get the men aboard," Black said softly. "The lieutenant will come later."

The sergeant obviously didn't understand, but he gave his hand signal, and the other two Hotdogs moved toward them.

"Where do you think the lieutenant might be?" Tiny Bechler asked.

"Let's get aboard," Black told him. He waited until the others had loaded, then swung through the door and sat on the web seat as the crew chief closed and latched the door. When the chopper lifted off, then dipped and hurried toward Nakhon Phanom, he continued to stare out toward the east.

2045L—Tan Son Nhut Officers' Club

Lieutenant Colonel Pearly Gates

Their routine had changed. After work they now went to their individual rooms and changed into civilian clothing before meeting at the club for dinner. In uniform he was Colonel Gates and she was Lieutenant Dortmeier. In civvies he was Pearly and she was Lucy. And each evening they'd do something, like bowl a game at the base recreation center or take in a movie—or just talk over after-dinner drinks, sharing private jokes that would be funny to no one else.

Afterward, when he'd walked her to her room, the door always remained cracked open, for they were proper about such things.

Tonight was an after-dinner drink evening, because they'd both worked even later than normal, and the Grand Marnier helped bring them down some. They sat alone in a corner of the lounge.

"I saw the general in the hall today," Lucy said. "He's been looking concerned lately."

Pearly sipped his drink. "It's General McManus," he said in a lowered voice. "He had another heart attack yesterday."

"A bad one?"

"I don't think so, but he's in the hospital again."

"Could it affect . . ." She stopped herself, but they both knew she meant the LINE BACKER JACKPOT plan.

"No way to tell. Probably not, I'd guess. Now it's all up to the big man. All it will take is a phone call and we're on."

Lucy stared out at the room. "It's too normal here, Pearly. Like a dinner club in the States. It's hard to believe there's a war going on—that people are dying violently so close to us."

"In Saigon, just six miles from here, they're still finding infiltrators from the Tet offensive. A block away from the fighting, the stores are open for business."

"That's what I mean."

"Yeah. No front lines or anything, and you don't know who the good guys and the bad guys are. All of that makes me know we're on the right track with our plan."

Lucy was looking at him with an odd, soft expression. "Let's go, Pearly."

"To your room?"

"Yes, please." No hesitation.

He stood and waited as she gathered her purse, adjusted herself, and slung the strap over her shoulder. God, but she was petite and feminine. She gave him the intimate and sharing look once again, and Pearly felt a small pang of apprehension.

Lucy Dortmeier was a virgin. She'd told him that. She was also very correct.

She touched his arm in a fond and territorial way as they walked toward the entrance.

Tonight, he knew—they both knew—the door wouldn't be left cracked open.

Wednesday, February 21st, 1100 Local—Mountains, Northeastern Laos

GS-15 Linda Lopes

The vehicle was like an oversized, ancient American pickup with a canvas-covered cab and wooden bed, and there was only the sublieutenant driver, the assistant commissioner, and herself. Linda shared the truck bed with several large containers of diesel fuel that jostled and slid about, leaking noxious fluid which permeated the flooring. The other two rode in the cab.

Linda was naked but not really exposed, for she was covered with a gummy mixture created by the oil and the rust-
colored dust that boiled thickly over her. Pain coursed
through her body in a hundred places as she was bounced
about. Slivers from the wooden truck bed, both large and
small, had become firmly embedded in her flesh. It had
been laborious going, but the truck had relentlessly crawled
its way along the tortuous path that climbed ever upward
through the thick jungle. The driver had stopped dozens of
times to clear the crude roadway where it had become
blocked. Other times the two men had gotten out to eat or
urinate. Initially when they halted, they'd checked on her
condition and given her water, but then they must have run
low, for the practice was discontinued. When they'd spoken
to her during those first stops, she'd only grunted responses
and begun the low, howling sounds of madness. Since Sergeant Gross wasn't with them, they couldn't question her or
interpret her words, but she remained fearful of any communication.

Was she truly mad? She thought so.

Twice day had dwindled into cool and welcome darkness,
but then the relentless sun had returned to parch her. At
first she'd been blindfolded, but the cloth had slipped up
and became tangled in her hair, and they hadn't made an effort to reposition it.

Before the magical event happened, Linda had also been
trussed securely with ropes.

Periodically she'd waft into unconsciousness, and it was
during those times when she came closest to peace. Despite
the ever-present suffering, she'd feel herself slipping as she
lost lucidity, and at first wondered if her prayers were being
answered and death was finally coming. After several times
she decided that respite would come only later, perhaps
from dehydration but certainly after other, longer periods of
unconsciousness.

Please don't let me wake again, she pleaded each time she
drifted into unconsciousness.

Then it happened. The rope tying her elbows together
was the first to loosen, then the cord binding her hands. It
was not something she helped along, but was caused by the
constant jostling, bouncing, and sliding about the truck bed.
Linda moved her shoulders forward and briefly felt the

wonder of freedom before a shock of severe pain coursed
through her upper body. She wanted to scream from the agony, but contained it. She'd been through so many hells. She
would also endure this one, created by the return of circulation to her torso and limbs.

It was an answer to her prayer to die in some place other
than this, with her tormentors looking on. She wished to
find a peaceful place, perhaps beside a pleasant stream,
where she could drift off to dreams of her childhood.

Looking forward at the cab, she saw that both men were
peering ahead at the road, and the Thin Man was grunting
terse directions to the driver. Linda rolled and crawled toward the back of the truck bed, withholding a cry of agony
as a two-inch splinter pushed deep into a bare and bony
buttock.

At the rear of the bed now.

The truck accelerated some as they entered an open area
of road. She tried to lift herself, paused to pant and collect
her energy. Tried again.

She couldn't do it.

Linda cautiously looked around at the cab, but couldn't
focus well enough to see the men there or whether they
were observing her. She grasped her way slowly up the tailgate, clutched the rim, and pulled harder.

A voice shouted from the cab and she hesitated. It was
not for her, she decided. They called her Whore.

Linda adjusted her position and pulled again. She found
that with great effort she could claw her way farther. She
levered herself even with the top of the tailgate, pushed
again, teetered, and shoved forward with all her remaining
strength. As she went over the side, she grasped for a hand-
hold to slow the fall, but once she'd passed the balance
point and her weight had shifted, there was no stopping.
She flailed and tumbled, struck an arm on the back of the
truck, then bounced hard onto the hardpack roadway.

The truck's engine revved, then down-geared, but kept
going.

When they discover I'm gone, they'll come back, she
thought dully, and knew she must get off the roadway and
out of sight. She crawled, favoring the pain-numbed arm,
slithering, for her legs were still bound together, toward the
side of the road. She paused, then turned and tried to

smooth out signs of her body's passage as she backed into grass and brambles.

Now clear of the roadway, she stopped and listened as the truck's engine grew fainter. She heard the slow tinkling sound of water in the distance. A drink would be wonderful, Linda decided. Then she'd wash herself thoroughly and find a nice place to die.

She crawled toward the source. The sounds of the truck engine became muted and even. Suddenly the engine revved.

They were coming back for her.

She continued crawling.

1247L

Assistant Commissioner Nguyen Wu

Wu shrieked at the sublieutenant for allowing it to happen.

"Find her!" he cried angrily.

The driver was working the truck back and forth, trying to turn about in the narrow roadway.

"Hurry! I think she is in the open area we just passed through."

"I do not believe she can go far," the sublieutenant said cautiously, fumbling with the gears.

Chuka-chuka-chuka-chuka . . .

"A helicopter," said the sublieutenant.

"Perhaps it is ours," Nguyen Wu muttered. He peered skyward through the tree canopy.

Chuka-chuka-chuka . . .

"I do not think so. Ours are louder." Wu chewed on his lip, wondering. If they returned to the open area, they could be seen from the air, but he definitely didn't wish to wait around until the helicopter had gone.

Chuka-chuka-chuka-chuka . . . The sound of the helicopter was growing louder.

He glanced down at the leather courier's pouch that contained the woman's secrets.

The sublieutenant crunched the gears again in his efforts to turn around.

Chuka-chuka-chuka . . .

"Stop," Wu demanded. The woman was only a burden, and was dying anyway.

The sublieutenant stared.

"We shall go on without her," Wu decided.

CHAPTER
THIRTY-EIGHT

Monday, February 26th 0750 Local—HQ Seventh Air Force, Tan Son Nhut Airbase, Saigon, South Vietnam

Major Benny Lewis

Benny walked down the stairs slowly, mindful of his back and the stiffness he felt there. It wasn't that he was not getting better, simply that he had pushed himself too far during the Tet offensive, then as the pace of the Pave Dagger testing had increased. He prudently strapped on the light brace each morning, and twice daily took time for the simple, relaxing exercises the Nellis physical therapists had trained him to do, like sitting on the floor with his back held rigidly against a wall, or lying on a hard floor, knees up and arms at his sides. The stiffness was a handy danger signal, and whenever he felt it, he backed off—like now, taking his time coming down the stairs. He showed his badge to the security guard, then nodded to Moods, who waited impatiently at the main entrance of the headquarters building. The entire Pave Dagger team had come to Saigon to await a decision from General Moss on the future of the combat test program.

They were several feet down the sidewalk, still walking

slowly, heading back to the visiting officer's quarters, when Moods Diller burst out with his question. "So what did you tell the general?"

"Same as you and I talked about, Moods. I told him PACAF had shut us down without reason, and that we want to continue the tests."

"And?"

"And I asked if he'd help."

Moods waited, then exploded. "Dammit, Benny, what happened?"

"General Moss agreed that Pave Dagger's a good idea. Hell, he was acting like he'd agreed all along, even though you know how he fought it. When you knocked down the bridge with the single bomb, I think it convinced him."

"So the test's back on?"

"Yeah, Moods. But not here. He said to quit pushing for more combat testing . . . to go back to Nellis and finish your work there."

Moods looked crestfallen, and Benny wanted to tell him the rest, how General Moss had sent out a flurry of back-channel messages to all the LINE BACKER JACKPOT people, telling them the Pave Dagger smart bombs were perfect for use when they started going to Hanoi in earnest—how they'd solve a lot of the problem of collateral damage and threats to civilians and foreigners. Benny wanted to tell him that Pearly Gates was writing a new annex to the OPlan, which included Moods's smart bombs, designating an F-4 squadron at Ubon as the first to be equipped and trained, and planned to use as many of the weapons as could be produced in the JACKPOT bombing campaign.

General Moss had told Benny to return to the States via the Pentagon and visit the chief of RDQF, the fighter-requirements office, who was one of those briefed in on JACKPOT. The Pentagon contacts there and in procurement would have things ready and waiting. When they got everything rolling, it would likely be one of the largest nonnuclear weapons-acquisition programs in the post–World War II era.

Moods was frowning.

"You've proved your concept, Moods. You've won. Be satisfied with it."

"It feels like we're being chased out of Dodge City."

"You all packed and ready?"

"Why?"

"The general's secretary's got you and your military team members scheduled out on a civilian contract airliner at fourteen hundred."

"Damn! Now I really feel like I'm being chased out of town." Moods looked at him oddly. "How about you? You're going with us, aren't you?"

"I'm taking another flight. I'm going to drop by my ex-wife's place in Oregon and see my kids, then go on to Washington."

"The Pentagon?"

"Yeah. I'll see you back at Nellis in a couple of weeks."

"How about Julie? What do you want me to tell her, with her moving and all."

Benny stopped cold in his tracks. "Moving?"

"When I talked to Pam on the phone last night, she told me about running into Julie Stewart again, and how she said something about a move. She was kind of hesitant, so Pam didn't press her. Where's she going?"

"New Jersey, I guess."

"You didn't know she was going? Jesus, Benny."

"It doesn't matter." Although he'd expected it, he was amazed at how much it did matter.

"Is there some kinda trouble between you two or something?"

Benny began walking again. "We'd better get ready to catch a plane."

Moods was often slow to catch on to the mundane features of life, but he knew when someone changed the subject that abruptly not to pursue it. Especially when it was his boss.

"Yeah," said Moods. But he still wore a puzzled expression. He'd thought Benny and Julie were a shoo-in for a trip to the altar, maybe even before he was dragged there by Pam.

Benny didn't enlighten him.

1000L—355th TFW Commander's Office, Takhli RTAFB, Thailand

Colonel Buster Leska

The Deputy for Operations had come to see him with a problem and had brought along the weapons officer. The Wild Weasel crews were raising hell because they were about to run out of AGM-45 missiles. There were only seven left in the munitions inventory at Takhli, and the Weasels fired a lot of them to keep the North Vietnamese SAM operators' heads down during strike missions.

"So how many Shrikes are we going to have to airlift in?" Buster asked the Deputy for Operations.

Jerry Trimble turned to Manny.

"I think about forty," DeVera mumbled too hesitantly, looking even worse than the last time Buster had seen him. Manny had the puffy bags under his eyes and looked both nervous and tired, and now he was getting blotchy patches on his swarthy skin.

Buster quelled an angry response that he didn't want guesses.

"We better make it sixty," Trimble said. "More if we can get 'em."

"How the hell did we get ourselves in a corner like this?" Buster asked, not politely. "Didn't someone advise us about the surface shipment being slowed down? Hell, if we'd started the airlift a few days earlier, we wouldn't be in this fix."

Manny said something vague about maybe he'd screwed up. Buster shook his head morosely, trying to pin Manny's eyes, but DeVera wouldn't look at him directly. Something was definitely wrong.

Jerry Trimble motioned to Manny. "Get with logistics and tell them we need an emergency airlift of sixty Shrikes, and we'll need 'em as soon as they can get 'em here. Then have 'em call Korat and see if we can borrow a few until the airlift arrives."

"Tell the loggies that I'll sign the requests," Buster growled angrily.

"Yes, sir." DeVera quickly left the room.

"Something wrong with him?" Buster asked when DeVera had gone. "He doesn't seem his old self."

"Probably working too hard. But you're right. He's nervous and he's looking bad."

"Maybe he's flying too much."

"I'll check into it."

"Do that. Now, you said you had something else you wanted to talk over?"

Jerry Trimble hesitated for a moment. "More of a generalization than a real problem, but I thought you should know before it gets worse."

"Shoot."

"It's George Armaugh and his people. The overall status of our aircraft is going downhill fast. My pilots are starting to raise hell about all the maintenance problems, and I've got to agree."

Buster's brows knitted. "What do you mean?"

"Well, some days we're barely getting enough aircraft to meet the frags. We go out there and get our asses shot off, and the fucking maintenance people—"

Buster rose angrily from his chair. "I don't want you *ever* saying those words together again. They aren't *fucking* maintenance people. They're guys trying like hell to give you the aircraft you need." He had a flash of déjà vu . . . he'd heard the recording before.

Jerry Trimble flashed an agreeable expression. "Yes, sir. Sorry about the word. It's just that I don't think Armaugh understands our needs."

Buster Leska worked hard to maintain an even tone. "Colonel Armaugh and his people are doing their damnedest."

"Maybe it's because he's new to maintenance, but—"

"Stop!" Leska roared.

It was more of the same crap—the continuing argument between maintenance and operations that slowed things down and created unnecessary antagonism.

"Jerry, go on out there and do your job, and stay the hell off George's back."

"I just thought you should—"

"Damn it!"

Trimble's resolve melted. "Yes, sir." He left.

After a moment of smoldering inwardly over the return of

the infighting, Buster pulled out of his top drawer the message he'd received just before the meeting.

A JACKPOT message from General Moss. General McManus was still in the hospital, having suffered yet another in a series of minor heart attacks, but he'd dictated a back-channel message through his aide to Moss. President Johnson was having a bad time in the polls. Strident outcries from the media about communist successes during Tet, however contrived, were creating a backlash. There were unconfirmed speculations by the press that Westmoreland wanted massive numbers of additional troops sent to the war zone—which provided fodder for the end-the-war people. The public was growing weary of the conflict half the way around the world.

An obscure antiwar senator named McCarthy was running against L.B.J. in the New Hampshire primary, and his numbers in the polls were rising daily. It was conceivable that Johnson, a serving president, might lose his own party's nomination.

The UN secretary-general had called for a unilateral halt to the bombing of North Vietnam, saying the North Vietnamese would surely respond with meaningful talks. Although intelligence sources revealed that U Thant was not the unaligned figure he purported to be—he'd been raised in a Red Chinese family in Burma and was a communist sympathizer—numerous members of Congress said they'd like to give his plan a try.

All of those things combined to make McManus believe L.B.J. would very shortly call for the LINE BACKER JACKPOT campaign to be initiated. It was his only real option to end the war quickly and get out of the quagmire. The CSAF said he'd be out of the hospital and back on the job in another week to facilitate things. He'd press to begin deploying air combat forces as soon as possible.

General Moss wanted a report from his contacts at the bases: a final, thorough review of their ability to fly the sustained sortie rate required in the LINE BACKER JACKPOT OPlan and a complete list of resources they'd require when they were augmented by the units from the States. Since Lieutenant Colonel P. S. Gates was away on temporary duty to PACAF Headquarters, all responses were to be forwarded directly to Moss himself.

Buster pondered the last paragraph. That report would require a dedicated effort from the contacts at each of the bases. He wanted to put Manny DeVera in charge of the project, but was hesitant. Something was troubling about the way the Supersonic Wetback was acting, at a time he needed him most. He decided on Lucky Anderson, who seemed to be emerging from his grief.

Buster took a call from Jerry Trimble. He spoke in a humble voice following the ass-chewing. "Boss, I checked with the 333rd where they keep track of Captain DeVera's sorties. He's not flying much at all . . . down to a flight every four or five days."

"Thanks."

Buster decided to deal with Manny's problem directly. Before he could pursue it, he received a phone call from George Armaugh, who argued that Jerry Trimble was working his crew chiefs unduly because of unreasonable requests to have the Gatling guns aligned better.

Captain Manny DeVera was mentally shuffled to the bottom of the list of priorities.

1255L—Over Channel 97, Laos

Lieutenant Colonel Lucky Anderson

The TACAN was back on the air, and its presence was reassuring as they approached.

The join-up was done in silence—an easy one, just as they'd been before the nav station had been overrun. When the TACAN needle swung about, showing station passage, the strike force was already tucked into position.

No surprises or tardy flight members. He liked the feeling.

He'd been growing accustomed to the fact that he'd never see Linda again except in the stack of photos. With time the sharpness of his anguish had lessened as the likelihood that she was dead had grown. There had been no further word from Sergeant Black at Nakhon Phanom, and his latest discussions with Richard at the Bangkok embassy had been gloomy.

"I don't think we can be optimistic any longer," Richard

had told him flatly. That had been two weeks ago, and nothing had changed in later conversations.

Lucky had trouble accepting it, but there was no alternative. To continue hoping would mean to continue life in a turmoil, and the men who served beneath him deserved better.

He checked his flight instruments carefully, then began to set up his switches as the strike force approached the Ma River, which, from 20,000 feet, looked like a tiny dark ribbon. He paused, eyes drawn to the river so far below them.

An uneasy feeling settled over Lucky as he continued staring, and he couldn't dispel the feeling that something was wrong. Ridiculous, he told himself, and dragged his attention back inside the cockpit.

"Scotch force, let's green 'em up and turn on the music," he announced. But he couldn't keep an odd sadness from his voice.

1500L—Ma River, Laos

GS-15 *Linda Lopes*

She'd made it to a freshet and then followed that for a hundred yards to a gentle river whose banks were green and lush. In her previous life Linda had enjoyed plants and had developed a knack for gardening, but her mind was now too filled by constant agony, too clouded and numbed by malnourishment, to comprehend anything beyond the fact that it was a more pleasant surrounding than she had known for a long while.

A much better, almost gentle place to die.

As the days and nights passed, she huddled in a tiny copse of trees beside the river, awaiting death and experimenting with the vegetation. Each morning at sunrise she'd crawl to the river and wash herself. She would scrub and carefully attend each scab, wound, and tiny pore. Her skin was a profusion of welts and open abscesses, created by the abuses of the past months and the fact that since she'd left the Pathet Lao's care, she'd not been provided with a sleeping net to ward off the constant swarms of insects. Her hair came out in bunches at the slightest tug. Her nose, broken and rebroken so many times by Sergeant Gross, had healed some in the time since her last beating, but she knew it must be an unsightly thing. She could breath only through her mouth, and the sounds of her respiration were harsh and ragged. Her rib cage, where they'd beaten her so thoroughly, felt as if it might collapse, and she could feel bones protruding unnaturally there.

She ached in so many places. Her left arm, where she'd struck the back of the truck when she'd tumbled out, presented the newest constant pain, but there was much more. Her left foot had been agonizingly tender since the sergeant had beaten there, and she could take no more than a few steps before crawling. Both breasts were misshapen by knots of scar tissue and ached continuously.

She was ready to accept death and knew only it could release her from the constant agony.

Although long past hunger, Linda tried eating the various vegetation she found in the area. *If you're unsure, place a tiny amount in your mouth to see if they're edible,* Paul had cautioned her.

She'd found juicy bright-red berries growing on a bush in her dying place, and after cautiously mouthing one, retched and spat it out. They were obviously poisonous. Next she tried delicate yellow shoots from young plants growing beside the water. When there was no reaction, she ate them by the handful, ignoring the sharp pain from teeth broken off at the gum line. Half an hour afterward her stomach began to grumble. She didn't know if it was a sign of rejection or the simple fact that she'd been starved for so long, but she ate more of them. She couldn't take many at once, but as she ate and her stomach gurgled, she became even more famished, as if her body finally realized that it must have nourishment.

There was a sort of lily pad floating on a small pond fed by the stream, and she pulled out a few and tried their tender roots.

Shoots and roots.

Paul had told her that young shoots and tender roots were lifesavers in wilderness camping, which was his hobby. The roots were tasty, sort of like eggplant. She ate as many as she could keep down and again developed a stomachache, but that time it hadn't been nearly as bad.

The fourth day at her dying place was the first that she

heard and saw soldiers making their way along the river-bank. There were not many, but by the next day their numbers had grown. They were unkempt and appeared dazed and dispirited. Some were wounded and bloody. They moved quietly, periodically casting fearful gazes at the sky. She remained in her dying place and looked out upon them with dispassion.

It was on the sixth day that she realized that dying might not be as easy as she'd anticipated. Her body was broken and sick, but simply refused to stop functioning. She awoke early and bathed, attended to her wounds and sores and new profusions of insect bites she'd collected during the night. Then she smeared mud over her wet nakedness to keep away at least some of the mosquitoes and gnats, and crawled back toward her dying place. Two straggling soldiers passed nearby, but they ignored her.

Perhaps, she thought, there was nothing to fear from them now that they had problems of their own. She ate more of the tender water-lily roots, carefully because of her throbbing mouth, and contemplated the disturbing fact that she was gaining strength, which was sure to prolong her existence.

What would Paul do? Linda wondered, then realized she knew the answer. He'd cling to life. His enemy was death. Paul was the ultimate survivor. She pondered the question and thought of him fondly as she ate more shoots and roots.

At noon she looked up for some inexplicable reason and tried to focus in the distant sky. She saw fuzzy specks and shortly heard the rumble of aircraft engines. It was awful to know that Americans were so close, yet were oblivious of her. As she stared, a sure thought possessed her. *Paul was there.* Strong and wonderful as ever.

A trill passed through her. Another distant formation passed over, but somehow she knew that he'd been in the other, first one.

She slept for a while, and then awoke. She could feel someone's presence.

Four men were hunkered and watching her closely. A captain and three soldiers had invaded her dying place . . . contaminating it.

"Go . . . away," she whispered angrily.

When the captain reached forward and grasped her by

the left arm, pain shot through her so intensely that she cried out. He pulled her roughly to her feet by the broken arm, and she squealed louder.

The soldiers chattered among themselves, calmer and better disciplined than others she'd seen previously.

The captain motioned toward the river with the muzzle of his rifle.

She shook her head. She wasn't going.

The captain shrugged and aimed the rifle at her head.

Linda took a breath and calmly looked about her dying place. She would go no farther. It would end here.

A shot sounded and she stiffened, trembled, waiting for the pain, then heard a dull sound and looked to see that the captain had crumpled. She heard a shout.

The soldiers fled.

A Vietnamese lieutenant came into her dying place, looking about carefully before regarding her. He was followed closely by several squat and tattooed men in loincloths, one of whom picked up the dead captain's assault rifle.

Linda sighed, then sucked in another breath and held it pensively as the lieutenant examined her with his eyes. He looked vaguely familiar. It didn't matter who killed her, she was going no farther.

"Missy Lopes?" he said.

She was startled by the words.

"You hokay now, sistah." The lieutenant's voice was gentle, and she felt she'd heard it before. He motioned to one of the tribesmen, who brought forth a swatch of dark material.

"You make . . ." He searched for a word, but could think only of a Vietnamese one. Finally he pointed to his clothing. Linda stood her ground firmly. Her nakedness no longer bothered her, and she was going absolutely nowhere.

The lieutenant came closer, fumbling in his pack, and came up with a small ball of rice, which he cautiously offered.

She paused, then took it with her good right hand. He nodded. She ate.

"You hokay now," the lieutenant repeated. "Go see Kunnel Lokee."

What had he said?

"Kunnel Lokee ver' worry." He nodded again and formed a shy smile.

"You mean Lucky?" she croaked incredulously.

"Kunnel Lokee Anduhson."

"Oh, God!" she wailed, and could take no more. She crumpled, sobbing.

The lieutenant knelt and patted her shoulder. She winced, and he hastily pulled the hand back. Regardless of how she tried, she couldn't stop crying for a long while.

"We bettah ged gone, sistah," he finally said, gently draping the cloth about her nakedness. She didn't fight him, and let him tuck it into place.

When they finally left the dying place, the dark cloth draped about her like an Indian sari, she hobbled so badly on the broken foot that the lieutenant held up for a while longer and fashioned a huge bandage, which he tied about her foot. Then they went very cautiously, a tiny, barrel-chested tribesman supporting her good, right arm, another with his arm about her midriff. The lieutenant led the way and looked very professional about it. He peered back periodically to observe her. His look was sad and kind, but it also held a glimmer of triumph.

2130L—Trailer 5B, Takhli RTAFB, Thailand

Captain Manny DeVera

"I'm not doing my job well," he told her.

They were naked. He was sitting upright on the bed, and Penny was rubbing his back with gentle hands, providing the peace Manny could experience only in her trailer. He'd been tense, and she was trying to soothe him as she did every night now.

"I feel bad . . . like I'm letting the guys down."

"I feel wonderful because I know you're going to live. We're going to have a good life together. I know we will." She said it almost fiercely.

"I dunno, Penny." He shook his head. "I don't think I can stay in the Air Force."

"That's up to you. I'll follow you wherever you go, Manny DeVera."

"I don't think it's up to me, staying in the Air Force, I mean. I took an oath to protect and defend. I take that sort of thing seriously." He almost added, *At least I used to.*

"You've given all that a man should ever have to. You've done your share and more. Look at all the draft dodgers and peace marchers back in the States. They refuse to give anything."

Manny had thought of them a lot the past few days. It hadn't made him feel better at all. He'd decided it was only fair to go to Colonel Leska and let him know what he was doing. Maybe tell him he wanted to quit flying altogether, as Penny wanted.

There were times when he felt he was going nuts . . . others when he thought he was doing the right thing . . . and sometimes he told himself to quit being a cowardly jerk and letting his buddies down—that if someone took his place on the schedule and got killed, it would be his doing. And just perhaps, if he went back to flying the tough missions, there would be no more terror. Maybe . . .

But it had already gone too far . . . hadn't it?

"Penny . . . ," he started, but she was nuzzling his back with soft lips, and her arms were moving gently on his chest.

She leaned her face against him and whispered. "God, I love you, Manny."

The peace she offered slowly returned, and he could feel the wetness of tears on his skin.

He pulled her around and caressed her.

As they made gentle love, he forgot about the promise, about flying, about everything except his feeling for this woman.

CHAPTER
THIRTY-NINE

Assistant Commissioner Nguyen Wu

The roadway through the mountains was treacherous and exasperatingly long, and Wu had grown weary of riding in the foul-smelling, balky truck. He was also tired of listening to the sublieutenant's constant chatter about his family, who lived in Lao Cai, near the Chinese border, and how dedicated they were to the Enlightened One and the war effort. Every hour or two he'd tell the man to be quiet and drive, but a while later the sublieutenant would make a comment, then begin to expand upon it. On five separate occasions he'd taken wrong turns on the series of unmarked mountain pathways, and they'd had to backtrack for hours.

Yet he intended to have him promoted and decorated—for serving a Hero of the Republic, as Wu was sure he'd become. The sublieutenant was awed by Wu's position as the right hand of the Commissioner of Death, and would spread the story of his heroism. Nguyen Wu would become a legend, the reed that had withstood the terrible American attacks to accomplish his task. They would be among the first few to emerge from the chaos at Ban Sao Si, and there would be no one to refute his deeds—how he'd left the bunker and walked calmly through hails of American bullets, determined to bring his important information to the Lao Dong party.

The sublieutenant was parroting the proper words, and glowed with the promise that he'd be allowed to serve Wu during his rise within the party.

In the early morning of the ninth day, they passed women bearing baskets on their heads, and the sublieutenant learned they were approaching the village of Yen Chau, and that there was a military outpost there. Wu felt a great flood of relief. They were safe! The Thunder planes attacked trucks on roadways, but never villages inhabited by civilians. As they drove past the first huts, Nguyen Wu assumed the haughty look he felt a Hero of the People should wear, ignoring the disgusting, rancid smells of the dismal, small community.

"Find the camp where the soldiers live," he barked with authority. He wished he was more presentable and hoped they'd find a radio so he could notify Hanoi. As they passed more hovels, Wu wanted to blurt out a shout of thanks for being saved, but knew it did not fit into his new image. He maintained the stoic look of a Hero of the People.

There was no encampment, only a handful of ragged militia, and those lived in miserable huts beside a crude, stilted observation tower at the edge of the jungle. Yet Wu's pulse quickened, for an antenna extended from the top of the tower. When they halted in a thick cloud of dust, Nguyen Wu swore he would not go a kilometer farther in the wretched Chinese-built truck.

They dismounted, and the sublieutenant called up to the tower. Yes, there was a radio, a soldier in a ragged uniform laconically responded.

"The assistant commissioner must speak with Hanoi."

"Assistant commissioner?" When he was told Wu worked for the Commissioner of People's Safety, the man immediately became obsequious and began to bow and chatter nervously. "Of course!" he spouted. They'd do anything for a representative of the Commissioner of Death.

The sublieutenant shouted that Wu was a hero, fresh from battle with the Americans. They would hear much about this great man in the future, he said. The soldier was so overcome he could scarcely speak. Wu interpreted the silence not as fear, but awed respect. He knew he must grow accustomed to such treatment. When they arrived at Hanoi and revealed what he'd brought them—the list of agents in locations throughout Thailand, as well as the power structure of the Mee intelligence effort in Laos and Cambodia— he'd be acclaimed by the Lao Dong party. He had attended parades and proud speeches in Ba Dinh square honoring men who had done far less.

No one would dare withhold his rewards. His beloved aunt would see to it.

As Wu crawled up the tower's ladder, he wished his uniform was in better repair. He'd have time to have it washed and mended, he decided, because it was unlikely they'd send a helicopter before nightfall. Daytime travel would be dangerous, and his information was invaluable. A moment later he was briefed on the operation of the ancient and bulky radio. When the thing had warmed, and the fearful soldier had adjusted the tuning and volume, Wu spoke with an operator at the People's Army headquarters in Hanoi. He identified himself and asked to be immediately connected with a Lao Dong party representative.

He was told to stand by. The voice was cool and efficient, and made Nguyen Wu yearn for the sophistication of Hanoi. Several long minutes passed before a jumble of static sounded. It was not the party liaison officer, but the same voice asking him to tune to a new radio frequency.

The soldier made the change, and Wu again made contact. He was surprised when a distinctive, rasping voice responded. Xuan Nha first cautioned him not to use names on the radio, then congratulated him for making it safely out of Ban Sao Si. He asked how many of the 900 men at Ban Sao Si had survived the air attacks.

Wu said there were few who remained alive. He told him how he'd fought his way gallantly through hails of American bullets and ignored the bombs that were exploding nearby.

Xuan Nha said he must have been very brave, and Wu could hear no derisiveness in the rasping voice, so he remained appropriately quiet. *"We have assigned this frequency to you, so long as you remain at Yen Chau,"* Xuan Nha said.

Wu asked if that would be necessary, since he'd be there for such a short time.

Xuan Nha replied that there were too many Mee aircraft flying in the area during the daytime to attempt to extract him right away, and that the Soviet helicopter pilots weren't proficient at night flying in the mountainous regions.

Nguyen could not keep a tremor from his voice. *"When will they come for me?"*

"Shortly," Xuan Nha answered vaguely. He asked if Wu had been successful with his mission.

"More successful than anyone can imagine! I have served my party and country with courage and honor. I have ..." He stopped himself, remembering that he must be stoic.

Xuan asked if he wished to give the information of his findings over the radio, so People's Army intelligence could begin working with it.

"It is far too sensitive," Wu responded. *"When I arrive in Hanoi, I will personally brief the Lao Dong party intelligence chief. My information is for him, not the People's Army,"* he said with appropriate disdain.

Xuan Nha didn't press the subject. He welcomed him back again—repeated that future communications between Hanoi and the Yen Chau outpost should be made only on the new frequency—and told him to call back in another week, and to ask to speak with only him.

"A week?"

"That is how long intelligence believes the bombardments will continue. The Mee Thunder planes are bombing targets between your position and Hanoi."

Wu's spirits plummeted. His former elation had completely disappeared.

"I will tell everyone how brave and honorable you have been. You are too important to be placed in jeopardy, and the information you possess is undoubtedly critical to the party."

That helped some.

"The Mee must not discover your location or know that you are carrying critical secrets. Remain out of sight as much as you can, for their spies are everywhere in that area. The fewer people who see you there, the better."

That seemed reasonable. The Mee would surely want the secrets he carried.

"From now on, when you speak on the radio, do not tell

*your name. Use your code name ... which we have assigned
as Brave Hero. Do not tell even the people in Yen Chau who
you are.*"

"*Brave Hero,*" Wu repeated, liking the sound of it.

"*You may also assume command of Yen Chau, since you
are the ranking official there.*"

"*I will do so immediately,*" Wu said happily.

Xuan Nha said they'd talk again in seven days, then he
terminated. Nguyen Wu handed the microphone to the soldier, wondering if he shouldn't have been more adamant. He
already felt like a captive in the mountain village so far from
Hanoi, and now he must spend seven more days here? He
determined that his stay would not last a moment longer
than that.

When he leaned out of the tower, he noted that another
slovenly soldier was speaking to the sublieutenant. When
Wu asked, he called in a tremulous voice that he commanded the outpost.

"I am now in charge," Wu barked. "That was Colonel
Nha I spoke to on the radio."

The soldier gawked up at him.

"Surely you have heard of Colonel Xuan Nha, in temporary command of the People's Army of National Defense.
That includes the militia, you know."

"No longer temporary, honorable comrade. He is our
general now. The promotion was announced several days
ago. General Giap himself issued the bulletin."

Xuan Nha a general? Wu started to boast that General
Nha was his aunt's husband, but suppressed the words, remembering that he must remain anonymous.

The soldier at his side spoke out. "I heard General Nha
on the radio myself. This important visitor is to be called
only Brave Hero, and no one is to know he is here. The general said so."

There were gasps at the significance of their visitor. The
soldier below bowed deeply. "We are honored that you now
command our humble outpost, Brave Hero."

"The sublieutenant and I shall take rooms in the largest
and finest house in this miserable place while we wait for
the helicopter."

The sublieutenant smiled wider.

"That is my home," said a man who was marginally better

clothed than the others. He introduced himself as mayor of
the patriotic and grand city of Yen Chau. "We will be honored to have such a great and brave hero stay with us."

While the humble village of Yen Chau was neither grand
nor a city, Wu glowed at the description of himself. *Ah well,*
thought Wu as he descended the rickety tower. His glorious
return to Hanoi would come soon enough.

A troublesome thought arose. With Xuan Nha now a general, his trysts with Li Binh must be more discreet. Perhaps
Wu should even begin to curry his favor.

0740L—VPA Headquarters, Hanoi, DRV

General Xuan Nha

It had been a fine week for Xuan. He'd thoroughly enjoyed
attending the ceremonies—one when General Giap and Li
Binh had looked on quietly as General Dung read the honors, the other when he'd read the orders promoting his own
subordinates as they assumed new responsibilities. *Colonel*
Tran Van Ngo, replacing him as Commandant of Rockets
and Artillery, *Captain* Quang Hanh, aide and communications officer. Eight others, all trusted subordinates, were also
advanced to new positions, replacing his predecessor's staff.

When the Americans attacked at Ban Sao Si, communications had been lost. Finally there'd been radio contact with
a forty-man company that had hidden in a Lao village where
no bombs had been dropped. They confirmed that the
Strelas had proved useless against Thunder planes and
Phantoms. The 900 defenders in the area were estimated to
have suffered 80 percent casualties.

Xuan Nha had directed the company commander to establish a camp east of Ban Sao Si, to report on enemy activities on the mountaintop. He'd dispatched a train of pack
horses to resupply them, for their radio was weak and their
provisions were already dwindling.

He'd hoped Nguyen Wu had suffered a lingering and
painful death. But the man lived, and harbored thoughts of
being received in Hanoi as a hero. That wasn't out of the
question—upon his arrival Li Binh would likely arrange an
observance for her nephew's heroism.

It had been fortunate Quang Hanh had been monitoring the Yen Chau frequency for word about stragglers arriving from Ban Sao Si. No one in Hanoi but he and Xuan Nha knew about the conversation with Nguyen Wu. Xuan felt he must handle this latest challenge discreetly. He couldn't simply order Wu to be executed, for if Li Binh heard of it, her wrath would be lethal. Yet as a member of the general staff, he could no longer tolerate Wu's shameful dalliances with his wife. Which was why he'd delayed Nguyen Wu's return. Xuan Nha could have dispatched a helicopter to Yen Chau that very evening, for the Mee air attacks had dwindled in numbers and intensity in the northern regions of the country.

The frequency he'd told Quang Hanh to tune to had made the new captain raise a questioning eyebrow. Xuan Nha nodded, and Quang Hahn made the change, although the channel was known to have been compromised, and to be monitored by the Mee. Afterward he'd told him to remain secretive about the matter and knew the order would be obeyed.

Xuan told him to raise Air Regiment Commandant Quon at Gia Lam, using yet another compromised frequency.

He spoke a few niceties to Quon, who in turn congratulated him on his promotion.

"The important official with the code name of Brave Hero is now at the village of Yen Chau, in the western mountains," Xuan Nha said very slowly and clearly.

"Brave Hero?" Quon almost strangled on the words, and couldn't suppress a short laugh.

"That is the code name I assigned him," Xuan Nha said. *"He has broken the American spy woman and has her secrets there at Yen Chau with him."*

"The spy woman who was first captured by the Pathet Lao?"

Well spoken, Xuan thought. Surely the Americans would understand that. *"Yes. That woman. Brave Hero is carrying her secrets with him. It would be unfortunate if the Mee decided to attack there with their airplanes."*

"Very unfortunate," Quon said in a clear voice over the compromised frequency as they'd agreed.

Neither of them knew that monitoring of that frequency had been shifted to a lower priority at the American listening station at Danang Air Base, since nothing of intelligence interest had ever been found there. That particular channel of the tape, one of hundreds being recorded at the time, would not be interpreted for several days.

0930L—355th TFW Commander's Office, Takhli RTAFB, Thailand

Captain Manny DeVera

As he passed Penny's desk, Manny gave her a final look before proceeding into the wing commander's office. He'd told her what he must do and knew it pleased her. He could no longer continue the lie, living among his friends and acting as if he were betting his ass just as they were. It was only right that Leska be the first one to know. He'd been the one to trust Manny after he was branded a lair. He shouldn't be told by others that his faith had been misplaced.

Manny could live no longer with the constant shakes and jangles, unable to face his friends, wondering if one of them was going to fly in his place and not return. He'd not been able to sleep, or lately even to make love with Penny. He was utterly exhausted, both physically and mentally, and felt that only by making a clean breast of it all would he be able to rest. Manny was going to lay it all out, then stand to attention and face the consequences—do whatever the wing commander felt was appropriate.

Leska was on the phone, but he waved him into a chair at the side of his desk. Manny sat gingerly and rubbed at his eyes.

So fucking tired.

"George," the wing commander was saying in a strained voice, "I don't give a damn if you feel they're tearing up your birds, you don't bitch at Jerry Trimble in front of crew chief and pilots. I won't have any more open arguments, dammit."

He listened for a moment, then shook his head as if Armaugh could see him over the telephone line. "No! Dammit, you will not forward a report like that. Any such bickering we'll keep in house. I don't want you exposing our dirty laundry to the world."

As Leska continued to chew his Deputy for Maintenance's ass, Manny fidgeted, thinking about the colonel's temper and how it would be directed toward himself in a couple of minutes.

He deserved the worst. He'd betrayed the man's trust.

"See me in fifteen minutes. No, here in my office." A pause. "Bring your write-ups with you. I'm going to sit you and Jerry Trimble down together, and we're going to settle this damn arguing once and for all." He slammed the telephone harshly into its cradle, then turned his eye on Manny. "You didn't hear that."

"No, sir," he replied.

Leska was reduced to muttering. "One of those cases where everyone's right and everyone's wrong, and there's no good answers." He buzzed Penny and told her to prepare the conference room for a private meeting between himself, operations, and maintenance. Just those three, he told her.

Leska leaned back in his chair, relaxing some. "It ain't easy, Manny." He examined his weapons officer's face with a concerned look.

DeVera could keep it in no longer. He blurted his words. "I want to quit flying, sir."

Colonel Leska continued staring. "You want to *what*?"

Manny swallowed hard, shifted his eyes to the all. "I want to quit—"

"Just a second," the wing commander interrupted, and picked up the telephone. "I've got to make a phone call, Manny."

DeVera looked on grimly. Leska was probably calling the legal people to have him court-martialed—maybe Colonel Trimble to have his wings ripped from his chest, or whatever they did with cowards.

Leska hesitated, then dialed and spoke with the civil engineer about a problem with runway lighting. "Send one of your guys over to check 'em out, okay?"

Manny relaxed. Apparently the colonel's mind had been preoccupied when he'd told him. After a few more words Leska hung up, rolling his eyes. "Can you believe there are four lights out and they didn't even know it? That I'm the first one to tell them?"

Manny mumbled a response, not minding the delay, willing to grasp at any small lifesaver so he could put off telling about his cowardice. It was the shittiest thing he'd ever had to do. Yet he had to get it said and over with.

Leska was writing something on a notepad. "I've found if I don't write these things down, I tend to forget them."

"Yes, sir," Manny muttered, savoring the small talk. "I know what you mean."

The intercom buzzed, and the colonel took a call, this one from the wing commander at Korat, obviously a good friend, because he called him Willie and made little private jokes. After ten minutes of banter, Leska hung up. "Now there's a leader of men. His people think he's right up there with God, and I can understand why. He's one of the guys, know what I mean, but he's still able to make the tough decisions and he doesn't take any crap."

"Yes, sir, I've heard that."

The colonel looked back at his notepad and shook his head. "Damn."

"Something wrong, sir?"

Leska grimaced and looked up at him. "You won't like it, Manny."

"Sir?"

"Doc Rogers spoke with me about you yesterday after the staff meeting."

Manny couldn't remember the flight surgeon being at the staff meeting. But, then, lately he'd been missing a lot of what was going on around him.

"Remember when you punched out of the airplane and hurt your shoulder? It seems a colonel physician from PACAF reviewed the case and decided you've gotta have more tests."

It didn't make sense. He'd been put through a thorough medical examination before Doc Rogers had cleared him to start flying again. "What kind of test, sir?"

"Got me. But Rogers told us to have you report to the clinic at zero-nine-hundred this morning, and it's already past that time. You'd better get over there ASAP."

"My shoulder?" His shoulder felt just fine.

"Go on over there now, Manny. Don't keep the Doc waiting any longer than necessary."

"Yes, sir."

Manny got to his feet and saluted awkwardly, then went out the door. He didn't see Buster Leska grab for his telephone the second he was gone. He didn't hear the words spoken to the flight surgeon or the urgency in the voice.

Manny passed Colonel Trimble and Colonel Armaugh in the outer office, and both men were glaring nastily at one another.

DeVera had to wait out in the small lobby for half an hour before Doc Rogers came out and waved him into his office.

"Bunch of bullshit, you ask me," Rogers huffed as he closed the door.

"What's that, Doc?"

Rogers peered at his face. "Jesus, what the hell's happened to you?"

"What do you mean?"

"You look like shit, Manny."

"I've been tired lately."

The Doc scribbled on a prescription pad. Manny peered but couldn't read his writing. Rogers handed the sheet to him. "Go back to your room, take one pill, and get some rest."

"Sleeping pill?"

"It'll knock you out for a few hours. But don't be late for your plane in the morning."

"What are you talking about, Doc?"

"The surgeon general at PACAF says you've gotta go to the hospital at Hickam so they can run some tests. The people at wing headquarters are typing up your travel orders right now."

"My shoulder's fine," Manny argued.

"It's not just the shoulder. They've got a whole series of tests they want to run. They'll tell you when you get there."

Manny was confused by everything that was going on. He started to argue, then remembered what he'd gone to see Colonel Leska about in the first place and decided he wouldn't mind the delay.

"How long am I gonna be gone, Doc?"

"Oh, I'd say ten days or a couple weeks."

It would be nicer if Penny could go with him, he thought as he took the prescription out to the pharmacy window, but a trip to Hawaii didn't sound half-bad.

Friday, March 1st, 0645 Local—Royal Hawaiian Hotel, Honolulu, Hawaii

Colonel Tom Lyons

The alarm rang with its shrill howl, and Tom groped, then slapped at the off button to silence it. Normally he slept in longer, but this morning was special. At ten o'clock he'd meet with General Roman. It was to be an interesting day. With luck it would be a good one for him and get things back on a proper track.

Roman hadn't called him to his office in a month—not since Tom had returned from his trip to tell what he'd learned about the "fucking cowboys'" stupid plan. Since Margaret had left, and with her the considerable leverage of Senator Lingenfelter, there'd been no reason for the general to meet with a lowly colonel. There'd been no more mention about his being a trusted staff officer, or of his chances for a star when Roman moved to Washington.

But Tom had devised a new plan designed to impress the general, and he'd also gotten onto his busy calendar—a feat which had taken sweet-talking the nymphomaniac bitch secretary who'd given him the dose of gonorrhea and said it had been *he* who'd given it to *her*.

Roman had once told him he needed an in with the new Secretary of Defense, whom he'd never met. And that was precisely what he would offer, for Tom Lyons's father had grudgingly agreed to arrange a private meeting between Roman and the incoming SecDef. His father was still angry that he'd fucked up his marriage to Margaret Lingenfelter so thoroughly, but he'd done *one last* favor for his youngest son.

Ever since Tom had been so indiscreet as to, as his father put it, "foul his own nest," he'd been on the old man's shit list. A man could fuck any number of common women—it was one of the privileges due the privileged—but it should *never* be indiscreet or come to his wife's attention.

Indiscretion, not fornication, was a mortal sin.

Senator Lingenfelter had been so incensed that the odious disease might have been passed to his daughter that he'd ended the long-standing and mutually beneficial relationship with the senior Lyons. Redemption from his father would be a long time coming unless he made things right.

Tom had sent a continuous flurry of contrite and groveling letters to Margaret. She hadn't responded for a long while, but finally she'd answered. Her note was short and fraught with anger, but at least she'd taken the time to write it. He continued with loving letters and barraged her with flowers, for he now knew that Margaret Lingenfelter was the key to his good life.

If it hadn't been for the damn form being forwarded to his home, he'd still have her. The situation begged for retribution against the incompetents at the Takhli medical clinic, but there was no way to chastise the flight surgeons unless Tom revealed that he'd contracted the disease—and *that* indiscretion was sure to harm the career of a full colonel on the inspector general's team. The situation was frustrating.

When he'd finished showering and shaving, Tom slipped on a satin dressing robe, padded back to the sitting room, took a seat at the small desk, and opened a folder made of soft Florentine leather—a present from Margaret. Inside he kept notes from his inspection trips, data about certain projects, as well as a few official messages and the list of his contacts at the various bases. It didn't concern him that the folder held classified information that was supposed to be secured in a safe. Such ridiculous rules were for others.

On the pad of gray paper, he outlined suggestions about how to approach establishment of a rapport with the new SecDef. He wanted to be well prepared for the meeting with Roman.

0850L—CINCPACAF Office, Hickam AB, Oahu

Lieutenant Colonel Pearly Gates

Pearly entered the outer office and presented himself to the brunette secretary, hefting a stack of vu-graphs and carrying a briefcase in his other hand.

"Oh, yes," she said, flashing a smile. "You have a nine o'clock with the general."

He sat across from her in one of the brown leather chairs there, and looked about.

"You just came in from the combat zone?" the secretary asked.

"I've been here for a couple of days," he replied. Surely she knew that the general had already postponed the briefing three times. Pearly had forwarded a message, labeling the subject as Contingency Operational War Plans, and General Moss had even called ahead to get him onto the schedule. Obviously General Roman hadn't been impressed. Either that or he was making Pearly cool his heels to teach the "fucking cowboys" another lesson.

Pearly had known Roman from his days in Strategic Air Command, and the delay surprised him. While he often lashed out at briefing officers, Bomber Joe Roman had seemed satisfied with Pearly's presentations. He thought it unlikely that he didn't remember him. Roman had a prodigious memory—he could even remember the first names of all of his subordinate's wives.

Pearly glanced up and saw that the secretary was observing him with cool eyes. Her voice was melodic. "Where are you staying, Colonel?"

He gave her a cautious smile. "The BOQ."

"Have you had time to visit the city?"

"Some." He'd walked Waikiki Beach, watched the surfers, and bought a couple of pukka shell necklaces and a few knickknacks for Lucy.

The secretary went on with her conversation, as if sincerely interested in his well-being. She asked where he went in the evenings for drinks, recommended a couple of hotel lounges, and told him he needed to take a drive to the windward side if he *really* wanted to see the island. She hinted that she'd be pleased to accompany him, and Pearly faltered awkwardly.

Lucy would take him apart if she got wind of his spending time with another woman. She might be tiny, but she was extremely perceptive, and had a fierce temper and a possessive attitude. Pearly was not a good liar when she pinned him with her soft, serious eyes. He told the secretary he had to get back to Saigon immediately following the briefing, although that wasn't true. He wouldn't depart until the day after tomorrow.

She looked at some sort of signal on her desk and told him the general was ready for him. Pearly rose, hitched his

trousers and smoothed his shirt, then pushed his glasses into
position and entered the lion's den.

Roman was staring at papers on his desk, fastidiously
avoiding looking up as he motioned him forward with a
brusque wave of his hand. Pearly looked about vainly for the
vu-graph projector he'd requested in his message.

Roman grunted. "Just hand 'em here and get on with it.
I don't need a fucking machine."

"Yes, sir."

"I'm giving you fifteen minutes."

Pearly had asked for half an hour. He blew out a ragged
breath, then began to speak, opening by stating the name of
the OPlan. "My subject is LINE BACKER JACKPOT."

"JACKPOT?" Roman's eyes came alive at the mention of
the word, and Pearly knew they'd been right. The general
knew of the plan. After ten minutes Roman stopped him for
the first time. "Ten squadrons of B-52's?"

"Yes, sir. We feel that would be the minimum number
necessary to do the job."

Roman's eyes narrowed. "Go on," he snapped. He had
him go over the target list in depth, but neither indicated he
agreed or disagreed as Pearly explained the rationale behind
each. When he described projected loss rates, Roman didn't
flinch. Pearly remembered that Major "Bomber Joe" Roman
had flown twenty-five combat missions over Germany in
B-17's, before the advent of P-51's when the Eighth Air
Force was in its most vulnerable hour.

When Pearly mentioned the ways they planned to limit
collateral damage, the general was especially attentive. He
first explained the various aircraft to be used on the sensitive targets near built-up areas, and their relative accuracies.
Then he mentioned the Pave Dagger tests and the phenom-
enal accuracy that had been displayed, and showed BDA
photos of the Canales bridge, with its center knocked down
by a single bomb.

The general asked for more information on Pave Dagger,
and Pearly explained what he knew about the laser designator and the bomb kits with their seekers. Roman asked an
odd question about blinding people, and Pearly reiterated
what he knew, showed more bomb damage photos, and explained the superb accuracy the smart bombs had shown
during the tests.

He finished in a little over half an hour, but then Roman had him start over from the beginning. When Pearly Gates finished the second time, Roman slowly stood and walked to the window overlooking the entrance to Pearl Harbor.

"Sir, I think—" he began.

"Be quiet for a moment, Gates."

"Yes, sir."

A full minute passed before the general spoke. "Why wasn't I briefed on this from the first?"

"I'm not really at liberty to say, General. I don't know."

Roman gave a terse grunt. "Give me your gut feel. Why was I kept in the dark?"

Pearly wondered if the explanation would enrage the general, who had been known to vent his fury on briefing officers in the past. He decided the stakes were too high to lie. "I'd say it was because General McManus knew you were going around him to the SecDef."

"Why the change of heart?"

"General Moss felt you should be included, sir. I think he was uneasy that you didn't know about it, and as your subordinate, he did."

Roman turned and cast a look of surprise. "*Moss* suggested that I be included?"

"Yes, sir. I saw the message he forwarded to the Chief of Staff."

Roman pursed his hips thoughtfully, then gave a brusque nod. "This your OPlan, Pearly?"

It was the first time the general indicated that he remembered him. "I wrote part of it, sir."

"Send me a copy."

"I've brought one for you, sir." Pearly removed the tome from his briefcase and placed it on the general's desk. "General McManus asks that you safeguard it."

Roman didn't respond.

"I can leave the vu-graphs and photos, too, if you wish."

"Do that."

He placed those on the desk beside the OPlan as Roman took his seat. "I've got a busy morning," he muttered, glancing at his watch in such a way that Pearly knew he was dismissed. As he prepared to leave, Pearly realized that the general had not once indicated whether the OPlan was to his liking. He wondered if he hadn't just made a grand mistake. If Roman decided to, he could likely have the entire project killed.

Colonel Tom Lyons was waiting in the outer office, being thoroughly ignored by the brunette secretary. He gave Pearly a glance, but he seemed preoccupied, and there was no recognition in the look. When Pearly stopped for a moment to straighten the papers remaining in his briefcase, the secretary took a brief call, then spoke to Lyons in an icy tone. "The general says he's too busy to see you just now."

Lyons looked as if he'd just choked on something. He asked for the new date.

"He didn't say."

"Surely you can look at his calendar and find out when he'll be available?"

"I'm not free to discuss the general's schedule with anyone outside the command section."

Lyons went closer, smiled and whispered something in a smooth voice.

She said she as already meeting someone for lunch. As Pearly left, the secretary eyed him, and her expression changed to a smile. "Give me a call if you need anything at all, Colonel Gates." Her voice was melodious and inviting.

1630L—Mahlon Sweet Airport, Eugene, Oregon

Major Benny Lewis

When the shuttle bus stopped in front of the airport terminal, Benny gingerly hefted his two gray issue bags and started toward the door. He'd stayed with his kids too long and would have to hurry to make the connecting flight to Portland.

"Hey!" The driver yelled at him.

Benny turned.

"You an Air Force pilot?" He'd noticed the stencils on the bags.

"Yeah."

"Keep 'em flying over in Nam. My brother's a dog-face with the Big Red One."

"Will do." Benny entered the small terminal and found the proper line.

He'd spent two days with his kids, three-year-old Laurie and Little Benny, who was five and a half. Not five. If you said he was five years old, he'd point out that he was in kindergarten and was *five and a half.* The kids were doing well, which was not the doing of his ex-wife, who spent her time with her boyfriend. The previous day they'd left for San Francisco for a vacation of some kind or other.

Bets had spoken to him only once, asking if he and his friends weren't tired of fighting an immoral war. Her boyfriend had slunk around in the background, looking sullen whenever Benny glanced his way.

Bets's wealthy parents doted on their grandchildren as much as they blamed Benny Lewis for screwing up the marriage. If he'd gotten a proper job and settled down, instead of dragging Bets around to godforsaken places around the world and chasing off to war, Bets would have been happy and stayed put. His former father-in-law thought military people were those who couldn't get honest work and chose to live on handouts from taxpayers. He'd told Benny all of that. Enduring the criticism was the price Benny paid for seeing the kids.

Today he'd spent the day with Little Benny and Laurie—had driven them out past Springfield and up the beautiful McKenzie River for a picnic in a forest glen park. When he'd taken them home, grandpa had quizzed both children to see if they'd been abused, or if he'd implanted improper thoughts in their minds. Little Benny had gushed how they'd seen a chipmunk and tried to capture it in a box. Grandpa told him chipmunks were a kind of rat, and to stay away from them lest he get some filthy disease. Laurie told how she'd gotten to ride in front, which she didn't normally get to do. Grandma told her the backseat was much safer.

Divorce is shitty, Benny thought as he edged forward in the line at the airline counter. His back seemed to be doing well, even though he'd lifted the kids often during the last two days. Although they'd known that he'd broken his back, no one, not even his ex-wife, had even once asked about it.

He was on his way to Washington, D.C., where he'd visit with the Requirements Office as General Moss had told him to do. There he'd talk about the future of the smart bomb project.

His mind switched, as it often did, to Julie Stewart and

their last night before his departure. How he'd looked forward to such an evening with her for months, and then, when it finally happened, how he'd screwed up the entire thing. One night of love . . .

That's bullshit, his inner voice said. *You've loved her since the first night you saw her, and just haven't known how to go about getting her.*

She and the baby would be in New Jersey now, living with her mother in much better surroundings than the simple apartment he'd found for her in Las Vegas. He knew he should have written. He'd also told her he'd phone when he got back to the States. But he didn't have her mother's address in New Jersey, and if he did, he didn't know if he'd have the guts to place the call.

He'd come to peace with the specter of her dead husband. Bear Stewart had given his approval. His last words on the radio had asked him to take care of his wife and unborn child.

God how he loved her! And he'd lost her because of a single, lousy night followed by doubts and foolish righteousness. Benny would give anything for a chance to start that evening over, but he was unsure how to make that happen. He wasn't a polished lover. When women were attracted, which happened often enough, he'd redden and turn away, or hastily move his mind to something else. Like Bear Stewart had once told him, he might be a great fighter pilot, but he was also an old-fashioned square who could hardly cope with the fact that his wife had left him, and didn't even wish to get revenge.

He hoped Julie Stewart would be happy wherever she was. Maybe he should try to track her down and give her a call after he got to Washington.

2040 Local—Pirate's Den, Honolulu, Hawaii

Captain Manny DeVera

He met the aging hooker the second night, while nursing a drink in a quiet bar not far from the beach. She was on the sundown side of forty, but she had a pleasant face and a sort of sophisticated air about her, even stuffed into the tight, flashy dress. She'd approached his table with a come-on smile that made her profession obvious, asked if he minded if she sat with him, then gave him a sideward smile as if she wouldn't mind if he bought her a drink.

Manny, being a gregarious type, enjoyed the company, even if he wasn't interested. He hadn't thought about chasing women, because of Penny back at Takhli and the way they felt about each other. But he enjoyed the woman's chatter. She said her name was Ann. To put her off, he stretched the truth some, saying he was convalescing at the base hospital because he'd been shot down in combat. It was the right thing to say, because the aging hooker's fierce patriotism surfaced. She had a son who lived with her ex back on the mainland. He'd just been drafted into the Army, and she was scared he might be sent to Vietnam. Then she'd bought *him* a drink, insisted on it even when he made it clear he wasn't interested in sex, paid or otherwise.

They chatted. Manny treated her like a real person instead of a whore. Ann responded warmly and once said that her son smiled the same rascally way he did. She introduced him to her girlfriend, who came over from another table.

It was a slow night for a Friday, the friend said.

They worked together, Ann told Manny, and when her friend tried to come on to him, she told her to lay off.

Ann looked at him closely. "You sure got some ham-sized bags under your eyes, Sweetie. That from getting shot down, or you got woman problems?"

She was astute. "I'm feeling better," Manny confided, and realized it was the truth. The nights of forced sleep were steadily improving his outlook and health.

They alternated buying drinks, and Manny broke his promise to lay off the alcohol. After an hour passed, they'd gotten down to telling tales, and he remembered and told them about this rich colonel who lived at a big hotel suite there in Honolulu—which he'd learned from a phone call to Tom Lyons's office—and what the guy had done to a nice girl back at his base and how he mistreated his subordinates. Ann listened carefully, her mouth taut.

The girlfriend bristled at what the colonel had done to Penny.

"And he oughta treat his men good," Ann added. "We

don't send our kids to war to be fucked over by their own bosses. Sounds like a real asshole."

"He is," Manny confirmed.

After a few more drinks Ann brought the subject back around to Lyons. She asked which hotel the bastard lived in. She'd like to meet him.

"Naw you wouldn't," Manny told her, shaking his head with his growing intoxication. "He's a real bastard. Ask that girl back at my base."

"Which hotel's he in?" she demanded.

"The Royal Hawaiian."

The girlfriend said the Royal Hawaiian was the grand lady of the beach resorts. It had been the first big hotel to be erected on Waikiki, and in her estimation was still the classiest. She bragged that she'd hustled a number of big-spending tourists there in her younger years.

Ann had him repeat the asshole's name and what he looked like, and she listened hard.

When he finally went out to catch a cab to the base, Manny was feeling little pain.

He didn't get back to the hospital until late, and a morose floor nurse chewed him out before allowing him into the ward. She said he was to be discharged from the hospital in the morning, to full out-patient status, and could check into the BOQ for the remainder of his stay, where he wouldn't disturb the *real* patients. As soon as she left, Manny DeVera pulled off his outer clothes, crawled onto the bed, and immediately fell asleep, as if he had no troubles at all.

CHAPTER FORTY

Saturday, March 2nd, 0930 Local—Royal Hawaiian Hotel, Honolulu, Hawaii

Colonel Tom Lyons

Tom slowly came awake, but he kept his eyes closed, afraid to open them lest the pulsing headache split his head open. He heard a loud rasping sound that reverberated through the room. Remembrance was slow in coming—how it had taken a goodly series of mai tais to get the woman tourist into the sack.

He squinted toward the other side of the bed. She was lying on her back, mouth agape, sheet pulled down to expose large breasts which splayed across her chest. It was hard to imagine, but the terrible racket that filled the room was her snoring.

He vaguely remembered the two women coming out onto the lanai bar and taking a table beside his. More memory cautiously filtered into his tortured, pounding brain. She was the shy, buxom wife of a California state senator, visiting Honolulu with her sister, both of them sporting cameras and chattering about how delightful the beach had been. The breasts had looked full and inviting when she'd been clothed, even if she was little stout about the middle. Tom had worked hard at impressing her, then talking the suspicious sister into returning to their hotel alone.

When she'd finally agreed to come up to his suite for a drink, he'd had to sweet-talk her into bed. Then she'd stepped out of her dress and loosened her girdle and the flab had swelled free, and she'd released the bra and the breasts flopped down to rest on the generous stomach. But he'd been drowsy and inebriated and wanted to curl up with her anyway. He remembered everything being fuzzy and how he had trouble getting it up and . . . had she laughed about it? That was all he could recall. He'd been so damned sleepy! It didn't matter if he'd fucked her. She wasn't worth a notch on the old musket.

His head pounded unmercifully. She shifted, smacking her lips obscenely in her slumber. *Jesus!* he thought, angry at her for last night's false advertising with the girdle and uplift bra. When he got to his feet at the side of the bed, his head felt as if it would explode. He shook her.

"Wha . . . ?"

"Get your clothes on . . ."

She blinked about suspiciously.

". . . and get the fuck out of here," he snarled.

She crawled out, yawning, and gave him a sleepy-eyed inspection. Then she grunted and methodically began to stuff herself into the elastic girdle and cast-iron brassiere.

Tom felt sheer disgust as he padded into the bathroom, took three aspirin, and washed them down with water. He decided it was time to stop with the women, since it would be only another few days until Margaret arrived with her father at their vacation home. He planned to act as contrite and caring as he possibly could. Maybe then she'd agree to see him.

Indiscretion was a mortal sin. He would be *very* discreet from now on.

Tom fumbled with the brush and shaving mug, wondering at his clumsiness as he finally stirred up a good lather and daubed it onto his face. His head pounded mightily as he scraped the beard away, cutting himself in several places.

He prayed for the aspirin to take effect and promised there'd be no more women, except for Margaret if she'd have him back, for a long time.

Tom finished shaving, wet a face towel, and scrubbed his face. Finally he padded back out and peered cautiously into the bedroom. The woman was gone. He heaved a sigh of relief as he returned to the bathroom and showered. While he bathed, something plagued him—there'd been something subtly different about the bedroom. Was something missing?

He rejected the idea. The woman was a well-respected senator's wife, and she'd acted just as gaga as all the other women he'd pursued when he described life with his family's old money. Her sister had eyed him angrily when the woman had whispered tipsily that she would stay at the hotel and dance for just a while longer, and Tom had known she was in the bag.

No way it could have been an act. Yet . . . he hastily shut off the shower and trailed water as he hurried to the bedroom.

There was nothing left on the dresser. She'd taken it all—his wallet, the wafer-thin watch, the gold money clip, the three-carat diamond pinkie ring he wore to impress women at the bar—everything except a single scrap of paper. The thieving bitch!

Tom immediately reached for the house telephone, then just as quickly paused, his hand wavering in midair, remembering. *Indiscretion is a mortal sin!*

He thought of something else and walked into the sitting room to stare with open mouth and dead eyes. The soft leather folder was gone.

Tom Lyons sat heavily on the couch, slumped and groaned, and felt extremely sorry for himself. In the past month his world of honey had turned to vinegar.

After a bit he rose and dressed, fingers shaking violently as he buttoned his shirt, rationalizing that all would be okay. The woman would likely toss the classified papers out . . . probably had no idea what they were. He prayed that was true. The rest of it was replaceable.

Anyway . . . how the hell could he have known she was a thief?

Before leaving the suite, he paused to read the words scribbled on the scrap of paper.

A mutuel frend sayed to look you up cause you are a rich no good shit. I dont wory about you saying any-

thing to the cops cause you are chickenshit. I took a
lot of nice pictures. Look in the drawer. I left you one.

He opened the top middle drawer.

The Polaroid photograph showed him lying on his back
with the woman astride him, hunkered as if he were fully inserted. The woman's face wasn't shown, only her grotesque
body. His face was very identifiable. He was smiling se-
renely, and it wasn't apparent that he was asleep.

"Oh, God," he moaned aloud. It was obviously blackmail.

When she called, he decided that it was worth everything he possessed to make sure the photos—and the classified documents—were returned.

Wednesday, March 6th, 1145 Local—Command Post, Nellis AFB, Nevada

Captain Moods Diller

The connection was made with the scrambler phone in the
basement command post of the Pentagon, and the sergeant
handed the phone to Moods and nodded. Moods remembered that he was also supposed to relay an important message from Julie Stewart.

"*Captain Diller?*" Benny's questioning voice sounded as if
it were coming down a long, hollow tube.

"*I'm reading you three by three, Benny. Go ahead. Over.*"

"*I'm here with a civilian from procurement, Moods. She
needs some information so she can complete a quick reaction
contract. Over.*"

Moods grinned. "*I'll try to provide it. Over.*"

"*Number one. How many bombs per month are we talking
about, if we modify and dedicate an entire squadron of F-4's?
Six illuminators and eighteen shooters. Over.*"

"*What kind of sortie rate are we talking about? Over.*"

"*Let's say sixteen sorties per day, average. Over.*"

Moods's excitement mounted as he did a quick mental
calculation. "*Nine hundred and sixty bombs per month.
Over.*"

"*We get the same here. We're adding four percent for
training and rounding at one thousand bomb kits per month.*"

The big question now is how can we get them? Your Texas company rep said they can only crank out eight a day, if I recall. Over."

Moods didn't understand. *"How many total are you talking about? Over."*

"An initial order of three thousand bomb kits, with a ten-thousand-kit minimum follow-on. Over."

"Jesus!" Moods was staggered by the numbers. His voice became weak. *"When do you need the three thousand? I mean . . . how long do we have, Benny? Over."*

"We want eighteen designator pods and three hundred bombs in place at Ubon one month from start production. Six weeks at the latest. Then one thousand bombs per month thereafter. Over."

"One thousand a month?" Moods's tone was shrill. It was obvious that something very big was about to happen. *"So when's the projected start production date? Over."*

"Two weeks from today. Over."

Moods almost strangled. *"That's impossible! They're going to have to hire and train people, get a facility, and . . . Jesus. Two weeks? Over."*

"If we don't jump at this opportunity, it may not happen for a long time, Moods. Maybe a year or more. This is their big chance. Over."

His big chance. Moods related very personally with his project. He made up his mind. *"I'll fly down there tomorrow. Over."*

"No. I want you there at Nellis. We're sending in a cadre of F-4 instructor pilots who'll specialize in smart bomb tactics, and they'll instruct aircrews on their way to Southeast Asia. By the way, the Pave Dagger code name's being changed. The laser-guided bombs will be called Pave Way, and the illuminator pods will be Pave Knife. Over."

It was all coming very fast for Moods, who three months earlier had been unable to generate official interest outside the world of R and D academia.

"Colonel Mack MacLendon is going to fly a procurement team to the Texas company tonight, to tell them what we need and look things over. If they can't handle the contract, they may lose it, Moods. Over."

"They'll do it," Moods said confidently. *"The Texas team's dedicated. Over."*

When he'd hung up, Moods stood there for a long while, his mind racing with the startling developments.

Whatever was about to happen was damn big.

He'd forgotten about the message he was supposed to pass on to Benny Lewis, and did not remember it until that evening when his fiancée Pam questioned him. And even then it hardly registered. His long effort to give the Air Force a new and more efficient way of conducting conventional warfare was about to bear fruit.

Friday, March 8th, 1845 Local—Command Post, Takhli RTAFB, Thailand

Lieutenant Colonel Lucky Anderson

He made his calls from the command post, where they had the most lines and could get through easiest, but he ran into an old and familiar brick wall. Just as before, even though he used the number Black had given him, he was told by the man who answered the phone that there was no such person as Sergeant Black at the Special Forces field headquarters.

"I know the man," Lucky tried. "I've talked to him on this number."

The man at the other end was increasingly patient and would have become angry if it hadn't been for his rank. "I guarantee it, Colonel. There's no one here by that name."

"Well if there's someone even close, have him give me a call," Lucky finally tried.

"Sorry, sir."

Lucky replaced the receiver, frowning and shaking his head with frustration.

He went out to the status boards and reviewed how the birds in his squadron were faring.

Of twenty-six assigned aircraft, eighteen were operational. Not a good ratio. They'd flown them into the ground the previous month and were feeling the effect.

"Colonel Anderson," a master sergeant called out. "You've got a call on line three."

"Who is it?" he asked. He had a squadron pilots' meeting to conduct in ten minutes.

"A Captain Dillingham, sir."

He didn't know him. "Take his number and tell him I'll call back in . . ." Lucky paused. "Where's the call from?"

The sergeant spoke into the phone. "From NKP, sir."

"I'll take it," Lucky grumbled. He picked up the nearest phone and punched the proper button. "Anderson here."

"Captain Dillingham, sir." But it was Sergeant Black's voice.

Lucky was confused, but then he recovered. Though he still wondered what the hell was happening. "You're a strange bunch there."

Dillingham laughed. "Yes, sir. I would say that's so. Can I help you?"

"Anything new about the lady in question?"

The voice came back slowly, the tone guarded. "Nothing. If there is, I'll make sure someone contacts you, as we agreed."

Lucky sighed. "It's been a long time."

"I don't believe we'll hear anything positive, Colonel."

When Lucky walked out the door of the command post, he was sorry he'd called. Each time he heard that the situation was hopeless, he grew more despondent. He'd done that the last time he'd talked with Richard at the Bangkok embassy. As he hurried toward the 333rd squadron meeting, Lucky decided not to telephone either of the men again. The calls simply hurt too much. Linda was dead and gone, now only a memory to cherish.

2200L—Mountains, Northeastern Laos

GS-15 Linda Lopes

For twelve days they'd traveled very slowly, avoiding the straggling soldiers on their way toward Hanoi, stopping often to allow her to rest. As a result they'd not come far. Just fifty kilometers, the lieutenant estimated, and they still had almost forty to go to reach safety.

Linda gained strength each day, but the broken foot and arm hindered her.

The squat, barrel-chested Ma tribesmen were tireless and treated her with great deference, offering fresh fruits,

and making sure she didn't have to move once she was settled each evening.

When she asked the lieutenant about it, he related in his
pidgin English that he'd told them she was the woman of a
great warrior. He made it plain that he considered Linda to
be that, as well as a very brave individual in her own right.

Linda liked the lieutenant and was humbled to think of
what he'd done for her. He'd walked a hundred kilometers,
searching day and night along the way, to find and retrieve
her. Yet each time she tried to thank him, he apologized for
not rescuing her sooner.

They were now at the foot of a mountain range. Tomorrow they'd go a few kilometers south and intercept a path
used by the Ma tribesmen when they traveled to markets in
North Vietnam. From that point on they'd be safer, the lieutenant said. It was doubtful the Viets knew about the path.

They'd delayed a day at their present bivouac, for a company of enemy soldiers had established a camp directly in
their path and sent out random patrols. Once they'd passed
by them the next morning, they'd move faster, the lieutenant
explained. Linda would be placed in a makeshift litter and
carried along the small, hidden path.

Linda and the lieutenant spoke together often. He'd been
difficult to understand at first, but he tried very hard with
his pidgin, and it was becoming easier each evening. She
supposed they were both adjusting, she to his strange language and he to simple English.

He'd explained the Hotdog team to her. He said there
were others in the People's Army who would fight communism if given the chance. He also told her about an American named Sarge Brack, and what a good man he was. How
he was going to arrange it so they could also become Americans and go to Ha Wa Eee.

"It's beautiful there," she said.

He nodded slowly, his eyes intense, although he'd seen it
only in descriptions from others.

"I went there with my fiancé," she told him. "We loved
it."

The lieutenant told her how, after she'd first been taken,
Kunnel Lokee had come to Nakhon Phanom to ask for their
help in finding her. That was before the lieutenant had
crossed the Mekong into Laos, to the camp at Ban Si

Muang, and found her the first time. She said she remembered the NVA lieutenant who had told her it would not be much longer, and he apologized that he'd taken so long. The lieutenant thought highly of Lokee Anduhson. He told her they were a good team, she and Kunnel Lokee, like Hotdog.

Linda grew pensive. It hadn't occurred to her that she'd get out of the terrible situation. Now that there was a ray of hope that it might happen, she wondered about her relationship with Paul. A quiver of fear embraced her. *Whore,* they'd called her after so many men had—

"Kunnel Lokee need you," said the lieutenant, interrupting her thoughts.

She remained silent.

"You need Kunnel Lokee, sistah. Mebbe bo'f need same-same."

"I miss him so much," she whispered wistfully.

"Kunnel Lokee same-same."

A serenity settled over her as she thought of it. The lieutenant was a sage man, and she decided he was likely a very good leader of his people. When she prepared to sleep, the lieutenant carefully checked her mosquito netting, as he'd done every night of the trek, and reminded her again that she was safe.

Saturday, March 9th, 0915 Local

They had to cross the roadway to get to the Ma tribe's hidden market path, but the lieutenant said that for the past two hours it had been periodically traveled by enemy soldiers from the camp, as well as by a train of horses and men who'd brought them supplies.

The tribesmen wanted to go back eastward for a couple of klicks to try it there, but he doubted it would be better. They'd post a lookout and wait for a lull in the foot traffic.

"Perhaps we should wait for darkness," she suggested.

"Mebbe," he replied. He was anxious to get her to safety. He'd told her that the previous evening during their conversation.

She waited as the lieutenant left to observe the road again. Twenty minutes later he returned. No one had passed during that time.

"Led's ged gone, sistah," said the lieutenant.

She pushed to her feet and was immediately assisted by two tribesmen.

There was only fifty yards of open area, but she moved so slowly that it took far too long. Their luck ran out when they were smack in the middle of the clearing. A group of soldiers came trotting down the roadway, a dozen or more of them, all in clean field uniforms and looking very military, quite unlike the stragglers they'd seen.

The Ma panicked at the sight and set up a chatter, but the lieutenant spoke sharply and they quieted and continued helping her along.

When the soldiers were twenty paces away, one of them called to the lieutenant.

He answered in an authoritative voice.

The leader of the group called out something. He looked at them suspiciously and was not at all subservient. As the lieutenant spoke with them, the Ma tribesmen and Linda continued to make their way across the clearing. They were almost to the trees when the lieutenant called out and trotted up behind them.

The militia soldiers demanded that they wait until they'd conferred with their officers, the lieutenant told first her, then the Ma leader in his tongue. They'd sent a runner to their camp, he said.

The tribesmen stared at the soldiers anxiously and again babbled among themselves, for the militiamen held their weapons in a ready position, and seemed suspicious.

As the lieutenant looked at the soldiers, he quietly told Linda she must go ahead with the tribesmen. He didn't wait for a response, but immediately spoke with the Ma leader.

The headman glanced at the soldiers, weighed the words in his mind, then nodded.

"See ya ladah, sistah," the lieutenant said crisply. His eyes were narrowed, his face hard.

As Linda started to respond, two tribesmen swept her off her feet, as if suddenly uncaring about her injuries, and began running with her. She tried to twist about and see what was happening with the lieutenant, but it proved impossible.

She heard the loud sounds of automatic weapons fire as she was borne into the dense forest.

From their first step Linda felt sharp pains shooting

through her injured limbs, but she gritted her teeth and endured. Another Ma tribesmen joined the first two, and three were now carrying her. Two others dropped behind, and she heard their weapons fire joining the first group's. Bullets whispered through the trees. One of her bearers staggered and went to his knees and she was almost dropped, but another tribesman took his place and they continued at a trot, one man at her shoulders, another at her midriff, the third at her legs, all grasping her tightly. On and on they went, their route through the dense jungle sure and swift. They continued like that as the weapons fire at the clearing grew faint and distant—then stopped.

They emerged finally, almost magically, onto a narrow but traffic-smoothed path, turned onto it, and ran faster yet.

They'd borne her for half an hour when, as abruptly as they'd begun, the small men stopped, edged off the path and into the trees, and carefully deposited her. Then they collapsed about the periphery of a tiny clearing, panting and catching their breath as they waited for the others.

CHAPTER FORTY-ONE

Monday, March 11th, 1200 Local—VPA Headquarters, Hanoi, North Vietnam

General Xuan Nha

Captain Quang Hanh had summoned him from his office, down the hall to a small room where he'd set up the long-range radio. Brave Hero was calling from Yen Chau.

"*Go ahead,*" Xuan rasped into the microphone.

"*It has been twelve days,*" Nguyen Wu lamented. "*Surely it is safe to send a helicopter now.*" His voice was plaintive and anxious.

"*We must wait longer, Brave Hero. The Mee aircraft are still attacking.*"

There'd been no bombardments in the area for the past several days.

"*How long?*" Wu tried.

"*Until it is safe, Brave Hero. You are too important for us to take chances. Everyone agrees. Even your aunt and the Lao Dong party officials. They are planning a fine reception.*"

Even that did not seem to impress Wu. He ended the radio call with yet another plea.

Xuan immediately radioed Quon on the other compromised frequency.

"*Brave Hero has called again,*" he told him. "*Why has nothing been done about him?*"

They'd both believed the Americans would attack the village after intercepting their daily conversations, but they'd waited in vain. The matter was increasingly worrisome to Xuan Nha.

"*Perhaps he is safe there because the Americans do not attack civilians,*" Quon tried.

"*Don't they know that it is not a village, but a hidden military base?*" Xuan spoke the lie easily, hoping to encourage the Americans. It didn't bother him that a few hundred civilians might be killed if the Mee believed him. Not only did he despise his wife's nephew for what he had done, but if Nguyen Wu returned and Li Binh learned that Xuan Nha had placed him in jeopardy and delayed the revelations of his secrets, she would destroy him.

Tuesday, March 12th, 1600 Local—Waikiki Beach, Honolulu, Hawaii

Captain Manny DeVera

The sun had been just right, casting just the appropriate amount of light and heat to make him feel lethargic, as if he had not a care in the world. It had been another great day in paradise, the way to cap off a grand stay. Tomorrow morning he'd climb into a contract airliner bound for Toyko, then on to Don Muang airport in Thailand. He had mixed emotions about returning. He'd like to stay another week, but there was unfinished business back at Takhli. Not that he'd spent much time thinking about the place—he hadn't—but there were things he had to do.

He rose from the sand and brushed himself off, staring at a pretty blonde a few feet away. She gave him a pleasant smile before demurely looking away. Life was good.

"Hi, there. You're a hard guy to find."

Manny swiveled his head, still wiping sand from his feet. It was the aging hooker he'd had the drinks with the previ-

ous week. What was her name? Oh, yeah. He smiled. "How
are you, Ann?"

"Not bad for an old broad." She nodded at a cabana bar
nearby. "Buy you a drink?"

"Best offer I've had all day."

He slipped on thongs and joined her.

"I saw your friend Lyons."

Manny remembered they'd talked about him.

She told him the way the night had begun.

"You give him a mickey?" He was horrified at the
thought before he remembered who they were talking
about, then he changed his mind. Lyons had deserved it.

She told him about the photos she'd taken.

"Jesus, you're not going to blackmail him, are you?"

"Not my style, but I hope the asshole's sweating bullets.
I thought of making about a thousand copies and spreading
them around town, but I . . . ah . . . wasn't looking my best,
and my vanity couldn't take it. I was pretty foxy when I was
younger, Manny."

"I wish I could have met you."

"Me too, you handsome devil. You look a lot better, by
the way."

"I feel better. They couldn't find anything wrong at the
hospital. Maybe I was just tired."

She lowered her voice. "I robbed the asshole."

Manny held up his hands. "Hey. I don't wanna know
about that."

"Couldn't resist it." She waved him toward an umbrella-
shaded table. "I'll bring us something to drink. What would
you like?"

"How about a Bud?" He waited, thinking about Lyons
being robbed, and almost felt sorry for his part in it.

Ann brought two opened bottles of beer, then sat and
groaned. "I've walked all over hell looking for you. Been
looking for a whole week."

"Good thing you caught me today. I'm leaving first thing
in the morning." He thought about Lyons again. "I hope to
hell you didn't catch anything from him."

"He never got that far." She smiled. "Nice of you to
worry, though."

"You're okay, Ann."

Ann lifted a painted eyebrow. "You sure remind me of my

kid—the way you grin. I'll bet you're a real ladies' man, like he is."

Manny laughed.

"There's something I think you oughta see."

"What's that?" He sipped the beer, going slow with the booze. Everywhere he'd been, they'd served mai tais, zombies, and other tasty rum drinks, and he'd drunk entirely too many of them.

She reached into her purse. "Something I took from the asshole's room."

He held up his hands again. "I told you, Ann, I don't want to know anything about it."

Ann pulled a sheaf of papers from her purse and handed it over. "Take a look."

"Dammit." Manny started to push her hand away, then paused and took them. On top was an onionskin stamped SECRET. He went to the next page, which was filled with notes. He looked closer . . . and found the word JACKPOT.

"Whattaya think?" Ann asked.

"Yeah," Manny breathed. "I'll take 'em."

"I didn't read 'em or let anyone else see 'em. I wouldn't do that."

He nodded absently as he looked through the papers.

"Maybe you oughta burn 'em," Ann said.

"Just forget you ever saw them."

Manny didn't stay downtown. Instead he returned to his BOQ room, found a large envelope, and with his left hand scribbled on the outside FOUND IN THE BAR OF THE ROYAL HAWAIIAN HOTEL. He inserted the classified messages along with some of the notes with Lyons's name on them, and carefully burned the remainder in the ash tray. When it was quite dark, Manny walked to the headquarters building, which was not far, made sure no one was looking, and dropped the envelope at the entrance where the security-police guards would find it.

On the way back to his BOQ room, Manny DeVera whistled a lively tune and thought about how much better he was feeling. Damned good, in fact. There was no more blotchy skin, and no more bags under bloodshot eyes. His hands were steady, and he felt as if he could take on a grizzly.

And . . . the retribution against Lyons felt sweet. The least he'd get would be an official reprimand.

Yeah, he felt a lot better.

After the first couple of nights, which he'd spent sleeping soundly in a hospital bed, the docs at the Hickam Hospital had placed him on outpatient status. Then they'd given him the longest, most drawn-out physical examination he'd ever experienced.

Manny wondered what they'd been looking for that had taken so long.

1855L—Trailer 12, Takhli

Lieutenant Colonel Lucky Anderson

He answered the rapping on the door.

"Hi, Yank." Lucky held it wide so Donovan could come inside.

Recently Yank had become a regular at the Officers' Club, hanging out there almost every night and drinking with the men from his squadron. It was certainly not a bad thing to do, but seemed out of character for the surly instructor pilot he'd known back in the States.

Tonight Donovan was brooding about something, his face still marked from the oxygen mask he'd worn on the afternoon combat mission.

"Whiskey?" asked Lucky on his way to the kitchen.

"Vodka on the rocks, if you've got it."

"How was the mission?"

"Okay. No losses." He'd led the Takhli strike force to pack four, where they'd bombed a petroleum-storage area.

"Defenses?" Lucky was leading the morning go, back into the same area.

"Three SAM sites and a lot of guns. We were fortunate."

Lucky handed him his drink, then went back to pour a Scotch for himself. He seldom drank alone, so visitors gave him the excuse he needed. He poured three fingers of Chivas over a single ice cube and returned to the sitting area, swishing the liquid about in the glass to cool it.

"I've been thinking a lot recently about the way we're flying here."

Lucky smiled. "That's about all any of us think about."

The old Yank would have snapped back. The new one just brooded. Finally . . . "We're losing too many young guys. Kids who don't know what it's about."

"Maybe, but they learn."

"They shouldn't let the kids go up to pack six at all."

Lucky narrowed his eyes, started to respond, but held his tongue.

"I mean, guys like you and me, we've been there. We know how to fight and survive, Lucky. These kids—"

"Not kids, Yank. They're men, and they sure as hell prove it."

Donovan wouldn't be baited. "Okay, young men. Guys who don't know where it's at yet."

"Being young means their reflexes are better. You heard the old man. Leska won't even lead missions anymore, because he knows his eyes and reflexes aren't what they used to be."

Yank snorted. "I disagree a hundred percent. Young eyes and reflexes are fine and dandy for a basketball game. In combat it's experience that counts. Knowing what to do when the chips are down. Which way to attack from and which way to recover, and how to do them both and survive. I think it ought to be only the guys with experience who go to packs four and six. Let the kids . . . the young men . . . fly where it's safer."

Lucky shook his head. "It's a young man's war, just like all other wars have been. If we did what you're saying, we'd just lose all the old heads. Buster's right."

"I disagree."

"Then let me put it this way. Buster Leska's our wing commander. He plays something, the rest of us march to the tune."

They spoke of other things, and Lucky poured them both another drink. But he knew that Donovan hadn't been convinced about keeping the younger pilots from harm's way. When Yank left an hour later, Lucky quickly forgot about the conversation. He would remember it a few days later.

Wednesday, March 13th, 2100 Local—McCarren International Airport, Las Vegas, Nevada

Major Benny Lewis

The Boeing 727 flew west of the city, parallel to the strip, and the passengers talked about the gaudy lights and how anxious they were to get to the action and try their luck. Benny stared with them, but his mind was on something more poignant.

The captain moved the flaps from half to full down position, and they flew slower yet.

He'd gotten everything done at the Pentagon he'd gone to do. Not only with Moods's smart bomb project, but also with coordinations between the various forces which would be required to ensure LINE BACKER JACKPOT went off smoothly.

At the Pentagon, Colonel Mack MacLendon was General McManus's front man for the OPlan, and the project could not have been placed in more capable hands. He was working relentlessly to make sure everything went off without a hitch. By the time Benny had left, Mack had briefed in more than a hundred officers and NCOs, and they were giving their all, just as others had in his squadron at Takhli. Mack was a leader.

Benny had continued at the Pentagon until there were no more excuses to stay away. He'd not tried to called Julie Stewart.

The desert city of lights would be a dismal place without Julie. He'd gladly put up with her mother's interference if he had the chance to do it again. At least he'd known she was there—and he believed she'd sincerely cared for him. His heart ached dully, as if it were weighted with lead, as it did each time he thought of her and what he'd missed.

The airliner made a wide, looping 180-degree turn and descended on final approach. The landing gear squealed as they lowered.

In his latest message to Nellis, he'd given his flight number and requested that someone from the office meet him. It would likely be Moods, for he'd want to know details of how things were going with the smart bomb procurement.

Good man, Moods. The Air Force needed his intellect and spirited dedication.

The 727 flared slightly, then the tires squeaked at touchdown. A little long, Benny thought, but not really bad. He rated the landing a seven out of a possible ten.

He waited until most of the other passengers had deplaned before joining the line and trudging along with the flow. Out the raised hatch and down the boarding ramp, helping an elderly gentleman who had trouble with the steps. Into the terminal, and looking around for Moods.

He paused and stared at the face that had become etched in his mind. Julie Stewart hurried forward—stopped just out of arm's length. Her eyes were wide, her expression shy.

"I thought you'd moved," Benny said awkwardly.

"That's what Moods told me. Are you disappointed?"

He shook his head, struck wordless.

"Mom went back to New Jersey. She was the one I told Pam was leaving. She misunderstood."

"Oh?" He wanted to hold her.

Julie pulled in a breath, turning her eyes toward the crowd. "Been here an hour so I wouldn't miss you if your plane was somehow early. Hell, I work here. You'd think I'd be smarter than that."

As they started down the corridor toward the baggage-claim area, Benny realized she was alone. "Where's the baby?"

"She's with Pam and Moods for the night. I told them we'd want to talk."

"Your mother's gone?" he asked.

"We had a long discussion. I told her I didn't have a chance with you unless we had more time to ourselves. She argued, but that's Mom."

A chance with him?

"God, I missed you, Benny Lewis," she whispered as they walked.

He put a hand on her shoulder and stopped her. The crowd milled past, but he didn't care.

She looked up at him, tears welling. "I realize you were too busy to write or call—at least I hope it was because you were busy. It was awful not hearing from you all that time."

"I thought—"

"After that dumb night when I acted so silly, I felt you might want out. Tell me if you do. I'll learn to live with it."

He shook his head wordlessly.

"I'm sorry I was such a klutz. Give me another chance, okay?" Tears were flowing freely.

He gently pulled her to him and held her. He wanted to protect and shield her from harm as he'd wanted to do since he'd first seen her more than a year earlier and every time since when he'd thought of her and felt the warm and comfortable sensation. She made a small sound, grasping on to him as if he were a life preserver.

"I thought I'd lost you," she whispered.

He found his voice, and it was determined and sure. "You'll never lose me, lady."

They stood, hugging fiercely as the tourists continued past.

An impatient couple jostled them and Benny glared, then regarded Julie. His voice was gravel rough. "After we get my bags, let's go somewhere."

"I've cleaned the apartment constantly for the past month, waiting for you to get home."

Home. "Yes," Benny said, "let's go home."

CHAPTER FORTY-TWO

Thursday, March 14th, 0730 Local—HQ Seventh Air Force, Tan Son Nhut Air Base, Saigon, South Vietnam

Lieutenant Colonel Pearly Gates

As soon as he took his seat in the general's office, Moss handed Pearly the JACKPOT message. The general's look was studiously neutral, yet the back-channel message was the most encouraging of all those sent to date.

```
SECRET—IMMEDIATE—JACKPOT
CC EYES ONLY—NO FURTHER DISSEM
DTG: 13/1840ZMAR68
FM: CSAF/CC, HQ USAF, PENTAGON
TO: CINCPACAF/CC, HICKAM AB, HI
CINCSAC/CC, OFFUTT AFB, NEB
CINCTAC/CC, LANGLEY AFB, VA
HQ MAC/CC, SCOTT AFB, ILL
HQ 7 AF/CC, TAN SON NHUT AB, SVN
HQ 13 AF/CC, CLARK AB, PI
USAFTFWC/CC, NELLIS AFB, NEV
USAFTAWC/CC, EGLIN AFB, FLA
SUBJECT: STATUS REPORT
```

1. (S) MET WITH J THIS A.M. HE IS OUTRAGED
OVER LEAK TO N.Y. TIMES ABOUT
WESTMORELAND'S REQUEST FOR
200,000 MORE TROOPS & BLAMES THAT
FOR THE 40 PERCENT VOTE GAINED BY E
MCCARTHY IN NH PRIMARY. HE BELIEVES
RFK W/BE ENCOURAGED TO ENTER
RACE. THAT WAS TONE WHEN HE CALLED
ME IN.
A. J'S 1ST QUESTION WAS "WILL LINE
BACKER JACKPOT END THE WAR?" MY
ANSWER WAS "IT WILL FORCE NVN TO
RECALL THEIR FORCES, & THAT WILL
QUICKEN END TO THE WAR."
B. J GAVE TENTATIVE APPROVAL FOR
IMPLEMENTATION, PENDING HIS FINAL
GO-AHEAD WHICH COULD COME ANY DAY
NOW.
2. (C) CONTACT ON PRES STAFF SAID
NEXT WK J WILL NAME W.
WESTMORELAND AS NEW CHAIRMAN OF JCS
(NO SURPRISE). HAS NOT YET DECIDED UPON
OTHER REPLACEMENTS (SUCH AS MINE).
J WILL AUTH 7 AF CC AS 4-STAR
POSITION.
3. (C) MY FEELING IS THIS TIME THE
APPROVAL IS REAL. J CANNOT SEND
200,000 TROOPS TO COMBAT ZONE
WHILE CRITICISMS ARE MOUNTING. LINE
BACKER JACKPOT IS ONLY HONORABLE WAY
OUT.
4. (S) FOR ALL: REVIEW & ENSURE THAT
THE I'S HAVE BEEN DOTTED ON THE OPLAN,
NOW GIVEN OFFICIAL STATUS AS AF OPLAN
68-1011, SHORT TITLE: LINE BACKER
JACKPOT.
SECRET—IMMEDIATE—JACKPOT

When Pearly had finished reading, General Moss pointed at
the address block. "Notice all the big boys are included
now?"

"Yes, sir. And he wants you promoted to four stars."

"It says this *position* will be elevated to a four-star billet. There's no mention of my name. They may bring in someone from the outside."

"But the President said he wanted you running the effort."

"I suppose he did." The general played it with the neutral expression, but Pearly noted he was in a jovial mood. "By the way," Moss added, "I finally received a phone call from General Roman yesterday regarding the briefing you gave him."

Pearly leaned forward, listening hard.

"He said, 'Tell Lieutenant Colonel Gates that I concur with his plan.' That's all. He just spat out those words like they were bad-tasting medicine, then hung up."

Pearly heaved a sigh of relief. "Then he's aboard."

"It would seem so." Moss stared moodily at the shuttered window, and Pearly knew what he was thinking. He still did not trust Roman. Not a bit. And Roman, Pearly knew, did not trust Moss. It was an odd world, his Air Force.

Half an hour later Pearly was going over the LINE BACKER JACKPOT inputs from the various bases. All units would be ready to fly the sustained sortie rate, given the four weeks of preparation time noted in the plan for the buildup. Everything, from top to bottom, was ready to go. All they needed was the nod from the President of the United States to begin deploying stateside units to beef up their numbers.

He was placing the messages in his safe when Major Friday Wells came into the office and asked to speak with him. Pearly spun the knob on the safe to secure it, then went back to his desk and faced the Special Operations rep.

"Whatcha got?" he asked, feeling upbeat.

"I just came from MAC-V intell. What does it take to get an air strike authorized in North Vietnam, Pearly?"

"If its around Hanoi or Haiphong, it takes an executive order."

"Nope." The C-130 pilot went to the large-scale wall map of North Vietnam, searched, and placed his finger on a spot in the mountainous region of pack five. "How about here?"

Pearly pushed his glasses into position and peered. "I don't see anything but a village."

"It's called Yen Chau."

"We don't bomb villages, Friday."

"What if it's a military camp?"

"General Moss can authorize a strike in route pack five."

"Good." Friday tapped the tiny black dot. "We want an air strike."

"Come on, Friday. I can't go to the general and say we've got this place that's shown as a village, but it's really not and the good guys at MAC-SOG want to bomb it. First place, General Moss doesn't think the people at MAC-SOG are much good at all. He keeps saying they stole his airplanes. Second place, you haven't proved it's anything except what it looks like, which is a medium-sized village."

Friday looked troubled.

"What's there?"

"I'm not supposed to say."

"Then the answer's no. You can't get an air strike. I won't even take it to the general."

"Nice guy."

"I want to keep my job."

"What if I tell you what it's about? Will you help getting it authorized?"

"Try convincing me. If you do, I'll call for a recce mission and we'll send an RF-4 up there. If the photos come back showing it's a military base, I'll go to the general and try to convince him. If he says yes, I go to the TACC and they write up an air tasking order and send it out to the units."

"Jesus, and I thought we had a bunch of bullshit red ink in Special Ops. How long does all that take, from convincing you until the fighters drop their bombs?"

Pearly pondered. "A week. Longer sometimes."

"You've gotta be shitting me!"

"But if you're really nice, and everything goes smooth . . . we can do everything on an immediate basis."

"How long for that?"

"Twenty-four hours or less."

Friday looked happier.

"So convince me. I'm a busy man."

"First of all, everything I'm going to tell you is sensitive, okay? Like Top Secret plus."

"I'm cleared for anything you've got."

"Yeah, I know. Anyway, there's this North Viet bastard who specializes in getting information out of people, and he's cooling his heels in this place." He tapped Yen Chau. "He's carrying all the secrets he beat out of one of our people. An American."

"What's your source of information?"

"I can't say."

Pearly pondered. The case was weak and recce flights were expensive.

"Send up your RF-4, Pearly. Check out the village."

"And you think this North Viet's there with information he beat out of one of our men."

"Not one of our men. It was a woman."

Pearly stared.

"He got the information from Clipper. He doesn't have her with him, so we think he killed her."

Pearly's jaw clenched. He searched around in a drawer for a RECONNAISSANCE PHOTO SORTIE REQUEST form.

He filled it out, making a check mark in the IMMEDIATE block. The sortie would be flown that afternoon.

1730L

Pearly led the way into the photo lab—one of a dozen such rooms along a long corridor.

"That was quick," Friday said. "I take back some of what I said about you headquarters pukes taking a week to pick your nose."

A staff sergeant in a white smock looked up. "The film came out okay, Colonel Gates."

The two officers leaned over the table at eight-by-ten blown-up prints.

"Be careful," said the photo interpreter. "They're still drying."

"Looks like a village," Pearly said.

"It is a village," said the PI. "I'd say a thousand people there. Maybe a few more or less."

"Dammit," Friday muttered. His face was drawn into a hostile grimace. "You're *sure* it's not a military camp?"

"It's just a village, sir."

Friday glowered at the photo, as if trying to change what he saw.

The PI used a small pointer. "There's this. Looks like an observation tower of some sort. Probably part of their manual air-defense system where they call in aircraft that fly overhead. And I'd say the adjacent huts there are where the militia guys live."

"How about the rest of it?" Friday said, pointing to the remainder of the buildings. He wouldn't give up.

"Just your run-of-the-mill, everyday village, Major. Those are no-shit women, children and puppy dogs running around. There's a Chinese-built weapons carrier parked next to this large house, but that's the only military vehicle in town, and I couldn't even find any antiaircraft guns."

"After they've all dried, mark the photos and send 'em to my office," Pearly told the PI.

"Anything else, Colonel?"

"Not right now. Thanks, Sarge."

"Anytime. We aim to please."

As they walked back toward the headquarters building, Friday remained in a dark mood.

"We win some, we lose some," Pearly said.

"I'd still like you guys to take the fucking place out," Friday muttered. "There's a no-good bastard in there, Pearly. He specializes in torture."

"It's a village with noncombatants. We couldn't hit it if Jack the Ripper was in there giving us the finger."

"How about the observation tower? How about bombing that fucker? Maybe he'll be in it."

"Too close to the town. Look, Friday, if we bombed or strafed the place, even if it isn't a village and it's the best case of camouflage in the world, the gomers would say we'd bombed innocents, and someone would sure as hell be all over our asses."

"Not this one. No one gets in trouble no matter what we do there."

There was no one around them. "What makes you think that?"

"Remember when I told you about the sensitive sources?"

"Yes."

"Dammit, I can't tell you more, Pearly. Just believe me, okay? It involves MAC-V intell and the Army Security Agency, and it's real."

Pearly chewed on his lip as they walked.

"No one gets in trouble if we bomb the village, Pearly."

Pearly shook his head, remembering the noncombatants in the photos. "We can't do it."

After a few more steps Friday said, "What if my general took it straight to General Moss?"

"Tell him to go ahead." They both knew that Moss was distrustful of both MAC-SOG and Special Operations.

Friday sighed. "Yeah, I suppose I agree we can't go around bombing villages. It's a crying shame, though, that we're just going to let this character get away."

As they approached the headquarters building, Pearly slowed, then stopped. "The guy's gotta get out of there some way, if he's going to get to Hanoi. If your sources can tell us when and how, we can try to take him out while he's traveling."

"That's a hell of a long shot."

"It's all I can come up with."

Friday remained discouraged. "I'll see if they can get the information. I don't see how they can, but I'll try."

"If he's going out by chopper, we'll need the takeoff time and route."

"That's probably too much to hope for. I think we've lost our chance, Pearly."

"Wish I could have helped more, Friday. I'll send a recce bird over the place every couple of days and see if anything changes."

Wells gave him a highball salute and trudged off toward the BOQ. Pearly returned to his office, certain there'd be another hour's work stacked in his in-basket.

CHAPTER
FORTY-THREE

Saturday, March 16th, 0830 Local—Nakhon Phanom RTAB, Thailand

Major John Dillingham

It hadn't been a bad morning so far for the man who'd once called himself Sergeant Black. The first thing he'd done when he'd risen at 0500 was remove the captain's railroad tracks and pin new gold oak leaves onto the collar of his jungle fatigue shirt and admire them. After a leisurely breakfast he'd reported to the outgoing XO and told him he was ready to start his two-week understudy of the position. When he assumed the job on the first of April, he wanted to be ready.

For the next two hours he'd followed the guy around, listening hard and thinking life was pretty damned good.

He was sitting outside the XO's office at half past eight, sipping java and waiting for the major to get through with a private chewing on an A-Detachment commander's ass over a difference of opinion when the admin sergeant asked if he'd take a phone call from the comm center.

Larry, who was manning the Buffalo Soldier HF radio, requested that he come over.

Dillingham took his coffee along. The guard at the entrance to the comm center was attentive and passed him quickly through to the inner room where Larry manned his HF radios.

"Sorry to bother you, Captain . . . whoops, make that Major. Sorry all to hell, sir."

"Don't sweat the small stuff." Dillingham grinned.

"Razorback's on the line. Says he has a situation. Since the XO and the old man were both busy, I thought you'd wanna take it." Razorback was the code name for the A-Detachment at the Channel 97 mesa, so Dillingham took the mike quickly, hoping to get word about the Hotdog lieutenant.

He had to think for a second to remember his new radio call sign. *"Razorback, this is Lobo. Go ahead with your transmission."*

The guy on the other end also hesitated because of the unfamiliar call sign. *"Ah, Lobo, this is Razorback leader. Some Ma tribesmen just brought in a . . . ah . . . female."*

"Go ahead."

"She claims she's an American national."

Dillingham sat bolt straight in the chair. *"Her name?"*

"Says she's a Miss . . . ah . . . Linda Lopes."

Clipper! It took a moment to respond. *"What's her condition, Razorback?"*

"Not good. She's emaciated. Teeth missing, can hardly walk, like that. My corpsman's looking after her now. He'll give me a better rundown when he's through."

He didn't hesitate. *"Do what you can for her, Razorback. We'll get a bird up there ASAP."*

"You know anything about her, Lobo?"

"Yes." He remembered the classification. *"Let's not talk anymore about it over open radio, except give me an update on the package's physical condition."*

"Ah, roger."

Then Dillingham drew a breath and asked the other question. *"Was she accompanied by my team member, Razorback?"*

There was an audible sigh as the A-Detachment commander realized who he was talking to, and the conversation they'd had at the mesa. *"Negative, Lobo. Just the one package and the Ma's."*

"Roger, Razorback. Before they get away on you, question

*the tribesmen who brought the package in and try to find out
anything you can, okay? Send the report back with the package.
And remember to tell the Ma they've got a reward coming.
I promised them."*

"*Will do, Lobo.*"

"*Buffalo Soldier out,*" said Dillingham, tingling with the
good news.

"You think it's really Clipper?" Larry asked excitedly.

"Yeah." He stood. "Phone over to the Air Force command
post and see if they've got a chopper flying up there, Larry.
If they don't, tell 'em we're requesting a flight, pronto."

"We're supposed to clear it with Vientiane Control."

"Just do what I ask, okay? I don't want the contractors
getting anywhere *near* her."

"Yes, sir."

"I'll pass it along to the old man. Give me a call at his office when Razorback gives a new reading on her condition."

"Gotcha. One more thing. The directive on Clipper said
we're supposed to contact a guy at the embassy in Bangkok
the second we get word on her. You want me to do that?"

"Yeah, go ahead," Dillingham called over his shoulder
from the door.

1125L

The State Department had a man on the ground at NKP two
and a half hours after Larry's call. As the old man had
directed, John Dillingham met him at base operations when
he crawled out of the embassy jet. He was tall, with closely
shorn gray hair, and wore a seersucker suit complete with
tie, which looked out of place at the forward base. He introduced himself as Richard and smiled, but you could tell he
was constantly evaluating what he saw. Somehow
Dillingham knew the guy had his crap together in a single
bag.

They went to the base-operations snack bar and waited,
drinking coffee and chatting about things like the weather
that was getting warmer and the fact that the summer monsoon was just around the corner. After ten minutes of it
Black knew he was some kind of high-ranking spook with
the State Department. He very studiously avoided talk

about Clipper, except to ask for the estimated time en route for the Jolly Green chopper that the Air Force had diverted to pick her up, and to briefly discuss her physical condition.

Dillingham checked with the base-ops sergeant and found that the Jolly Green was only fifteen minutes out. He told Richard, and they walked out to observe the sky to the north.

He stood beside the man in the seersucker suit and waited, wondering about the woman. "Her fiancé's stationed at Takhli," he told the official.

"I know," Richard said. "He used to call the embassy quite often."

"You want me to phone him?"

"Others will take care of notifications. Once she's safely on the med-evac aircraft, I'd appreciate it if you and everyone here forgot all about the Clipper operation."

Dillingham decided he was with State Department Intelligence, which made the CIA look like pikers when it came to secrecy. They had access to resources and information no one else had, and exercised clout that could water eyes and destroy military careers. Regardless of her title, Clipper was one of them. All of that combined to make Dillingham listen attentively.

1245L

The big HH-3 Jolly Green clopped in from the north, entered the helo-approach pattern, and swung around to land thirty yards in front of them.

Dillingham walked out toward the chopper, Richard close behind.

A sergeant in jungle fatigues emerged from the door and placed chocks fore and aft of the wheels while the rotors idled. Finally the engines wound down and the blades clattered to a halt.

A captain jumped out of the thing and came over to Dillingham. "You Lobo?"

"Yeah."

He handed him a sealed envelope. "We got your package in the chopper." He looked around the parking ramp. "Where's the med-evac bird?"

"Be here in a few minutes. They'll park right next to you." Dillingham said. "How is she?"

"Medic pumped her full of antibiotics, and he's got an IV running. Needs a general overhaul, he says. Med-evac people have their work cut out."

"Is she lucid?" asked Richard.

"Sure is. Keeps saying she wants to talk to someone named Sergeant Brack. Know anything about him?"

"I do," said Dillingham, feeling a jolt of adrenaline. She'd had contact with the lieutenant.

"Maybe you ought to get him. She's pretty definite about wanting to see the guy."

"That must be the med-evac aircraft," said Richard, eye-balling a bird on final.

"I'll talk with her," said Dillingham, and the civilian followed him as he crawled into the chopper. A paramedic was sitting beside a litter, talking to the patient.

She didn't look at all like the pictures he'd studied of a pretty woman in her early thirties with a clean-cut, almost regal look. This one looked old and unkempt, even though they'd cleaned her up. She was very dark, likely burned that way by the sun, and her skin was cracked like old leather. Her hair was stringy and sparse. Her face was battered, the nose mashed and lopsided, knotted with gristle. Dillingham approached cautiously. Her eyes stared. Deep, sunken eyes that held no trace of happiness.

"I'm Sergeant Black," he said in a quiet voice.

"Sarge Brack?"

"Yes, ma'am."

She regarded him somberly, then glanced at the civilian, and after a moment recognition flickered. "Richard?"

"Leave me alone with her," said the civilian.

"No," she croaked in a sandpaper voice. "I must speak with Sarge Brack."

"Just a quick status report, Linda," the embassy spook said. "We'll get a debriefing when you get to the hospital, but I need a synopsis so we can relay it to the field people."

"They broke me," she said. "I told them ... everything, I think. I can't remember all of it, but I told them a lot. I held out as long as I could so you could protect the networks, but I finally gave them names, procedures ... everything."

Richard nodded. "That's the way we played it, like all your nets were compromised."

She moved her eyes to stare at Dillingham. "You're Hawaiian, aren't you?"

"Yes, ma'am."

"Lieutenant Phrang said you were going to take the Hotdog team to Hawaii."

Dillingham's adrenaline surged again. "You saw the lieutenant?"

"The North Vietnamese were going to kill me, and he took me away from them. He found me, fed me, and saved my life."

"Where is he now?" Dillingham blurted.

Even in her condition she managed to look sadder. "Dead. He stayed behind to hold off the soldiers so the Ma people could get me away. He was very determined."

John Dillingham heaved a long, tortured sigh.

The roaring of jet engines grew louder as the med-evac bird taxied up outside. Both he and Richard moved close to hear her whispers over the noise.

"The lieutenant said you are a brave and good soldier, and he was proud you were his friend."

Dillingham opened his mouth to speak, but words wouldn't emerge. He ignored the moisture gathering in his eyes.

"He said when you took him and his men to Hawaii, they were going to work in a big hotel in Honolulu until they bought a boat. Then he said they'd take haoles fishing and make lots of money. He said they were very tired of war."

John's request for asylum for Hotdog had been denied. In two weeks the remainder of the team were to be turned over to the South Vietnamese ARVN Rangers. Only his persistant delaying tactics had put them off this long.

"Tell his men about him, please. He was very proud of them."

Dillingham forced out words. "Yes, ma'am. I will."

"He also said you were a friend of Colonel Lucky. He was talking about Paul Anderson."

"Yes."

She nodded weakly. "Tell him about me. I don't want him to worry."

The PJ corpsman interrupted. "The med-evac bird's

ready. Gotta get the lady over there. You gentlemen are going to have to wait for another day to talk." Two medical technicians and a flight nurse, all wearing sage-gray flying suits, boarded through the opened door of the helicopter.

Then, for no reason he could think of later, John Dillingham reached out and touched the woman's cheek.

Her tense expression softened.

The nurse edged him out of the way and motioned to the techs. "Get her over there and into the emergency cab." She glared once at the two men, and both Dillingham and Richard scrambled to get out of the chopper.

They watched as Clipper was removed from the Jolly Green, the two techs carrying and the nurse shepherding the way toward the big med-evac cargo aircraft.

Dillingham stared after they'd disappeared through the door. His voice was gruff. "That lady's got balls."

The embassy official mused for a moment, then nodded. "Linda's a very special woman."

"You heading back to Bangkok?"

"First thing I've got to do is find a secure telephone and make a couple calls."

"I brought a jeep. I'll take you to our compound. I can phone Colonel Anderson from there too."

"You forget everything about Clipper and this incident. Like I told you, we'll take care of notifications. I'm sending a team of agency people from Manila to meet her when she gets to Clark. They'll handle all of that."

"You're CIA?"

Richard paused, then smiled. When he spoke, Dillingham knew he'd passed some sort of inspection. "No. They're useful sometimes though. They'll be told what we want and make appropriate notifications. There's her family to consider too."

"I wasn't looking forward to telling the colonel about her condition, anyway."

They watched the med-evac bird's doors being closed and secured, then as the pilot throttled forward and crept in the path of a pickup bearing a large, yellow Follow Me sign.

"How come she called you Sergeant Black?" Richard asked.

Dillingham started to say it was classified, but changed his mind. "Back about a year and a half ago I started work-

ing with North Vietnamese Army deserters in a new program a colonel at MAC-SOG thought up for recon teams.
The policy was that anyone who worked with them used a
fake name and rank, so if the NVA were ringers, they
couldn't get hard information. We had a Captain Marvel, a
Captain Midnight, and a Sergeant Mickey Mouse. I decided
on Sergeant Black."

"I heard about the program. I thought it was unsuccess-
ful."

"My team worked out fine. I helped train 'em, and we
went out on some hairy long-range recons. The code name
was Hotdog, but the brass never trusted them and called
them Black's renegades." His voice trailed off sadly. "They
were rather spectacular, my bunch of renegades."

"This Lieutenant Phrang she was talking about, was he
one of them?"

"He was their leader, my second in command. A goddam
good man. Hell, they were *all* good men. There's only three
left now."

They watched the aircraft taxi toward the runway, then
John led the spook toward the jeep. The emotional scene
with Clipper had somehow built trust.

The civilian was thoughtful as he took his seat beside
Dillingham. "Tell me more about the lieutenant who saved
her life. Him and the team you were talking about."

"I've been trying to get them some kind of asylum so
they can go to the States. I promised them, but a couple
days ago I was told it's been turned down."

1855L—Third Regional Hospital, Clark AB, Philippines

Major Marty Mikalski was a hefty, florid woman and, as the
hospital commander once said, was the nurse he wanted in
attendance if *he* was ever hospitalized. As he put it, she was
the kind of hardheaded nurse who wouldn't back off until
her patients received the best treatment possible. As chief
duty nurse for the evening hospital shift, she'd been given
the task of sealing off a room and preparing for an incoming
VIP. An incoming, *very secret* VIP. To Marty, who fastidiously treated all patients alike, the VIP part was pure bullshit. The secrecy cloaking the patient's arrival was a pain in

the butt that had better, by God, not interfere with proper treatment.

As soon as the comedy twins, Mr. Smith and Mr. Jones, arrived to honcho the VIP's arrival, they'd demanded a meeting with all medical personnel who would be involved with the incoming patient.

Smith gave a fifteen-minute spiel to the assembled staff on how he wanted them to treat her. No questions other than of a purely medical nature. No notifications of next of kin or anyone else. They'd handle that. No inquiries about how injuries had been incurred or where the subject—he called the patient a "subject," for crap's sake—might have contracted any diseases she might have. No visitors. No casual conversations with the subject. No one allowed *near* the room. Two security policemen to be stationed outside her door at all times. Upon her arrival, and especially before sedation was administered, she was to be interviewed by them, with no one else in the room.

At the end of the talk Nurse Marty, as she was known to her patients and co-workers, snorted to a doctor that the twins had put on a pretty good comedy act, which Jones overheard and which made him glare.

When she walked back to the third-floor room they'd designated for the special patient, she thought about the fact that Smith, the intelligence agent, which was surely what they were, had called the subject a "she." Which meant that it was a female coming in, and that aroused her curiosity.

The room was deemed ready half an hour before the patient was scheduled to arrive, and as Marty made her final examination, a tech walked in past the agents, who were busy briefing the full-colonel base provost marshal and a couple of security policemen. He handed her the report routinely radioed ahead by the med-evac crew whenever a patient required special or emergency treatment. So much for secrecy.

NAME: LINDA MARIE LOPES / RANK: GS-15 / DOB: 27 DEC 36 / SINGLE / ROMAN CATHOLIC / MEDICAL RECORDS: REQUEST FROM U.S. EMBASSY CLINIC IN BANGKOK / INITIAL OBSERVATION: GENERAL DETERIORATION FROM PROLONGED LACK

OF NUTRITION, DEHYDRATION, AND
EXTENSIVE PHYSICAL ABUSE. IN
CONSTANT PAIN FROM MULTIPLE
BROKEN TEETH, BROKEN AND CHIPPED
FACIAL BONES, BADLY DAMAGED AND
DETERIORATED NASAL CARTILAGE,
FRACTURED AND POORLY MENDED
LARGE METATARSAL IN RIGHT FOOT, AND
MULTIPLE FRACTURED AND POORLY HEALED
RIBS. BOTH SHOULDERS HAVE BEEN
REPEATEDLY DISLOCATED. SUSPECT
FRACTURE OF UPPER LEFT ARM. RAPE
VICTIM WITH INFECTION COMPLICATIONS.
SUSPECT SHE IS PREGNANT (PATIENT
NOT TOLD). MENTALLY ALERT, BUT
EXPERIENCING EXTREME DEPRESSION &
SELF-CRITICISM. SUSPECT SHE IS
WITHDRAWING. WILL REQUIRE
EXTENSIVE PSYCH SUPPORT. ETA AT
CLARK: 2045 HRS LOCAL.

Marty ground her teeth a bit before telling the tech to get his ass down to the ranking doctor on duty and tell him she had to see him about the incoming patient ASAP.

Mr. Smith looked over inquisitively. "How long before the subject arrives, Nurse?"

She gave him a withering stare. "You fellas clear out. The lady's going to need immediate medical attention, and you'll just get in the way."

"Didn't you hear my briefing? *We* talk to the subject before *anyone* sees her."

"Look, fella, you're in the wrong place and talking to the wrong person. Now trundle your butt out of here so we can do our jobs. Soon as the lady's well enough to talk, and soon as she *wants* to talk, I'll come get you. The way things look right now, I figure that'll be a day or two, so you might as well go get yourself a drink. We'll follow your silly rules as best we can unless they interfere with our job. Then we go by our own."

Smith shook his head, sighed, then motioned to Jones. "We got a little problem here. Give the hospital commander a call and straighten things out."

"You talking about me?" The chief on-duty physician, a full-colonel flight surgeon who was also the acting hospital commander, pushed past the special agents and came into the room.

"I'd like a word with you, Doctor," Smith said angrily.

"Just a moment, please."

Marty handed him the printout and he scanned it.

"Jesus," he muttered.

Smith tried to get his attention.

"Dammit, just a moment!" the doctor said.

Smith snapped his mouth closed. Marty glared at him, her nostrils flaring angrily.

The doctor nodded. "When she gets here, I want her taken to the emergency room for a full workup."

Marty relayed that to the hospital tech, who hurried out. He would radio the ambulance attendants on their way to pick her up, so they'd take her directly to the ER.

Mr. Smith frowned as he watched the tech leave.

Marty thought about the pregnancy. "How about a quick D and C while you're at it?"

"Sounds appropriate. That'll be in the morning, when we know we've got her stabilized." The flight surgeon reread the message. "Have 'em set up a dental surgeon for tomorrow morning, soon as she comes out of the OR. I'll sedate her until then, so she'll not be in pain."

"Doctor?" Smith tried again.

"Should I contact the mental-health clinic?" Marty asked.

"Yeah. Have a doctor set up to talk to her tomorrow afternoon. Until then you'd better keep someone with her at all—"

"Doctor!" shouted Smith, frantic to regain control.

Marty had had enough. She turned slowly toward the agent, her face flushing brighter with each second, and began to stalk toward him, her finger pointed at the door. "Get out of my room! Get off of my floor!"

The agent stubbornly stood his ground, trying to look past her at the doctor. "Doctor, this is a special case, and I—"

"Get out!" yelled Marty.

"Doctor?"

"You heard the nurse," the flight surgeon said conversationally, still reading.

"Dammit, Doctor—"

The full-colonel provost marshal came into the room and motioned to his two cops, then to Smith and Jones. "The doc and the nurse asked you to leave. They're in charge here."

"This is an agency matter, and we're—"

That was another error, for now he'd angered the provost marshal, who interrupted with a frosty edge to his voice. "Let me remind you that this is a Department of Defense installation. Soon as you guys start paying the rent for our bases, you can tell us how to run our hospitals." He nodded to the door, and the security policemen started forward.

The entourage left noisily, the agents arguing that the matter would go to the ambassador, to Washington, to the director, to generals.

Nurse Marty stared at the doorway for a moment after they'd gone. "Assholes."

The doctor was oblivious. "Make damned sure the ER knows about the damaged ribs and the foot, so they'll handle her appropriately. I'll want X rays from top to bottom."

"We'd better get on down there," Marty said. "They'll be bringing her in anytime now."

2030L—O' Club Stag Bar, Takhli RTAFB, Thailand

Captain Manny DeVera

Manny had arrived back at Takhli on the late shuttle flight from Don Muang. As soon as he'd dropped his bag off at his BOQ room at the Ponderosa, he'd called Penny at work and said he'd meet her at the club.

Smitty had joined them for dinner, then accompanied them into the bar.

"How's the flying going?" Manny asked. It was the first chance he'd gotten to ask. So far all the discussion had been about what he'd gone through at Honolulu. Smitty wanted to know all about Waikiki, which he planned to visit after he finished his combat tour. Penny wanted to know what the women were wearing, and whether maxidresses were really catching on.

"Not many sorties going up to pack six lately. Mostly to

the lower packs." Smitty grimaced. "Damn! I forgot to tell you. We thought you were getting in earlier, so I put you on tomorrow's flying schedule. Colonel Donovan's leading, and you'll be number three in his flight."

Penny's face fell, and Smitty caught the expression.

"Since you got in so late," he said lamely, "why don't I take your place tomorrow?"

Manny didn't answer, so Smitty just nodded and the deal was done.

Lieutenant Smith had changed considerably since Manny had met him upon his arrival at Takhli. He looked the same, with his cherub's face and guileless expression, but he was a different man. The guys liked to joke about being steely-eyed, TAC-trained killers. When he flew, Smitty came close to the description. He was calm, professional, and extremely aggressive. Smitty not only loved to fly fighters, he savored flying them in combat. After the toughest missions, where the SAMs flew and MiGs swarmed about the sky, he de-briefed in such a manner that you could tell he'd enjoyed pitting his skills against those of the enemy. His flight com-mander, Captain Billy Bowes, swore he was the best wing-man at Takhli, and Manny thought he was likely right.

Bowes joined them at the bar. "You guys holding a meeting without me?" he grumbled good-naturedly.

Smitty waved to Jimmy the bartender. "Give my boss here a drink, so he'll stay off my back."

"Good seeing you made it back from the ravages of Ha-waii, Manny."

"Good to be back, Billy."

Penny eyed them all. "You guys go ahead and talk shop. I'm going to my trailer." She gave Manny a not very subtle look that said she expected to see him later.

"Don't let me run you off, Pen," said Billy Bowes.

"Don't be silly. Just don't let this guy drink too much," she said, motioning at DeVera.

"Why's that?" Smitty asked innocently, the sparkle of a grin threatening to surface. Everyone knew she and Manny were sleeping together.

Penny gave Smitty a mock glare and left through the side door.

"That's too nice for you, Manny," Billy observed.

"Okay, now you can tell us what you *really* did at Waikiki," Smitty said.

"I *really* got a lot of rest and laid around on the beach. I'd check in at the hospital and some medic would run a test, have me pee in a bottle, take a blood sample . . . stuff like that. Then they'd tell me to go off and relax and check back in in a couple more days."

"For two weeks?"

"Damn near."

"Wonder how I could get a deal like that." Smitty asked; then he grinned. "How'd the women look?"

"They looked like females anywhere, except they didn't wear many clothes."

Smitty's smile widened.

Billy Bowes cautioned. "You better not let the Thai base commander's daughter hear you asking about other women, Smitty. You just got paid, so she'll be in love again."

"We've got a date tomorrow."

"Gonna spend all your money on her again?" Manny asked.

"Not this time. We're going to a Thai boxing match. She's a nice girl."

"That," Billy said, "is probably true. I'll bet you haven't gotten a sniff of her snatch."

"I like going out with a nice girl. She's teaching me how to speak Thai."

Billy regarded Manny DeVera. "Smitty's getting it free from the girls at the Takhli Villa now. The hookers like him so much they're buying him dinner."

Smitty was noncommittal, so Manny decided it was true. "What does your sometime girlfriend think of you whoring around?" he asked.

Smitty colored. "We don't talk about it."

Billy shook his head, muttering something about if Smitty got it free, then the whores had to raise their prices for the rest of them to make up the difference.

Yank Donovan came in, looking weary. He sidled up to an open spot at the bar beside them and motioned for the bartender to bring him a drink.

Billy came up with an idea. "Since Smitty's driving the price of fucking up for the rest of us, he ought to subsidize our prices. We oughta bill him every time we get a short time."

"That's dumb," Smitty said. "You're just jealous."

"Damn right I am. Hell, you're king of the hookers. A real potentate. You oughta see it, Manny. Smitty walks in and the place gets quiet. Then the girls start deserting the rest of us so they can go over and try to impress him."

Smitty shrugged and grinned. "I can't help it if you guys are ugly bastards."

Manny was enjoying himself thoroughly, being with the guys he'd shared so much with when they'd been in C-Flight under Lucky Anderson. It was a sort of clique. They'd learned a lot from Major Lucky. Like how they could rely upon one another.

Manny reflected on other things they'd learned. Like it was the guys with the aggressive attitudes who survived, that the ones who didn't display steel nerves and big balls were more likely to screw something up and get hammered. To make a plan and stick by it. To fly the mission as you briefed it. To put the enemy on the defensive and keep them there. *Yeah*, he thought. All of that had been life-saving advice, but the biggest thing they'd learned was to know and rely on one another. To support your flight mates. Like Smitty saying he'd fill in for him tomorrow? The thoughts rolled around in his mind.

Yank Donovan was talking to Billy Bowes, one of his flight commanders, asking how his pilots were holding up and how proficient he felt they were. The squadron commander was a case in point: aggressive and sure, he constantly took the fight to the enemy. His problem was that he didn't rely on others and wanted to do it all himself. He hadn't built up that level of trust that Lucky Anderson had taught them was so critical.

Yank started a discussion with Smitty then, asking about the status of the squadron aircraft. It was some sort of additional duty he'd assigned the lieutenant, to keep track of which birds were going tits up and breaking most often, and which had write-ups that kept recurring. It was a task handed down by Colonel Trimble, to keep track of maintenance's screwups.

Billy asked Manny how many missions he'd flown.

"Eighty-five," he immediately answered. All the pilots

kept track of the precise number of counters, which were the ones flown over North Vietnam.

"Won't be long until you're done," Billy observed.

Manny looked at Billy's Aussie bush hat, which had a series of vertical marks that reached halfway around the brim. Those were for counters. Red lines marked the significant missions, black ones the easier ones. "How about you?" Manny asked.

"Smitty and I have the same number—ninety-six," Billy said. "We've got our orders. Both of us are going to Luke to check out in F-4's. Then I'm going to Hahn Air Base."

"How about Smitty?"

"He's going to Bitburg. We'll be neighbors."

"Germany will never be the same," Manny muttered, but he was thinking about the fact that Smitty, with only four missions to go, had volunteered to fly in his place.

What if . . . He frowned, half listening in on the talk between Yank Donovan and Smitty. He squinted at Billy Bowes. "What's the target tomorrow afternoon?" he asked.

"Can't say. It's a big one, though. First big mission we've had in a week. Colonel Donovan's going to be force leader."

Smitty had finished his rundown for Yank Donovan, so Manny tapped his shoulder.

"I'll fly the afternoon go tomorrow," Manny said.

"You sure?" Smitty looked let down. He'd likely looked forward to flying one last big one.

"Yeah," Manny said, "I'm sure." He felt a small tingle of nerve ends, as if a cool breeze had passed over the hairs on his hands and arms. He was breaking the promise to Penny, but it was something that had to be done. He didn't try to explain it to himself.

A Wild Weasel pilot, a dark-haired guy with a great curled mustache, began to pick at his banjo. He was seated near the jukebox on a bar stool, and Manny remembered when Animal Hamlin would sit beside him and they'd play together, entertaining the others and leading the songs.

He wished Animal was there with them. He'd been one of the good ones.

"You guys ready?" the Weasel pilot asked, plinking out a chorus. A couple of pilots were beside him, anticipating.

They sang the one about the Doumer bridge first, Animal Hamlin's favorite.

"*Come on down!*" was the chorus, and it raised goose bumps on Manny's arms, for he remembered flying to the big bridge on the northern side of Hanoi. They'd lost good men, trying to relearn the difficult secrets of destroying bridges, as other pilots had done in other wars.

When the song ended, there was a short moment of silence; then someone decided they should sing "Throw a Nickel on the Grass."

Yank Donovan remained at the bar, staring without expression as the rest of them sang. Manny DeVera went out and joined in.

> *Cruising down the Red River,*
>   *Doing five and fifty per . . .*
> *When I call to my flight leader*
>   *Oh won't you help me, sir?*
> *The SAMs are hot and heavy,*
>   *Two MiGs are on my ass,*
> *So take us home flight leader,*
>   *Please don't make a second pass!*

Manny especially like the chorus.

> *Hallelujah, oh hallelujah,*
>   *Throw a nickel on the grass,*
> *Save a fighter pilot's ass.*

> *Hallelujah, oh hallelujah,*
>   *Throw a nickel on the grass,*
> *And you'll be saved!*

Manny stayed late at the stag bar, singing and carousing with his friends—the best ones, he knew, that he'd ever have. There was a sense of camaraderie among men in combat you'd never find anywhere else. They relied upon one another. They could do that and never be let down.

It was after two A.M. when he left the bar with Smitty and Billy Bowes, and they began to walk toward the Ponderosa, half a mile distant, singing other songs and laughing together as they remembered funny things that had happened when they'd been in C-Flight together.

Manny thought fleetingly about the promise in Penny

Dwight's look as she'd left, and about the vow he was breaking. He didn't linger on it, though, because Smitty started singing about the "Sexual Life of the Camel," and that was one of his favorites.

A security vehicle stopped, and a cop looked them over to make sure they were okay. He drove away, shaking his head with mock disgust as they began to sing about "Mary Ann Burns," who was "queen of all the acrobats."

Sunday, March 17th, 1230 Local—Yen Chau, Western Mountains, DRV

Assistant Commissioner Nguyen Wu

The town was an awful place in the growing monsoon winds—boiling with fine dust that permeated every pore and clogged nostrils on dry days, awash with muck when it rained. Each day Wu became more downcast and despairing.

When would they come for him? Had he been forgotten? The dream of his grand return to Hanoi, his rendezvous with greatness, was dwindling.

That morning a convoy of three canvas-clad trucks had rumbled into the village from a crude path to the north. They'd been diverted there, said the senior sergeant who commanded the forty militia men, by orders from Hanoi. The senior sergeant was greatly impressed when he was told about the man with the code name of Brave Hero, called that by the same general who was his own ultimate superior.

Nguyen Wu spoke excitedly on the radio, asking over the specially assigned frequency to be connected with General Xuan Nha, wondering if the convoy hadn't been sent for him.

"The general will be here shortly, Brave Hero," was the brusque reply. The mention of the code name no longer made him puff up with pleasure.

As Wu waited, he thought of the teeming streets of the capital city, and how wonderful it would feel to walk on pavement once more . . . to go to Ba Dinh square and watch the people celebrate victories, cheering the Lao Dong party's wisdom. Survey the fools as they listened to loudspeak-

ers announcing the gibberish spoken by Ho Chi Minh.
Watch them cast careful looks in his direction, for they knew
he was an official of the Commissioner of Death, looking for
those who were insufficiently exuberant. Before his silly
mistake with Quon, he'd been known and feared. It would
be that way again.

The radio crackled with Xuan Nha's croaking voice.

Nguyen Wu told him about the Phantom reconnaissance
flights that had passed overhead three days before, and wondered if Mee fighters might come to destroy the village.

That was not likely.

When would they send the helicopter?

He was told the same maddening things as before. He
was too important to be placed in danger. All VIP travel was
postponed. Be patient. Perhaps next week . . .

Wu told him about the convoy, and how it would leave in
two days for Yen Bai.

Xuan Nha told him it would be too dangerous to accompany them. Be patient. Wu was told that his aunt Li Binh
wanted very badly to see her nephew. There was a great celebration coming up in eight days, and she felt it would be
a perfect time to present his proud achievements to the Lao
Dong party officials.

Wu's heart beat faster as he thought of it.

Too bad. There would have to be another time.

Nguyen Wu's mind raced as he considered his aunt's desire. She would know the best time to present her nephew's
achievement, for she was very good with such things. Was
she trying to relay her impatience to him?

Yes! he decided.

Xuan Nha asked if he was being treated well in Yen
Chau.

Wu burst out that it was a dismal and despicable place.

Xuan closed the conversation on that unhappy note, saying he had matters to attend to.

Wu stared at the radio for a long while. He knew that he
must hurry to Hanoi. Xuan Nha was no longer to be trusted.
His aunt had spoken through his stupid lips to tell her
nephew that he should come immediately. As soon as he
reached Hanoi, he would tell her about the maddening and
ridiculous delays Xuan Nha had imposed, placing him in

such danger. She'd know how to deal with the man they both disdained.

A short time later Nguyen Wu spoke with the senior sergeant commanding the convoy. He told him that he'd talked with Xuan Nha. The general wanted them to leave at first light the next morning and proceed with haste to Yen Bai. Wu and the sublieutenant would travel with them in the weapons carrier they'd brought from Ban Sao Si.

He was pleased when the senior sergeant readily agreed. Wu asked how long the trip to Yen Bai would take.

Traveling cautiously, only at night as was normal, would take them as long as ten or eleven days over the treacherous mountain roads.

He thought of the celebration in eight days. What if they traveled during daylight hours, at a faster speed?

The senior sergeant frowned, then dutifully replied that the trip could be made in four or five days of hard travel, if there were no serious breakdowns.

Which meant that Nguyen Wu could be in Hanoi six days hence. In time for the great celebration Xuan Nha had spoken of.

Wu briefed the village militia leader and the mayor of Yen Chau. They were to tell absolutely no one about his departure, and that included even the highest-ranking generals. He then ordered the sublieutenant to prepare to leave. The officials in Hanoi, he said, were preparing a welcome for him.

A great rumbling sound passed overhead—another visit by the Phantom reconnaissance jet.

Nguyen Wu shuddered, thinking he was leaving the place none too soon.

1255L—Brown Anchor, Gulf of Tonkin

Captain Manny DeVera

The mission was to destroy POL storage tanks and a large warehouse at Nam Dinh, which was in pack four, and they would attack from the water side. Which meant they'd flown across the panhandle of North Vietnam and were refueling over the South China Sea.

It was, as Billy Bowes had told him the previous evening, a big mission. Two flights of Wild Weasels, and two flights of MiG-CAP F-4's to protect them from defenses. A sixteen-ship force from Korat was to attack the petroleum-storage tanks first, and just behind them a similar force from Takhli, theirs, would bomb a nearby warehouse. The intell briefing had warned them there'd be SAMs and hundreds of big guns. It was classified as a heavily defended area, and those pilots who had flown into the area were believers.

Yank Donovan, Bear Force leader, had remained quiet during the flight, but Manny, flying as his number three, ascribed that to the man's strangeness. The squadron commander was a loner and had difficulty interrelating. Yet he was entirely changed from the prima donna who'd arrived at Takhli with an ego as big as a Mack truck.

Bear flight had twice cycled through the position on the KC-135's boom, topping off their fuel tanks the second time through.

"Good luck, Bear flight," the tanker pilot radioed as they dropped away.

Yank answered with two clicks on his radio button.

One by one the other flights in the strike force, Wolf, Wildcat, and Bison, checked in on frequency and joined into the large formation.

"Bear Force, this is Bear Force leader. Check your switches and turn on the music," Donovan called. No response was required. The formation tightened some as the ECM pods came on. Manny ran through his familiar mental drill. *Remain calm—stay on the offensive—think of the next move.* He was not overly apprehensive, as he'd feared he might be.

"Wolf lead has the MiG-CAP in sight at four o'clock high," came an unnecessary radio call.

Manny was surprised that Donovan didn't comment. He was a stickler for radio discipline.

The force flew northward toward pack four, slowly accelerating to 600 knots, maintaining 18,000 feet altitude.

At thirty nautical miles from coast-in, Donovan made his first odd radio call. *"Bear Force, this is Bear Force leader. When we get to the target area, I want you to proceed on past for ten nautical miles, then turn back inbound, holding your altitude."*

Wolf, Wildcat, and Bison all radioed that they understood the instruction.

Manny DeVera wondered what the hell was coming off. He also wondered when Donovan would have them begin the step-down descent, for although they were getting ever closer, they remained at altitude.

Donovan finally began the descent.

Lucky Anderson, thought Manny, would be coming unglued if he were on the mission. He was fanatical about flying a mission precisely as it had been briefed. He wondered again about Donovan's directive to fly past the target and double back.

Red Dog, a Wild Weasel flight flying several miles out in front, called that two SAM sites were active near the coast-in point.

Yank leveled the force at 15,000 feet, higher than they'd normally be this close in.

They were at the coastline. *Too high,* Manny thought. It would be difficult to see the target.

"THIS IS DAGWOOD. SPOTLIGHT AT BULLSEYE ONE-SIX-ZERO FOR FORTY." The EB-66 electronic countermeasures bird had called a SAM launch near the target area.

"This is Red Dog leader. Disregard the launch. No threat to the force."

Yank Donovan didn't respond to either call. The sixteen-ship strike force continued. The Korat formation passed them, outbound, headed back to the tankers.

Manny felt a tingle of apprehension sweep through him. He fought the rising fears by busying his mind, thinking of how he would sight the target from their high altitude.

As they approached Nam Dinh, black bursts erupted in clusters as batteries of 57mm guns welcomed them to town. White puffs of smaller popcorn flak puffed above the city, growing thicker as they approached.

"Bear three, assume the lead," Donovan said in an easy voice.

"Bear three," Manny acknowledged, wondering that his own tone was so calm. As his last word was uttered, Donovan abruptly rolled inverted and disappeared from view.

Then Manny knew. Yank was going to bomb the target alone.

Dammit! Manny raged to himself. The gomer gunners would have a single target to concentrate upon. He rolled ever so slightly, but Donovan's Thud was out of sight.

He continued ahead for another minute, then ordered the turn. Halfway through he saw an enormous explosion below. *The warehouse?* The dark shape of a lone aircraft jinked southward. Donovan, surrounded by thickets of fierce flak bursts. Scores of guns tracked the single target.

"*This is Bear Force leader,*" came the radio call. "*The target is destroyed. Proceed outbound. I repeat pro—*" The radio transmission was abruptly cut off.

More flak bursts tracked the Thud. Manny eyed the target area, so far below. Another, smaller explosion there created another column of back smoke. Donovan had indeed taken out the target.

The single bird belched a dark puff. An engine compressor stall? A hit? The Thud continued to climb, issuing a dark trail.

"*Bear lead,*" Manny radioed, "*you're hit!*" and immediately began to descend toward the coastline, followed by the rest of the formation, so Donovan's stricken bird could rejoin more quickly. He got no response from his radio call.

The lone aircraft continued toward the coast, still trailing smoke but now free from the reach of the big antiaircraft guns. Bear Force continued to descend, and to accelerate; Manny hoped to catch up as quickly as possible.

The coast was not far ahead.

Donovan's Thud torched brightly aft of the cockpit.

"*Eject, Bear leader,*" he called. "*Your main fuel tank's on fire!*"

The aircraft torched brighter, then exploded. The wingless fuselage slewed and began to tumble.

"*This is Bear three,*" he radioed to the others. "*Anyone see a chute?*"

There was no response.

1555L—Takhli RTAFB, Thailand

Colonel Leska attended the debriefing.

Manny went over the sequence of events carefully, supported by Captain Billy Bowes, who had led Wildcat flight on the mission.

At the end of Manny's recital a captain said it was one of the most heroic things he'd ever witnessed, and wondered if Yank Donovan shouldn't be put in for an Air Force Cross or even a Medal of Honor. He deserved it, he said.

"No." Leska emphasized his remark with a single curt shake of his head and left the room.

The captain looked after the departed wing commander with a reddening face. "Colonel Donovan did it for us," he said. "Why doesn't he deserve a medal?"

"The whole idea," Billy Bowes said as he carefully marked another line onto the brim of his hat, "is to kill the other guy. You don't get medals for committing suicide."

CHAPTER
FORTY-FOUR

Tuesday, March 19th 0704 Local—HQ Seventh Air Force, Tan Son Nhut AB, Saigon, South Vietnam

Lieutenant General Richard J. Moss

Moss and Pearly sat in the commander's office, sipping coffee and talking over the back-channel message which had just arrived from the Chief of Staff of the Air Force.

1.(S) MET WITH J THIS A.M. HIS MOOD WAS
DOWNBEAT & IT WAS A SHORT MTG SQUEEZED
INTO TIGHT SCHEDULE. J ASKED IF WE
ARE READY TO PROCEED. I ASSURED HIM
ALL PLANNING HAS BEEN COMPLETED &
WE ARE PREPARED FOR KICKOFF. I ALSO
CONFIRMED THE CAMPAIGN WOULD BE
SHORT, SWIFT, & SURE.
2. (S) AFTER MTG WITH J, I SPOKE WITH
A MEMBER OF PRES STAFF FOR FURTHER
BACKGROUND:
A. RFK'S ENTRY INTO DEM RACE ON AN
"END THE WAR" THEME FIRMED J'S RESOLVE
TO WIN S.E.A. CONFLICT AS EXPEDITIOUSLY

AS POSSIBLE & CERTAINLY BEFORE
NOVEMBER ELECTIONS.
B. TWO RECENT POLLS SHOW THAT
ESCALATION OF BOMBING TO END THE WAR
IS FAVORED (63 & 66 PERCENT) BY U.S.
PUBLIC.
3. (S) HE BRIEFED THE FOLLOWING
"FIRM" SCHEDULE:
A. 31 MAR: J WILL HOLD PRESS CONFERENCE
& "SPEAK TO THE NATION." HE WILL
ANNOUNCE (1) A BUILDUP OF AIR
FORCES, (2) NO MORE GROUND FORCES WILL
BE SENT TO WAR ZONE EXCEPT THOSE
REQUIRED TO ENSURE PROTECTION OF
U.S. FORCES. (3) HE WILL "STRONGLY
SUGGEST" THAT NVN IMMEDIATELY
WITHDRAW ALL GND FORCES FM SVN OR
FACE "PROBABILITY" OF "HEAVY
BOMBARDMENT." (4) HE WILL SUGGEST
TO USSR & PRC TO REMOVE ALL PERSONNEL
FM NVN.
B. 30 APR: J WILL TELL THE NATION
THAT A MASSIVE BOMBING CAMPAIGN
HAS BEGUN SINCE NVN HAS NOT RESPONDED
TO REASON. HE WILL TELL NVN THAT
TALKING IS NO LONGER ENOUGH, THAT
THE BOMBING WILL CONTINUE UNTIL
THERE ARE VISIBLE SIGNS THAT NVN TROOPS
HAVE CEASED OFFENSIVE OPERATION & ARE
BEING WITHDRAWN.
4. (S) DEPLOYMENT UNITS HAVE BEEN
NOTIFIED TO INSPECT AND UPGRADE
MOBILITY KITS AS REQUIRED. MILITARY
AIRLIFT COMMAND IS PREPARING FOR
DEPLOYMENT AS PER AF OPLAN LINE
BACKER JACKPOT, BEGINNING 1 APR 68.
CIVIL CARRIERS WILL BE ADVISED AS OF
KICKOFF DATE.

"Short, swift, and sure," Moss muttered. "Those were the
words we used when we wrote the original ROLLING

THUNDER campaign. Now it's going to happen. Got a nice ring to 'em, don't they?"

"Yes, sir."

"Contact the wing commanders on the scrambler and give 'em the kickoff date."

0820L—355th TFW Commander's Office, Takhli RTAFB, Thailand

Colonel Buster Leska

Buster had been reading his latest letter from home when he was summoned to the command post to take a classified phone call.

Carolyn was still troubled by everything that had transpired with their son, but was becoming resigned. Marcus had made his way to Canada. He'd called her from there, exuberant about a new circle of friends. His pal was a U.S. Army deserter who'd received orders for Nam and decided that dying in a foreign civil war was ridiculous. He had no complaint with North Vietnam's desire to reunite their country and bring efficient government to South Vietnam. Ho Chi Minh wasn't a communist, but a patriot who should be compared to George Washington. Marcus said they might head for Sweden and ask for sanctuary, since they'd heard it was a nice place.

As Buster walked the short way to the command post, he realized how dramatically his personal life had been altered since he'd left the Washington scene. And just as his family had been divided and weakened, Buster believed, so had America.

He did not understand everything that was happening, but he knew the wounds of both would take a long time to heal.

The scrambled telephone call was from Lieutenant Colonel Pearly Gates, and was a short one.

Before leaving to return to his office, Buster told a duty sergeant to notify Lieutenant Colonel Anderson and Captain DeVera and have them meet with him. As he walked back, he could see both men emerge from their respective buildings and hurry his way.

.   .   .

Penny Dwight served coffee as they spoke of inconsequential things, then closed the door to leave them to their privacy.

Buster didn't delay. "LINE BACKER JACKPOT's ready to go, with a kickoff date of April first. That's when the other units will begin deploying over here. Thirty days later we'll initiate the around-the-clock bombing campaign."

Both men became subdued.

He turned to Anderson. "I checked the books, Lucky. You'll have ninety missions when you land this afternoon. Only ten to go. Yet I haven't seen orders come in reassigning you."

"I've been talking to the Personnel Center in the States, sir, and I finally got an answer. If you'll concur, they've agreed to let me stay in place for another couple of months."

"A hundred missions is enough stress for any human."

"I'd like to see the thing through, Colonel. No use to break in another new squadron commander in the most critical phase of the bombing campaign. I was hoping it might be started before this, but since it didn't . . ." He shrugged.

Buster pondered his answer. What Lucky said made sense. He decided to agree. "The second you decide you want out, I'll approve the orders. And the first sign I see of strain, I'll do the same. Is that fair?"

Anderson nodded.

"How about you, Manny? You've only got thirteen missions to go."

DeVera didn't hesitate. "I'd like to extend my tour until JACKPOT's over."

Manny's position would also be critical. Things would go smoother if both men were aboard when the campaign began. "Same deal as for Lucky. If I see signs of fatigue, you go home."

"Yes, sir."

"Well, now there's nothing left to do except wait, gentlemen."

"When will it be releasable?" Lucky asked. "I'd like to brief my flight commanders."

"It remains close hold until after the President makes his announcement."

Anderson rose to leave. Manny DeVera asked to have a few words in private.

Captain Manny DeVera

The door closed quietly behind Lucky Anderson.

Buster Leska's eyes betrayed his amusement, and DeVera knew the answer to his question.

"You're looking good, Manny."

"I feel a lot better, sir."

"You needed the rest. You were intense for too long."

"When I came to see you last time, I was going to tell you I wanted to quit."

"I was working you too hard. I tend to do that with my best men."

"I chickened out for a while there."

"That's too harsh. You drove yourself until you were so tired and confused you ran out of answers."

Manny thought about that, then slowly nodded. "That's a nice way to put it. I could have gotten someone killed, though, and I apologize for that."

"Don't be hard on yourself. We all have our fears. Any man who faces what we do up there and isn't apprehensive is a damned fool. We just learn to control it. Next time you'll know the symptoms. You start getting too nervous when you're flying hot and heavy, slack off some, and when you can, take an R and R."

"I'll remember, sir."

"How about your flying?"

"I'm handling it just fine now."

"You're a good combat leader, Manny." Leska paused with his sermon and softened his voice. "How are things between you and Penny?"

"She doesn't understand."

"Or maybe she does and we're wrong. It doesn't really matter, does it?"

"No, sir."

"There'll be someone else out there you'll cherish just as much."

This time Manny knew the colonel was wrong. He'd never feel the same toward another woman . . . but as he'd said, it didn't matter. He could cope with the heartache. He couldn't live with the alternative. Manny got to his feet. "That was all I wanted to say, sir. That I'm okay now and thanks for the help."

"You're going to be in my shoes someday, Manny. At least I hope they pick people like you. And you'll have a young person come before you who's about to make the worst mistake of his or her life."

"Send 'em to Hawaii, sir?"

"Yeah. Then kick yourself in the butt like I did, because you didn't see it coming and fix the problem before it went that far."

Manny closed the office door and started toward the entrance, thinking the colonel was just as astute as he'd always thought him to be. Then he stopped and looked at Penny Dwight.

Their eyes met. Since he'd made his decision she'd carefully avoided him. She appeared in command of herself. Not at all like the wide-eyed girl they'd first seen come to Takhli. It had been easy to shun other women in Hawaii; he knew they couldn't compare with what he already had. Emotion surged, but he summoned courage and quelled it. He was locked into his role, and that would not change.

Penny believed fighter jocks were uncaring. He wanted to explain that they felt just as intensely as anyone—that they formed bonds that were more love than camaraderie— that they wanted very badly to mourn when those friends were lost, but the numbness they forced upon themselves was the only way to avoid being consumed by grief. Taking death in stride was the only way to remain rational. A touch of madness was the only way to avoid insanity.

He turned and walked out. As the colonel had said, it didn't really matter. A flight of Thunderchiefs flew overhead, then one by one pitched out to land. He watched.

When he'd been in his fatigued fog, searching for truth, he'd written Sister Lucia, the elderly nun who had guided him through his youth. She was living her final years in a small convent in San Antonio, no longer the energetic dynamo he remembered so vividly. Her body was old and she moved slowly, but her mind was clear and her resolve steady.

He'd hinted how he might quit—refuse to fly combat any longer. Told her he'd met a woman he wanted more than anything in the world, who cared about him and despaired each time he flew into mortal danger.

He'd received her response that morning.

Not once did she mention Penny, although she'd often urged him to find a mate. Except for priests, bachelorhood was unnatural, she'd said.

She related a story told her in her childhood, about two men in a small village, one who dared, the other who did not. The one who dared was met with difficulty, pain, and sorrow, while the other led an untroubled life and was always warm and comfortable. When the two men lay dying, the man who had not dared had few visitors, for the townspeople were occupied with memories of the man who had done so much. They named the village for the man who dared. The name of the other man? No one could remember, for it had long been forgotten.

Some men would be remembered for their toil, triumphs, and tragedies.

Others were best forgotten.

A tough taskmaster, was Sister Lucia.

0915L—VPA HQ, Hanoi, DRV

General Xuan Nha

Captain Quang Hanh handed him the microphone. "The Yen Chau observation post. The operator there is very nervous, as you thought he would be."

Xuan Nha spoke into the radio, asking for Brave Hero.

Silence.

"*Do you know who I am?*" he asked.

"*I believe so,*" a tremulous voice responded.

"*Does anyone else have my voice?*" Xuan rasped.

"*No, comrade General Nha.*"

"*When did he depart?*"

"*Brave Hero ordered us to be silent, comrade General.*"

Xuan Nha's voice lowered to a dangerous whisper. "*When?*"

After a final pause the soldier blurted out the information Xuan asked for.

"Good. Now tell me about the convoy."

Alone in the radio room, Xuan changed radio frequencies and called for Quon, who was visiting his MiG pilots at a base near the Chinese border.

"Brave Hero departed Yen Chau with the convoy, just as we planned, but a day earlier."

"When did he leave?"

"Yesterday at oh-six-thirty." Xuan enunciated as clearly as he possibly could. *"He is in the second vehicle in the group."* He described the convoy in minute detail.

"They will be vulnerable to air attack," Quon said slowly.

"Very vulnerable." Xuan Nha described the convoy's light defenses. *"They are traveling very fast, in the daylight hours, and will not use normal precautions."*

"It would be a terrible thing if the Americans discovered him, since he is carrying their secrets."

"He is in the second vehicle." Xuan Nha reiterated. Then he described the precise route he knew they'd take.

0937L—Monkey Mountain, Danang AB, South Vietnam

The Army Security Agency Spec-5 linguist/operator removed the headset, rubbed his ears vigorously, then called over his immediate supervisor, another young NCO who was also his best friend.

His supervisor grew increasingly excited as he read what he'd written on the pad. "Shit. Rerun the tape and get a transcript."

"Don't have to." He pointed at the pad. "That's verbatim. Our buddies talked even slower than before, like they were dictating a letter. The guy with the frog's voice said Brave Hero's probably gone thirty klicks by now. Bad road all the way. Said it'll only take him two more days to get to Yen Bai if the convoy keeps up their speed. Three at the outside."

His boss mused. "MAC-V intell thought he'd go out by chopper."

"They screwed up again," he said happily. The Army Security Agency delighted at proving the bureaucrats at Tan Son Nhut wrong.

"Either way, they wanted an immediate message when we got word he was leaving."

"Message?" he despaired. He was an awful typist. "How about a secure phone call and then I send 'em the transcript?"

His supervisor rummaged in a cubbyhole, found a message form, and offered it. "They want a message, we send 'em a message."

"Folks in hell and Nam want ice water too." He grimaced, then awkwardly rolled the form into the typewriter and positioned it in the carriage. "They want it so fast, you better tell the major so he'll be ready to sign it out." He referred to the words on the pad and began to hunt and peck.

His supervisor departed. A few minutes later he returned and peered over his shoulder. "Major says to forward an info copy to the MAC-SOG liaison officer at Seventh Air Force."

"Think the Air Force will try to take this Brave Hero guy out?"

"Ours is not to reason, asshole. Just send the message."

The linguist/operator continued his laborious typing. "I got a buddy over at the base says the Air Force can't hit their butt with a hand towel. Betcha they miss him."

"You ever seen a fighter strafe a target?"

"Nope."

"Some of 'em carry Gatling guns. Bullets come out so fast you get dizzy. Big twenty-millimeter rounds that explode on contact. I sure as hell wouldn't wanta be this poor bastard if they get him in their sights."

"If they find him. That won't be easy where he's traveling." The operator peered at his typing, grimaced, and corrected an error with a ballpoint pen marked U.S. GOVERNMENT. "Sure makes me wonder what our two North Viet buddies are up to."

"That's your problem, you keep trying to think."

The operator finished, drew the message form from the typewriter, read it over and handed it to his friend.

Wednesday, March 20th, 0640 Local—Military Assistance Command-Vietnam HQ, Tan Son Nhut Air Base, South Vietnam

Lieutenant Colonel Pearly Gates

The previous morning, when Friday Wells had relayed a MAC-V intell request for fighter sorties to find and destroy a convoy in North Vietnam, General Moss had balked. It hadn't been as easy to convince him as Pearly had thought, even when he'd told him about Clipper being involved.

Find out more, the general had told him. The whole thing sounded fishy to him.

Pearly had all the right clearances—they were required in his job. It was the need-to-know prerequisite that made the Army major hesitate to provide the nitty details of a priority–one, no-shit, sensitive project. He'd flatly refused to come over to the Seventh Air Force headquarters building and talk in his classified vault.

If they decided to speak with him, it would be on their turf, at 0615 the next morning, they'd said.

Why so early? Later, Friday had told him how the Army did everything at uncivilized hours. Those strange people liked to get up at two or three A.M., hump around a course in full packs, and work until noon. They turned into pumpkins shortly after lunch.

No wonder the Air Force had broken away from the Army, Pearly had groused, but he'd agreed to the early briefing time.

Now Pearly awaited the major's arrival in the vaultlike briefing room in the annex to MAC-V headquarters, the private domain of the recently departed General William C. Westmoreland. It was said that since Westy mistrusted the CIA and their cautious estimates, he'd created his own set of spooks, involving MAC-V intell and much of MAC-SOG, but that they'd quickly become just as bureaucratic as the agency.

Pearly was forming his own opinion on their efficacy. At 0620 a clerk had poked his head into the room and said the briefing had been delayed fifteen minutes. Now the major was ten minutes late for *that* meeting time. Pearly decided to give him five more, until a quarter till seven. He would then return to his headquarters and tell the United States Army and Military Assistance Command–Vietnam to go screw themselves.

He was rising from his chair when a serious-looking gnome who stood no taller than five-five entered the room and nodded.

Pearly sat back down.

"Good day," said the dour major. From first eye contact, antagonism grew between them.

Pearly removed his glasses and stared moodily at the blurred vision. These people knew how to start a meeting on the wrong foot, he decided.

"I've been cleared to brief you in," the major said abruptly, "but keep in mind that everything I'm about to discuss is compartmented Top Secret, Sensitive Information."

Pearly nodded absently as he carefully polished the lenses, then pushed the spectacles back into place. The major proffered and he signed a U.S. Army form stating he was in receipt of special information regarding source-sensitive material.

"Have you heard of a man called Le Duc Tho?" the major began in his clipped speech.

"Sure," said Pearly. "He's the guy who coordinates the war and the politics in South Vietnam for Hanoi's Lao Dong party."

"He is Ho Chi Minh's personal emissary. A very important man."

"You're not trying to tell me that Le Duc Tho's been passing you information, are you?"

"Have you heard of Quon?"

"He's a senior officer in the VPAAF. No one knows if he's a colonel or general, because he doesn't wear rank. Real mysterious-type guy."

"He's also a national hero and Le Duc Tho's son-in-law. A few months ago Quon became a bit sloppy in his work as the air regiment commandant at Phuc Yen and angered his boss, who not only runs their Air Force but is even better politically placed than Quon. It seems the Lao Dong party thought Quon needed to be taught a minor lesson, so . . ."

Another minute passed before a light bulb came on for Pearly Gates. He raised his hand and said, "Whoa!"

The major grew silent.

"Are you telling me that Quon's trying to use us to eliminate one of their own government officials?"

"We believe so."

"And he's cooperating with you?"

"On this matter at least, that appears to be the case. He's using a known compromised frequency, and he speaks very distinctly. The second voice on the frequency belongs to a senior officer in their Army of National Defense."

"Militia or the air-defense side?" The VPAND was a large organization.

The major sighed, as if speaking with Pearly were a hardship. He obviously did not like answering questions and paused for a long while. "He's influential over the entire VPAND structure."

Pearly tried to remember the name of the general who commanded the VPAND.

"This second person also speaks slowly and clearly, which makes us think he too knows the conversations are being monitored. His voice is distinctive and easily identified."

"What's the VPAND commanding general's name? Luck?"

"General *Luc* hasn't been seen in public recently. We've got photos of a colonel with one arm, a patch over one eye, and a small beak, who's attending all the right meetings. According to the intercepts, he was recently promoted to general, so the rank is also correct. The new guy's name is Nha ... General Nha."

"And he and Quon are cooperating with the United States military? It seems preposterous."

The runt major hesitated. "It may not really be a matter of cooperation as much as expediency. Perhaps we provide the only way they've got to get rid of this official."

"So why should we help them?"

"Three reasons. One, we might get more cooperation in the future. Two, the initial contact, the radio transmission from General Nha to Quon, stated that the VIP is carrying intelligence material that we believe is important to our interests and should be destroyed. Our third rationale for intercepting the convoy and eliminating the VIP is that we believe it's good policy to keep as much infighting as possible going on up there."

Pearly was in agreement with that reasoning. With LINE BACKER JACKPOT about to begin, any cracks in the North Vietnamese hierarchy would work to their advantage. "Why don't you go through normal channels?" he asked. One of General Moss's several hats was as the Deputy Commander for Air, MAC-V, meaning he worked for General Abrams.

"There's very little time, and this matter is simply too sensitive for normal channels." The major collected his notes and grew silent as he looked to Pearly for a response.

"I'll have to brief General Moss about all of this."

"We'd rather you didn't, but if that's the only way we can get the missions authorized—"

"It is," Pearly interrupted. He was irritated at the major's lack of courtesy, his asshole attitude, and could likely come up with a few more irritants.

"Will you comply?"

Pearly would have loved, just then, to tell the major to go fuck himself. Instead he asked about the convoy and any air defenses they might have.

"Four vehicles. Three two-ton four-by-fours and a utility vehicle about the size of one of our weapons carriers. That one's second in the convoy, and the one we're interested in. They'll have two 12.7 and two 14.5 millimeter machine guns, and one rapid-fire 37 millimeter towed gun."

"Where are they?"

"Then you'll do it?"

"I think the general will go for it."

The major spread a map onto the tabletop, then pointed out a line that snaked through mountainous terrain. "General Nha described the route of travel very carefully."

Pearly noted the United States Military Academy ring on the major's finger, and his antagonism dwindled. As a West Pointer, the guy couldn't help being an asshole. American taxpayers had spent a lot of money to educate him that way.

At 0810 hours Pearly Gates went directly from General Moss's office to the Tactical Air Control Center, where he made out an addendum to the current air tasking order, which had been sent to the combat flying units the previous evening. He tasked the wings at Korat, Ubon, and Takhli to search out and destroy a four-vehicle convoy enroute from the village of Yen Chau to Hanoi, describing the route of travel as well as other physical details.

CHAPTER
FORTY-FIVE

Thursday, March 21st, 1145L—Command Post, Takhli RTAFB, Thailand

Lieutenant Colonel Lucky Anderson

Lucky was leading Scotch flight; Manny DeVera, Brandy.

There were only eight aircraft involved, but most of the pilots thought even that small number was a waste of time and effort on another bullshit mission to locate and destroy trucks under a jungle canopy. This one was unique in the amount of information they received and the mystery over why they were going at all, but it didn't alter the fact that they were being sent on another useless wild-goose chase. Korat Thud pilots had discovered that the previous afternoon when they'd thoroughly scoured the area and found nothing. That morning Ubon had sent out eight F-4 Phantoms, with the same results.

Four vehicles in the convoy. A two-ton truck in front with a canvas-covered bed, hauling a thirty-seven millimeter gun. Next was the target vehicle, a weapons carrier transporting whatever it was Seventh Air Force wanted destroyed. Bringing up the rear were two more two-tons, with mounted automatic weapons.

They'd be traveling the eastern slope of the mountainous region of route pack five. Much of the area was covered with dense foliage.

"Like looking for a rabbit in a briar patch," Manny DeVera grumbled. "If they don't want to be seen, they won't be. They hear an airplane and they just pull over and hide. Or more likely, they're holing up in the daytime and only traveling at night."

Lucky's response was quickly given. They'd received the tasking and they'd fly the mission. He pointed out the route they were to search between a mountain village and Yen Bai, on the Red River. He also pointed out the forty-kilometer stretch of road they were to concentrate on. The median point for their search was three quarters of the way to Yen Bai.

"We'll alternate," he briefed. "Captain DeVera's Brandy flight will start out by flying low along the track, and we'll sit up at three thousand feet overhead, looking down. After twenty minutes we'll drop down, and Brandy flight will take our place on top. After twenty minutes of that, if we have any time remaining, we'll split up and search different segments of the route."

Manny was examining the monocular he'd bought in Saigon. Lucky started to tell him the things were unauthorized and potentially dangerous to use in flight, but he stopped himself. Finding the trucks would take every trick they could think of. He went over it all again.

His audience listened with half an ear, unimpressed with the mission.

"What the hell is it we're after?" a pilot groaned.

"They didn't tell us in the frag order. But whatever it is, it's in the second vehicle."

The Thuds would each carry two BLU-1B napalm canisters—bluies—and a full load of high-explosive incendiary cannon rounds. The frag order directed them to burn the convoy.

1355L—Route Pack Five, North Vietnam

Captain Manny DeVera

They were fast approaching the end of their fuel endurance and had seen nothing at all on the mountain road, which was seldom visible beneath the tangles of trees and brush.

Brandy flight had flown for twenty minutes down low, then another twenty up higher, as briefed. At the slow speeds they'd used little gas, so the two flights had split up and would continue to search different parts of the road until they were "bingo fuel," meaning they had to return to the tanker and gas up for the trip home. Lucky was looking at the western twenty-kilometer stretch, and Manny had taken Brandy eastward along the road, to search closer to Yen Bai.

Manny had his four birds flying in a trail formation, throttled back to four hundred knots, each half a mile behind the next so the individual pilots could make their own observations. He bunted over a rise, then settled at five hundred feet above the terrain and pulled the monocular back into place.

He looked through it with one eye, keeping the other squinted but open for safety's sake. Manny didn't want to smack into a mountain while looking for a two-bit truck.

He saw a glint, decided it was from a mountain stream, and continued. They were getting close to Yen Bai. Ten miles at the most. Since he didn't want to wage an air battle with the antiaircraft guns at Yen Bai over a few stupid trucks, he decided to give it thirty more seconds before reversing course.

Manny started a slight pull-up over a knoll and saw another glint, this one brighter and near the apex, where the trees were more sparse. A windshield?

"Brandy lead's making a two-seventy-degree turn to port," he announced. The turn slowed him even more. He stared toward the knoll as he drew closer, then noticed brown bees zipping past the canopy.

"Brandy lead's taking small-arms fire," he said, and jinked away to his right as he pushed up the throttle.

"Lead, this is Brandy three. You got the trucks?"

"Maybe," Manny responded. He looked again, through

the monocular. Something was there. He could see angular shapes that were obviously not natural.

"*Yeah,*" he finally announced. "*I think I've got our convoy.*" He'd seen two of them, stopped on the roadway near the hilltop. Just beyond, to the south of the trucks, was dense jungle.

More brown bees zipped past as he approached. It was coming from a position immediately west of the trucks he'd sighted.

Manny checked his fuel. Enough for a couple of passes, no more. He turned outbound again, to set up to release the bluies. The other three Brandys were circling off to his left.

"*Brandy lead, this is Scotch leader,*" Lucky radioed. "*We're bingo fuel. You're going to have to destroy 'em by yourselves.*"

"*Roger.*"

Manny double-checked his weapons-release switches. "*Brandys,*" he called, "*Lead's got two of the trucks in sight near a small hilltop, and I believe the others are in the trees just to the west of 'em. Stay in trail and follow me in for a nape drop. Then we'll go around for a low-angle strafe pass.*"

Assistant Commissioner Nguyen Wu

Nguyen Wu sat in the truck's cab, subtly coaching the sublieutenant on how he should tell the world of Wu's heroics at Ban Sao Si. The sublieutenant was a willing subject, sufficiently intelligent to realize that his future rested in Wu's hands.

They'd been pressing hard toward Yen Bai and had stopped at the hilltop for a short rest to let the overheated truck engines cool.

Nguyen had heard the first Thunder plane pass overhead and make a lazy turn toward the north, but he was not worried, for they'd heard the sounds of other aircraft in the past two days and none had discovered them. The trees here were sparse, but they were enough to hide them, he decided. Then he heard the ear-shattering sound of gunfire from one of the automatic weapons.

"The fools are going to attract the aircraft," he told the sublieutenant as he peered through the dust-caked window. He heard the senior sergeant outside, screaming that they'd been seen, and for his soldiers to man the other truck-mounted machine guns. They began to fire even more wildly, entirely without a disciplined plan.

"Stop shooting!" Wu screeched, for he saw three more Thunder planes in the distance.

Soldiers worked frantically to set up the small towed antiaircraft gun.

"Don't shoot!" he implored.

The first Thunder plane had now turned inbound, directly at them. Nguyen Wu immediately scrambled out of the cab and began to flee toward the jungle.

The sublieutenant called after him in a loud, frightened voice, but Wu didn't pause. Heart pounding wildly, he looked around at the oncoming Thunder plane, then back forward—and ran smack into a tree. He squealed with the pain from his nose and scrambled on into the brush.

WHHOOOOOOM!

The fighter roared overhead, and he fell, flattening himself as close to the ground as possible, expecting the awful concussive blast that came from bombs. Instead there was a bright flash and wave of searing heat. *What?* He heard terrified screams and began to whimper, although he'd not been hurt.

WHHOOOOOOM! Another aircraft passed over, and a second later there was another flash and heat-wave, that one farther away and not as intense.

He looked back and saw the sublieutenant staring at the sky, then turning to search the edge of the jungle. "Brave Hero!" he called plaintively.

Nguyen Wu started to yell for him to hurry, but was mesmerized with horror. Another Thunder plane approached—two shapes tumbled free—an immense ball of orange fire engulfed the forward-most truck. Tendrils of liquid fire spewed onto a tree ... and onto the sublieutenant. He screamed and leapt about, trying to put out flames that engulfed his upper body. He stumbled drunkenly toward the truck, blinded, still screaming.

The fourth Thunder plane also dropped, but by then Wu held his head flat against the ground. He was shivering violently and trying to dig into the earth with clawed hands.

Sounds of the jet engines receded, and he slowly relaxed.

The shrieks were now coming from many sources as other humans burned. He raised up to survey the aftermath.

Several fires roared. Bright figures staggered about, igniting everything they contacted. Two trucks were burning fiercely, thankfully not theirs, for in his haste Wu had left the precious courier pouch on the vehicle's seat.

The pouch! He must have it! He slowly stood and walked ever so cautiously back toward the truck. He gingerly avoided the sublieutenant where he lay burning from head to fiery toe, body fat crackling, arms clawing beseechingly upward from the flames.

"They are returning," a soldier shrieked, and began firing his rifle.

Wu immediately spun about and ran toward the protective jungle.

There was a roar of an aircraft passing overhead, immediately followed by a loud *BRRAAA-AAAAAT*. Wu ran on wildly; he'd heard the sounds of Thunder planes firing their awesome Vulcan guns before.

BRAAA-AAAAT!

He felt a stinging sensation in his abdomen as he stumbled headlong for the ground.

BRRRAA-AAAAA-AAAAT!

Nguyen Wu cried out in terror, crabbing farther into the trees, leaving a trail of bright blood. Another Thunder plane fired its gun, and he continued to sob hysterically and crawl ever deeper into the jungle.

Again the sounds of the aircraft receded, but Wu knew not to trust them. He found a tree and cowered low behind it, pulling his knees to his chest and hiding his head between them. Crying out for someone . . . *anyone* . . . to save him. Even when all became silent except for his own wimpering, he was oblivious to the fact that the Thunder planes had departed.

More than half an hour passed before he decided the fighters weren't waiting to attack again. He examined his throbbing lower abdomen, where the blood had now congealed. A thin shard of metal had been wrenched from a truck by the shower of exploding bullets and thrown forth with such great velocity that it had skewered him. He stared at the sharp, jagged metal that protruded front and rear, and his shoulders convulsed as he began to cry.

1900L—Regional Hospital, Clark AB, Philippines

GS-15 Linda Lopes

The two agents from the Manila agency office had interviewed her again that afternoon, and she'd told them the same thing she'd said the previous times. She'd not revealed anything to her captors for a long period, but in the end she'd broken and given the North Vietnamese the names of her network people in Thailand, as well as names of American intelligence personnel in the embassy, including that of Richard. She wasn't precisely sure how many names she'd given, for her physical and mental condition had been deteriorated, but she was certain it was enough to compromise a lot of people.

Mr. Smith repeated the same questions over and over, as if he were trying to pry a confession from a criminal, and she'd become frightened of him. She hadn't told anyone, including the psychiatrist who visited daily, but she was beginning to put Assistant Commissioner Nugyen Wu's face on Smith when he spoke to her. He even used some of the same phrases Wu had used through his interpreter. Smith said they needed to know what she knew, so they'd be able to tell what might have been compromised.

Might have been compromised? She'd begun to give vague responses to Smith's questions, as she had at first with Sergeant Gross. He had become the enemy, and Linda was increasingly confused about such distinctions when Smith and Jones visited.

When she timidly asked if they'd notified her parents and her fiancé that she was alive and well, they said sure they had, but they'd told them she was isolated and not to correspond. When they were finished with the debriefing, she'd be able to speak with them on the telephone and receive letters.

She was afraid to ask when that might be.

Linda was miserable each time the agents visited, and the rest of her hospital life was not much more pleasant. She'd been examined and reexamined, scrubbed, purged, rebroken, and reset in a several places, had a cast on her right foot and left arm, bandages covering much of her chest and face, and both arms were suspended in front of her by an aluminum device. There were no more intravenous feedings, though, and in a few more days she'd be able to eat more than mushy pap that looked like baby food. The dentist had pulled all but eight teeth, cut away diseased gum tissue, and told her he'd be installing partials.

She was confined to the guarded room, so the specialists had to come there to see her, although she was recovered sufficiently to hobble about on the walking cast.

The evenings were best, because every night Nurse Marty came and spent time with her. She'd brush her hair and talk about nice things, like how she liked flowers and gardening, and how pretty her hair was, even though Linda knew it wasn't true. Then she'd have a Filipina girl bathe her while she went out on her rounds, and return to rub moisturizing lotion into her skin and talk again. Nurse Marty was the first person since Lieutenant Phrang had been killed that she trusted. She made her feel almost feminine.

Sometimes Nurse Marty would talk about boyfriends she'd had, and try to get Linda to talk more about Paul Anderson, whom she'd slipped up and told about on their third brushing session. She said he sounded nice, and that she'd once known a special guy from Takhli too. Linda didn't talk much about Paul after the one time, just said she wished she could get his letters. Thinking about him made Linda uneasy, and increasingly ended with terrible guilt. She wanted to forget the things that had happened to her during her captivity, but whenever she thought of Paul, her mind would soon wander to their moments of intimacy. Then, however much she fought it, he'd be replaced by the pudgy sergeant huffing and blowing as he labored on top of her. She'd recall his squeals when he'd finish, his watching and orchestrating with the others . . . so many others.

Whore.

"I'm sorry, Paul," she'd whisper.

She couldn't afford to think of Lucky Anderson often if she wished to retain the fragile string of sanity to which she clung so desperately. Today the psychiatrist had brought up his name, and she'd stiffened and refused to answer any more of his gently probing questions.

So Nurse Marty was not to be trusted either! She was the only one here who knew about Paul, and she'd obviously told the doctor.

That night when the big, florid-faced woman came into her room, Linda looked away and refused to answer her cheerful greeting.

Nurse Marty came to her bedside anyway and sat. "I know what you're thinking, hon. I talked to the psychiatrist, and he said you were upset when he spoke about your fiancé. And you're right, I told him. But I did it because I thought it might help."

Linda didn't answer.

"See, hon, the shrink thinks you're withdrawing further from reality. He wants you to be able to put everything in perspective, and you can't do that if you don't face up to the facts."

"There are things I'd like to forget," Linda whispered.

"Hon, you mustn't forget. You've got to remember what happened, and then you've got to put it all in its proper place. Like the fact that those bastards raped you. Someday you've got to look back on that and hate them for doing that to you, but you've also got to realize that they didn't take a damned thing away from you. You won."

She mused on that. "I think most of them are dead."

"See. And you're here alive and getting better. You won. You're free."

"You sound like the psychiatrist."

"Sure I do. I talk with him every day after he finishes with you. See, I care, and I want to make damn sure everyone's giving you the best treatment possible. He's trying to do that, you know."

Linda sighed. "Sometimes it's hard for me to trust people, Marty."

"I know. It'll come, though, once you realize you're back in charge."

Linda was silent.

Nurse Marty ran the soft brush through her hair, then withdrew it. "Do you mind if I do that?"

"No." It felt good.

The big nurse continued with the gentle strokes. "I don't want you seeing anyone who upsets you, but the shrink's one of the good guys. Let me tell you something about him since he's an awfully big guy, and he might look scary to you. He played football for the University of Texas, and he even had a chance at the pros. But know something else?

He's henpecked. His wife stands about five two, and she lays down the law. He worships the ground she walks on, so he lets her do it. Just stands there and grins when she chews his ass out. He's big and he's a pussycat. She's tiny and she's a fire-eater. Kind of a strange relationship, but they're good for one another."

Linda thought about the psychiatrist. He seemed more human after Nurse Marty's explanation.

"They're like that. Other people are different with each other, but there's something special between a couple in love. That's the way of boys and girls. You know that. You've got a man."

Linda *almost* thought about Paul Anderson, but made herself stop. "How about you?" she asked Marty, to steer the conversation away.

Nurse Marty chuckled. "I'm a pushover. Show me a man with nice buns, and I break into a sweat. He says a couple slick words and I start purring. I may not be beautiful, but I sure like guys and what they do for me. If I get a chance to land one like you have, I'd be happy for life, and you can damn well bet he'd be happy. I'd keep him tuckered out and grinning."

"Paul and I went to Hawaii last fall." She'd uttered the words before thinking.

"I like the islands," Nurse Marty said in her quiet tone. "You visit Waikiki?"

Linda hesitated a long time before responding. "Our hotel was right on the beach."

"I spent a few days at the Hale Koa."

"That's where we were."

"Kinda like heaven, isn't it?"

Did she dare remember? "Did they really notify Paul and my parents?" she asked.

"The comedy twins? They *said* they would."

"I thought Paul would have come if he knew about my being here."

"I'll ask them again. They don't like answering questions."

Linda started to tell her how frightened she was of them, but held her tongue.

The big nurse paused in her strokes. "We're gonna have

to get some new rinse for your hair, hon. I've got some at home I think you'll like. Brings out highlights real nice."

Friday, March 22nd, 1400 Local—Western Mountains, DRV

Assistant Commissioner Nguyen Wu

He'd spent the night and morning huddled at the base of the tree. He had licked moisture from a damp spot in the earth, for he'd become very dry, his throat so parched that he could hardly swallow.

He prayed for rain.

In the past hours the wound caused by the metal shard that protruded from his thin abdomen had begun to throb with a deeper sensation that reached into his very core. Red streaks reached out from the wound like fiery fingers. Periodically he'd touch the rusted metal, but he did so cautiously—fearful that if he moved it, he'd cut himself worse inside.

If they'd only come for him, he was sure he could survive it.

As for the woman's secrets, he had memorized much of what the major had written on the pad. They'd soon find him, he decided, and take him to the Bach Mai hospital in Hanoi, where doctors would operate and perhaps heal him with penicillin and sulfa.

You are a brave and great man, Lao Dong officials would tell him as his aunt looked on.

His mouth was so dry!

The churning sounds of a helicopter passing overhead roused him, and he held his breath, knowing it was theirs and not the Americans. He looked up, but it was gone.

Hope welled anew in his chest as the helicopter returned twice more, then once again, hovering long enough for him to see the huge green body with the blood-red star.

They'd come for him! He rejoiced, weakly waved his left arm to attract them, felt the powerful down-draft cool him. The helicopter moved away once more. The engine surged, then the blades clattered and settled to a steady clopping sound. They'd discovered the trucks and landed!

It was just as he'd thought. He would live! Wu tried to stand, but the pain from the wound was too intense. He whimpered and settled back into a crablike crouch.

He tried to cry out so they could hear him, but the sound was more like a single, low cough. His throat was so dry.

He must reach them and be rescued. Wu began to crawl on hands and knees, ever so slowly, toward the noise of the idling rotor blades. There were also other sounds . . . distant voices. He trembled in anticipation as he continued to crawl, remembering that he must act brave when they found him. Nguyen Wu would return to Hanoi, to his beloved aunt, in glory. The wound would be proof of his dedication.

A shot of pain seared through him, and he gasped and stiffened at its intensity, but didn't cry out. He must be brave. And he must conserve the little sound remaining in his parched throat. After a long moment he continued to crawl for another meter or two, then stopped to rest, taking short breaths as he settled onto the earth.

A voice and a distant laugh. The sound of movement as someone came into the forest.

So close. He waited patiently, for the sounds were moving in his direction.

A man appeared not ten meters distant, wearing the green overalls of an aviator, staring down at the trail of dried blood Wu had left the previous day.

Nguyen Wu tried to utter a word to attract him, but nothing emerged from his lips.

The man approached closer. "Brave Hero," he said in a mocking voice.

Wu stared. It was his former prisoner, Quon. Nguyen Wu forced a weak smile. Quon pursed his lips thoughtfully as he eyed him, then crouched and examined the wound.

Wu summoned his resources, and the sounds were more breath than speech. "Take . . . me to . . . helicopter."

Quon reached forth and touched the skewer.

"My aunt . . ."

Quon pushed harshly on the metal. Pain coursed though him like a fiery lance, but he could issue only a low croaking sound.

"You are dying," Quon casually observed.

"Please."

"You are quite filthy, Brave Hero. Did you know that there are leeches on your neck, sucking your blood?"

"The helicopter," Wu gasped with the last ounce of his energy.

Quon smiled. "Tomorrow I will send a rescue team from Yen Bai to search the forest for survivors, Brave Hero. It will take another day for them to get here. I don't believe you can live that long—but, then, who knows?"

Wu tried to whisper more words, but could not.

"I came to shoot you. But that would be a terrible thing to do to a . . . hero." Quon stood and gave him the mocking look, then reached out with his boot and kicked harshly at the skewer.

"Annnghh." The pain was unbearable.

"You are bleeding again. What a shame." Quon laughed once, a soft yet brittle sound, then turned on his heel and departed in the direction he'd come.

Wu managed a final, pleading gasp. Later he heard the distant voices and the helicopter's engine surge as it lifted off.

The world about him wavered indistinctly, but he could see that the sky was growing angry with large, dark clouds. It would soon rain and he'd be able to drink.

Help would arrive in two days. They'd find him and he would be taken to Hanoi.

Spots danced in his eyes as he slowly lost vision. Blood seeped from his opened wound. The last coherent thoughts of Nguyen Wu were of his hatred for Quon and an image of the Mee woman whose secrets had promised so much.

His body was still functioning when the torrential rain began to pour upon the mountainside, running in small cascades, gathering here and there in great puddles. When the water covered his mouth and nostrils, there were a few small bubbles, but they soon stopped.

Sunday, March 24th, 2010 Local—O' Club Dining Room, Takhli RTAFB, Thailand

Captain Manny DeVera

Smitty wanted to borrow a few dollars until payday. "It's just a week," he said.

"Dammit, quit spending everything you've got on that gold-digger," Manny said, pulling out his wallet.

"Maybe you're right," Smitty muttered. It was the first time he'd admitted he was being taken.

"Stick with the hookers at the Takhli Villa," Manny counseled. "They're more honest, and they'll take care of you. Shit, Smitty, you could start a bank with all the money you've spent on that broad." He handed over twenty bucks.

Smitty looked thoughtful as he finished his rubbery tapioca pudding.

"Maybe you oughta take me downtown with you," Manny said. "I'd like to learn your secret with the hookers."

Smitty frowned. He didn't like to discuss his prowess with the ladies of the evening.

Penny Dwight came in then, escorted by the red-haired major from supply who seemed to go out of his way to give DeVera lessons in bureaucracy. She laughed and said something in a low voice as they took a table at the opposite side of the room. Manny couldn't help staring, or stop the feeling of loss. Penny returned the look for a single moment before returning to her major. She was bossy and demanding with him, but the supply officer seemed to accept the situation.

"How come you extended your tour?" Smitty was asking, but Manny ignored him.

"Wonder what she sees in that guy," Manny muttered, although he knew.

"You'd think you liked this place. Some of the guys think you're crazy, Manny."

"What the hell are you talking about?"

"Why don't you go some place they're not trying to kill you? You got a thing about being shot at?"

"Let's change the subject," Manny growled, looking again at the other table and feeling queasy. Penny had reached over and was holding the major's hand on the tabletop.

"Okay," Smitty said happily. "Let's go to the bar. It's my big night."

Smitty had finished his hundred missions the day before, but he'd waited until today to celebrate, when Billy Bowes had also finished and they could share the tab and have a *really* big blast. Both men would be leaving within the next couple of days.

Manny got to his feet. Smitty followed him. "You mind paying for the meal, Manny? Me being short of cash and all?"

"No sweat." He paid at the counter, eyeing Penny Dwight and listening to the sound of her laughter. When he finally turned to join Smitty, he felt truly miserable.

As they joined the mob going into the stag bar, Manny remembered something. "Hey. If you're so fucking broke, how're you going to pay for your hundred-mission party?"

"I borrowed around. Like when you gave me the twenty bucks in there."

Manny gave him an incredulous glare. "You mean the rest of us are paying for your party?"

"Yeah." Smitty turned on his shy grin.

"Well, you tricky bastard."

"You want, we'll go downtown and celebrate when we get done here. Some of the girls at the Villa asked me to drop by. I think they're planning something."

Manny let his imagination rove freely as he thought of what the hookers might be up to. He decided he wouldn't miss it for anything in the world. Maybe he'd stop thinking so much about Penny Dwight and what they'd shared and lost.

CHAPTER
FORTY-SIX

Wednesday, March 27th, 1829 Local—Tactical Fighter
Weapons Center, Nellis AFB, Nevada

Major Benny Lewis

Benny finished his briefing for Major General Gordon S.
White.

They'd done all they could to assist in the preparations
for LINE BACKER JACKPOT. Helped with the planning
for deployments. Coordinated with Strategic Air Command
about how F-4 and F-105 flights would escort B-52's when
they bombed targets near Hanoi. Sent their best air-to-air
and air-to-ground instructor pilots to the fighter units that
would deploy, to give insights into anticipated enemy defensive reactions and brush them up on their tactics. Accelerated operational test and evaluation on new weapons and
aircraft avionics. Ensured the logistical train was prepared
to accept the surge of weapons and supplies required by five
additional combat wings of aircraft.

"Can you think of any loose ends?" the general asked.

"Nothing, sir. We've done our part. Now all we can do is
sit back and watch. It's up to the unit pilots."

"What's your impression there?"

Benny shook his head. "We're still not training them properly, sir. When the units are in place and fly their first missions, we'll take unnecessary losses, like we do with all new pilots who deploy to Southeast Asia. They're trained to fight another World War II, but when they get to combat, it's an entirely new show and they're not prepared."

"You keep telling me that, but we don't have time to train as realistically as you'd like to. Maybe we'll be ready for the next war, Benny."

They talked as if the ongoing conflict were about to end, because they sincerely believed that to be true. LINE BACKER JACKPOT would be bloody for both sides, but it would force the North Viet Army out of South Vietnam, and that would be the beginning of the end for communism there. Left to their own devices, the Viet Cong would fold in short order. The ARVN had proved they could fight effectively during the Tet offensive.

The general stood and stretched, shuddered, and blew a weary breath. Gordie White had worked hard to bring things to the present state. "Let's get out of here," he said.

Benny looked at his watch. "Damn! Julie's supposed to pick me up in fifteen minutes. I've gotta get over to my room so I can change."

"Going somewhere?"

"I'm taking her to dinner at the Ranch House. She likes their piano bar."

"Tell Julie hello for me." General White and his wife were partial to both Benny and Julie and were prone to act as matchmakers. "You could do a lot worse than that lady, you know."

That was precisely Benny's view of things.

Benny was ten minutes late getting out to the parking lot, where she waited in her new Ford Mustang. He leaned in the window and gave her a light kiss.

"You want to drive?" Julie asked.

"No," Benny said. He went around and crawled into the passenger's seat. "I'll criticize."

She put the car into gear and eased out of the parking lot and onto the main street of the base. He watched her closely.

"Quit looking at my nose," she grumbled. "That's my bad side. That's why I wanted you to drive." She was in a mood.

"You don't have a bad side," he tried.

"You're blind. My nose looks lumpy from the right side." She glanced in the mirror as if to confirm her statement, then slowed as they went through the gate, dog-legged down Las Vegas Boulevard for a block, and accelerated onto Craig Road.

"How was work?" he asked casually, wondering how he should approach what he really wanted to say and hoping her mood would get better.

"Same as always," she said. "Stews complaining they're getting too much or not enough flying time or because they're put on crummy routes. No one's happy with my scheduling, which means I'm probably doing a fair job."

"You miss flying?" Before the baby, Julie had been a stewardess.

"I'll let someone else handle the sick kids and the drunks wanting a quick feel."

"I visited the flight surgeon today."

"Oh?"

"They've finally agreed to evaluate my back. I go in next week for a physical. If I pass, they'll forward a request to get me back onto flying status."

"That's great, Benny." She knew how much he missed flying. "We'll celebrate."

Now she was improving. He thought of a way to approach his subject. "General White said to tell you hi."

"He's nice."

"He . . . ah . . . also said I could do a lot worse than . . . ah . . ."

Julie waited.

Benny took a deep breath. "Let's get married," he said. "Go downtown and . . . you know."

"No!" Julie's response was quick and emphatic.

The ensuing silence was awkward. He'd not expected immediate rejection. They spent most of their nights at her apartment, and she'd repeatedly told him how happy she was.

He approached the subject again. "I . . . ah . . . want to spend my life with you, Julie."

She pulled onto the Tonopah Highway, heading north toward the Ranch House turnoff. Still no response.

He was getting desperate. "I'd be good to you, Julie. And the baby."

"I know."

Benny deflated. "But you don't want to get married?"

The silence in the vehicle was complete. He looked glumly out the window.

She turned onto the dirt road leading to the restaurant, bumped along for a bit, then pulled into the crowded lot and parked.

He started to get out so he could go around to open her door.

"Wait," she said. She leaned toward him and gave him a slow kiss with her full, soft lips.

They kissed again.

"I will not go downtown to one of those fake wedding chapels to be married. I refuse to."

He began to understand.

"Now," she said, "would you please ask me to marry you in a proper church, any church in the world with a real pastor? If you do, I'll laugh and I'll cry, and I'll tell you I love you more than anything I've ever imagined. I'll tell you you're the most wonderful man in the world, which you are, and I'll promise to make you the best damn wife any man has ever had."

He laughed.

She glared. "Ask me, damn you Benny Lewis."

He did.

Thursday, March 28th, 0707 Local—HQ Seventh Air Force, Tan Son Nhut AB, Saigon, South Vietnam

Lieutenant General Richard J. Moss

Moss went over his notes from the previous night very carefully, examining them one at a time and pondering each at length. Twice in the early hours he'd received phone calls over the scrambler unit in his quarters from General McManus, and he'd scribbled down an unnerving mix of notes containing good news–bad news–good news.

CINCSAC, CINCTAC, CINCPACAF, and MAC were ready. Everything was in position and poised. Appropriate key personnel, including all affected unit commanders, had been briefed.

The air staff were prepared, both physically and mentally, to commit the most powerful air armada in the history of aviation to battle. Hundreds of C-141's and civil airliners would join surface ships in moving thousands of airmen and their equipment into position at forward bases. Thirty days later KC-135 tankers, EB-66 jamming aircraft, and C-121 command-and-control aircraft, would launch to provide their critical support. B-52's, F-4's, F-105's, even the new F-111's, would bomb relentlessly to destroy the infrastructure of a nation that refused to discuss peace or accept reason.

The military was ready.

But the CSAF hadn't been able to get in to see Johnson as scheduled. The President had sent word that he was busy.

Was that a bad omen? McManus couldn't say.

SecDef and SecState had been briefed in detail about LINE BACKER JACKPOT, then told simply that it was a viable option. Neither had betrayed their inner feelings to the briefing officers, but both men had recently been increasingly reluctant about even the slightest degree of escalation.

The President had asked the U.S. ambassador to Moscow about the potential Soviet reaction to a stepped-up bombing campaign, and he'd urged against it, saying that Moscow would "react vigorously"—but of course he hadn't said how they'd do that.

Next Johnson had convened a panel of "wise men," including former top Army generals and statesmen, and offered the LINE BACKER JACKPOT OPlan as one solution, and the Westmoreland request for additional combat troops as another. Unfortunately, there'd been no Air Force generals or air-power advocates on the panel. Their response had not mentioned the air campaign. They'd urged the President to send no more combat troops and seek a negotiated peace.

The other tidbit of bad news had been uttered by McManus with none of the acrimony that Moss felt. The CSAF had been provided with an information copy of a message forwarded directly from CINCPACAF to the new Secretary of Defense. General Joseph Roman had worded it cautiously, saying that he was "not opposed" to the LINE BACKER JACKPOT air campaign. But he also stated that if the OPlan was *not* implemented, he agreed with the "immediate cessation" of bombing north of the 20th parallel in North Vietnam.

When Moss had bristled, McManus had quietly told him that the Secretary of Defense had obviously asked Roman the question and requested a response. It likely had to do with selecting a candidate to replace him as Chief of Staff of the Air Force.

That was all the news that had been given during the two A.M. telephone call, and Moss had not returned to bed with a good feeling. At four A.M. his aide knocked again at his bedroom door and told him General McManus was on the classified line again.

The CSAF had spoken with the White House contact who had engineered his meetings with Johnson, and had been presented with an entirely different story.

The President was determined to get the war behind him. Yet another poll had confirmed that the American people wanted the war over and done with, but they wanted to do it by *winning*. Johnson was damned angry at the milquetoast recommendations of the wise men.

Best of all, the President had reconfirmed that he wanted to reserve prime time on all three major television networks on 31 March, when he'd make an *important* announcement. He was very secretive about his speech and wasn't allowing anyone, including his closest friends and advisors, access to the words. He was sick and tired of leaks to the press.

Moss and McManus chatted a bit about the fact that as soon as the President made the announcement, everyone on the fence like General Joe Roman would very quickly shut up and get aboard the train. The CSAF said he felt that by sending the message that ran counter to the President's desires, Roman had lost his chance to take over his position.

The evening of the 31st in the States would be the morning of April first in Saigon.

Sunday, March 31st, 1950 Local—O' Club Stag Bar, Takhli RTAFB, Thailand

Captain Manny DeVera

The bar was overflowing with pilots, for it had been an easy day, with interdiction missions concentrating in the Mu Gia Pass—looking for convoys hidden under the jungle canopy. The frag for the following day was more of the same. They'd flown few missions to pack six recently, which was okay by most of the pilots, who didn't relish having mach-3 SAMs fired at them.

Lucky Anderson, seated at Manny's side, was uncharacteristically grim, as he'd been during the period after Linda Lopes had been ambushed. There had been absolutely no word for a long time, and he'd long since stopped making queries. Whenever the bad times like this returned, his friends gathered and tried to be upbeat, and it usually worked.

He said he'd received a confusing letter that morning from a lady he didn't know, and he had to make a phone call, but he didn't seem to be in a hurry about it.

Manny tried conversation. "Who's gonna replace Colonel Trimble?" The Deputy for Operations was leaving next week.

"A colonel named Hoblit. Tall, good-looking guy, sorta the John Wayne type. He's known as a mean bastard if you cross him, but he's a good pilot and takes care of his men."

"How about the 354th? Who's gonna take Donovan's place as squadron commander?" he asked.

"New guy named Sparks," Lucky said. "It's his second tour. A smooth, quiet-spoken guy who never raises his voice. Good reputation and lots of Thud time."

Lucky was getting tipsy. He was also opening up.

"You gonna listen to the President's speech in the morning?" Manny asked. They couldn't talk about Jackpot, not even this close to kickoff, but he was in an upbeat mood about it.

Lucky was looking toward the door. "I'm surprised at you, Manny. I thought you'd be going after that young lady with a vengeance."

DeVera turned. It was the Deputy for Operations' pretty,

young, and large-breasted blonde secretary, the one he'd taken to dinner to make Penny jealous.

He shook his head. "Took her out once. She's a nice kid, but she wasn't happy when I went back with Penny. Anyway, I promised myself I'd stay away from round-eye females. I've learned my lesson. You see me even talking to a round-eye, kick me hard, Colonel."

"I'd still say she's the best-looking girl on base."

The secretary was stuffed into a party flight suit like the one Penny had worn, and it stretched in all the right places to show off her attributes. As Manny stared, a second female came in to join her and looked shyly about. She was slender and dark-haired, with a nervous but nice smile. She remained close to her friend, ignoring the men in the room.

"Who's that?" Manny asked.

"The new donut dolly. Just got here last week."

Manny had trouble dragging his eyes away. There was something about her that intrigued him. He wasn't alone in the feeling. Half of the men in the room were eyeing the two women.

"I've gotta make that phone call," Lucky said. He drained his glass and left.

Jimmy the bartender had finagled himself into a dice game, so Manny waved to get the assistant bartender's attention.

Smitty edged up beside him, grinning. "Want to go downtown tonight?"

"I thought you left this morning for the States," Manny said.

"I had it put off for a couple more days."

"So you could be with the Thai base commander's daughter?"

Penny Dwight came into the room, escorted by her redheaded major friend. She paused and spoke to the two other women, then followed her date toward the rear of the room. It was a different turn of events, because the nonrated major seldom ventured into the stag bar, which was regarded as a flyers' domain, and Penny fastidiously ignored fighter jocks. She ordered the supply officer major around as if she were boss in the relationship, and Manny did not doubt she was. He remembered how she'd once taken over a large part of his own life. The memory was bitter-sweet.

"Nope," Smitty was saying. "I'm broke and she won't go out with me." He nudged Manny. "You sure you don't want to go downtown? The girls at the Villa liked you the other night."

Manny snorted. As soon as they'd entered the Takhli Villa, several girls had immediately escorted baby-faced Smitty to a room in back, and he'd not been seen again until morning. The next day Smitty had told him the ladies had thrown a private going-away party for him back there, but he wouldn't give details. He'd had bloodshot eyes and walked very gingerly and a bit bowlegged.

"You go ahead," Manny muttered, looking again at the shy and dark-haired newcomer who was changing his image of Red Cross reps. She wasn't as well stacked or vivacious as her secretary friend; she looked to be more the steady kind.

As her eyes swept the room, they paused for a moment on Manny. Nice eyes.

Jesus! He felt as if he were blushing. He smiled and the girl averted her gaze.

"You sure?" Smitty was asking, sounding forlorn.

Manny sighed and pulled out his wallet, then handed him a ten.

Smitty grinned. "I'll give it back tomorrow when I get paid."

"Yeah, and remember the twenty I gave you the other night."

A couple of fighter pilots were looking at the two girls and edging closer.

Manny DeVera immediately picked up his drink and pushed his way past the two would-be suitors. The secretary gave him a frown, but Manny's attention was zeroed on her friend. "Hi," he said to the Red Cross representative. "They call me the Supersonic Wetback."

2045L—Command Post

Lieutenant Colonel Lucky Anderson

That morning he'd received an odd two-liner letter from a woman he couldn't remember meeting, requesting a telephone call. She said it was important. Lucky had been perplexed, but decided he might as well phone her. It wouldn't hurt to find out what it was about.

It had been a good day, but for some reason he'd not been able to shake a rotten mood. That hadn't been the case with Buster Leska and Manny DeVera when they'd met in the wing commander's office. Pearly Gates had called Buster on the secure telephone and repeated that tomorrow morning the President would make his announcement to the American public. Get ready, he'd said, for hot and heavy activity. The war was about to take a definite turn for the better.

"Help you, Colonel Anderson?" asked a command-post sergeant as he entered.

"I've gotta make a call. Autovon to Clark."

The sergeant waved him toward a seat at the rear of the command center. "Lines to the States are all jammed up, but you should be able to get through to the Philippines."

Except for another sergeant posting numbers on the plexiglass boards and an airman manning a phone, the room was empty. Lucky stared at the maintenance board and noted the status of his squadron aircraft before picking up the hot line phone and telling the autovon operator he wanted to call Clark.

After the third try the Clark operator came on the line. Lucky read her the number shown in the letter.

"Third floor," answered a sullen male voice.

"I'm Lieutenant Colonel Anderson, and I'd like to speak to a Major . . . Mikalski."

"She's with a patient. It'll be a minute."

"I'll hold." A patient? Again he wondered what it was about.

"This is Major Mikalski." The woman's voice was businesslike.

"I'm Paul Anderson. I got your letter this morning, and—"

"Just a moment, Colonel." He heard her go off-line and give terse instructions about someone getting his ass in gear and responding to room 302. Couldn't he see the damn call-light?

"Sorry about that, Colonel Anderson."

"Anyway, I got your letter this morning."

"Have you been notified about the status of your fiancée?"

Lucky's heart thumped hard in his chest. "No," he blurted.

"Well, those bastards!" She cursed a bit, then paused. "I think I've got something you'll want to hear."

CHAPTER
FORTY-SEVEN

Monday, April 1st, 0800 Local—VIP Quarters, Tan Son Nhut AB, Saigon, South Vietnam

Lieutenant General Richard J. Moss

Except for the morning when he'd been so down with the stomach flu that he hadn't been able to take more than a dozen steps without rushing to the bathroom, Richard Moss had never arrived a single minute late at his office. Not once. Some thought it a peculiarity. He felt it was setting a proper example. Fighter pilots were not late for flight briefings. Fighter-pilot generals were not late to man their desks. This morning was an exception—it would be a day of note.

He sat at the large kitchen dinette table with his full-colonel chief of staff and Lieutenant Colonel Pearly Gates, all sipping coffee from mugs kept refreshed by Moss's captain aide and all listening intently to the Armed Forces Radio and Television Service network station. Radio Saigon.

During the previous fifteen minutes Lieutenant Colonel Gates had filled in the captain and the colonel on what the President was about to announce. Those three were appropriately exuberant. Moss's own spirits were moderated only slightly by the natural cynicism that comes with age and experience.

The *Good Morning, Vietnam* show, which Moss disliked thoroughly because of the awful music, was interrupted for a "live report from the White House."

Pearly Gates slowly pulled off his ridiculous Coke-bottle-bottom glasses and began to fastidiously wipe them.

The radio grew quiet. There was a rustling of paper.

Moss asked the aide if he'd get him a glass of tomato juice. A wedge of lemon, please.

"The President of the United States of America."

Pearly Gates stopped the polishing motion. The colonel's chair scraped as he moved closer to the radio. The aide hurried so he could finish his task before the President got to the meat of his speech.

"My fellow Americans," Johnson began in his distinctive down-home drawl. His tone was grave.

For the next twenty minutes there was absolutely no sound in the room as the Texas politician ordered a "unilateral" halt to both air and naval bombardments of North Vietnam except in those areas north of the DMZ where the continued enemy build-up . . .

He called for similar restraint by the North Vietnamese, and for them to sit down and negotiate in good faith.

He would send 13,500 more troops to Vietnam and would request expenditures to . . .

He would neither seek nor accept the nomination of his party for another term as President, but would concentrate his energies upon seeking a negotiated end to the war.

Richard Moss switched off the radio.

The colonel cleared his throat to speak, but Moss waved a hand to quiet him. Without speaking, for he did not trust his words, he stood and stalked silently out to his car and the driver waiting there.

"Another beautiful day, sir," the sergeant said cheerfully, holding the door open.

Moss did not answer. He crawled inside and sat stiffly as the door was closed.

They rode toward the headquarters building in silence.

The driver commented that it was April Fools' Day.

It was indeed the Day of Fools.

1000L—Ministry of External Affairs, Hanoi, DRV

Deputy Minister Li Binh

There were happy shouts, laughter, and sounds of joyful celebration throughout Hanoi as the word of the American
President's statement was read by gleeful announcers over
Radio Hanoi. Sirens wailed and klaxons and automobile
horns brayed, and many thought it was a Mee air attack until they were told differently.

When Li Binh had gathered her office staff to tell them
the news, they'd been jubilant. The Minister of External Affairs might receive a degree of credit, but it was known
among those who counted that, more than any single individual, it had been Li Binh's doing that had forced the announcement from the hated President *Riddin Jah-soh*.

She'd repeatedly told the party leaders that the work of
her agents in America and Europe was eating away at public
confidence. The continued and increasingly strident demonstrations her office nurtured and encouraged had produced
the desired effect upon Washington politicians. Her office's
efforts had turned the bleak and awful defeats of the Tet offensive into a perceived victory. And that had been just as
effective as the success on the battlefield that had been denied the People's Army. The final, deciding factor, had been
subtle promises her offices relayed to the American President that if he stopped the bombing, the Democratic Republic would immediately and without precondition enter
negotiations to withdraw *all* foreign military forces from the
South.

Now all they had to do was act as if they would negotiate. Go through the motions and demand every advantage.
America had blinked and been branded a coward. They'd
blink again.

Hanoi was safe! The bombing respite would embolden
the most cautious Lao Dong leaders to pursue the war vigorously.

It was a wonderful day. Nothing could possibly mar it.

She took a telephone call from the office of Le Duan,
Secretary-General of the party. Her presence was requested
at an afternoon planning meeting. She hung up slowly, feeling numbed. Le Duan wanted her there—had *requested* her

presence at a meeting that was likely to decide the future of the nation.

Upon a whim she telephoned her husband's office and asked to speak with the general. Since his promotion he'd gained stature in her eyes. Xuan Nha came on the line. The first words that came from his mouth were of praise, for he knew she was the one most responsible.

Li Binh preened as she told him about the planning meeting, and how she'd speak for External Affairs. Xuan told her he was very proud. He said that he'd also be busy with meetings, determining new dispositions of the defenses presently massed around the capital city.

Then he made a statement that shook her, and she had him repeat his words.

Her nephew's body had been found in the mountains west of Yen Bai. Nguyen Wu had escaped Ban Sao Si only to be killed by an American air attack on his convoy.

She was stunned and unable to speak. A trill of rage swept through her, and she silently vowed to make the despised Americans pay in every way possible.

Xuan Nha spoke of his sadness at the death of her nephew.

After the telephone call, Li Binh remained despondent for more than an hour, until she received a written note from Le Duan's office.

They were sending her to Paris, to supervise their delegation there and orchestrate negotiations with the Americans until Le Duc Tho's arrival. The afternoon meeting was set up to discuss the matter and gain her insights.

Ways to negotiate, yet work toward the defeat and subjugation of South Vietnam.

Li Binh felt she would be very good at such things.

CHAPTER FORTY-EIGHT

Wednesday, April 3rd, 0705 Local—HQ Seventh Air Force, Tan Son Nhut AB, Saigon, South Vietnam

Lieutenant Colonel Pearly Gates

He'd been surprised that there'd been another JACKPOT message. But Flo had called from the general's office and summoned, asking him to pick up a special comm on his way, which was the way she acted when the back-channel communications arrived during the night. Pearly took the message into Moss's office and waited until the admin chief of staff finished his summary of the night's events. Nothing of any real note had occurred.

When the colonel had departed, Moss motioned at Pearly and reached for the message.

He read quietly, face impassive until he was almost finished. A tiny curl grew at his lips. Pearly couldn't tell if it was a sign of sarcasm or satisfaction.

Finally he pushed the message across to Pearly, then spoke to Flo on intercom, asking her to connect him with the chief of personnel.

"General Abrams's meeting at ten o'clock," she reminded him.

Pearly read the final message slowly.

SECRET—IMMEDIATE—JACKPOT
7 AF CC EYES ONLY—NO FURTHER DISSEM
DTG: 02/1800ZAPR68
FM: CSAF/CC, HQ USAF, PENTAGON
TO: HQ 7 AF/CC, TAN SON NHUT AB, SVN
SUBJECT: STATUS REPORT
1. (C) MY OFFICE HAS TAKEN
APPROPRIATE ACTIONS TO TERMINATE
IMPLEMENTATION OF AF OPLAN 68-1011,
SHORT TITLE: LINE BACKER JACKPOT.
2. (C) I HAVE SUBMITTED MY
RESIGNATION AS CSAF EFFECTIVE
05APR68 DUE TO HEALTH REASONS. SEC
DEF HAS NOMINATED GEN JOSEPH R. ROMAN
AS MY REPLACEMENT. THE CHANGE
WILL BE ANNOUNCED TOMORROW.
3. (C) IN A CONGRATULATORY PHONE CALL
TO JOE ROMAN, I SUGGESTED THAT YOU BE
NAMED AS CMDR OF TACTICAL AIR
COMMAND, AND HE AGREED. HE WILL
MAKE THAT APPOINTMENT, AND OTHERS,
THE DAY AFTER ASSUMING HIS NEW
POSITION.
4. (U) GOOD LUCK, AND THANK YOU FOR
YOUR SUPERB SUPPORT. SUGGEST YOU
DESTROY COPIES OF PREVIOUS MESSAGES.
SECRET—IMMEDIATE—JACKPOT

It was the job General Moss had wanted most, the best position a fighter-pilot general could hope for, and he'd get his fourth star to boot.

"Congratulations, sir," Pearly Gates said, but his words were lost because Moss began to speak on the phone with his chief of personnel.

Pearly heard his own name mentioned by Moss, along with other members of the small inner group the general called his mafia. General Moss was preparing for his move to Langley Air Force Base, Virginia, pulling his best men with him to the new assignment.

"Lieutenant Dortmeier," Pearly whispered during a

pause, and Moss made an *oh yeah* raise of his eyebrows and added her name to the list.

1055L—Clark Regional Hospital, Philippines

GS-15 *Linda Lopes*

"Why do you keep asking the same questions over and over?" she pleaded.

Smith was his nasty self. "Because there's such inconsistency between what you've told us and the response we're getting from the enemy, Lopes. So far there's nothing at all to support your statement that they know *anything* about the networks."

"Do you think I would lie about it?" she cried. "Do you think I'd say I told them secrets if I hadn't? I hate myself for telling them. Why should I lie?"

Jones spoke up. "Would you be willing to take a polygraph test?"

Linda bit her lip to hold back another surge of fear. Nurse Marty had told her she was in charge of herself. Each time Smith and Jones visited, they made it clear who was *really* in charge.

"You see," said Smith, "there are some who believe you could be telling us ... ah ... misinformation which might cause us to unnecessarily dismantle important networks."

She looked at him with disbelief. Her fear intensified.

"A polygraph test would show these ... individuals ... that you're telling the truth, and that the—"

She interrupted. "Why in the world would I want to lie about something like that?"

Smith raised an eyebrow. "Well—we know that you were under their control for some three months, Miss Lopes. A lot of things could happen during that time."

"A lot of things," echoed Jones.

Male voices could be heard from the hallway beyond the closed doors. Smith frowned and looked there, then turned back to Linda.

"So, you see, it's imperative that you take the polygraph," Jones said. "We'd have the device brought to the room so it wouldn't be an inconvenience."

Linda studied her hands. Her fingernails were growing back. The metal brace had been removed, so she could move her arms now, but her range of motion was not meeting the doctors' expectations.

"Are you listening, Miss Lopes?" It was Smith's voice.

Linda didn't want to meet his eyes. Nurse Marty called them the comedy twins and told Linda to think of that name whenever they bothered her, but it didn't help. She'd also said to ring the nurse-station buzzer whenever she felt at all threatened. She'd always been too frightened to do that.

"If you refuse to take the test," Jones began, "we'll have to assume—"

Someone rapped insistently on the door. The agents stared with matching, irritated expressions. The knocking came again, louder.

"We're busy," Smith growled.

Male voices out there again. The rapping stopped. While the two were looking away, Linda edged timidly toward the buzzer, grasped it, and held it in her hand.

Jones looked back. "What the hell are you doing with that?" he asked in a loud, irritated tone, reaching for it. She pushed it away as if it burned her hand, then couldn't help uttering a terrified sob.

Smith glared. Jones shook his head. She'd angered them. "I'm sorry," she cried out, cringing.

"For Christ's sake, we're just—"

The door pushed open and a face peered inside.

Smith turned back. "What the hell do you—Jesus!"

Linda looked, but was so upset that it took a moment for her to digest what she saw. Then her heart lurched.

Smith and Jones both stared at Lucky Anderson's ruined face with horrified expressions.

Paul stepped inside, fixed the men with pale blue eyes, then looked at her.

"Who the fuck are you?" whispered Smith.

"Are you okay, Linda?" Paul asked.

She made an involuntary whimpering sound.

Lucky took two steps inside and grasped both men by their arms. They gave sharp yelps.

"Oh, God! Paul!" she cried.

"Did either one of you touch her?" His deep voice was angry.

"No!" both men wailed.

Paul gave a curt motion with his head. "Out."

They fled.

Paul Anderson came close and reached down to touch her face with a strong, gentle hand. Through the door Linda heard Smith's quavering voice ordering the security policemen into the room.

A staff sergeant peeked around the door at her with a quizzical look. "You okay, ma'am?"

Linda couldn't speak, but she nodded vigorously.

"Get him out of there!" Smith demanded.

The staff sergeant obviously didn't like the agent. "The colonel says he's her fiancé, and I believe the lady *wants* him in there. I'm not so sure about you, though."

"He is *not* authorized to go into that room."

"Maybe we'd best call the provost marshal about this."

"Sergeant, could you close the door?" Lucky said.

"You can't do that!" screeched Smith.

The door closed.

"I'm sorry," Linda said in a low voice.

He just shook his head very slowly from side to side. "God, I've missed you."

Linda Lopes reached up and clutched the hand stroking her face, and smiled for the first time in five months. She was safe.

1400L—Base Operations, Nakhon Phanom RTAB, Thailand

Major John Dillingham

The gooney bird hovered over the end of the runway, then landed gracelessly.

The three men before him wore new civilian clothing: outsized brightly colored shirts, shorts, tennis shoes, and baseball caps. Dillingham had made the purchases and told them that was how they'd dress when they arrived at their new home. The senior sergeant even had a Japanese camera hung around his neck. They peered at him soberly and listened hard.

"You guys just stay put after you land at Don Muang.

Someone from the embassy's supposed to meet you, but if they're late, don't go rushing off anywhere and get lost."

Two of the Hotdogs looked puzzled at the English words, so he repeated his instructions in Viet.

"Hokay, Sarge," said Nguyen, as the lieutenant used to do. Nguyen was the youngest of the group. He also understood English best.

Dillingham had instructed them thoroughly and repeatedly on what to expect, from their arrival in Bangkok right down to how to recognize his sister, who would meet them when they landed in Honolulu. He'd given them a picture of her lest they forget. Still he was nervous and fidgety, as if he were seeing kids off to camp for the first time.

The request for special consideration for immigrant status had been speedily approved. Richard the Spook had done that for them, and he'd apologized that he wouldn't be there to meet the Hotdogs when they arrived in Bangkok. He'd received a call from a nurse in the Philippines that a couple of guys were giving Clipper a hard time, and he was leaving for Clark *tout suite.* When he was done with them, he'd said in an angry voice, the too-young and too-eager CIA agents would be grateful that they were being posted to a consulate in the Cameroons. Dillingham said he didn't know where that was. Richard just chuckled.

He'd told Dillingham all that before he'd left Bangkok, when he'd also given his final instructions about the Hotdogs. They'd spoken so often on the classified line recently, they were getting to be regular telephone pals. Richard said he'd have an embassy representative pick up the renegades and process their paperwork. As soon as he returned tomorrow, he'd make sure everything was on track and get things started for their flight to Hawaii.

A good man, was Richard the Spook.

Dillingham realized the senior sergeant was speaking to him.

"What?" he asked, leaning forward. The gooney bird was creating its normal racket as it taxied toward base operations.

"We are very happy to be going to Ha Wa Eee. We thank you, Majah Dir-rin-hum."

"I rike Sarge Brack bettuh," said Nguyen, wearing an impish look.

"You all earned it."

"We will be good Americans," said the senior sergeant gravely.

"You've already shown that. There's nothing left to prove."

The left engine on the goon clattered to a halt. They shut down only the one engine on the round-robin flight, and kept the other propeller turning. As soon as the passengers were loaded, they'd depart.

John drew a deep breath. "I guess you'd better be going." One by one he shook their hands and looked each man in the eye. The Hotdogs turned together and started hesitantly toward the gooney bird.

Nguyen turned and waved. "See ya, Sarge Brack."

Major John Dillingham stood at attention and rendered them the sharpest salute he could muster. He watched as the hatch was closed behind them, then as the left engine coughed and caught. The goon revved once and taxied back toward the runway. He stared for another moment, then turned and strode toward the jeep he'd left at the side of the building.

When he reached the vehicle, he stopped and could not help turning and watching the takeoff. A moment later he crawled in and started the engine.

"C'mon bruddah," the lieutenant's voice echoed in his brain. "Le's ged gone fum heah."

Thursday, April 4th, 1700 Local—VIP Quarters, Hickam AFB, Hawaii

Colonel Tom Lyons

His call was patched to Lowry Air Force Base, in Aurora, Colorado, then to his parents' home in Cherry Hills. His mother answered and was alarmed at the discouraged way he sounded. "Are you okay?" she asked.

"I need to talk with Dad," Tom said, trying to firm up his voice but not succeeding.

She paused, then dropped her voice. "He's still not happy with you, Tom. The thing over Margaret, you know."

"I'm in trouble, Mom." His voice caught.

"I'll try," she said, but she sounded dubious.

Tom waited, praying softly to himself.

His father finally answered in a gruff tone. "What's wrong *this* time?"

"They've got me confined to quarters, Dad. Some classified papers were found in the bar at the hotel with my name on them."

"Jesus," his father muttered. "Can't you stay out of trouble?"

"I wouldn't be calling, but they're talking about a summary court-martial."

"I don't think you're going to learn, Tom. How many times is this going to make that you've wanted me to pull you out of the crapper?"

"This is the last time I'll call for help. I promise."

"That's what you said last time."

"Dad, I swear I didn't leave the papers there. I swear it to heaven."

"Tom, I'm going to do you a favor. Something I probably should have done a long time ago."

Lyons breathed a sigh of relief. "Thanks, Dad. You won't regret it."

"I'm going to let you get out of this one all by yourself."

The telephone went dead.

1945 Local—O' Club Dining Room, Takhli RTAFB, Thailand

Captain Manny DeVera

Manny motioned their waitress over.

"I thought you were getting married?" he asked her.

The cute Thai *puying* smiled, her pencil tucked behind an ear as she'd seen in some old American film. She didn't answer, just shrugged and smiled wider, then hurried off toward the kitchen.

"No Hab's fiancé just left for the States," Manny explained to the base Red Cross representative.

She murmured something low about how she wouldn't let Manny get away if *he* proposed. She was starry-eyed with newfound love, and Manny wasn't in much better shape. He was certain he'd never felt this intense about a woman.

"Ready to go?" he asked.

"Whenever you are." Her eyes followed him as he got to his feet and came around to get her chair.

It was going to be another great night, Manny thought happily. As they started toward the entrance, Penny Dwight came in with her red-headed major, and Manny nodded pleasantly but drew no response.

Friday, April 5th, 1850 Local—Las Vegas, Nevada

Major Benny Lewis

Benny let himself in and immediately smelled the aromas of her cooking.

"Hi, hon," he called toward the kitchen.

"You're late," she fussed.

They normally had a glass of wine and conversation before eating at seven. Benny went in and found her peeking into the oven. He put his arms around her and kissed the nape of her neck.

"Mmm." Her whiskey voice. "If you want dinner, you'd better stop that, Benny Lewis."

"I'm back on flying status." Benny said it casually, as if it were no big thing.

She squealed with delight and turned to hug him.

He grinned. "I bought a bottle of wine. Good stuff."

"I can get Pam to watch the baby if you want to go out to celebrate."

Benny shook his head. "I'd rather just stay home with my two women."

He didn't have words to tell her how happy he was every night when he came home to them. He'd come a long way to find precisely what he had.

"Benny?" Julie started as he began to open the bottle of wine at the counter. She said his name as if she wanted to tell him something she'd spent some time thinking about.

"Yeah?"

"When we get married next week, I want you to know

that I love you more than anyone or anything in the world. There'll be no more ghosts between us."

He began to turn the corkscrew into the cork, thinking how wrong she was. The ghosts would be around for the rest of their lives. Not between them, he hoped, but they'd be there.

Julie would try, but she'd not be able to forget. He knew he could not.

"I want you to know I'm not giving you half my love," she said.

He pulled out the cork and sniffed it. "Good stuff," he repeated.

"I just thought you should know," she said awkwardly.

He thought of her husband, who'd been his closest friend. About so many others whose lives had been wasted because a group of politicians and generals thought they could fight a war without trying to win. Such an awful, terrible waste of fine men.

As far as military contests went, the war in Southeast Asia was minor, Benny thought. More combat losses had been suffered in single battles of other conflicts. But American fighting men had never before been more dedicated than those who fought this one, and never so utterly betrayed by their leaders.

Since the morning after the President had made his announcement, Benny's work telephone had been busy. Calls from the different fighter bases, from the Pentagon, and from the various headquarters. Others who thought like him, who were terribly discouraged, and suddenly so determined. They made a quiet pact. To hell with promotions, careers, or whatever the generals or politicians might want. They'd work together to change things.

There was much to be done before they could be certain that it could never happen again.

The telephone calls would continue, and their numbers would keep growing, encouraged by the memories of the men who had fallen.

The ones who lived couldn't afford to forget.

CHAPTER
FORTY-NINE

In April of 1968, following the speech by the President of the United States of America, an entirely new spirit was perceived among American fighting men, who had come to realize they were not in the war to win.

An embittered headquarters puke at Seventh Air Force Headquarters in Saigon, a lieutenant colonel whose spectacle lenses were so thick they looked like Coke-bottle bottoms, shelved the no-longer sensitive details of an OPlan that had initially been called Total-Forces Utilization, the phonetic initials for which were Tango Uniform. Later the program had been changed to Line Backer Jackpot, but the Tango Uniform name seemed more appropriate.

A master sergeant in his office joked humorlessly about the OPlan at the Tan Son Nhut NCO club.

"This whole fucking war," he growled, "has gone tits up."

The Seventh Air Force headquarters lieutenant colonel was reassigned to Tactical Air Command, at Langley Air Force Base, Virginia, as General Moss's Chief of Plans and Programs. Captain Moods Diller, from Nellis Air Force Base, was also assigned to TAC, to work in the Requirements Directorate. Lieutenant Lucille Dortmeier was approved to attend the University of Virginia, to finish her law degree. Upon graduation General Moss promised her a position on the TAC headquarters legal staff.

At PACAF Headquarters, as General Bomber Joe Roman prepared to leave for the Pentagon, he ensured that his own most trusted staff officers would follow him. Colonel Tom Lyons was not among that group.

At Takhli Royal Thai Air Force Base, the F-105 Thunderchief pilots continued to fly combat missions under the superb guidance of Colonel Buster Leska, but only in South Vietnam, Laos, and cautiously selected targets south of the twentieth parallel in North Vietnam.

With reassurance that the Americans would no longer bomb targets near Hanoi and Haiphong, the North Vietnamese, under the canny leadership of General Xuan Nha, deployed SAM and AAA defenses to the mountain passes and troop build-up areas where the fighter-bombers were now attacking, and the killing skies were moved southward.

In the Spring of 1968, Madame Li Binh traveled to Paris. A few months later she was joined by Le Duc Tho, and together they orchestrated the first official meetings with American negotiators. For more than a month they argued vehemently about the shape of the table.

And in the musty cells of prisons in and around Hanoi, more than four hundred pilots were repeatedly beaten and told they were common criminals, and tried hard to reject the idea that they'd been forgotten by their countrymen.

TRUTH & FICTION

Missing Man Formation

TRUTH & FICTION

The characters herein are fictitious. Descriptions of bases, units, and locales are generally accurate for the period. While Takhli Royal Thai Air Force Base is the setting, the air-combat stories are adaptations of war tales of men stationed there as well as Korat, Ubon, Udorn, Danang and other airbases. A number of the Hotdog tales were related by men of the U.S. Army Special Forces, as well as aircrews of Air Force Special Operations.

The awful songs? Yeah. They're real, and we still sing them at gatherings—too loudly perhaps, but of course always on key.

Laser-guided bombs—proven around the period of the novel—were the brain child of a canny engineer at Texas Instruments, promoted by two Air Force officers whose intelligence quotients made the rest of us look like Stone-Age bumpkins. I have simplified the weapons system and the grueling development test and evaluation process, and moved test locales for purposes of the novel. The most telling combat test was at the heavily defended Thanh Hoa Bridge, which had survived the attempts of hundreds of Air

Force and Navy fighter pilots using gravity bombs. The bridge was dropped using a single smart bomb.

American women were finally assigned to Takhli in November of 1967. I've taken great liberty here. The real-life ladies were intelligent and lovely, and quite understanding of the crazy fighter pilots they so graciously endured.

The Linebacker plan was not new. Aircrews were told to prepare for such a contingency in 1965 and several times thereafter. By the time of *Tango Uniform,* the conflict was dividing America by being allowed to continue entirely too long, and there were strong indications that a plan such as Line Backer Jackpot was about to be implemented. Polls indicated that the American people would overwhelmingly (more than sixty percent) support such an option. In late 1967 President Lyndon Johnson visited the war theater. Whether he spoke privately with the Commander of Seventh Air Force, I do not know, but rumors proliferated that something very big was afoot. Finally, confused by barrages of conflicting advice, L.B.J. chose to trust the word of the North Vietnamese, who had relayed (through U Thant) that they would negotiate if the bombing was stopped without precondition.

Tango Uniform (with *Termite Hill,* and *Lucky's Bridge*) completes the fictional trilogy about the F-105 Thunderchief and the resolute pilots who flew her in combat during the intense air war years of 1966 and 1967. I have studied war and have never known, and cannot imagine, braver men. I also cannot think of a more honest war steed than the Thud.

The period was a bleak one for the military, and not only because they were forced to look on helplessly as American politicians almost gleefully engineered our first major military defeat. Enlisted families lived below the poverty line, and yearly were told that pay raises were again deferred due to the high costs of the Great Society and the Vietnam War. Acquisition of new weapons systems were also delayed. Since the USAF knew they must wait for new aircraft to challenge the superb MiG designs coming off Soviet production lines, they looked desperately at the alternative: to upgrade an older model. The choice was narrowed to two fifteen year old designs. Republic Aviation promoted a lighter, more maneuverable version of the rugged F-105 Thunderchief, while McDonnell Douglas fought for an improved version of their versatile F-4. The Phantom had two pilots and two engines, and a thunderous voice went out from the Pentagon that the redundancy made it safer. As is done entirely too often, arguments for the single-engine, single-seat Thunderchief II (F-105G) came to be viewed as heretic, and proponents within the Air Force found their careers in jeopardy. The following decade became the era of the Phantom, extolled as the multi-mission champion of the free world.

In December of 1972, when Linebacker II was finally initiated at the direction of a bolder President, F-4 crews used laser-guided bombs to destroy point targets in downtown Hanoi, and no damage was done to adjacent civilian housing. B-52 crews took out area targets with their massive bomb loads, and P.O.W.'s reported that the earth shook and their North Vietnamese captors were terrified. After only eleven days of intensive bombardment, North Vietnamese negotiators in Paris acquiesced to American demands. The agreement was signed shortly thereafter, and the P.O.W.s brought home. It is easy to play what-if: like what if we'd done it in 1965. Would we have avoided those other years of conflict? Would America now be a quite different country? Who knows. It did not happen. But what if . . .

ABOUT THE AUTHOR

TOM "BEAR" WILSON was a United States Air Force officer with more than three thousand flying hours, mostly in fighters. During his five hundred hours of combat flying, he earned four Silver Star medals for gallantry and three Distinguished Flying Crosses for heroism. He also served in roles as instructor, flight examiner, tactician, staff officer and unit commander. After leaving the military, Wilson enjoyed diverse careers, including: private investigator, gunsmith, newspaper publisher, and manager of advanced programs for a high-tech company in Silicon Valley. Mr. Wilson is the author of TERMITE HILL, LUCKY'S BRIDGE and TANGO UNIFORM. He is presently working on BLACK WOLF.

Now there are two great ways to catch up with your favorite thrillers